CHILDREN OF THE BLESSING

BOOKS BY PERRY MORRIS

THE LEMURIAN CHRONICLES
Children of the Blessing
Chaos Rising

LEGENDS OF LEMURIA
(Novella Series)
Renn and the Bounty Hunters
Shamael and the Battle at the Well of Sacrifice

Get a free copy of *Renn and the Bounty Hunters* by subscribing at www.perrymorris.net/free.

BOOK I OF THE LEMURIAN CHRONICLES

CHILDREN OF THE BLESSING

PERRY MORRIS

Copyright 2015 © Perry Morris. Seventh edition.

ISBN 978-1099164217

All rights reserved. No part of this publication may be reproduced, distributed, or transmitted in any form or by any means, including photocopying, recording, or other electronic or mechanical methods, without the prior written permission of the publisher, except in the case of brief quotations embodied in critical reviews and certain other noncommercial uses permitted by copyright law.

This is a work of fiction. Names, characters, places, and incidents either are the product of the author's imagination or are used fictitiously. Any resemblance to actual persons, living or dead, events, or locales is entirely coincidental.

Cover image artwork copyright 2015 © Joe Shawcross

Map artwork copyright 2015 © Cornelia Yoder; rights assigned to Perry Morris.

Flag artwork copyright 2015 © Perry Morris
Assistance with flag artwork provided by Joe Shawcross

Editing, typesetting, cover design, and ebook production provided by Writer Therapy.

TABLE OF CONTENTS

Map of Lemuria viii
Banners of Lemuria x
The Red Bear 3
Discovery 15
The Bear Wakes 24
Demon Fire 30
Snake and Wheel 44
The Council 59
The Road to Basilea 67
The Blessing 89
Ambush 97
Visitors 110
Confrontation. 119
The Mob 132
Shadows and Despair 142
The Box 152
Thorn 162
Skull Fire 171
Demon Spawn 179
The Tahsz Codex 183
Disappearing Act 190
Avaris 205
Bone and Fire 213
Lekiah 222
The Mighty Muk'gula. 230

The Hunt	238
Hail, Great Warrior	248
The Bold Plan	256
Return to Leave	263
Return of an Old Friend	272
City of the Avuman	284
Aleah	294
King Achal	303
Princess Tristan	311
Bitter Betrayal	325
The Kiel-Don	330
Lorum Root	341
Return of the Shadow	350
The Wanderove Divide	359
Truth Revealed	371
Tiaro Devi	380
The Battle	388
Escape	396
Dinner Party	403
Oracle of Tanith	413
Anytos	423
Winter's First Festival	430
Prison	438
Revenge	447
Elahna's Gorge	457
Elder Island	470
The Crystal Towers	477
The Staff of Greyfel	487
The Well of Sacrifice	494
The Red Bones Inn	503
Gifted Healer	508
Azur's Acropolis	518
Shadowsplitter	527

Wind	533
Race across Elder Island	545
Unwelcome Guest	558
Earthmaster	573
Presentation	584
Pandemonium	589
About the Author	596

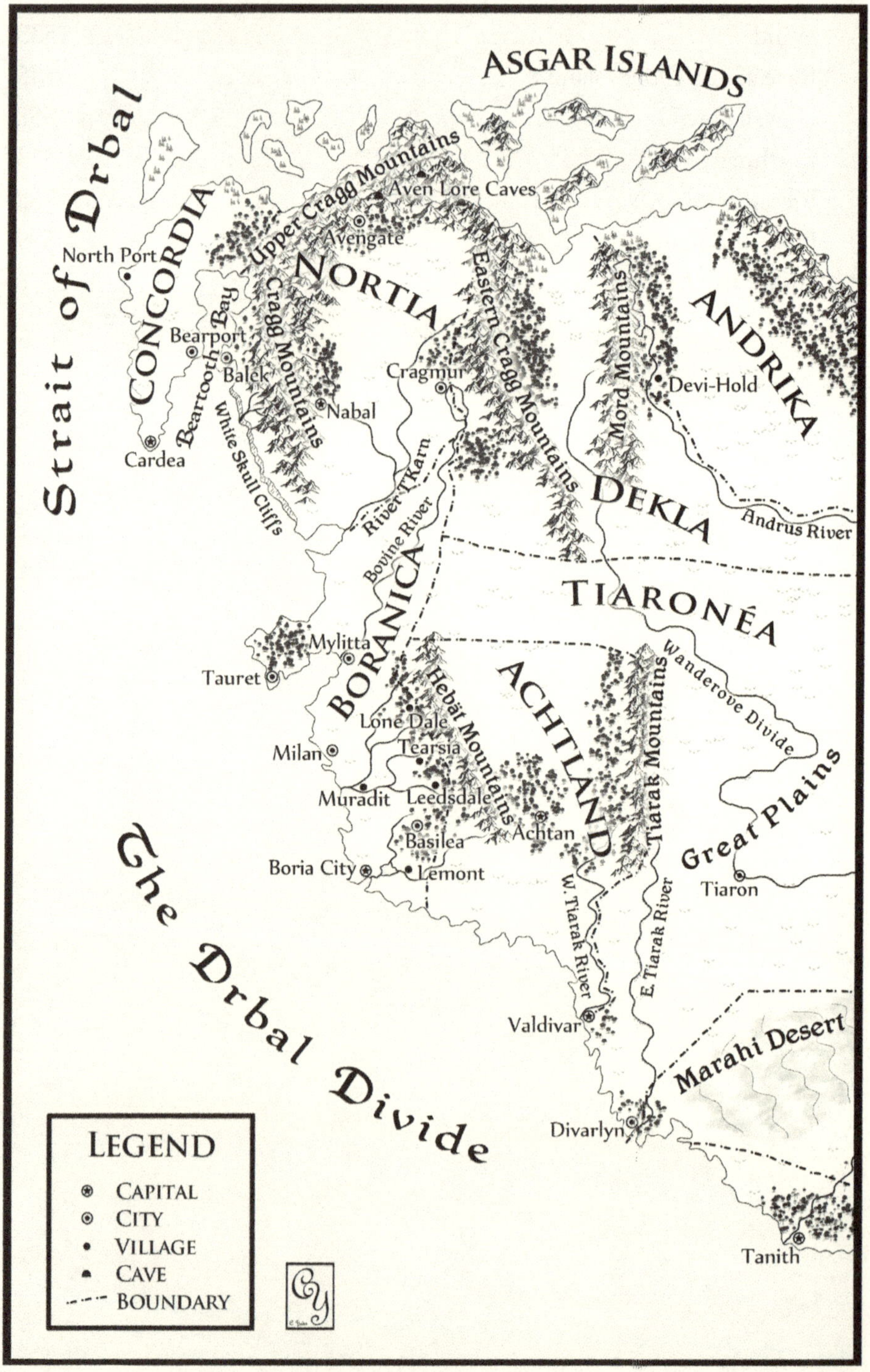
ASGAR ISLANDS
Strait of Drbal
CONCORDIA
North Port
Upper Cragg Mountains
Aven Lore Caves
Avengate
NORTIA
Eastern Cragg Mountains
Mord Mountains
ANDRIKA
Devi-Hold
Bearport
Beartooth Bay
Balek
Cragg Mountains
Cragmur
Nabal
Cardea
White Skull Cliffs
River T'Karn
Bovine River
DEKLA
Andrus River
TIARONÉA
BORANICA
Mylitta
Tauret
Wanderove Divide
Hebät Mountains
ACHTLAND
Tiarak Mountains
Lone Dale
Milan
Tearsia
Great Plains
Muradit
Leedsdale
Basilea
Achtan
Boria City
Lemont
W. Tiarak River
E. Tiarak River
Tiaron
The Drbal Divide
Valdivar
Marahi Desert
Divarlyn
Tanith
LEGEND
CAPITAL
CITY
VILLAGE
CAVE
BOUNDARY

The Lands and Seas of Lemuria

BANNERS OF LEMURIA

Achtan	Anytos
Avalian	Aven City
Basilea	Boranica
Elder Island	Menet
Mordrahn Clan	Tiaron

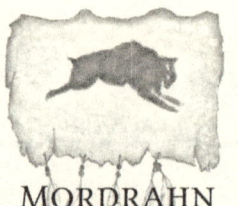

PROLOGUE

Artio looked up into the moonless sky and tried to catch his breath. His heart still pounded from the implications of what occurred earlier this evening. The warm air smelled of pine and felt good as it blew gently across his wrinkled face. His thinning hair, usually neatly combed, was pressed with sweat against his forehead, and his dark eyes peered anxiously into the night sky—he almost expected to see that the stars themselves had changed constellations. The old Mage had served as the Meskhoni for the people of Leedsdale for more than forty years. Most of his work was dull and tedious, but for the first time since taking this position, excitement, tinged with traces of fear, coursed through his veins.

He turned toward the rocky bluff in front of him, quickly traced a triangular rune in the air with his middle and index fingers close together, and touched the rough stone surface with his staff, opening a secret door that revealed the cave beyond. The small cavern was well lit by an Enchanter's Orb hanging from the ceiling. The walls were lined with shelves filled with books and trinkets—items gathered by Artio during his eighty-two years. He hurried toward the crude stone table in the center of the room, dipped his ragged feather quill into the black inkwell, and scratched out a letter.

To my dear friend, Salas, High Lore Master of Elder Island,
You no doubt felt the power of the gods tonight during the first night of midsummer's Azur-Aven festival. I'm certain all lore users throughout Lemuria felt it. You should know that a child I blessed was marked in the most astonishing fashion. The gods left a visible mark—an eagle in flight—on the baby's chest. This child may or may

> not be the fulfillment to prophecies found in the Tahsz Codex. As such, many will want to use or kill the child. I respectfully request your urgent guidance in this matter.
>
> Your fellow servant in the lore,
> Artio

He reread his words, then quickly folded the parchment, waved his staff toward the Enchanter's Orb to douse its light, and left his small cave.

Letter in hand, Artio sealed the cavern door behind him. He wound his way through the pine and aspen groves that concealed his rocky study and headed to the small chicken coop behind his cottage.

Artio opened the door and ducked in. The coop smelled of dusty seeds, and the rooster and hens complained loudly, but he wasn't here to steal eggs. Instead, the old Mage hurried to a beautiful peregrine falcon perched stately on a branch set near the roof in the back. *I don't know how Phaedra gets her birds to be so patient,* he thought, tying the note to the falcon's leg. *It isn't natural for a falcon to roost among chickens and wait months at a time until it's needed.* But Phaedra had a special way with her birds. They may act unnaturally, but they were her messengers and they were fast and reliable; tonight he was thankful for that. Artio raised his staff to the perch and the bird hopped on. Artio carried the falcon out into the night and quietly spoke the command, "Elonitha Elder Island." With that, the bird launched itself into the sky and disappeared over the Hebät Mountains as it headed northeast on its long journey to Elder Island.

THE RED BEAR

Renn Demaris let out a deep breath, took a careful step forward, and stopped to listen. A light breeze brought the clean scent of pine but no sound. He looked behind him. He was alone. Renn would be long gone before his parents realized he'd run away.

The full moon and starlit sky had made it easy to find his way across the family's freshly plowed field. But as Renn stood at the edge of the forest, the light was reduced to intermittent shafts struggling to break through the thick canopy. He took a few more steps and stopped. Up ahead, Renn heard something rustle under a bush and scratch against a boulder. He stopped breathing. *Maybe it's a mountain lion,* he thought. Renn's heart beat like it would break through his tunic. He held still and waited.

A scratching sound came from behind the boulder again, and then a rabbit hopped away. Renn breathed a sigh of relief and muttered, "Stupid rabbit." He tiptoed his way forward. *Maybe some of the monsters Jomard saw in the Cragg Mountains live here in the Hebät Mountains,* he thought.

A twig snapped on the ground behind him, and his stomach pulled up in knots. He spun around and found himself face-to-face with the Red Bear.

"Whatcha doing out here all alone, boy?" The Red Bear—Raul Lucian—fastened his big hands around Renn's shoulders.

"I . . . uh . . ." Renn knew if he said the wrong thing the Red Bear was liable to beat him like a stray dog.

"Yer old man never disciplines you boys," the Red Bear slurred. "I bet you ne'er had a switch to yer backside, eh, runt?" He pulled Renn's face so close, the tobacco stains on the Red Bear's teeth were visible through his thick red beard and forced grin. A fit of coughing that smelled of alcohol broke the Red Bear's grin, and Renn turned his head to keep from retching.

Through clenched teeth, the drunken man hissed, "Ya never were punished proper fer lettin' the dogs in on my chickens. So I'm gonna teach ya manners the right way, ya worthless piece of rat meat."

Renn started to cry. More than once, the Red Bear had beaten his son, Renaul, until he was black and bloody. Renn still had a vivid image in his mind of a morning a couple months ago when he saw the Red Bear screaming and flogging Renaul with a board. *If the Red Bear would do that to Renaul, his own blood-kin, what's to stop him from killing me?*

"Quit yer wailing, whelp!" the Red Bear said. "You'll have plenty to bawl about soon enough."

He turned Renn around and pinned him against a big willow tree, unsheathed his knife, and cut a switch as tall as Renn. The Red Bear examined the knife for a moment, running his thumb along the sharp blade. He shifted his beady eyes to Renn, shook his head once, grunted, and slid the knife back into its sheath.

Renn tried to twist away from the man's powerful grasp, but the Red Bear grabbed a fistful of Renn's tunic and held him in place.

"Oh, no you don't," the Red Bear growled. He threw Renn to the ground and pressed him against the cold dirt with his muddy boot. He whipped the switch a couple of times against a rock. It whistled as it passed by Renn's head and slapped against the stone with a sharp crack. The Red Bear pulled back the switch, and Renn knew this time the man intended to strike him.

Renn grabbed the muddy boot that held him against the ground and kicked up as hard as he could at the Red Bear's groin. The man howled, thrown off-balance as he tried to bring the switch down. The Red Bear's shifting weight allowed Renn to push the man's foot up enough to roll away. Instead of hitting Renn, the branch hit the Red Bear's knee, and he fell to the ground.

Renn scrambled to his feet and ran. He slid past bushes and under fallen logs, between boulders and around trees. The Red Bear's heavy feet crashed through the bushes behind.

"Get back here," Raul boomed. "The farther I gotta chase you, the more switch you're gonna get!" The angry man shouted a lot of other things, too. Renn didn't understand most of the words, but he was sure his mother would give him a good dose of soap if he repeated them.

Scratches stung Renn's hands, and his clothing ripped as he stumbled heedlessly forward. During the day, he could've successfully navigated the twists and turns, but the dark and his panic turned him around. His legs felt like wet hay, and the Red Bear was gaining on him.

Renn hurried through a small grove of aspens that opened into a ravine that grew narrower the farther he went in. Soon the walls of the ravine stretched into high cliffs. The ravine took a sharp turn to the right, and Renn found himself stranded in a small, grassy box canyon. The moon cast enough pale light on his surroundings to reveal that cliffs rose high on all sides. Renn scanned the walls for a cave to hide in or a boulder to get behind—but found nothing. He turned to double back, but the Red Bear lumbered through the trees, still cursing and madder than ever.

When the Red Bear saw Renn, the man stopped and held his right hand over his heart—his face bright red, his shirt dripping with sweat and clinging to a belly that was overly large from too much ale and not enough farming. He bent over and between gulps of air wheezed, "Ha, there's nowhere to run, and you're gonna pay double now." The Red Bear's mouth turned up into an eager grin and his small round eyes grew narrow. "I'm gonna enjoy this more than you're gonna hate it, runt."

"Help!" Renn screamed and looked side to side, desperately hoping to find a way out of the box canyon that he may have missed before. His heart raced, and he couldn't stop shaking. A burning sensation stirred in his chest. Like a spark smoldering in a wad of tinder, it jumped to flame as though fanned by massive billows. He didn't want to focus on the growing fire—he wanted to scream and run—but the burning had a seductive lure that gathered him in until he felt his very soul would be scorched.

"Yell all ya want." The Red Bear laughed and picked up a dead branch. "No one'll hear way out here."

The Red Bear's words sounded like they came from deep inside a well. Renn felt sound ripping through his throat and knew it was him screaming, but that, too, sounded distant, because he was immersed in the burning in his chest. Noises and dark images filled the sky, but it felt like a dream. The Red Bear advanced toward Renn, and his sense of everything around him became obscure: the cliffs, the canyon, the sounds, even the Red Bear slapping the branch into his palm.

The Red Bear let out a howl, and Renn thought the man was sounding a battle cry, ready to charge. But it wasn't a scream of anger, and the Red Bear wasn't charging.

The world jerked back into focus, like a flash flood crashing down a dormant riverbed.

Birds of every kind filled the sky—sparrows, ravens, falcons, hawks—and dove down with talons extended to attack the Red Bear. The man was covering his face with one hand and swinging his stick above his head with the other. The birds picked at the Red Bear with their sharp beaks and beat at him with their wings. When one wave flew out to make another pass, they were replaced by a dozen more . . . and a dozen more . . . and, soon, hundreds more.

Renn felt a sharp pain in his head. A small sparrow fell to the earth near his feet, dead. Its head crushed from one of Raul's wild blows. An empty pit of darkness grew in Renn's heart as he considered the lifeless creature. He was responsible for altering the destiny of this tiny animal. Another bird fell, and Renn's sorrow deepened. The thought of the sacrifice these animals made to protect him became a sadness so palpable he believed he would lose himself to despair.

"Please!" Renn shouted as loud as he could. "Please stop!"

The Red Bear was on one knee, blood streaming down his face. But he kept swinging. And the birds kept attacking . . . and kept dying.

A large bald eagle screeched and dove, talons extended, and the other birds paused. Instead of attacking, however, the great eagle landed on the ground, positioning itself between the Red Bear and his assailants, and continued to screech at the birds.

The birds listened, then with cries full of pain and rage, returned to their attack on the Red Bear—Raul Lucian.

The trees rustled, and a wave of wild animals appeared to join the battle, each sounding a unique battle cry and running at the flailing man in the center of the grassy clearing. A fox, a badger, and several squirrels and rabbits joined with the birds—strange allies to destroy a common enemy.

The Red Bear fell, still kicking and clawing as he rolled on the ground. Renn stood helpless, horrified as he watched the relentless assault unfold. And every time the Red Bear landed another blow, Renn's pain and sorrow increased.

The eagle started to grow, and the animals paused. A torrent of green light brightened the moonlit sky, and the magnificent bird transformed into an old man holding a long wooden staff. The strange crystal on top of the staff glowed with pale emerald light that lit the clearing with an eerie green glow.

Renn had only seen Artio, the local Meskhoni, a couple of times, mostly at the midsummer festival of Azur-Aven. But even though the man wore breeches and a lightweight tunic instead of his customary red robe, there was no mistaking the short gray hair peppered with black—remnants of color from years past. The Mage looked to the sky and chanted a monotonic rune song in a deep voice.

Even amid all the chaos, it occurred to Renn he was going to be in big trouble. *The Meskhoni, he'll save the animals . . . He'll tell Momma and Da.*

The pale green light from the Meskhoni's staff pulsated and swirled with the rhythm of his rune song. The power flowing from the staff took on a life of its own—like living energy slowly twisting around and through the melee.

By the green light of the Mage's staff, Renn saw the Red Bear more clearly. Dark bruises covered his body, and blood dripped from gashes in his skin.

The green power from the Meskhoni's staff increased in intensity, and the animals howled and chattered. They were clearly fighting between the Mage's will and a driving obsession to attack Raul. Finally, the light from the Meskhoni's staff flickered and died.

Once more, the animals screamed their unique battle cries, and the ferocious attack on Raul Lucian resumed.

The Meskhoni turned and stumbled to Renn, who stood watching numbly. The old man tossed his staff on the ground and dropped to his knees. He took Renn gently by the shoulder. "Renn, you must call them off!"

Renn stared blankly at the old man. *What does he mean?* he thought. Renn wanted to run again, but the Meskhoni's dark eyes were filled with compassion as they locked onto his. Renn felt that, despite the trouble he'd caused, the Meskhoni could fix it. Still, he couldn't bring himself to speak.

"Renn! Snap out of it, boy." The Meskhoni pushed Renn's dirty blond hair out of his eyes, then pulled his face close to his own. "You *must* call them off!"

The old Mage trembled a little, and perspiration ran freely over his creased brow and down his worn face. He sighed, released Renn, and picked up the Mage's staff. The Meskhoni placed his calloused hand on Renn's forehead. The crystal on top of the staff glowed green once again, and a ribbon of mist circled Renn's head. It smelled like fresh grasses mixed with flowers when he breathed it in. The burning in his mind subsided.

"Now, Renn," the Meskhoni repeated, "call them off."

"But *I* didn't call them!" Renn protested.

"Yes, you did. Listen carefully. Think of peace and safety, and then project that feeling to the minds of the animals."

"I can't! I don't know how!" He felt hot tears stream down his face and tasted salt as they wet his lips.

The Meskhoni looked past the Red Bear to the opening of the box canyon, where a mountain lion bounded with a loud cry. It quickly scanned the area and then charged toward Raul, who no longer moved. The mountain lion ignored the birds and smaller animals, which continued attacking the Red Bear with no apparent concern that a large predator was now in their midst.

"Renn, you must try," the Meskhoni said. "Relax. Let me help you."

Renn closed his eyes and tried to forget everything happening around him; then he felt the Meskhoni's presence in his mind. His instinct was to fight the intrusion and force it out.

"Renn, no!" the Meskhoni shouted. "Don't fight me . . . You must relax."

Renn held back the wall building in his mind and allowed the Meskhoni to guide his thoughts. Renn saw his family's farm on an early spring morning, the peaceful serenity of a sunset on a warm summer's evening. He saw himself playing and laughing with friends and family—swimming in the river with his brother, Tavier. Feelings grew in his heart, and then he felt a gentle outward push. Though he didn't see anything, he knew the Meskhoni helped him to cast the thoughts out to the minds of the animals.

The battle ended as quickly as it began. Renn opened his eyes. The Meskhoni rushed to the side of the Red Bear, who lay unconscious on the ground. The animals ran in circles, darting first one way and then another, trying to find a way to escape both the small box canyon and the mountain lion, which snatched up a rabbit in its powerful jaws. Several of the smaller creatures hid beneath bushes and in the grass, while the rest, including the mountain lion, disappeared back into the trees that grew in the ravine beyond the opening of the box canyon. Escape for the birds was much easier; they simply launched into the air and flew away into the moonlit sky.

Renn cautiously walked toward the two men. The Meskhoni opened a small leather pouch hanging from his belt and produced pieces of brown cloth and various liniments. The Mage cleaned and dressed the worst of the Red Bear's wounds. Renn silently looked down at the mangled figure lying on the ground. An occasional moan escaped the Red Bear's lips while the Meskhoni's hands rushed to apply herbs and ointments that smelled like a mix of pine, mint, and alcohol. After completing each wrap, the Meskhoni passed his hand over the bandage in a circular motion and murmured strange words before turning his attention to the next wound.

Renn knelt and picked up a sparrow. Its soft feathers were still warm, but its neck was broken. While it still made him sad, he didn't feel the personal anguish like before. There were many other animals lying motionless in the clearing. Renn looked at each one for a moment and then wiped at the tears on his cheek with a dirty hand.

Renn stood back up when he heard a dog barking in the distance, the bark growing steadily louder. He recognized the bark and looked anxiously toward the opening of the box canyon as his dog, Coy, bounded through the trees.

Not far behind the dog, an exhausted Ehrlich Demaris—Renn's father—came stumbling after. He held a floppy sleeping cap in one hand, and his nightshirt hung well past his waist and looked a bit silly with his brown breeches and work boots. Renn ran to his father, who bent over and took Renn into his arms and held him tight. Renn wasn't sure if he should be relieved or worried his father had come. His father was always fair and measured in dealing out punishment, but Renn had never run away before—or nearly killed a man.

His father stood, looked down at Renn, then at the Meskhoni—who paused from attending to the Red Bear long enough to acknowledge Renn's father—and back at Renn. Still breathing heavily from the long run, his father gasped, "What in the world happened here? Is that Raul Lucian?"

"Yes." The Meskhoni finished the last wrap. "I need you to help me get Mr. Lucian to his home. Renn can explain what happened on the way."

"Renn can explain?" Renn's father's brows scrunched together and his mouth dropped open. He looked to Renn to the Red Bear to Renn and back to the old Mage. The Meskhoni motioned for Renn's father to move to the opposite side of the Red Bear.

"Are you sure you can do this?" Renn's father asked the Meskhoni. "I mean, Raul is pretty heavy and . . ."

"And I'm an old man," the Meskhoni finished for him.

"I didn't mean to be offensive, sir, but—"

"Don't worry about me. Four score and ten is young for a Mage."

Together, they lifted the Red Bear's heavy, limp frame off the ground. The two men held the Red Bear between them with one of his arms over each of their shoulders and let the man's feet drag on the ground behind them.

Each time they went through brush or over a log, the Red Bear moaned. The Meskhoni breathed easily as they dragged the unconscious man, but Renn's father had to stop periodically and rest. During the first of these brief respites, the Meskhoni said, "All right, Renn, tell us what happened."

"And what were you doing out of bed?" his father added.

Renn's heart raced and his palms began to sweat from anxiety. This was a no-win question. He knew a punishment would be coming, but how he responded would determine the magnitude of his penalty. Renn built up the courage to answer, but his lower lip quivered when he spoke.

"He was going to whip me," he finally managed to say, "so I ran. And then the animals—"

He stopped talking. He wanted to say more but lost control when he remembered the sacrifice of the animals on his behalf.

"This won't do at all," the Meskhoni muttered, and he reached once again into the brown leather pouch at his side. He produced a small piece of hard candy and handed it to Renn. "Here, suck on this for a while."

Renn stuffed the treat in his mouth and stopped crying. Not just because he had some candy—a rare treat for sure—but he felt soothing warmth as a sweet mint flavor filled his mouth. The warming sensation coursed through his body limb by limb, until even his toes and fingers felt light and detached. He touched his thumb to his fingers a couple times and stared in wonder at the odd sensation. He knew he controlled the movement, but it felt like he was watching someone else's hand.

"Feel better?" the Meskhoni asked. Renn stood and nodded enthusiastically.

"Good," the Meskhoni said. "Now, tell us everything that happened. I want to hear every detail, no matter how insignificant it may seem."

"I snuck out the back door of our house and looked around to be sure I was alone. Then I ran through our field to the river and crossed over to the forest."

Renn's father interrupted him. "Wait a minute. Why did you sneak out of the house?"

Renn knew he should make up a good excuse, but he couldn't stop talking long enough to think of one. "I was running away," he said matter-of-factly. "Once I got to the forest, I looked back and saw the Red Bear coming out of—"

"Why were you running away?" his father interrupted again.

The Meskhoni stopped walking and looked down at Renn. "What's this about a red bear?"

"That's what the boys call Raul," Renn's father said. "Now, why were you running away, Renn?"

"I heard what Jomard said to you and Momma last week," Renn said. "You thought I was asleep in the loft, but I wasn't. I thought something bad would happen to everyone if I didn't go."

Renn's father looked at him for a long time and then at the Mage. The Meskhoni's thin, dark eyebrows were drawn down, and he rubbed at his chin. At last, Renn's father breathed out slowly and said, "Eavesdropping is a bad habit, Son."

As they continued through the forest, Renn related everything he could remember—which was quite a lot. His mind felt so clear it made him want to tell everything that popped into it—he simply couldn't think of anything without saying it out loud.

He told them his fears as he entered the dark woods and how startled he was when Raul appeared. When he told them of the chase that transpired once he freed himself from Raul, he included every word the big man said—even the bad ones. His father wore a sort of pained expression on his face during that part.

When they finally reached the edge of the forest, Renn was still chattering away. A single lantern burned at the Lucian farm in the distance to the left, but a light was also flickering in his own home across the field. That could only mean one thing—his mother was waiting up. Although part of his mind worried about the severe tongue-lashing she would inevitably give him, he heard his voice continue to repeat every word he thought.

His father was winded by the time they reached the Red Bear's dilapidated farmhouse. A bead of sweat running down the Meskhoni's tan, leathery face was the only indication he was beginning to tire. Inari and the Lucian children, Renaul and Genea, ran out the back door and met them near the chicken coop. Renn looked at the feathers scattered everywhere and felt a stab of guilt. Inari held an oil lamp above her head in one hand. When the flickering light revealed her husband's bloody form, she gasped and covered her mouth with a long, slender hand.

Genea dropped the black-and-white family cat and let out a cry. "Father!" She ran forward, quickly looked him over, turned to the Mage, and—with tears running down her face—asked, "What happened? Is he going to be all right?"

Renaul stopped short behind his mother and watched his sister. He wasn't crying.

"He just needs some rest, child," the Meskhoni promised the little girl. "Why don't you hurry in the house and help your mother get warm water and clean rags?" The Meskhoni looked from Genea to Inari and nodded.

Inari lowered the lamp, but instead of hurrying to the house, she walked forward and considered her husband. In the closer light, Renn saw a swollen bruise on her cheek. Inari briefly looked up to the men holding her husband but then cast her eyes back down to her feet. "Follow me."

She led them to a cluttered sitting room that smelled faintly of mildew and strongly of ale. She motioned them toward an old, battered bench where the Meskhoni and Ehrlich laid Raul's broken body.

The gray-haired Mage turned to Inari. "Put some water on the fire and find me some clean rags."

She nodded, pulled back a strand of long black hair from in front of her eyes, and turned to follow his instructions.

"Go help your mother, child," the Meskhoni said to the sobbing Genea. "We can discuss what happened later." He turned back to Renn's father. The Meskhoni's face was rigid as chiseled stone, but his dark brown eyes gleamed like wells of deep water. "You'd better get this boy home. His mother's probably beside herself with worry by now."

When Renn and his father walked to the front door, the Meskhoni said, "Master Demaris?"

Renn's father stopped and turned. "Yes?"

The old man rubbed his chin and looked up as though he were gazing beyond the ceiling. He looked back at them and said, "Thanks for your help tonight. May I stop by after I finish here?"

Renn's father's lips pulled into a sad smile. He nodded once, rested his hand on Renn's shoulder, and led him out the door.

DISCOVERY

Renn spoke nonstop from the Lucian's deteriorating cabin to the family farmhouse. His ceaseless chatter must have announced their arrival to his mother, because Renn saw her stop pacing and look out the shutters as he and his father walked through the gate and into the yard. She threw open the door, lifted her white cotton nightgown above her bare ankles, and ran out to meet them.

"Renn, I've been worried sick!" She pulled him close and wiped tears from her cheeks. "Are you all right? Where have you been? You know better than to go out at night!"

"I saw a big eagle, but it was really the Meskhoni, and all the animals came—where's Tavier, I've got to tell him—and the Red Bear tried to get me . . ."

His mother raised a single eyebrow.

"The Meskhoni gave him something to make him talk," his father said. "Now he won't stop long enough to take a breath."

Her green eyes grew wide. "The Meskhoni? What was Renn doing with him?" His mother looked up at his father and noticed his bloodstained nightshirt. "What happened? Are you hurt?" She let Renn go and hurried to examine his father.

"Let's go inside." Renn's father put his arm around her shoulder. "I'm all right, but it's a long story."

The front door of their small farmhouse opened into the sitting area of a great room with a long wooden bench in the center that divided the room into equal portions. A smaller bench rested against the opposite wall, next to the back door that led to the field behind the house. Renn's father's favorite chair sat against the wall next to the main door. A small table rested between this chair and a matching chair for Renn's mother.

Renn's mother made him lie down on the center bench and rest his head on one of the straw-filled pillows, which she kept there so a person could sit with a modicum of comfort. The warmth and smell of the small fire coming from the hearth in the kitchen portion of the great room was a comfort after the ordeal with the Red Bear.

Whatever the old Meskhoni gave Renn began to abate, and by the time his father related the story to Renn's mother, Renn's disposition had changed from wide-eyed frenzy to drowsy half consciousness.

Renn heard a soft knock. His mother opened the door, and the Meskhoni stepped inside. She looked at the blood staining his shirt and caught her breath.

"Please, sit down." She directed him to a pillow on the bench next to Renn. "Let me get you some tea, Meskhoni."

"No need to be so formal," the Meskhoni said. "You can call me Artio if you wish."

Renn's mother hurried to the opposite side of the bench where she selected a pair of iron tongs from the assortment of pots and cooking utensils that hung above the kitchen table.

As she removed the teapot from the fireplace, she called over her shoulder, "Ehrlich, would you like some as well?"

"Thank you, dear." Renn's father sat in his reading chair, rubbed wearily at his tired eyes, and pushed his fingers through his sandy brown hair.

While Renn's mother poured the hot drinks, Renn yawned and closed his eyes, pretending to be asleep; however, he kept one eye barely open to see what was happening. His mother covered him with a wool blanket. He struggled against drifting off because he had a feeling the Meskhoni was going to tell them something important—something about him.

"I wanted to speak with both of you tonight." The Meskhoni's deep voice sounded dry, and he cleared his throat. "I was afraid something like this might happen before Renn had proper training. I intended to speak with you before it did . . . I just didn't think it would happen while he was so young."

Renn remained still. If he drew any attention to himself, his mother would surely send him to bed.

"What exactly did he do?" his mother asked.

"He drew upon the *aeon myriad*, but how is not entirely clear to me yet." The Meskhoni tapped his finger on his chin. "Ehrlich, tell me how you and the dog found us so quickly."

"Coy started growling and barking like he'd eaten a bucket full of crazy root. I got up and looked out the back window but couldn't see a thing. Still, Coy kept scratching at the door and growling. Obviously, something was wrong. About that time, Tavier looked down from the loft and asked where Renn was." His father pointed to the loft above the room Renn's parents shared with Chria—his baby sister. "My first thought was someone had taken him, so I threw on my boots and let Coy take the lead. It's strange, come to think of it, but Coy never stopped to get the scent or anything. He ran across the field, through the river and forest, and straight to the box canyon where I found you and Renn."

During the silence that followed his father's tale, Renn slowly opened his eye to see a little better.

"How did *you* know Renn was in danger, Artio?" His mother stood by her husband with one hand on his shoulder. Her blonde hair hung in a long braid instead of up on her head, the way she wore it during the day. "And how did *you* know where to find him?"

"Huh? Oh, I heard him." The Mage vacantly stared past Renn's parents and rubbed at his chin.

Her eyebrows raised. "You *heard* him?"

The Meskhoni turned his attention back to Renn's mother. "Well, I suppose *heard* might not be the best way to describe it, Delphia. It's kind of feeling and hearing him at the same time. Not his voice—his power."

"You heard his power?" his father pressed.

"Oh yes . . . I'm sure every accomplished user of the Azur-Lore within one hundred leagues or more sensed it." The Mage cleared his throat again and took a long sip of tea. His dark eyes grew narrow, and he stared into his cup. "Renn drew upon a great deal of the aeon myriad tonight." He looked up and stared into the distance. "Not many lore users can tap into so much power at one time . . . maybe not any."

Renn barely heard the last few words, even though he was lying right next to the Meskhoni.

Renn's parents stared at the Mage, wide-eyed.

His father took his mother's hand. "I was under the impression that to use *real* sorcery, you had to be schooled in the lore of El Azur. Renn's had no training."

"Knowledge of the lore does come from training," the Meskhoni said, "and the ability to direct the power comes from that knowledge. But the power comes from a person who has been marked by the gods, drawing upon the essence of life itself. It's called a lot of things: the pool of existence or the essence of life. Most often we just refer to it as the aeon myriad. If all it took was knowledge of the runes and symbols, then anybody could be a lore user. One must combine knowledge with power that lies within existence. I've never heard of anyone being able to tap into their power without first being shown how, but, then again, no one has ever been marked as dramatically as Renn, either."

Renn didn't remember being marked during his naming blessing at the midsummer Azur-Aven festival. But he'd heard people talk about it when they didn't think he was listening, and the white eagle on his skin above his right breast made it obvious he was different.

"So Renn was able to call on the power," his father said methodically—the way he did when he was guiding Renn or Tavier through a math problem or helping them solve a riddle. "But because he lacked the knowledge, he couldn't keep it under control."

"Possibly." The old Meskhoni rubbed his dark eyebrows. "However, that doesn't explain how the animals knew where to go. If Renn wasn't in control, the animals wouldn't have known where to find him." The Mage looked back and forth between Renn's parents. "You see, for the animals to know Renn's precise location, he had to project an image into their minds. That would take mental control. The animals saw the box canyon through Renn's eyes, and they saw Raul as a dangerous enemy. Even more, somehow, Renn compelled the animals to attack because, normally, woodland creatures would simply run or hide from an enemy."

Forgetting about pretending to be asleep, Renn sat up and stared at the Meskhoni. He didn't quite follow the Mage's reasoning, but it sounded like he'd done something wrong.

His mother looked at the Meskhoni, whose face remained the same as when he finished giving his explanation—tired, yet resolute. His eyes were solidly fixed on Renn's parents as if waiting for a response.

Renn's mother's voice was barely above a whisper when she finally spoke. "What are we supposed to do? How can we make certain something like this won't happen again?"

The Meskhoni shifted slightly in his seat and cleared his throat. "I don't believe you can do anything. The only alternative I see is to put the boy in the care of someone who can help him learn to control his power." He looked at Renn and added, "And protect him."

"Are you suggesting we give him to you?!" Ehrlich's eyes opened wide, and he leaned forward in his rocker.

"Me? Oh no, no . . . not me." The old man held his hands up and shook his head. "Me raise a child?" he said softer and chuckled. "An old badger like me wouldn't have time or patience for such nonsense. No, I suggest I write to Salas—the High Lore Master of Elder Island—and apprise him of the situation. I would recommend that Renn be sent to live with suitable godparents. Frequently, students at the school of lore fall in love and marry. I'm sure Salas could find a responsible couple—"

"No!" Renn's mother interrupted the Mage loudly and stepped forward. "I have to give my son up soon enough as it is. I refuse to lose him while he's still a baby!"

"I'm not a baby," Renn protested, and immediately realized his mistake.

His mother pointed to the loft. "To bed, young man."

Renn's mouth dropped open. "But, Mother—"

"Now!" Her lips, which were usually full and a bit pouty, were pressed into thin lines. Her green eyes were alight with fire.

Renn stomped up the ladder. He stopped halfway and looked back to argue, but thought better of it when his mother impatiently added, "Go on."

Renn's older brother, Tavier, was lying near the edge of the loft, listening to the conversation. He raised a finger to his lips when Renn climbed over—signaling for him to be quiet. The light from the fireplace in the great room below interrupted the darkness of the loft so that flickering shadows allowed the boys to see one another. They kept far enough from the edge that their parents wouldn't see them if they looked up.

"I understand how you must feel, my good lady—"

"No, you don't! How could you? *You've never been a father. You've* never had to love and raise a child, knowing all the while that in a few short years you'd have to send him away." She was crying. Renn heard it in her shaky voice.

Renn and Tavier looked at each other in the half light of their attic-like bedroom. Neither of them had ever heard their mother so upset. The only other time they'd seen her cry was when their grandmother had died. Renn's stomach twisted in knots.

"I apologize," the Meskhoni said. "Of course you're right. I cannot completely understand your feelings. However, the situation is urgent, and there's more involved than you realize."

"What do you mean?" Renn's father asked. "What else is involved?"

"It's *who* else that's involved really," the Meskhoni said, "not *what*. Do you remember the evening of the festival after I performed Renn's naming blessing, Ehrlich? I told you there would be those who would seek his life."

"Yes," their father admitted. "I remember."

"You never told me that." Their mother's voice was sharp and a little louder.

"There was nothing either of us could do about it. I didn't want you to be worried."

"I wasn't referring to the likes of Raul," the Meskhoni continued. "There are ancient prophecies that speak of certain events and a great shifting of power that will occur when these events take place. Some people believe the time is now or very soon. Some want to help these events move along and place themselves in a position to benefit from the circumstance; others would like to stop it altogether."

"What does any of that have to do with Renn?" Renn's father pressed.

Artio paused a moment before answering, then said deliberately, "He is the reason many feel the time is soon. When the gods marked him on midsummer's Azur-Aven, every magic user in Lemuria knew someone with great power had been born. When the gods do something, you feel the power everywhere. When Renn used the power tonight, it marked his location to anyone skilled in the Azur-Lore. Although they won't know for certain it was Renn who wielded the power, they will be curious enough to investigate."

"Just who are these *others*?" Renn's mother asked.

"Certainly, the demons under the Cragg Mountains will be interested when they learn of it, and they'll likely send Kirocs to investigate—"

"Come now," Renn's father said. "Demons and Kirocs are just a myth—children's stories told around campfires."

"Are you so sure?" the old man replied.

Renn swallowed deeply and cast a scared glance toward his older brother.

"Just because you don't see something," the Meskhoni continued, "don't assume it isn't real. Still, the most likely enemies will appear to be ordinary men and women. The worst part about it is we won't always know whom we can trust. Friends and relatives can become enemies and spies when power and riches are involved. The Tahsz Codex prophesies of a great shift in the balance of power, and there are many who lust for that power."

Tavier stared at Renn like he was a stranger who had crept into the house.

"Stop that!" Renn whispered. He inched a little closer to the edge of the loft, careful to not cause the hardwood slats to creak, and turned his attention back to the conversation below.

"You said certain events have to take place before this . . . shift in power occurs," their father prodded. "What are the other events?"

"'*But two shall come with strength in their wings—being marked great—and then will great evil be destroyed and the dark side rule.*' That is a passage from the Tahsz Codex, the prophecy that speaks of the shift of power."

"That doesn't make sense," their mother said. "If great evil is destroyed, how can the dark side rule?"

"Well . . . the prophecies aren't usually very clear."

"What about the other one?" Renn's father asked with hope in his voice. "The prophecy mentions *two* with great strength."

"Another was born up north in Andrika and marked on midsummer's Azur-Aven two years after Renn's blessing," the old Meskhoni replied gravely. "His blessing, I am told, was similar to Renn's, but instead of an eagle above his right breast, he has a spear."

Several moments passed before Renn's father spoke again. "In light of what Artio has told us, maybe we should reconsider, dear."

"No." She didn't even hesitate to consider it. Renn felt ashamed. Even after all he put his mother through tonight, and even though he was a danger for the whole family, she still loved him. The fervency of her answer made that clear. "I think if someone were looking for Renn so hard, they would have found us already. It's no secret Renn's blessing was unusual. I'm not giving up my son just because people *might* be looking for him."

"Not just people, Delphia," the Meskhoni said. "Very powerful people. And for all we know, they have been watching since the day he was blessed and just biding their time, waiting for the right moment to make their move."

"Is there any way you can protect him while he's living here?" Renn's father asked the Meskhoni.

Again, the old man paused, looked up, and rubbed at his chin. "I could place a shield around your home to keep out intrusion from sorcery; however, that would be like putting up a beacon. And it wouldn't do anything to stop a person with evil intent from just walking right through the front door. All we can really do is keep our eyes and ears open and be prepared to act in a moment's notice." Renn heard the bench squeak as if somebody stood up. "You know where I live if you change your mind?"

"My mind is made up, Artio," their mother answered firmly. "Renn stays with the family until his fourteenth birthday; then he can go to Elder Island like every other Apprentice."

"We appreciate your concern, great one," Renn's father said. "We'll be very careful."

"Very well, Ehrlich. If you change your mind, please let me know."

"We will," Renn's father said.

Renn heard the door close, and his mother burst into tears again. He heard his father softly comfort her.

Renn tried to sleep, but the image of his crying mother played in his mind as he tossed and turned.

THE BEAR WAKES

"Mother," Renn said as he and his mother walked through an opening in the Lucian's fence where a gate used to be. "How come I have to play with Genea? You're supposed to be tending her. Why don't you play with her and let me go play with Tavier and Renaul?" All that remained of the gate lay broken and rotting on the ground, along with several other battered sections of what was, at one time, a white picket fence.

"I am tending her, dear," she answered, and her full lips turned up slightly. "I'm tending both of you. Besides, Genea's not a bad girl. In time, you may learn to like her."

Renn doubted that very much, and he made a show of sulking as they walked past broken and discarded tools and dusty pieces of ripped canvas. Swarms of flies attacked a large pile of decomposing garbage that smelled like a mix of rotting food and manure. The front door of the small wooden shack where the Red Bear and his family lived was in desperate need of paint. When Renn's mother knocked, a stream of dust and dirt fell from the doorframe.

Someone on the other side of the door struggled to open it, first with the rusty latch and second with a loose hinge that caused the door to drop at an angle. When the door finally opened, the sun hit Genea's face, and she squinted and gave them a sad smile.

"Thank you for coming," she said politely. Her face flushed, and she looked down at her feet. She stepped aside to let them in.

The home smelled of alcohol, sweat, and cat urine. Renn's eyes slowly adjusted to the dim light that seeped through a partially opened shutter and several thin cracks between the planks of wood in the walls, and he saw a big lump lying on a straw-covered pallet in the front corner of the room—the Red Bear.

A few moments later, Genea's mother walked in from a door at the back of the room that led into the backyard. When she saw Renn and his mother, she set the basin of water she held on the lone table and crossed the room to greet them.

"Delphia, you're so kind to offer to help," she said softly, "but it really isn't necessary. I'm sure you have many things to do at your farm."

Renn agreed wholeheartedly. They had plenty of other things to do, and he would rather be doing *any* of those other things. He looked at his mother with hope. They did their duty by offering to help, and now they could just leave.

"Nonsense," his mother said. "You would do the same for me, were I in need of help."

Renn let out a sigh and scowled.

His mother started issuing commands as though the matter were settled. "Genea and Renn, go feed the chickens and clean the coop. And don't let any of them get out." She looked pointedly at Renn, as if to say, *That's what started all this trouble to begin with.*

Renn felt awkward working with Genea. For a long time, neither of them spoke. When Genea finally did talk, she went straight to the subject Renn wanted to avoid.

"What were you doing with my father last night in the forest?" she asked.

"Nothing."

She stopped working, placed her hands on her hips, and gave Renn a hard look. "Really? You expect me to believe that?"

Renn shrugged his shoulders, resumed shoveling a pile of chicken mess, and tried to ignore her. She stomped across the small coop and punched him in the arm.

"Ow!" Renn was surprised by how hard she could hit.

"Renn Demaris, my father is almost dead, and he was with you last night! What happened?"

"It wasn't my fault," he protested and took a step back. "He was trying to beat me for letting the chickens out, so I ran. The next thing I know, he got attacked by a bunch of animals."

She pursed her lips and put her hands on her hips once more. "How come the animals didn't attack you?"

"I don't know."

She glared at him, and Renn kicked at a pile of manure. Genea harrumphed and stomped away to the seed bin. She didn't say another word. She simply finished scattering seeds for the chickens.

⁂

The next day, after they finished cleaning the mess in front of the house—including burying the pungent garbage pile—Renn and Genea were allowed to go play. "Just stay nearby and don't get into trouble," his mother warned, and they quickly left before she changed her mind and assigned them another job.

Renn still didn't want to play with Genea, but it was better than doing chores. They walked through the field behind Genea's home to the river that ran along the back of their fields and separated the farms from the Hebät Mountains, and they sat on the bank.

"See that stump on the other side of the river?" Renn asked.

Genea looked to where he pointed and nodded.

"Betcha I can hit it more times in a row than you can."

"You practice throwing more than I do, Renn," Genea said. But she picked up a handful of stones and stood to take up his challenge. After playing that game for a while, they changed it up to see who could skip a stone the most times down the lazy river.

Genea beat Renn four tosses in a row. He held up his hand, and she stopped in the middle of a laugh because she just skipped a stone eight times—three more than Renn's best.

"Wait a minute," Renn said.

"What's wrong?" She grinned. "You can't take being bested by a girl in a dress?"

"No, I'm serious. Be quiet." He signaled for her to stay still, and he stared across the river into the forest.

"What are you looking at?" she whispered, stepping closer to him and following his gaze.

Renn shook his head slowly. "I'm not sure, but I think . . . something is in the shadows . . . like unseen eyes staring."

"Are you trying to frighten me, Renn?"

He squinted, but he couldn't see anybody. Still, he felt malevolence emanating from a dark shadow under a thick stand of pines.

"Come on." He backed nervously away. "Let's go play somewhere else."

"Okay," she said happily. "I'll race you to your barn!" She shoved him to the ground and took off running across the field toward Renn's farm. Renn stared at the shadow for a moment longer, and then scrambled to his feet and ran after Genea.

Renn's favorite place to play was his family's barn. It wasn't large, but it had a hayloft, rafters to climb, a wagon, and their two workhorses—Dusty, with her light brown coat, and Ranger, a dappled gelding. After playing hiding games, they put a tall pile of musty-smelling straw on the ground below the loft door and took turns jumping into it.

"Your hair looks like a raccoon just raided a bird's nest." Renn laughed and pointed at the stiff pieces of yellow straw sticking out in every direction from her brown curls. Genea punched him in the arm and stuck her tongue out at him.

"Ow, what was that for?"

Genea didn't answer. She rolled out of the stack, brushed herself off, and picked straw out of her hair. She looked at the wagon and got a strange, excited expression on her face.

"Let's pretend we're going to a ball at the king's palace!" She ran to the wagon and climbed on to the seat. "You can be the driver, and I'll be a lady of the court."

Renn didn't like the sound of that idea, but he did fancy pretending to drive a team of powerful steeds as they charged over the countryside.

"Renn, we aren't chasing villians," Genea complained when he yelled at the imaginary horses and drew his pretend long sword, prepared to charge into battle. "We're going to a fancy ball."

When they arrived at the palace, she made Renn get off first and help her down, as though he were a servant, and then he had to announce her as Lady Genea of Leedsdale when they entered the ballroom.

"Okay, now you are a lord who has noticed me," Genea said, "so you have to bow and ask me if I'd like to dance."

"*Dance?*" Renn protested. "I don't know how to dance. Besides, you said I'm your driver."

"I can teach you. It's easy," she answered.

"Forget it. I am not dancing!" Renn said. "Especially not with a girl."

By the time the end of the week arrived, Renn was surprised to realize that he was beginning to enjoy Genea's company—although he wasn't about to admit it to the other boys.

One morning, as he and his mother knocked on the Lucians' door, Renn thought about how he would take Genea to his secret fishing hole. The main room of Genea's house no longer smelled bad—in fact, it smelled like fresh bread and fried eggs. Renn's mother had spent the last several days cleaning the entire home, repairing much of the chinking between the wallboards, and helping Genea's mother get caught up with laundry. Genea's mother was cheerful and greeted them with a hearty smile as she opened the door to them.

When they walked into the room, the Red Bear groaned and opened his eyes. His face was bruised. An angry, fresh scar ran from his left eye to his chin. Renn and his mother paused at the foot of the pallet the Red Bear rested on.

"Raul!" Genea's mother hurried to his side. "You're finally awake. How are you feeling?"

Upon seeing Renn, he coughed and in a hoarse whisper demanded, "What's that demon child doing here? *Get out!*"

Renn's stomach felt sick, and he quickly moved behind his mother. His heart pounded in his chest, and he was afraid to even breathe.

Genea's mother knelt by her husband's side and changed the hot towel on his forehead. "They've been so helpful to me while you were sick, Raul." She adjusted the blanket covering him, and the Red Bear reached up and slapped her across the face with the back of his big hand, sending her sprawling onto the floor.

"How could you be so foolish? You stupid wench! This boy is *possessed*! How do you think I got injured in the first place?"

Renn felt his mother tense up, and Genea cried out and ran to her mother's side. The Red Bear struggled to sit up. He glared at Renn and, in a voice dripping with venom, hissed, "*Get out!* I never want to see you on my land again!"

Renn looked up at his mother. Her jaw was rigid, and her eyes were narrowed. She took a deep breath, and for a moment he thought she was about to lecture the Red Bear. But instead, Renn's mother took his hand, turned around, and walked out the door.

DEMON FIRE

Avaris Mordrahn laced his thick, knee-high moccasins and tied them tight. The warm fur lining tickled his feet in a good way. He pulled on his favorite buckskin shirt and then slipped a bone knife under the leather strap he used for a belt. He didn't put on the new buffalo coat he'd received on his eighth birthday the week before. This he would carry with him until he and his father, Akusaa—the high clan chief—were near the peaks of the Mord Mountains. With his finger, he traced one of the black buffalo dyed into the coat; there were several, which his mother had arranged into a circular pattern around the front and back of the garment. The charging black buffalo was his family's insignia, and he was proud to wear it—no matter what the warriors from the other clans said about his father. His father and his grandfathers had been the high clan chiefs of the Andrikan Devi for more than one hundred and twenty years. No other family had held that honor for so long in the history of his people.

He placed a necklace that held five white dove feathers around his neck, and pride swelled in his chest. The necklace signified he was the son of the high clan chief. The feathers symbolized courage, honor, bravery, strength, and rule. Only his family was allowed to wear five dove feathers. His younger brother, Toci, chose to wear his in a headdress, but Avaris found that too cumbersome.

After he braided his long black hair and tied it off with a leather thong, he stepped out of the large tent into the center of the Devi-Hold. Although it was still morning, the hold was busier than usual. All the Andrikan Devi tribes were gathered for the summer months at the main hold—the only permanent year-round settlement for the Andrikan Devi. Avaris's clan lived here all the time because his father was high clan chief, but the other clans were only here during the four warmest months of summer. It wouldn't be long before the last Azur-Aven of summer, so people were busy making preparations.

Avaris stood on the platform just outside the door of their tent and scanned the crowd for his father. Akusaa was in the center of the inner circle of tents—not far from where Avaris stood—and he was shouting at Lokia, one of his advisors. Avaris hurried down the steps and crossed to join them. His father's hair was black like Avaris's, but not nearly as well-kept. It looked as though he hadn't washed it in months. It was mostly pulled back from his face and tied in a braid that hadn't been loosed for days, but several matted strands worked free and hung in his eyes and around his ears.

Avaris heard his father shouting as he approached. "I don't care about tradition! I am the high clan chief. I make my own traditions."

"Yes, you are, and you are completely within your rights to do as you wish," Lokia calmly replied. His hair was black, too, but cut short and receding some on both sides of his head. Unlike Akusaa, he was always clean and well-dressed. The orange and brown patterns in his shirt complemented his buckskin pants nicely. "But what about the Mordvins?" he continued. "They would not hesitate to attack a single man and a small boy—and it doesn't matter to them that you are the high clan chief."

Avaris knew little about the Mordvin tribes who roamed the Mord Mountains. He'd never seen them, but everybody knew they were cannibals. They were a small people. It would take several of them to defeat a single Devi warrior, but they were ruthless and quick. Akusaa's mouth worked silently for a moment, and then he stopped, a distant look in his eyes. He mumbled to himself and turned to look toward the Mord Mountains across the river. Avaris couldn't make out what his father was saying—he never could when he got like this. But he did pick out "might work" and "better" among the unintelligible ramblings.

"Father?" Avaris said cautiously, tugging on his father's coat. "I'm ready."

Akusaa looked at him for a moment, then turned back to Lokia. "I am taking my son on a hunt," he spat. "I don't need any protection. Extra men will just make more noise and scare the prey." Avaris noticed his mother and brother, Toci, were standing to the side—also listening to the exchange.

"Please, my husband," his mother said, her voice shaking slightly. "I know you are strong, but I fear for Avaris."

"Ha!" he shouted, and the veins in his forehead and neck bulged. "Fear for Avaris? Is he not the *great one*? Is he not the *promised child*? If the gods love him, they'll protect him!"

Avaris was a little embarrassed by being referred to as the "great one" and the "promised child." And the way his father emphasized his words, it sounded more like a curse than a blessing. And now others were looking.

"Yes, Chief, your son is special," Lokia said. "All the more reason you should not go alone."

"I am the clan chief!" Akusaa's face was red, and spittle clung to his thick mustache and dripped onto his wiry, unkempt beard. "You all worry more about a boy than your leader! My son and I go alone, and that's final." With that, he picked up his pack and threw it over his shoulder, grabbed the three spears he'd leaned against a tree, and headed for the gate that led to the banks of the Andrus River. Avaris's mother watched his father leave, and the boy saw tears rolling down her cheeks. She looked at Avaris and hurried to him. She embraced him so tightly he had difficulty breathing.

"I'm just going on a hunt, Mother," he said, a little confused. "I'll be back."

"Avaris!" Akusaa shouted over his shoulder. "Come now."

His mother released him and took a step back. She looked like she was drinking his image with her eyes. Then she burst into tears and ran to the tent. Avaris watched her vanish behind the tent flap and then turned to Lokia, whose face looked like a warrior who had just lost an important battle. None of this made any sense. *We're just going on a hunt,* he thought. *Warriors go on hunts all the time.*

"You'd better join your father," Lokia said. "He doesn't take well to waiting."

Avaris picked up the pack his father left for him and, with Lokia's help, got it onto his back. After he'd fallen into step beside his father, he said, "Father, why is Mother so sad?"

His father grunted a bit and mumbled something under his breath as they walked out the gate and toward a large canoe tied by the river's edge.

"Does she think I'm going to get hurt or something?" Avaris asked while they threw their supplies into the canoe.

"No one can know the mind of a woman," his father said. He untied the rope from the tree holding the canoe in place. "Might as well learn that while you're young." He pushed the canoe into the current, pointed for Avaris to climb in, and then hopped in after him. "Not a trustworthy one among 'em . . . Stab you when you're down, they will, and throw you out like a husk, only to reach for the next ripe fruit." He continued mumbling to himself and ignored Avaris, which was just as well. None of what he said made any sense, and Avaris didn't like where the conversation was going.

The river level was down from what it had been a month ago, but whitecap rapids still churned with snowmelt from the Mord Mountains. His father didn't need to paddle as much. Instead, he used the oars for a rudder to steer them through the rapids. The occasional spray of cold water felt good on Avaris's cheeks. They continued this way for about an hour and then put out on the west bank near the base of the mountains. After a meal of dried meat and nuts, they started up a path that led into the thick pines. The forest floor was soft with old pine needles, but fresh new pine needles filled the air with their scent.

It seemed to Avaris they would never stop hiking. At least the shade from the trees and mountain air kept him somewhat cool, but the mosquitoes were thick and he couldn't wait to make camp and eat a good meal. His father hadn't spoken to him since the canoe ride, and Avaris wasn't about to start a conversation. When his father got withdrawn this way, Avaris learned from experience that it was best to keep quiet and stay out of the way. He didn't want to say something that would make his father regret taking him on a hunt. This was Avaris's first time on a real hunt, and he wanted to be sure he was invited on many more.

When the shadows of the mountain peaks were so long they reached as far east as Avaris could see, he asked, "Father, should we look for a place to make camp?"

"Hmm?" Akusaa said and turned to look at his son as if he wondered how long he'd been following him. After a moment, his father looked up at the sky and then scanned their surroundings. "Yes . . . camp . . ." He kept mumbling, turned, and walked toward a thicker stand of pines. Avaris followed. The brief stop made him realize how tired his legs were. His pack was light compared with his father's, but he'd never walked this far before.

"We'll sleep here tonight," Akusaa said, dropping his pack against a large, flat boulder set into the mountainside.

"Shall I gather wood for a fire?"

"No!" his father shouted, his face momentarily flushed with anger. "If there are any Mordvins in the area, that will draw them like dogs to a carcass. Use whatever brain you've got in that skull of yours, boy."

Avaris looked to his feet and wished he'd just stayed quiet. He set his pack down and dropped beside it.

His father tossed Avaris some dried meat and a skin of water. "Here. Have something to eat and then sleep. We have a long way to go in the morning."

The next two days were a repeat of the first. Avaris tried a couple of times to start up conversation but was always met with a curt response. The air grew colder now. They were high enough in the mountains they occasionally passed unmelted patches of snow. Avaris wore his coat in the mornings and evenings. The first two days, he wished he'd left the coat behind but now he was glad he hadn't.

That night, as they sat across from each other eating their ration of dried meat, nuts, and water, his father finally relaxed and began talking. "You know," he said, biting into a chunk of dried meat, "a lot of people have disappeared in these mountains."

Avaris looked at the trees and the dark shadows created by the setting sun. His father took a long drag of water and wiped at his wiry, thin beard. "They get lost . . . can't find their way home. Killed by wild animals . . . maybe eaten by the Mordvins—who knows." He quit looking at his food and stared at Avaris. "If you were alone out here, I doubt you'd last more than a day." He watched Avaris a moment longer and then returned to his meal.

Avaris swallowed hard and scanned the trees to see if anything was moving. "But, you're with me . . . so I don't have to worry . . . huh?"

His father took another bite of meat and a long drink from the waterskin, but his eyes never looked away from Avaris.

"Right, Father?" Avaris asked again. "You're with me and you know the tricks to surviving in the mountains . . . so we'll be okay."

"Just pray we don't get separated," he answered and tossed a handful of nuts into his mouth.

The next day, they walked beyond the tree line. The snow grew deeper, and the air colder.

"Father, when are we going to start hunting?" Avaris asked at one point. He realized he wasn't even sure what animal was to be their prey. His father only glared at him and continued his relentless march. That night, they took shelter by the side of a cliff under an outcrop that offered scant protection from the elements. Sometime during the night, it snowed, and no matter how tight he pulled his buffalo coat and blankets around him, Avaris was still cold.

He must have fallen asleep at some point, because he awoke to the bright glare of the sun reflecting off a new layer of snow. He shook the remnants of snow from his blanket and sat up. He looked around but didn't see his father.

"Father?"

His father's sleeping mat was missing. Avaris stuffed his blanket into his pack, and it occurred to him that his father's pack was missing. His heart raced. *Why wouldn't Father wake me?* he wondered. *What if wild animals or the Mordvins find me alone?*

"Father!" Avaris ran out of from under the outcrop. *Maybe he woke early and went to scout for game,* Avaris thought. "Father!" he shouted. His father must have left some time ago because there were no footprints—the fresh blanket of snow had covered them.

Slowly, Avaris walked back to their campsite and sat. He would just have to wait until his father returned. He pulled his buffalo coat over his knees and traced one of the charging buffalo with his finger. When the sun was high overhead and his stomach grumbled, he decided he would try to find his father after all. Perhaps his father couldn't find his way back to camp since the snow covered his tracks. Avaris tightened the laces of his boots, grabbed his pack, took one last look at the campsite, and then trudged out into the snow.

As the sun was getting low, another storm rushed in. Avaris was stunned by how quickly it changed from sunny warmth to windy darkness. The snow flurries whipped at his face, and he shouted repeatedly, "Father! Where are you?" His voice grew hoarse from shouting. He topped a small ridge, and his footing gave way. The other side was steep, and he slid for a good fifty steps before he grabbed on to a bush and stopped himself.

He dug snow out of his boots and from under his cloak, and then blew on his fingers and rubbed his hands together to try to warm them. His stomach growled, but the pockets of his buffalo cloak were empty and his father had taken the pack with all the food when he left. The storm was building strength, and he had no idea where he was or what he was going to do. Avaris's eyes filled with tears, and he cried. He missed his mother so badly. He would give anything at that moment to be home in their warm tent right now. She was probably eating supper with Toci and his older sister, Kalisha, at that very moment. Thinking about it made him cry even harder.

"Avaris."

He heard a woman's voice speak his name. He looked up but couldn't see far through the snow and his tears. He must have imagined it.

"Avaris." Someone placed a hand on his shoulder, and he whipped around, hoping against hope it was his mother. However, the saggy, round face staring at him from beneath the brown wool hood was spotted with red marks. He screamed and fell back.

"Don't be frightened, Avaris," the ugly woman said. "I won't harm you." Her large nose and thin mouth twitched in an odd fashion. She was nearly as wide as she was tall, and under her cowl a few dark moles dotted her round face.

"H-h-how do you know my name?" he asked. He tried to back away farther, but he was pressed up against a scrub bush that scratched the back of his neck.

"I know many things." She hesitated for a moment, and then said, "Like I know your father abandoned you to die in these mountains."

"No, he didn't!" Avaris shouted. "He just went to scout, and I'm trying to find him!"

The woman pulled her hood back and leaned closer. Her hair was red and thinning and much shorter than any women he'd seen—it barely covered her neck.

"Come with me, Avaris." She reached to take his hand. "You'll die if you stay out here."

He flinched away. "No. I can't. I have to find my father."

"Your father is gone, Avaris. He's not coming back."

Avaris stood and sidestepped around her. She wasn't much taller than he was, but she was easily three or four times as wide. "I don't even know you," he yelled over the wind. "You're lying to me!" He turned and ran through the storm, clutching his coat and dragging his pack behind. He didn't know where he was going, but he knew if he went down the mountainside, he would eventually reach the Andrus River. From there, he could make his way back home.

He stumbled frequently as he ran, but he kept getting back to his feet and pressing forward. Night fell, but he didn't dare stop. Maybe once he was below the snow line he would stop. It would be a little drier and warmer there. He stumbled again, but this time he wasn't able to regain his feet. Something had wrapped around them and he couldn't stand up. Before he realized what was happening, he felt a stinging sensation on each wrist, and then his arms were yanked outward in either direction. He looked at his right wrist and saw a whiplike cord wrapped around it, and then he saw his attackers. Dozens of small men, not much bigger than him, jumped out of the bushes and tied his hands and legs to a long wooden pole. Their skin was only slightly darker than his, but they shaved their heads, and their faces and bodies were tattooed with white patterns. His captors picked up the pole, two men on each end, and carried him away.

"Help!" Avaris shouted over and over, but he knew his cries were lost in the wind. His face stung as bushes whipped across his cheeks. He saw by the position of the stars they were taking him north and angling down the mountain slopes—at least they weren't headed back into the snow. Not that it mattered anymore. It occurred to him this would probably be his last night alive. His father was right. He wouldn't survive a day out here on his own.

Where is my father? he wondered for at least the hundredth time. *Maybe the ugly woman was right.*

"No!" he shouted out loud. He wouldn't believe his father left him on purpose. *But then . . . a lot of people think Father is mad . . . maybe . . .*

Avaris remembered his mother crying just before he left, and it occurred to him that the dumpy old woman in the mountains was right. *But why?* he wondered, and a new stream of tears burned his eyes and ran down his cheeks. And why did his mother let him go if she knew his father was going to kill him? But he knew the answer to that: she had no choice. It wasn't a woman's place to go against her husband. Especially if her husband happened to be a crazy high clan chief.

Avaris didn't pay attention to where the little savages were carrying him. He knew they'd been traveling for hours, and he knew his wrists and ankles burned, but it didn't matter. Even if he did manage to get away, he had nothing and no one to go to.

They entered a large clearing in the forest with a bonfire raging in the center. Because of the way he dangled from the pole, Avaris felt the heat and smelled the burning wood before he saw the flames. Circling the fire were dozens more of the Mordvins—dancing, singing, and beating on drums. Behind the little cannibals was a cluster of tents. They carried Avaris toward the center of the clearing, closer to the flames. He saw two wooden stands that would hold the pole he was tied to above the fire. His captors marched to the beat of the drums toward the fire. *They aren't even going to kill me first,* Avaris realized. He would be roasted above the fire like a pig on a spit . . . but at least the pigs he'd seen cooked this way had been killed before being placed over the hot flames.

Avaris screamed and wiggled as much as his bonds would allow. The butt of a spear jabbed him in the ribs, knocking the wind out of him. His eyes grew wide. The fire drew nearer, and he felt like his heart was going to pound out of his chest. From the very pit of his stomach, a burning sensation rose. It was small at first, but expanded as quickly as fire through the dry, grassy plains during an Andrikan summer. His wide eyes saw only the burning flames of the bonfire; his body felt only the burning sensation building in his chest and spreading throughout his limbs. The burning grew until he hurt with the immensity of it. He heard screaming and felt the sound rip from his throat, but he was somehow separated from it. He sensed his body was falling and his limbs were no longer tied. He hit the ground, and it jarred him back into his immediate surroundings.

He lay on the ground a good five paces from the bonfire, the wooden pole he'd been tied to burning on the ground only an arm's length away. The three Mordvins who had been carrying him now screamed, rolling in the dirt around him, trying to extinguish the flames that consumed their bodies. But the flames wouldn't be extinguished. The three who had been holding the pole writhed and screamed. Other Mordvins doused them with water until the three could writhe and scream no more. They stopped moving, but the flames continued until their bodies were entirely consumed.

Avaris still had a burning sensation in his chest, but instead of pain, he felt intoxicating power. Flames that smelled of sulfur licked the ends of his fingertips, but rather than consume his flesh, the flame begged to be freed. He looked up to see a dozen Mordvins cautiously advancing toward him, spears raised and ready to be thrown.

"No!" He pointed his hands at them and yelled at the top of his lungs. "You're not going to take me again!" Angry torrents of fire shot from his fingertips.

The cannibals who had stood in front of him only moments before were now writhing on the ground as flames ravaged their bodies. The tents and trees behind them had also caught fire from the force of Avaris's attack, the flames eagerly jumping to the surrounding trees and bushes. The rest of the Mordvin tribe screamed as they rushed toward the sections of forest that weren't on fire.

"Avaris, stop!" a woman shouted from behind him.

Avaris turned and saw the ugly old woman. She was waddling down the mountain slope toward him. In one hand, she held a human skull and, in the other, what looked to be a human leg bone. She waved the leg bone above the skull in a circular pattern, drawing closer and chanting in a monotonous voice. The skull glowed an eerie red color that expanded with each pass of the leg bone. She stopped at Avaris's side, and her chanting grew louder as the red glow expanded around her body. She held the skull high above her head and pointed the leg bone toward the section of trees that were engulfed in flames. Red energy shot from the eye sockets of the skull and encircled the burning trees. Once all the trees were surrounded by the strange red glow, she made a cutting gesture with the leg bone, said a few strange words in a guttural-sounding tongue, and sat on the ground.

She was breathing heavy, and Avaris saw perspiration running down her forehead and chin. He looked back at the trees. The red glow still surrounded them and the fires still burned. Avaris no longer felt the burning sensation in his chest or intoxicating power, but he felt something else . . . a different burning pain. As he watched each tree get consumed by fire, the pain intensified until it felt his very soul was being seared.

"Ohhh—" he cried out, and he fell to his knees. "Can't you make it stop? It hurts."

"What hurts?" she asked.

"The trees. Please, put out the fires."

"Avaris, I can't," she said, shaking her head. "That isn't just ordinary fire you unleashed. That's Demon Flame. It has to burn itself out—I can only keep it from spreading."

Avaris's eyes opened wide, and his stomach felt twisted and sick as what she said sunk in.

"You mean, I'm going to feel their pain until the trees burn to the ground?"

The old lady stared at him from under the cowl of a cloak that was too large for her, then looked to the trees and back to him. "You *feel* the pain of the trees?"

"Yes!" he screamed. "They're burning because of me—I burned them when I burned the Mordvins."

"I've never heard of such a thing, Avaris," she said, pulling out a dirty red handkerchief and wiping her forehead. Her mouth twitched spastically for a moment while she considered him. Then she took out a waterskin and handed it to him. "Drink this," she said. "It might help."

The cool water wetting his tongue and throat did help a little, but Avaris sat hunched in a ball for the next thirty minutes, crying and burning up inside until finally, mercifully, the last tree was entirely consumed and the pain died with the fire. The ugly woman was still there when his suffering ended. She handed him some berries and dried meat, and he greedily ate. Never before had food tasted so good. It felt like years since he'd eaten. When he finished, he wiped at his eyes and pushed his long black hair off his face.

"Why?" he whispered, and tears started to fall again. "Why did he leave me?"

The old woman shook her head for a moment, and then said, "Fear."

Avaris stopped crying and looked up at her. "What do you mean?"

"You were a threat to him," she said. "You are a great Child of the Blessing . . . perhaps one of those prophesied by the Tahsz Codex." The last words she spoke softly, thoughtfully.

"But . . . I'm his son," Avaris said. "Why would he fear me?"

"*Because* you are his son, he fears you." She passed Avaris a handful of nuts, but he didn't eat. Now that his hunger wasn't gnawing at him like an infected wound, he had no more appetite. "You will soon be so powerful," she continued, her mouth and nose twitching again, "you'll be able to do almost anything you can imagine. Then he wouldn't be able to keep you from taking his place as high clan chief, if that's what you want."

"But I don't want that," Avaris protested.

"No. Probably not," she agreed. "At least . . . not yet."

Avaris stared at the dirt and kicked at stones lying on the ground. After a little while, something else occurred to him. "Who are you?"

"Myrrah. My name is Myrrah."

"I mean . . ." Avaris struggled for the right words. "Are you . . . a . . . Witch or something?"

She stood, walking to the fire where the Mordvins had intended to cook him, and warmed her hands. The fire was much smaller now than when Avaris had been tied to the roasting pole.

"I'm a Necromancer," she said. "In the Aven-Lore, that's one level beyond Witch."

In the light of the fire, the red blemishes that marred her round face really stood out. Her puffy cheeks and thin mouth reminded him of a prairie dog with its cheeks stuffed with nuts and no hair on its face. Watching her warm herself made Avaris realize he was cold, too. He stood and joined her.

"What does that mean, Necro . . . whatever and Aven-Lore?"

"I'll explain it to you in time. For now, you only need to know that you will become a powerful Warlock of the Aven-Lore." She peered into his eyes. If she was looking for some reaction, she would be disappointed. Avaris was numb. In less than a day he'd been abandoned by his father, been captured by cannibals, and produced enough fire to destroy his enemies and lay waste to dozens of majestic trees. These revelations from Myrrah paled in comparison. At length, she added, "That is, if you let me help you."

With that, she turned and waddled down the mountain. The predawn sky gave up scant light, and soon she was little more than a shadow. Avaris watched her pick her way through the smoldering ash and disappear into the thick trees beyond. The ground was charred where the Mordvin warriors had once stood. The drums and spears still lay where the frightened tribe had left them to flee from the Demon Fire. Avaris had no idea how he'd called upon such power and wasn't sure he could do it again. His heart raced at the thought of being alone. If he returned to the hold, his father would find another way to kill him. If he tried to survive in the mountains on his own, the Mordvins, wild animals, or starvation would kill him.

Avaris took a deep breath, squared his shoulders, and then ran to catch up with Myrrah before he lost her, too.

SNAKE AND WHEEL

Renn climbed halfway down the ladder from his bedroom loft and jumped the rest of the distance to the floor.

"You're up early," his mother said from the kitchen. The smell of bacon and hotcakes filled the great room of their farmhouse. "I didn't even have to holler to wake you up. I can't imagine what's gotten into you."

"It's my birthday!"

"Really?" His mother's mouth dropped open, and she brought both hands to her cheeks. "I completely forgot."

"Then why did you make my favorite breakfast?" Renn cupped his hand and placed it next to his mouth. "Tavier! Chria! Da!" he shouted. "Breakfast is ready!"

The back door opened, and Renn's father tossed his straw hat onto the bench that ran along the wall. "Perfect timing," he said. "I just finished saddling Dusty and Ranger, the saddlebags are packed, and our bedrolls are tied in place."

Tavier peeked his head over the edge of the loft and rubbed his eyes. His hair stuck out in several directions. "It's not fair," he said. "I want to go with you, too."

"When you turned eleven, your father took you on your first overnight hunt, Tavier," Renn's mother said. "It's Renn's turn now."

Tavier scowled, climbed down the ladder, and stomped his way to the table and sat between Renn and their father. Chria appeared next. She stopped at the threshold of their parent's room, rubbing her eyes with one hand and holding a blanket in the other.

"Come get your breakfast, sweetheart." Their mother lifted Chria into a high chair their father built when Tavier was a baby.

"We need to hurry and finish our breakfast, Renn," his father said. "I want to be to my secret fishing hole before it gets too hot and the fish stop biting."

Renn rode Ranger, and his father rode Dusty. Ranger followed Dusty everywhere, so that made staying close behind his father simpler. They took the road toward Leedsdale for a couple miles before veering off onto a small game trail that led through a wooded area toward the Hebät Mountains. The sun still hadn't crested the peaks of the mountain, so the air wasn't blistering hot yet. Renn breathed deeply as they passed a copse of sweet-smelling honeysuckle bushes. Bees were already hard at work buzzing around the blossoms and collecting nectar.

It was another hour ride up the mountain, and thirty minutes of leading the horses around dry fallen logs, through dense brush, and over cold streams, before Renn's father announced they had arrived.

The secret fishing hole was a calm pool downstream from where two brooks joined under the shade of an aspen grove. Green coin-shaped leaves rustled overhead with the light summer breeze.

Renn's father threaded a thick, slimy worm to the end of a barbed hook. "The trick," he whispered, "is this lead weight." He used a pair of pliers to pinch a small piece of lead around the line a couple hand widths behind the hook. "This water is a little murky, so we want the fall rate of the worm to be fast enough that the fish don't get too good a look at it, but slow enough they can see it and strike before it hits bottom."

His father pitched the worm out into the center of the pool and waited a few moments before pulling it back to the surface.

He handed the rod to Renn. "Now, you try while I prepare my line."

Renn lightly cast the worm into the center of the pool the way he'd seen his father do it. He pulled it back to the surface and pitched it again. His rod jerked, and Renn nearly dropped it into the river.

"Da! Da!" he shouted. "I think I've got a fish!"

"See! I told you this is a great fishing hole. Pull it up slowly, and I'll catch it with the net."

The fish was only ten inches long, but Renn couldn't stop grinning when he looked at his catch.

"Do you have more worms?" Renn asked. "I want to catch another one!" His father laughed and threaded another slimy worm on the hook.

Before noon, the fish stopped biting. But Renn and his father had caught more fish than they could eat. His father cooked two for their lunch and strung a rope through the rest and set them in the cold river to stay fresh.

"The fishing won't be good again until this evening," his father said as he licked his fingers. "So, this afternoon I'm going to teach you how to set a simple trap to catch small game." Renn licked the fishy grease off his own fingers and wiped his hands on his shirt.

Using small branches, twigs, and twine, Renn and his father constructed an open-top box with the heavier branches on the bottom. They turned the box upside down and held one side of the box in the air using a twig as a support post. Renn's father tied a long piece of twine to the supporting twig and strung the twine to a stand of bushes that was downwind from the box and covered the twine with soil.

"Let's try to catch a bird first," Renn's father said. "We'll put a small pile of bread crumbs under the box and make a trail of crumbs leading to this tree." Birds fluttered and chirped in the upper branches of the aspen his father pointed at.

"Now, we hide behind the stand of bushes and wait." His father took off his straw hat, wiped sweat from his brow, and put it back on his head. "When a bird follows the trail of bread to the pile under the box, pull the string, and the box will fall and trap the bird."

It felt like hours to Renn as he crouched behind the bush, peering through the leaves and holding the twine. Sweat trickled down his back, and his tongue was dry. He was about to suggest to his father that they should try a different trap when a large robin dropped to the forest floor and snatched up a piece of bread. The bird launched back into the tree with its booty, but it soon returned to the forest floor followed by two more robins. They pecked and chirped at each other as they tussled for the small white morsels. Renn placed his supporting hand farther into the bush and leaned forward in anticipation—ready to pull the twine as soon as one of the unlucky birds hopped under the box. A twig snapped under his hand, the birds flew away, and Renn felt a sharp pain.

"Ow!" Renn fell backward, rubbing his wrist. "Something bit me!"

A flat, triangular head rose from underneath the bush and hissed. Renn's father grabbed Renn and pulled him back before the snake could strike again.

His father threw a rock at the snake, and it slithered away. It was light brown with a series of darker brown spots ringed with black.

"A chain viper!" his father said. He made Renn sit with his back against a tree and pulled out a leather flask filled with water.

"Keep your wrist and arm below your heart." His father's hands trembled as he ran water over the bite mark. "How do you feel?"

"My wrist stings."

"Do you feel sick or dizzy?" His father studied Renn's eyes.

"No."

"Okay, stay still for a moment."

His father ran in the direction of their campsite and returned a few moments later with the horses in tow.

"Do you feel strong enough to ride?" his father asked.

"Of course," Renn said. "What about our bedrolls and supplies?"

"I'll return for those later."

"Really, I'm fine, Da," Renn said. "Let's try trapping some more animals."

His father smiled, but his eyes darted to the bite on Renn's wrist. Renn's arm ached, and he noticed the skin around the bite was turning red.

"Up you go," his father said as he helped him mount Ranger.

His father took Dusty by the lead rope, and Ranger dutifully followed as they retraced their steps around bushes, over fallen branches, and through streams. Once they reached the game trail, his father mounted and pushed Dusty into a trot.

He looked back at Renn. "You still okay?" Renn nodded to reassure his father he felt fine, but winced at a stabbing pain that twisted his stomach.

"Can you ride?" Again, Renn nodded.

His stomach clenched with another stab of pain, and he doubled over onto the saddle horn. He saw the grass and dirt under Ranger's hooves, but they grew blurry and began spinning.

"Whoa!" he heard his father shout, and Ranger stopped. Renn vomited onto the trail. His father caught him as he fell from the saddle.

"Hang on, Renn." His father carried Renn to Dusty, placed him on the saddle, and climbed up behind. With one hand he held Renn against his warm body, and in the other he held the reins.

His father spurred Dusty to a trot. Bushes and tree branches rushed by, making Renn dizzy. He closed his eyes, but his head still felt like he was spinning. He opened his eyes and watched the ground race past—that was a mistake. He leaned to the side to avoid puking on Dusty's neck but instead managed to get it all over his leg.

He felt weak. He wanted to lie against his father and sleep, but the jarring movement kept him awake.

They rounded a boulder and saw a dark-haired man with a goatee bending over the trail, apparently studying animal tracks, judging from the way his fingers were moving over the soil.

"Jomard!" Renn's father called. The man stood and stepped off the trail as the horses came to a stop in front of him. He was tall and thin, but Renn knew from experience that Jomard was agile and lithe despite his lanky frame.

"Renn's been bitten by a chain viper," his father said. "I need to take him to the apothecary in Leedsdale. Would you take Ranger and ride to my farm to let Delphia know what's happened?"

Jomard lifted Renn's face and peered into his eyes.

"Open your mouth, Renn," the man said, and Renn did as instructed.

"I can do better than that, Ehrlich," Jomard said. "Set him down. I have something in my pack that will help."

Renn's father carried him to a boulder and rested him against it. Renn tried to lie down, but his father's calloused hand held him in place.

"Renn, we have to keep the bite below your heart," his father said. "You can't lie down right now."

"Pour some water over the bite," Jomard instructed as he unstoppered a small bottle of black powder. He gently dried the wound and dumped some of the black powder into his hand and mixed a little water with it. He put the mixture on the bite and wrapped it with a clean cloth. The dark paste felt cool and soothing, but the ache in Renn's arm didn't subside.

"I've got Domerian Mongoose plant at my home." Jomard put the stopper back on the bottle and placed it back into his pack. "It's much closer than Leedsdale. We can treat Renn there."

Renn's father lifted him back to the saddle and climbed up behind him. Jomard swung onto Ranger. Once they left the wooded area, his father spurred Dusty to a run.

Jomard's homestead was smaller than Renn's family's, but it was well maintained. A quaint wooden fence surrounded a yard that contained a flower bed and vegetable gardens. Jomard's wife stood when the horse skidded to a halt, and Renn's father pulled him from the saddle and pushed through the gate with Renn in his arms. Renn felt like he was in a dream. He saw and heard everything going on around him, but it felt distant and blurred.

"The boy has a snakebite!" Jomard took the horses' reins and headed for the back of the small house. "Heat some water, Clarid," he said to his wife over his shoulder.

Jomard's wife was a petite woman with long red hair and fair skin. She dropped the weeds she had pulled, wiped her hands on her green work dress, picked up her little son, and ran to open the door for Renn's father.

Jomard's home reminded Renn of their own, except there was no loft. Just a great room that served as a kitchen and a sitting room, and a bedroom to the left of the main door.

"Set Renn on this chair." Clarid pointed to a chair with a brown pillow on the seat by the wall. She grabbed a teapot and headed for the back door. "The coals should still be hot." She pointed to the hearth. "Get it burning for me, Ehrlich."

By the time Renn's father placed small logs on the coals and stoked it back to a flame, Clarid had returned with water in the teapot, and she hung it over the fire.

Jomard came in through the back door moments later with a handful of long green leaves and twisted white roots. He shoved the leaves and roots into a mortar he grabbed off a shelf and ground them with a pestle. He removed the dressing from Renn's arm and washed the black powder away.

"What was that powder?" Renn's father asked.

"Charcoal," Jomard answered, "but I got it from the smithy—his fire is much hotter than normal and it changes the charcoal so it adsorbs toxins."

Jomard made a paste with some of the crushed mongoose plant and handed the mortar with the remaining crushed leaves and roots to his wife. "Make tea with this, Clarid."

He put the Mongoose leaf paste on Renn's bite and rewrapped it with a clean strip of cloth. When he finished, Clarid brought a steaming clay mug of tea. It smelled like mint but tasted bitter and made Renn's lips pucker and nose scrunch.

"Drink it all," Clarid instructed.

Renn finished the tea, and Jomard reexamined his eyes and mouth.

"You're lucky, Renn," Jomard said. "You'll feel weak for a couple days, but after that you should be good as ever. Although your arm will be tender in the bite area for a couple weeks."

"How do you know so much about medicines?" Renn's father asked.

"My father was an apothecary, and he taught me. I'll give you some Mongoose plant to take home with you. Apply it to the bite three times a day, and have Renn drink the tea morning and night."

"I thought you said your father was a farmer." Renn's father's brow creased, and he scratched his chin. Renn saw Jomard shoot a glance at Clarid, whose eyes widened almost imperceptibly.

"Oh, he inherited the apothecary from my grandfather." Jomard smiled wanly. "But things took a bad turn, and he lost it. He had to become a vassal after that and farm for a lord near Mylitta."

"Oh, I see." Renn's father smiled. "Well, lucky for us he passed the knowledge on to you. I can't tell you how thankful I am we came across you in the forest today."

"A blessing from the gods, for certain," Jomard said.

Renn's father bent down to be eye level with him. "I'm sorry our outing was ruined, Renn. I should have been more cautious."

"It was still the best day ever, Da," Renn said.

His father swallowed hard, smiled, and rubbed Renn's hair. "Come on. Let's go home."

⋈

Three weeks later, Renn had all but forgotten about the snakebite. His arm still itched now and then, but there were much more exciting things to focus on. The sun hadn't yet crested the Hebät Mountains when he and Tavier nearly fell over one another as they raced down the ladder from their bedroom loft. Their mother only had to call them for breakfast once today because the sooner they were done eating, the sooner the family could leave for midsummer's Azur-Aven. The smell of hotcakes and sausage already permeated the small farmhouse.

The boys bounded to their seats, and their father walked through the front door with Coy panting excitedly around his legs.

"Well," he said as he set his straw hat on the arm of his chair. "The wagon is loaded and the team's hitched and ready." He sat next to Tavier, took a drink of goat milk, and put a hotcake on his plate. "Renn and Tavier, I expect the two of you to help sell fruits and vegetables for at least a few hours during the festival."

"Ah, Da, do we have to?" Tavier groaned. "Me and Renaul had the whole day planned already."

"I don't know if that's such a good idea," their mother said. Her full lips pursed together and she wiped her hands on her apron. She sat next to Chria and cut her breakfast into bite-sized chunks. "You know how Raul feels about you playing with his children."

Their father grunted and shook his head but didn't comment.

"Don't worry about him, Mother," Renn said. "The Red Bear will be drunk by midmorning and unconscious by early afternoon."

"That's not nice to say, Renn," their mother chided.

"Maybe not," Ehrlich agreed, "but probably accurate."

"It's not fair," Tavier complained. "Renaul's my best friend, and I can hardly ever play with him." Tavier's eyes grew wide, and he clapped his hands. "Hey, Renn, I've got a great idea. Why don't you use your power to make the Red Bear like us? Then he'll let us play with Renaul again."

"I don't know how to do that," Renn said.

"Maybe Artio could teach you a couple spells before you go to school," Tavier said. "You're supposed to be some powerful magic boy—you might as well use it to our advantage."

Renn thought about that for a moment. It made pretty good sense—which was unusual for one of Tavier's ideas.

"Get that look off your face, Renn," Delphia said, finally eating her own breakfast. "Using the lore to force people to like you isn't the answer."

"Why not?" he asked.

"Well . . . because . . . people . . . It just isn't," she said. "Besides that, Artio isn't going to teach you spells that will let you manipulate people for your own enjoyment."

The ride to Leedsdale was unbearably long. Renn was so anxious to get to the temple grounds that every mile along the road seemed to stretch forever. When they finally entered the little village, the main thoroughfare was so crowded they could barely maneuver their small wagon through the melee. And the closer they drew to the center of town, the more crowded it became. Merchants and farmers lined the streets with colorful carts filled with fruits, vegetables, sweets, pots and pans, knives, tobacco, and clothing. They rode by a cart selling fresh pastries, and the smell made Renn's mouth water.

Jugglers and acrobats were performing anywhere they found an open space. Several small crowds surrounded the performers, clapping and laughing and tossing coins at their feet.

"This is ridiculous," his father said to Renn's mother, loud enough to be heard over the din of the crowded street. "At this rate, we won't get to the temple grounds for another hour."

"Da, can me and Renn run to the temple grounds and meet you there?" Tavier asked. Then he hurriedly added, "We could find a good spot to set up the wagon before they're all taken."

Their father and mother looked at them suspiciously. Then their father grinned and said, "Be careful."

They jumped down from the wagon and ran into the crowd. "Remember to save us a good place," Renn heard his father call out.

The two boys made much better time on foot. In minutes, they found themselves in the middle of the temple grounds. They grinned and stared wide-eyed at one sight after another. A clown wearing tall stilts strapped to his legs towered over everybody else and walked through the crowd juggling apples. A man with long dark hair, wearing a leather vest and covered with tattoos, slowly swallowed a long sword as a group of children and adults stood watching, dumbfounded. A bald man, also covered in tattoos, put a flame on his tongue and then blew fire across a torch he held in one hand, causing it to light. Puppeteers performed at a small stage for a group of children, while live actors performed *Greyfel and Elahna* on a larger stage.

"Wow," Renn said in amazement. "This is even better than last year."

As Renn took in all the sights, Tavier fell into him, and they both tumbled to the ground—Renaul stood over them, pointing and laughing.

"I knocked you both down with one shove." Renaul's sister, Genea, walked up next to him and covered a grin with her hand. "Good thing I just barely tapped you," Renaul said.

"Oh yeah?" Tavier dove at the other boy's midsection and wrestled him to the ground. They were both laughing, but it wasn't long before Tavier twisted Renaul into a position that looked very uncomfortable.

"Okay . . . okay," Renaul cried out. "I give up—you win."

"Honestly, you two look like a couple of street beggars." Genea waved the dust from in front of her face. Renn had to admit they did look pretty messy. "Mother isn't going to be happy when she sees your clothes, Renaul."

Renaul grabbed a handful of her dress and wiped his face on it.

"Cut it out!" Genea shouted and twisted away from him.

"There." Renaul stood and brushed off his trousers. "Now, she'll be unhappy with both of us."

Renn and Tavier broke out in laughter, and Genea stuck her tongue at them.

"Where's your da?" Renn asked. "If he sees you playing with us, you're going to get it."

"He started drinking hours ago," Renaul answered. "I don't imagine we'll see him for a day or two."

"Renaul!" Genea chastised him in her best grown-up voice. "You shouldn't talk about Father that way."

Renaul and Tavier looked at each other and rolled their eyes.

"Let's go through the Hall of Horrors," Tavier said excitedly, pointing to the other side of the temple grounds. "I've heard it's the best thing here."

The others agreed, and they made their way through the throng.

Renn felt a prickly sensation that ran up the back of his neck and stopped walking.

"What are you doing?" Genea asked.

He held up a hand to halt her from asking more questions and rubbed at his neck. But the feeling didn't go away. If anything, it grew stronger. He felt like someone was hanging above him in the air and was about to pounce on him. He looked up but saw nothing. He turned in a circle, scanning the crowd, but other than Genea, everybody hurried about their business and paid him no mind. Still, the sensation of being watched by unseen eyes was very real. After a moment, Renn shrugged his shoulders. "Nothing . . . I just thought . . ." He shook his head. "Nothing."

The Hall of Horrors was a bit disappointing. It was only townsfolk dressed in costumes, jumping out to scare them around every corner. The Room of Mirrors was much better. Although the hall was only a few highly polished pieces of brass bent in strange shapes to contort your reflection—it was entertaining.

"Look, Genea." Renaul pointed to her reflection in a tall, convex-shaped piece of brass. "Now you know how you'll look after you've grown up and had a few babies."

Her reflection was short and fat. The boys all broke out in laughter, and Genea gave them a dark scowl and punched Renn in the shoulder.

"Ow!" Renn rubbed his arm. "I didn't say anything."

"That's for laughing." She turned on her heel and marched out the exit into the sweltering sun. When Renn and the others came out, she had apparently forgotten about the little exchange and beamed with excitement.

"Renn! Renn!" She waved him over. "Look at that."

The boys all stared with open mouths and wide eyes.

"What is it?" Tavier asked.

"Look how high it goes," Renn said.

"They must've finished putting it up while we were in the Hall of Horrors," Genea said.

The ride looked like a pair of giant wagon wheels raised side by side. Seats with backs and armrests, big enough for two people, were fixed between the big wheels. Near the base of the ride, a team of oxen was yoked to a wooden wheel with grooves carved in a circle around the top. The teeth of a cogwheel rested in the grooves. Ropes and pulleys connected the cogwheel to an axle at the center of the ride. As the oxen walked in a circle, the gigantic wagon wheels also went in circles—carrying people high in the air and back down again.

"I'm going for a ride," Renaul said and ran to the long line, with the other children on his heels.

A thrill of excitement ran through Renn when he sat down. The ridemaster tied a rope over his and Genea's waists and onto the armrest next to Renn. The oxen walked, and the great wheel turned, lifting them effortlessly backward and up into the air. Genea let out a slight whimper and clutched onto Renn's shoulder.

"Hey," he protested. "What are you doing?"

Genea flushed and loosened her grip, but the wheel took them higher, and she held on to Renn even tighter than before. He was about to protest again but decided it wasn't that bad. Besides, Tavier and Renaul couldn't see them because the seat with the two boys was in front of and slightly below him and Genea. So long as the two boys didn't look back, they would never know.

The wheel took them back down and up again, and Renn felt the hair on the back of his neck rise. At first, he thought it was just the excitement of the ride. But the feeling didn't go away. He felt like he was standing in the center of a fight pit with a thousand eyes watching him with twisted anticipation. His skin crawled and his heart raced. He looked above him, but just like before, there was nothing there. He scanned the crowd below. The sword swallower was entertaining a boisterous crowd. The line of people waiting to ride the giant wheel stretched all the way to the Hall of Horrors, and a procession of gray-clad priests marched into the temple. He leaned forward and scanned the faces of the crowd directly below. Hundreds of people were looking up and watching the riders on the giant wheel, but those weren't the unseen eyes that caused his anxiety.

He scanned the tree line on either side of the massive temple grounds, but it was impossible to tell if anybody watched him from that distance. However, the shadows in the forest *did* appear darker than they should. He focused back on the fairgrounds and noticed the shadows cast by the tents and rides *felt* foreboding and dark. Almost as though malice emanated toward him from unseen eyes within the shadows.

"What's the matter?" Genea asked.

"I feel . . . darkness." Renn stared at a particular shadow on the edge of the forest that seemed to grow darker. "Someone evil is watching me—someone that . . . someone who hates me."

The ride jerked to a stop, and they fell forward. Genea screamed. If they hadn't been secured by a rope, both Renn and Genea would have fallen out.

Renn looked down, and the oxen stood still. The animals' handlers shouted and cracked whips above the oxen's ears, but the animals refused to move.

The ride jerked again.

But instead of turning, the giant wheel tilted to the side.

Renn gripped the edge of his seat, pulling himself away from falling into Genea. He grabbed her around the waist to keep her from falling out.

Renn heard Tavier and Renaul shout in alarm. People below were running into each other and falling over tables in their rush to get out of the way. The wooden braces that held the ride together creaked and groaned, and Renn knew they would break soon. His arms ached from the strain of holding himself and Genea.

Below, the handlers had stopped yelling at the oxen. Instead, they were tying thick ropes around the biggest beams of the wheel and struggling to pull the ride erect.

The malice Renn felt from the unseen eyes twisted into . . . sadistic anticipation. The feeling that he was in the center of a fight pit flooded back into his mind. The unseen eyes were savoring the killing blow.

There were at least half a dozen ropes tied to the big wheel, and thirty or forty men straining to pull it upright. The ride jerked again. Renn heard the wood crack and break.

The wheel fell sideways. Genea's hair whipped around Renn's face as the ground rushed toward them. A man and woman on the ride but closer to the ground fell out and rolled to avoid being crushed by a falling beam. Renn's grip finally gave way, and he fell into Genea, pressing her hard against the armrest. The armrest broke away. Renn grasped Genea's hand and caught the rope in his other hand as they fell.

The air around them turned green.

Renn still held on to Genea's hand, but her weight no longer pulled against him.

A green, glowing light surrounded the wheel, and they stopped falling.

Renn saw the Meskhoni gripping his staff firmly in both hands, pointing it at the wheel. Green energy poured from the end of the staff and circled the ride and patrons. The Meskhoni was down on one knee and, even from where Renn was, he saw the veins standing out on the old man's neck and forehead.

The wheel continued its descent but at a controlled pace. The green force pressed Renn against the seat, holding him in place. Once the ride was horizontal to the ground, the wheel stopped and hovered about six feet in the air while soldiers of the Basil's guard helped the patrons to safety.

As Renn waited his turn to be helped from the ride, the malice he felt from the unseen eyes turned into rage. In the ink-black shadows, Renn detected a hint of red as the rage intensified.

Once the soldiers had herded Renn and the other riders a safe distance from the wheel, Artio slumped over, dropped his staff, and lay on the ground, gasping to catch his breath. The green glow surrounding the giant wheel vanished, and the massive ride crashed to the ground, sending clouds of dust and debris into the hot summer air.

Renn turned in a circle, looking at shadows, trying to identify where the unseen eyes were hidden. The rage he felt directed at him grew so intense Renn was certain another attack was imminent. But as abruptly as the jerking of the ride had been, the prickling sensation in his spine went away. The sense of being watched by unseen eyes vanished completely.

THE COUNCIL

It rained very little the remainder of the summer, and the river that ran through the back of Renn's family's farm was reduced to a small stream.

One morning, Renn went with his father and Tavier to irrigate and found it impossible. The river was too low to pass through the floodgate into their irrigation ditch.

Renn's father walked into the middle of the riverbed, took off his straw hat, and wiped the sweat from his forehead. He looked up and down the dwindling stream a few times and cursed under his breath. Renn looked at Tavier, whose face probably matched Renn's—wide-eyed and slack-jawed. They almost never heard their father use foul language.

The hair on the back of Renn's neck stood on end—and not because he was surprised at his father's language. Renn felt a strange presence. Just like the unseen eyes at the festival. The shadows in the forest across the riverbank were irregular and, in places, darker than they should have been. It felt like an evil presence filled with malice was hiding in the shade of the woods.

"Tavier," Renn whispered. "Do you feel that?"

"Feel what?"

"Like someone evil is watching us?"

"What are you talking about?"

"Across the river. In the shadows of those trees." Renn pointed past their father, who still studied the water problem. Tavier squinted his eyes and peered to where Renn pointed.

"There's nothing over there."

"But I feel unseen eyes in the shadows *themselves*." Renn realized it did sound a little strange. But the sensation was so strong; how could others not feel it?

"You're making my skin crawl, Renn," Tavier said. "There's nothing over there. It's just your imagination." Their father placed his hat back on his head and started up the riverbank, and Tavier called out to him. "What are we going to do, Father?"

"I'm not sure yet," Renn's father said. "One thing is certain, though: the crops won't last more than a week without water—probably not even that long in this heat."

After lunch, Renn's father went to organize a town meeting with the other farmers who shared the river. Renn knew they were in a bad situation, but he and Tavier were still happy to have the day off. They played games together, pretending to be valiant knights and great warriors. They even managed to sneak away to the forest with Renaul and Genea where they took turns hiding and finding each other.

Shortly before sunset, Renn's father returned with Jomard. His skinny neck, sharp nose, and lanky frame gave him the appearance of an uncoordinated dolt—but Renn had watched Jomard participate in footraces and other games at Azur-Aven festivals, and the man always won.

Renn's father and Jomard looked upset when they walked into the small home, and Renn saw the worry in his mother's green eyes as she led them to the sitting area of the main room and brought them both a glass of tea.

"I take it things didn't go well in town." She twisted at the ring on her finger.

"I don't understand," Jomard replied. "The town council has changed so much in the past six months. You used to be able to talk sense at these meetings."

"What happened?" Renn's mother's voice had risen in pitch.

"It doesn't make sense, dear," Renn's father said. "Jomard and I tried to inform them of the water situation, and they didn't seem to care. In fact, Raul started blaming the drought on . . . on . . . uh, ridiculous superstitious stuff." He glanced toward Renn.

Renn knew what his father wouldn't say. The Red Bear had tried to blame everything on him.

"Raul even convinced several of the men he was right," his father continued. "After that, the whole discussion deteriorated."

Renn's mother stood and paced. Her jaw was rigid.

"Something strange is going on." Jomard pulled his fingers through his dark hair and said, "They're not being rational. They didn't even want to discuss the water situation. Most of them are farther upriver, so it hasn't hit them as hard yet, but they should still be concerned."

"Wasn't *anybody* willing to talk about it?" Renn's mother stopped pacing and folded her arms.

"A few. But the major landowners, particularly Hevor Shoen, seemed uninterested. They seemed . . . hostile . . . almost to the point of rioting."

"Rioting?" his mother exploded. "Over what?"

"They complained a lot about the Basils, and how we should have a local man govern us instead of distant lords."

"They always do that," she said.

"Yes, but they were openly hostile this time," Jomard said.

"Right," Renn's father agreed. "Something's going on, and I don't like it."

"So what do we do about our crops?" Jomard asked. "They wouldn't even talk about the water situation, let alone work out rationing plans."

"Maybe the two of you should pay a visit to the Meskhoni this evening." Renn's mother rubbed her palms on her apron and paced again. "Maybe he can get the council to address the problem, and he might have an idea about what's going on."

"That's not a bad idea," Jomard said.

"If we hurry," Ehrlich added, "we can get there and back before midnight."

Soft voices woke Renn. Flickering light reached the loft from the room below. Renn lay on his back on the straw-covered sleeping pallet he shared with Tavier and looked out the window. The waxing half moon had already set, so it was after midnight. He crawled over his brother and to the edge of the loft, careful not to make a sound. Renn couldn't see anyone, but he saw shadows on the far wall. No fire burned, so the light must've been coming from a candle. He positioned himself so he could hear the conversation below but wouldn't be seen if somebody looked up.

Renn recognized his father's voice. "Artio didn't act surprised. Apparently, the Mage has been watching Hevor and the other landowners, and he knew many of them were regularly corresponding with someone in the north."

"Does he know what they're up to?" Renn's mother asked. A splinter poked through Renn's nightshirt, and he shifted his weight. He winced at the creaking noise of the boards beneath him.

"No. But he said they aren't working on their own. He thinks one of the Warlocks from up north is calling the shots. Artio thinks a Warlock is trying to position himself to take over when the 'prophesied events'—as Artio puts it—begin to happen. He said people aren't being corrupted just in Leedsdale. Other cities and villages are being affected as well."

"What's going on?" The floorboards squeaked again, and Tavier joined Renn at the loft's edge. Renn held a finger to his lips and pointed below with his other hand.

"That would account for some of the confusion at the council meeting today," Renn's mother said. "But why would they be so irrational? I'd think if someone were trying to take over, they'd be discreet until they were ready to make their move."

"I asked the same question. The Meskhoni said whomever they're working for uses subtle forms of mind control. Hevor Shoen and the others probably don't realize how foolish they're acting. They've been promised power and riches for helping, and they apparently think they're going to be rewarded fairly soon."

"Or," Renn's mother said, "maybe they've already been rewarded, and that's why they don't care about their crops."

"Good point," Renn's father said.

"So, what now? Can the Meskhoni do anything to help us?"

"He claims he already has been. According to Artio, for the past six months someone has been watching Renn—almost constantly. He thinks it's a Warlock named Kahn Devin, but he isn't certain; there are other powerful Warlocks as well. But whichever Warlock is doing this, Artio thinks that person may have been responsible for the giant wheel collapsing at the festival. Artio said he's been involved in a magical struggle of some kind with a powerful person who isn't physically here but is able to cast his influence a long way. Artio has been trying to keep that someone out of Renn's mind."

Renn caught his breath. He wasn't imagining things after all. He elbowed Tavier. "See?" he whispered. "I told you something was in the shadows."

Tavier elbowed him back.

"Why does Artio suspect this Kahn Devin person rather than one of the other Warlocks?" Renn's mother asked.

"Artio said that Kahn is the most powerful Warlock of the Aven-Lore. The Meskhoni isn't sure if any of the other Warlocks could exert so much power from such a great distance."

"What are we supposed to do?" Renn saw the shadow of his mother stand and pace.

"I'm taking Tavier and Renn with me in the morning to inform Lord Danu. In the meantime, Artio and Jomard will try to work out an agreement with the farmers and keep an eye on things in town and around our farms."

Renn looked at Tavier, and they both grinned. Neither he nor Tavier had ever been outside of Leedsdale, and going to Basilea to the Basil family castle sounded like a great adventure.

"Why take the boys?" his mother asked.

Renn held his breath. He knew it wouldn't take much for her to persuade his father to reconsider.

"Cover," his father said. "The Meskhoni doesn't think the conspirators are very organized yet, but if Kahn Devin is behind it, they may be more prepared than we know. If anyone asks, we'll say we're going to help my mother in Basilea for a couple of days."

"But if you leave now, won't that raise suspicion?" his mother asked. "Who is going to work the farm while you're away?"

His father breathed a loud sigh. "I've done everything I can in the fields. There is no water for irrigation. All we can do at this point is pray to the gods for rain."

Renn saw the shadow of his father rise, walk to his mother, and place a hand on her shoulder. "I asked Jomard to mention to a few of the other farmers that my mother needed help and how I thought now is the only time I could get away in the next several months. Hopefully we won't arouse any suspicion that way."

"This whole business just makes me mad." Their mother's voice rose, so Renn didn't have to strain to hear now. "How does this Kahn Devin have so much power? If Artio believes Kahn is behind all this, can't Lord Danu and his father the duke do something about it? After all, if Kahn attacked innocent citizens at the midsummer's Azur-Aven, that should be grounds for arrest."

"Kahn lives *far* north," Renn's father said. "In a network of caves in the Upper Cragg Mountains of Nortia. King Thrakus of Nortia is basically his puppet and has armies to defend him. Kahn is a powerful Warlock. He once studied the Azur-Lore on Elder Island but then defected to the Aven-Lore." Renn's father paused for a moment, then added, "He's also the Grand Warlock—second only to Lord Monguinir, according to Artio."

Despite his efforts to remain quiet, Renn gasped when he heard the name of the demon lord. Everyone said demons were only make-believe, but after hearing Artio talk about them, Renn wasn't so sure. One thing he did know was that he didn't want to find out from firsthand experience.

"When will you leave?" His mother's voice was shaky and soft.

Renn waited for the answer. He turned and looked at his brother. Tavier was holding his breath, likely just as impatient as Renn to find out when they would be leaving on this grand adventure.

"At dawn," his father finally said.

Renn couldn't go back to sleep. He kept thinking of a great, shining city with smooth streets and beautiful gardens. He envisioned knights in gleaming armor and gentry on the palace grounds and merchants and commoners in the town square. He was certain Basilea would be wonderful.

Renn and Tavier were up before the first crow of the cock, excited and ready to go. Instead of wearing their everyday breeches and loose linen shirts, their mother dressed them in hose and sturdy leather shoes with leather thongs that laced over the hose to about midcalf. Under their short leather tunics, which were belted high on their waists, they each wore a light cotton shirt.

"Mother, these clothes are going to be too hot," Tavier complained.

"Maybe," she replied. "But they'll protect you from the sun and insect bites."

"Can't I just wear my breeches and a shirt?"

"Your breeches are filthy. Besides, they're not practical for travel."

"Can't I at least take off the tunic?"

"Stop arguing with me or you can stay home. And leave that tunic on."

"Everything is loaded and ready to go." Renn's father brushed the dust off his hands as he walked across the yard. He wore the same style of clothing Renn's mother made the boys wear, and his sandy blond hair blew fitfully in the early morning breeze.

"Are you certain you have everything?" his mother asked. Renn's father pushed back a strand of her flaxen-colored hair and kissed her cheek.

"I've already checked the list twice: blankets, food, extra clothing, canvas, tools, an ax, rope—you don't need to worry. We'll be all right."

The wagon was uncovered, but Renn had to climb on the spokes of the wheel—careful to not get slivers from the rough wooden planks—to see over the the side. The items his father listed were neatly arranged along the back and sides of the wagon bed. Two bales of straw were set lengthwise in the center of the wagon bed to keep things from sliding around. A wool blanket rested across a third bale of straw set directly behind the driver's seat.

The high wooden driver's bench at the front of the wagon was only wide enough for two, so one of the boys would have to sit on the bale of straw with the blanket. Renn argued a good bit with Tavier over who would sit next to their father—until their mother stepped in and told them to take turns.

The horses that were to pull the wagon were the same two that worked the fields each day. Dusty and Ranger. They weren't show horses to envy, but they were reliable and strong; to Renn, those workhorses were second only to their dog, Coy.

While he climbed onto the bale of hay, his father crossed the small yard back to the porch and gave Renn's mother another kiss. His father took his straw hat from her and placed it on his head.

"We will be home before you know it," he said.

She nodded and blinked several times—presumably to hold back her tears.

"It's only twenty leagues to Basilea," his father said. "Even with resting the horses every few hours, we will be home in five days. Six at the most."

"Be careful." She gave him a smile, and he kissed her again.

Renn's mother's face flushed, and she turned her head and rubbed at her eyes. Renn's wide grin melted as he watched her struggle to keep from crying.

"Don't worry, Mother!" Renn shouted. "Tavier and I will be good, and we'll bring back something special for you and Chria."

She stood on the porch, holding Renn's little sister, who was still rubbing the sleep from her blue eyes. Their mother forced herself to smile. She pushed Chria's blonde curls off her forehead, pointed toward their wagon, and said, "Wave bye-bye."

Chria looked to where their mother pointed, then quickly turned her head and buried her face into her mother's chest.

Renn watched the little farmhouse slowly grow smaller as the wagon rolled down the dusty road, until it finally disappeared behind a small hill.

THE ROAD TO BASILEA

The early morning air smelled fresh and clean, and the sun slowly crested the Hebät Mountains directly behind Ehrlich.

The small farms they passed on the road to Leedsdale were already teeming with activity. Farmers were working in the fields, anxious to take advantage of the cool morning air. It was long past planting season and still too early to harvest. Ehrlich assumed most of them were probably trying to irrigate. That's what he would be doing now if he were home . . . that is, if there were water in the north fork of the river. The south fork of the river that ran through these farms started higher in the Hebät Mountains and still flowed. He looked behind him to the east horizon. *The sun will be high before long*, he thought. *I'd better enjoy the cool morning while it lasts.*

By the time Ehrlich and the boys reached the small village of Leedsdale, the refreshing dawn had been completely burned away and replaced by the midmorning heat typical of southern Boranica.

I'd rather be sitting under the big oak behind the barn reading a book and watching the boys swim in the river—except the river is just a muddy stream right now, he thought.

"Da," Renn said from behind him. "I'm hot. Can I take my tunic off now?"

"I don't know," he replied. "You heard what your mother said about the insects."

"I'd rather get a few bites than die of heat," Tavier said.

"So would I," Ehrlich said. "All right, boys, the tunics can come off. But if your mother gets after me, you've got to back me up. There'll be no leaving your da to suffer the consequences alone."

The boys laughed, stripped off their tunics, and discarded them in the wagon bed.

Patrons crowded the narrow cobblestone thoroughfare of the village, pressing into shops on either side of the road. The old cobbler wearing spectacles and a worn apron stood just inside his door, examining a boot. His customer wore a dirty sock on one foot and the matching boot on the other. The customer didn't appear dangerous, but Ehrlich didn't recognize the man. That, however, wasn't unusual. Leedsdale was a crossroads to other cities and towns, and merchants would stop here to sell their goods. This, in addition to the permanent stores, attracted folks from outlying farms and villages.

A bell tinkled as the tailor opened his door for the day. A man with a long scar on his face, wearing a beard but no mustache, followed the tailor into the shop. *Probably a Nortian,* Ehrlich thought. But the man held a cloak, so perhaps he was visiting the tailor with legitimate business.

Stop that, Ehrlich thought. *You'll go crazy if you start suspecting everyone you see of being part of a conspiracy.*

The press of customers on the thoroughfare caused Ehrlich to drive slowly, but he found it nearly impossible to navigate his wagon through the crowded open market in the village square.

A merchant with rosy cheeks and a big belly stood under a red-and-white-striped canopy and pointed at designs on the glass vase a potential customer was scrutinizing, insisting that the handcrafted detail justified the asking price. Next to a cart painted blue with gold trim, a finely dressed merchant sold "every spice known to man." A brute wearing bracers and a sword at his waist stood with his arms folded next to the spices. *Probably hired by the merchant to protect his expensive goods,* Ehrlich thought.

A baker and his apprentice pulled handcarts through the crowd. The smell of fresh bread and pastries tempted Ehrlich to call them over. He resisted the urge, because if he stopped to buy one item, he'd soon be surrounded by other peddlers.

"Good morning, sir." A young woman in a bright green dress, carrying a basket of flowers, approached Ehrlich's wagon. "I'm sure the missus would fancy fresh flowers, and mine are the best in the market."

"I'm sure they are." Ehrlich tipped his hat to her. "But not today."

The local farmers peddled their fresh fruits and vegetables in a tight ring in the middle of the square, and their carts were surrounded by customers trying to get their produce before it was all picked over. One farmer shouted above the din, "Get back here, you little thieves!" and two small boys pushed their way out of the circle of people and ran off with apples in their hands toward the Azur temple just east of the village square.

Ehrlich watched them dart past gray-clad priests and the ancient statue of the goddess Avalian. Water from the underground hot springs flowed up and through her cornucopia and landed in the reflection pool that surrounded her. People traveled from all over Boranica, and even from other countries, just to wash their faces in these waters. Most would pray and collect water to take home to a loved one who was sick. Many believed the water possessed the magical healing powers of the goddess. Ehrlich never told any of the travelers it was all superstitious nonsense. Anything that brought additional commerce to the area was a good thing.

A narrow viaduct, cut into the center of a broad stone walkway, carried a steady flow of warm water from the reflecting pool toward the temple, where it disappeared underneath the first of a series of great stone steps that climbed to the grand oak doors. Japhet, the high priest who instructed initiates in theology and natural healing in the temple, stood at the top of the steps watching a procession of priests file past him.

The thoroughfare on the far side of the village square was less crowded. The road was no longer cobblestone, but hard-packed dirt. A large man with long black hair and a beard that followed his jawline, but no mustache, walked out of the swordsmith's shop, rubbing his thumb across the blade of a knife that he likely just purchased. Ehrlich slowed because the man stepped into the street without looking. The stranger's crooked nose had clearly been broken at least once.

"Does it seem like there's a lot of Nortians in Leedsdale today?" Renn stuck his head forward between Ehrlich and Tavier. Ehrlich pursed his lips, scratched his chin, and tried to think of an answer that wouldn't alarm his sons.

"There's always strangers in Leedsdale," Tavier said. "Everybody knows that."

Ehrlich wished he shared Tavier's cavalier opinion.

"Yeah." Renn's tone was thoughtful. "But these guys aren't dressed like Nortians. It's like they're trying to disguise themselves."

"That's cause it's hot, you dolt," Tavier said. "Even a Nortian wouldn't be stupid enough to wear thick leather and fur in this heat."

"That's enough, Tavier," Ehrlich said.

Renn's right, Ehrlich thought. The man slipped the blade under his belt and hurried down the road. *It is odd for so many Nortians to be here at one time. And buying knives . . .* Ehrlich watched the man walk away. *Then again,* he thought, *we all buy knives. Maybe the man just needed a new one.*

He was about to pass it off as coincidence, but the Nortian approached two men standing in the shade of a dirty canopy in front of the Lion's Tooth Tavern—a two-story building with greasy windows that marked the edge of town. A carved lion's head above the door held a sign between its teeth that was in sore need of a fresh coat of paint. The tavern was a favorite destination for those wanting to pass their time with a game of cards or with a woman. One of the men the Nortian approached was not a stranger—Hevor Shoen. The man Hevor was talking with stood a head taller than him and wore dark leather armor with a sword on his hip and one in a scabbard on his back. His skin was pale, and long black hair fell to his shoulders. He wore a thick beard with no mustache.

"That man talking to Mr. Shoen isn't trying to hide where he's from," Renn whispered.

The strangers and Hevor Shoen looked up as Ehrlich and his boys approached and watched until they passed. Ehrlich pretended not to notice them, but he saw from the corner of his eye that Renn stared openly. Ehrlich suppressed the urge to flick the reins and push the horses into a trot.

He looked over his shoulder as they left Leedsdale behind. Both Hevor and the distinguished stranger were gone. As Ehrlich turned to face the road ahead, he had a bad feeling in his gut. He hoped it was nothing more than him being overly cautious.

"Father?"

"Yes, Renn?"

"Do you think anybody might be following us?"

Ehrlich swung around in his seat and studied the road. A merchant wearing a blue felt cap was in front of his wagon, pulling on and cussing at the donkey that didn't want to move. The man should've been to the market with his wares a good hour ago. A farmer and his wife were leaving the village with an empty wagon. That was odd, but they weren't following Ehrlich and his sons.

"I don't see anything out of the ordinary," Ehrlich said, trying to convince himself as much as Renn. "What makes you think somebody is following us?"

"There were a lot of strangers in town. You saw that big man Hevor was with."

"Yes."

"I think they were up to something."

"What makes you say that?" Ehrlich asked.

"They looked sneaky, and they were making some kind of a deal."

"How do you know they weren't just passing time?" asked Tavier.

"Because they exchanged money. Besides, why would Hevor just be passing time with some stranger who looks like a soldier from Nortia?"

Ehrlich stopped watching the people on the road behind and looked at Renn. "You saw them exchange money?"

Renn nodded.

"You're very observant, Renn," Ehrlich said. Tavier gave Renn a sour look, which Renn returned with a smug expression. It bothered Tavier that Renn was so quick to pick up on things. Tavier was a lot stronger than Renn, but Ehrlich knew it was embarrassing for the fourteen-year-old that his eleven-year-old brother was smarter. It wasn't that Tavier was unintelligent; he was brighter than most boys his age. Renn was just precocious.

Ehrlich didn't want his boys to worry, so he said, "I really don't think anybody would be following us. Nobody except your mother, Artio, and Jomard know where we're going."

"Where *are* we going, Father?"

"If anyone asks, we're going to Basilea to visit your grandparents."

"Where are we *really* going?" Renn pressed.

As usual, Renn saw past the surface and suspected something more. *It's very unnerving at times,* Ehrlich thought. *Almost like the boy can read minds.*

"To Basilea," Ehrlich repeated. "That's all you need to know."

The brothers looked at each other and smirked, but they didn't ask him again.

They stopped to water and rest the horses and eat a light lunch of cheese and bread with jam about an hour out of Leedsdale. Ehrlich wanted to keep the horses fresh because it was already hot and dusty, and it would only get worse as the day wore on. When they resumed traveling, Renn took his turn sitting on the driver's bench with Ehrlich while Tavier sat in the back on the hay.

Ehrlich checked the road behind several times. There were other travelers, but none seemed out of place. He kept watching. Hour after hour, nothing but brown and green rolling hills sporadically covered with orchards and an occasional farm or ranch. The only travelers they passed were farmers, ranchers, or pilgrims on their way to the temple. There were a few stretches of forested land that provided shade from the angry sun, but the road only passed through the edges of the woods. Drake Basil, the Duke of Basilea, found it was much less expensive for his men to maintain a straight road in the grasslands than a winding road in a forest.

"Da, I'm hot and thirsty and bored," Renn said.

"Me too, Son," Ehrlich answered. "I'm also sore. Riding on a hard seat all day isn't my idea of fun." Ehrlich shifted his weight and checked the road behind once again. "I'll tell you what," he said. "Get my lute, Tavier, and I'll sing to help pass the time. Do you think you can handle the reins, Renn?"

Renn looked at him wide-eyed and nodded eagerly.

"Hey, no fair," Tavier protested. "I didn't get to hold the reins."

"That's 'cause you'd probably run us off the road." Renn laughed and scooted into a better position behind the horses.

"Next time you're up front, you can have a turn, too, Tavier," Ehrlich promised. Then, turning to Renn, he mussed his sandy blond hair and said, "Try not to bounce me out. It's hard to hold on when I've got both hands on the lute."

He tuned the lute as best he could without his pitch pipe, then, crossing his legs to steady the instrument better, he strummed and picked a classic folk song. The strings were old, which gave the lute a dark, mellow sound. He played a tune—"The Legend of the Wizard Greyfel"—which was a favorite of the boys. It told the story of Lemuria's most legendary hero, Greyfel the Wizard, and how he saved the land from a terrible beast, trapped the demons in another realm, and saved his lover—the princess Elahna—from a horde of Kirocs. Ehrlich had sung this song so often the boys joined in singing. It reminded him of the many nights he sat in his small farmhouse, playing for his children and wife as she knit or sewed.

As Ehrlich reached the last stanza of the song, the part where Greyfel and Elahna jump into the massive gorge east of Anytos and disappear forever, he noticed two riders on the road behind them. He stopped singing and studied them. *Where did they come from?* he wondered. Although the road passed over rolling hills, he could see a long distance in both directions—except those places where the road crossed through a section of forest. If these riders came from Leedsdale, they'd ridden hard to catch up. But, if that were the case, he'd have seen them before now.

The riders weren't pulling a wagon, so they weren't peddlers or farmers, and their horses were galloping. They wore dark clothing, but from this distance Ehrlich couldn't distinguish many details about the clothing style. But he saw the glint of sunlight reflect off what could only be polished steel.

These riders had weapons.

"Tavier, put my lute away." He handed the instrument to his oldest son. "Thanks for manning the team, Renn. I'll take it from here." Ehrlich kept his voice calm as he took the reins from his youngest son. No need to alarm the boys; he was just being cautious. After all, the two riders may just be regular travelers. *But what kind of traveler carries weapons and pushes his horse that hard in the heat of the day?*

Ehrlich flicked the reins and made a clicking sound to signal the horses to move faster.

"Father?" Renn asked after a moment. "Are you nervous because of those two men behind us?"

"What makes you think I'm nervous?"

"What men?" Tavier asked.

"You don't pay attention to anything," Renn said to his older brother. "Those two riders weren't there before, and now they're trying to catch up to us."

"We don't *know* they're trying to catch up to us, Renn." Ehrlich still tried to keep his voice steady. "For all we know, they could be Duke Basil's men."

Renn and Tavier watched them for a few moments before Renn said, "The duke's men don't wear black leather armor."

Ehrlich looked over his shoulder. The men were close enough now to see the dark clothing they wore was, in fact, leather armor. At this rate, the travelers would overtake them in another ten minutes.

"Yhah!" Ehrlich shouted, and he gave the reins a hard snap. The workhorses lurched into a trot. "Yhah!" he shouted again, pushing the horses faster down the dirt road.

"Why are they chasing us, Father?" Tavier shouted above the noise of the wooden wheels and pounding hooves. He sounded as scared as Ehrlich felt. He couldn't outrun whoever was behind them. Not with a couple workhorses pulling a farm wagon. And where was he going to run to? Basilea was still a good seventeen leagues away. Even if the horses could run the entire distance without resting, it would take at least five hours to get there. The riders behind would catch them long before that.

Ehrlich made a quick decision and pulled up hard on the reins. The horses whinnied and shook their manes. Their front legs dug into the dusty road, and the wagon slid to a stop.

"Quickly," he shouted to the boys. "Grab a few blankets and the pack with our foodstuffs."

Ehrlich saw the fear in their eyes as they followed his instructions. He jumped down from the wagon and yanked the yoke and harness off the horses. He cut the long rein lines so they could be used while riding horseback and left the bridles in place.

Ehrlich laid the blankets on the horses' backs and then cupped his hands so Tavier could climb onto Ranger—he was the stronger of the two horses, and he would follow Dusty. He lifted Renn by his waist and set him on the blanket behind his older brother.

"Tavier, follow me," Ehrlich said. "No matter what happens, don't get separated from me. Renn, hold on to your brother."

Ehrlich hoisted the pack with their food onto his own back and prepared to mount Dusty but noticed his lute case in the back of the wagon. His father had given it to him. It had belonged to his grandfather and his grandfather's father. He reached over the side of the wagon bed and grabbed it. Delphia would definitely have words for him wasting valuable seconds at a time like this—that is, if he lived to tell her the story.

Using a piece of the line he'd cut earlier, he fastened the instrument to the loop on the girth strap and pulled himself onto the horse's back. Ehrlich shouted and kicked at Dusty's flanks.

He hated the thought of abandoning the wagon on the side of the road. He wasn't too concerned with leaving clothing and the few tools it held; they could be replaced over time. But the wagon would most likely be gone by the time they returned—*if* they returned—and he needed it for work around the farm.

He looked over his shoulder; the boys were right behind him. Renn held tight to Tavier's waist. The fear in their eyes filled Ehrlich with determination. *There must be a way out of this*, he thought. He looked past the boys to the riders in black armor. Dust kicked up from the hooves of their horses as the men spurred their horses into a hard run.

Ehrlich tried to calm himself, but he kicked at Dusty's flanks again. He drew a map in his mind of the surrounding area. Large ranches were the only homesteads out here. He even knew a couple of the ranchers. But what could they do? They were no match for two armed soldiers. He would only be bringing trouble to their houses.

As they crested a small hill, a forested area stretched down from the north. The road cut into the southern edge of the forest. Ehrlich knew from previous trips that the forest was only a mile wide, but it stretched several miles northward. Perhaps they could leave the road and hide in the forest. But Ehrlich was no woodsman, and he had two small boys with him. The forest would just as likely trap them as hide them.

A trap! he thought with alarm. *What if there are others hiding in the forest, and the two riders behind are driving us into a trap?*

Ehrlich pulled left on the reins, leaving the road and charging into the grassy hills to the south. He and the boys would skirt the trees and meet up with the road again where it left the forest on on the far side. Ehrlich led the horses up and down the small rolling hills, careful to avoid unwittingly running Dusty into a hole or sudden ditch. He didn't want to think about what would happen if one of the horses got injured.

He looked behind again.

The cloud of dust left a trail behind them and partially obscured his view. But he could still see an outline of the two riders chasing them—now closer than before. At this rate, they would overtake them within a half hour.

El Azur, he prayed, *did you bless Renn with great power only to let him be killed as a child? Help me, please!*

Dusty was slowing, her breathing getting more labored with each step. The animal needed rest and water. Ehrlich had no time to give her, either.

He glanced over his shoulder again. Only one rider had followed them into the grassy hills, the other staying on the road. Ranger kept the boys close behind Ehrlich and Dusty. The boys bounced up and down on the horse blanket. The blanket, however, was slipping to one side.

The rider entering the forest would be waiting for them on the other side, where the road left the woods. Maybe Ehrlich should make a stand now. When would he have better odds than one-on-one? *Sure,* he thought sarcastically, *my lute against his sword.*

He urged Dusty to run faster. Maybe they could reach the road on the far side of the forest before the other rider. Just a little farther and they would be around the edge of southern tip of this forest, and they could meet back up with the road.

Cresting a rise on a hill that was larger than most, he saw the road—still a good half mile away. From here, it looked like a brown ribbon leaving the woods and winding up and around the rolling hills beyond. He urged Dusty onward. If they could reach that before . . .

Three riders emerged from where the road left the forest. Ehrlich didn't know if one was the same rider from before, but all three wore black leather armor. They spotted Ehrlich and his boys at the top of the hill and spurred their horses toward them.

Ehrlich wouldn't reach the road now.

He couldn't continue forward or turn back. He pulled left on the reins, angling away from the forest and the three riders. The breeze hitting Ehrlich's face did little to dry the sweat dripping down his cheeks. He clenched his legs against the horse's rib cage to keep from falling sideways.

The only option was to flee southwest through the hills. Basilea was in that general direction, but even if their horses could run full speed with no rest, it was still three hours away—four, considering they wouldn't be following an actual road. Dusty and Ranger couldn't keep this pace up for another half hour, let alone four hours. The riders would overtake them in minutes, not hours.

I should've never left Leedsdale, he berated himself. *When I saw Hevor and the Nortians, I should've turned around and gone straight to Artio for help.*

They crested another hill and surprised a small group of grazing cattle. The animals looked up and scattered. Ehrlich led his boys in a straight line through the brush and grasses where the cattle had grazed only moments ago, not daring to veer left or right lest he give their pursuers a better angle to intercept them.

He looked back again. Two riders chased them from behind, one flanked them on the east, and the last was hurrying to flank them on the west. Tavier and Renn rode just behind, on his right side.

Ehrlich kicked at Dusty's flanks. They had to move faster; they were losing ground.

Scanning the horizon ahead, he looked for anything that could give them a chance for escape. There was nothing but rolling hills as far as the eye could see. He clenched his jaw and leaned into his horse as it charged up a small rise. Ranger still kept pace. They reached the crest, and Ehrlich saw a line of dust in the distance. There were only a few things that could raise so much dust: a windstorm, a herd of animals, or a caravan of some sort.

The dust hung in the air like a brown mist, so it couldn't be a windstorm. *Probably just more cows,* Ehrlich thought. But if it was a caravan, it might give him and the boys the chance they needed. Then again, a small caravan might not be able to protect them against four armed fighters.

He had no other choice. He flicked the reins and headed straight for the cloud of dust.

"Is that smoke ahead?" Tavier shouted above the noise.

"No," Ehrlich yelled. "I hope it's dust being kicked up by horses."

Their pursuers must have come to the same conclusion because they shouted at their mounts to close in.

The riders chasing them drew their swords. The pounding of their horses' hooves joined with the frantic thudding of Dusty's rhythm.

The riders were only a hundred yards away, and Ehrlich could make out details. They were definitely Nortian soldiers. There was no mistaking that now. Nortian soldiers this far south could only mean one thing: they wanted Renn.

Maybe if I charge directly into them, Ehrlich thought, *I could slow them down enough for the boys to escape.*

He quickly dismissed that idea. They would just kill him and still capture Renn. And he didn't know what they would do to Tavier.

Ehrlich crested another hill and, indeed, there was a line of horses marching southwest in the direction of Basilea. It looked like a legion of soldiers. Ehrlich shouted, but they were too far away. They couldn't hear him.

Ehrlich chanced another look over his shoulder.

The Nortians were no more than ten horse-lengths behind them. Ehrlich could see the excitement of bloodlust mixed with anger in their eyes. They would overtake him and his boys before they reached the legion ahead. The closest Nortian raised his sword above his head and shouted a battle cry.

Shapes and figures became easier to distinguish the closer they got to the legion. Ehrlich guessed there were a hundred or more mounted soldiers.

If only the army was marching toward us, he thought.

But he and his boys were coming from behind. The army still couldn't see them.

Ehrlich kicked at Dusty again. He shouted and flicked the reins. He felt the horse's muscles tense and shake as Dusty gave everything she had. Ehrlich felt a stab of sorrow; he realized he may be driving the poor girl to kill herself.

But Dusty managed to find enough strength to lunge forward and gain another horse-length on their pursuers. True to character, Ranger kept up with her.

"HO THERE!" Ehrlich shouted, and his boys joined in. "HELP!"

A trumpet sounded in the distance ahead—three quick notes—and the army came to a halt. Whether a scout spotted the approaching riders or had heard his call, Ehrlich wasn't sure. He didn't care. A dispatch of a dozen soldiers peeled away from the calvary, wheeled around, and trotted out to meet them. Ehrlich looked over his shoulder once again. The Nortian soldiers had turned around, and their horses were kicking up clumps of dirt as they fled. Ehrlich pumped his fist and shouted up at the sky in case El Azur really was listening. "Thank you!"

Behind the dispatch of soldiers coming to meet them, the legion stood waiting. At the head of the legion—far enough away that Ehrlich could make out the banners but not individual features of the men's faces—five soldiers rode as vanguard, ten paces in advance of the main company. The vanguard rode in a triangle pattern with one man leading at the head of the formation. The others in the vanguard had turned, some standing in their saddles, to see what was happening. Soldiers on either side of the leader

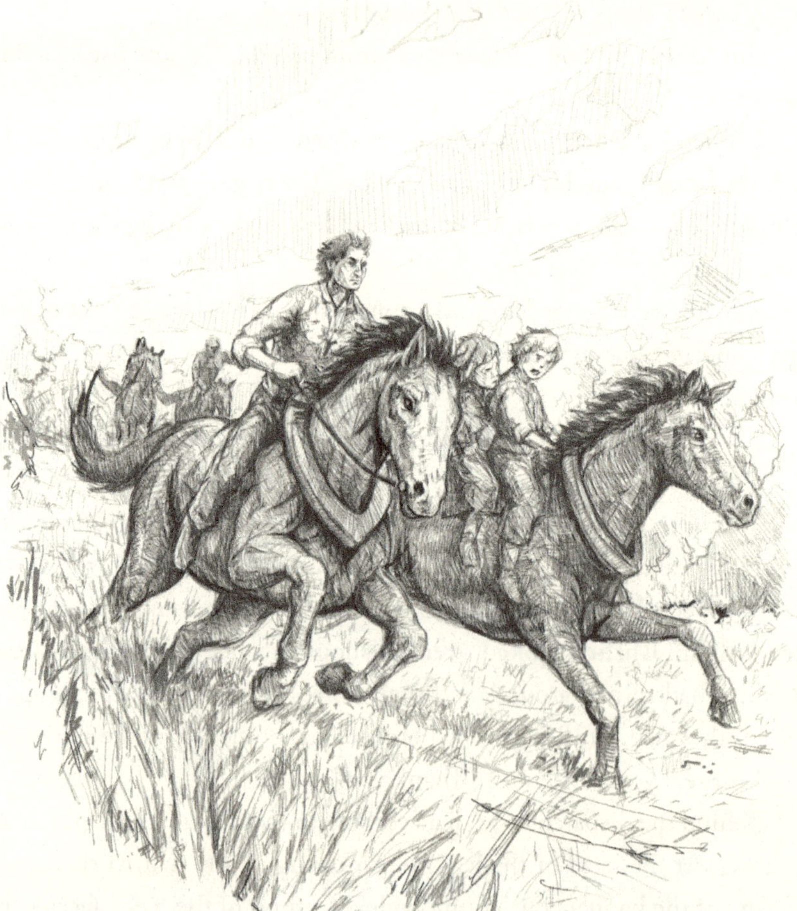

carried a long pole with a colorful flag attached to the end. The banner on the right was deep red with the figure of a silver lion in the center. The other banner had a royal blue field with a gold-colored sickle and three shafts of golden wheat in the center.

"The red flag is King Kimael's banner," Ehrlich told his boys with relief. "The other is the banner of the Basil lords."

"They sure scared those guys chasing us," Renn said. He turned and shouted at the fleeing men, who were almost out of view, "Serves you right, you stinky cowards!"

"Too bad they didn't catch 'em before they ran off," Tavier added with a look of indignation on his face.

The boys' mood changed with the danger behind them, and they gaped in admiration at the army. A wave of relief crashed over Ehrlich as the small detachment approached. Only a few moments ago, he was certain his boys would be dead before the day was out. The thought that Delphia and his little Chria would never have known what happened nearly brought tears to his eyes.

"This is a stroke of luck!" Ehrlich said, trying to help calm himself as much as to reassure the boys. "That's Lord Danu's band of strangers. Now we don't need to travel all the way to Basilea—by the way, don't repeat that part about a band of strangers." Ehrlich suddenly had visions of one of his boys asking Lord Danu why they were called a band of strangers.

"But, Father," Tavier said, "I wanted to see Basilea."

"Yeah," Renn chimed in. "Me too. I've never seen a real city before."

"I know, boys. But the reason we were going to Basilea was to see Lord Danu and ask for his help," Ehrlich explained. "Once things return to normal, we'll take some time and go to Basilea to visit Grandma." He wiped the sweat from his forehead and realized, for the first time, that his straw hat was gone. It must have fallen off during the chase.

The detachment of soldiers coming to greet them pulled back on their reins and brought their horses to a halt just in front of Ehrlich and the boys. A man with brown skin and short black hair advanced toward them on his horse. A curved scimitar hung, sheathed, from his hip, and a sling was looped around his belt next to it. He studied Ehrlich for a moment with intense brown eyes before looking at the boys with interest and then back to Ehrlich.

"I am called Aidan," he said with a thick accent.

Ehrlich knew there were various nomadic tribes in the central plains and southern deserts of Lemuria, but he didn't know much about them. However, by this man's features, choice of weapons, and accent, Ehrlich surmised he was a Marahi Devi from the desert country of Sarundra.

"Thank the gods we found you, Master Aidan," Ehrlich said. "My name is Ehrlich, and these are my boys, Tavier and Renn."

"You and boys in trouble, no?" He used his chin to point in the direction their pursuers had fled and said, "Why men chase you and who they be?"

"Yes," Ehrlich said. "We are definitely in trouble. I believe they were Nortian soldiers."

The men with Aidan broke into a murmur of discussion, and Aidan raised an eyebrow and looked over his shoulder at them. The men were of different ages and various backgrounds. Ehrlich knew this, not just because of how they looked and spoke, but also by reputation. It was the reason people referred to Lord Danu's division as the band of strangers.

"Follow me. Lord Danu want to know this." Aidan turned his horse. The other soldiers parted as he trotted for the front of the legion.

Ehrlich looked at his boys. "Stay close. And remember, Lord Danu is the marquis, so mind your manners." They were good boys, but they had no experience with how to act around the noble class. Come to think of it, neither did he.

The men in the vanguard at the front of the legion saw them coming. The one who led the vanguard was Lord Danu. The son of the grand duke, Drake Basil. Lord Danu was nearly thirty and still a bachelor—a fact that was commonly known to irritate his father. Two other men from the vanguard accompanied the young lord to meet Ehrlich, his boys, and their escorts. One looked a lot like a Nortian: big with dark hair and a beard with no mustache. However, he wasn't wearing black armor. The other wore all black, even his horse was black, but he was clean-shaven and his lithe form looked more like a traveling acrobat than any Nortian Ehrlich had seen before.

"What is this, Aidan?" Lord Danu brought his muscular gray steed to a stop. Raising his right hand, he signaled the others to halt. Lord Danu had thick blond hair that didn't quite reach his shoulders and was a bit mussed from riding. His broad, natural smile reached all the way to his eyes.

"Farmer say Nortian soldiers chasing them," Aidan said.

The young lord examined Ehrlich and his boys with a look of sudden interest. "Greetings, my good man. I am Lord Danu. Is this true?"

The man wearing black moved his horse closer and scrutinized Ehrlich and his boys with eyes that were also nearly black.

"Hello, my lord." Ehrlich made his best bow from horseback and said, "I am Ehrlich Demaris, a farmer from Leedsdale. Yes, it is true. Had my sons and I not come across your legion, I fear . . . well, I don't want to think about what would have happened."

Lord Danu turned and addressed the soldier in black. "Raven, are you aware of Nortian soliders this far south?"

Ehrlich wondered if the man's name was truly Raven, or if he was called that because of his penchant for all things black. The only part of him that wasn't dark was his milky-white skin.

Raven didn't speak. Instead, his expression turned grave, and he shook his head.

Lord Danu considered this, and then he looked at the boys and raised an eyebrow. Their faces were smudged with dust and dirt, but they stared, slack-jawed, at the lord and his men. Danu's entire demeanor softened, and he smiled.

"Lucky for those Nortians they didn't catch you, Master Ehrlich," the young lord said. "I'm sure your boys would've given them a good, old-fashioned, Boranica-style beating."

The soldiers laughed, and Ehrlich relaxed a little. He'd always heard that Lord Danu was easygoing and good-natured. He shot a glance at the soldier with no mustache. He didn't seem to be bothered by the jab

Lord Danu had made at Nortia's expense—if anything, he laughed harder than the rest.

"I apologize for delaying you and your men," Ehrlich said. "But my mission is urgent and very important . . . The Meskhoni, Artio, sent us."

"On an urgent mission with two small—but obviously strong—boys?" Lord Danu asked as he surveyed them. Renn was holding on to Tavier, while the older boy still gripped Ranger's reins. The boys were staring at the soldiers and grinning.

"A disguise to avoid suspicion," Ehrlich explained quickly. "This is my eldest son, Tavier, and this is Renn." Renn tried to bow and nearly fell off Ranger.

"Of course! No wonder your name and face is so familiar, Ehrlich." Danu looked directly at Renn and said, "You must be the famous young man who was marked so noticeably on midsummer's Azur-Aven ten years back."

Ehrlich heard a chorus of murmurs break out among the ranks of soldiers. Raven shot a look at the soldiers, and the talking immediately stopped.

"Last time I saw you, Renn, you were just a little baby," Lord Danu continued, as if he hadn't noticed the commotion among his men. "You certainly have grown well."

"Thank you, my lord, but I'm really not very famous," Renn politely replied, and then added, "In fact, most people avoid me."

Lord Danu broke out in cheerful laughter, and Renn's cheeks colored a deep red. The men within hearing distance also chuckled. Raven, who had silenced the soldiers a moment ago, now acted as though he hadn't heard this remark at all. Ehrlich found this peculiar because, although Raven's dark eyes were constantly searching the horizon, the look on the man's face made it clear that he was alert to his immediate surroundings.

Lord Danu stopped laughing. "You don't have to be well-liked to be famous. If people avoid you, it's only because they're afraid of what they don't understand. Take my father, for example. Everyone avoids him out of fear, and yet he's the most famous duke in all of Boranica. I, on the other hand, am a nice, friendly type of person, and although people like my company, they don't jump at my voice like they do with my father."

"What makes you think people enjoy your company?" the Nortian-looking soldier, sitting on a horse next to Raven, chided. "We only associate with you because nobody else will have us!"

"You see what I mean? No respect unless you're feared." Lord Danu winked at Renn. "By the way, allow me to introduce my 'band of strangers,' as many call us."

Ehrlich felt his face flush, and he quickly glanced at his boys—hoping neither would say anything about him using the same phrase only moments ago.

"That overgrown, under-disciplined ape you just heard from," Lord Danu said, pointing to the large man who had just baited him, "is Lieutenant Kivas of my personal guard."

Kivas nodded to Ehrlich and his boys and said, "Good to meet you."

"Thank you," Ehrlich answered. "The pleasure is ours."

"Are you from Nortia?" Renn asked.

"Why, yes. I am." Kivas saluted Renn. "You're quite observant for one so young."

"Kivas is one of the few Nortians I trust—or even like, for that matter," Lord Danu said. Then, gesturing toward the quiet man on the black stallion, he continued. "This is my trusted advisor and Captain of the Guard, Raven."

Raven gave a curt nod.

"I can't place your nationality, sir," Renn said. "Aidan is obviously from Sarundra, and Lieutenant Kivas—"

"That's enough, Renn," Ehrlich interrupted Renn, and Tavier elbowed him.

"I'm impressed you figured out Aidan's origins so quickly, Renn," Lord Danu said. "Most people aren't sure which plains tribe he is from."

Renn smiled and said, "I apologize for speaking out of turn, my lord."

"On the contrary," Lord Danu said, "I'm glad you did. I'd be quite interested in hearing where you think Captain Raven is from."

Ehrlich watched Renn screw up his face in concentration as he looked the captain over. Raven cocked his head a little and raised an eyebrow—as if tempting Renn to try.

"His face is too angular to be Boranican or Nortian, but his skin is too light to be from the plains tribes. And if he were from down south, I'd expect his skin to be tan. So, I'll guess he's from Achtland."

All eyes turned to Raven to see if Renn was correct. The corner of the captain's mouth turned up into what might have been the beginning of a smile. "I'm from Achtland . . . and many other places as well."

"Ah, c'mon, Raven," Kivas said. "Why do you always have to be so mysterious?"

"You know the rules among our band," Danu said. "Our past is ours to keep or to share as we please. Now, tell the soldiers to take a short rest while I speak with this good man."

Kivas sat taller in his saddle and gave Lord Danu a smart salute. "Yes, sir," he said, and turned to carry out Lord Danu's order.

"Thank you, my lord," Ehrlich said.

Lord Danu dismounted. The young lord took off his dark leather riding gloves and tucked them into his saddle. Then he untied his riding cloak, laid it in front of his saddle horn, and walked over to Ehrlich. The young lord wore high sturdy riding boots, well-tanned leather riding pants, and a deep blue shirt that billowed at the sleeves. Ehrlich noticed Renn staring at Lord Danu's eyes as the young lord approached—his right eye was blue and the left was brown. *By Azur's light*, Ehrlich thought, *I hope that boy doesn't blurt something out about Lord Danu's eyes being different colors!*

Ehrlich climbed off Dusty, handed the reins to Renn, and took a couple steps away from the boys with Lord Danu. Raven didn't dismount, but instead he pressed his black boots into his horse's flank to urge the animal closer.

Raven made Ehrlich uneasy. He sat in stony silence on his horse. Like a statue of onyx towering above them. His dark hair was parted to one side to keep his long bangs out of his eyes, which were slightly narrow and shadowed with dark, graceful eyebrows.

"I assume," Lord Danu began, "Artio's concerns and your run-in today with those men from Nortia are related?"

"It's a rather long story," Ehrlich answered. "To be honest, I am shocked that armed men would attempt to overtake us on the open road. I believed the Meskhoni when he told me things were urgent, but I never thought I'd be running for my life when we set out to find you. The Meskhoni believes there is a conspiracy between the town leaders in Leedsdale and a man named Kahn Devin in the north. I don't know if there is a connection with that and the men who were chasing us, but I did notice a few Nortians watching us as we left town."

"Hmm . . ." Lord Danu shook his head. "That man is really beginning to bug me. I've just been to Tearsia, putting down a rebellion caused by Kahn Devin's conspirators in that area. Tell me what's been happening in Leedsdale."

Ehrlich proceeded to tell Lord Danu about the water difficulty and the responses he and Jomard had received from the town council. He also told him of his visit to Artio later that night.

"Artio thinks it's getting out of hand," Ehrlich said. Then, softer to make sure his boys wouldn't hear, he added, "There is one other thing. Apparently, Kahn Devin has somehow been watching Renn. At the festival last month, there was an . . . accident that nearly took Renn's life. The Meskhoni believes Kahn Devin was somehow behind that. The Meskhoni believes he may be getting ready to 'make his move'—Artio said you'd understand what that meant."

"Yes . . . I do—open rebellion." Lord Danu rubbed his beardless chin and looked up at Raven, who now seemed to be concentrating completely on Lord Danu and the story Ehrlich had just told. "Raven, choose five of my best men to accompany us to Leedsdale. Send the rest back to Basilea with Sergeant Andron in charge. Instruct him to inform my father of our situation and that I will return as quickly as possible with my report."

Raven simply nodded, his black hair falling over his left eye, turned his powerful stallion, and galloped toward the legion.

"Thank you, my lord, for giving ear to our plight," Ehrlich said in the same formal manner he used to narrate his story. He hesitated a moment and then added, "I mean no disrespect, Lord Danu, but perhaps you should bring more than five soldiers. I fear there may be more men from Nortia looking for us. What if they set a trap?"

Lord Danu's eyes gleamed, and his lips curved into an adventurous smile. "I hope they do."

THE BLESSING

Ehrlich watched as the legion formed back into ranks and began riding southwest toward Basilea with Sergeant Andron at its head. Lord Danu turned and introduced the soldiers Raven had selected to accompany them on the trip back to Leedsdale. Soon their small group was traveling northeast, retracing the path Ehrlich and his boys had recently blazed. Raven spurred his horse ahead and quickly became a black speck on the horizon. Knowing the captain and his black stallion were scouting the trail ahead helped Ehrlich relax a bit.

Ehrlich, with the boys riding on his left side, followed behind Lord Danu. Ehrlich was startled when Tellio, who rode on the other side of Renn and Tavier, started to sing in a deep bass voice. *"Pass me a pint, and play me a jig. Bring me a wench to feed me figs—"*

"Tellio," Lord Danu interrupted. "We all love to hear you sing, but don't you think that song's a bit much for young boys?"

Tellio looked at the boys for a moment, and his bald head flushed slightly. "Beggin' your pardon, boys. You're both so big and strong-looking, I thought you were full-grown men."

Renn and Tavier sat a little taller on Ranger, and Ehrlich had to chuckle and shake his head. Like so many others of Lord Danu's band of strangers, Tellio wasn't originally from Boranica. It was obvious he was from Anytos—his thick, waxed mustache that curled to a point at both ends gave that away.

"That's our Tellio," Cole said. He rode on Ehrlich's right side and leaned forward to glance down the line at the big man from Anytos. "He can always turn a criticism into a compliment and make you laugh at the same time." Cole was a good-looking young man with light brown hair that looked like it hadn't seen a comb in weeks—but it framed his face in such a way as to make him appear rather fashionable. He wore the same blue jacket and light mail armor as the others, but in addition he had a leather cord around his neck with multiple bone pendants, each carved with a strange rune.

"Turning a criticism into a compliment is a nice trait to possess," Ehrlich said. "Probably wins him a lot of friends."

"It might if he could stay in one place long enough to make any," Lord Danu said over his shoulder. "Tellio's not happy unless he's on the road."

"True. True." The bald man twisted his mustache between his thumb and index finger. "There's something about the open road that makes a man feel free."

"Renn—Tavier?" Lord Danu dropped back to be a little closer to the conversation so he could talk without shouting. "Do you want to hear the story of how we found Tellio?"

"Why do you always have to tell that story, Danu?" Kivas complained from behind Ehrlich. "Tell them something else."

"I'm sure they'd much rather hear about Cole, my lord," Tellio said with a big smile. "What with him being noble and dashing, trying to stay free of all the ladies who chase him . . . He's got much better stories to tell than I."

"See what I mean?" Cole said to Ehrlich. "Always turning attention away from himself to compliment someone else."

"I don't know if I'd call that a compliment," Radien said through a big, toothy smile. He rode directly behind the boys and was fixing the feathers of an arrow resting on his thigh and saddle horn. "I've heard some of your stories. Not very flattering if you ask me."

Cole grabbed a handful of nuts out of his saddlebag and threw them back at Radien. The boys laughed because one of the nuts got hung up in Radien's coarse red beard.

"I want to hear the story," Renn said to Lord Danu.

"Yeah, me too," Tavier joined in. Kivas muttered something under his breath and sighed in defeat.

"About four years ago, Kivas and I finished inspecting some of my father's troops near Tauret—in fact, that's when we met Cole, come to think of it."

"Now that's a story!" Kivas boomed out with a laugh. "Cole was running from a lady and a ghost! Let's tell that story instead."

Cole's eyes widened, and he drew a quick breath. "Don't mock the spirits, Kivas." Cole took one of the bone pendants between his thumb and forefinger and rubbed it while he looked to the sky and mumbled some words Ehrlich didn't recognize. Kivas rolled his eyes and shook his head. Radien chuckled quietly.

"We finished inspecting the troops early," Lord Danu said loudly, bringing the discussion back to his story, "and Kivas wanted to head into town for some entertainment."

"Wholesome entertainment," Kivas added quickly. "Maybe see a play or something."

"I didn't know you fancied the theater," Micha said to the big Nortian as he pushed his horse from the rear to join the conversation. He brushed a strand of his thinning hair away from his hooked nose. "If it's fine arts and wholesome entertainment you want, I'll make sure you find it next time we have leave."

Kivas stumbled to reply, and the others laughed. Micha had an innocent expression, but Ehrlich thought his eyes had a hard look about them.

"Would you louts stay quiet long enough for me to tell the story?" Lord Danu looked back and winked at the boys. "Let's see . . . Where was I?"

"Going to Tauret," Renn said.

"Oh, yes. Well, on the way we came across a gypsy circus."

"Not a circus," Tellio interjected. "A carnival. There's a big difference."

"Okay. A gypsy carnival. Since Kivas was rather thirsty, and sure he could find . . . uh, wholesome entertainment with gypsies, we decided to stop and have a look around."

Kivas joined in. "There was a big crowd of people in a circle near the center of the circus—uh, carnival. So we went to see what was so interesting."

"Wait a minute," Lord Danu said. "You're skipping some important parts."

"That's not important," Kivas said. Then he threw his arms in the air and looked to Ehrlich. "Okay. So I had a few pints of ale. Nothing extreme, mind you." He turned to Lord Danu and the other men. "There, are you happy?"

"Well, if you hadn't had a *few* pints," the young lord replied, "we probably never would have met Tellio. You see, the crowd was gathered around the 'Strongest Man in the World.' That's what a big colorful sign said on the wagon behind Tellio."

The big bald man blushed a little at that, and Tavier said, "You're not really the strongest man in the world, are you?"

"That's what Kivas asked him at the carnival," Lord Danu answered with a laugh. "Except he wasn't quite so polite when he asked. In fact, he challenged Tellio to an arm wrestle."

"Who won?" Renn asked anxiously.

"They arm-wrestled for more than a half hour, and neither could best the other. Then they tried stick pulling. And finally, they had an all-out wrestling match. They ruined a wagon and a bunch of supplies, but there was no clear winner. In the end, Kivas had to admit Tellio was at least tied as the strongest man in the world."

At this, all the men broke out in raucous laughter—all but Kivas.

"I didn't say that," Kivas said, trying to defend himself, but nobody would listen.

As they traveled and joked, Ehrlich felt better than he had in weeks about their prospects. The lighthearted attitude of Lord Danu's men was infectious. Ehrlich's spirits raised even more when, just before dark, they found his abandoned wagon—still on the side of the road where he and the boys had left it earlier that day, with all their belongings inside.

Cole and Radien helped Ehrlich fix the leading lines and yoke Ranger and Dusty back to the wagon, then the boys climbed in—Tavier took the seat up front next to Ehrlich—and they headed toward Leedsdale as the sun was setting behind them.

Raven selected a campsite about a hundred steps off the main road in the center of a grove of aspens on the far side of a small hill. He obviously wasn't pleased with the location but told Lord Danu there was nothing better. As soon as the canvas tents were up, Raven disappeared. Tellio made a small fire and began preparing supper using a large, flat stone a short distance away. Renn and Tavier sat near the fire on a fallen tree, opposite from where Tellio worked. Ehrlich finished setting up their tent, picked up his lute, and noticed Renn watching the big bald man as he cooked and sang songs from his homeland.

"Strange, isn't he?" Renn said quietly to Tavier, as Ehrlich walked past the boys.

"What's that?" Tavier said without looking up from the stick he was whittling.

"Tellio." Renn nodded toward the muscular soldier, and Tavier paused to stare at the man. Tellio was busy peeling potatoes and dropping them into a pot of water. He had taken off his jacket and mail shirt, and underneath he wore a rust-stained, tattered undergarment that left his arms bare. Ehrlich wasn't surprised by the big man's affinity for tattoos; it was another common trait among the men living in the Anytos region. A tattoo on his right bicep was shaped in a heart with an arrow through it and something written inside—probably a girl's name—and two battle-axes crisscrossed each other on his left forearm.

"What's so strange about him?" Ehrlich asked and sat on an adjacent log by Micha, who played softly on a lute of his own.

"It doesn't seem to fit him," Renn said. "You know . . . he looks tough and mean. It's a little funny to see him singing and cooking. Don't you think?"

"I suppose," Tavier replied and then went back to whittling his stick.

Ehrlich nodded and watched for a moment.

"Ho, Tellio!" Radien shouted as he and Kivas approached the clearing. "You got room in that pot for a couple rabbits?"

Tellio's eyes lit up, and he dropped a spoon into the pot as he hurried over to inspect the fresh kill Kivas held up. "There's always room for rabbit on the menu. I see you shot these in the head."

"Don't bring up how they were killed, Tellio," Kivas complained. "I've been listening to Radien brag for the past twenty minutes about how good he is with that bow of his."

"Well, I did hit the rabbits on the run. At over a hundred paces. With only one shot each," Radien said with an exaggerated bow.

The boys looked at each other, clearly impressed. Ehrlich chuckled—although he had to admit he could never come close to a shot like that.

After dinner was long over, Ehrlich sat next to Lord Danu and the dying fire and looked at the stars. Kivas was snoring—passed out against a tree trunk with an empty mug lying next to him in the dirt. His black beard had bits of food tangled in it. Insect song filled the night with chirping and light buzzing noises. The night air smelled clean with just a hint of juniper. The boys were finally asleep in the tent Ehrlich had set up earlier. After all that had occurred that day, Ehrlich was grateful for a few minutes of peace and relaxation. Although Lord Danu hadn't said as much, Ehrlich figured the young lord felt the same way.

"Shall I keep first watch tonight, my lord?"

Ehrlich's heart skipped a beat when the voice sounded behind him, and Lord Danu jumped to his feet with his sword half-drawn. Raven seemed to have materialized out of nowhere.

"Don't do that, Raven," the young lord said. "You're going to drive me to an early grave."

The corners of Raven's mouth turned up slightly. "Shall I keep first watch tonight, my lord?"

Lord Danu made a show of shoving his sword back into its sheath. "Put Cole on first watch, then meet me at my tent. I want to discuss some plans before tomorrow."

Raven disappeared into the darkness, and Lord Danu took a deep breath and brushed himself off.

"Well, Ehrlich, will you tend to the fire before turning in?" Lord Danu asked, nodding toward Kivas as if to say, *He won't be doing it.*

"Of course, my lord." Ehrlich watched the young lord walk away and then pulled out his pipe, packed it with his favorite Domerian tobacco, and turned back to studying the stars and his thoughts. Millions of tiny lights crowded the night sky. He could never look at them for long without thinking about Renn's blessing ten years ago during midsummer's Azur-Aven.

Six babies had been blessed before Renn—including Genea Lucian, whom the Meskhoni said was marked by the gods. Raul Lucian had shouted with pride, but Ehrlich was happy. It was unusual for a baby to be marked, and never had two been marked by the gods in one night. Ehrlich figured Renn wouldn't be marked now, which meant his son would be able to grow up with the family and help around the farm.

But when the Meskhoni placed Renn on the Earthstone and applied the ointments and started the blessing, sound came from everywhere all at once. It moved like a rushing wind with hurricane fury through the trees and over the fields, yet there was no breeze. The crowd's attention scattered as everyone looked around to determine the source of the disturbance. Somebody close to Ehrlich shouted, "Look . . . up in the sky!"

Ehrlich looked up and saw a massive concentration of light, as though all the stars in the sky were converging and joining strength. The light consolidated high above the earth to form a single conduit that surged to the ground like lightning and completely enveloped the Earthstone and Renn in brilliant white flames.

The light gathered together and focused on a single point on top of the altar. Ehrlich tried to rush to his son's side, but the heat from the energy was too intense. He fell back and shielded his eyes. Then, as abruptly as it began, the light withdrew into the dark night sky and the sound stopped.

The ensuing silence was deafening. Ehrlich stumbled to the Earthstone.

Artio came forward and stood on the opposite side of the stone, his eyes wide and his hands trembling.

The fresh flowers that had been so lovely and colorful were reduced to blackened ash and no longer resembled an arrangement of any kind. The earth surrounding the stone, which had been laden with food and gifts, now smoldered and steamed. The scent of roses and pansies was replaced with the smell of burned dinner.

Renn lay in the center of this carnage unscathed, looking up at Ehrlich as though nothing had happened.

Ehrlich searched Renn's body for signs of injury and was shocked when the only change he found was a flying white eagle above Renn's right breast. Renn kept that mark still. It hadn't dimmed in time, and nothing could remove it.

Artio took Renn and examined the mark, then gave the baby back to Ehrlich. "I have never seen or heard of such a marking by the gods," he said. "He will possess awesome power. Keep him safe. I suspect there will be those who will seek his life."

That seemed like only yesterday, but it also felt like ages ago. And today, the old man's prophecy came true.

AMBUSH

The group broke camp early the next morning. As Renn was helping his father take down their tent and put away bedrolls, Raven walked past him. He must have gotten up quite a bit earlier, because his things were already packed and he was sweating as though he'd been doing hard work for some time.

"Did you have a good workout, Raven?" Lord Danu asked the mysterious man.

Raven nodded once and took a long drink from the leather flask tied to his saddle.

"You're going to kill yourself, Raven," Kivas bellowed from the far side of the clearing. "You need to learn to relax. A couple mugs of strong ale will do you more good than all that sword practicing you do."

Raven actually smiled and said, "One day, when you're too intoxicated to protect yourself, you'll be glad I left the drinking to you."

Although the other soldiers laughed, Renn wasn't sure if Raven was joking or being serious.

By sunup, they had eaten a good breakfast of fried pork and bread and were back on the main road heading toward Leedsdale. Ehrlich brought out his lute and played a light tune while Micha played harmony on a wooden recorder. Renn listened to the music but found himself watching Lord Danu's dark-haired captain with profound interest. Raven, Renn noticed, acted and looked the same as he had the day before—silent and wrapped in black clothing.

Curiosity got the better of Renn, and he turned to Tellio, who rode alongside the wagon, and in hushed tones asked, "Why is Raven so quiet all the time?"

The big man twisted his waxed mustache as he considered Raven. "He's had a difficult past, I think."

"What happened to him?"

"I don't think anyone knows. He doesn't talk about it much."

"Then how do you know he had a difficult past?"

"You sure ask tough questions for a little guy." Tellio laughed. The big man rubbed his bald head before speaking again. "When I traveled with the gypsies, I learned a lot about men and life on the road. I think Raven is sad."

Renn watched the dark-haired captain's back and thought about Tellio's explanation. "He doesn't seem sad," he whispered to the bald man. "He seems . . . cold."

Tellio got a philosophical look on his face and said, "Every man has secret sorrows that are hidden from our view; oftentimes, a man seems cold or angry when he is really just sad."

Lord Danu had been riding in the back of the small group, talking with Radien, and heard the end of their conversation as he rode toward the front. "How could anyone be sad on a beautiful day like today?" The young lord was in good spirits, as usual, and soon Tellio was laughing as Lord Danu exchanged sarcastic remarks with the burly Lieutenant Kivas. Lord Danu also entertained Renn and Tavier with stories and rides on his horse. Radien, Cole, and Micha brought up the rear; they were arguing about longbows and swords. With seven men talking over each other, Renn couldn't make out much of what they were saying—nor did he try.

"Lord Danu, how did you get to be a lord?" Tavier asked at one point.

"A cruel joke of the gods, Tavier," Kivas answered before Lord Danu could reply.

"Yes," Lord Danu said without missing a beat. "And to make matters worse, they cursed me with this loud Nortian barbarian for a lieutenant." Lord Danu cast a mock glare at Kivas and then winked his blue eye at the boys. "Actually, I didn't do anything . . . I was born into it. Generations ago, my family colonized Basilea and has ruled this part of Boranica ever since. Basilea, of course, is named after the Basils."

As Lord Danu explained his bloodline to Renn and his brother, the small group entered one of the shaded wooded areas that the boys and their father had passed through the day before. The break from the persistent sun was welcome, but Renn felt a foreboding darkness. Like the shadows of the forest had unseen eyes. The hair on the back of his neck stood on end, and he looked up to make certain nothing was about to pounce on him. He hesitated to warn the group, however, because in the past only he could feel this strange sensation.

At the head of the group, Raven stopped and raised his hand. Lord Danu fell silent and studied the woods on either side of the road. Radien took out his bow and nocked an arrow in the string.

"What is it?" Lord Danu asked Raven.

"We've got company," the dark-haired captain said—as if it explained everything. Apparently, to Lord Danu and his men, it did. Tellio pulled out a large ax while the others drew swords.

Renn felt anticipation from the unseen eyes. He took quick, short breaths to try to slow the pounding of his heart.

"How many are there?" Kivas asked, squinting as he peered into the dark forest.

Raven only shook his head.

A burly man who was dark-haired like Kivas stepped out from the trees about twenty-five paces ahead of the small party and blocked the road.

"There are enough to take care of you if necessary, traitor," the man said to Kivas.

Ten other large men in dark, studded leather armor materialized from the woods on either side of the road and joined the first man to block the way forward.

Renn moved to the side of the straw bale that was immediately behind his father and watched from over his father's shoulder. He was thankful that Raven, Lord Danu, and Kivas were between him and the newcomers.

"Krilahn," Kivas said lightly. "What brings the madman's mindless cronies so far south?"

Krilahn and his men had long, dark hair and full beards with no mustaches—typical for Nortian warriors. Their armor was split at the waist to hang down and protect each thigh. In one gauntleted hand, they each held round wooden shields that bore the figure of a rabid-looking black dog. They brandished swords or long-handled maces in their other hands.

"Clever, Kivas," Krilahn said through clenched teeth. "Laugh while you still can because eventually you will hang."

"What difference does it make?" Kivas asked with a mocking grin. "King Thrakus already has a reward on my head. Did he send you all the way down here just to fetch me?"

"Don't flatter yourself," Krilahn replied. "Your little rebellion at Nadgala was only a minor setback. It should please you to know the villagers you fought to save have been rounded up and given a nice warm home"—Krilahn flashed a wicked grin, and some of his men started to laugh—"deep in the slave mines under the Cragg Mountains."

"They were innocent farmers," Kivas said. Renn couldn't see the lieutenant's face, but from the way Kivas emphasized each word, it was obvious he was angry.

"There are no innocents in war, you fool," Krilahn spat back at him. "You choose a side and fight, or you become a resource to be used as the victor sees fit."

"There is no honor in using the weak."

Krilahn's face reddened as he shouted back at Kivas, "Don't lecture me about honor, you hypocrite. You went against orders, and a lot of good men died by your treachery."

Kivas didn't respond. In the strained silence, Renn heard the faint cry of a hawk from somewhere high above.

"Oh, and the *innocent* farmer you stabbed in the back," Krilahn continued, "his wife and child were gathered with the others, but they weren't sent to slave in the mines—it was the Well of Sacrifice for them."

Kivas ripped his sword from its scabbard, and a metallic ring sliced through the air.

Lord Danu placed his hand on his lieutenant's shoulder. "Easy, my friend."

Krilahn's eyes narrowed and darkened. "You're insignificant as far as King Thrakus is concerned." Turning his attention to Lord Danu, his tone grew condescending. "Lordling, give me the boy, and you and your soldiers will be free to run along."

Radien, Cole, and Micha moved forward to help shield Renn, his father, and Tavier.

"You said you've brought enough men to take care of us, if necessary," Lord Danu answered. "I only count eleven. That's not even enough for two of us. You'd better scurry on home for more help."

"Ha ha," Krilahn said. "I see Kivas's bad habits have rubbed off on you, lordling."

To his right, Renn heard movement from behind the trees. But before he could react, someone grabbed him from behind. Renn was yanked off the straw bale, and his leg slammed into the side of the wagon.

"They have Renn!" Tavier shouted.

The man holding Renn dragged him toward the cover of the woods. Renn kicked and wiggled, but the man's powerful grip dug harder into the back of his neck.

He reached behind to try to pry the man's hand free. Renn dug his heels into the dirt, trying desperately to stop his captor from making it into the cover of the trees.

Renn heard a whistling sound and a low thud. His captor dropped Renn facedown onto a small bush at the side of the dirt road and then, with a groan, fell directly on top of him, crushing Renn through scratching twigs and filling his mouth with leaves and dirt.

"Get the boy!" The body of the man on top of Renn muffled the voice, but Renn knew it came from Krilahn. The sounds of metal hitting metal and men shouting was also muted by the body on top of him.

Renn tried to push himself up, but his abductor was too heavy.

Renn squirmed and wiggled until he could squeeze out from under his captor. The man had a dagger buried deep in the back of his skull. Blood dripped down the hilt.

Renn pushed himself up, spit the dirt and leaves from his mouth, and turned to run back to the wagon.

Raven blocked the way. The captain fought two paces in front of Renn against four of the big northerners.

The captain held a dagger in his left hand, and in his right he wielded a short sword. As one man lunged at him, he gracefully parried the attack, slicing into the man's throat with the dagger while his sword pierced the eye of a second attacker.

Raven swept the feet out from under the man whose throat he'd slashed, forcing him to fall into the man immediately behind. Renn's eyes widened when Raven used the falling men as leverage to flip over the fourth attacker. The captain twisted in the air and rammed his dagger into the back of the man's neck and then shoved his sword into the forehead of the falling man he'd used as leverage to flip into the air.

The dark-haired captain whistled, and his muscular black horse charged in. In a single, swift motion, Raven was on his great horse and riding toward Krilahn and the two remaining warriors who stood by his side. Krilahn and the two men ran behind the trees with Raven close behind.

Lord Danu was pulling his sword out of a soldier's chest near the side of the wagon when Renn ran back for safety.

Where was his father?

Radien was wiping off his sword; his bow was now neatly hanging over his right shoulder, and Tellio was examining the blood on his ax. Both men were still on their horses in front of the wagon. Renn couldn't see Micha, but Cole was in the wagon with Tavier attending to his father.

"Father!" Renn shouted as he climbed into the wagon.

"He's all right, Renn," Cole assured him. "He took a nasty blow to the head, but he doesn't appear to be hurt too badly."

"What happened?"

Cole pointed to a dead man who had one of Radien's arrows sticking out of his chest and was lying on the road next to the wagon. "That man hit your father in the back of the head when the other one took you."

Renn looked at his brother. Tavier watched as Cole tended to the boys' father. Tavier's wide eyes were glazed with tears and his face was pale. Renn clasped his hands over his head and watched as Cole flipped through the bone pendants of his necklace until he found the one he was looking for and began to pray and rub the rune.

This is my fault, Renn thought. What would he do if his father never woke up? What would his mother do? How could she take care of the family without their father?

Renn looked around at the bodies littering the road, and his hands trembled as he saw the carnage. Pools of blood oozed from the wounds of the dead northerners. Arms had been severed from two bodies, and a detached head stared into the sky.

Renn felt a sickness grow in the pit of his stomach, and he became light-headed. He fell over the side of the wagon and then pushed himself to his knees and heaved onto the dirt road.

Everything turned black.

※

Renn was lying flat on his back when he awoke. Faces towered over him, gradually coming into focus, but the blue sky overhead was spinning.

"He's coming to," Lord Danu said. "Tavier, fetch the canteen of water from my saddlebag."

I fainted, Renn realized. He sat up too fast, and the faces and sky spun in faster circles. He felt hands catch his shoulder and lower him gently back to the ground.

"Sorry," Renn said. "I'm fine . . . really."

"It's okay, Renn," Lord Danu said with a light laugh. "We're not in a hurry. Lie here for a few moments, and you'll feel better soon."

"None of us like the sight of blood, boy," Tellio remarked. "We're just more accustomed to seeing it."

Renn pushed himself to his elbows and took a drink of water from the canteen. He managed to sit properly, and then he dumped a little water into his hand and splashed it onto his face. Still, Lord Danu had to help Renn into the wagon. The young lord gave him a cup of water and a blanket and told him to watch over his father. Renn knew Lord Danu was just being kind. Renn had been no help at all in the battle, and to make matters worse he'd fainted in front of everyone. He punched the bale of straw and looked at his father. Someday Renn would be able to defend his family. Someday he would be so strong that no one would ever be able to harm those he loved.

Lord Danu turned to his men and said, "All right, how many shovels do we have with us?" Without waiting for an answer, he proceeded to pull Renn's father's shovel from the back of the wagon and announced, "We'd better get digging if we're going to bury this trash before nightfall."

"We're going to bury these guys?" Radien asked incredulously. "Why not throw them off the side of the road and be done with it?"

"Their spirits would wander the land in a state of in-between," Cole said with conviction.

"Dead is dead," Kivas grumbled. "You're too superstitious."

"Spirits haunt us in many different ways—even if it's only in our dreams."

"What's that supposed to mean?" Kivas narrowed his eyes, and Renn worried there might be another fight any minute.

"That's enough talk of ghosts," Lord Danu cut in. "I don't want common citizens accidentally stumbling upon dead Nortians. El Azur knows what kind of rumors that would cause."

Renn rubbed his shoulders and looked around for spirits. He'd never seen a person die before. He'd been told that spirits of the dead return to Valhasgar to wait for rebirth, but he wondered if you could see them when they left the body. If you couldn't see them, maybe you could *feel* them. He wondered what the sensation of being surrounded by spirits would feel like, and it occurred to him that the unseen eyes no longer watched.

Using swords and shovels, the young lord and his men dug a large pit on the side of the road and committed the bodies to a common grave. While they were throwing dirt onto the bodies, Renn heard two separate screams come from deep in the woods. The men stopped working and looked in the direction of the sound.

"I hope one of those screams came from Krilahn," Kivas said.

Renn hoped it wasn't Raven or Micha who'd screamed.

As Renn watched his newfound companions work, he realized two unusual things: First, Lord Danu was working as hard—or harder—than any of his men. Renn didn't consort with gentry often, actually never, but it seemed strange to him a lord of the House of Basil would engage in manual labor. Second, none of Lord Danu's men were seriously injured. Lord Danu and his six men had fought Krilahn and the ten men with him, plus the man who had grabbed Renn and the man who had hit his father—thirteen would-be assassins. Yet the worst injury among them was a small cut underneath Cole's left eye.

Hopefully Raven and Micha weren't hurt. The captain certainly hadn't been injured when he'd charged off into the woods after the retreating attackers.

Micha emerged from the trees. His wispy hair was plastered to his forehead with sweat. The sword in his right hand was dripping blood, and Renn felt nauseated. He took a deep breath and punched the straw again. He would not show weakness any longer at the sight of blood.

Lord Danu stopped working, looked at the young guard, and raised a single eyebrow. Micha simply nodded, wiped and sheathed his blade, and joined his comrades as they completed the burial.

The group traveled the rest of the afternoon in silence. Renn sat on the straw behind the seat of the wagon so he could watch his father, who was covered with a blanket and laid out on the two bales of straw that ran lengthwise in the center of the wagon bed. Tavier drove the team. Renn didn't argue with his brother about who should drive. He wanted to be by his father's side.

Before they left the shade of the woods, Renn felt the unseen eyes return. The watcher was angrier and more vengeful than before—Renn could feel the hair rise on the back of his neck and looked behind him and into the shadows of the woods. *What if there is another ambush waiting to be unleashed?* He was about to warn Lord Danu when the unseen eyes retreated.

Renn sat in silence as the wagon moved forward, contemplating the events of the last two days. When he and Tavier left on their trip only a day ago with their father, he was excited for the adventure. Now, he realized adventures weren't always fun. And battles *definitely* weren't glamorous. The vision of men lying in pools of their own blood kept replaying in front of his eyes. Renn felt his father's forehead and bent over to listen to his breathing. He was alive but still unconscious. Despite Lord Danu's reassurances, Renn didn't know if his father would ever wake up. And if he did, would he ever fully recover? Fortunately, none of Lord Danu's men were injured, but what about the next time? And Tavier was different now. His eyes held a far-off look, and he'd barely said a word to anybody since the battle.

When Renn and the small group finally left the woods, Raven and his horse were waiting off the side of the road. He had undoubtedly been riding all day, chasing—and perhaps killing—Krilahn's men, but he didn't seem battle-weary like the others. His face showed no emotion, and his dark eyes betrayed no sign of victory or regret.

Behind Raven, nine branded horses were grazing contentedly on tall grass. All the horses wore saddles and were picketed to a rope tied between two scrub oak trees. Renn was relieved. Not only because the dark-haired captain had returned without injury, but also to be back in the open. It was hotter and dustier, but at least they wouldn't be surprised by another ambush.

Lord Danu rode beside the wagon now, and Renn saw him wipe sweat and dirt from his face. His smile looked forced to Renn as the young lord waved to his captain. "Raven! I'm glad to see you. What happened?"

"Krilahn escaped," he replied flatly. "I caught the two who were with him trying to mount their horses. They don't need them anymore."

"Where did you find the other horses?" Lord Danu asked.

"They were picketed in the forest."

"Nine horses. We were attacked by thirteen men," Lord Danu said, "and we buried eight. You and Micha killed three more in the forest, so that means one other escaped in addition to Krilahn. Tavier," Lord Danu called, "do you recognize this brand?"

Tavier handed the reins to Renn, jumped down from the wagon seat, and hurried to where Raven had the horses picketed.

"Yes, my lord. It belongs to Hevor Shoen."

"That's what I thought." Lord Danu dismounted and walked to the horses, looking through their saddlebags. The young lord rubbed at his chin as he studied a document he found. He turned to Raven and said, "I think it's time we paid Hevor Shoen's estate a little visit. You and Radien go and watch his home and wait until he leaves. His new maid is a friend of ours. She's only been with him for two weeks now, but I think she will have information for us. If nothing else, she can let you in to search the place."

True to form, Raven simply nodded.

※

Renn's father woke as they approached Leedsdale. Renn wiped a tear from his cheek before anybody saw his emotion and gave his father water and something to eat.

His father cringed as he sat and rubbed the back of his head. "What happened?"

Renn spent the next hour retelling the story of the battle and answering his father's questions.

About one league outside of town, they turned off the main road, and Lord Danu led them to a small farmhouse of weathered wood. A dirty rope held the door of the small house to the doorframe. As their company approached, an old man and his dog came out to meet them.

"Greetings, Conrad," Lord Danu called, and he signaled for a halt. "And how is Dex these days?" He dismounted and stroked the ears of the old sheepdog that ran up to greet him.

"That lazy dog thinks he's retired. I got mice running everywhere, and he just lies on the porch, wagging his tail as they run by."

"That's because he's been taking lessons from Lieutenant Kivas. Haven't you, boy?" Lord Danu asked.

Tellio burst into laughter. Renn's brother jumped a little at the sound of Tellio's booming laugh, and that made both Renn and Tavier start laughing with the big bald man.

"Why work if there's someone else around to do it for you?" Kivas turned his palms upward. "That's why I accepted the position of lieutenant. So I could make everyone else do the work."

Renn took a deep breath and let himself smell the dry summer air and take in the scene around him—something he hadn't done since the battle.

The old barn behind the tired farmhouse was rickety and in shambles. Renn's father always said you could tell a lot about a farmer by how he kept his barn. Conrad didn't look like a farmer to Renn. He wore a patch over his left eye, and his white hair, dark eyebrows, and mustache gave him a rather distinguished look, despite his ragged breeches and stained tunic. He had a garden on the side of his home, but it was much too small to completely support him. He either lived off savings or was currently engaged in some form of business.

"Conrad, I need a favor," Lord Danu said.

Conrad leaned heavily on a cane, and he pushed Dex out of the way with his foot. "What else is new?" The old man pulled out a flask and took a long pull of whatever liquid it contained.

"These horses belong to Mr. Shoen," Lord Danu said. "We have a surprise for him, but I don't want him to know we have his horses just yet. I'd like to leave Cole here with the horses until tomorrow afternoon."

"Sure, why not? Of course, I will have to charge you extra this month—my salary doesn't include livery expenses."

"Just don't inflate the bill too much." Lord Danu placed his boot in the stirrup and remounted.

After the men secured the horses, Lord Danu gave Cole and Conrad some final instructions, and then the rest of the group continued to Leedsdale. Instead of taking the main route, they chose a route seldom traveled to avoid being seen. They circumvented the village by traveling along the base of the Hebät Mountains and occasionally cutting through fields. It took longer, so by the time the small group reached the Demaris farmhouse, the sun was nearing the horizon.

The farmhouse had never felt so wonderful to Renn. The smell of the dry wheat, the clucking of the chickens, and the small stream of smoke climbing into the evening sky from the chimney made his heart swell. He couldn't wait to sit around the table with his family again and share a loaf of his mother's fresh bread and jam.

When his mother came out of the house to greet them, it was all he could do to not bolt for her arms and cry. But he had to control himself. He wouldn't let these brave men see his weakness again, and so he remained in the wagon until they stopped.

Renn's resolve to be manly by maintaining control of his own emotions didn't stop his mother from taking him and Tavier in her arms and treating them like children. So, much to his chagrin, he was embarrassed in front of Lord Danu and his men anyway. Still, it was good to be home and great to be in his mother's arms.

VISITORS

"Lord Danu, welcome to our humble home," Delphia said with a curtsy. "I apologize for not being prepared to receive you and your men. I didn't expect my husband to return for several days."

Ehrlich smiled. He knew the home would be tidy. Along with a fire in the hearth, there would most likely be a vase of fresh flowers on the kitchen table. Delphia looked lovely, even though a loose strand of blonde hair fell over her cheek and she was wearing her work dress and apron. *I am a lucky man*, Ehrlich thought.

Lord Danu dismounted and signaled for his men to do the same. "No need to apologize, my good lady. Fortunately, your husband's path crossed ours a few leagues outside Leedsdale. We came as soon as he explained the situation to us."

Ehrlich was glad the young lord skipped over the details of their journey. He didn't want his wife to worry over what was now in the past.

"Momma, we were attacked by men from Nortia!" Renn exclaimed.

Delphia shot look of questioning concern at her husband. Ehrlich let out a sigh and slowly shook his head in resignation.

"And father got hit in the head and was knocked out for a whole day," Tavier added.

"Okay, that's enough, boys," Ehrlich interjected. "I want you to take all the horses to the corral and see to their needs."

"Thank you, good man Ehrlich," Lord Danu said.

The excitement on the faces of Renn and Tavier changed to sullen resignation, and they glumly took the reins of the horses and led them to the corral.

"Is it all right with you if we come inside?" Lord Danu asked. "I'd rather not be seen by any passersby."

"Of course," Delphia said with a small curtsy. "Follow me."

As Ehrlich had surmised, their small home was tidy and clean. His wife indicated to the chairs at the table and the long bench that divided the room into two equal sections for Danu and his men to sit. She said, "Please, make yourselves at home. Ehrlich, you lie down on this bench while I prepare some food." She fluffed up the pillows on the bench that sat against the wall.

"Really, I feel fine," he said. "It was just a bump, but I'm okay now." He tried to stand, but Delphia pushed him back down.

"Just a bump doesn't render a person unconscious for a day," she said.

Ehrlich lay on the bench and watched his wife work. He was grateful his small family was safe. He'd never been a pious man, but perhaps the next time he visited the village he would give extra alms to the temple of Azur to show his thanks to the gods. The mission to find Lord Danu turned out to be much more dangerous than he'd imagined. While he'd always believed the Meskhoni when he'd said that Renn would play a part in the future of Lemuria, Ehrlich hadn't fully realized how much danger they were in. The Meskhoni's presence nearby was probably what kept the conspirators in check this long. But things were getting worse. Men had attacked Lord Danu in broad daylight, right in the heart of Basil lands.

Ehrlich watched Lord Danu's men interact as they waited for Delphia to serve them food. Kivas and the young lord were engaged in a quiet conversation and sitting in the chairs opposite where Ehrlich was lying down.

Renn and Tavier finished with the horses and hurried back inside. Ehrlich shook his head. The boys normally would've taken twice as long to feed and brush so many horses. No doubt they hurried because they wanted to spend time around the young lord and his men. The boys surveyed the room and sat down at the kitchen table to see what game Micha and Tellio were playing. Ehrlich frowned. He wasn't sure what game it was, but coins were stacked on the table and cards were involved. Probably not a game he wanted the boys to learn.

"Renn and Tavier," Ehrlich called from his reclined position. The boys looked up from the card game. They'd been through a lot the past few days, and it showed on their dirty faces. Tavier and Renn had behaved like young men and not children while on the trip. Ehrlich was proud of them, and it made him sad to realize they would never be innocent again. "Why don't you go out to the well and draw some water for your mother?"

"Aw, Da, do we have to?" the boys complained in unison.

At least they were starting to act like their normal selves again.

"Yes," Ehrlich replied. "And wash your faces and hands, too."

As he watched Renn shuffle out behind Tavier, he thought about all the things he wanted to teach his youngest son before he left for the school on Elder Island. Fourteen short years wasn't enough time, and much of that had already passed. *What if I'd died in that battle yesterday?* he thought. *There's so much I need to say to Renn before it's too late.* He promised himself that soon, very soon, he would have a heart-to-heart with him.

"I'm so thankful you were with Ehrlich and the boys when they were attacked, my lord," Delphia said to Lord Danu as she busied herself over the kettle in the hearth. "I can't begin to repay you for saving my family."

"Repay me?" Lord Danu's right eyebrow arched. He stood and walked toward the kitchen area. "The thought of repayment never occurred to me. Your husband risked his life doing what he felt was in the best interest of Basilea. I'd say he's the hero, and it is I who should be thanking you." He hit Tellio on the head with his riding gloves and said, "Put those cards away. You're not at a tavern. We're guests in the home of friends."

How could Lord Danu be so different from his father, the grand duke? Ehrlich wondered. *Lord Drake Basil would probably start listing the ways we could repay him.* When Ehrlich had lived in Basilea before he and Delphia married, he'd often heard stories of the grand duke's disdain for those beneath him. Ehrlich once saw him confiscate an old peddler's wagon because the man was selling without a permit. The man tried to explain he was new to the area and didn't know a permit was required. Lord Drake laughed and said, "Now you'll never forget it." Ehrlich could still see the image of the peddler, his face in his hands as he knelt on the hard street while the grand duke's men took away all he possessed. Lord Danu gave Ehrlich hope there were some in the noble class he could have faith in.

Raven was another matter. He owed Renn's life to the strange man, but Ehrlich still wasn't entirely sure he could trust him. It was impossible to tell what the dark-haired captain was feeling. During the short time Ehrlich had spent with these men, he realized they all respected or feared Raven, but only Lord Danu was completely comfortable with him.

Raven and Radien arrived as Delphia was dishing up the stew, and she quickly filled bowls for each of them. They graciously took them from her and leaned against the wall to eat because all the seats at the table were taken.

"Head hurting?" Radien asked Ehrlich when he saw him lying on the wooden bench.

"Queen's orders," Kivas answered for him, nodding to Delphia.

Radien nodded and gave Ehrlich a knowing grin. At this, Ehrlich stood up and said, "I don't suppose my queen will object to her subject getting out of bed to eat a hearty meal, will she?"

Delphia scowled and handed him a thick piece of bread with his stew.

⋈⋈

"My good lady," Lord Danu said, "I don't recall when I've last eaten so well." Kivas was eagerly cleaning out the last remnants of stew from Delphia's pot, and Tellio was topping off his fifth mug of ale.

Ehrlich beamed with pride, knowing the compliment from Lord Danu was genuine. Delphia had a way of making everyone feel welcome and comfortable—she was certainly his better half. She still hurried around the kitchen while the four men sat at the kitchen table.

"I apologize there isn't more," Delphia answered, and her cheeks reddened. "Had I known you were coming so soon, I would have prepared a larger pot."

"May I impose further upon you, Ehrlich?" Lord Danu asked as Delphia set a plate of cobbler in front of him.

"All we have is at your disposal, my lord," Ehrlich answered. With a glance toward Kivas and Tellio, he added, "At least, all that has not been disposed of already."

Lord Danu laughed as he looked toward the two big men, who were oblivious to the quip made at their expense. Kivas, with bits of food clinging to his dark beard, was still scraping away at the empty pot of stew, and Tellio, with white foam on his waxed mustache, was looking mournfully at the now-empty keg of ale that sat next to the kitchen wall.

"You should try keeping them fed in the field," Lord Danu replied, shaking his head in mock disbelief. "If they don't get triple rations, they truly believe they're going to die of hunger!"

Tellio must have heard the last bit of conversation and realized he was the brunt of a joke, because he looked up, apparently embarrassed that Delphia was laughing at him as well, and said, "Lord Danu rations food so frugally even the lovely lady here would starve if she were forced to live on them."

After they stopped laughing, Ehrlich asked, "What did you need me to do, my lord?"

"Raven and I need to pay a visit to Artio," Lord Danu said. "In the meantime, do you feel well enough to go back to the village and organize another town meeting? I'll leave Kivas and the other men here to watch over Delphia and the children."

"I think I can manage," Ehrlich said. "I'll stop down the road first and solicit Jomard's assistance—he's a close friend of mine."

"Good. We'll meet you back here later tonight. One more thing—"

"Yes?" Ehrlich asked.

"Do you mind if my men and I stay here tonight? I'd like to keep our presence in Leedsdale a secret. Don't worry about extra beds. My men and I have bedrolls. We can sleep on the floor if necessary."

"I'm afraid our humble home isn't as comfortable as your father's castle," Delphia said, "but we'd be honored to have you stay."

Tellio looked up from his empty mug, and with feigned aristocracy—and slightly slurred speech—he said, "Do not apologize for your home, my lady. It is said that a home's greatest ornament is the friends who frequent it."

"What's that supposed to mean?" Kivas asked as he picked up a piece of bread. "If you think our staying here is their greatest ornament, then they'd do well to move."

Everyone laughed, and Kivas stuffed the entire piece of bread in his mouth.

Delphia looked at Tellio and Kivas but addressed Lord Danu when she added, "For breakfast, I'll be sure to cook enough to satisfy your men." She shook her head and grinned as Kivas put the pot aside, now focused on finishing the last of the bread.

It was well past dark when Ehrlich and Jomard returned and walked through the front door of the Demaris home to find Lord Danu and his men sitting on the benches in the great room and visiting quietly with Artio. Delphia was busy with a pot of hot water and a sack of tea at the table. The boys and Chria were in bed asleep. The Meskhoni wore a concerned look on his weathered face as he sat on Ehrlich's reading chair, sipping the tea Delphia made for him.

"How did it go in town?" Lord Danu asked.

"Fine," Ehrlich said. "I think we got word out to most of the town council."

Lord Danu stood and walked toward Ehrlich and Jomard. "Good. Do they suspect I'm here?"

"We were in the tavern for a while, and no one *said* anything about you," Jomard answered, "so it isn't likely. But Hevor looked nervous when he saw Ehrlich. By the way, my name is Jomard," he said with a bow. "I bought a farm down the road from here a few years ago. It's a pleasure to meet you in person, my lord."

"It's good to meet people who are loyal to the crown, Jomard." Lord Danu indicated for Jomard to rise, and he shook the farmer's hand. "I trust the land ownership experiment suits you well? I think we may expand it because it's been quite a success here in Leedsdale."

"Yes, Lord Danu," Jomard said. "It gives a man pride to own and work a piece of ground."

The blond lord faced Ehrlich and pointed to the Meskhoni. "Artio and I had a long talk, and I think he'd like to discuss some things with you and Delphia."

"Oh thanks, Danu," Artio said sarcastically as he looked up from his tea. "Ehrlich, I think you'll agree now that we need to do something more to protect Renn."

Ehrlich pulled Delphia to his side, and she wrapped an arm around his waist. He knew that she feared the Meskhoni might suggest Renn be given to someone else to raise. Now it would be more difficult to refuse because Lord Danu was on the Mage's side. The young lord already risked himself and his men to keep the boy safe once; obviously, something had to be done before another attack came.

"I know we've spoken about this before," Artio continued, "but things are getting worse. Kahn Devin and his allies have infiltrated much more than we've realized. The attack yesterday shows they are getting bold. Soon there will be open rebellion if something isn't done to stop them. The more we counter them and try to put an end to their plans, the more desperate they'll become."

"I've got spies throughout most of southern Boranica now," Lord Danu interrupted. "And we are making progress apprehending traitors and conspirators. But I believe one of their prime objectives now is to capture Renn and deliver him to Kahn Devin."

Artio quickly added, "I think we've found a solution that will allow Renn to stay with you."

Ehrlich felt Delphia relax somewhat. Up until the Meskhoni's last comment, he was certain she was about to protest at any moment.

"What did you have in mind?" Ehrlich pressed.

Lord Danu picked up the explanation. "We can't protect you very well out here on this farm. However, if you move your family to Basilea, I can set you up on a farm near the castle and protect Renn myself. Our court Meskhoni, Ishtar, will be able to protect against magic users, much the way Artio has done here."

Ehrlich looked at Delphia. The pain of defeat in her eyes mirrored what he felt. This part of Boranica was about the only place a man could be a landowner and make a name for himself. Ehrlich still remembered the excitement he had felt as a boy when King Kimael first announced he was going to try an experiment with individual land ownership in the southern district. Ehrlich's father always dreamed of purchasing land but was never able to gather enough funds. He farmed as a vassal on a lord's land until the day the lord died. But what he'd saved he'd given to Ehrlich; together he and Delphia had saved enough money to purchase the small farm after they married. The farmland in Basilea was worked by vassals, so he'd be giving up the dream by going back. But if it meant being able to keep Renn in the family for a few more years, he also knew that she, like him, would make that sacrifice.

Kivas, no doubt trying to lighten the tension of silence, said, "Basilea isn't so bad. There are plenty of good taverns about—not as many as in Nortia, mind you, but enough—so we'll keep you entertained."

"That's quite all right, Kivas," Delphia said with a scowl. "There are lots of things to keep Ehrlich entertained at home. He won't need to join you in the taverns."

Radien elbowed Kivas in the ribs and gave him a disapproving glare—but the exchange did lighten the mood a little, and Ehrlich managed a wan smile.

"Do you trust Ishtar?" Ehrlich asked Lord Danu. He knew it was presumptuous to ask the lord if he trusted one of his family servants, but he'd heard a lot of strange rumors about the Mage in Basilea.

It was Artio who answered. "He's a bit eccentric. But I believe he can be trusted."

"Is there no other solution?" Delphia asked, looking at the old Meskhoni.

"I have considered this problem at great length. The only other solution is godparents who are well-trained in the Azur-Lore."

Ehrlich looked down at his wife; he knew she was fighting back her tears, and he drew from her strength. "Then we will move to Basilea."

CONFRONTATION

A ray of sunlight stabbed Ehrlich's eyes. He groaned, rolled to his stomach, and buried his face in his pillow. He told himself the reason he slept past dawn was exhaustion from yesterday's activities, but he knew it was a lie. Today Lord Danu would confront the conspirators. Men whom Ehrlich had known for years. He'd helped some of these men raise barns and clear trees, and now he was setting them up to be judged for their crimes. He'd rather stay home and work in the field—even though the river was dry.

He blew out a deep breath, pushed himself out of the blankets, and splashed cool water on his face from a large wooden bowl; Delphia must have placed it by the bed earlier that morning. Ehrlich pulled on his breeches and his favorite loose-fitting shirt. He took his straw hat from the bedpost, placed it on his head, and ambled into the great room.

"Good morning, dear," Delphia said with a forced smile. "Everybody else has already eaten. The eggs are cold, but they should still be good."

"Morning," he mumbled. He tipped his hat to Lord Danu and Raven. They looked up from the long bench that divided the sitting area from the kitchen.

"It's about time you got up." Lord Danu smiled and raised the brow over his blue eye. "I was under the impression farmers woke with the sun."

"So was I," Ehrlich said, and he rubbed the spot on his head where he'd been clubbed two days before. It didn't hurt anymore, but it made for a good excuse. "I guess that hit I took made me more tired than I realized."

The aroma of eggs, sausage, and buttered bread filled the room like Delphia's breakfasts always did, but Ehrlich had difficulty chewing and swallowing his meal. He pushed a sausage link around the plate with his fork and watched Delphia wash the same dish three times.

"Kivas and Radien"—Lord Danu stood and pulled on his riding gloves—"put those cards away and help Ehrlich's boys finish saddling our horses."

Kivas and Radien were sitting on Ehrlich and Delphia's reading chairs, and a few coins were scattered on the small table between them.

"Yes, sir." Radien jumped to his feet, scooped up the coins, and headed for the back door.

"Hey!" Kivas protested. "I was just about to win some of my money back."

Lord Danu cocked his head and folded his arms.

"Yes, sir." Kivas saluted the young lord and followed Radien.

"I hope your head doesn't bother you too much, Ehrlich," Lord Danu said. "We have a busy day ahead of us."

"I appreciate your concern, m'lord," Ehrlich said. "I'm sure I'll be fine." He grimaced, shoved a scoop of cold eggs into his mouth, and forced himself to chew.

⋈⋈

On the way to the village center, Ehrlich couldn't help but feel nervous. He was about to accuse a man he'd known for years of treason. Ehrlich remembered the first time he met Hevor. The man was working on his fence near the road when Ehrlich and Delphia first rolled into town with their meager belongings and hope for a bright future in Leedsdale. Hevor had stopped what he was doing to give them directions and wish them luck. He then kicked the hired hand who'd been helping him mend the fence and cursed him for splitting the wooden post.

Ehrlich didn't approve of the way Hevor Shoen treated his hired staff, but he never would've thought the man would become a conspirator. True,

Hevor was self-aggrandizing, but it's a long way from ornery, pompous farmer to traitor.

What had happened to make Hevor decide to join forces with Kahn Devin? And why were conspirators suddenly crawling out of the woodwork like an army of feeding termites? Lord Danu claimed that there may be as many as a dozen traitors in the area.

Is Kahn Devin offering more than just money to make my neighbors change so quickly and completely? Ehrlich wondered.

Maybe he was offering them power. Or maybe Artio was right in his assessment that the Grand Warlock was somehow using magic to coerce these men into doing things they otherwise wouldn't do. And if that was true, was it right to try Hevor for treason?

Ehrlich, Lord Danu, and his men arrived at the edge of town an hour before the meeting. At Lord Danu's request, Radien stayed at the Demaris home to provide protection if necessary. To avoid being recognized, Lord Danu and his men wore nondescript clothing and hid their weapons. To anyone who didn't know their faces, they would appear to be regular travelers. Still, Ehrlich pointed out the best back alley for Lord Danu and his men to follow so they could enter the meeting unobserved through a door in the back of the barber-apothecary shop—the location of the room where the council held their meetings.

Ehrlich watched them ride down the alley until they rounded a bend and then continued down the main road alone, heading for the front of the apothecary shop like he would for any other town meeting.

A bell above the door jingled as Ehrlich walked into the shop. An elderly man with a slight hunch was staring at a jar of red powder that rested on the top shelf of a bookcase in the back of the shop.

The old man turned and smiled. "Ehrlich, I'm glad you're here." He pointed at the jar and asked, "Would you mind pulling that down for me?"

"Of course, Witzen, no problem at all." Ehrlich walked past the barber chair, around the scrivening desk, and joined the old man in the apothecary section of the shop. "Has anybody else arrived?" Ehrlich asked as he handed the jar to Witzen.

"Nope, you're the first." Witzen placed the jar on his desk and brushed off his hands. "In fact, you're a good thirty minutes early—time for a haircut and shave if you're interested."

"Thanks, Witzen, but I think I'll just take a seat in the back and wait for the others."

"Suit yourself." The old man probably didn't expect Ehrlich to take him up on the offer because he knew that Delphia cut Ehrlich's and the boys' hair.

The meeting room in the back of the barber-apothecary shop was fairly large. A solid oak table was placed at the far end, with three chairs set behind it. Several sturdy log benches were lined up on the near side, facing the table—enough to comfortably seat fifty men. The floors and walls were wooden, and a sky window allowed a generous amount of sunlight into the dusty room. There were two doors on the right side of the room—one near the big oak table that led outside and one in the center of the room that led to a smaller room.

Ehrlich took a seat on the back row and waited. It wasn't long before Lord Danu and Raven entered through the door near the oak table. Raven set the papers he had retrieved from Hevor's home onto the table while Kivas stood guard at the door.

"Did you see anything out of the ordinary as you rode through town, Ehrlich?" Lord Danu asked.

"Nothing, m'lord."

Ehrlich heard the jingle of the bells from the shop, and moments later Artio walked into the room. After a brief hello to Ehrlich, he took Lord Danu, Raven, and Kivas to the side room. Ehrlich still waited.

The shop bells announced another visitor had arrived. Ehrlich heard a noise that sounded like pots clanging to the ground and the muffled voice of Witzen saying, "Be a bit more careful, would ya?" and then a red-haired, bearded man stumbled in. It was Raul. Dirty, unkempt, and barely sober.

"What is the meaning of this, Demaris?" Raul asked. "Why do we need an *emergency* meeting?"

"I wouldn't know, Raul," Ehrlich lied. "The Meskhoni didn't tell me." Raul grunted and sat on the front bench—the seat farthest from Ehrlich.

Fortunately, Ehrlich didn't have to entertain Raul for long. Jomard arrived moments later and sat on the bench next to Ehrlich. The bells jingled and several other townspeople began filing in. Hevor Shoen sauntered in, wearing a white shirt that clung to his belly and was already wet with sweat under his arms. Of course, he also had that silly red sash tied around his waist. As usual, he took his place at the table next to the other two council members—Regin and Samsin.

"Do either of you know what this meeting is all about?" Hevor asked. Ehrlich had to watch the man's lips as he spoke to make out what he was saying above the din of the other voices in the room.

Samsin, who was the wealthiest rancher in miles and a personal friend of King Boran, sat in the center seat with his arms folded. He pursed his lips and shook his head in response to Hevor's question.

"What about you, Regin?"

"Nobody ever tells me anything," Regin answered. He wore a scowl on his sun-weathered face. The man was a farmer, and his children were all grown and had moved on with their lives. Regin was left to work his farm with just his wife, so he probably resented spending valuable morning time in a meeting.

"Do you think Regin or Samsin are involved in this mess?" Ehrlich whispered. Jomard scratched at his dark hair, and Ehrlich was tempted to suggest that his friend take advantage of Witzen's services at the barber's chair after the meeting, but he held his tongue.

"Both men were on the council long before Hevor," Jomard said. "I don't think they associate with him outside of these meetings . . . at least I hope not."

Ehrlich nodded and rubbed his chin. He hoped that, of the three, Hevor alone had sold himself to Kahn Devin.

As the men of Leedsdale entered the room, the seats were quickly taken, and soon people stood lined against the walls, waiting for the meeting to begin.

"Listen to them all." Jomard looked across the gathering crowd as he spoke. "There are a hundred different guesses as to why Artio would call a special meeting."

"Do you blame them?" Ehrlich whispered. "The Meskhoni hasn't called a meeting in years. Plus, we just had a meeting last week to discuss the water. They probably wonder why he didn't just come to that meeting."

Finally, Artio came out of the adjoining room, wearing a loose brown woolen robe with the hood down. His staff clicked on the wooden floor as he walked to the front and nodded to the three council members. Samsin and Regin smiled broadly and stood as the Meskhoni approached them. Hevor saw them rise, and he scowled before following their lead. The council members sat, and Artio turned to face the crowd and raised a hand to call for silence. His face looked tired, but his eyes were unyielding as he scanned the men in the room.

"Thank you, good men of Leedsdale, for attending today," the Meskhoni said. "We are living on the edge of dark times."

Whispers erupted at his announcement, but the old Mage raised his hand to silence them.

"There are certain prophecies," the Meskhoni continued, "that speak of the balance of power in our world and warn that one day that balance will be disturbed. Many believe the time is at hand. Even in our small village, there are those who conspire against our king and would make Kahn Devin of the Cragg Caves our ruler."

The room broke into a cacophony of separate discussions at this announcement.

"How can that be?" one voice said.

"Are you certain?" asked another.

"Why would anyone want the Grand Warlock for a king?"

"Who would be so foolish?"

Artio rapped his staff against the floor to bring order back to the meeting.

"I know this is a shock, but I wanted you to be aware of schemes like this so you can help us stop it." The crowd quieted as the Meskhoni scanned the room. "I have invited someone else to speak to you about this problem."

Artio nodded toward the side door as it opened, and all eyes turned to see Lord Danu walk out, confident and bold, with Raven and Kivas close behind. Some of the men at the meeting who had appeared skeptical at the Meskhoni's news looked at each other with open mouths and wide eyes as the young lord took the floor.

"Look at Hevor and Raul," Jomard whispered.

Hevor shifted in his seat and wiped sweat from his forehead. Raul's beady eyes darted from the young lord to the side door that led outside, as though he were wondering if he could leave the meeting without being noticed.

Lord Danu nodded to the council, who all quickly stood and bowed. Kivas and Raven took their positions in the front of the room, standing on either side of the table. Lord Danu signaled for the council members to sit and turned to face the crowd.

"I extend greetings from my father, the grand duke, and from the king," Lord Danu began. "I wish this were a routine visit, but it is not. I know most of you are loyal and true to the king; however, Artio speaks the truth. Some among you have committed treason. You know who you are. And I am learning who you are.

"I recently visited Tearsia to investigate a conspiracy, and I uncovered secret plans. I found records of transactions that I'm certain some of you would like to pretend never occurred. So far, we haven't been able to decode the fake names used in the transactions, but we will. Treason is punishable by death. But should you surrender and save us the trouble of hunting you down, your punishment may be reduced to exile."

As Ehrlich glanced around the room, he saw wide eyes and gaping mouths. But he thought he saw a few men shift in their seats and bite their lips. The door at the back of the room opened and closed with a bang. He turned to see who had entered. Cole filled the doorframe, holding papers in his hand.

"By the way, Hevor." Lord Danu's voice had a smooth lilt to it as he paused, like a mountain cat ready to pounce.

"Yes, my lord?" Hevor squeaked like a mouse.

"Krilahn of Nortia failed in his mission. My men and I are still alive, and he was unable to confiscate the package we were transporting."

"I'm sorry, my lord . . . I . . . I don't believe I know to what you refer."

"That's odd. Krilahn and his men were riding *your* horses when they attacked us."

"That means nothing, my lord! Several of my horses were stolen just last week!" Hevor licked his lips and looked around the room for support . . . or perhaps for a clear path to attempt to flee.

"Cole," Lord Danu said, "come forward, please."

All eyes in the room watched as Cole walked to the front of the room.

"Would you show Hevor the letter we found in the saddlebag of one of his *stolen* horses?"

"Gladly, my lord." Cole walked forward and, with a grim expression, placed a letter on the table in front of Hevor, whose face changed from red to white as he read the note.

Men sitting in the first couple rows sat a little straighter and leaned forward as though trying to catch a glimpse of what the note said. Ehrlich knew it was a note from Hevor—the *Red Sash*—saying that once the boy disappeared and his father and brother were dead, Hevor would incite anger and fear among the village because of the lack of protection from the Basil family.

"We found other letters similar to this at your home, *Red Sash*, if you need more evidence," Lord Danu said.

"I-I—we—" Hevor stammered. Then, with a passing breath, his expression changed from fear to rage as heat poured into his face and a vein bulged in his forehead. "How dare you break into my home and rummage through my personal belongings. Have you no decency?" Hevor stood and pounded the table with his fist.

"We didn't break in." Danu's calm demeanor was a stark contrast to Hevor Shoen's anger. "We knocked on the door and were invited in to search your entire house."

Hevor's mouth dropped open, and he turned to run, but Raven and Lord Danu's big Nortian lieutenant—Kivas—blocked escape on both sides of the table.

"You should get to know your hired help better, Hevor." Danu's eyes narrowed, and he set his jaw. "Hevor Shoen, you are guilty of treason. By the authority of my father, the grand duke, your property is hereby confiscated and will be sold to repay the government for the expense we've incurred investigating your crimes." Lord Danu motioned for Kivas to restrain Hevor. "You will be executed tomorrow morning at sunrise."

Lord Danu's eyes scanned the room. From the back row, Ehrlich couldn't see the faces in the crowd, but the way some of the men appeared to crouch as if hiding behind the person in front of them made him wonder how many others were involved.

"If anyone else is found guilty," Lord Danu said, "they will suffer the same fate. And know this: we *will* find you. This meeting is now adjourned."

Lord Danu held his shoulders high and looked straight ahead as he walked through the silent room toward the main entrance. Artio, Raven, and Cole followed in his wake. Ehrlich sat in his seat and stared at them as they passed by, stunned. Lord Danu was so good-natured. He joked with his men and was playful with Ehrlich's boys. It was unnerving to see him deal out punishment without hesitation or any apparent remorse.

"You can't just kill me!" Hevor cried. "Give me a chance to explain . . . Can't we strike a deal of some kind? I could help identify other conspirators—you can't execute me."

Men shifted in their seats, and a chorus of murmurs broke out at Hevor's sudden willingness to name other conspirators. Lord Danu paused midstep and then turned and scrutinized the traitor squirming in Kivas's powerful grip.

"You would turn on your friends so quickly?" Lord Danu frowned, and his eyebrows drew together into a scowl. He looked as though he'd just smelled rotting flesh. "I don't need your help identifying others. Your letters and records will be sufficient once I've had time to review them. You have committed treason and will die at sunrise." Lord Danu let his words sink in for a moment and then turned to the others in the room. "Good men of Leedsdale, we have nine horses and saddles for sale outside. If you wish to purchase one, speak with Cole. The rest of Hevor's estate will be auctioned off next week." Lord Danu walked out the door, and

Raven and Kivas followed him out, dragging with them a cursing, red-faced Hevor Shoen.

Ehrlich sat for a long time, considering all that had just occurred. Raul glared at him as he walked out of the room. Ehrlich figured it was only a matter of time before his neighbor's name turned up in the documents Lord Danu had confiscated. Ehrlich felt a pang of sadness for Raul's family. His wife and children deserved better.

He watched the other men file out of the room and wondered how many more would hang in the coming weeks. There was no mistaking Lord Danu's resolve to stamp out the conspirators after what he had done that morning. Certainly, Hevor deserved to die. He'd committed treason and attempted to kidnap Ehrlich's son. But it still amazed Ehrlich that Lord Danu, the laughing, loveable, hardworking young lord, could offhandedly order another man to die and not think twice about it. His youth and laughter concealed what he was truly capable of.

Fortunately, Ehrlich thought, *he's one of the good guys.*

I think.

Ehrlich left Delphia and the children at home, and he came alone to see Hevor Shoen hanged at dawn in the town square. His two boys had witnessed enough death for one lifetime, and Delphia had no desire to watch someone die.

Ehrlich stood at the back of the crowd, holding on to Dusty's reins, and wondered if maybe he should have stayed home as well. A hanging was a very disturbing thing to witness. Though he knew it wasn't logical, he couldn't help but think he was partly responsible. Certainly, he had no control over the power the gods gave to Renn, but it *was* his son's blessing that people pointed to as evidence that a power shift would soon occur. It was Renn's blessing that Kahn Devin used as leverage to convince power-hungry men to conspire with him to overthrow the kingdom. Now, the first conspirator had been hanged. Although nobody had come forward to turn themselves in and Hevor didn't name any of his coconspirators, more hangings would soon follow. Ehrlich had no doubt about this.

Nearly a hundred people came to view the execution. Maybe because it was the first hanging in over a decade. Maybe from morbid curiosity. Nevertheless, word traveled quickly throughout the night, and farmers, ranchers, merchants, and peasants alike traveled from well before dawn to see Hevor dragged to the gallows.

The gray-robed priests of the temple, under the high priest Japhet's direction, had performed the death march and completed the cleansing rituals invoked to wash the people clean of the criminal's blood. Now Hevor's lifeless body swung slowly in the morning breeze—his red sash blowing gently as though it had taken on a life of its own.

The crowd slowly dispersed. They left in groups of twos or threes, heads huddled close as they quietly discussed the events of the last twenty-four hours. Some nodded kindly to Ehrlich as they walked by him; a few wouldn't meet his gaze and intentionally walked the other direction. He thought he could probably identify some of the guilty simply by the way they had acted at the meeting yesterday and at the execution today.

The morning sky was dull with leaden clouds as Tellio and Kivas cut Hevor's body down, tossed it onto a wooden cart, and covered it with a tarpaulin. Lord Danu handed some coins to the undertaker, who flicked his reins and took the body away to be buried in an unmarked grave outside of town.

Cole stood next to the gallows, watching the undertaker's wagon roll away. He ran his fingers over a bone-carved pendant and chanted a death prayer that would make sure Hevor's spirit wouldn't walk the land and haunt those who had put him to death. Once they finished this task, Lord Danu and his men prepared to leave. The blond-haired lord motioned for Ehrlich to join them.

"Thank you for your help these last few days," the lord said as Ehrlich led Dusty to the side of the gallows where Lord Danu and his men were making their preparations. "How soon can you and your family be ready to move to Basilea?"

A sharp pain stabbed at Ehrlich's heart as he thought, once again, of leaving the farm he and his wife had worked so hard to build. They wouldn't get a harvest this year—of course, if it didn't rain soon, few farmers would. He would be dependent on Lord Danu to feed his family this coming winter. The young lord had generously offered them land to farm in Basilea, but Ehrlich would be a vassal. He wondered if he would ever be able to save enough to purchase his own land again. He smiled sadly, then finally answered, "My wife has already begun packing, my lord. We should be ready in three days' time."

"That's good," the young lord said as he mounted his gray horse. "I will send fresh men and horses to escort you and your family so you will be protected as you travel. With Hevor out of the picture and the loss of all Krilahn's men, you should be safe for the time being. But we won't take any chances."

"Thank you, my lord. May the hand of El Azur guide your path."

"And yours." Lord Danu turned, signaled to his men, and galloped westward down the hard-packed dirt road that led out of Leedsdale and toward Basilea. Ehrlich watched them go until they rounded the bend and only a settling cloud of dust marked their passing. Then he mounted his farm horse Dusty and headed slowly toward home. He smiled ruefully as he watched a line of gray-clad Azur priests walk out the massive temple doors as they set off to begin their morning chores—or perhaps they were on their way to some religious observance.

As he rode eastward from the village square through the narrow cobbled road that led down the main street of Leedsdale, merchants were just beginning to open their shops and carts. He found them annoying most days, but today he realized that in Basilea the markets were much larger, more crowded, and not nearly as personable.

As he continued home, he saw farmers milking cows, gathering eggs, trying to irrigate; his heart sank even more. He would miss this life and the people. Jomard had been like a brother at times, and Artio was always there in moments of need. The beautiful Hebät Mountains, towering to the east like a mighty fortress behind his home, would be traded for the buildings and walls that dotted Basilea like flies on a carcass. It wasn't a welcome exchange, but one that was necessary if he wanted to keep his young family together.

As he rode, he thought of the day he and Delphia had first came to Leedsdale. They were just kids themselves, and Delphia was pregnant with Tavier. The people had been so accepting and kind then. After Renn's blessing, their family was the pride of Leedsdale. Nobody had ever been blessed as favorably as Renn had been. It wasn't until the incident with Raul that people's opinion began to turn against them. Some of the people began to fear Renn, and Raul made no attempt to conceal his contempt for the boy. On the contrary, he took every opportunity to persuade others that Renn was a societal menace.

Ehrlich took a deep breath. A lot had happened during the past ten years. And now his dreams and plans were being altered and changed without his control. Less than four years remained before Renn would be taken to Elder Island. That didn't give Ehrlich much time to teach Renn the valuable life lessons he'd need to know. Maybe after Renn was safe on Elder Island, things would return to normal. Maybe then Ehrlich could move his family to another small village with the renewed dream of owning land. He wanted to believe it could happen; he wanted to have hope for a peaceful and prosperous future, but the realist in him said things would never be the same.

He looked at the Hebät Mountains straight ahead; his little farm was nestled in its shadow. He smiled sadly as he pictured it in his mind, and a low rumble of thunder sounded on the horizon. He looked up into the gray sky as rain began to fall. It sprinkled for a moment before it turned into a steady drizzle.

"Really?" Ehrlich said to whatever gods might be paying attention. Then he sighed and spurred his horse to a gallop.

THE MOB

After Hevor Shoen's execution, the tasks of tending to the children and making household arrangements were left to Delphia. Her husband focused his attention on selling the farm and the large equipment that would be too difficult to move. Their three children behaved well. Much better than many children, Delphia supposed. Still, her nerves were raw by midafternoon, and as she stared at the pots and pans hanging from the ceiling that needed to be packed, she felt like she'd been run over by a stampede of wild horses.

She liked to think of herself as a young woman—after all, she was only thirty-one—but Tavier, Renn, and Chria had the ability to change her from feeling young and strong to old and exhausted within the space of an hour. Today, she felt even older and more tired than usual. Maybe the heat of the day had caused her to sweat as she worked, or perhaps it was merely the stress from all she had to do. *Probably a combination of the two*, she thought as she once again brushed the long strand of blonde hair off her cheek that kept falling in her eyes and sticking to her skin.

There was so much to do and so little time. Lord Danu wanted them to move to Basilea immediately, and while she knew it was unwise to stay in Leedsdale any longer than necessary, she still resented it all. She knew it was irrational. Lord Danu was only trying to help. He'd saved her husband and sons from certain death, but she needed more time to adjust; as it was, she hardly had time to sleep. All they owned had to be packed or taken care of in some way.

Fortunately, Ehrlich had found a buyer for the home, and he and Jomard would both be back soon to help. The family planned on leaving the following morning, but the house still needed cleaning and the wagon needed to be loaded.

Delphia turned around. "Chria! What are you doing?" Her two-year-old daughter was sitting on the floor, white from head to toe and engulfed in a cloud of baking flour. "Mother just cleaned the floor, and you've made it all messy again." She opened the back door. "Tavier!" she yelled. "Where is that boy when I need him?" she muttered under her breath. She picked up Chria and took her outside to the well. "Tavier!" she called again and began drawing water. Tavier and Renn came bolting around the corner of the house, Tavier in the lead, laughing, and Renn close behind, red-faced and angry.

"Stop! All right, young man, I thought I asked you to keep an eye on Chria while I did some work."

Tavier was breathing hard and still smiling. "I was, but Renn—"

"I don't care what you or Renn did," she interrupted, unamused. "I asked you to watch your little sister, and now she's covered with flour. And so is my clean kitchen!"

"I didn't do anything!" Renn said angrily. "Tavier—"

"I said I don't care who did what!" Delphia snapped. "The both of you better quit playing around and do as I ask, or you'll find yourselves cutting a switch! Do I make myself clear?!"

The boys looked at her with their mouths wide open. She had never whipped them with anything before; she didn't believe in it. However, she was ready to change her beliefs. Taking a deep breath to calm herself, she continued. "Tavier, finish cleaning your little sister and then watch her *closely*. I don't intend to follow you children around all day long cleaning up your messes. Renn, you come with me."

The children were much more helpful after her outburst. Delphia felt a little guilty for losing her temper with them, but she didn't have time for them to be children today. As she and Renn finished cleaning the kitchen and putting the sack of flour away, Ehrlich walked in with Jomard.

"Am I glad to see you," she said, greeting her husband. "I'm exhausted."

"I see the children are behaving themselves," he said cheerfully as he walked up and gave her a quick kiss. "I'm glad they're helping you." She didn't respond to that; talking about her day would only make her mad again.

"I made the final arrangements for the sale of the farm," Ehrlich continued. "I had to practically give it away. Nobody has any money, and the drought has made things worse. Frankly, I'm amazed to have found a buyer at all."

"At least you sold it," Delphia conceded. "Jomard, I can't thank you enough for helping us. You're such a good friend."

"You're welcome, Delphia. But, of course, my help isn't free . . . It will cost you some dinner."

Delphia laughed and gave him a hug. "You're a good man."

Preparations to leave went much faster with the men helping. Still, it was dark before all their belongings were packed. Delphia couldn't wait to get the kids in bed and turn in for the night. However, as she and Ehrlich were thanking Jomard for his help, a quick, hard knock sounded on the back door.

"Mr. Demaris!" a little voice urgently called through the door. Another desperate knock sounded before Ehrlich and Delphia could answer. They opened the door to find little Genea Lucian standing with tears streaming down her face. She was out of breath. Her hands and knees were dirty, and messy brown curls fell in front of her eyes.

"They're coming! You have to leave—"

"Who's coming, Genea?" Delphia asked as she knelt in front of the frightened girl. "Calm down and tell us what this is all about."

"There's no time. Some men are coming to burn down your house and take Renn!"

"How do you know?" Ehrlich demanded.

"I heard them . . . I was at our well, and a man came to the barn and spoke to my father . . . They didn't know I was there. He said they were ready to burn the house and take the boy. I know they were talking about your house—my father and his friends are very angry. I'm so frightened." She cried harder and began shaking.

Delphia pushed Genea's brown hair back and wiped her eyes. "Thank you, Genea. You're very brave. You need to stop crying now and go home. You can't ever let your father know you warned us, all right?"

Genea nodded, sniffed, and tried to regain her composure. "Okay." She started out the door. Then, with an audible gasp, she darted back into the house.

"I can see torches down the road!" Genea was near the point of hysteria, shaking all over and crying harder than ever.

Ehrlich looked out the door, trying to see how large the crowd was and how soon they would reach the farm. Based on the way the twenty or so torches moved, the mob appeared to be on horseback.

He bent down, held Genea by the shoulders, and, looking into her face, said, "You need to get home before your father sees you. Run through the field. Once you get home, go straight to bed and act as if you don't know anything at all about what your father is doing. You've already put yourself in danger by warning us."

Genea struggled to calm herself, nodding as she dried her eyes on the sleeve of her dress and sniffled. After giving Renn a look that Delphia found rather odd for such a young girl, Genea ran out the back door and through the field toward her home.

"They're not being very cautious, are they?" Jomard observed as he looked out the front window at the approaching mob.

"They don't need to be," Ehrlich answered. "There's nobody around to challenge them. Only us."

"What are we going to do?" Delphia asked, steadying herself by gripping the kitchen table with one hand and holding the other against her pounding heart. Why wouldn't they just leave her family alone? She'd thought the likes of Raul would be content to see them leave.

Ehrlich paced back and forth in front of the large bench in the center of the great room while Jomard watched the progress of the mob through the window in the kitchen.

"They're still a mile down the road." Jomard let the curtain drop back over the window and turned to face Ehrlich. "We might be able to scare them off."

"Jomard, you've been wonderful," Ehrlich said, "but I don't want you getting involved. You should leave before they see you."

"I'm already involved, Ehrlich, and I can help."

"The only help you can give now is to leave!" Ehrlich insisted, obviously losing his patience as he walked toward Jomard. "We can't stand against them; we have to run! If you try to help, you'll only be killed. I don't want to watch one of my only true friends die fighting an impossible battle."

Jomard stared at the angry man, but Ehrlich held his gaze and didn't retreat. "All right," Jomard said at last. "Have it your way. But be careful."

"Thank you, Jomard. I will," Ehrlich replied, and he took his friend's hand in a firm grip. "Delphia, take the children through the field and over the river, and then work your way through the forest to Artio's place. He'll be able to protect you."

"What are you going to do?" she asked her husband. Her heart raced, and she wanted to scream and cry at the same time. But she had to be strong for her children.

"I'm going to draw their attention and hopefully lead them away from . . . from you and the children."

Delphia knew her husband had almost said, *Lead them away from Renn*, but he didn't want their son to blame himself. But Renn was observant. She looked at her youngest son and could see guilt written on his face like letters chiseled on a gravestone. She longed to comfort him, but there was no time. First, she had to take her children to safety, and then, if she still had any strength left, she would try to heal his emotional wounds.

They gathered some necessities that wouldn't slow them down, blew out the candles, locked their home, and went to the barn. Ehrlich and Jomard had only finished loading the wagon an hour earlier, and now they worked frantically to unload it so the horses could pull it faster. Ehrlich put a torch near the driver's bench so the mob would be sure to see him leaving.

Delphia looked down at her hands, and her long, slender fingers were shaking. She quickly clasped them together and forced herself to hold them still—she had never been so afraid in her life. She felt like a helpless child and was too tired to travel all night in the mountains. She knew she would have to carry Chria most of the way, and Delphia didn't think she possessed the physical strength to make it. She looked at Tavier's face—his eyes were wide with fear, but his jaw was set in determination. He was trying so hard to be the brave man since his father wouldn't be traveling with them. Chria didn't understand what was happening, but she could sense the apprehension and fear in her mother, and Delphia had to hold her constantly so she wouldn't cry. Renn wore a blank stare—like he had to harden himself for whatever was coming. But guilt and the weight of self-inflicted blame haunted his eyes as he stared down the road in the direction of the mob.

Last, she looked at her husband. He was looking at her as if he were drinking in her every last detail. She set Chria down and embraced him as long as she dared, and then she looked up into his sad blue eyes. "I love you. Please be careful."

"Delphia, if I don't—"

"Stop." She put her finger to his lips and shook her head. "Don't say it. Everything will be all right."

"I love you, Delphia." Ehrlich kissed her gently and then, giving each of his children a quick kiss and a hug, instructed them to behave for their mother and told them he would join them as soon as he could. He paused for a moment after he hugged Renn and looked at his son like he wanted to say something more. He took a deep breath and turned to leave but then changed his mind and dropped to one knee in front of him.

"Renn, listen close," he said as he gripped their youngest son's shoulders tightly and looked fervently into his blue eyes. "Sometimes in life you have to make difficult choices. The best time to make those choices is before you're ever confronted with them. Does that make any sense, Son?"

Renn nodded, but only slightly.

"Ehrlich, you'd better make it quick," Jomard cut in and pointed toward the fast-approaching torch fire of the mob. "You don't have much time left." Ehrlich looked over his shoulder and then turned back to Renn.

"Sometimes it's hard to tell right from wrong, Renn. The dark side tries to imitate the light—they'll try to confuse you." He licked his lips, quickly glanced over his shoulder toward the mob again, and then spoke even more deliberately. "Make your decision to follow El Azur before you're ever confronted by the agents of Ba Aven. That way, you don't have to make your choice during the pressure of the moment."

Delphia listened with wonder as she watched her husband. Why, of all times, was he taking time to say this now? Especially with an angry mob getting closer by the minute. Then Ehrlich stood and looking at each of his children said, "That's good advice for all of you."

"Honey," she said with a nervous laugh. "Stop talking that way. You act as though we'll never see you again." She kissed him quickly once more and then gathered the children together and started to leave. "Now get out of here and don't keep us waiting long at the Mage's cottage."

The torches of the approaching mob were no more than half a mile away, so with one last look at the small farm, Delphia hurried her children out into their fields away from the road and toward the Hebät Mountains.

Tavier and Renn were silent as Delphia led them quickly through the dry wheat field. The nearly full moon in the clear sky cast a pale glow on the ground. Strands of Delphia's hair blew gently in the warm south wind. She normally loved evenings like this. But this was a nightmare. Chria was crying softly in her arms, and Delphia had more than a league to travel through rough terrain before reaching the safety of the Meskhoni's cottage. The only one among them who wouldn't mind the difficult journey was their dog, Coy. He lopped back and forth through the wheat as they made their way through the field.

As they neared the bank of the river that marked the end of their small farm and the beginning of the woods, Delphia heard Ehrlich shout to the horses. As she turned, she could see the outline of the wagon and her husband as he charged from the barn and burst onto the road. The mob, seeing the wagon leave and presuming it was carrying Renn to safety, began shouting and quickened its pace. They paused at the farm long enough to make sure no one was hiding and then condemned it, along with the barn, to fire. Hearing the commotion, Coy looked back and began barking. He would have run back, but Tavier grabbed hold of the fur on his neck and held his muzzle to keep him quiet.

The dry wood of their home caught quickly, and Delphia watched as flames rose high into the air. Through the light cast by the inferno, she could see the mob consisted of more than twenty mounted men; however, she was too far away to recognize any of them.

"They're burning the barn!" Tavier exclaimed angrily. "All of our things are in there! One day I'm going to kill him."

Delphia realized he was referring to Raul Lucian. Although she knew she should say something to Tavier about his oath of vengeance, Delphia remained silent. She brushed a tear from her cheek and watched the fire devour her hopes and dreams as it greedily devoured her little home.

She pulled her eyes from the fire, wishing she'd never turned to watch. But it was too late; the burning image of everything they'd worked so hard for was imprinted forever into her memory. She wiped her eyes and looked down at her sons. Tavier continued watching the mob and holding Coy. His brow furrowed as his jaw turned rigid, the hate in his eyes so thick it was palpable. Renn said nothing. He stood silently and watched. His bleak face was still void of emotion, but in the pale moonlight Delphia saw tears rolling down his placid cheeks.

"Come on," Delphia said, bracing herself for the long trek ahead. "There's nothing we can do about it now."

Her two sons looked at her and slowly nodded.

The long walk through the night was exhausting in and of itself, but the added strain of carrying Chria made it nearly impossible. Tavier helped some; he was big for his age, but he tired rapidly and was only able to give Delphia brief respite. Renn remained silent, even when they stopped to eat the bread and cheese Delphia had managed to salvage before their hasty escape.

As the moon rose higher in the night sky, Delphia grew more exhausted. Determination and concern for the safety of her children were all that kept her from giving in to the overwhelming urge to stop and sleep. Her arms and legs burned, and her lower back ached from straining to hold herself and Chria erect as she worked her way up the forested hills. Her feet were blistered and seared with pain, but still she pressed forward. The thought of the mob discovering their deception and following them drove her forward.

She thought many times through the night of Ehrlich and wondered where he was and how he was doing. The emotional strain of not knowing his situation was worse than the physical strain of putting one foot in front of the other.

Did he get away from them? Will he be waiting for us once we get to the Meskhoni's cottage? Or did the mob . . . No! She wouldn't allow herself to consider that possibility. Ehrlich had to be all right. She needed him too badly now—the family needed him. He had to be okay.

After hours of stumbling in the dark through the woods—climbing, slipping, and aching—she began to see her surroundings blur together like props in a dreamworld. Delphia felt like a mind-numbed, disjointed figure wandering vaguely through a barely recognizable world of trees, rocks, and hills. She persisted only by some instinctive drive to continue. She was aware that two others were walking by her side, and for some reason she needed to be sure they didn't leave her, but it was difficult to remember why.

She felt her knees hit dirt and rock as she stumbled on something, and she struggled to rise and continue. She tasted salt on her lips but wasn't sure if it was from tears or blood. She tripped again . . . and pulled herself up again. The process repeated itself over and over, hour after hour.

Somewhere within her, a voice cried out in despair—a frantic voice of warning. As she walked, her vision narrowed and grew dark. She wanted so badly to stop and lie down. All she had to do was stop walking and close her eyes . . . just for a few moments. But the voice in her mind cried out loudly, *"No! Wake up!"* However, her mind spiraled deeper and deeper into a beckoning dreamworld that promised to lock out the surroundings threatening to destroy her world. She could find safety in sleep. No fear . . . no pain . . . no sorrow . . . only peaceful, safe bliss.

SHADOWS AND DESPAIR

Something smelled terrible. Extremely acrid, like rotten eggs. No, worse. Delphia woke with a start, coughing and gasping for air. She was lying on her back on cold, hard earth, and a few fading stars peeked through a canopy of tree branches overhead . . . Then her memory came flooding back like a sudden burst of wind.

"Tavier!" she yelled as she sat up. She hoped her oldest son had protected Chria and Renn while she had lain unconscious. Blood rushed to her head, and she felt dizzy for a moment.

An old man hovered over her, holding a brown leather pouch in his left hand and a vial containing the foul-smelling elixir that had brought her back to consciousness in his right. It was Artio, the Meskhoni.

"I'm here, Mother," Tavier reassured her as he stuck his head around the Meskhoni's shoulder.

"How are you feeling?" Artio asked as he handed her a steaming cup of liquid. She took the cup and nodded as she quickly drained its contents. It must have been some kind of tea, but Delphia couldn't name it. The taste was unfamiliar but not unpleasant.

"I'll manage. Where are Chria and Renn?"

"They are sleeping soundly in the cottage, my good lady. Had you walked but another hundred yards, you would have fainted on my doorstep."

"How did you find us?" she asked, looking past him, hoping to see her husband.

"I didn't," the Meskhoni replied absently. He poured water from a leather skin into the empty cup, placed a pinch of powder from his pouch into the liquid, and chanted in a strange language while he stirred the contents. Light green energy surrounded the cup, and steam began to rise from it. He handed the fresh cup of hot tea back to Delphia and smiled encouragingly. "The children found me."

She drank the contents of the second drink Artio had concocted, her eyes scanning the surrounding trees. "Have you heard from my husband yet?" she asked anxiously as she handed the cup back to his thick, rough hands.

The old man shook his head. "Tavier has informed me of the situation. Let's get you to my cottage, and I'll go search for him."

"Thank you," she said politely as he helped her stand. Her feet were sorer than she remembered, still blistered, and her body was still tired. But at least she and the children were alive and safe—for now.

Dawn began to make its entrance while they walked, revealing a thickly wooded forest of tall white aspens and stately oaks intermixed with the occasional pine. Birds began singing, but the music did nothing to ease Delphia's fear and anxiety. Artio led them past a rocky bluff, and they approached a small clearing where Delphia saw the back side of a stone cottage. A white, wispy trail of smoke rose from a chimney, and a small, well-kept garden flourished along the left side. A rooster crowed and chickens clucked from a nearby coop. A small, arched wooden bridge spanned a little gurgling stream that separated the home from the forest. Any other time the scene would have been welcoming, but as Artio led them over the stream, Delphia was beside herself with worry.

With Tavier supporting her on one side and the Meskhoni on the other, she limped past a round stone well and through the back door of the Mage's home. They entered into a large room with a sitting area directly in front of them. A small fire crackled in the hearth on the left end of the main room. Renn was sitting at a table in the kitchen area near the fire. He looked up as the three walked in the door, his face pale and void of emotion, and he stared at them with swollen red eyes before burying his head in his arms.

Delphia swallowed and bit her lip as she looked at her youngest son. She stared at the room behind Renn as she tried to think of something to say. The brown-colored stones that made up the floor and the bottom four feet of the walls were neatly cut, placed, and mortared together. The upper part of the walls and ceiling appeared to be made of finely crafted oak. The cottage wasn't much larger than her home—

She forced herself to end that line of thought as it brought a vision of fire and devastation. She took a deep breath and walked to the table.

"Why aren't you asleep, dear?" Delphia asked Renn as she sat down next to him.

"I'm not tired. Are you feeling better?" Renn pulled his head out of his arms, but his eyes remained on the table, his expression never changing.

"I think so. Why don't you lie down and try to sleep? It's been a long night, and you really should get some rest."

"What were you doing?" Tavier asked Renn, walking up behind his brother and pointing at a piece of charcoal and scrap of parchment that lay on the table next to Renn. Delphia hadn't noticed it before Tavier pointed it out.

"Nothing." Renn picked up the parchment and wadded it into a ball. "Just . . . drawing."

Delphia picked up the crumpled paper and carefully smoothed it out, watching her youngest son for any sign of objection. He made none. He didn't even take his eyes off the table as she and Tavier looked at his work. It was a crude drawing of their farm in flames and a stick figure in a wagon riding away with a group of men following him.

Artio stepped up behind Tavier, set another cup of something in front of Delphia, and looked at the drawing. "I'll go look for him now. I know you're all very anxious, but try to sleep while I'm gone. There's a large bed in my room"—Artio pointed to a door to the right and near the front door of the cottage—"and the settle is quite comfortable as well." He nodded to an ornate wooden bench against the far wall. "Chria is asleep on a cot in the small room," he said, indicating to a second door on the right wall, near the back door they'd just entered through.

"Thank you again, Artio," Delphia said. "You've been so kind to us."

"After I find Ehrlich, we *will* find whoever is responsible for this. I promise you that."

Tavier looked up from the drawing and said, "It was Raul. Genea told us so."

"Is this true, Delphia?" the Mage asked. "Was Raul involved?"

Delphia blinked rapidly to keep tears from falling and swallowed. "I didn't see anyone well enough to recognize them." Delphia looked at the Meskhoni's weathered face, and she could see the anger growing in his dark eyes. "But his daughter, Genea, did come to warn us and said her father was involved. If it hadn't been for her, we'd all—"

She couldn't finish her sentence, but she didn't need to. The old Meskhoni paced back and forth, rubbing his chin and looking at the stone floor. Then he sighed. "I better get going. The sooner I find Ehrlich, the sooner we'll get to the bottom of this. I shouldn't be too long. Make yourselves comfortable. There's a little food in the cupboard and vegetables in the garden." He turned to Delphia. "Try to rest. You've been through a lot of trauma. Your body needs all the sleep it can get."

"Be careful," she called as he walked out the door. She fell back a step and shielded her eyes when he shimmered with a green hue, changed into an eagle, and flew off into the new morning.

She turned to her boys. Tavier was watching the eagle fly away, but Renn continued to stare at the table. Delphia's hands trembled as she thought about her husband. She wanted to curl into a ball and cry but knew she had to be strong for the children. She folded her arms to still her hands, forced a smile, and said, "Well, you heard him. Let's get some sleep."

Despite being exhausted, Renn couldn't sleep because the light from the morning sun was streaming through the windows. He lay on his back, staring up at the wooden ceiling of the Meskhoni's cottage as he played the same scene over and over in his mind: His father charging from the barn, yelling and shouting to draw the attention of the mob. The only home he'd ever known bursting into flames, turning to smoldering ashes on the ground.

It was *his* fault. His mother, father, Tavier, Chria—all of them were suffering because of him and his stupid blessing. He never asked to be one of the "prophesied events." It wasn't fair that everyone he loved had to suffer abuse and hatred because he was "special." He didn't feel very special—he felt cursed. He should be helping comfort his mother, but he couldn't bring himself to even look her in the eye. He hoped she would feel a little better when his father returned with the Meskhoni.

After hours of tossing and turning, he quietly got out of the large bed, careful not to wake Tavier, softly walked across the cold stone floor, stole around Coy—whose senses weren't what they used to be—and slipped out the door to wait for his father and the old man. The brisk mountain air felt cool and refreshing. He walked behind the cottage to the stream that meandered noisily behind the Meskhoni's home and, kneeling down, splashed cold water on his face. The water felt much colder to his face than to his hands, but the shock was exhilarating. He walked to the garden, pulled out an unusually large orange carrot, and, wiping it off, sat down on an old oak stump to think.

What should he do? It was too late to run away; the damage was already done. Besides that, all his current problems could very likely be traced to the last time he attempted to run away. Maybe Raul wouldn't hate him so badly if it hadn't been for the incident with the animals on that night so long ago. Maybe Raul wouldn't have tried to kill his family if Renn hadn't run away. But that didn't make sense. Why would Raul burn down their home and try to kill their family just because he'd been attacked by animals that had come to Renn's defense? No, Raul's actions certainly went beyond simple revenge. *He must be part of the conspiracy Lord Danu spoke of,* Renn thought.

As he sat eating his carrot, he became aware of the shadows in the trees. Something was watching him. Again. Some odd presence hiding in the trees and bushes. It was there, and yet at the same time, it wasn't. Renn jumped to his feet, suddenly angry beyond control, and ran toward the trees, shouting, "Come out, you coward! Come out and fight! I'll kill you, whoever you are!" He stopped and picked up a stout stick and a handful of rocks and began throwing them across the stream at the shadows in the forest. He could feel the presence laugh at him, and it made him furious. Yelling and shouting challenges, he picked up bigger stones and threw them with greater force into the empty shadows.

"Renn!" his mother called from behind.

He ignored her and kept throwing rocks at his invisible enemy.

"What are you doing! Calm down, Renn." His mother took him by the shoulders and turned him around.

Tears of frustration were running down his face. He pointed back to the trees and cried, "It's in there again! The shadow is making people do mean things to us!" He grabbed another rock from the ground, turned back to the trees, and threw it as hard as he could as he screamed, "I'm going to kill you!"

His mother peered past him and into the trees, her eyes searching. "Who, Renn? Who is in the shadows? I don't see anyone."

"I don't know who. And nobody can see him." Renn relaxed a little as his mother pulled him to her. "He laughed at me. He thinks it's funny."

"Renn, listen to me." She pulled his chin up and looked into his eyes. "The shadow cannot hurt you. Just ignore it. If you get upset, you're only giving it what it wants. Ignore it, and it will get no satisfaction."

Renn could see the concern in her eyes. Even though he was to blame for everything bad happening to their family, he could see she still loved him. He slowly nodded, walking with her as she led him back inside.

Neither Renn nor his mother slept. He sat at the table, eating biscuits that she managed to put together from the poorly stocked cupboards in Artio's kitchen.

Noon was fast approaching, and they still hadn't received word from Artio . . . or his father. Renn could tell his mother was worried about his father because she hadn't eaten anything all morning, she'd said very little, and she rubbed her hands together as she paced back and forth—stopping frequently at the window to stare down the poorly maintained dirt path that led down the mountain, twisting through the forest until it eventually met up with the main road.

"I wish they'd hurry." His mother opened the door, presumably to see farther down the road. "I hate all this waiting."

Renn didn't answer; she wasn't really talking to him anyway. Instead, he wondered what had become of the mob. *Did they give up chasing Father? Maybe they are still chasing him.* He imagined his father leading them on a wild-goose chase all night, and when the mob realized they had been tricked, they would have howled and cursed. His father might have abandoned the wagon and ridden bareback on one of the horses to gain speed and outrun the attackers. Or maybe he had stopped and set traps for them. Whatever had happened, he just wished his father would hurry. Like his mother, Renn was tired of all this waiting.

He wondered what Lord Danu and Artio would do to the conspirators once they were caught. Renn hoped the young lord would exact vengeance upon those who so violently forced them from their home and destroyed their property. That was something to look forward to—watching the mob pay for what they did to his family.

Sometime after noon, Chria woke up crying, and that, of course, woke Tavier. Renn's mother stopped pacing long enough to cook more biscuits and make a pot of tea, and then she turned her attention back to pacing and watching the dirt road.

Tavier busied himself by gathering wood, building a fire, and keeping Chria company. Renn knew he should probably help his brother, but he didn't feel like doing anything except sit at the table and wait.

The day continued to drag on, minute by minute, until the reddish haze of the evening sun burned through the front window and permeated the room with a dusty orange glow. Renn still sat at the table, his arms folded and his head resting on them, when abruptly the front door swung open.

His mother caught her breath as she turned to the door—she apparently had not seen anybody approach the cottage from the road. Looking up,

Renn saw the Meskhoni standing in the entry. The old Mage looked tired and worn. His tan tunic, green cloak, and loose breeches were stained with dirt and sweat, and he leaned heavily on his staff. He didn't say a word as he walked in, but his expression spoke volumes. His mouth and jaw were set rigidly, yet his eyes looked sad. So much so, Renn almost thought the old man was struggling to hold back tears.

His mother hurried toward the old man but stopped two strides short of where he stood. She gasped and brought her hand to her mouth as her eyes met his, and she began shaking her head.

"No . . . no . . ." she breathed. She dropped to her knees, and Renn saw tears well up in her eyes. "No!" she cried louder, and tears began streaming down her cheeks.

"Oh Azur, father god, please no . . . no . . . What am I to do?!" She sobbed as she buried her face into her hands, her body shaking violently as she knelt on the stone floor. Her hands muffled the sounds of her anguished supplications, and Artio stepped closer to place his hand on her shoulder.

As he did, the realization of what happened hit Renn like a bolt of lightning. His father was dead—the mob had killed him—and he would never come back. His mother wept uncontrollably at Artio's feet, shaking her head back and forth as she pled and prayed to the gods to bring her husband back. His baby sister, Chria, upset by her mother's tears, was crying in Tavier's arms, who had tears running down his own cheeks, contrasting with the anger flashing in his eyes.

"Tell me," his mother implored through her tears. "I must know."

"I'm sorry." The old Meskhoni's voice cracked like dry autumn leaves as he spoke. "He's . . . gone. I was too late."

His mother dropped her face into her hands. Her shoulders shuddered as though waves of utter despair were passing through her bent body. Renn forced himself to watch. He wanted to run—wanted to vanish or crawl under a rock. But he stayed and forced himself to watch the anguish he'd caused.

"What happened?" Renn's mother asked through her tears. "How did he die?"

The old man looked down at her, then looked at Renn and his brother. Tavier still held their little sister—her blonde hair hanging in thin ringlets in front of her tear-streaked face.

"Perhaps I should tell you later," the Meskhoni suggested.

His mother looked up and wiped her eyes. The Meskhoni nodded to the children and raised his eyebrows. "He's their father," she insisted. "It wouldn't be right to hide anything from them."

The old man let out a long breath and then turned and stared blankly out the window.

"They hanged him," he finally said.

Hearing those words from the Meskhoni caused a vivid image to shoot into Renn's mind. He felt burning tears stream down his cheeks as he imagined his father's limp body swinging from a lone tree. He turned and sat at the table, buried his head in his arms, and cried. It felt like somebody had reached their hand into his chest and ripped out his heart. His insides ached all the way to his gut. He would never see his father again. And it was his fault.

Artio reached into a pocket inside his cloak and took out a small silver amulet attached to a tarnished silver chain. Renn immediately recognized it as the good luck charm his father had always worn around his neck—it had been in the family for years, an heirloom handed down from father to son for many generations. It was one of his father's most prized possessions and one he would have eventually given to Tavier. The old Mage put the talisman into Renn's mother's hand as he helped her to her feet and, supporting her by the arm, led her to the ornate bench against the far wall. Delphia examined the charm for a moment, holding it close to her breast as she sat down. She dropped her head into her hands and sobbed like a lost child.

Renn shook his head as he watched his mother and said, "No . . . no . . . This can't be true!"

He ran out the back door of the Meskhoni's cottage, splashed through the small stream that separated the yard from the forest, and ran into the trees. He picked up a rock and threw it as hard as he could at the first shadow he could find. He picked up more rocks and screamed as he threw them over and over at shadows in the trees. He dropped to his knees, pounded the dirt with his fists, and cried.

THE BOX

Renn saw his father, standing on the back of a horse beneath a large tree. His hands were tied behind his back, and a noose rested loosely around his neck, its other end wrapped around a sturdy branch overhead. A faceless shadow appeared and pointed at Renn, laughing hysterically. Renn ran through the shadow to get to his father before the horse walked out from beneath him, but no matter how fast Renn ran, he couldn't get closer to his father and the horse. The faceless shadow appeared once more and laughed harder than before. Renn screamed at the apparition and ran through it again, but his father was gone. A red sash twisted on the branch where the noose had been and then blew away into the wind.

Renn opened his eyes and bolted upright. He was in a cold sweat, and his heart pounded so loudly he thought it would wake Tavier, who lay next to him in the Meskhoni's bed. He could tell by the color of the sky through the window it was nearly dawn, so he got up and walked into the main room.

He could hear the steady breathing of his mother as she slept on the settle, so Renn walked quietly to the kitchen table where a candle was burning next to a note. Renn was proud of the fact he could read, but that thought caused a stab of pain because it was his father who had taught him that skill—a skill that was normally found only among the wealthy. The note read:

I have gone to get Lord Danu. I shouldn't be long. You'll be safe in my home until we return.
    —Artio

    Renn walked to the window and looked up at the early morning sky. He wondered if his father was in Valhasgar, resting in a beautiful garden and looking down on Lemuria, waiting to be born again. Moments passed before he realized tears were running down his cheeks. He turned away and wiped his eyes with his shirtsleeve. He looked at the kitchen table where he'd spent so many hours sitting and waiting. If he spent another minute doing that he would lose his mind, so he decided to investigate the little house instead. Certainly, the Meskhoni would have some unusual books or potions or trinkets that might prove to be interesting and help take Renn's mind off the events of the past few days.

    Renn first investigated the Mage's bedroom that he and Tavier now shared. The iron-bound chest at the foot of the bed contained wool blankets, and the wooden desk held some old letters, blank parchment, a few quills, and a bottle of dark ink. A large wooden wardrobe stood against one wall, but it held only clothing and an extra pair of boots.

    He left the bedroom and then carefully opened the door to the little storage room where Chria lay sleeping, wrapped in a blanket on a small cot. Renn quietly sifted through the items on the shelves, careful not to wake his sister, but found only wheat, sugar, lard, empty earthen jars, a few wooden buckets, a broom, and other boring household items.

    Renn went back into the main room, which reminded him of the main room in his home. The large room was divided into a sitting area and a kitchen area, except there wasn't a long bench in the middle of the room separating the two spaces. The settle rested against the far wall, where his mother lay sleeping.

    Renn was impressed by how clean the old man kept the place; however, it was even less interesting than their farmhouse. He found only one book—a book of history—some candles, matches, oil, the basic things any house would have. Where were the bat wings, potions, spell books, and talismans? He looked for a secret room or hiding place but found nothing.

The next couple of days Renn spent his time outside. He still didn't find any secret books or magic items—only an old toolshed and a chicken coop with a falcon perched on a branch in the back corner, which was very odd—but investigating the Mage's little homestead helped to pass time and keep him from thinking too much. Tavier joined him in some of his expeditions, but neither of them laughed and played like before. His mother stayed inside, coming out only to draw water from the round stone well behind Artio's home and to call Renn and Tavier when it was time to eat. She quietly went about taking care of Chria, but her eyes had a distant and vacant look to them, and her face was bleak.

On the third day, Renn saw a small change in his mother. She was still sad, but she began assigning him and Tavier chores—much to Renn's chagrin—and playing with Chria while she cleaned and cooked.

That evening, as Renn sat on Artio's porch swing, practicing his reading skills with the history book he'd found, he heard horse hooves coming up the dirt road. Looking up, he saw Lord Danu on his familiar gray mare, Raven and Artio riding on either side of him. Closely behind them rode Tellio, Kivas, and Micha, but instead of their normal laughter and jokes, their faces were serious and somber.

"Mother," Renn called into the house. "They're here."

He set down the book he was reading and walked toward the men. Renn tried to smile but only managed to turn up one corner of his mouth. Under usual circumstances, he and his brother would be anxiously running down the seldom-used road to greet them—but these weren't usual circumstances.

"Hi," Renn said as they got within range of his voice. "Did you catch Raul yet?"

"Not yet, Renn," Lord Danu answered as he climbed off his horse. "We rode straight here from Basilea as soon as Artio gave us the bad news. How is your mother?"

"Lord Danu!" Tavier's jaw was rigid and his brow clinched as he walked briskly toward them. "Will you let me go with you to catch Raul?" He wore a permanent scowl on his face lately, and he placed his hands on his hips as he waited for Lord Danu's reply.

"That's very brave of you, Tavier," Lord Danu said, "but I'll need you to stay here and protect your mother."

Tavier's hands remained on his hips, but his scowl lifted a little, and he seemed to be considering Lord Danu's answer.

"She's doing a little better now," Renn said, answering the lord's previous question as Tavier began to pace.

Delphia waited on the porch while Chria hung on her leg, watching them ride up the road. She looked tired but somewhat relieved.

"Tavier and Renn," she said. "Take the horses around back to the stream and then remove their saddles. I'm sure they will welcome the rest. Lord Danu," she continued with a slight bow toward the young lord, "you and your men look hungry. You must have ridden very hard to get here so quickly. If you will give me some time, I'd be happy to make dinner for all of you."

"Thank you, my good lady," Lord Danu replied. "However, you needn't worry about us—you've been through enough as it is."

"I insist. Staying busy helps keep me from thinking about . . . things."

Renn and Tavier took care of the horses and hurried back inside. Neither of them wanted to miss what Lord Danu or Artio might say.

"—and so we came as soon as Artio told us. I'm truly sorry, Delphia." Lord Danu sat at the table with his back to the door, while their mother stood looking out the back window. The room fell silent. Lord Danu's men shifted on their feet as they stood around the small room; they looked back and forth at one another as though they'd rather be anywhere else than trying to console a new widow. Raven, Renn noticed, was the only one whose eyes didn't dart from face to face and then back to his mother. Instead he sat opposite of Lord Danu, watching the front entrance, alert as always.

"Lord Danu," Tavier said, breaking the uncomfortable silence. "When are you going to go catch Raul?"

"Soon. After dark." Lord Danu turned his attention to Tavier. "Why do you ask?"

"Are you certain I need to stay here when you go after Raul? I may be able to help."

"No, Tavier." Lord Danu smiled. "I think you'd be better off staying here."

"When he hangs," Tavier said in a determined voice, "I want to be the one to do it."

"What do you mean, Tavier?" Lord Danu asked, and all eyes, including Delphia's and Raven's, turned to Tavier.

"I mean that when you hang him, I want to be the one to pull the horse out from underneath him."

Renn's mouth dropped open at Tavier's request. Renn knew his brother had never been more serious in his life. Renn hated Raul, too, but wasn't sure he could kill him. Tavier, however, showed no sign of backing down as everyone looked at him. Kivas scratched at his beard and Tellio twisted at his mustache as they studied Tavier and then looked at Lord Danu.

"I'm not sure that would be wise, Tavier," Lord Danu finally responded.

"Taking someone's life," the Mage said, "even a murderer's life, can be very . . . disturbing."

"Let him do it." Raven shifted his gaze from Tavier and fixed it on Danu, who sat across the table from him.

While Tavier's request had stunned Renn, Raven's sudden interjection was even more surprising.

"It isn't good to keep such intense anger locked inside."

The way Raven spoke made Renn feel like the captain knew precisely what he was talking about. Maybe he was always quiet because he bore such burning hate for someone that it consumed his every thought and haunted his every waking hour.

During supper, the only sounds were spoons scraping against wooden bowls and mugs clanking on the table. Renn noticed that everyone carefully avoided his mother as she cleaned up the dinner. Lord Danu and Artio busied themselves making plans to capture Raul and the other men who were involved in the mob. Captain Raven and Lieutenant Kivas stood next to them as they sat at the table discussing the best strategy. The men set out as the sun touched the horizon, hoping to surprise the conspirators during the night.

Renn lay on the Meskhoni's bed and stared at the dark ceiling. Tavier lay next to him. Renn knew his brother was awake because Tavier kept shifting, but neither of them spoke. Instead, Renn wondered if Lord Danu and his men had caught the conspirators yet. He imagined Tellio and Kivas busting down the door to Raul's home and dragging the man out of his bed to face justice. But then it made him sad to think that Genea and Renaul would have to watch their father be arrested by Lord Danu. Maybe Raul would be at the Golden Goblet instead, drinking with some of the other bad men, and Lord Danu and Artio would capture them all at the same time. He hoped all the men in the mob would be hanged for what they did to his father . . . but he wasn't sure he wanted to watch their executions.

Renn must've dosed off because he woke to voices coming from the other room, and he sat up in bed. Tavier must've fallen asleep, too, because his breathing was slow and steady and he didn't move. Renn opened the thick curtains that covered the window and saw by the position of the moon that it was still a couple of hours until dawn. Quietly, he crept to the door and listened. Listening in on conversations through a door was much more difficult than from his loft at home, but he could still make out most of what was being said.

"What are you doing?" Tavier asked, giving Renn a sudden start.

"I thought you were asleep," Renn whispered.

"You woke me when you got up."

"Shhh." Renn put his finger to his lips. "Lord Danu's back, and he's talking to Mother."

"Scoot over," Tavier whispered. "I want to hear what they're saying."

". . . and someone must have warned them." It was Lord Danu's voice.

"But who?" Kivas asked. "We came immediately, Lord Danu. How could anyone have known? Besides those of us in this room, the only people who knew anything were your father and Ishtar. Unless they—" Kivas left his words hanging, and for a moment, no one spoke.

"Who's Ishtar?" Renn asked Tavier quietly.

"I think he's Lord Drake's Meskhoni."

Micha's voice broke the silence in the other room. "There must be another answer."

"Do you mean to tell me Raul and *all* the other suspects simply . . . disappeared? Vanished into thin air?" Delphia sounded upset. "Can't you track them or something?"

"Yes," Lord Danu said in a gentle tone. "We can, and we will. But we need more men. As soon as we return to Basilea, Raven will take a group of men out and—"

"Why didn't you bring more to begin with?" Delphia demanded. "What were you planning to do if they were still here?"

"It is easy for us to arrest twenty men, Delphia," Tellio replied. "But tracking twenty outlaws in the forest is another matter. We need trackers and dogs to aid in our search."

In the ensuing silence, Renn imagined his mother was looking out the window, pondering the situation, and the men were probably watching her, afraid to say anything that might further upset her.

"When do we leave?" Delphia inquired, so quietly that Renn barely heard her.

"At daybreak," Lord Danu answered. "There is one other thing—"

"Yes. I know!" Delphia snapped. After a pause, her tone turned defeated. "What am I going to do with Renn?"

Renn drew a sharp breath and looked at Tavier. The moonlight revealed the concern in his brother's furrowed brow and the question reflecting in his eyes. *What does she mean?*

It was Artio who spoke next. "I've thought about it for the past three days, Delphia. The danger to him and your family is simply too great to ignore. I don't believe you'd be safe, even in Basilea with Lord Danu to protect you, if Renn is there also."

"But what else can I do? If I give him up, I may never see him again." She was struggling to hold back tears—Renn could hear it in her voice—and he was busy fighting to hold back his own.

"If you don't, you may all be killed," Lord Danu said.

"What if Renn were to stay with me? Here at the cottage," Artio suggested. "I could keep him safe, and you'd be free to visit him as often as you please."

"I thought you said once that you weren't cut out to raise children?"

"Renn was younger then, and . . . I'm a bit older now. A little companionship might be good for me."

Renn wrestled with a myriad of thoughts and emotions in the long pause that followed. Did he like the idea of living with the old Meskhoni? He wasn't sure. It might be fun and exciting, but then again it might be very dull. And he'd miss his mother, Tavier, and Chria. One more cruel hand that fate would deal him because he was "special." Renn's heart beat so hard it hurt as he waited to hear his mother's decision.

"I don't know what to say," Delphia reluctantly confessed. "I'm so confused. I don't know whether I should thank you or curse the gods. But I suppose it's for the best."

"I will, of course, still make arrangements to see you are taken care of and protected in Basilea," Lord Danu announced, obviously relieved to have the matter settled. "I have a place in mind I think you might like . . ."

They continued talking, but Renn rose to his feet and climbed slowly back in bed. He didn't sleep—he wasn't even tired.

As the first hint of dawn touched the sky, Renn crept out of the house. The dew-soaked grass on his bare feet made him shiver, but he decided against returning for his boots—he didn't want to wake anybody. He knelt down on the bank of the stream, splashed his face, and took a long drink.

He walked around the little cottage, staring at the ground and kicking at pebbles with his toes. As he rounded a corner, he walked straight into a wagon, one he was certain hadn't been there the day before.

A tarpaulin covered the wagon, but Renn could see there was something underneath. He looked around, determined he was alone, and slowly lifted one corner of the tarpaulin and peered underneath. The wagon was empty except for a long, narrow pine box positioned in its exact center. Renn discreetly pulled back the canvas tarpaulin and climbed into the wagon to get a closer look at this unusual box and possibly its contents.

The long sides of the box each had a handle—as did the lid—and two ropes were tied around the box holding it closed. Renn began working the knot in one of the ropes as he looked around him once again to make certain he was still alone.

Once he got the knots undone, the lid pulled off easily, and Renn peeked inside. The lid fell out of his hands with a sound that, in the still morning air, sounded like a thunderclap, and Renn jumped back gasping for breath. He sat with his back against the side of the wagon and a hand on his racing heart.

He'd never seen a casket before, but he should have guessed what it was. He cursed himself for being so inquisitive and nosy, wishing he would have just walked past this wagon without a second look. His hands and shoulders were shaking, and tears rolled down his cheeks as he reached to straighten the lid. He tried not to look at his father's gray face and the rope burns around his neck, but he had seen it, and the image would be etched permanently into his mind. He would never be able to remember his father again without remembering how he had looked at that moment.

As he finished tying the last knot in the ropes, he heard voices coming around the corner. Not wanting to be caught snooping where he shouldn't be, he quickly pulled the tarpaulin back over the wagon, hid underneath, and waited.

"Yes, my lord, but I wouldn't make such accusations lightly."

"I know you wouldn't, Kivas. But Ishtar is my father's closest advisor and a trusted friend. Charging him with conspiracy practically implicates my father as well. They counsel with each other about everything."

Renn held his breath as the Lord Danu and his lieutenant walked around the house and stopped next to the wagon. He knew he was in no trouble, but he didn't particularly want to suffer any embarrassment, either. He peeked through a knothole in the side of the wagon and saw the sword at Kivas's hip.

"Maybe Ishtar is keeping secrets. Maybe he *is* aligned with Kahn Devin. I'm not saying your father is involved, but I don't trust Ishtar. You have to admit, your father's Meskhoni is very strange. All I ask is that you keep a wary eye on him."

"You know I watch everyone," Lord Danu said, and the men began walking again. "If Ishtar is involved, I'll find out . . ." Lord Danu's voice trailed off as they walked around the front corner of the cottage.

Renn scampered out of the wagon, adjusted the tarpaulin, and ran off in the opposite direction of the two men. He paused to pluck a ripe bunch of grapes from a vine in Artio's garden. He sat on the oak stump behind the Meskhoni's home and watched the inevitable rising of the sun.

THORN

Renn only ate a few grapes before getting lost in thought and just staring at them. It was nearing autumn, yet in the foothills of the Hebät Mountains, the early morning sun quickly burned away the dew that had cooled Renn's feet only an hour before. Coy joined Renn at the stump and pushed at his hand with his wet nose and licked his fingers. Renn smiled sadly, dropped the grapes on the ground, and scratched distractedly at Coy's ears while the dog ate the grapes.

Lord Danu's men had each walked by Renn several times as they prepared to leave, stopping momentarily to ask why he was up so early or how he was doing. Each time Renn would force a smile and claim to be doing fine, but he felt hollow inside. Lord Danu even stopped to check on Renn before going back inside to help Renn's mother with his brother and sister.

All these preparations to leave made the hollow feeling in Renn's gut feel worse. He knew his family wasn't safe as long as he was around. His father's gray body lying in the casket was proof of that, but Renn wasn't quite ready to admit that him being left to live with the Meskhoni would be best—at least not out loud. The thought of anyone else dying was intolerable. However, the thought of being left behind was unbearable. Being abandoned by his mother right after his father's murder added a black hole in the emptiness he felt. *Why can't we just move far away where nobody would know us?* he asked himself a hundred times as the day wore on. *We could start over and pretend I was the same as every other ten-year-old boy.*

But he would never be the same as other boys. No matter where he went, there would be people sent to find him. He silently cursed the pain, sorrow, and now death that seemed to follow him like scavengers waiting for another victim to fall prey to their indiscriminate hunger.

He was so focused on his thoughts that he didn't notice his mother walk up until she was standing right in front of him.

"How are you doing?" she asked.

Renn didn't look up. He only shrugged his shoulders and continued rubbing Coy's coarse black-and-gray-speckled fur.

"I know you heard us talking this morning when the men came back." She folded her arms and cocked her head, but when Renn made no reply, she continued. "Please try to understand, Renn . . . I don't like it either, but I have no choice. Don't make this more difficult than it has to be."

Her voice began to shake; the past week had taken its toll on her. There was a time, not so long ago, when she never cried. Now, she wept frequently, and each time she did, it stabbed at Renn's heart like a dagger.

Finally, he stopped scratching Coy and looked up at his mother's fatigued face. She seemed to have lines that weren't there before, as if she had aged ten years in the past week. Renn took a deep breath. "I just . . . I wish . . ." He wished she would take him with her, but he couldn't ask that. Not after his father was killed because of him. He dropped his shoulders and looked down at Coy. "Do whatever you have to. I guess it doesn't matter what I want anyway."

"What would you have me do?" she asked painfully. "If you have a better idea, I'm listening. I'm willing to try just about anything at this point."

Renn shrugged and resumed scratching the old dog lying at his feet. His mother just stood there, watching him. He could feel her eyes on him. He knew he was acting selfish and should say something to ease her pain, but he had no idea how to put his feelings into words. She was going to leave him—she had to—and nothing he could say would change that. So he sat with a grim expression on his face and kept petting the dog.

Without warning, his mother bent over and took him in a strong embrace. "I love you, Renn. I'm sorry, but you must stay here. I'll visit you . . . I promise." Then she turned and walked back into the house. Renn watched her go. He wanted to call her back and apologize for everything, but the words wouldn't come.

A few moments later, the back door of the Mage's cottage opened and Tavier marched toward Renn. "We're about to leave."

Renn looked at him and shrugged.

"Aren't you going to at least see us off?" Tavier asked, his face turning red.

"What difference does it make?"

"It makes a lot of difference!" Tavier shouted. "Maybe you don't care, but Mother is very upset and you're making it worse! Here." He thrust their father's good-luck amulet out to Renn. "Take it. Mother gave it to me. She said it's always passed down to the oldest son. I ought to give you a swift kick in the backside instead."

Renn took the talisman from his brother's outstretched hand, surprised. "Why do you want me to have it? Father would want you to keep it." Renn held the talisman close to his eye and examined it. The long tarnished chain held an oval amulet that was bright silver with the emblem of a flying eagle etched into the center. Renn turned it over in his hand and examined the strange runes on the back.

"I want you to have something to remind you of the family—something special. Besides, you need all the good luck you can get. Now, come on." He pulled Renn to his feet. "At least kiss Chria goodbye before we leave."

⋈⋄⋈

It had been twenty-nine days since his family had left with Lord Danu—not that Renn was counting. Twenty-nine tedious, boring days with nothing do to and only a quiet old man to do it with.

The Meskhoni plopped a spoonful of boiled and mashed squash onto the pewter plate in front of Renn. "Lord Danu set your family up on a small farm near the castle." He shoved a wooden bowl with butter toward Renn and a cup with water. Squash. Artio loved the stuff, and it grew like weeds in the small garden. If Renn never ate it again in his life, it would be too soon.

"That's nice, Meskhoni," Renn mumbled.

"I thought you'd be happy to know about it . . . that's all. And you can call me Artio. We've lived together now for a few weeks, so there's no need to be so formal."

"That's nice, Artio." Renn still mumbled his response.

Artio fidgeted with a bowl that had some crushed spices in it and looked at Renn like he wanted to say something more. Finally, he simply said, "The field was already planted, so they'll get a crop this fall." Then he passed the spices to Renn and awkwardly turned his attention to his own plate of squash and eggs.

At least they were safe now, but Renn couldn't help feeling a little jealous. He stole a quick glance at the Meskhoni—Artio. The old man's brows were narrowed as he concentrated on his food. Renn felt a little guilty for not talking more to the Mage. It wasn't that he didn't like the old man. He just didn't feel like talking.

On more than one occasion, the Meskhoni tried to draw him out of his shell, make him smile or laugh, but it was for naught. The pain of all Renn had lost was just too consuming—his father, his home, and his family . . . it would never be the same again.

He spent many long nights either tossing in bed or waking in a cold sweat after a bad dream. When he did sleep, it was a restless slumber that did very little to lessen his fatigue.

The weeks passed, but as the cool, wet months of winter began, Renn still rarely smiled. His family only came to visit him twice during the first four months he lived with Artio, and despite the Mage's attempts to cheer him, Renn couldn't bring himself to drop his guard and let the old man past his defenses. What if he got too close to Artio and then the Mage left him, like his mother . . . like his father?

It rained for two solid weeks. The ground became saturated and muddy, the stream that ran behind the Meskhoni's cottage turned into a viable river, and the upper half of the Hebät Mountains were capped in white.

Artio made frequent trips to town to buy supplies or to bless babies at the monthly Azur-Aven festivals; he had always done so, but during good weather Renn didn't mind staying back at the cottage. At least, not *much*. But now, anything seemed better than staying cooped up doing nothing all day. However, the old man still wouldn't let Renn accompany him because he said it wasn't safe. Renn argued it wouldn't be very safe if someone came to the cottage while the Mage was gone, but Artio didn't seem too concerned with that possibility. So, Renn stayed shut up in the small cottage with nothing to do but the writing and reading drills Artio made him practice; he even learned to cook a little to pass the time.

How could going to town be more dangerous than staying alone at the cottage? he wondered as he cooked himself some rabbit and vegetable stew. Certainly, no one would dare attack him if he were with the Meskhoni. But who would protect him if someone came to the Meskhoni's home when the Mage wasn't there? It didn't make sense. There had to be something else the old man wasn't telling him, and that made him mad. He'd decided he didn't like living alone with the Meskhoni. He was a boring old man who wouldn't let Renn go anywhere or do anything fun. *This is like being in the town jail,* he thought. *No, it's more like being alone in a dungeon. At least in jail there are other prisoners to keep you company.*

It rained almost every day during the winter months, so Renn cherished the few days when the storm clouds passed and the sun shone brightly overhead once again. In the middle of winter, even in the foothills, the sun was quick to warm southern Boranica, and Renn anxiously took advantage of the opportunity to do some outdoor exploring. It was the only escape available to him, the only *fun* thing Artio would let him do. But even his exploring was hampered because the old man had set limits to how far he could go.

He had no true friends, although he did listen to the animals frequently as they sang to one another and imagined they were his friends—he could imagine anything he wanted when he was out in the forest behind Artio's cottage. On this particular day, he pictured himself to be a great warrior chasing the minions of dark. He charged up the hill, around great boulders, and through thickets of trees—he had the cowards on the run. As he rounded one particularly large boulder, he heard a loud whinny, skidded to a halt, and let out a startled yelp. Renn looked toward the sound and saw a frightened young horse down a steep drop on the mountain.

The yearling was white, except for a light brown patch on his forehead in the shape of a diamond and some brown around his hooves. His dull coat was riddled with small lacerations and spotted with dried blood, and his ribs were visible underneath. He looked as though he'd been out in the rain with no food for days. Looking closer, Renn realized one of the horse's hind legs was stuck in a large thornbush.

Renn gathered a handful of long grass and climbed cautiously down the short, steep hill, careful not to knock rocks onto the trapped animal. Upon reaching the horse, Renn gave it some of the grass in his hand. The animal eagerly ate the peace offering and clearly wanted more. Renn noticed nothing grew out of the rocks on which he and the horse stood, and behind the colt there was nothing but a dense patch of thornbushes.

"How did you get yourself into this mess?" Renn asked as he rubbed the horse's cheek. It was obvious he couldn't take the horse back through the thorn patch, and the hill was so rocky and steep it would be a dangerous climb. But that seemed the best option of the two.

After picking another handful of grass, Renn leaned over the hill, just out of the horse's reach. "Here, boy, come on. It's all right. I'll take care of you now."

The horse struggled a little, but it couldn't move. Instead, it whinnied a couple of times, snorted, and looked longingly at the grass in Renn's hand. Somehow, Renn understood what the problem was. Its hoof was stuck between rocks under the thornbush, and it had no way of getting out. It had struggled for days to no avail.

Renn needed help; he couldn't save the horse alone. He gathered more grass, placed it in front of the horse, and said, "Don't worry. I'll be back with help." Renn didn't know how, but he was sure the young horse understood him. He scrambled back up the hill and ran to find the Meskhoni.

When he got back to the house, the old Mage was on the roof, fixing a leak that had developed during the two weeks of winter rain.

"Artio!" he yelled, breathing heavily. "Artio, come quickly! I need your help."

"What is it, boy?" The old man hurried down the wooden ladder leaning against the small cottage.

"I found a young horse. It's stuck down a steep hill and needs help," Renn quickly explained.

"Wait a minute. Let me get some rope."

Artio came out of the house a moment later with his staff in one hand, a leather pouch in the other, and a rope around his arm.

"Hurry up." Renn waved to the Meskhoni as he waited for the old man to climb over a group of large boulders.

"Just a minute," Artio gasped. "Let me catch my breath."

"It's not far from here," Renn said. "You can rest when we get there." Renn led Artio through the forest, up the hills, and over the logs to where the colt was waiting.

Renn grabbed a fistful of grass and carefully climbed down to the horse. "See, I told you I'd come back for you, boy. Everything will be all right now."

"Renn, tie the end of this rope around his body just behind his front legs so I can help him climb up the hill!" Artio hollered as he threw one end of the rope down the steep incline.

"We need to get his back leg free first," Renn replied. "His hoof is trapped under some rocks."

Artio tied his end of the rope around a large oak near the top of the drop and, using it to control his descent, climbed down the hill.

"How do you know that? It's completely covered by the thornbush."

"He told me."

Artio raised his right eyebrow and looked quizzically at Renn. "He *told* you?"

"Well, not in words. I don't know *how* he told me," Renn said defensively. "He just did."

Still holding the rope in one hand, Artio climbed behind the horse and used his staff to pull back the thorns to reveal that, in fact, his hoof was trapped between two large boulders. From where Renn stood, he could see the horse's fetlock and shank were scraped badly, almost to the bone, and he had lost a lot of blood.

"I don't think it's broken," Artio announced, "but we'd better be careful getting it out so we don't make it worse. I wonder how he got into this predicament."

The young horse whinnied, jerked his head a few times, and then Renn replied, "He was attacked by wolves. His mother died fighting them off so he could escape. He ran up this hill and halfway into the thorn patch before he realized his mistake. He was too afraid to turn back, so he kept going until he got stuck in those rocks. That was two nights ago."

Artio's mouth dropped and his eyes widened as he listened to Renn's narrative.

"I suppose he *told* you all of this?" Artio asked, astounded.

"Well . . . yes," Renn answered, not quite sure how he understood the horse.

"When did he tell you all of this?"

"Just now . . . after you asked about it."

"You mean to say that he can understand me?" Artio asked.

"I guess so."

"You wouldn't be playing games with me?" Artio asked suspiciously. "Because if you are, I'm going to be mad."

"No," Renn said. "How do you think I knew about his hoof?"

Artio thought for a moment, rubbing his gray-stubbled chin, then turned his attention to the horse's hoof. "I guess we'd better get busy or we'll be here all night."

Renn and Artio worked side by side with the horse for more than an hour before they managed to get him safely up the hill. The sun was already a large orange ball on the western horizon when they approached the cottage.

"I'm going to name him Thorn," Renn announced as he brushed the horse's coat. Artio was busy applying salve and bandages to the horse's hind leg, while Thorn eagerly munched on the abundant supply of grass Renn had placed on the ground.

"This is a wild horse, Renn," Artio replied without looking up from his work. "Once he gets better, he'll want to go free. I wouldn't get too attached to him if I were you."

"Thorn likes me," Renn said. "He wants to stay."

"I suppose he told you that, too?"

"Actually, he did."

Artio stood up and brushed the claylike mud off his breeches. "I'll tell you what. As long as he stays without being picketed or fenced in, you can keep him. But if he runs off, you let him be. Is it a deal?" he asked, extending his hand.

Renn's heart leapt; he knew Thorn would never leave him. With a smile, he took the Meskhoni's hand and shook it. "Deal."

SKULL FIRE

When Renn first began working with Thorn, the Meskhoni went through his shed and found a currycomb and brush. Renn used them religiously to help Thorn's coat improve. With daily care, the young horse grew strong and fit. Thorn's coat, which had been dull and dingy when Renn found him, was now as clean as fresh snow, and powerful muscles corded in his legs and breast.

Their ability to communicate also grew stronger with each passing day. Renn understood Thorn through a combination of thoughts; facial expressions; ear, nose, and eye movements; and the occasional whinny or snort. Thorn didn't understand words or phrases—he grasped basic concepts through facial expressions, tone of voice, and body language.

I'm amazed I didn't recognize the language of animals before, Renn said to Thorn one morning.

I do not find it amazing, Thorn replied. *Men assume animals have no language.*

Perhaps I could teach others how to understand, Renn suggested.

I don't think ordinary men will ever understand.

Thorn snorted, shook his mane, and looked across the meadow. Renn followed the horse's gaze and saw Artio walking across the long brown grass.

"Good morning," the old man said. "How is he today?"

"Fine. I just finished inspecting his leg," Renn said. Artio nodded, rubbed his chin, and walked slowly around Thorn.

"You've done a good job, Renn," he said. "The horse looks healthy and strong." Artio never called him Thorn; he told Renn giving the horse a name would just make it that much more difficult when it came time to let go. "I'm surprised he's still around, though."

"Thorn and I are best friends." Renn said. "He doesn't want to leave."

Thorn pranced around, testing his healed leg. *My leg feels much better now,* Thorn told Renn. *I wish to run. Do you wish to ride?*

Renn's heart leapt. He'd had dreams of riding on Thorn and racing through the mountain meadows, but he wasn't sure the horse would want to carry a rider.

"This is great." Renn smiled broadly at the Meskhoni. "He wants me to ride him."

Artio laughed. "Renn, the horse hasn't left yet—and I'll grant you that I was wrong about that—but you don't just climb on a wild horse and ride. It takes a lot of work and time to break a horse for riding."

Why does the old one call me wild? Thorn asked Renn. *And how could you ride me if I was broken?*

He doesn't mean it that way, Thorn, Renn thought back. *Let's have some fun with the old one. Bend down to help me climb on your back.*

When Thorn bent his front legs to make it easier for Renn to mount, Artio's jaw dropped, his eyebrows rose, and he stammered before speaking.

"I guess I was wrong again," he said. "It would appear you and Thorn are going to be great friends."

Renn laughed and patted Thorn on the neck, and Artio chuckled and shook his head as he turned to go back to the cottage.

"Yee-haw." Renn held Thorn's long white mane, and they sped off across the meadow and into the forest.

Renn and Thorn rode well into the evening. Unlike when he rode the big, plodding farm horses his family had owned, Thorn's gait was effortless, and he could run for miles without tiring. Renn noticed a large eagle in the sky above them in the morning and figured the old Mage was scouting for danger, but he didn't see the bird after that.

When he finally returned to the Meskhoni's cottage, the sky was growing dark. Renn gave Thorn carrots and combed his coat once again, then washed up and ambled to the door. Normally, he would just walk in and sit—well, sit and sulk if he was going to be honest with himself. But he'd been doing a lot of thinking as he rode on Thorn's back today, and he knew he needed to say some things to Artio that weren't going to be easy. He took a deep breath and walked inside.

The smell of rabbit stew drifted from a kettle over the fire, and a bowl and spoon waited for Renn at the table. He could tell the Meskhoni had already eaten because his bowl was cleaned and put away.

"So, you decided to return." Artio sat on the settle with a thick wood-bound book on his lap. Renn was certain he'd never seen that book in the cottage and wondered idly where it came from. "I knew no one dangerous was near," the old man continued, "but I thought you'd lost your way or fallen off and been injured. I was just about to go looking for you."

"Sorry," Renn said sheepishly. "I was having so much fun I lost track of time."

"Well, you haven't had much fun since coming to live with me, so one splurge now and again is probably all right." The Meskhoni set his book down, filled Renn's bowl with stew, and set it on the table.

"Are you going to eat," the old Mage asked, "or just stare at your dinner all night?"

"Artio." Renn laid his spoon aside and looked up. "I've been thinking."

"Uh-oh, this sounds serious."

"Not really. But . . . well . . . I guess I wanted to tell you I'm sorry."

"What for?"

"I haven't been easy to be around since my father was . . . since my . . . since things changed. And I wasn't very nice to my mother, either. I guess I've been feeling sorry for myself and not thinking about anybody else."

The old man just swallowed and nodded. Renn picked up his spoon and stirred the soup in his bowl. "Thank you for letting me live here with you."

Artio cleared his throat and turned to the window. "It's been good for me to have the company, Renn," he said gruffly. "I enjoy having you here."

After supper, Artio lit a candle and set it on the table between them. The Mage poured ale into a large pewter tankard for him and handed a glass of goat milk to Renn. Sipping his ale thoughtfully, Artio began talking about history—at least that's what he called it.

"Thousands of years ago, gods walked the hills of Lemuria—long before even the Wizard Greyfel's time. Did you know that, Renn?"

"I don't know much of anything about the gods," Renn said.

"No, I guess you wouldn't. That's the problem these days . . . parents don't teach their children about history. How can you expect kids to grow up and not make the same mistakes their ancestors did unless they know something about them?"

Renn shrugged. He didn't know who his ancestors were, and he knew less about what they did.

Artio picked up his staff and made a circular pattern in the air above them. Green mists began to follow the pattern of his staff and form images that acted out the story the Mage was telling.

"The most powerful gods are El Azur, the creator, also called the god of light, and Ba Aven, the god of chaos. Ba Aven accused El Azur of being a thief because he organized life out of chaos. Ba Aven's desire is to return all things to chaos. So, he created six children—lesser gods—and sent them to destroy Lemuria. El Azur then created six children of his own to protect his creations. The most notable of these lesser gods was Avalian, the eldest daughter of El Azur, and K'Thrak, the eldest son of Ba Aven. These two lesser gods and their siblings battled back and forth for thousands of years."

"I thought gods were good. Why did they fight so much?" Renn interrupted.

"Good? All gods?" Artio dispersed the green mist, set down his mug of ale, and rubbed at his gray-stubbled chin. "Good and bad are sometimes terms that change depending on your point of view. What you and I call *good*, the gods of chaos call *weakness*. They don't see it as 'good and evil.' They respect strength. Those weaker are viewed as necessary chattel. They exist to provide for the strong." The old Mage picked up his pewter mug and took a long draw before he continued. "For the purpose of this discussion, however, we'll say the gods of dark are not good. For example, do you know about demons?"

"Not really, but I have heard awful stories about them. Are they the evil lesser gods that fought against Avalian and the gods of light?" Renn cocked his head.

"Close. The demons are the children of the dark gods, and they're nice compared to their parents."

"What happened to the gods? Why is Monguinir the lord of the demons instead of K'Thrak?" Renn asked.

"If you'll stop interrupting me, I'll tell you what happened to the gods. Incidentally, Monguinir is K'Thrak's son. That's why he rules under the Cragg Mountains." Artio once again waved his staff in a circular motion, and the green mist shifted into images. "K'Thrak decided he needed a bigger army, so he and his brothers and sisters copulated with humans, and the result was demon spawn—Monguinir and his siblings."

"What's copu—copulate?" Renn asked, his brows furrowed.

The old Meskhoni flushed and said, "It means they had children together."

Renn scrunched up his nose. "That's gross."

"Yes, well, their children are pretty disgusting, I'll grant you that," the old man agreed. "Of course, the children of El Azur responded by joining themselves with humans and created the Avalians, and so the forces remained equally balanced. Their battles lasted hundreds of years, and they were destroying the land and mortals along with it.

"Finally, El Azur and Ba Aven intervened and called a war counsel. El Azur was frustrated because life wasn't progressing, and Ba Aven was furious that instead of destroying life, his children created new life. They gathered the twelve lesser gods together in one place to decide what should be done. After much arguing, they decided to combine their will and place enormous power into a special stone. This rock became known as the Godstone, and the gods charged it with maintaining balance and order. Then El Azur said, 'Let us leave this world to be ruled by the children of men, lest we resume this war and both our purposes are frustrated. The Godstone will ensure a balance of power, and the inhabitants of this world will have free will to follow the path of life or the path of chaos as they see fit.'"

"Where did the gods go when they left Lemuria?" Renn asked.

"The story goes that three of Ba Aven's children returned to a state of chaos with their father, and three of El Azur's children returned to him. The demons and the Avalians remained and continued the battle on a smaller scale—that is, until Greyfel invoked the binding."

"What about the other gods?" Renn pressed. "You said there were six of each, and yet only three each returned to their . . . father gods."

Artio smiled. "Very good, Renn. You've been listening. The others remained on Lemuria, but under the agreement they take no active role in its destiny. K'Thrak became the essence of darkness, Danisyr—one of Ba Aven's twin daughters—remained as the power of storms, and Necrosys became the Necro Sea, or sea of death. The three children of El Azur who remained are Avalian, Bremen and Lunaryn. Avalian became the forests surrounding Alfheina, and she is the patron goddess of the Avalians. Bremen's essence remained as the forests of Bremenon, and Lunaryn became the moon.

"The children of chaos and light despise each other. Neither side can bear the thought that the other should become more worshipped and praised than they, so the battle still rages on among their followers—and that is what you and I are mixed up in."

"Is that why you hate Kahn Devin so much? Because he changed sides and now worships chaos?" Renn asked.

"That is one of the reasons, I must concede, but there are many."

"Why did he do it?" Renn asked. "Switch sides, I mean."

Artio stood, walked toward the window, and looked out at the night sky.

"The dark gods promise easy power," he said. "They use cunning words to make evil sound good. Kahn Devin once told me he wanted Lemuria to be a land of peace and safety." The Meskhoni turned and walked back to the table. "The Azur-Lore teaches restraint and prudence—respect for everyone's free agency. Kahn Devin didn't care much for that. He thought we should force obedience to law to ensure his idea of peace and safety for all. So, after he became a Mage, he went to the caves under the Cragg Mountains and offered himself to Lord Monguinir. Now, he is a Warlock in the Aven-Lore as well as a Mage in the Azur-Lore."

"You mean he's still a Mage?" Renn's eyebrows shot up. "Why don't they take away his staff or something?"

"I wish it were as simple as that." The old Meskhoni shook his head sadly. "Kahn Devin doesn't use *tools* of the Azur-Lore, such as a staff; he twists the knowledge he has of it, combines it with the Aven-Lore, and uses it to further his bid for power. It's his knowledge that can't be taken from him."

Renn was lying in bed that night thinking about what the Meskhoni told him when he heard a clicking sound, like a door latch, then soft footsteps walking across the main room floor.

Renn slipped on his breeches and boots, then cracked open his door and peered out. He saw Artio put on his cloak, pick up his staff, and slip out the back door.

Too curious to ignore the Meskhoni's midnight venture, Renn pulled on his shirt and followed. The Mage was crossing the little stream behind the cottage when Renn gently let the door close. He waited until the old man disappeared into the trees, then followed, keeping a safe distance between him and the Mage.

Artio walked for ten minutes around boulders and trees before stopping in front of a high, rocky bluff. Renn hid behind a large pine as the Meskhoni turned to look around, probably making sure he was alone. A burst of soft green light illuminated the area, and when Renn peeked around the tree again, Artio was gone.

Curious, Renn thought. *It's as if he disappeared into thin air.* At the base of the cliff, he could see footprints on the soft earth; however, they didn't lead anywhere. Renn *had* seen the man change from an eagle more than once. He looked up to the sky but saw no birds.

As Renn was scanning the sky, he heard faint rustling from within a copse of aspen trees to his left.

"Artio," he whispered, "is that you?" The soft rushing of the cool breeze as it blew across the coin-shaped leaves was the only reply. Renn strained to see into the dark thicket and took a step closer.

"Hello? Artio, is that you?" His heart pounded in his chest.

"Yes, Renn," the old man replied. "Come here . . . I have something I want you to see."

Renn breathed a sigh of relief and walked toward the sound of the Meskhoni's familiar voice.

"I was getting worried for a moment," Renn said.

The elderly man was bending down as Renn approached. He appeared to be studying something on the ground underneath a particularly large tree.

"What is it?" Renn asked, looking over his mentor's shoulder.

The Mage wore a strange grin when he looked up. It wasn't Artio!

Renn gasped. He wanted to run, but fear rooted him firmly in place. This creature didn't even look human! Its deformed face was pale green, and its eyes were blood-red. Instead of a nose, it had three large holes set in a triangular shape. The creature pulled back its cavernous mouth into a wicked grin revealing two rows of razor-sharp teeth and dark saliva that dripped thickly down its chin.

"Glad you could join us, *Chosen One*," it rasped in its true voice.

DEMON SPAWN

Renn overcame his temporary paralysis and spun around to flee, but he found himself face-to-face with a massive black dog. He screamed and jumped backward.

Even crouched, the animal was so large it stood eye to eye with him. It curled back its upper lip and snarled at Renn, revealing a set of long fangs that also dripped with thick, dark saliva. It had bright red eyes and shiny black fur.

The creature behind Renn grabbed him. Renn screamed, and it covered his mouth with long bony fingers.

"We'll have none of that, little Renn," it hissed and turned the boy to face him once more. "I won't have you yelling all the way to the caves."

Renn struggled but couldn't break free from the creature's powerful grasp. A blinding flash of green light illuminated the clearing, and the giant dog yelped. The creature covering Renn's mouth threw him to the ground.

Renn looked up and saw the Meskhoni standing on the opposite side of the clearing, holding his staff high in the air. Green light surrounded the old Mage like a shroud of power, and in a loud voice he ordered, "Leave this place or die."

The massive dog crouched and snarled—saliva and froth dripped from its teeth. The other creature pulled a white human skull from under its cloak and chanted something in a guttural tongue. A red glare sprung to life from the skulls' vacant cavities, shielding the hideous creature in its own aura of power, and with a hissing shriek, it said, "You're not strong enough to fight us both, old man."

The giant dog leapt toward Artio. A torrent of red fire shot through the air from the skull, forcing the Meskhoni to his knees. With his staff in one hand, the Mage made a circular pattern and pointed it toward the creature commanding the skull. The Meskhoni sent a river of green fire at the red attack to keep it at bay. In his other hand, Artio held a dagger that also glowed green. The Mage stabbed at the dog with the blade as it attempted to penetrate his defenses.

The skull glowed more brightly in the hand of the grotesque creature, and the green Mage fire faltered. Artio grimaced and sweat trickled down his face as he struggled to maintain his shield.

The giant dog seemed to sense the old Mage was weakening. It circled Artio with demonic fury, lunging and recoiling to get past the shining green dirk.

Renn's heart raced, and his eyes darted between Artio and their attackers. The old man had become more than just a friend—he was Renn's mentor and protector. And now, just like his father, Artio would die trying to protect him.

Renn found a large stick lying on the ground. He snatched it up and swung it at the creature that was attacking Artio with red power, striking it in the side. The red fire quavered, and the creature cursed and sent Renn reeling with a solid backhand across his face.

Renn tasted blood in the corner of his mouth. He wiped it on his sleeve, rolled to his knees, and looked back to the battle. Artio had regained his feet during the brief respite Renn's interference provided, but Renn didn't think the old man could hold on much longer. Battling two at the same time was more than the Mage could handle.

As Renn searched the ground for another weapon, he heard a pounding noise. Thorn burst out of the trees and charged the giant dog. The dog was focused completely on the blazing knife in Artio's hand. The horse rose on its hind legs and, with all its weight, struck down with its front hooves on the back of the enormous beast.

The giant dog collapsed and yelped in pain. But to Renn's horror, the beast rolled to its feet and leapt toward the yearling with surprising agility. Thorn whinnied and jumped backward but was too slow. The rabid beast had the horse in its grasp and dragged him to the ground.

Artio took advantage of the diversion and, with deadly accuracy and speed, threw the flaming dagger at the huge dog's back. The dagger buried deeply into the animal with a dull thud and pulsed and radiated an intense emerald color. The giant dog howled in pain and turned to green smoldering ash before their eyes.

"*By the dark of K'Thrak*, I'll destroy you all!" the creature vowed in a raspy voice, and red lightning shot from the skull toward Artio.

Renn grabbed another large stick and and struck the inhuman creature with all his strength on the arm holding the skull. The beast dropped the glowing cranium and turned to Renn with a raised fist.

Renn braced for the strike, but a green flame ripped into his attacker, throwing it forcefully against a tree. Artio held the Mage fire on the creature's chest, keeping it pinned against the aspen until it shrieked in anguish.

The green power swirled as the Meskhoni sustained his attack. Renn recalled seeing a similar effect years ago—the night Raul attacked Renn, Artio's green power had looked alive.

The creature let out one last scream and exploded in a flash of green light. The skull on the ground met a similar fate under Artio's green Mage fire. The old man sunk to his knees in exhaustion.

Renn stared, open-mouthed, at the ashes of the giant dog. The knife no longer burned with emerald light. It looked quite ordinary as it lay on the ground next to the remains of the vicious beast.

All that remained of the creature who wielded the skull was a smoking dark spot on the tree and the acrid stench of its power that hung in the air like rotting eggs.

Renn looked down and saw that his hands and legs were shaking. He jumped with a start when Thorn's moist muzzle nudged the back of his neck.

Are you injured? the young horse asked him.

Renn's heart pounded under his shirt. He barely comprehended the question but managed to shake his head.

The old one looks very tired, Thorn said, nodding toward Artio. *He fought valiantly to save your life. He saved my life, too. He is good—for a human.*

Renn looked at Artio. His face was pale, and he leaned on his staff as he struggled to pull himself to his feet. Renn thought about Thorn's comment but was unable to respond. His entire concept of the world had just been drastically altered. Creatures like what he just saw existed only in fairy tales and nightmares. Oh sure, Artio had told him that demons and other strange beasts were real, but Renn wasn't ready for what he'd just witnessed.

Artio stumbled toward Renn, still using his staff for support. He looked into his eyes as if pondering some momentous dilemma. The Meskhoni wiped the perspiration off his forehead and set his jaw.

"Come with me, Renn," Artio said. "I think it's time you learn a few things."

THE TAHSZ CODEX

Renn stared at Artio's back as he followed him to the rocky bluff on the edge of the copse. He felt like he was walking down a tunnel surrounded by blurred-out trees. Minutes ago he stood by this same small cliff looking for the old man—it seemed a lifetime ago now.

The Meskhoni raised his staff, tapped the side of the cliff, and spoke some words in a strange language. The staff came to life, and a rough opening appeared in the rock wall.

Artio has a secret cave, Renn thought. Somewhere in the deep recesses of his mind, he knew this was an exciting discovery.

"Don't just stand there staring into space," the Meskhoni said. "Come inside."

Artio led him to a wooden chair next to a crude stone table in the middle of the cavern, then set a goblet of foul-smelling liquid in front of Renn. "Drink this," he said.

Renn picked up the elixir, stared vacantly at the dark, steaming drink, and raised it to his lips. He only managed three swallows before he coughed and spat it out.

"What is this stuff?" He scrunched his nose and put the goblet on the rock table, far away from himself. His surroundings rushed into focus. "Wow," he said. "This place is incredible."

The walls were high and arched toward the center, as though they had been carved by hand. Stone shelves, cut into the back wall, were lined row after row with books. Some were bound in leather, some held together with twine—all of them had seen much use and appeared to be ancient. Tables and strongboxes lined the sides of the room, and a variety of maps, brown with age, hung above them on the walls. Scrolls, vials, books, and containers were stacked neatly on the tables and three of the iron-bound chests were locked and labeled: Weapons, Talismans, and Trinkets, respectively. This was more like what Renn expected to find in the Mage's cottage.

Renn got to his feet and walked around the Mage's lair to get a closer look at the strange objects.

"A bit overwhelming, is it?" the Mage asked, the corner of his mouth raised in half a smile. "I built it some time ago, when I first came to Leedsdale to serve as the Meskhoni."

"You *built* this . . . all by yourself?" Renn imagined it would have taken several men years to carve out this room.

"The cave was already here. I made some changes, of course—I hid the entrance, carved the shelves, and added the furniture—but the cave was ideal when I found it."

"How does it stay light in here?" Renn didn't see any candles or lamps.

"Look up." The Mage pointed to the center of the cavern's ceiling. A round ball embedded in the stone radiated brightly, illuminating the entire vault with a soft white light. Renn's mouth dropped open. He'd never heard of light without fire.

He stared at the glowing ball. "How does it burn?"

"It's called an Enchanter's Orb, and it doesn't burn. It's a simple spell. You'll learn how to do it early in your studies at Elder Island—but that isn't why I brought you here." The old man set his staff against the wall, clasped his hands behind his back, and began to pace.

"Renn." Artio turned toward him. "You've been through a lot for someone so young, but you've never been in as much danger as you were tonight."

The hideous face of the vile creature that attacked them only moments ago flashed in Renn's memory. Leaving the cottage to spy on Artio nearly got them all killed.

"Those . . . things that attacked you," the old man continued, "are not like Raul or the group of northerners Lord Danu and his men fought. The one with the skull was a Kiroc Shapeshifter, and the other was a Demon Dog."

"A Kiroc what?" Renn furrowed his brows and tilted his head.

"Shapeshifter. It's one of the levels of power a user of the Aven-Lore must pass through on their way to becoming a Warlock. It's confusing at first, but the two lores are similar in some respects. In the Azur-Lore, you begin as an Apprentice. Once you master that level, you become an Enchanter, then Sorcerer, Healer, Druid, Mage, and finally a Wizard. Seven Wizards are chosen to return to the school to teach and are called lore masters—the leader of those Wizards is Salas. The Aven-Lore has a comparable system. Beginners in their craft are called Demonologists. Once they master that, they become a Magician, then Witch, Necromancer, Shapeshifter, Warlock, and finally Grand Warlock. There are few Warlocks and only one Grand Warlock at any given time."

"Is Kahn Devin the Grand Warlock?" Renn scratched his head and squinted up at Artio.

"Yes. In the Aven-Lore, only strength is respected. Kahn killed the previous Grand Warlock to gain his current position. He's the most powerful Warlock now. But if someone else became more powerful than Kahn Devin, that person—or thing—would become the Grand Warlock and rule the Cragg Caves for Lord Monguinir."

"What's a *Kiroc*?" Renn asked.

"Half demon and half human." Artio crinkled his nose like he had just smelled dead fish. "Long ago, before the Godstone maintained balance, the demons would rape the daughters of men and the resulting offspring were called Kirocs. Since the binding, Kirocs have been forced to interbreed, and now, as a result, most of them are mindless brutes."

"Why does Kahn Devin want to take me, Artio? That *is* why the Kiroc and Demon Dog came . . . isn't it?" Renn asked, cutting to the question that plagued him most. The old Mage took a deep breath and patted Renn gently on the shoulder.

"I'm getting to that, but you need to understand certain things first." The Meskhoni tapped at his chin. "The lore of the gods—both the Azur- and Aven-Lores—have been studied by man since the beginning of his existence. One man, however, did more for the study and understanding of the Azur-Lore than any other: Greyfel, the first lore master. He set up the school on Elder Island and studied with the Avalians to master the art."

"The Avalians are the children of the good gods, right?" Renn asked, following along as best he could.

"That depends on your point of view," the old man said. "To you and me and anybody who values freedom and life, the Avalians are the children of the *good* gods. But to those who follow Ba Aven, the Avalians are the children of a thief—that's how they label El Azur. Let's just say the Avalians are children of the gods of life. Remember that, because Kahn Devin will try to convince you that the gods of chaos are the first and most powerful and should be the ones you follow. He will tell you there is no good or evil, only power. But that's a lie. Now, let's get back to the story at hand. Let me see . . . Oh yes, Greyfel. He did many great things and had many adventures as he traveled, searching for different artifacts and ways to unlock the potential of the Azur-Lore. One of the most curious discoveries he made was an ancient scroll he found in the city of Tahsz."

"What's *Tahsz*?" Renn interrupted.

"If you keep stopping me, we'll be up all night." The Meskhoni rubbed his temples. "However, since you asked, Tahsz was once a great city in the country of Domeria, built by a people long forgotten and now lost to the jungle. It hasn't been seen for hundreds of years. At any rate, Greyfel called the scroll the Tahsz Codex, after the ancient city. We don't really know who wrote it, possibly a group of mystics—it appears to have more than one author—but it speaks of the creation of the world, the war between the gods, the Godstone, and to Greyfel's astonishment, it prophesied of him and some of the things he would do. There are many prophecies in the Codex, and they seem to be accurate in every case. One prophecy in particular stands out, and many people, Kahn Devin included, believe it is about to be fulfilled."

Artio's lips pressed into a tight line, and he stared into Renn's eyes.

"Maybe it would be best if I read the prophecy directly from a copy of the Codex itself." Artio walked toward a table standing against the wall. He rummaged through some papyrus scrolls, pausing several times to examine the ancient texts. "Ah, here it is."

He laid the writings in front of Renn. "I made this copy myself from the original while I was a student on Elder Island. It's a very arduous task—which you shall discover once you become an Apprentice."

Renn was proud of the fact that he could read; most people could not. But the markings on this scroll looked more like scribbles and scratch marks than letters.

"What does it say?" He strained his eyes and cocked his head to the side, trying to make sense out of the odd characters.

"It says: *Balance shall be set by the gods, infused into a stone, and it shall protect the creations of the gods, maintaining between them a natural order of things. But, when two children of the blessing shall come with strength in their wings—being marked great—then will darkness be destroyed and great evil rule. Oh, fear and tremble, nations of Lemuria, for its taskmaster is pain and anger, and thy deliverer death.*"

The Meskhoni stopped reading and stared at Renn. *It doesn't make sense*, Renn thought as he repeated the prophecy in his mind. How could darkness be destroyed *and* evil rule? If darkness is destroyed, wouldn't the evil be destroyed as well?

"Are you sure you read it right?" he asked.

"Of course," Artio snapped. "I've read it a thousand times."

"Maybe you copied it wrong," Renn suggested, attempting to subdue the Meskhoni's growing impatience.

"I didn't copy it wrong." Artio's voice rose in pitch, and he waved his hand dismissively in the air. He folded his arms and took a deep breath. "It's difficult to understand; even the lore masters at Elder Island disagree over the interpretation. The only clear thing about it is that two powerful lore users will rise up, and they will somehow cause a great shift in the balance of power that has been ensured by the Godstone. When that shift occurs, Kahn Devin, as well as others, want to be in place to usurp whatever control and domination they can."

Renn wondered what this prophecy had to do with him and the attack that just happened, but then it clicked. Not just the attack tonight but all of the horrible things that happened to his family were linked to this prophecy.

"People think I'm one of the powerful lore users." Renn clenched his teeth and stared at the markings on the parchment.

Artio nodded and sat down across the table from Renn. "It is very likely. No one before you was ever marked so significantly. The connection with the gods and the aeon myriad is very strong in you, Renn."

"The prophecy said two would rise up," Renn said. "Maybe the time isn't now. You said yourself that no one else has been marked liked me."

Artio held up his hands to stop Renn's questions. "I *did* say no one *before* you was marked so significantly, but I didn't say no one *after* you was."

Renn's heart dropped. He'd hoped he'd found a loophole in the prophecy.

"When you were two," the old man said, "a child in Andrika was blessed and marked on midsummer's Azur-Aven; his blessing was much like your own. I'm not saying you two are the children the prophecy refers to, but it is a good possibility. However, Kahn Devin is so certain you are that he will stop at nothing to make you his ally."

"His ally." Renn jumped to his feet and threw his arms in the air. "I wouldn't be his ally if the entire world were falling apart and he was my last hope for survival. It's his fault my family left me. It's his fault my father is . . ." Renn couldn't finish his accusation. He could feel his voice beginning to break and had to fight to keep the tears from his eyes.

Despite Renn's efforts to mask his pain, the Meskhoni must have seen through the anger. He rose, walked to Renn, and pulled him into an awkward embrace. At first, Renn wanted to push away, but his need to be comforted by someone he could trust overcame his embarrassment. The idea of being magic and special was exciting when he was younger. But it brought nothing except pain and loneliness, and no amount of magic could change that.

Renn pulled back from Artio, who looked into his eyes and placed a hand on his shoulder.

"It is good you have made your decision to follow the Azur-Lore, Renn. Because you've made that choice now—before you've been confronted with the situation—it will be much easier to resist the persuasions of Kahn Devin."

"Why did he leave me alone for the past six months, then suddenly send those creatures to get me?"

"Since you came to live with me," Artio said, "Kahn Devin and his people have been looking for you. He wrongly assumed you went with your mother to be protected by Lord Danu. I placed a shield of sorts over my cottage and the surrounding area to keep you hidden. Because I am a Mage, a shield around my home didn't arouse suspicion.

"Since your family left, you may have noticed you haven't sensed shadows in the woods either—that's because he could not find you. Kahn Devin must have recently realized what I was doing and sent the Kiroc and the Demon Dog here to capture and take you to him." The Mage stroked his chin and looked up at the glowing orb on the ceiling. "When his messengers don't come back," he said, "I imagine he'll get suspicious and either send someone else or wait for a better opportunity to get you. Either way, that will take some time."

"That's real comforting. What am I going to do if someone else *does* come—someone even more powerful than the Kiroc?"

"That is the reason I showed you this cave. My strongest magic is here. I sensed something breached my defenses tonight, and that's why I came here—to make sure the shield was still intact and discover who trespassed its boundary. Fortunately for you, the Kiroc was noisy. Otherwise, you would be riding to Nortia right now on the back of that Demon Dog."

"I don't see how this cave will protect me," Renn wondered out loud. "Am I supposed to hide here?"

"You could . . . I suppose. I don't know what Kahn will do next, but he doesn't know what we'll do, either. I still think you're safest living with me. But just in case Kahn sends others, I have decided to teach you to protect yourself. Starting tomorrow, this cave will be your schoolroom."

DISAPPEARING ACT

"Do it again, Renn," Artio said. The old man set the scroll he was studying back on the rock-hewn shelf in the cave. "This time, try to visualize the energy from the aeon myriad coming into your body. Let it come in through wherever it makes the most sense to you—your fingers, your eyes, your ears—and then imagine it all flowing into a shield protecting your mind."

Renn put his feet shoulder width apart, pursed his lips, and narrowed his eyes. "Should the shield be round like the kind knights use," Renn asked, "or square like the infantry uses? And what color should it be?"

"Hmm . . . don't think of it like that kind of shield," the old man said, tapping his chin. "Instead, think of it like a bubble of energy encompassing your mind so there is no part left exposed. And let it be any color you want—except not red. I don't know if that makes a difference, but when the energy manifests itself as red, it's because the intelligences from the aeon myriad are angry."

Renn concentrated and did as the Meskhoni said. A moment later, he felt the calm and intoxicating power of the aeon myriad soaking into his body and then he focused it on protecting and surrounding his mind. He decided to let it be blue.

"Okay," Renn said. "I'm ready."

"That was fast," the Mage replied. He didn't sound surprised anymore by the speed at which Renn picked things up. Since Artio had started training him more than six months ago, the only thing Renn did besides study the lore was ride Thorn every day.

"It's blue."

"What's blue?"

"My shield," Renn replied. "I decided to make it blue."

Artio shook his head and laughed. "It takes most people years to learn to create a shield with the power and hold it this way. You've been working on it for a week, and not only can you do it correctly, but you want to make it different colors."

"It makes it more fun."

"If you say so," the Mage replied. "I just want to make sure you can protect yourself if something happens. At least long enough for me to arrive and help you. Now, you're going to feel pressure against your shield as I try to enter your mind. Don't let any holes appear in it."

It felt like fingers poking at him. At first, the touch was soft and slow, but after a few moments the poking became harder and quicker, and he felt it at different places in his shield.

"That's very good," Artio said. "I can't enter your mind, but I can still sense it. Go ahead and release the power. Tomorrow we'll begin working on how to protect your mind and hide it at the same time."

"When are you going to teach me to turn into an eagle and fly, like you do?"

Artio stared at him for a moment and then laughed. "I'm only teaching you enough basics to keep you safe, Renn," he answered. "I'm almost through teaching you how to use the lore. I'm already going to have to explain myself to Salas and the other lore masters at the school when you show up to be presented and you can already do all the things I've taught you. There are strict rules about showing people how to use the lore before they are properly accepted at the school on Elder Island." Artio rolled up a scroll he'd made Renn read earlier and returned it to the rock shelf, where he filed it next to several other spell scrolls.

"Can you teach me how to fight with the power like you do? That would come in handy if I were attacked." *Then maybe I could live with*

Ma again, Renn thought. *My family wouldn't have to worry about mobs anymore.*

"No. You just need to be able to protect yourself long enough for me to find you. And my warding spells will notify me the moment you are in danger."

Renn looked around the cavern. Artio had already refused to teach him how to use anything in the trunk marked Talismans. About the only thing the Mage didn't put limits on was the amount of history he could read. He looked up at the Enchanter's Orb lighting the room and sighed.

"How about teaching me to make an Enchanter's Orb, then?"

"For the last time, Renn—no."

"Well, can you at least explain to me what the aeon myriad is?"

The old man looked at him with exasperation, and Renn thought he was going to get another no out of the Mage. But then his face relaxed and he said, "I suppose that would be all right. Believe it or not, the power we harness comes from the same source as those who follow the Aven-Lore."

"How is that possible?" Renn asked. "When the Kiroc battled you, he used a skull and the energy was red. The power you used was green."

"We draw upon the life around us for our power," the old man explained. "All life has intelligence—even this rock." He pointed at the walls of the cavern to emphasize his point. "Without intelligence, the elements within all things would cease operating in the order and motion El Azur gave to them, and they'd fall apart . . . Life would cease to exist, and all things would revert to chaos. These intelligences exist everywhere to one degree or another. That great ocean of intelligence is often referred to as the aeon myriad." Artio scratched his chin and looked up at the Enchanter's Orb on the roof of the small cave for a moment. "Those marked by the gods can access the essence of the aeon myriad that exists in all elements, because those intelligences recognize the touch of the gods upon us—and they respect the trust the gods have placed in us. When you use the power in a way that is consistent with the advancement of life and creation, the intelligences lending their power do so freely. But when you force them to act in a way that opposes life and creation, they grow angry at being used against their nature. This anger is manifest as red color in the power."

"So, when Kahn uses the power, is it green or red?"

"Red."

"Even if he is using an Azur-Lore spell?"

"Probably," Artio said. "He forces and bends the intelligences to his will and has done so for so long they recognize and despise his touch."

"Why do they keep responding to him, then? Why don't the intelligences just stop obeying him?"

"Because the aeon myriad is in a state of chaos until the intelligences are organized into something more by El Azur. Ba Aven is the god of chaos, and he rules in chaos. El Azur took them from Ba Aven and organized them into life. When a child is marked by the gods, he or she has been marked by both gods."

Renn stared at Artio, wide-eyed and slack-jawed. He ambled to the rock table and lowered himself into the chair.

"Have I been . . . tainted by Ba Aven?"

"No," Artio said. "But all of us who have been marked by the gods have the same choice to make: which path to follow."

Renn remembered what his father said the night the mob attacked them. *Make your decision to follow El Azur before you're ever confronted by the agents of Ba Aven. That way, you don't have to make your choice during the pressure of the moment.*

"I've already made my choice," Renn said.

※

Renn turned twelve that summer, and Lord Danu, Raven, and Kivas brought Renn's family up from Basilea to celebrate with him. He couldn't believe how much his siblings had changed. Chria spoke much better and ran around like a young filly, and Tavier's voice frequently cracked when he spoke—especially when he was excited. His mother laughed and smiled like she used to, and she seemed stronger and more independent than ever. Renn learned she had helped establish a school in Basilea and made it accessible to the general public—the first of its kind—while Tavier spent his time working their small farm.

At the end of that week, Lord Danu helped Renn's mother and Chria into his carriage, then with Tavier seated next to him at the front, they waved goodbye and started back down the dirt road to Basilea. Raven disappeared first down the road, and Kivas rode alongside the carriage on a large brown mare. Renn stood with Artio in front of the Meskhoni's little cottage and watched them leave.

"I wish I could ride by Lord Danu like Tavier."

"Not many boys get that opportunity, Renn." Artio rested his hand on the boy's shoulder. "Lord Danu has done a lot for your family. He's a special young man."

Renn looked at Artio and considered the Meskhoni's words. When he looked back to the road to watch the young lord drive the carriage away, it dawned on him that he never really thanked Lord Danu for everything he'd done. In fact, until Artio mentioned it, Renn hadn't realized anything unusual about the way Lord Danu treated them.

"I guess I should write him a letter. You know, thank him for everything."

"That's an excellent idea. Most noblemen wouldn't concern themselves with commoners. I think you owe a lot to Lord Danu."

Renn didn't care much for being referred to as a commoner, but for the time being that's all he really was. One day he might be a great Wizard, but for now he was the son of poor farmers—they had once been landowners, true, but even that was due to the good graces of the king.

The days before midsummer's Azur-Aven passed slowly as the summer wore on. Artio finished teaching Renn about the Azur-Lore; he said Renn knew enough to protect himself and that he would have to wait until he went to the island before learning any more. The only thing that made Renn's life bearable was Thorn. The horse was a loyal companion, and Renn truly believed that without him he would still be moping around.

When the night of midsummer's Azur-Aven arrived, Renn was sitting at the small table in the main room of Artio's cottage, staring blankly out the window as evening storm clouds rolled in. Despite Renn's most persuasive arguments, Artio refused to allow him to attend the festivities.

The Meskhoni was in his bedroom, preparing to leave for the festival, grumbling noisily about rain, mud, and his miserable duties. Renn's attention snapped back as the old man walked out of his room carrying a wooden box of supplies that he apparently intended to take with him to the festival.

"Help me with this stuff, Renn," he said in a grumpy voice as he nodded toward a smaller wood box on his bedroom floor.

"Lord Danu and Raven will be here any minute to take me to the festival, and I still need to go to the cave to get some things."

The mention of Raven gave Renn an idea.

"Artio?" he said. "If I stay next to Raven the whole time, do you think—"

"No," the Meskhoni answered before Renn finished his question. "Raven would be able to protect you, but I don't particularly want a fight on my hands during the biggest festival of the year."

Renn breathed out a loud sigh and stomped over to get the small box for the Mage.

"Look, Renn," Artio said when he came back into the room. "I know how hard this is for you. I don't like it either, but we must be careful. You're safer here at the cottage. I still have a shield surrounding the area, and if anybody trespasses, I'll know. As long as you stay quiet, an intruder wouldn't know you were here . . . even if he were standing right next to you. He'd look right past you as though you were a chair or a desk."

"What if Kahn Devin comes?" Renn asked, trying to persuade Artio of his point of view. "*He* wouldn't be fooled by a shield, would he?"

"No, but Kahn Devin isn't going to come this far south right now. According to Lord Danu's sources, Kahn Devin is too busy up north. If someone does come, I'll know they're here as soon as they pass through the barrier. Should that occur, I'll be here within a few minutes."

Artio turned, walked out the back door, and started toward his cave as the first drops of evening rain began to fall. Renn watched him go until he was out of sight. He considered disobeying the Meskhoni. He could disguise himself and ride Thorn into town once Artio left. Nobody would be the wiser. He deliberated the idea for only a moment before deciding against it. He had caused the Meskhoni enough trouble in his life and decided he would listen to the old man this time.

Shortly after the Mage returned from his cave, Lord Danu and Raven arrived with an extra horse in tow. After Artio gave Renn a few last words of instruction, the three men mounted and rode down the road toward Leedsdale.

Now what? Renn wondered as he watched the graying dusk swallow them. The rain made the outdoors dismal. He had read the history book Artio kept in his room three times and didn't feel like starting on his fourth. He could explore the cave . . . but he'd already done that many times during his studies. Everything in the cave that looked interesting had been securely locked with some type of magic, and Artio wouldn't teach Renn how to unlock them.

Renn didn't keep track of the time as he sat staring at the growing darkness outside the window of the back door. An hour, maybe two, passed away, and all he could think to do was sit and think. Finally, the summer storm broke, and the stars appeared through patches of clear sky. But with no moon, the night was still very dark.

He stood to make something to eat, but as he turned toward the kitchen, he saw a shadow cross swiftly in front of a clear patch in the night sky. He turned to the window, his heart pounding, and slowly advanced for a closer look.

He wondered why he was so nervous all of a sudden. *It's probably nothing but a fast-moving cloud,* he thought.

He hid behind the wall, peered out the window, and looked up into the sky. The clouds *were* moving rapidly, but there were no clouds in the area where he'd thought he saw the shadow. The wind sighed and moaned as it gently bent the willows and aspens back and forth.

"Stop being such a baby," Renn muttered, trying to convince himself it was only his imagination.

He turned back to the kitchen but stopped short. Every muscle in his body froze, and he held his breath. Something enormous stood by the oak stump, looking directly toward the cabin. Renn's heart thumped hard in his chest. He had been concentrating so hard on the clouds and the trees that he failed to look on the ground. He hoped the shadow hadn't seen him yet.

Renn slipped to the side of the window, dropped to his knees, and crawled along the cold stone floor and crouched in the corner. He didn't move as he held his breath. He hoped Artio was right about his shield. Had Artio sensed that the creature had crossed the shield's barrier? If so, how long it would be before the Meskhoni could get here?

The door burst open, and a gust of wind filled the room. Renn nearly gasped in astonishment and fear, but he held it in check. He even kept enough concentration to shield his mind the way Artio had taught him.

A dark figure stood in the doorway, filling the entire frame. In the darkness, Renn couldn't pick out specific features, but he knew the creature wasn't human. Although it stood somewhat erect on two legs and held the door back with a strong human hand, the floor-length, hooded black cloak it wore bulged out over its back. *Probably concealing large wings,* Renn thought.

He couldn't see its face, but the hissing of its breath sounded like the thing was breathing through clenched teeth. A hood covered its ears, but a pair of glowing red eyes peered out from within the darkness and looked around the room. Something about the odd creature sent cold fear through Renn's bones, and yet, he felt a strange compulsion drawing him toward the beast.

"Rrrennn," the creature hissed as it walked into the cottage. Renn covered his nose and mouth to eliminate any sound from escaping, and he watched the creature until it stopped in the middle of the room.

"I know you are here. Don't be alarmed . . . I won't hurt you. Come to me, and I will show you your destiny."

Its soft voice was compelling. It drew Renn out of his fear much like a beautiful melody; his legs almost involuntarily rose to walk toward the creature, but somewhere in his mind, he resisted. It felt like something was tugging at him, begging him to rise and give in to the destiny the thing in the black cloak promised.

The creature chuckled softly, then in the same breathy voice said, "The old man is clever, but I know you're here, Renn . . . I can feel it. You feel the bond between us, don't you? Let me help you discover your true power, Renn. Open yourself to me, Son."

Renn was confused. Did he feel a kinship with this thing? Why couldn't he just go to it? It promised to help him . . . but *something* was wrong. He couldn't tell the difference between his own feelings and these intruding ideas. Part of him longed to rise up and go with this creature, but something in the back of his mind warned him to stay still and quiet. Still, what could it hurt to just talk with the creature? It'd said it wouldn't hurt him.

Renn felt a prodding at his mind. It felt like tiny fingers were trying to get past the wall that Artio had taught him to place as a barrier around his mind.

"Ahh, there you are. Yes, Renn, open up to me. You can do it. Let yourself go, and I will teach you. I will be your mentor, and you, my pupil."

The prodding turned into prying as an immense force fell down upon Renn and tried to burst through his shield.

This creature did not have Renn's best interests at heart. It had been lying all along. In the corner of his memory, something snapped, and Renn remembered what Artio had taught him.

Perspiration beaded on his forehead, and his palms grew wet with sweat as he struggled against the invisible force. He focused his mental control on the fingers prying at his mind, then pushed against them with all the cerebral strength he could summon.

The creature flew backward, and a wailing shriek burst from its throat as it smashed through the back wall, sending splinters flying everywhere. It landed in a heap on the wet ground, twenty paces away from the cottage.

Renn stared in amazement. He hadn't expected that. According to Artio, the trick was only supposed to force an intruder out of your mind, not throw him through walls.

Renn climbed to his feet and crept toward the dark pile that lay motionless on the ground. Broken glass and fragments of wood snapped under his boots as he walked across the floor and peered out the aperture that, only moments ago, had been the back door and wall of Artio's cottage. What was left of the door frame dangled from the top of the breach. The old man wouldn't be happy about the damage.

As Renn moved across the yard toward the dark, lifeless mass, he heard the cry of a bird. He snapped his head to look up, afraid the creature wasn't alone. He saw a large eagle flying toward him. He almost turned to run, but then recognized the enormous bird. *Of course,* he thought. *It's the Meskhoni.*

The bird landed and, with a bright green flash, turned into the old Mage painted and dressed in ceremonial robes and holding his staff in his right hand. Artio looked at the black figure lying on the earth, then looked with wide eyes and a dropped jaw past Renn toward the wreckage in the back wall of his cottage.

"What in Azur's name happened here?" the Meskhoni asked with slow emphasis on each word.

"I'm . . . not sure," Renn replied in a puzzled tone. "I did what you told me to do . . . but it didn't work quite right."

"No, I guess it didn't. I don't recall teaching you to blast holes through my walls."

Renn heard hooves pounding across the meadow and knew Thorn was coming to his aid. Thorn stopped by the creature lying on the ground, sniffed at it a moment, then, looking at Renn, said, *You are fortunate. Where did this creature come from?*

Renn told them how he thought he saw a shadow fly across the night sky, but it turned out to be the creature now lying motionless on the earth. He told him how it'd looked when it threw open the door and everything it had said. He recounted the way it'd made him feel, how it'd tried to reach inside his mind, and finally, the way he'd pushed it out.

Artio took a deep breath and rubbed his chin with his left hand as he looked up to the sky. This expression, Renn knew, meant the old man was entering deep contemplation. It must have occurred to the Meskhoni that he still was wearing ceremonial paint because he jerked his hand away, looked at it with pursed lips, and wiped it on his robes. Even though the circumstance was quite serious, Renn had to stifle a laugh because the paint on Artio's chin was smeared together, and it looked more like a bruise than ceremonial makeup now.

Artio walked toward the motionless shadow still piled on the earth and rolled it over with his boot. Renn looked over Artio's shoulder and let out a sharp gasp when he removed the hood, revealing the hideous face.

The creature's skin was hairless and pale red. Its ears, nose, and mouth resembled those of a jackal. Two long, sharp teeth grew from its lower jaw and curved up the sides of its muzzle. What took Renn by surprise even more than the grotesque features was how its eyes were wide open in horror, its lips were curled back and twisted—as if in a permanent scream—and it breathed in quick, shallow breaths.

Artio backed up a step, nearly knocking Renn down. "It's still alive."

Renn stared at the beast from behind the Meskhoni's back. "What is it?"

Before the Mage could answer, the pounding sound of horse hoofs caught their attention. They both looked up to see Lord Danu and Raven come charging around the cottage, full speed, to stop in front of Renn and the old Mage.

"What's going on?" Lord Danu jumped off his mount. "You gave the crowd quite a shock when you yelled at me to meet you here, then changed into an . . ." He stopped short when he noticed the hole in the side of Artio's home and the strange-looking beast lying on the ground.

"What happened here? What in the world is that thing?" Danu pointed at the hideous creature, his brow arching and his nose scrunching.

"That *thing* is a result of a man giving his soul to Ba Aven. I heard Monguinir did this type of thing to men, but this is the first I've actually seen."

"Seen what? What is it?" Lord Danu asked.

"It used to be a man," Artio said. "Probably a Nortian—judging from its size. Those who study the Aven-Lore but aren't adept enough to become Warlocks will sometimes submit to being transformed into a creature Monguinir deems more useful in exchange for greater power."

"You mean someone would willingly be changed into something like that?" Lord Danu asked.

"Sometimes. I was told they're given a choice between this or being sacrificed to Ba Aven. He apparently decided this was preferable to death."

"I don't know," Lord Danu replied. "I think I'd prefer death myself."

"If you knew how they sacrifice their offerings to Ba Aven, you might think otherwise."

"Oh? How do they kill the sacrifice?"

"You don't want to know." Raven spoke for the first time since the two men arrived. Lord Danu looked up at his dark-haired captain with one eyebrow raised. Renn thought he saw Raven cast a quick glance in his direction, as if he were telling Lord Danu he would tell him when Renn wasn't around. Renn almost objected but decided maybe he didn't really want to know how the worshippers of Ba Aven sacrificed their victims after all.

"You still haven't told us what happened." Lord Danu looked back at Artio.

Artio repeated what had happened, and when he finished, Lord Danu, and even Raven, stared at Renn with wide-eyed amazement.

"That was a . . . pretty good throw for a beginner, Renn," Lord Danu said, looking at the jagged hole in the side of the cottage.

"I think I did it wrong or something," Renn replied, rather sheepishly. "It wasn't supposed to do that."

"You didn't do it wrong, Renn," Artio said. "You just don't know your own strength. We'll have to have a discussion about excessive force later."

Renn felt his cheeks flush with embarrassment, but he was proud that, for once, he'd defended himself. Lord Danu, Raven, and Artio all had risked themselves in the past for him. Now, all three of them saw he could take care of himself.

"Well, what are we going to do with this . . . this thing?" Lord Danu asked.

Artio considered the creature on the ground. He placed the heel of his staff against the creature's forehead, and the staff vibrated lightly in his hand and a soft green glow escaped from its ends. After a moment, the Mage opened his eyes, stepped back, and shook his head.

"Its brain is mush. I doubt it could speak now if its life depended on it. Most likely it will be a babbling dolt for the rest of its years." Artio looked skyward and began rubbing his chin. A wicked grin formed on his lips, and he chuckled.

"I think we should send it back."

"Do what? Why?" Lord Danu asked.

"Even though this thing had a limited use of magic," Artio explained, "it still should have been able to protect its mind from almost any assault. Sending it back in this condition will give our northern friends something to think about."

"How are we going to do that? Send it back, I mean," Lord Danu asked. He bent over and looked closer at the deformed face. "Even if you can get it to stand, I don't think it could find its way back to the hole Renn blew it through, let alone the Cragg Caves."

"I should be able to give it a little assistance. Just enough for it to fly back home." The Meskhoni pulled his brown leather pouch out from beneath his cloak, knelt beside the creature, and went to work.

Minutes later, with eyes still wide with terror, the hideous man-beast rose and flew awkwardly toward the north.

"It looks like you'll have plenty to keep you busy for the next little while, Artio." Lord Danu laughed, put his hand on the Mage's shoulder, and pointed toward the hole in his cottage wall. "Renn's little battle didn't sit so well with your home."

"Actually, I've decided not to fix it."

"What?" Renn and Lord Danu asked at the same time.

"We'll be flooded with rain this winter, Artio," Renn said.

"That's assuming we stay here this winter."

"What are you saying, Artio?" Lord Danu asked.

"Kahn Devin is sure to send more of his pawns here, especially once he sees what happened to the last one. I think this would be a perfect opportunity to lose him."

"How so?" Raven sounded interested for the first time.

"The next creature Kahn sends here will find nothing but a rundown cottage with a hole in the back wall. Kahn will know something happened here—something big—but he'll have no way of knowing the outcome.

Renn and I will disappear, that creature we sent back will be no help to Kahn, and it will drive him crazy wondering what happened."

Lord Danu laughed, and the corners of Raven's mouth actually turned slightly upward.

"Let's get back to the festival before the townsfolk go crazy, and finish blessing the babies," Lord Danu said. "First thing tomorrow, we'll get you some supplies, and you and Renn can disappear."

"No," Artio said. "You and Raven will return without me. You don't know what happened. When you arrived here, the cottage was ruined, and Renn and I were gone. You'll have to find a new Meskhoni for the area."

Lord Danu bit his lip and ran his fingers through his blond hair. He looked up at Raven, who nodded once. The young lord extended his hand to Artio. "You're right, of course. Good luck. We're going to miss you."

TWO AND A HALF YEARS LATER

AVARIS

A light autumn rain fell on the plains below, but winter had already made its chilling entrance in the Mord Mountains. Avaris Mordrahn sat silently next to Myrrah, crouched and huddled on his haunches, as snow gently fell from the Deklan sky. The vantage point from atop the bluff, halfway up the mountainside, caused the young warriors training in the valley below to look like a hundred insects busying around their colony.

"One day I'll oversee their training," Avaris commented, more to himself than to Myrrah. "One day soon."

The boys were learning about snow cutters on the grasses located outside the piked wooden walls of the Devi-Hold. Clusters of tents, erected by the Andrikan Devi tribes, created dozens of temporary villages in the plains surrounding the field where the boys trained. Smoke from hundreds of cooking fires rose like gray tendrils into the sky.

"Be patient, Avaris. You're only into your twelfth season," the dumpy, old Necromancer replied with a twitch of her mouth and nose. "You are not yet powerful enough to challenge your father."

"You mean I'm not yet powerful enough to challenge Mindahl, my father's Meskhoni," Avaris corrected smugly. "Besides that, I don't think I'll have to challenge him in that way. Sooner or later, the Andrikan Devi are going to realize my father is mad. Then, if I handle things correctly, I can step in as clan chief in his stead . . . without a fight."

"Humph," the red-haired Myrrah snorted. "You underestimate the task, child. The only way the tribes will recognize you as clan chief is if you destroy your father for dishonoring you. The only way you will claim your rightful position is to seek revenge against him. They will only respect strength."

Avaris turned and met the old woman's cold stare; her mouth and nose twitched sporadically. Anyone else would be repulsed by her mannerisms—but not Avaris. Myrrah had been a mother to him for the past four years. She rescued him when he was only eight years old—abandoned by his father in the perilous Mord Mountains—from freezing to death in the middle of a harsh winter. Yet despite his youth, he knew she had her own reasons for hating his father, the Mordrahn of the Andrikan Devi, and she sought to exact her revenge through Avaris.

Myrrah had served for a short time as the Meskhoni to the Andrikan Devi before Avaris was born. For reasons Myrrah never fully explained to him, she lost favor with his father, and Akusaa banished her from their lands.

Akusaa Mordrahn—just thinking of his father's name and how he abused his position made Avaris angry.

"If I destroy him, as you say I should, those who love him will not follow me," Avaris said. "Sometimes revenge has to wait."

"That man deserves to suffer. Don't be so kind to him," she snapped. She looked back on the young Andrikan Devi warriors below. "He would not be so generous with you."

She snorted and spit into the snow. "Remember, he left you to die. If I hadn't stumbled upon you when I did, either the Mordvins or the winter would have killed you."

Avaris made no reply. What could he say? His father *had* left him to die. Had Myrrah not found him, he *would* have fallen victim to the cannibalism of the Mordvins . . . or the winter cold.

He followed her gaze back to the valley below across the Andrus River, where his boyhood friends were learning to be warriors of the Andrikan Devi. Each year, a fresh group of boys trained to become men of the Devi. Every summer and autumn he would watch them, but this year was different. As a twelve-year-old, he should be down in the valley training with them—but he was dead. At least, his people thought he was dead, and for the time being, that was the way it had to be.

Avaris had trained himself with the sword, the bow, the ax, and the sling during his exile. He felt he could hold his own with any of the other boys when it came to hand-to-hand combat; however, he had no training with the snow cutters.

"I wish I could get close enough to see how they maneuver those things," Avaris muttered under his breath. "If I could watch them up close, I'm sure I could figure it out."

He hated the idea of getting behind in anything, particularly something as vital as using a snow cutter. The mountains and northern plains of Andrika were covered with snow more than half the year, and a snow cutter was best for travel and fighting.

The snow cutters were a kind of sled. Two different types were designed for battle. One, shaped like a crescent moon, allowed the two warriors it carried to stand. The other was fashioned to carry a solitary warrior kneeling down.

Avaris had only seen them up close as a small boy, but he remembered the body was crafted of strong wood that rested on two smoothly polished rails made of bone. A smaller bone—a scapula—was shaped and placed as a rudder underneath and near the back of the cutter. The rudder attached to a leather binding, which they fastened to the warrior's boot. This allowed him to fight with both hands and still control the snow cutter.

When used for travel, a team of strong dogs pulled the sleigh. But in battle, warriors were pulled by snow wolves. This intimidated their opponents and spooked their horses—giving the Devi warriors a big advantage.

"This is their last week of training, Myrrah." Avaris wrapped his arms around himself and sniffed. "Next week they'll go through induction ceremonies and—"

He couldn't finish the thought out loud. The other boys his age would be honored and received as men of the tribe, while he was forgotten. His guts twisted at the thought. He wondered if his mother was thinking about him now. Did she remember this would have been the year her oldest son became a man? And what of Kalisha, his older sister? Did she remember the games they used to play as children? Would she recall that her younger brother, if he were still alive, would have become a man this week? He doubted that Toci, his younger brother, could even remember what he looked like. But perhaps Kalisha or his mother would tell Toci stories about his older brother and how they thought one day Avaris would have been great and powerful.

"I hate Akusaa Mordrahn," Avaris shouted. "How could my own father leave me to die and then act as though it were an accident? Why did he do it, Myrrah? Why . . ." A lump developed in his throat. He turned once again to face his adopted mother as the cold breeze blew his long black hair across his eyes. Absently, he brushed it aside and slowly rose to his feet.

"I wish I could ease your pain, Avaris," the old Necromancer said. She grunted and pushed against the ground. "Don't just stand there while a lady's trying to get up. Give me a hand."

Avaris couldn't help but grin as he helped the struggling woman to her feet. She was wrapped in old buffalo skins, and a matted fur bonnet covered her head; the additional clothing forced the portly Myrrah to waddle rather than walk.

"I suppose most of the tribe clans will be leaving the Devi-Hold soon for the winter," Avaris said as he looked back down the mountain, across the Andrus River, and past the men in the valley to the only permanent settlement of the Andrikan Devi.

The entire Andrikan Devi nation gathered to this hold during the summer because they were most vulnerable to attack from outsiders after the snow melted. Festivals and contest made the Devi-Hold a lively place in summertime. During the gathering, the young men learned to hunt and fight, and the girls learned to cure meat and tan animal hide. The life of the Devi was harsh and demanding, but they were a proud, tough people because of it.

Once winter took the northern lands firmly in its grasp, the family tribes of the Devi would go back to the plains of Andrika and follow the gazelle and buffalo herds. Food was scarcer in the winter, so of necessity, the Devi separated into smaller units during these months. Although the Devi were separated in the winter, they were safe from outside attack because warring nations learned that to war with the northern tribes during winter was suicide. The worst enemy during the winter months, for the Devi, was the cold and lack of food.

Only the clan chief's tribe, Avaris's family, remained at the hold during the winter months. They maintained the hold and protected it during the winter months and, if necessary, called the other tribe leaders back for council.

"Come, Avaris," Myrrah said as she started up the ledge. "We need to get home before it gets too late. You know I don't like being out past dark when it's snowing. The Mordvins get desperate for food, and they may decide to see how we taste."

Avaris followed her. "The Mordvins are scared to death of you. They wouldn't dare attack us."

"Maybe. But in the dark, they may not recognize me and try to ambush us anyway."

By the time Avaris and the old woman reached her cabin, the snow had stopped, the sky had cleared, and the first stars of evening had appeared overhead.

"You'd better get extra wood from the pile tonight, Avaris," Myrrah said. She peeled off her bonnet—revealing her matted, stringy red hair—shook her head, and stomped the snow off her boots. "It's going to be cold tonight."

Avaris grumbled under his breath and headed back out the door into the cold evening. The wood shed behind the run-down cabin between two pine trees was still full. It seemed to Avaris that he spent most of his time gathering wood, stacking it in the shed, then retrieving it again and bringing it into the cabin. He'd suggested, on more than one occasion, that it made more sense to stack it against one wall inside the cabin to begin with. The cabin was a wreck inside anyway; a little wood wouldn't make much of a difference. Myrrah didn't take too kindly to his idea—besides, she'd said, it gave him something to occupy his time.

He piled the small logs into his arms and wondered why Myrrah continued to stay in the run-down shack. As a Necromancer in the Aven-Lore, she would likely have friends or relatives in Nortia, and yet, she chose to live on the border of Dekla and Andrika like a hermit in her small mountain cabin.

Did she hate his father so much that she was willing to sit around for years just waiting for an opportunity to get even with him? She had grown close to Avaris during the past four years; maybe her decision to stay was because of him. But that seemed unlikely for a Necromancer of the Aven-Lore. He wondered if he would ever find out what really motivated her.

Each day during the following week, Avaris watched the activities of his estranged people and cursed his father. But today, Avaris watched the young warriors until after the sun had set. Tonight, once the moon was directly overhead, the tribes would gather for the ritual feast and dance of manhood. The other boys his age would be named warriors. He brushed a tear from his eye and started back for Myrrah's cabin.

Pulling his buffalo robe closed against the brittle gusts of wind that shot down the mountain, he trudged up the incline, considering his options. Maybe he *should* go to the Cragg Caves when he turned fourteen and study the Aven-Lore with Kahn Devin, like Myrrah wanted him to, and then he could come and destroy his father by force. Certainly, that Wizard of the Azur-Lore who protected Akusaa would be no match for him once he became a Warlock.

As Avaris crested the mountain and started down the other side into the thick pine growth, the sun completed its descent, and the moon cast its tree-filtered light across patches of the crusted snow. He knew the path back to the cabin by heart, so instead of thinking about where he walked, he played scenarios through his mind of how he could return to his people in a way that would gain their trust.

He didn't notice movement in the trees, and he didn't pay attention to the snapping of a twig nearby. He *did* notice the two short men who appeared immediately in front of him. Startled out of his reverie, he instantly recognized the mazelike white ink patterns painted on the brown skin, their ornamented quarter spears, and the colored head wraps.

He turned to run, but two more of Mordvin cannibals cut him off. The trees came alive with the thin little mountain natives, and he found himself encircled by more than a dozen of the painted savages.

His mind raced as he tried to recall the lessons that Myrrah had given him. The Mordvins were superstitious—maybe he could scare them and give himself a chance to run. However, he was limited in the choice of spells at his command, and the most impressive ones required the use of an animal bone, which he didn't have.

Avaris looked down at the ground and saw a medium-sized rock. He bent over, picked it up, and focused his will on it. The stone began to glow, and the Mordvins stepped backward, staring open-mouthed at the rock.

Knowing he could do nothing more and realizing the cannibals would soon get over their fear, he threw the stone as hard as he could at the forehead of the nearest one. The rock hit with a deep thud, and the Mordvin fighter fell to the ground.

The little men pointed at their fallen comrade and took another step backward. Avaris took advantage of their shock and ran over the top of his victim and through the gap he created in the circle.

The filtered moonlight made for poor visibility, and Avaris tripped several times on roots, rocks, and bushes as he ran frantically toward home and Myrrah's protection. She would scold him for staying out after dark, but right now he didn't care.

His heart pounded in his chest, pumping against the strain of his exertion. His throat burned from swallowing gulps of cold air and exhaling clouds of steam.

He could hear the thudding of footsteps closing in behind him. It felt as though a hundred men were breathing down his neck. He pushed his legs to run harder, but they felt like wet grass as he stumbled up and down the snow-covered, rocky terrain.

He glanced over his shoulder and brushed his sweat-dampened hair aside. They were about to overtake him. He had to do something quick or he would be captured—just like the night Myrrah first found him in the mountains four years ago.

He kept running, and fear rose in his breast, causing his lungs to burn even more. Fear consumed him and begged to be released. Time and space seemed to stop until the only thing that existed was his fear and the burning that now moved to his mind.

Cords struck his ankles, wrapping around them. The ground rose to meet him. Avaris held out his hands to break his fall, but more cords struck and wrapped around his wrists. He saw a blinding flash of light as his head hit the frozen dirt, and everything went black.

BONE AND FIRE

D^{rums . . .}
   Pounding louder and louder.

Avaris couldn't move. His throat was parched, and his lips were cold and dry. The wind cut through his buffalo-hide coat as though he wasn't wearing it.

Where am I? Avaris wondered.

He forced his eyes open and discovered he wasn't wearing his buffalo coat. He stood in nothing but a loincloth, with his wrists and ankles strapped to a wooden pole.

Mordvin men, some shorter than him, danced in a circle around a large bonfire only ten paces from where he was bound. On the far side of the fire, men with painted faces and colorful roaches in their hair sat cross-legged, beating a solid, droning rhythm on drums. Mordvin villagers sat in a wide ring encircling Avaris, the dancers, and the drummers. The fire illuminated enough for Avaris to see crude huts beyond the villagers and trees surrounding the entire clearing but nothing beyond that.

His head pounded, but whether from the constant beat of drums or the blow he took when it hit the ground, he wasn't sure. His hands and feet tingled from the tightness of the cords, and his long black hair hung in matted clumps in front of his face.

Avaris strained to look up at the night sky. The moon was low in the western horizon; he must have been unconscious for several hours. He wondered if Myrrah was searching for him. Certainly, she would have been worried when he didn't arrive for supper—unless she was in the middle of studying her grimoire. If that were the case, she might not miss him for a few more days.

Two Mordvin warriors left the circle and cut Avaris loose. They dragged him to the front of the celebration, and the drummers stopped their endless rhythm. An old man, painted with white designs from head to toe and wearing a colorful array of feathers, horns, and furs, stepped forward.

In the sudden silence, Avaris could hear his heart pounding. A hundred eyes stared at him, unblinking.

He fell to his knees when the men at his side let go of him. The old man, who Avaris guessed was the leader of this tribe, flipped the base of his staff into Avaris's side without warning. Avaris doubled over on the cold, packed dirt.

The chief laughed. "You honor us with your presence, young Devi." The rest of the tribesmen laughed in response to their leader's remark. "Unfortunately, you won't be able to stay with us long. However, in keeping with the Mordvin tradition of hospitality, we *insist* you stay for dinner."

Avaris didn't like the emphasis the old man placed on the word *insist*. He knew he had no choice; he would stay for dinner because he was to be the main course. He struggled to his knees and felt another sharp blow to his side. This time, he fell forward onto his stomach, nearly hitting his face on one of the wooden drums. His eyes watered, his side ached with pain, and despite the huge bonfire, he was bitterly cold.

This was not meant to be his fate. Surely the gods wouldn't mark him so vividly and then allow him to die like this.

As Avaris struggled to rise to his feet, he saw a pair of buffalo thighbones on either side of the drum. The ends and sides were smooth, as though they had been hit together repeatedly. *Bone and fire*, he thought.

Avaris grabbed the two bones, rolled toward the bonfire, and thrust the ends of each bone deep into the coals. Avaris turned his face from the intense heat and focused his will on drawing the power of fire into the animal bones.

Shouting filled the air, but Avaris ignored them as best he could. Myrrah had taught him bone and fire, but it took all his concentration to summon the power, even when there was no outside noise to distract him.

A Mordvin warrior dove into Avaris. The impact caused them both to roll away from the fire, but Avaris held on tightly to the bones.

The warrior came up on top, and the man's fist caught Avaris on the side of the head. Avaris cried out in pain and anger. His attacker raised his fist to strike again, but Avaris swung the bone in his right hand and hit the half-naked warrior on the left shoulder.

The blow didn't connect well, but an explosion of white power sent the little man careening through the air. Avaris pushed himself onto one elbow, and his mouth dropped open. The chief's eyes grew wide, and he stared at Avaris. Recognition passed unspoken between Avaris and the Mordvin chief. The man realized Avaris was the boy the Mordvins had captured years ago.

The chief shouted orders in a language Avaris didn't understand. Mothers picked up their children and ran for the huts. The warrior's eyes grew wide as the chief continued to shout and point at Avaris.

Warriors raced toward Avaris, and he rolled to the side to avoid being run through by a short spear. He came up on his knees and released the power of white fire in a circular pattern to drive the warriors back.

He climbed to his feet, waving the bones dangerously in front of him, threatening any who might try another attack. He pointed one bone directly at their leader and said, "Give me back my coat and let me go, or I'll kill him."

Avaris heard a snap and felt a sharp sting on his wrist. His arm jerked backward, and the bone he pointed at their leader flew out of his hand.

Avaris tried to turn and call up the power of fire from the remaining bone, but his other wrist and both of his ankles were also wrapped with Mordvin whips, and he was yanked to the ground.

A mob of angry Mordvin warriors piled on Avaris almost before he hit the frozen ground. *This is it,* he thought. He could handle one or maybe two in hand-to-hand combat, but not all of them.

Just before resigning himself to unconsciousness, Avaris heard shouting. The shouts weren't like the threats directed at him by the attacking warriors. These were shouts of alarm and cries of pain.

As fast as the warriors had piled on top of him, they scrambled off. One of the warriors hit him on the head as he climbed off. Avaris wiped the blood from his eyes and watched the scene through blurred vision. Villagers ran around in confusion, huts were on fire, and the leader of the tribe lay prostrate near the bonfire.

On the far side of the clearing, red power surrounded Myrrah. She held a skull in one hand and a thighbone in the other, and she systematically destroyed the small village and anyone foolish enough to oppose her.

Avaris watched the Mordvins pour out of their huts. They carried possessions in their arms and ran into the forest opposite the angry old woman. Several men fell to the red bolts of power that shot from the eyes of the skull as they tried to flee.

Avaris closed his eyes. The screams of women and children faded into the distance, and he slipped into unconsciousness.

⋈

The smell of fire penetrated Avaris's sleep. His eyes shot open, and he breathed a sigh of relief as he recognized Myrrah's one-room cabin. He lay on the hutch on the far side of the room, wrapped in warm furs, and Myrrah was asleep on the hutch near the door. An old fire smoldered in the fireplace, and the hot coals radiated welcome warmth throughout the cabin.

A glass of water had been placed on the table. Avaris's parched mouth reminded him that he hadn't had anything to drink since early the day before, so he quietly rose and took a long drink. Although warm, it tasted as sweet as if it came fresh from a mountain stream. By the position of the sun shining through the single dusty window of Myrrah's hut, Avaris knew he'd slept most of the day.

The events of the previous night seemed more like a dream to him now, but the sores on his wrists and ankles, as well as the tender bump on his head, told him the experience was very real. He finished the glass of water, lay back down on the hutch, and fell back into a deep sleep.

He awoke a second time to the smell of mint. Myrrah was sitting by his side, rubbing ointment on his head and mumbling to herself.

"It's about time you woke," Myrrah said. "I thought you were going to sleep forever." Avaris looked out the dusty window, but he couldn't judge the time because it was dark.

"What time is it?" Avaris asked. He sat and rubbed his eyes.

"It's near midnight," Myrrah said. She stood and placed the jar of mint-smelling ointment on the table. Her grimoire was lying open in the center of the table along with vials, powders, and bones. A thick candle burned in the center of the table, but most of the light in the cabin came from a small fire that crackled in the hearth.

"I haven't been asleep long then." He calculated the hours in his head. Myrrah found him near dawn, so he'd been asleep for maybe sixteen hours.

"I found you three mornings ago, Avaris. You've been asleep nearly the entire time."

"Three days? I've been asleep for *three days*?"

"Don't get so upset," Myrrah said as she turned back around and handed him a cup of odoriferous liquid. "It's not as though you've missed any great event. If you hadn't been sleeping for the last three days, you would have just spent them watching the Devi-Hold anyway."

Avaris started to protest but reluctantly admitted to himself she was right.

"What made me sleep so long?" he asked.

Myrrah walked toward her iron cooking pot hanging over the fire and stirred its contents. "I'm not sure. Your injuries weren't severe. Probably a combination of physical exhaustion and the mental and emotional strain of using your power."

"But you used more power than me—why didn't you sleep for a long time?"

"I drew upon the power of the skull and of bone and fire."

"I used bone and fire also," Avaris said. He remembered that part of his experience vividly. He took two bones, held them under the coals, and focused his will on them.

Myrrah turned and stared at him and slowly shook her head. "The power you used came through you, Avaris." Her face looked paler than usual.

"But I saw the fire come from the bones I held," Avaris said.

"What color was the power?" She waddled back to the table.

Avaris hadn't had time during the battle to think about the color of the power he used. "It was . . . white."

"And the color of my power?"

"Red." He also remembered that when Myrrah drew upon power, it left a stale, acrid smell in the air. The power he used left no such odor. If anything, it smelled fresh and felt alive.

"The power you wielded was unlike anything I've ever felt. You have a strong connection with the aeon myriad, Avaris Mordrahn, and that is why we must prepare you for service to Ba Aven."

Myrrah walked to the dusty wooden bookcase that lined the wall opposite the fireplace. The shelf held experiments, vials, jars of odd specimens, scrolls, and, ironically, a framed painting of a beautiful, young Nortian woman—Myrrah's sister. She took a stack of parched scrolls from the shelf, thumbed through the yellowed pages, and sat back down at the table.

"There is great power in the Aven-Lore, Avaris. Greater power than you can imagine. No one has ever, to my knowledge, brought to their studies the connection to the aeon myriad that you possess. Maybe not even Nefarion Drakkas. You will be a great disciple for Ba Aven . . . perhaps the greatest."

"Nefarion . . . who?"

"Drakkas," she said. "He was the most powerful Warlock in history, but he turned against Lord Monguinir."

She flipped through the pages until she found what she was looking for, then compared it to something in her grimoire. "In a few years, you'll go to the catacombs under the Cragg Mountains and learn to master your powers. Kahn Devin himself will be your personal instructor."

Avaris ran his fingers through his hair and pursed his lips. Myrrah talked about Kahn and the caves like they were the greatest thing, yet she kept Avaris hidden away. It didn't make sense.

"Why did you leave, Myrrah?" he asked.

"I didn't leave," she snapped. "Your father exiled me."

"I mean, why did you leave the caves under the Cragg? And why didn't you return once my father made you leave the clan?"

She took a deep breath and looked across the room at the painting of her beautiful younger sister. Her nose twitched, and she sniffled, then shifted in her chair and gave Avaris a tight-lipped smile.

"I . . . can't go back." She struggled to keep tears at bay. She never cried. Avaris had thought the stout woman wasn't capable of it.

"What do you mean? Why not? Don't you miss your family and friends?"

"Of course I do. It's just . . . the Aven-Lore is sometimes . . . harsh. I left the caves—left the service of Ba Aven—to serve a tribe of men. I can't go back now; I made that choice when I decided to serve as the Meskhoni to the Andrikan Devi. Now I don't even have that."

No wonder she hated his father so badly, but it didn't answer why she made the choice to follow a different path than most Aven-Lore users.

"Why did you leave the Cragg Caves in the first place?" Avaris pressed. "If you'd stayed, maybe you would have become a Shapeshifter, or even a Warlock."

"No, I went as far as I could in the lore. I don't have . . . what it takes for the higher levels."

"But that doesn't explain why you left," he said.

"Avaris, you are young. It's hard to explain. I made my choice to leave . . . for many reasons. I didn't like the death rituals of the Aven-Lore, and I felt like my calling was elsewhere. Who knows?" She shrugged her shoulders and smiled. "Maybe the gods wanted me here to keep you out of trouble and make sure you get to the caves for your training."

"What happens if I don't go to Kahn Devin for my training?"

"You must." She shot to her feet, and her cheeks flushed. She took a deep breath, cleared her throat, and sat back down. "The Aven-Lore is the way of strength and power. You need that power to rule your people and fulfill your destiny. Kahn Devin will help you reach your potential. He is the most powerful man on earth; he knows both the Aven-Lore and the Azur-Lore. He chose to follow Ba Aven because the other path is too weak, too passive."

"But if you didn't like some of the rituals," he argued, "maybe I won't like them, either. What is the death ritual anyway?"

Myrrah stared at him. Her mouth and nose intermittently continued their habitual spasm, then she stood and walked toward the picture of her younger sister.

"She was so beautiful." She took the painting off the shelf and traced the lines of her sister's face. "Ba Aven requires human sacrifice, Avaris. It is the ultimate offering, and the ultimate talisman is the skull of someone whom you have offered to the dark god. Maybe it's a cruel thing, but it is the only way to gain favor with the gods."

A sick feeling moved into the pit of Avaris's stomach. Had Myrrah sacrificed her own—no, she wouldn't do something like that. But, still, he had to know for certain.

"Is that what happened to your sister? I mean . . . did someone sacrifice her?" he asked carefully.

"No." Myrrah set the picture of her sister back in its usual place, then walked to the little window and stared out into the darkness. "No, she's still alive."

"Where do they find people to sacrifice? Who would want to die for that?"

Myrrah spun away from the window, walked to the table, and began to gather her things. "You've learned enough for one night," she said. "Some things you won't be able to understand until you've experienced them. I have already revealed more than I should have."

After putting her grimoire and other trinkets back on the shelf, Myrrah gave Avaris water, bread, and the stew she'd been making. Then, taking a blanket out of her hutch, she wrapped herself and went to sleep.

Avaris stirred his stew and watched the shadows from the small fire dance on the old crone's face while she slept. He had more questions now than when he started prying for answers. If she left the Aven-Lore because she had problems with it, why would she encourage him to study it? What if he didn't like the death ritual either? It didn't sound very pleasant.

However, he longed for power; he needed it to fulfill his goal of supplanting his father.

I will be a great leader, he thought. *Nobody will sacrifice any of my people to the gods when I rule. I will end all wars against us and make sure the Devi people live in peace.*

If the Aven-Lore was the most powerful, Avaris knew he would do whatever was necessary to master its skills.

LEKIAH

Lekiah looked at his reflection in the shined brass plate he kept in his circular tent. He looked and smelled as though he'd just returned from a hunting excursion. His angular face and slender hands were dirty, his pelt clothes were damp from mud and sweat, and his long black hair looked as though it hadn't been combed for days.

Like every other day during the four months of summer, he'd been helping his father, Lokia, train young Andrikan boys to become warriors. Now, with the first snow covering the mountains in a blanket of white and the ritual of passage only a week away, they were training from dawn until dusk.

Lekiah sat on the fur mat that served as his bed and chuckled to himself while he removed his fur-lined boots. He remembered how sore he was five years ago after his first day of training to be an Andrikan Devi warrior. Since that time, he'd fought in numerous battles and been on so many extended hunting trips that being sore and tired seemed a normal part of life.

Lekiah removed his clothing, tossed them near the small fire in the middle of his tent, and washed himself with the water he'd drawn from the well in the center of the Devi-Hold. Akusaa Mordrahn, the high clan chief of the entire Andrikan Devi, had invited him to eat the evening meal with his family, and although Lekiah's father was Akusaa's closest advisor, Lekiah was not given that honor very often.

He naturally wanted to impress the clan chief, but even more so because he hoped to one day be his son-in-law. Lekiah smiled as he contemplated that prospect. Akusaa's daughter, Kalisha, was fourteen now—old enough to marry—and Lekiah had been in love with her since they were children. He remembered the games they would play with the other children when they were younger. Somehow, he and Kalisha always managed to hide together or play on the same team. Whatever the game was, they found a way to be with each other.

Lekiah dressed in clean clothes and walked the fifty-four steps to his parent's tent. Families always stayed close together in the hold. When he arrived, his father, Lokia, and his mother, Llianen, were already dressed and waiting.

"What took you so long, Lekiah?" his father teased. "Have to make sure each fingernail is clean and every hair is in place?"

"Just tired. You've been making me do all the hard work in the training fields while you sit and watch," he joked back, attempting to change the subject.

"Lekiah," his mother said, "have you been doing well? Are you keeping your clothes and tent clean?"

"Of course, Mother." She still worried about him living alone. "I've been taking care of myself for five years."

"Well, I'll feel better when you marry. A young warrior needs a good woman to keep his clothing mended and his tent comfortable. I think you should take Kalisha. She's marriageable age now, and I've seen the way you watch her when you think nobody's looking."

Lekiah looked down so his parents wouldn't see his wide eyes and open mouth. *Is it that obvious?*

"Oh, Mother—"

"Come to mention it," his father broke in, "I have noticed you watching her a lot lately. Is there something you're not telling, us?"

Lekiah blushed furiously, and his father burst out laughing.

"Come," Lokia said. "We can't keep Akusaa and his family waiting. I may be his closest advisor, but even *I'm* not above his temper when he's hungry."

The high clan chief and his family occupied a large multiroom tent in the center of the Devi-Hold. The walls and floors were lined with furs, colorful blankets, and throw pillows—giving the home a warm, comfortable feeling. Lekiah looked for Kalisha when he entered the tent and smiled when she entered from one of the adjoining rooms. She had been helping her mother, Lilisha, prepare the meal, and she carried hot bread on a wooden platter.

A silver-and-gold beaded headdress partially covered Kalisha's long black hair. The headdress wrapped around her forehead and then circled below her chin to form a loose necklace. She wore a colorful bison robe that fastened around her neck with an engraved silver clasp, and the long robe had small silver conches lined down the center. Her smooth dark skin and big brown eyes that rested beneath slightly arched eyebrows drew him in as they always did.

Akusaa and Lokia sat together on the opposite side of the fire, discussing the details of the passage ceremony, only a week away, and Toci, Kalisha's younger brother and heir to Akusaa, was pretending to be dignified—the way the child felt his father's heir should. Even though Toci was a nine-year-old boy, Lekiah thought he wasn't that bad. He could be a little arrogant at times, but at least he wasn't noisy and obnoxious.

Dinner consisted of buffalo meat, cooked roots, and mountain berry wine. It tasted good, but it was even better for Lekiah because he knew Kalisha had a hand in its preparation. He watched her during the meal and tried to catch her eyes whenever he could. For some reason, she kept them averted. *Unusual*, Lekiah thought. *Usually she likes playing this game.*

"Kalisha." Lekiah spoke to her for the first time since his arrival to dinner. "Is something bothering you? You don't seem to be your usual happy self today."

"Ha!" Akusaa stopped talking to Lokia. "That girl's never happy. She's always upset about something. You'll never win a warrior's heart that way, girl."

Kalisha flushed and looked down.

"She's sad because she misses Avaris," Toci said, answering Lekiah's initial question.

Kalisha raised her eyes and looked at Lekiah. "He would be going through the ritual of passage this week if he were . . ." Her voice trailed off as though she was unable to finish the thought. Lekiah looked at her as she turned her eyes to hide the tears. He wanted to take her in his arms and comfort her, but he had to maintain the demeanor of a warrior. Soon, Lekiah would ask her father to let him take her as his wife, and the clan chief was not likely to give his daughter to a man he considered weak. After they were married, he would comfort her and treat her the way she deserved to be treated. The ritual of passage ceremony was only seven days away, and Lekiah planned to use the occasion to ask Akusaa's permission to marry Kalisha.

The following week seemed to fly on eagle's wings. Lekiah was so busy completing the young warrior's training and helping his father with last-minute preparations he didn't have time to worry about anything else. It seemed one minute they were talking about ceremony plans, and the next minute he was dressing in his costume for the big event.

As Lekiah adjusted the feathers in his hair clip, it dawned on him that he still didn't know how to ask Akusaa's permission to marry his daughter. In fact, he had been so busy the past week he'd only seen Kalisha in passing. He hadn't even taken time to sneak off with her for an afternoon walk—something he always looked forward to. He laced up his midcalf buckskin boots. *Oh well,* he thought. *Next week, things will settle down and I'll spend more time with her.*

When Lekiah arrived at the ceremony grounds, he looked around for his mother and father. If it weren't for the fact that they sat with the high clan chief and his family, he never would have found them. Thousands of small fires surrounded by men, women, and children of the Andrikan Devi dotted the massive field. It looked as though an army had gathered. Every year, when he saw the size of his nation, he realized the wisdom in gathering during the summer months for protection. They were formidable when grouped together. When they spread out over the vast plains of Andrika—into their separate clans—they were isolated and vulnerable without the protection of snow.

He worked his way to the center of the noisy throng where the clan chiefs and their families sat in a large circle around a massive bonfire. Akusaa sat on one side of the circle on a large log so he was raised above everyone else. He wore a headdress of eagle feathers and a necklace of bear claws. His painted bison robe was clasped around his neck with a bone-carved broach, but the robe hung open to show the intricate and colorful patterns on his leather shirt. The red and black ceremonial paints on his face would have made him look evil, except that he constantly broke out in boisterous laughter from one of his own jokes.

The Wizard Mindahl sat next to Akusaa. He wore his usual light blue turban and a long wool robe that was dyed red. Thick white whiskers completely hid his cheeks so that, at first glance, his face looked like a long nose and two beady eyes cradled in a ball of white hair.

Mindahl was a mysterious man from a place called Sarundra. Along with Lokia, Mindahl was one of Akusaa's closest advisors. He also served as the Meskhoni for the entire Andrikan nation. Lekiah liked the man. More than once, Mindahl had given him valuable advice, and because his family was closer to the Meskhoni than most, he knew the Wizard possessed a great sense of humor as well.

Lekiah sat next to his mother and looked toward Kalisha. Their eyes met, and she flushed and looked away. Lekiah caught his breath when he noticed her long black hair no longer hung in braids but fell gently over one shoulder, signifying that she had reached maturity and the Devi Warriors could now court her.

"K'Thrak's dark heart!" he cursed under his breath. He'd hoped to quietly ask Akusaa's permission to marry her, but now he would be competing against all the other young, honorable warriors. After seeing the way she looked tonight, he knew every eligible warrior would want her.

"Raise your cups," Akusaa blared, taking Lekiah's attention off Kalisha and back to the festival.

"Friends, drink with me . . . to . . . for my daughter." He'd obviously had too much wine already. "Somehow the ugly thing turned into . . . an average-looking woman . . . I may be able to marry her off yet." Akusaa barely finished his toast before he burst out laughing. Several of the men joined him—whether because they thought him funny or because he was the high chief, Lekiah wasn't sure. He wanted to stand and say something, but he knew that by so doing he would lose any chance he had of marrying Kalisha.

Lekiah looked at Kalisha. She kept her head down and was trying to act as though she hadn't heard his comment, but Lekiah could tell she was deeply hurt.

Lilisha placed a hand on her daughters back and said, "Akusaa, please—"

"Silence, woman!" Akusaa glared at his wife. "It is not a woman's place to interrupt Akusaa."

Every eye in the circle watched the clan chief. Lekiah read both fear and anger in Lilisha's face, until she finally looked down, defeated by Akusaa's fierce stare. Akusaa raised his head, apparently recognizing the tension around him and, once again, broke into a raucous laugh.

"You see, my brothers. You must demand respect from those you lead."

Again, some of the men joined in laughing with the high clan chief. Lekiah felt a sharp jab in his side from his mother's elbow. "Quit shaking your head like that," she whispered. "And get that disgusted look off your face before your father sees it."

"It makes me sick the way he treats people," Lekiah said. "And what's worse is everybody just puts up with it and laughs."

"Well, many of the men feel the way he does."

"That doesn't make it right."

Akusaa's treatment of Kelisha upset Lekiah so much he barely noticed the dancers and performers as they rendered the traditional production of the ritual of passage, signifying not only the passage into manhood but also the passing of summer to winter.

Mindahl tapped his staff on the ground, and it glowed with green light. "Present the boys who wish to become men and warriors of the Andrikan Devi." The Meskhoni's voice echoed across the entire field, and the crowd quieted to a murmur.

Drummers beat a slow, rhythmic pattern, and the boys Lekiah had been training all summer began the customary *Dance of Warriors*. They circled the fire, wearing nothing but loincloths and faces painted with the colors of the tribe, and danced in time with the beat as the drummer's speed increased. Finally, each boy danced through the bonfire and then knelt before Akusaa and Mindahl.

The drums stopped, and in the silence Akusaa brought each boy to his feet and kissed both their cheeks. Lekiah couldn't help but notice Kalisha seated behind her father. Tears were streaming down her face as she watched. Her mother, Lilisha, was crying as well. Lekiah recalled what Toci had said a week earlier. Tonight, Kalisha's brother, Avaris, should have completed the ritual. But Avaris had died when he was only eight years old—a tragedy that tore at the heart of the entire Andrikan nation. He had been the hope and pride of their people, for none had ever been marked at their blessing as Avaris had. His death was hard for everyone to accept, but especially for Kalisha.

Akusaa kissed the cheeks of the last boy, then stood on top of the tall log so he could be seen by the crowd.

"Our nation has grown stronger by these new warriors." The Meskhoni must've used magic to amplify Akusaa's voice because it carried across the gathering. "Let us celebrate their manhood."

The drummers beat a steady rhythm and raised their voices in a droning song. This, too, must have been amplified by the Meskhoni. Those who refrained from too much wine during the feast now consumed it freely. Members of the gathered clans danced around the many fires.

Akusaa's face darkened, and he glared at his wife and daughter.

"What's wrong with you, women?" Lekiah could barely hear the clan chief over the singing and drums.

"Doesn't it bother you that Avaris would have become a man this night were he still alive?" Lilisha cried out.

Akusaa slapped her across the cheek. "How dare you speak to me that way," he shouted. "I was his father. But he's gone now, and Akusaa lives for today—not for yesterday."

Lilisha took her daughter by the hand, turned, and walked back toward the Devi-Hold. Lekiah started after them, but his father grabbed his arm and pulled him back.

"Let them go," he whispered. "You'll win Akusaa's favor if you want to marry her."

Lekiah jerked his arm free. "She needs me . . . I can't just watch while—"

"You can do nothing for her without Akusaa's consent—let them go."

Lekiah glared at his father. Lokia's face was set like stone. Lekiah glanced toward Akusaa to see if he'd noticed their interaction, but he was busy drinking and telling stories to the other clan chiefs. Lekiah looked back at his father, nodded, and tried to act as though he was having fun.

THE MIGHTY MUK'GULA

Lekiah wandered aimlessly through the paths that wound between the round animal-skin tents of the hold. It had been several weeks since the ceremony of passage, and the other Andrikan clans were roaming the plains now, but nearly every day a different warrior returned to the hold, hoping for an opportunity to curry favor with Kalisha and her father.

The tents in the hold were grouped by family and placed around cooking fires with enough area to carry out the daily chores of cooking, cleaning, and other domestic duties of Devi life. Lekiah ignored the small children that chased each other around the tents and the mothers cleaning dishes from their evening meals.

His long black hair protected his ears from the bite of the cold air while he walked. He kicked a rock protruding out of the thin blanket of snow, looked up, and found himself at the center of the hold in front of the Mordrahns' tent. He wondered for the hundredth time how he should ask Akusaa for his daughter. He pulled his buffalo coat tighter, kicked at another rock in the snow, and turned to walk down a different winding path.

"Where are you going, Lekiah?"

He almost walked right into his father, Lokia.

"Oh..." Lekiah looked up and blinked. "Just walking," he said. "I'm not hungry and it's too early to turn in for the night, so I thought I'd take a walk."

"Take a walk, huh?" Lokia raised his eyebrows and folded his arms across his chest. "Come with me, and we'll talk about it."

"Talk about what?" Lekiah asked, but he fell into step beside his father anyway.

"Young warriors don't go for evening walks . . . Old women do. You obviously have much on your mind."

"It's nothing," he said. "I'm fine." They walked in silence until they reached the dog kennels at the back of the hold. The snow wolves were kept separate from the regular sled dogs, and when Lekiah looked toward the wolves' kennel—a large fenced area on the side of a wooded hill, which was bigger than the hold itself—he didn't see any of them. That wasn't surprising, though. The snow wolves liked to hide behind trees and in caves rather than parade around in the open. The dogs, on the other hand, jumped and barked and wagged their tails as the two men approached.

"Help me with these dogs." Lokia opened the gate and worked his way through the excited dogs to back of the kennel where the Devi stored brooms and shovels. Lekiah found his favorite dog—a black-and-white, long-haired sled dog—and rubbed its ears and head. His father came back and handed him a shovel. "Help me clean up the dung." He pointed to the piles of dog feces that littered the kennel.

"Isn't this the younger boys' task?" Lekiah looked around and wrinkled his nose.

"Yes. But it needs to be done, and we have nothing better to do."

Lekiah thought he could find plenty of better things to do, but he went to work shoveling alongside his father.

"Kalisha is a beautiful girl," his father said.

Lekiah stopped shoveling and blew a puff of steaming breath into the air. His father had a way of cutting to the heart of an issue.

"She's more than beautiful." Lekiah stood and looked up at the moon rising above the horizon. If it hadn't been full, they wouldn't have been able to work because the sun had already set. But the light reflecting off the snow was bright enough to easily see what they were doing. "I really care for her . . . her soul. I don't care much for talking with women . . . but I look forward to talking with Kalisha."

"That is how I felt about your mother," Lokia said with a grin. "I still feel that way about her. So what's the problem? Why have you been moping around like someone took your favorite bow?"

Lekiah shook his heady. "I don't know. I know she cares for me, too, but I don't know how to ask Akusaa for her. I guess I hoped it would be easier than this." He looked down and kicked at the snow. "Warriors of other clans have been trying to win her favor now, too." Lekiah looked at his father and waited for him to speak, but he just looked at his son and waited.

"I've done everything I can think of to win her heart," Lekiah continued. "Yesterday, I took her on a walk to a beautiful meadow where you can see the eagle fly and the elk run free. I went earlier in the day and hid food. She was surprised. We ate our lunch and talked about many things." He smiled, remembering how it made him feel. But his smile only lasted a moment. "I don't know what else to do," he said.

His father took the shovels, set them aside, and stood directly in front of Lekiah. Lokia was a couple inches shorter than him, but Lekiah still felt like he was standing next to a giant.

"Perhaps you are trying to win the wrong heart," Lokia said.

"But I love Kalisha. I don't want any other."

"Yes. I know. That is why you must concern yourself now with winning the heart of Akusaa. He does not care who his daughter loves or does not love. He is concerned about one thing and one thing only—honor for himself."

Lekiah returned to his tent. *How can I bring honor to Akusaa?* he wondered as he removed his winter moccasins. Although he planned to give Akusaa a great gift for his daughter—as custom required—the fact that others would compete meant he would have to think of something wonderfully unique to gain the high clan chief's approval.

He ran his thumb over the point of one of his bone-carved arrowheads as he considered his problem. He looked at sharp edge and smiled, thinking of the perfect gift. A gift he could give to Akusaa that would not only ensure he acquiesce to their marriage but would also honor Kalisha more than any Devi woman had ever been honored before.

Lekiah left the Devi-Hold at dawn the following morning. A fresh blanket of snow covered the ground, and the wandering dawn star was still visible in the eastern sky. A light breeze bit into his face as he crossed the Andrus River, but once Lekiah reached the Dekla side, the tall pine trees and steep Mord Mountains provided some shelter.

He checked his weapons—he carried a sword, a knife, an ax, and a bow and arrows. He felt rather weighted down, and the extra equipment would make climbing the mountain trails more difficult, but this hunt would require his best. He'd hunted many times before, but this time he searched for an animal that lived only in the Mord Mountains, an animal that sensible people avoided: the great white bear, or as his people called it, *Muk'gula*.

Lekiah's heart raced with excitement and nerves. Only a small number of Andrikan warriors had ever fought a Muk'gula one-on-one, and most did not live to tell about it. But if Lekiah succeeded, he would be considered one of the greatest warriors of all time. Legends would be spun about him for many generations.

Lekiah hiked into the pine trees, searching the ground for tracks. He'd been on hundreds of hunts, but never for a Muk'gula. His tribe considered him to be one of the best hunters and warriors. He was the youngest warrior to train others in recent memory, and he had never been bested in hand-to-hand combat. He figured he stood as good a chance against the Muk'gula as any living warrior.

Lekiah stayed close to the Andrus River. Sooner or later, he reasoned, he would come across tracks of a Muk'gula that had come to the waters to fish. Fortunately, it had snowed during the night, so any tracks he found would be fresh and easy to follow. Also, he would be able to guess the size of the animal more accurately from prints left in fresh snow.

He had only been walking for an hour when he came across a set of bear tracks. He stopped midstride and looked around to make sure the animal responsible for the tracks was not still in the immediate area. Satisfied he was alone, he bent down to examine the impressions and inhaled sharply. The Muk'gula who left these tracks was probably more than eight feet tall.

Maybe I should look for a smaller animal, he thought. But then he realized how impressive it would be to make such a kill. Surely, no single warrior had ever fought against a beast that large and won. Also, the stronger the animal was, the more magic its bones possessed. If his estimate of the bear's size were correct, its bones would possess great power. The knives and arrows he made from a Muk'gula this size would be a valuable gift indeed.

Akusaa would probably make Lekiah his personal warrior for giving him such an offering. He cringed at the thought. He didn't like Akusaa, and the idea of being the high chief's personal bodyguard was not appealing. Still, it would assure he and Kalisha would have a good life together. That settled it. Lekiah checked his weapons and followed the tracks.

The Muk'gula were nearly invisible against the snow because of their white fur, and he wanted to surprise the beast—not the other way around. He guessed he was only an hour behind the animal. The tracks led him up the mountain, through pine trees, over a small peak, and down into a narrow canyon where a small river carved a twisted path down its center.

The river was audible but barely visible because of the large pines and thick undergrowth. The snow wasn't very deep in this area, however, and more than once, Lekiah had to stop and look in the brush for signs of the bears' passing. He walked silently as he studied the ground for signs and emerged from the thick foliage on the bank of the noisy river.

Lekiah looked across the river, and his heart stopped. He stared wide-eyed and his mouth dropped open. There, on the other bank, a boy who looked like Avaris Mordrahn crouched as though he'd just taken a drink of water.

No, that's impossible, Lekiah thought. *He's been dead for years.* The boy hadn't seen him yet, so Lekiah took a step backward to hide in the thick foliage and watch. He stepped on a bush and stumbled. The boy across the river must've noticed the movement because he looked up.

"Lekiah?" the other said as he stood. Lekiah couldn't hear him over the river, but he could read his lips easily enough. "Is that you?"

Lekiah froze. Avaris was dead. This must be his spirit come back to roam the woods where he died. Lekiah's heart pounded in his chest when he came to that realization. He turned and bolted back the direction he came.

"Lekiah . . . wait!"

Lekiah heard the phantom shout his name as he scrambled back up the narrow canyon on all fours. He grabbed at the undergrowth to help pull himself up the steep incline, but he stumbled and slid in the mud.

When he reached the crest, Lekiah lost his footing in the thin layer of snow. He tumbled and slipped down the other side, only stopping when his forehead hit against the base of a large pine. A blinding flash of sharp pain shot through Lekiah's head. He struggled to his feet, and a wave of vertigo sent him back to his knees. Something warm dripped into his eyes, blurring his vision. He wiped his eyes and saw blood on his hand. He looked up at the summit just as the spirit of Avaris ran over the crest.

"Wait!" the spirit shouted. "Lekiah, stop running . . . It's me, Avaris."

Lekiah grabbed on to the nearest tree and pulled himself to his feet. He stumbled to the next tree and then the next, working his way down the mountain from tree to tree. He leaned on a large pine and looked back. The spirit was only twenty paces behind him.

"Lekiah, please wait!"

Lekiah pushed away from the tree and ran recklessly down the mountain. He only made it ten steps before vertigo brought him down to the snow again.

"Lekiah, you're injured. Stop running before you kill yourself."

"What do you want with me, spirit?" Lekiah shouted. "Leave me alone."

The apparition furrowed its dark brows and scrunched its nose as if it were confused, then burst out laughing.

"Is that why you're running? You think I'm a spirit?" He laughed some more and then walked down the hill toward Lekiah.

"Look at my clothes—they're drenched from that stupid river. If I were a spirit, do you think I'd be wet? Or for that matter, if I were a spirit, why would I be drinking water in the first place?"

Lekiah's head was splitting with pain, but he still felt a little embarrassed. Everyone knew spirits could float in the air, yet Avaris was wet from running through the river.

"But you're dead. You've been dead for four years."

"Do I look dead to you?"

"But you never returned. If you're really alive, then—"

"Then what?" Avaris gestured for Lekiah to continue talking, as though he wanted him to solve a riddle.

"My head is killing me. It hurts to think right now."

"Can you walk?"

"I think so."

"Come on, then. We've got to clean that wound."

Avaris led Lekiah downhill to a stream where he cleaned and wrapped his forehead. As he worked, Avaris told the story of how his father left him to die in the mountains and how Myrrah found, saved, and raised him.

"I can't believe it." Lekiah shook his head. "Well, yes, I can. I hope it doesn't offend you if I say I have never thought very highly of your father."

"Not at all; he's not exactly my hero, either."

"I can't imagine leaving your own son to die in the middle of a blizzard. *Holy Azur*," Lekiah cursed. "He's pathetic. The way he treats people makes me so angry—he's always putting Kalisha down and . . ." Lekiah flushed, realizing as he rambled that he was saying too much. "Well, he just makes me mad, that's all."

"One day," Avaris said with a distant look in his eye, "one day, things will change. I'll see to that."

"What are you going to do?"

Avaris picked up a rock from the bank of the stream and tossed it in the water. "I don't know. But I do know I have been marked with great power by the gods and it is my destiny to put an end to injustice."

Lekiah wanted to believe Avaris would be the leader he claimed he would become, but he hadn't seen Avaris for four years. For all he knew, Avaris could be as crazy as his father. Yet, something about him drew Lekiah in, even though Lekiah was five years older. Avaris held himself with confidence and the look in his eyes was serious and sincere. It reminded him of the way Kalisha looked at him when she was sharing the deepest desires of her heart.

"I want to help you," Lekiah said.

"What?" Avaris leaned back and raised his eyebrows.

"You are the rightful heir and the Child of the Blessing. I want to make sure you become the next high chief."

"I don't know what to say. I wasn't expecting . . ." Avaris stopped, drew himself up, and in a serious voice said, "I swear to you, Lekiah, you won't regret it. Because you are the first to swear allegiance to me, I will oath myself to you as a brother."

Avaris pulled out a bone-carved knife and drew it across his thumb, all the while keeping his eyes fixed on Lekiah. Removing his knife from its sheath, Lekiah cut into his thumb as well. The pain was minimal compared to what his head felt, and he barely noticed the throbbing sensation in his thumb as he pressed the fresh cut against Avaris's.

The sun setting behind the Mord Mountains was turning the horizon mixed shades of orange, red, and purple while Lekiah walked back through the gates of the Devi-Hold. Dirty children and mangy dogs played noisily, as they always did, but he paid them no mind as he walked toward his tent in the compound.

He hadn't killed the Muk'gula he had set out to find, but the day had not been wasted. He made a critical discovery and made a sacred oath. An oath that would be considered treason by Akusaa.

He wanted to run to Kalisha and tell her the good news, but Avaris made him swear not to tell anyone, not even his sister. So, Lekiah walked in thoughtful silence through the scattered tents until he came to his own. Once there, he plopped down—without undressing—on the fur mat that served as his bed, and stared out the small circular vent hole in the top of his round tent.

THE HUNT

It worried Avaris that Lekiah had discovered he was alive. *Lekiah bound himself to me,* Avaris thought. *He is my oath brother now. I can trust him.* However, if Avaris's father learned he still lived, what action would the man take?

Avaris met Lekiah the next day at the same river where they first saw each other.

"Did anyone follow you?" Avaris asked.

"Don't worry, your secret is safe. There's nothing unusual about me going on hunting trips by myself."

"Good," Avaris said. "Tell me about our people and what it's like to live in the hold."

Lekiah talked about the celebrations, their battles, training boys to be warriors, and stories of great hunts. Avaris asked about his family and was pleased to learn that his mother, Kalisha, and Toci remembered him. When Lekiah told Avaris that his father hit his mother for crying over Avaris during the rite of passage celebration, Avaris pounded his fist into his hand.

"One day I will make my father pay for his crimes," Avaris vowed.

"I believe you," Lekiah said. "But you have a lot of training to complete before that time. Both in magic and with weapons."

Avaris stood and folded his arms. "I know how to fight. I bet I'm better than any of those boys who became warriors this season."

Lekiah drew his knife and cut a long stick into two even pieces. He tossed one piece to Avaris. "Let's find out how good you are with a sword, then."

Lekiah easily beat Avaris with the stick sword, but he also took time to help Avaris with his footwork. Lekiah bested him in knife throwing and hand-to-hand combat as well. But Avaris didn't mind losing. He was just thrilled to finally have another person to spar with. And better yet, Lekiah was a real trainer of Devi warriors.

"You're pretty good with a bow," Lekiah said after Avaris missed the mark by only a foot. "Especially considering you've had no one to train you."

"I practice with weapons many hours every day," Avaris said as he nocked a second arrow. "There's not much else to do when you live alone in the mountains with an old lady."

"I'd like to meet this Myrrah," Lekiah said. "She sounds . . . interesting. I think I vaguely remember an old woman acting as our Meskhoni when I was very young, but I'm not certain."

"If you didn't have a longer reach than me, I probably would have beaten you with the sword," Avaris said as he released his second shot. This arrow was only inches off the mark they'd drawn on the tree. He looked at Lekiah, grinned, and handed him the bow. "Being older and bigger won't help you win this match," he said, with pride in his shot.

"You're right about that," Lekiah said. He nocked an arrow and pulled it back to his ear. It seemed to Avaris that Lekiah barely took time to aim before he let the arrow fly, yet he hit the mark dead-on. Avaris stared dumbfounded at the target for a moment, and Lekiah lowered the bow. "Being better will," the older boy said as he handed the bow back.

Avaris hadn't realized until becoming friends with Lekiah how much he'd missed and longed for a friend he could relate to. Myrrah was a friend, but she was different; they had almost nothing in common. She was more like a mother. Whereas Lekiah was the older brother Avaris never had.

The next day, Lekiah brought an ax, a spear, a short sword, a knife, a bow, and some arrows and announced he was going to hunt for a Muk'gula. Avaris thought it sounded like a wonderful adventure, but he wasn't very pleased when Lekiah informed him that under no circumstance was he to intervene in the kill. Lekiah insisted he fight the bear alone.

"You're out of your mind, Lekiah." Avaris's voice rose. "Hunting for Muk'gula is one thing, but wanting to fight it alone? That's not courage, that's . . . that's stupidity."

"I'm not doing it to prove my courage," he said. "I realize how dangerous it is to—"

"Obviously you don't. You're going to get yourself killed."

"Look. You don't have to come if you don't want to, but this is something I *must* do and I've got to do it alone."

"Why is it so important that you have to risk your life? At least let me help if you're about to get—"

"No. That's final."

Avaris fixed a hard look on Lekiah's eyes, but Lekiah stared back just as determined. For some reason Avaris couldn't fathom, Lekiah was adamant about fighting the animal alone. Even if it killed him. Avaris could tell Lekiah wouldn't budge on this, so he let out a deep breath and folded his arms.

"All right. But at least tell me why it's so important to you."

Lekiah looked away but not before Avaris saw his face flush.

"Hey, I'm not blind. What are you trying to hide? Come on, you have to tell me—we're oath brothers."

"Umm . . . well, it's a gift for someone."

"You've got to do better than that Lekiah. A gift for who? That's a very big gift . . . Wait a minute. You're not planning on taking a wife, are you?"

Lekiah blushed even more. "Well, I . . . yeah I suppose—"

"Why didn't you tell me? That's different. Imagine that. Risking your life just for a girl." He chuckled at Lekiah's apparent embarrassment. "A Muk'gula would be a grand gift for the high chief and you're wasting it on a girl?" Avaris broke out in genuine, uncontrollable laughter. He hadn't laughed so hard in years.

"What's so funny?" Lekiah folded his arms and scowled. "If you were in love with a girl like Ka—uh, if you'd ever been in love, you wouldn't be laughing."

"Tell me," Avaris said as he wiped the tears from his eyes. "Who is this wonderful girl? Do I know her?"

Lekiah was silent. The corners of Avaris's mouth turned down as he waited for his friend's response. Lekiah shifted his weight, and Avaris could see he was desperately trying to control his embarrassment.

"You wouldn't be in love with who I think you're in love with, would you?"

"Uhh . . . probably," Lekiah stammered.

"Kalisha?"

Lekiah slowly nodded. Avaris blinked and ran his fingers through his hair. Kalisha was always a kind sister, and he loved her . . . but he didn't remember her being all that pretty. And what about Lekiah's oath to him? Was he going to forget about that now? He kept his gaze fixed on Lekiah's eyes as he thought about all this. Then it occurred to him that Lekiah was going to kill the Muk'gula so he could give gifts to Avaris's father—the Mordrahn.

"Wait a minute. You want me to help you track the Muk'gula so you can become a hero with my father! I thought you swore to help me—"

"I'm not doing it for Akusaa Mordrahn," Lekiah said. "I hate your father. I'm doing it for Kalisha."

Avaris glared at him, trying to decide why the idea bothered him so much.

"Yeah . . . but if you give him weapons made from Muk'gula bones, he'll be much more powerful."

"Weapons will be nothing once you've mastered your powers, Avaris," Lekiah said.

Avaris had to admit Lekiah had a point there. Avaris scratched his head and bit his lip. Then he smiled and got excited.

"Hey! If you marry Kalisha, that means we'll really be brothers."

"Yeah, I suppose it would. I never thought of it that way."

"All right, then, I'll help you. But if you get hurt—"

"Me get hurt?" Lekiah puffed out his chest and hit it with a closed fist. "I'm the best warrior in the tribe."

"Remind me to tell that to the bear when he's about to kill you," Avaris said.

The boys looked for more than two hours for any sign that might direct them in their hunt, but they found nothing. Avaris grew tired of hiking along the banks of the noisy Andrus River and wondered if they were just wasting time.

"Hey, Lekiah," Avaris said when they stopped for a drink, "don't bears sleep in the winter?"

"Yes, most do."

"Then what makes you think we're going to find any now? Winter is beginning, you know. It may be months before one comes to the river."

"Bears don't begin hibernating this early. Odds are on any given day at least one will come to the river to get a drink or eat a fish. Besides that," he explained as he wiped his mouth on his sleeve, "male Muk'gula are one of the few bears that don't hibernate in the winter." He grinned at Avaris, then looked around, studying their current surroundings as though he were searching for something.

"Maybe we should wait till spring is fully here," Avaris said. "It would be much easier then."

"Are you kidding? There are a dozen or more warriors competing for Kalisha. If I don't act soon, I'll lose my chance. Besides, I have to train new warriors again come spring."

"A *dozen* or more . . . Is she that pretty? I mean, I never thought of her that way before."

Lekiah laughed. "You're not supposed to. Brothers never think their sisters are pretty."

"Do you think she's pretty?"

Lekiah stopped laughing and got a distant look in his gaze. "She's the most beautiful girl in the Andrikan Devi nation. But more than that, she's tender, softhearted, and she's strong and a hard worker. She has deep feelings, too. She still misses you terribly . . . even after all this time."

"You haven't told her about me, have you?" Avaris asked.

"No. No I haven't, but I've wished I could many times during the past two days. It would make her so happy to know you're still alive."

Avaris longed to let Lekiah tell Kalisha and his mother the truth. His need for them to know was almost as strong as the hatred he felt for his father. He held his tears in check as memories of their faces rushed back into his mind. He thought of the many times Kalisha had held his hand and helped him cross streams or climb a large boulder when he was younger. He remembered his mother had always been there to comfort him or nurse him back to health when he was ill. He wished he could tell them the truth, but to do so would be a big mistake.

"No," he whispered. He shook his head and forced the memories from his mind. "They mustn't know. Not yet."

The two young warriors were pulled from their reverie by a faint, dry snapping sound.

"What was that?" Lekiah whispered, looking in the same direction as Avaris. Both had heard it. "It sounded like something moving in the forest," he said, answering his own question.

They were standing on the west bank of the Andrus River in a small clearing circled by big pines and thick underbrush. The still-fresh snow was about four inches deep where they stood. Avaris realized that the fact that only a trace of snow had penetrated the canopy of the pines probably saved their lives.

Once again, they heard a branch crack, as though something heavy was lumbering through the bushes. Lekiah pulled an arrow from his quiver and nocked it just as a large Muk'gula rambled into the clearing. As Avaris drew his sword, he heard the snap of Lekiah's bowstring and, almost simultaneously, heard the loud, surprised roar of the huge white animal. The beast rose on its hind legs, howling in pain and rage. Avaris suppressed the urge to run by keeping his attention trained on the massive animal. It stood more than eight feet tall, and its white coat now had a streak of crimson from its chest leading up to the arrow in its neck.

"Get back, Avaris," Lekiah shouted. He let another arrow fly, again striking the Muk'gula firmly in the neck. Before Avaris could reply, Lekiah pushed him aside, threw the spear into the animal's stomach, and charged toward the bear. His bow discarded, with a sword in one hand and a knife in the other, he met the angry beast near the center of the small clearing. The bear was injured badly—Lekiah's shots were both good—nevertheless, an injured Muk'gula was still more than a match for almost any man.

Avaris held his breath as he watched Lekiah lunge and dodge in fluid motions. Each time he attacked with his sword, the bear would swing one of his great paws at Lekiah's head, and every time he'd dive and roll out of the way at the last instant. As Avaris watched the battle, his nervousness and fear turned to amazement. He had worked on his own fighting skills, day after day for nearly four years, and considered himself to be good with the sword. But the graceful and precise moves with which Lekiah wielded the weapon, and the speed and accuracy of his attack, left Avaris in awe.

He'd thought Lekiah a fool for trying to kill a Muk'gula alone. Now, as he watched Lekiah's masterful assault, he felt sorry for the beast. One solid blow from the animal could kill Lekiah, but he moved too quickly for it to make contact.

Lekiah rolled out of the way from another swiping paw, then ran behind the animal and, using a tree trunk as leverage, launched himself onto the animal's back. He held his sword with both hands above his head and drove it into the base of the bear's skull.

The animal roared in pain, stumbled forward, and fell. Lekiah dove and rolled out of the way when the creature made one last desperate swipe.

Moments later, Lekiah leaned on his bloodied sword in the center of the clearing, trying to catch his breath. At his feet, in the trampled, scarlet-stained snow, lay the massive, lifeless form of the great white bear. Avaris sheathed his own sword and walked to his oath brother.

"I did it," Lekiah panted. "I killed it . . . by myself."

"How did you learn to fight like that?" Avaris tried not to sound impressed, but Lekiah's wide grin made it obvious he could tell he was. "I mean, we sparred yesterday, and you didn't move like that."

"That is because I wasn't scared out of my mind."

"That's the biggest Muk'gula I've ever seen—ever heard of," Avaris said as he examined the kill. "I'll bet it's the biggest any warrior has ever killed."

"You think so?" Lekiah raised his left eyebrow.

"I don't think so, I *know* so. Look at this thing. It's huge. You'll go down in legends as the greatest warrior ever. If I didn't see you fight it, I wouldn't have believed it. The way you moved was . . . it was . . . I don't know, but I was amazed."

Lekiah smiled and even laughed a little. Avaris knew he was feeding his friend's ego more than he should, but ideas came rushing to his mind, and he was too excited to hold them back.

"Do you know what I think, Lekiah? I think this is fated by the gods. Just think about it. Me, the most favored of the gods, and you, the *gifted warrior*." He pumped his fist to the sky, then smiled at Lekiah. "Don't you see? It's our destiny to become the greatest leaders the Andrikan Devi have ever known. Together we'll be able to accomplish anything."

"Maybe you're right." Lekiah raised his eyebrows and nodded.

Avaris looked over the animal once more and then looked toward the fast-moving Andrus River and scowled.

"Lekiah, how are you planning to get this thing across the river and back to the Devi-Hold?"

Lekiah's mouth dropped open, and he sagged to his knees.

"*Ba Aven's Breath!*" he cursed. "I knew I was forgetting something."

Avaris laughed and slapped him on the back. "You'd better stick to fighting and leave strategy up to me." Avaris looked up at the sky. "It's too late to start now. Let's come back in the morning and figure it out."

"No way," Lekiah said. "I'm not leaving the Muk'gula for vultures to ravage."

Avaris pursed his lips and looked around the clearing. "Then we'd better make a camp."

They built a lean-to, and after eating a meal of dried meat and water, Avaris took first watch.

Filled with stars, the clear night was beautiful, but without cloud cover, it was bitter cold. Several times during his watch, Avaris wondered what madness had possessed him to suggest they sleep outside. What had he been thinking? Camp in the clearing for the night? He was freezing to death.

He thought more than once about building a fire, but he knew to do so would attract the Mordvin cannibals. Instead, he shivered, huddled in his bison robe, and made do the best he could.

It occurred to him that Myrrah would probably skin him alive for staying out all night, especially after the recent incident with the Mordvins, but Lekiah needed his help. After all, they were oathed to each other.

When Lekiah took over the watch, Avaris didn't think he'd be able to sleep because of the cold. But he must have dozed off because Lekiah shook him awake shortly before dawn.

"Get up. We need to get to work if we want to get this thing out of here before nightfall," he said, pointing to the massive shadow in the center of the clearing.

The memories of the previous evening came rushing back when Avaris looked toward the dead Muk'gula. He grunted and pushed himself to his feet, so cold that his body complained against every movement.

"I think we're out of danger from the Mordvins now," Avaris said. "I'm going to build a fire before we freeze to death."

Lekiah rubbed his hands together and smiled. "While you're doing that, I'll locate the materials we'll need to get this beast out of here."

After another meal of dried meat—the last Lekiah had left in his small pack—they began working on a crude raft. Fortunately, Lekiah had remembered to bring rope on the hunt, and after a few hours they'd constructed a solid raft by tying large branches together.

Their plan was simple: Avaris would help Lekiah get the bear on the raft and into the water, and then Lekiah would float downstream to the Devi-Hold where he would make a grand entrance with his kill.

It sounded simple enough, but the bear weighed as much as seven strong warriors. It took them longer to get the animal on the raft than it had to build the raft. After securing the animal, Avaris and Lekiah added a few more logs to both sides of the raft, fearing it might otherwise sink under the bear's incredible weight.

As the sun made its descent in the western sky, Avaris shoved Lekiah and his kill out into the swift Andrus. Lekiah was equipped with a long pole to guide the raft, but Avaris knew it would be a difficult struggle until he reached the calmer section of river closer to the hold.

He watched Lekiah maneuver downriver until his friend was no longer in sight. Breathing a deep sigh mixed with relief and apprehension, Avaris headed for Myrrah's cabin . . . and her certain wrath.

HAIL, GREAT WARRIOR

Lekiah thought his makeshift raft would be torn apart by the swift current. He felt like he was fighting an impossible battle. The rapids pulled him toward jagged rocks that protruded dangerously near the shoreline and then sent him spiraling down narrow chutes. He soon figured out how to use his long wooden pole to keep him and the raft facing forward, but the current was still too swift for his liking.

A few miles before reaching the Devi-Hold, the land gradually became less steep and, in response, the river slowed. Lekiah sat on the dead bear and, despite the cold, wiped sweat from his brow. He couldn't decide which was the more difficult fight—the bear or the river. He set his pole across his lap and watched the Andrikan forest glide silently by on his left and the Mord Mountains on his right.

As the sun made its grand exit, turning the sky a myriad of soft reds and vibrant oranges, he rounded the final bend of his journey. The wooden wall surrounding the Devi-Hold was made of tall logs bound together and pointed at the ends to make them difficult to climb. A ditch had been dug around the base of the wall, and the dirt was piled in a long mound on the outside of the ditch so an invading army would first have to climb the mound and then cross the ditch before coming to the wall.

The only thing visible inside the walls of the hold was an occasional pointed tent roof and tendrils of smoke rising from hundreds of cooking fires. The smell of roasting meat made his stomach growl—reminding Lekiah that he hadn't eaten since breakfast.

Word of Lekiah's arrival spread quickly through the hold, and soon a group of young children gathered around to see his kill. They were followed by curious adults, and much to Lekiah's relief, he had more than enough willing hands to help him drag the Muk'gula off the raft, onto a large animal skin tarpaulin, and into the compound.

The procession wound its way through the snow-packed pathways between tents until it reached the wide path that led to the middle of the hold where a ring of tents—homes of the most important clan members—circled the Mordrahns' tent. Lekiah led the throng past his parents' tent. Their eyes grew wide as they smiled and joined the crowd. People cheered and shouted as they marched to the clan chief's tent, which sat in the middle of the circle on a raised wooden platform.

Akusaa emerged from his tent, pulling a colorful winter robe over his shoulder and watching the crowd approach. He pulled his shoulders back and thrust his chin forward. Lekiah silently cursed the fact that his beautiful kill would be given to a man who wasn't worthy of being honored with a weasel.

He had to remind himself that his gift was satisfying tradition. A man must present the father of the woman he wished to marry a gift as part of the marriage proposal. His gift honored Kalisha, not Akusaa, and she was more than worthy of the offering. As he dwelled on that idea, his anger subsided and was replaced by excitement.

The people of the tribe were already beginning to talk about the "Legend of Lekiah" as they followed him—certainly Akusaa would give him Kalisha's hand in marriage now that he was a hero.

As Lekiah took the last few steps toward Akusaa, Mindahl stepped from behind the tent flap and took his place next to the high chief. Mindahl's short snow-white beard, light blue turban, and long winter cloak was a stark contrast to Akusaa's dark hair and skin. Lekiah liked Mindahl. One of the few good decisions of Akusaa's reign was to hire him as the tribe's

Meskhoni. The only time Akusaa had shown good judgment was when the Wizard stood at his side, giving advice.

Lekiah stopped two paces before the ruler, bowed deeply—cursing silently as he did so—and rose again with a large smile etched onto his narrow face. A gentle breeze blew his black hair across his eyes as he gestured toward the men pulling his prized trophy. The men laid the Muk'gula at the feet of Akusaa and Mindahl, then disappeared back into the crowd.

Akusaa's eyes opened wide as he looked down at the enormous animal, but he gave no other sign to show he was impressed. Lekiah had hoped the leader would show a little more enthusiasm, and it aggravated the warrior that Akusaa would belittle his kill by acting as though it was nothing unusual.

Forcing the smile to remain on his face, Lekiah turned in a circle and spoke loud enough so all could hear.

"Great and revered leader, Mordrahn of the tribes," he shouted. "People of the Andrikan fields. This day, you are my witness. I fought and killed this animal with my own skill and strength. Now I humbly present it as a gift to you, great Akusaa."

Kalisha, Toci, and their mother stepped outside the tent as Lekiah turned once again to face Akusaa and Mindahl. Toci's mouth dropped open when he saw the carcass of the great white bear, but as he tried to squeeze between his father and the Wizard for a better look, his mother pulled him back. Akusaa shot a quick, angry glance at his young son, and Toci—likely recognizing the look from past experiences—cowered behind his mother, his eyes filled with fear.

What has Akusaa done to cause Toci to react in such a way? Lekiah wondered. Hating himself for having to fake allegiance to the one man in the world he truly despised, he dropped to one knee and continued in a voice that all could hear.

"I ask that you, great leader, would accept this gift and give me consent to marry your daughter, Kalisha, whom I love."

Lekiah heard Kalisha's gasp, no doubt at the symbolism of such a grand gift. No warrior had presented such a great offering to a father before. He heard excited murmurs behind him, and though he couldn't make out individual conversations, he knew they were marveling about his giving such a valuable gift for the clan chief's daughter. He hazarded a glance at Kalisha and her mother—both were smiling from ear to ear. Lekiah wished Avaris were there to share this triumph with him.

Lekiah's eyes slipped from Kalisha to her father as he stepped off the platform and walked around the bear. The crowd quieted, awaiting the high clan chief's response.

"Killed it by yourself, Lekiah?" he asked suspiciously.

Lekiah's heart dropped, and the crowd let out a collective gasp. Everyone took a Devi warrior at his word—to do otherwise was a bitter insult. Taken back by the unexpected question, Lekiah only replied with a slight nod.

"Father—" Kalisha said.

"Silence!" Akusaa cut off her weak protest with a sharp wave of his hand, his eyes bulging like they did when he was about to go on a rage. Turning back to Lekiah and the gathered crowd, Akusaa took a deep breath, but before he spoke again, Mindahl stepped down and whispered in his ear. As Akusaa listened, his eyes narrowed, and he glanced over his assembled people. When the Wizard finished, Akusaa nodded once and cleared his throat.

"You are an Andrikan warrior, Lekiah. If you say you killed this animal, then I must accept your word." It felt like the world had stopped except for the murmur that rose from the crowd. Lekiah kept his eyes fixed on the ground in front of him, afraid that if he looked up, the Mordrahn would see his desire to kill the man chiseled into every line of his face.

"Regarding the matter of my daughter," Akusaa said, "I will think about it."

Think about it? Lekiah's mouth dropped open, and he looked up.

The Mordrahn flipped his hand dismissively at the crowd. "Go back to your duties," he said. He pushed his chin forward and looked down his nose at Lekiah, turned, and walked into his tent.

Lekiah stared at the tent flap. How could Akusaa dishonor him like that, when he'd just paid the man the greatest honor of all time? No other warrior in history had so honored a man for the hand of his daughter.

Lekiah replayed the event once again in his mind. Maybe he said something wrong, or maybe he'd held himself too proudly and it offended the high chief.

Most of the tribe dispersed, although small groups still stood in the clearing, talking in low voices. Kalisha stood on the platform by the side of the tent. Her mother, Toci, and the Wizard had followed Akusaa inside. When their eyes met, Kalisha gave him an apologetic half smile, walked to him, and took his hand.

"I'm sorry, Lekiah. He's jealous, that's all."

Lekiah looked from Kalisha to the tent flap waving gently in the cold winter breeze.

"That's no excuse for treating a warrior this way, especially one who just paid him the highest honor." He turned to leave. Even though he loved Kalisha, he wanted to be alone to sort out his thoughts.

"Wait, Lekiah." She pulled him around and looked in his eyes as though she were looking into his soul. Her smooth face, high cheekbones, and soft brown eyes easily brought down Lekiah's defenses. "You paid me the highest honor, too. Never has a man given such a gift for a woman . . . I love you, Lekiah." She gently kissed his cheek and hurried back to her father's tent. Lekiah watched her go, feeling more emotions at one time than he'd imagined possible.

That night, Lekiah tossed and turned underneath his blanket. Physically, he was exhausted. He hadn't slept well the night before, and within the past two days he'd fought both a Muk'gula and a raging river. Still, sleep eluded him. The high chief should have graciously accepted the gift and even called for a celebration. Instead, he humiliated Lekiah in front of the entire clan. It infuriated him that he had to pretend to respect the man, but if he didn't, it would be a disgrace to Lekiah's parents. Besides that, if he ever hoped to marry Kalisha, he had to win Akusaa's respect. But he should already have his respect.

Lekiah eventually drifted into a restless slumber and dreamed about the day's events over and over. He awoke determined to confront Akusaa . . . alone.

Akusaa may be the high clan chief, he thought, *but I am the greatest warrior in the Andrikan nation, and he knows it. Certainly, that should be worth something to him.*

He walked confidently out of his small shelter and headed to the large tent in the center of the hold that served as Akusaa's home and meeting hall for the Mordrahn's council. As Lekiah walked down the paths that twisted around other tents and cooking fires, children pointed and stared at him and the adults watched him with broad smiles and gleams in their eyes. Lekiah suppressed a smile. At least the tribe gave him the respect he deserved, even if their leader didn't.

As he neared the center of the Devi-Hold, the sound of men shouting in the distance drew him out of his thoughts. Warriors ran toward the clan chief's tent with drawn swords. Lekiah forgot about Akusaa. His first concern was Kalisha. Was she inside the tent? Was she in danger? Images rushed into his mind of the girl he loved being attacked. He drew his sword and ran to join the fray.

Lekiah sprinted past the last row of tents that circled the central clearing where the clan chief's large canvas home stood. Burly men with white skin and dark hair ran out of the Mordrahn's tent and jumped off the platform. Some of them were injured, bleeding from superficial wounds, and each wielded a broadsword. The black-dog insignia on their round shields was new to Lekiah, but their beards with no mustache gave them away as Nortians.

The Devi aren't at war with the Nortians, Lekiah thought. *Why are they here fighting?*

Seeing scarlet blood drip from one of the big men's sword made Lekiah forget his questions. His heart felt like it had been gripped by a giant's hand. *Please, gods,* he prayed, *don't let that be Kalisha's blood.*

He let out a piercing war cry and attacked. The closest Nortian died before the man could turn or parry the attack. Two others faced Lekiah and charged even as he kicked the body of the first man off his sword.

The large Nortians were too slow. For every thrust and slice they made, Lekiah blocked and attacked twice. His sword pierced the abdomen of one attacker, then as he rolled and dodged the slice of the other's broadsword, he cut at the second man's thigh. The muscle severed, and the man dropped. Before he could howl in pain, Lekiah's sword went through his throat. He raised his blade to cut down the last man when a loud voice shouted: "Stop!"

Lekiah changed the arc of his attack at the last moment, and instead of delivering the killing stroke, he hammered at the base of his opponent's blade just above the hilt, disarming the Nortian. Three other Devi warriors who had been involved in the battle seized the man Lekiah had disarmed, and Lekiah turned to see who had commanded them to stop. Akusaa stood near the tent flap smiling, blood dripping from his sword as well.

"Very good, my warriors. Kahn Devin will think twice before threatening me again."

Lekiah's mouth dropped as the understanding of Akusaa's statement sunk in. These weren't Nortian thieves . . . They were messengers from Kahn Devin.

"The only thing the Grand Warlock will think twice about," the Nortian said, "is how he should kill you."

One of the Devi warriors slugged him in the face, knocking him to his knees. "Speak with respect when you address the high chief," he said.

The big man from Nortia spat on the bloodied snow. "I give respect to those who earn it and none else." The Devi warrior raised his fist to hit the man again, but Akusaa intervened.

"Wait, Rambha, there's no need to beat what little sense he has out of him. He needs to understand and remember my message." Turning his attention back to the sneering Nortian, Akusaa continued. "Tell Kahn I do not accept his proposal. The Andrikan Devi have managed to protect themselves for thousands of years without his help. Deliver that to your master and thank the gods I let you leave here alive."

Akusaa made a gesture for the warriors to release their grip on the man, who spat at the feet of Akusaa as he got on his horse and rode out of the hold.

Lekiah watched him go, and a tight feeling wrenched his gut. What had their foolish leader done? Was Lekiah the only one able to see his mad whims for what they were? Lekiah's attention on Akusaa broke when Mindahl ran, panting heavily, past him and up to the Mordrahn.

"What in the name of Azur happened here?" The Wizard flung his hands in the air. "Why did you kill these men? Don't you know who they are?"

He was so exercised that he was shouting, and the questions rolled like demands out of his mouth. Akusaa's brown face turned red, and his unkempt hair and scraggly black beard made Lekiah think that not only did Akusaa act like a madman, but he looked the part as well.

"You may be a Wizard, Mindahl," Akusaa hissed between clenched teeth, "but no one talks to Akusaa Mordrahn that way. No one!"

Lekiah looked back and forth between the Wizard and the clan chief, wondering who would give in first. Lekiah's father, Lokia, pushed past him and approached the platform where the two men were glaring at each other.

Akusaa pointed his finger in Mindahl's face, and Lekiah could see spit flying from Akusaa's mouth as he shouted. "Kahn Devin said we must ally with him. For that *privilege*, we would be required to give him one-fourth of our animals, food, men, supplies, and anything else of value. In return, he promised to allow us to live in peace. I killed his men because his offer is arrogant and dishonorable to our tribe."

"You shouldn't have killed his messengers." The Wizard didn't back down. "Kahn is vindictive."

"What do you—"

"Excuse me, great one." Lokia stepped between the two men and shot a glance toward the gathering crowd. "Don't you think it would be wiser for us to continue this discussion inside?"

The Wizard looked at the people. He took a deep breath, smoothed his blue robe, and forced a smile on his face. "Yes," he said. "That is good advice, Lokia."

Akusaa looked around, as though only now realizing more than a hundred people were watching. He pulled his shoulders back and puffed out his chest, then threw open the tent flap and disappeared inside, followed by his advisors.

THE BOLD PLAN

Avaris abruptly woke after a light knock sounded on the door of Myrrah's mountain shack. The old woman was already awake and lighting a thick, short candle. She walked to the door and placed her ear next to the crack.

"Who's there?"

"It's me. Lekiah."

"What in the world is he doing here so late?" Avaris said as he jumped off his hutch and threw on a bison robe. Myrrah pulled back on the cloth curtain that was covering the dusty window and looked outside to confirm the visitor was who he claimed to be.

"What are you doing out here in the middle of the night?" she asked as she opened the door and pulled him inside. "Don't you know how dangerous it is to walk through these mountains at night?"

"It's almost morning," he replied absently.

"What?"

"It's not the middle of the night any more. It's almost morning." His cheeks were red from the cold, but his hair was wet with sweat, and he had dark circles under his eyes.

"What happened to you?" Avaris asked.

"What do you mean?"

"What do you mean, what do I mean? Look at yourself. It's freezing outside, yet you're dripping with sweat. You look exhausted . . . What's happened?"

Myrrah set the candle on the table and headed for the hearth to put more wood on the fire while Avaris motioned for Lekiah to sit at the table.

"Thank you," he said as he sat on the wooden stool. "I *am* exhausted. I haven't been able to sleep for days."

Myrrah returned with cups of hot tea for each of them. The room was already growing warmer, and the smell of burning pine permeated the air. Avaris didn't bother to ask her how she heated the water so quickly—he'd seen her do similar things before, and Lekiah was apparently too worn out to notice anything unusual about it.

She handed Lekiah a cup of tea. "Drink this while you tell us about it." Her lips and nose twitched as she waited for him to begin. Avaris took a sip of the tea and tasted a hint of smooth mint—one of his favorites—and he settled back to listen.

It took less than a half hour for Lekiah to finish his story—it would have taken longer but Myrrah told Avaris to quit interrupting with questions. When Lekiah finished, the old lady stood up and paced. Avaris made a fist and pounded it into his hand.

"I can't believe my father would . . . well, yes I can. If he would leave me to die in the mountains, I guess he's capable of doing just about anything. It really bothers me he dishonored you in front of the clan the way he did. When I'm the clan chief, I'll make you my personal champion and give you the honor you deserve."

"That's the least of our worries, Avaris," Myrrah said, stopping in front of the two boys. "I know Kahn Devin; he won't take this well. I can assure you he will retaliate, and when he does, it won't be pretty. He'll probably kill every Andrikan Devi he can get his hands on. Or worse, sacrifice them to Ba Aven or make them slaves in the Demon Pits."

Avaris's heart dropped as he considered the horrors described by his mentor, whose nose and mouth continued to twitch.

"Why would he kill the whole tribe? It's my father who killed his men, not the Andrikan Devi."

"Kahn likes to use circumstances like this as object lessons." She walked to the bookshelf and looked at the picture of her sister. Her gnarled hand rose to her cheek, and she took a long breath. "He'll make an example of your tribe," she said and turned back to look at the boys.

"He shouldn't underestimate the Devi warriors," Lekiah said, his eyes narrowed. "No army has ever conquered us in winter, and none has defeated us for more than a four-month period in our entire history."

"Yes, Lekiah, but Kahn Devin is not like any enemy your people have ever faced. He won't fight like you do. He'll use his power and creatures from under the Cragg Mountains." She frowned, walked to the small dirty window, gazed out at the rising sun, and whispered, "Akusaa made a fatal mistake."

Lekiah jumped to his feet, knocking the stool over. "You mean, no matter what we do, Kahn Devin is going to kill our people?"

"Most likely." Myrrah shook her head and turned again to face the boys. "Let me think for a moment. We may be able to do something."

As she paced the small cabin again, Avaris began making his own plans. Now might be the time to make himself known to his people. Knowing how the Andrikan Devi love stories, Avaris suspected that even the tribes farthest from the hold have probably already heard about Lekiah's legendary kill. Akusaa had brushed it off as nothing, but the tribe's people would be impressed and look to Lekiah as a hero. Lekiah already held the nation's respect because he was the best trainer of warriors. If he and Lekiah could somehow save the clan from Kahn . . .

Myrrah snapped her fingers. "I've got it." She whirled to face the two boys. "Kahn Devin is certain to come personally to deal with Akusaa. When he does, Avaris, you need to talk to him before he gets to the hold."

"And say what?"

"Once we see his army coming through the mountains, the three of us will go into their camp and tell him it was all your father's fault. Avaris, you make an alliance with him. If you offer your support and promise to turn your father over to him, he may be willing to help you claim your rightful position as high clan chief."

"But what about all the minor clan chiefs?" Lekiah said. "They will resent Avaris if he allies with Kahn. It may even start a war among tribes."

"Kahn Devin is powerful. I think he can make the others see things our way," she replied with a twitching smile.

"I thought Kahn Devin doesn't like you, Myrrah," Avaris said. "Why are you so anxious to have me make a treaty with him? What if he kills you when he sees us?"

"Oh, he doesn't like me, but he won't kill me," she said. "The reason I think you should join him is because it's either that or let everyone at the hold be slaughtered, starting with your family."

"I will die before I let Kahn or any other man harm Kalisha," Lekiah said.

Myrrah stared in his eyes. "Then you will die."

Silence filled the room. Avaris considered Myrrah's plan as he looked back and forth between the dumpy, old woman and the strong, young warrior. It might work, but Avaris didn't like the idea of being in debt to Kahn Devin, or anyone else for that matter. He got up and paced. Myrrah, her nose twitching as she watched him, sat on his vacant stool. He always knew one day he would have to challenge his father, but he didn't think it would be so soon. However, if he waited, he might not have a tribe left to rule.

"I have an idea," Lekiah said, breaking the silence. "First winter's Azur-Aven is only a few weeks from now. Most of the tribes will be gathering back to the hold for the celebration. I could organize a rebellion. I'll tell the most influential warriors that Avaris is alive and his father is going to get us killed by his stupidity. With their help, we'll recruit the rest of the warriors to our cause. Then, during the festival, we'll take Akusaa prisoner and put you in his place. We'll let everyone know what happened and then ambush Kahn Devin with our army."

"Do you think that would work?" Avaris asked Lekiah.

"Of course not," the Necromancer answered for him. "Even if you convince your warriors to put Avaris in Akusaa's place, you won't catch Kahn by surprise. In the end, more people would be killed. My idea—"

"I don't think we'll do either plan," Avaris interrupted, even as a new plan formed in his head. "I don't want to be in debt to Kahn Devin, nor do I want to start a war with him. Instead, I think Lekiah and I should go to the festival together, and when everyone is waiting for Mindahl to bless the babies, we'll get on the platform and announce I'm still alive. My father will have to act pleased—he can't very well kill me in front of the thousands of people. Lekiah and I will warn them of the coming army and convince them to let us guide our warriors to meet and ambush Kahn in the Mord Mountains—"

"Wait a second." Myrrah cut him off. "I thought you said you don't want to start a war. And what makes you think they're going to let you guide the army? Your years are barely twelve, and Lekiah's seventeen. You think they'll trust a couple of kids to play scout for them?"

"I'm not a kid," Lekiah said. "I'm the best Andrikan warrior alive, and they know it."

Avaris had to step between him and Myrrah to be heard. "Quiet, you two, let me finish." Lekiah sat back down, and the Necromancer motioned for Avaris to finish. "Lekiah is one of the most respected warriors, and I am *still* the son of the high clan chief, and nobody knows these mountains like we do. I think we should be able to get them to agree. Even if they don't, they'll at least take us along to help in the fight."

Myrrah started to speak again, but Avaris waved her quiet and continued. "Once we find Kahn, we'll meet secretly with him and tell him who I am. I'll offer to . . . betray my father and promise to become his student when my time comes to be trained in the lore. In return, he must promise to leave the Andrikan Devi alone."

Myrrah's eyebrows turned up, and she pursed her lips. Avaris knew she was seriously considering his plan.

"We'd have to get your father into Kahn Devin's hands without anyone knowing you were involved," she said thoughtfully.

Lekiah folded his arms and tapped at his chin. "We can slip some of your powder that makes you sleep into his drink and, when he's asleep, take him to Kahn." He grinned mischievously, and his eyes lit up. "We'll leave a trail of animal blood in his tent along with a note from Kahn that says something like, 'I could have killed all of you, but I only wanted Akusaa.

Next time I send an emissary, treat them with respect or everyone dies.' We could even have Kahn put his seal on it."

"Once the tribe thinks Akusaa is dead, I'll be made high clan chief; no one gets killed, and the Andrikan Devi are still free." Avaris was rather proud of the idea. He could save his people *and* become the Mordrahn, and the only thing he would give up is his choice between studying at Elder Island or studying in the Demon Caves. But he'd already decided to study the Aven-Lore someday anyway.

"All right," Myrrah said. "We'll do it your way. But you're going to have a lot of work to do before the festival. There are more spells I want to teach you that might come in handy."

"What spells?"

"Well, how to make your voice carry over a large crowd, for example. It would be nice if people can hear when you introduce yourself."

"Oh yeah, I didn't think about that."

"I didn't think you had. Also, I want to teach you how to defend yourself with bone and fire and protect your mind from intrusion. Mindahl and Kahn Devin will both try to search your mind. You need to know how to block and keep them out."

"Won't they get suspicious if I do that?"

"I don't think so. It won't surprise them that someone with your talent is able to block them, and they certainly wouldn't let you roam around in their minds, either. If one of them does say something, just tell them you'll let down your guard if they let down theirs."

"What if Kahn Devin doesn't come and we lead them into the mountains for nothing?" Lekiah asked. "We'll look pretty foolish if that happens."

"He'll come," Myrrah said. "Trust me on that. I just hope we'll have time to get the warriors into the mountains before Kahn gets to the hold."

"We'll have time," Lekiah said. "Even on horseback, it'll take two weeks for the messenger to get back to the Cragg Caves. Then Kahn has to organize his troops and come back. We should have several weeks."

"Maybe, but don't bet on it. That man is full of surprises . . . full of surprises." She repeated the last phrase thoughtfully as if it brought back painful memories. Once again, Avaris saw her glance at the drawing of her sister. He considered asking her what her sister had to do with all this, but if she hadn't told him before, she wasn't likely to now.

"You both need to understand the risks we are about to undertake." Myrrah's beady eyes looked haunted. "If our plan fails to appease Kahn, he will be ruthless . . . I've seen his wrath before." She held up a hand to stop Lekiah's retort. "He will want your father to suffer, Avaris. Kahn will make Akusaa watch as your mother, your sister, and your younger brother are slowly tortured to death."

RETURN TO LEAVE

Renn hadn't been back to Leedsdale for more than two years—ever since the Kiroc attacked him. Yet, as he looked down upon it from a hilltop on the eastside of the village, he saw no noticeable change. It felt like he'd never left.

Renn had seen and learned a lot during his absence from the area. He and Artio spent their time in hiding during their self-imposed, two-year exile. That meant moving from town to town, city to city, and never staying in one place for too long as they tried to avoid being recognized. Before they left Leedsdale, Renn had never seen a city or even another town. But during their travels, he'd been from Tauret to Achtan and every place in between.

"One thing I didn't miss about this place is the blasted heat." Artio wiped sweat off his forehead and looked up at the noon sun. "It's autumn, *for Azur's sake*! It shouldn't be so confounded hot." The Mage looked down the hill at the village and then back at the sun. "What is taking them so long?"

Renn didn't bother to give an answer; the old man didn't really expect one. Instead, he turned and walked back to their small cooking fire and rotated the cottontail that was roasting over it on a spit.

"Lord Danu specifically said to meet him on this hill the first full moon of autumn," the Mage continued as he paced back and forth. "They're three days late now."

"Maybe they're gathering supplies or something," Renn said.

"Humph. I'm just anxious to get started, that's all. We have a long journey ahead of us, and the sooner we leave the better. If the northern part of the Ava River freezes over, we'll be trudging through several feet of snow for miles trying to reach Port Andrus."

A cough from behind made both Renn and the old Meskhoni jump. They turned to see Lord Danu standing with his arms folded across his chest and a wide grin on his face.

"How long have you been standing there?" Artio demanded.

"Just a little while."

"Why didn't you just come right out and tell us you were there instead of spying on us? Don't they teach you royals manners these days?"

Lord Danu laughed. "I was planning on it. But watching you pace nervously back and forth was irresistible."

Renn tried to suppress a laugh, but it came out as a snort. He coughed as though he had something caught in his throat—not wanting Artio to know he thought Lord Danu's joke funny. Normally, the old man was calm and cool to a fault, and Renn knew it irritated him to lose control. The fact Lord Danu made a joke of it clearly irritated the Mage even further.

"Amusing, my lord. Where are the others?" Artio slipped back into his subdued temperament and joined Renn by the fire.

"They're waiting for us in a meadow on the far side of the hill. We passed through the village during the night; I didn't want to start unnecessary rumors." Lord Danu must have anticipated a question as to why the Mage didn't see them pass.

"At least you showed some common sense in that regard. Have the others had lunch yet?" the Meskhoni asked, pointing to the small rabbit Renn was basting.

"Olosa was cooking it when I left."

"Olosa?" Artio slapped his lap and looked up at Lord Danu with raised eyebrows. "What did you bring that old windbag along for?"

"We've a long journey ahead of us, my friend. At least we can have good food along the way."

"Lord Danu?" Renn spoke for the first time. His upbringing taught him he should allow his mentor the courtesy of speaking to the young lord first. "How is my family?"

"Why don't you ask them yourself?" Lord Danu wore a wide grin as Renn jumped to his feet and grew wide-eyed.

"You mean they're here? With you? When can we go see them?"

"For the love of Lemuria, Danu. What in Ba Aven's breath are you thinking?" The old Mage threw his hands up in the air. "If anybody knows you brought them with you, they'll figure out Renn is still alive. We have to keep Renn and me a secret as long as possible."

"Why do you think we're three days late?" The young lord held up his hands to stave off more reprimands from Artio. "We traveled mostly at night with Raven scouting ahead. No one saw us. Besides that, I'm not about to send Renn off for who knows how long without letting him say goodbye to his family."

Artio pursed his lips and scratched at his chin. For the second time in less than ten minutes, Lord Danu had managed to make him upset. That was as many times as Renn had seen the Mage upset during the entire two years they spent in hiding.

"Let's hurry and eat this rabbit so we can get going then," the Mage said with a sigh and motioned for Lord Danu to join them.

When Renn, Artio, and Lord Danu rode down the hill toward the small camp, the evening sun cast long shadows on the ground. Renn was tempted to urge Thorn to a run as he thought of his waiting family, but he wanted to maintain some semblance of dignity in front of Lord Danu. Besides, there would be other boys and girls his age in the party who would be traveling with them to Elder Island, and he didn't want to look silly the first time they met him.

Children who were marked on their blessing day and had turned fourteen were supposed to be presented to the lore masters of Elder Island on either midsummer's or midwinter's Azur-Aven. Normally, a group left Boranica each spring to arrive by the summer celebration and was led by the fathers and older brothers of the future students.

This year, however, was unusual. For one thing, Lord Danu would personally lead the group along with a company of soldiers. Also, instead of leaving in spring, they were leaving in the fall to be presented to the lore masters on Elder Island during midwinter's Azur-Aven. Lord Danu and Artio determined some time before that if Kahn Devin still suspected Renn was alive—which he likely did—he would've expected them to travel in the spring like most parties headed for the island do.

A little girl stepped out from the largest tent in the center of camp. After turning to shout something to others still inside, she lifted up her dress and ran toward Renn.

"Renn's coming! Renn's coming!" she yelled as she closed the distance between them and the camp on the far side of the little meadow. Others emerged from the tents to see what was happening. Renn picked out his mother standing with her hands clasped over her mouth. Next to her stood a man that Renn didn't recognize. After a moment of squinting, he realized it was his older brother, Tavier. A dozen soldiers stood watching, as did a couple other young teenagers.

Renn recognized the small girl running across the meadow as his younger sister, Chria. She, too, had changed since Renn last saw her. Chria was tall for her age and, like her mother, she had golden blonde hair, the color of ripe wheat in autumn, that framed her soft blue eyes. She ran straight to Renn and climbed onto Thorn's back behind him, wrapped her arms around him, and gave him a long hug.

"I missed you, Renn. When are you going to come live with us again?"

"I missed you too, Chria, and I'll come back as soon as I'm done with my studies," he said, swallowing a lump in his throat.

"Can't you at least come visit us sometime?" she asked, leaning around him to look in his eyes. He gave her hand a squeeze. She wrapped her arms around his waist, and he started toward the camp again. He forgot how much he missed his family and didn't trust himself to answer her just then. He didn't want to start crying in front of Lord Danu.

As they reached the edge of camp, Delphia and Tavier could apparently no longer maintain their patient vigils. They hurried toward Renn with watery eyes. When Renn saw his mother and older brother shedding tears, Renn's tears flowed like water through a floodgate. He forgot about Lord Danu and the rest of the party. It didn't really matter what they thought anyway, he decided.

"What's going on?" a familiar voice asked. Tavier stepped aside and turned so Renn could see past him to the group of people watching their display. Genea Lucian stood among them. She must have been in one of the tents when Renn arrived because he didn't see her before.

"Renn is that . . . I thought you . . . were . . . but . . ." Her countenance changed from surprise to joy, then from relief to anger as she struggled for something to say. Finally, anger won out over the other emotions, and her face turned red as her eyes began to water. "I hate you, Renn Demaris!" She stomped away from camp toward a thicket of trees on the other side of the meadow.

"What was that all about?" Renn asked his mother.

Renn's mother ran a hand through her long golden hair and raised her eyebrows as she watched Genea walk away. "My guess is she likes you."

"What are talking you about? She doesn't like me. She just said she hates me."

"Get used to it, Renn." Lord Danu placed his hand on the boy's shoulder and laughed. "That's the way all women are." He pursed his lips, squinted, and nodded in the direction Genea left and said, "The only thing men can do is try to stay out of the way when they're mad."

"Oh?" Delphia folded her arms and looked at the young lord with one eyebrow raised. "*All* women, Lord Danu?"

Lord Danu flushed, and his soldiers grinned as he looked around for help. "Well, not you, of course . . . I mean . . ."

"You better quit before you get yourself in worse trouble, Danu," Kivas said. He and the other men stood in a semicircle behind Renn's mother, who was looking over her shoulder at Lord Danu. They all openly laughed at their leader.

"Laugh all you want," Lord Danu said. "Remember, I'm the one who gives the assignments around here, and the next man who laughs gets to clean dishes for the rest of the trip." The men quit laughing, although they all still wore a grin from ear to ear. Lord Danu looked them over one man at a time, waiting for one to slip back into a fit of laughter, and then winked at Renn and Delphia.

A skinny boy with dark curly hair and big ears pushed through the soldiers around Renn's mother and skidded to a halt.

"Wow! Are you really Renn? I heard about you, but Genea said you died when a Kiroc attacked you. I thought it strange for the gods to mark you so strongly and then just let you die like a—"

"Take a breath, Harlow," Renn's mother said with a smile. "We should probably introduce everybody before you get too carried away."

"Good idea," Lord Danu said. He raised his voice so everybody in the small group could hear him and motioned for them to gather in. "Since we're going to be spending the next couple months together, introductions are in order." Genea reluctantly rejoined the group, but she pointedly kept her distance from Renn and looked at the ground.

"This talkative young man is Harlow Gallim." Lord Danu messed Harlow's hair. "Harlow's family have been great workers on a beautiful farm just outside Basilea for two generations now. His brothers and sisters are a bit jealous they have to stay and work the farm while Harlow learns magic." Harlow's face turned red, but his smile reached from ear to ear.

"I think all of you have figured out that this is Renn Demaris and the Mage Artio." Lord Danu's shoulder-length hair blew across his brown eye, leaving only the blue eye visible. He brushed his hair aside as he continued. "Genea, I'm sorry we lied to you about why Renn's family came along, but the fewer people who knew he was alive the better."

"If it makes you feel better," Kivas said and furrowed his dark eyebrows, "his lordship didn't even tell me until last week."

"Like I said"—Lord Danu raised his eyebrows and looked pointedly at Kivas—"we kept the truth about Renn guarded for the past two years." Lord Danu turned and looked at Renn and Artio, who stood behind him and motioned to the line of men. "This bunch may not be much to look at, but they are my best soldiers. Some of them you met a few years back:

Raven, Kivas, Tellio, Cole, Radien, and Micha." As Lord Danu introduced them again, they each smiled or nodded to Renn and Artio.

"This is Durham of Mylitta." Lord Danu pointed to a large man with thinning blond hair and a prominent dimple in the center of his chin.

Durham nodded respectfully and said, "Pleased to meet you."

"Gunnar, here, is from Basilea." Lord Danu pointed to a skinny young man with meticulously combed, short blond hair. "Don't let his size fool you—he's fast and good to have at your back in a fight." The young soldier's face reddened at the compliment.

"Lahar is from Lemont, and soldiering is in his blood; his father and his father before him were great soldiers." As Lahar nodded, Renn couldn't help wonder why his hair and skin were so dark—at least dark for somebody from Lemont. He'd been to that town with Artio, and the villagers had fair hair and skin. But Lahar's skin wasn't as dark as the next soldier Lord Danu introduced.

"This is Aidan. He is from Sarundra and is of the Marahi Devi tribe." His hair was black and cropped short.

"I met young Master Renn before this day," Aidan said with an accent. "He and his father and brother running from Nortian soldiers."

"Yes, that's right," Lord Danu said. "I'd almost forgotten about that." Renn felt a stab in his heart as he remembered that day. It had occurred just before his father was killed by the mob. Lord Danu gave Renn a quick smile as if to say, *Sorry to remind you of painful memories,* and then continued with the introductions.

"Julius grew up on a farm outside of Basilea—he has been with my band of strangers since he was just a couple years older than you, Renn." The soldier smiled, and Renn thought he looked a little like Lord Danu—his hair was dirty blond and fell nearly to his shoulders, and he was good-looking.

"Last but not least is Beruth. He started out as a stableboy in our castle at Basilea but was so persistent in practicing the sword and trying to be like the soldiers, I finally decided to make him one—and so far I've not regretted that choice." Beruth looked mean even though he smiled at Lord Danu's introduction of him. His stubbled head of black whiskers suggested that he hadn't shaved in probably a week, and his eyebrows drew up in a kind of permanent scowl.

"I just realized why people call you a band of strangers," Renn blurted out.

"Renn." His mother scowled, and her face turned red. "That's not the proper way to refer to Lord Danu's legion."

Lord Danu raised a single eyebrow and some of the men chuckled. "Go on, Renn," Lord Danu said. "Why do folks call us a band of strangers?"

Renn felt his face flush, and he kicked at the dirt. "Well, most standing armies in Boranica are made up of knights and soldiers from wealthy or noble families. Most of your men aren't even from Basilea—some aren't even from Boranica at all."

"I sometimes call them stray dogs," Lord Danu said with a smile. "A bit unorthodox—my father only tolerates it because my men are the best division in his army. But they are fiercely loyal and they all have hidden talents."

A loud crash came from the opposite end of the camp. A large young man with disheveled blond hair and a whisker-shadowed face came running toward them laughing. A plump old man whose gray-stubbled face was flushed red chased after him. The older man shouted and waved a large wooden spoon menacingly above his head.

Lord Danu frowned and clenched his jaw. The young man noticed Lord Danu's expression and skidded to a stop in front of the group. The old man didn't stop in time and barreled right into the younger man, knocking them both to the dirt in a rolling heap.

Renn covered his mouth to keep from laughing and noticed his mother doing the same thing. Lord Danu shook his head but wore half a grin. Most of the other men laughed outright at the mishap.

"Stand up, you two," Kivas boomed out. "You're embarrassing all of us."

"I swear, Sela," the old plump man said as he tried to untangle himself and stand up, "if you mess around with my supplies—" He stopped midstream as he realized a dozen eyes were staring amused at him and his antics. He brushed the dust off his apron and said, "Begging your pardon, Lord Danu, ladies . . ." Renn noticed he didn't bother apologizing to the other men in the group—just Lord Danu, Genea, and his mother.

"If you two are finished making fools of yourselves," Lord Danu said, "I'd like to introduce you to our friends."

The older man hit the younger man on the shoulder with his spoon, painted a smile on his face, and stood at attention.

"This is Sela Nadgit," Lord Danu said with a scowl. "He is our blacksmith. I don't want to be slowed down by thrown shoes or broken wagons." This last explanation he directed to Artio, who had been about to protest bringing another person along. Now that Sela wasn't running or rolling in the dirt, Renn could see the sooty smudges on his face and in his clothes. His body had the common build of a blacksmith—barrel-chested with large shoulders and well-developed arms but with legs that were disproportionately thin.

Lord Danu pointed to the plump man with the wooden spoon. "And this is our cook, Olosa Sabulana."

The old man smiled and bowed—again, toward the ladies. "The pleasure is mine," he said in a formal tone. Sela snickered. Olosa's face reddened, and he hit Sela again with the spoon.

"You two, cut that out." Lord Danu leaned toward them and pointed his finger in their faces. "We have a long and dangerous journey ahead of us. We can't afford to be distracted with your squabbles the entire way."

RETURN OF AN OLD FRIEND

The following morning, Renn sat on a log finishing a plate of muffins, scrambled eggs, and ham cooked by Olosa. Renn closed his eyes and enjoyed the aroma of sizzling ham blending with the smell of campfire. He hadn't eaten so well since he lived with his mother. While he and Artio were in hiding the past couple years, most of the meal preparation had been left up to Renn. It would be nice to have somebody else do the cooking for a change.

Artio, Lord Danu, and his captain of the guard, Raven, had already eaten and now leaned against a wagon, studying a map. Renn couldn't hear them from where he sat on the log by the fire, but they were in deep discussion.

Kivas, the big lieutenant from Nortia, had bits of scrambled egg stuck in his dark beard. He'd finished his breakfast and was drinking a mug of ale and sitting on a log across the fire from Renn. Kivas sat next to Tellio, who twisted his waxed mustache while bragging about his feats of strength in a skirmish Lord Danu and his men had been involved in during the previous month.

"I love muffins. Of course, Ma makes them better—with blueberries and a bit of honey and butter. Not that I'm complaining, of course. These are great, too . . ."

Renn tried to ignore the constant chatter of Harlow Gallim, who sat on the log next to him. He, too, had been marked at his blessing and, along with Genea and Renn, was going to the school to study the Aven-Lore. The boy had unmanageable, curly dark brown hair and a permanent smile. Despite the fact that he never quit talking, Renn took an instant liking to Harlow. He constantly asked questions, said stupid things, and generally made a pest of himself—but he was happy and friendly.

Genea didn't care for Harlow much—a point she made obvious—and she still wouldn't speak to Renn. The previous night, she'd stomped to the opposite side of the fire from the two boys to eat her dinner. This morning, she shared the log with Tellio and Kivas but turned her back as she ate her breakfast and refused to even look at Renn. He watched her for a moment. She had grown into a young woman. Her dark brown hair still had a hint of red to it when the sun hit it just right. The day before, he noticed she was beginning to develop the curves of a woman. Just thinking about that made his face flush so he quickly looked away. He supposed she would probably attract the attention of boys at the school. That is, if she learned to control her temper.

The other soldiers that would be traveling with them had already finished eating and were busy preparing to leave. Beruth, who still hadn't shaved his stubbled head, helped Julius—a good-looking man with shoulder-length, sandy-colored hair—roll and pack the company's tents. Aidan and Lahar fed and saddled the horses.

One soldier impressed him the most: the well-built man named Durham, with calloused hands and a deep rumbling voice. He was helping Sela Nadgit, the barrel-chested blacksmith, shoe a horse that had thrown one the previous day.

"So, if Kahn Devin didn't kill you," Harlow said through a mouthful of muffins, "what happened to him?"

"What are you talking about?"

"Two years ago, I heard rumors that Kahn Devin had killed the boy from Leedsdale who was destined to be a great Wizard. But you're not dead, so what happened to Kahn? Did Artio fight him off? Did Danu's men chase him away? I wish I could've seen—"

"Slow down, Harlow," Renn said. "You talk too fast to follow. First,

Kahn didn't actually come to Leedsdale to kill me—he sent one of his Kiroc servants. As far as I know, he thinks the Kiroc killed me. We made it look like I didn't survive so he'd leave us alone. Although he did put a reward on my head, so we've had to move around to hide from bounty hunters."

"Oh, I see. Kind of." Harlow scratched his chin and squinted.

"Well, don't lose any sleep over it, Harlow. It really wasn't that big of a deal." Renn downplayed the ordeal, hoping Harlow would stop asking questions.

"If Kahn *didn't* kill you—"

Harlow stopped midsentence because Raven drew his sword and ran from the wagon to position himself between Renn and the trees. Renn heard a twig snap, and the other soldiers drew their weapons and stood. Artio and Lord Danu joined Raven, the Mage's staff emanating a soft green glow.

The leaves on one of the trees rustled, and a tall, thin man stepped into their camp. He wore a short beard—which was odd for one living in Boranica—but Renn recognized him immediately.

"Jomard!" He set his breakfast down, pushed between Artio and Lord Danu, and ran to his former neighbor. Jomard caught Renn in a strong embrace, laughing and crying at the same time. Renn's mother and siblings also set their meals aside and joined Renn in embracing Jomard.

Jomard stood back and looked at them all with a big smile. "When I saw your family out here with Lord Danu, I was sure something was afoot. I never dreamed Renn would be here, too. I can't tell you how happy I am to know you're still alive."

The Meskhoni cleared his throat and, with a dark tone in his voice, said, "No one saw you, Lord Danu?"

Lord Danu shot the old Mage a quick look and then turned to Raven, who was regarding Jomard through narrowed eyes. Lord Danu didn't have to say anything to his right-hand man. Raven shifted his gaze to the young lord, barely shook his head once, and then returned his attention to Jomard, who had his arm around Renn's shoulder.

"How did you know we were here, Jomard, and how did you slip past our watch?" As Lord Danu asked the last question, he motioned toward Radien and Cole. The change of expression from a smile to a frown on Jomard's face led Renn to believe the man didn't realize until now that he might not be welcome by these who he considered his friends.

Jomard shifted his gaze from Lord Danu to Renn's family and back to Lord Danu. "I live over the mountain, my lord, and frequently walk these hills at night. I simply noticed your camp yesterday evening and returned this morning for a closer look. I didn't intend to alarm you; I had no idea you were trying to keep your presence hidden. Your men probably didn't see me approach because I used a back trail that's well hidden."

Renn looked at Radien and Cole. Both guards looked back and forth between Lord Danu and Raven, but Renn couldn't tell if they were worried or simply trying to gauge their leader's reactions.

Lord Danu did not respond; his blank stare stayed fixed on Jomard as though he expected a better answer.

Jomard scratched at his trimmed beard and bit his lip. "When I got close enough to recognize Delphia and Tavier, I wanted to come and see my old neighbors."

Lord Danu sheathed his sword and signaled for his men to do the same. "Forgive my cold reception, Jomard," Lord Danu said. "Our mission is important. The fact that a simple farmer saw us and walked unobserved into my camp bothers me. Have you told anyone about us?"

Jomard shook his head.

"Good. When you return, you must remember to say nothing about us to anyone, no matter how innocent the inquiry may seem."

Jomard flushed and cleared his throat. "My lord. That shouldn't be a problem. I don't intend to go back for some time."

"Oh?" Lord Danu raised his eyebrows. "Why's that?"

"Renn's father, Ehrlich, was like a brother to me. Were he here, he would be escorting his son to Elder Island. I would be a poor friend if I did not personally stand in his stead to protect his son."

Raven whispered something to Lord Danu, and Artio and Kivas took a couple steps forward to join them. The other soldiers glared at Jomard. Renn realized it probably upset them that Jomard not only found their camp but also guessed where they were going.

Lord Danu nodded to something Kivas said, then looked up at Jomard with a warm smile. "That is a very generous offer, Jomard, but you have a wife and a child, and it is harvest time. Besides, we have plenty here to protect him should the need arise."

"My wife will enjoy some time to visit her mother. As for my field, last year was a good harvest, and I left it fallow this season."

"Still," Lord Danu said, "I think it better if you didn't join our group."

Jomard took his arm off Renn's shoulder and took a step forward. "Excuse my boldness, my lord, but I insist. Ehrlich would have done the same for my son."

No one spoke, and Renn could feel tension in the air like ropes being pulled tight, ready to break. Lord Danu raised one eyebrow and looked at Raven, who stood on his left. The captain's dark eyes stayed fixed on Jomard, and he shook his head. He obviously didn't think having Jomard along was a good idea.

"Artio?" Lord Danu looked at the Mage, who stood on his right. "Your thoughts?"

"Jomard has assisted at other times and proved to be a valuable ally. I see no harm in having him along."

Lord Danu took two steps forward and folded his arms. "Delphia, what do you think Ehrlich would want for Renn?"

Renn's mother licked her lips. He saw her glance at Raven before she made a small curtsy to Lord Danu. "Milord, Ehrlich would want Jomard to be with Renn." She looked back at Jomard and gave him a smile. "And I would feel better knowing Jomard is helping watch over him on this journey."

Lord Danu grinned with tight lips and nodded his head to Renn's mother. "That settles it, Jomard. It's probably best that you aren't left behind anyway. You can't reveal our secret if you are with us, so you may come."

"My lord, I would never betray this family or you." Jomard sounded offended at the notion that he wouldn't keep their confidence were he to be left behind.

Lord Danu walked forward until he stood chin to chin with Jomard. "Have you ever been tortured by somebody using the Aven-Lore?"

Jomard shook his head and swallowed.

"I didn't think so," Lord Danu said. "You'd be surprised at how quickly you might betray your friends and family."

Lord Danu motioned Raven to join them. "My captain will accompany you to gather your supplies and make the arrangements for your wife and child. You will have to think up some excuse to tell her about what you are doing for the next several months. She can't suspect the truth."

Jomard and Raven left while Renn and the others broke camp. They soon had everything lined up and ready to go. Delphia, Tavier, and Chria stood next to a beautiful white carriage that had at one time belonged to Lord Danu's deceased mother. Two soldiers, Clegg and Gunnar, sat atop the driver's bench, wearing the blue uniforms of Lord Danu's regiment, waiting to drive them back to Basilea.

Renn and the party traveling with him to Elder Island had changed into riding costumes provided by Lord Danu. The young lord was dressed as a wealthy merchant with fine, indigo-colored hose and a deep-red velvet doublet. His long navy-blue mantle, embroidered around the hem with gold, was clasped with a gold clip at his left shoulder. The soldiers in the company no longer wore the colors of the Basil lords. Now, they were mercenaries hired to protect Lord Danu and his cargo from thieves.

Artio wore hose and a doublet—though not nearly as rich-looking as Lord Danu's attire—and was instructed to act the part of Lord Danu's grandfather. Renn and Harlow were to be Lord Danu's pages—to which they both readily agreed.

Genea, however, was not so easy to please. She wanted to pretend she was a princess being escorted by Lord Danu and his men to Achtan on her way to visit her royal cousin, Princess Tristan, daughter of King Achal. Lord Danu and Artio smiled as she tried to sell them on the idea, but after all was said and done, she agreed to play the role of Lord Danu's niece.

Tellio and Kivas positioned themselves in the lead of the caravan. Harlow and Genea waited behind them on their mounts. Thorn stood between their horses, waiting patiently for Renn to say his final goodbyes to his family.

Renn blinked to fight back the tears that threatened to fill his eyes when he climbed on Thorn's saddle. He wiped his nose and turned to wave goodbye to his mother, sister, and brother as they rode west in the white carriage toward Leedsdale.

Thorn shook his beautiful white mane and whinnied in response to Renn's somber emotions. Renn sent a thought to turn and fall into formation with the others, and Thorn obeyed without a physical signal. No pulling of reins or pressing of his knees was necessary for the great white horse to respond to his wishes.

Lord Danu surveyed his small company from the back of his mount. "Is everyone ready?"

"What about Jomard and Raven?" Renn asked. "Aren't we going to wait for them to get back?"

"They will catch up with us on the way. We'll be staying on the main road until we reach Achtan, and I doubt Raven will be fooled by our disguises."

Lord Danu gave the signal, and the group began their long journey, heading directly into the rising sun until they hit the main road, then followed the thoroughfare southeast into the thick forest that covered the foothills of the Hebät Mountain Range. Lord Danu sent Lahar ahead to scout, and the solider and his horse disappeared into the trees. Tellio and Kivas told jokes and laughed while Lord Danu led the group at a steady, unhurried pace.

A beautifully unusual and dense forest crowded the road to Achtan—unusual because of the unlikely combination of both deciduous and evergreen trees growing side by side. The air was cool under the canopy of leaves and smelled of pine. In a month's time, the pine smell would be mixed with the musty smell of dried and falling leaves from the seasonal broad-leafed trees.

Renn looked down at the road. The hard-packed dirt was dark and rich with the nutrients that fed the roots of the beautiful forest trees. As he looked over the muscular shoulders of his young white stallion, he patted his horse on the neck. During the two years he and Artio were in hiding, Thorn had been his only close friend. The Meskhoni tried to be his friend, but he was more like a father to Renn, and he didn't always understand how Renn felt. Thorn, however, always listened to Renn talk about his fears, likes, dislikes, girls, and other things Artio didn't seem to understand too well.

The thought of girls reminded him of his experience the night before with Genea. He looked up and caught her watching him. Her face reddened, and she kicked her horse ahead of the two boys. Renn thought about what his mother said the day before. If Genea liked him, she sure didn't act like it.

Renn leaned toward Harlow to comment on Genea's strange behavior and realized his newfound friend was clinging, white-knuckled, to the horn of his saddle. The boy's eyes were wide with fear, and his stare was locked straight down at the gelding's neck.

"What's the matter with you?" Renn asked, chuckling.

"Huh?" Harlow jerked his head up to respond, then as if fearing for his balance, quickly looked back to his horse.

"Haven't you ridden before?"

"A little bit," he said.

"Would you like a few pointers?" Renn was glad to have something to do to keep his mind from wandering. Soon, Kivas and Sela Nadgit joined the effort to train Harlow. Before they knew it, they were nearly falling off their own horses with laughter as Harlow attempted the suggestions each offered.

They stopped shortly before sundown and set up camp a hundred paces off the main road in a small clearing surrounded by pine trees and thick shrubs. Lahar had found the location during one of his scouting excursions earlier that evening, and because a river was nearby, Lord Danu decided to stop there for the night. They organized their camp with the tents near one edge of the clearing in a semicircle around a fire pit.

Olosa broke out his pots and pans and began working on dinner once Sela and Durham got the fire going. Durham went about his work very stoically. He wasn't grumpy; he just didn't say much. And he always had a serious expression on his face. Sela, on the other hand, loved to joke and tease, and by the time the fire was ready for Olosa to use, the rosy-cheeked cook was at his wit's end.

"Sela," he said, shaking a stirring spoon at the young blacksmith. "If you don't get out of here and leave me alone, I'm going to burn your dinner to a crisp. Then we'll see how funny you are."

"You mean you do that to my food on purpose?" Sela said. "I thought that was just the way you cook."

"It's not my cooking that's at fault. The blacksmith who made these pots and pans didn't temper the metal correctly and everything sticks to them." He returned, knowing full well that Sela had made them.

"That's not what you said last—"

"You two, shut up." Kivas stepped between the young blacksmith and the cook. "I'm starving to death, and two of the horses need to have their shoes checked. You might have to replace one or two of them, Sela."

"Probably the same two shoes you replaced yesterday," Olosa said.

"Very funny, old man," Sela said and jumped aside to avoid the potato that came flying through the air at him. Renn laughed as he watched. It made him feel more comfortable to see this side of the men with whom he traveled.

"You got any of that coffee ready yet?" Kivas asked Olosa as Sela left to tend to the horses that were picketed on the opposite side of the clearing from the tents.

"That I do, Lieutenant," Olosa said as he reached for a pot and poured the dark liquid into a tin cup. "I always have a sack of good Valdivar coffee beans close by."

"I don't like the thought of supporting the Valdivar nobility, but pour me a cup of that, too," Lahar said as he joined them.

"What's wrong with the Valdivar nobility?" Renn asked.

Lahar took a sip of his coffee and studied Renn for a moment with his dark brown eyes. "For starters, they are arrogant and convinced they're better than the rest of Lemuria. King Reollyn doesn't really care about his citizens, and neither does the rest of the noble class. As long as they have their feasts and fine Valdivar wine, they are content to let the common folk starve."

"I didn't know you were so politically minded," Lord Danu said, joining the men at the fire and taking a cup of coffee from Olosa.

"I'm not," Lahar said. "My family left Valdivar when I was a boy because their farms kept getting raided by Tiaronéa Devi tribes and the Valdivarian nobles were too busy with their social gatherings to do anything about it. Of course, they still wanted their taxes."

"There you are, Renn," Harlow said, walking out of the trees from a path near the horses. "I've been down to the riverbank. You should come with me; there's a great swimming hole, and I bet we could catch lots of fish there—how long do you think we'll be staying here anyway?"

"Boy, you sure talk fast," Renn said.

"Yeah, I know. That's what everybody tells me. My ma and da always said one day—"

"You're doing it again," Renn said, cutting him off with a wave of his hand. Lord Danu and the others chuckled.

"Oh yeah, sorry." Harlow flushed. "Come on, let's go down to the river."

After a swim in the brisk water and a good meal of sourdough bread and stew, Renn was ready for bed. The long day of travel had taken its toll on him, and he felt as though he could fall asleep standing up. As he walked toward the tent set up for him and Harlow, a commotion in the trees behind camp caught his attention.

"It's only us, Beruth. Put down that sword before you hurt someone." Renn recognized Jomard's voice immediately.

"Jomard, I'm glad you found us," Renn said as he hurried to the farmer's side. "I didn't expect you and Captain Raven to catch up to us for a few days yet."

"How did you finish your preparations so quickly?" Lord Danu asked as he and the others left the fire to join Renn, Raven, and the tall farmer.

"Jomard is . . . unusually prepared," Raven said.

Lord Danu looked at his captain with one eyebrow raised.

"Preparation is a trait of all good farmers, milord." Jomard puffed out his chest and smiled.

"What did you tell your wife?" Artio asked as he joined the small gathering.

"I said I ran into Captain Raven while hunting, and he told me he was on his way to investigate claims of gold in the Hebät Mountains. I suggested she visit her mother while I try my hand at panning for gold this fall."

Artio harrumphed. "Sounds pretty good. Do you think she bought it?"

"Absolutely," Jomard said with an emphatic nod. "She knows I have a bit of wanderlust, and she's been at me to visit her mother for some time now."

"It's getting late," Lord Danu said. "We all need plenty of rest before morning. If we want to reach Achtan this month, we have to travel hard and long every day."

"Leave it to Lord Danu to remind us of duty," Kivas replied as he turned back toward the dying cooking fire.

"We didn't expect you tonight," Artio said, "so we didn't prepare a tent, Jomard. But my tent is larger than necessary. You're welcome to sleep there."

"Thank you, Meskhoni. I didn't feel like setting up camp after traveling all day." Artio and Jomard headed to the Mage's tent, and as the rest were dispersing for the night, Lord Danu gave assignments for night watch—assigning Beruth first shift.

Renn walked toward his tent, then realized he had some pressing business to attend to. He turned into the nearby trees, walked a short distance from camp, and relieved himself.

Renn looked up into the black sky and wondered at the billions of stars. The moon hadn't risen yet, and without the light of the cooking fire to hinder his vision the night sky became vividly clear. He walked aimlessly for a moment, then, finding a dead log, sat to gaze at the stars and think. Not long after, soft voices caught his attention. He knew eavesdropping was impolite, but after all, he was here first, and it wasn't his fault if he accidentally heard something he wasn't intended to hear.

"And all I know is either he's a very unusual farmer or he's hiding something." Renn had only heard Raven speak a few times, but even without seeing his face, he recognized the steady, confident voice. "You covered your tracks pretty good, Danu. Jomard followed my lead, but I could tell he could've easily found you without my help. And the last couple hours we tracked through the dark. No ordinary man could do that without training."

"Maybe you're overthinking this, Raven," Lord Danu said, chuckling softly. "Maybe he learned to track this well by hunting."

"And maybe Ba Aven's turning to the light." It surprised Renn to hear Raven answer with sarcasm. He didn't think the man had a sense of humor at all. Raven was, apparently, a different person when he was alone with Lord Danu. "I think we should watch him closely, that's all."

"You're probably right," Lord Danu said. "Just don't make it so obvious. Jomard has been a loyal subject, and he's always willing to help us out. I see no reason to upset him over our suspicions."

The two men left, and soon after Renn stole back into camp. Lord Danu and Raven didn't need to be so concerned about Jomard; Renn had known him his entire life. Jomard was only a simple farmer who wanted to help his friends. *He just knows these forests well enough to see things others would miss,* Renn thought as he crawled into his canvas tent.

CITY OF THE AVUMAN

Renn and the company traveled hard for the next three weeks, breaking camp at dawn and riding until well after sundown. As a result, they entered the forests surrounding Achtan in what Artio termed to be an acceptable amount of time. For the past several days, they had met more and more travelers on the road either going to or coming from Achtan.

Renn had been here once before, but still, for the last two days of the journey, he was overwhelmed with the beauty and health of the land. Even though Achtan's latitude was similar to Leedsdale's, Achtan's higher altitude made the climate much different. The forests surrounding the capital city of Achtland felt cool and pleasantly humid.

Renn watched Harlow's and Genea's reactions to the land with some amusement. He remembered how astonished he had been the first time he traveled this land. The trees crowded together in a combination of hardwood and pine that were taller and denser than at the beginning of their travels. The undergrowth teemed with lush ferns and flowering bushes. A kaleidoscope of colors and fragrances assailed them from every direction. The deep green of the leaves and undergrowth was dotted with dark red, purple, yellow, violet, and gold from blossoms that filled the air with rich, aromatic flavor. Bees and hummingbirds busied themselves around the flowers. Raccoons, beavers, squirrels, and other wildlife scurried in the trees and through the bushes. And what Renn's eyes missed, his ears heard—turning the woods into a symphony of birdsong and the drone of insects. Renn imagined Valhasgar of the afterlife must look a lot like the forests of Achtan.

Now that they were approaching Achtan, Genea rode on the wagon with Lord Danu and Artio. The soldiers all looked like hired mercenaries, half riding in front of the entourage and half trailing protectively behind. Although they didn't expect any trouble in or near the City of Avuman, Lord Danu wanted to keep their identity secret all the same. Renn and Harlow rode in front of the wagon but behind the front row of soldiers.

"What do the Avuman look like?" Harlow asked Renn. "I mean, are they tall and skinny? Do they really have pointed ears and high eyebrows, and do they run around in the trees and play practical jokes like all the legends say, or do they act just like we do? I heard somebody once say the Avuman never existed, but someone else swore that they saw them once and my ma said she didn't know, but I think—"

"Harlow, by the time you finish talking, I won't be able to remember your question," Renn said.

"Oh." Harlow flushed. "I'm doing it again, aren't I?"

"Yes, but that's just you, don't worry about it. As far as what the Avuman look like, I don't know. I don't think anybody really does. Artio said the Avuman disappeared from Lemuria a thousand years ago.

"Then why do people call Achtan the City of Avuman?"

"Don't you know anything, Harlow?" Genea piped in from the wagon behind them. "The Avuman used to live in the forests of Achtland; Achtan wasn't even built back then. Some of the Avuman married humans, and their children supposedly built the city after the Avuman disappeared. It's all a lot of nonsense, of course, nothing more than children's stories."

Renn looked at Harlow and rolled his eyes at Genea's pretentious explanation, and the two boys started laughing.

"What's so funny?" Genea asked, with a hint of accusation in her voice.

"Oh, nothing," Renn lied.

They rounded a bend in the road, and the towers of Achtan became visible for the first time. The tall, narrow spires emanated an alabaster gleam in the afternoon sun. Nestled between hills and surrounded by trees, the city disappeared and reappeared as the road wound its way through thick forest.

Before long, they drew near enough to make out the ancient-looking white stone walls surrounding the beautiful, tall spires. Sentries wearing green uniforms walked back and forth atop the parapets. Colorful flags adorned the corners of the walls, as well as many of the taller spires in the glistening city. They were close enough for Renn to see the flags were forest green and gold, but the design was still difficult to distinguish. From his past visit, however, he knew the flag brandished a golden eagle clutching an arrow in its claws—testifying of Achtan's legendary archers—with an oak leaf above each wing, symbolizing strength.

They emerged from the forest into a cleared area that encircled the city. A dozen or more other roads materialized from the surrounding forests to converge, like theirs, with the main road that led to the city gates. The enormous oak gates were drawn open, as they always were during the day in times of peace, and sentries stood on either side, supervising the comings and goings of the visitors of the great city.

"It seems to me they don't have nearly enough sentries," Lahar said, appraising the city's defenses. "A good-sized army could break out of the forest and overrun the gates before they could form any real resistance."

"They've been watching us for the past two days," Raven said. "They wouldn't be caught off guard."

"And you can bet they've got plenty of archers in the forest to mount a large-scale ambush," Cole added.

"I haven't seen anybody watching us," Harlow said.

"Raven's probably the only one who has, Harlow," Lord Danu said. "The archers of Achtland move like ghosts in these forests."

"These walls are solid enough to withstand a formidable assault should an army ever make it this far," Durham observed as they drew closer.

No one stopped them as they passed under the gatehouse, nor did they draw unusual attention as they made their way down the crowded, cobbled streets of Achtan.

Harlow's eyes went wide with apparent wonder from the moment they entered the city, and they never went back to normal. Each time they entered a plaza where roads converged, his black curly hair bounced and bobbed as he whipped his head back and forth to take in the colorful shop fronts and loud merchants peddling their wares.

"Oooh." Genea stood and pointed at a young lady carrying colorful bolts of cloth. "Look how pretty those are."

The woman saw her excitement and pushed up to the wagon. "Would the young lady like to see a sample of my cloth? It's made of the finest threads and dyed six times so the color will stay true."

"No, thank you." Lord Danu pulled Genea back into her seat.

"Look how pretty those flower bouquets are." Genea stood again, and the flower girl rushed to the wagon.

"Flowers for the pretty girl?"

"No, no. Thank you anyway," Danu said and pulled Genea back down. "Don't point at every pretty object or we'll be stuck in the markets for hours."

Artio chuckled. "Well, she is the niece of a wealthy merchant. I'd say she's playing the part pretty well."

"Look at all these people, Renn," Harlow said. "I've never seen such a crowd, and they all look so strange. My ma told me that people from other places looked different, but I never believed it until now, and just smell that fresh bread. Maybe we can—"

"Stop, Harlow," Renn said. "Didn't you hear what Lord Danu said to Genea?"

Harlow shook his head.

"I didn't think so." Renn pointed to a group of large men. "Those men are from Nortia. You can tell by how they wear dark beards with no mustache. Most of the people with tan skin and plain clothing are from Boranica—they probably look *normal* to you."

"What about the rest?"

Renn shrugged his shoulders. "I'm not sure."

"Where are all these people from?" Harlow turned and asked Artio. "I didn't know this many people existed in the whole world, let alone in one city."

"That's because you've been on a small farm your whole life, Harlow," Artio said. "They come from all over Lemuria; Achtan is a popular city. Merchants love it because there are always people willing to pay top dollar for their goods. Tourists come here simply because it's so beautiful and exciting, and it's the only big city for hundreds of miles in any direction."

"Where do you think those men are from?" Genea asked, pointing to three men wearing rich, dark, full-length tunics that had simple yet elegantly embroidered gold borders. Each wore a sword at his side with a jeweled pommel, supported over the shoulder by a dark leather baldric. They were average in height and size, but their thin, trimmed beards and mustaches were a distinctive trait that separated them from others.

"Those, if I am not mistaken, are emissaries from Kah-Tarku, Kahaal—the birthplace of Kahn Devin." Renn and others in the group tensed noticeably at the mention of Kahn Devin, but Lord Danu only chuckled.

"You don't need to worry about that. As Artio knows, most people of Kahaal aren't fond of our dear Mr. Devin. They see him as a traitor of sorts."

"Why is that?" Harlow asked. "Do they worship the gods of light in Kahaal?"

"They don't care much about any of the gods in Kahaal. Kahn Devin betrayed them, because had he stayed, he would have eventually been their king. He was heir apparent when he left for Elder Island to be trained in the Azur-Lore. Many thought he would one day be their greatest king ever."

"So when he abandoned the Azur-Lore and dedicated his life to the demon lord," Renn surmised, "they felt he abandoned them, too."

"Exactly," the young lord nodded.

Tellio let out a low whistle and rubbed his hand absently over his bald head. "Well, well," he said. "Where do you suppose they're from, Kivas?" Kivas, and everybody else in the company, looked in the direction of the big man's gaze to see a group of tall, beautiful women. They wore far less clothing than other women Renn had seen—loose skirts, reaching midthigh; cropped, sleeveless tops that left their stomachs bare; covered by a sheer, lightweight gown that fell just below their knees.

Their bodies were young, strong, and well-proportioned. Their skin was tan, their hair long and full, and their eyes were big—that was noticeable even at a distance. Renn felt himself blush and quickly averted his eyes. He noticed as he looked away that Genea practically glowered at the exotic foreigners.

"I think I'll go ask them myself," Tellio announced, twisting his waxed mustache to a tighter curl. "Care to join me, Kivas?"

"I wouldn't recommend it," Raven said..

Tellio cocked his head and looked at Raven with raised eyebrows. "Why not?"

"Watch." Raven pointed to a group of Nortian men who obviously had the same idea as Tellio and were heading toward the tall, captivating women. Four of them approached the scantily clad women, and although Renn couldn't hear them for the crowd, he could tell whatever the first man said to the women was not well received. The three women didn't even acknowledge him. The big man who spoke grew red in the face, grabbed the nearest girl by the shoulder, and swung her around.

"Hey!" Both Tellio and Durham shouted at the same time, and they jumped off their horses as if they intended to rush through the crowd and help the woman.

"Hold and watch." Raven held up his hand.

The woman let her arm arc with the momentum of being spun around by the Nortian and hit him across the cheekbone with a knife-hand strike. The man's eyes widened in apparent surprise at the counterattack, and he stumbled backward. Her bare foot came down on his knee, and he dropped to the ground.

"Great gods of light!" Kivas exclaimed. "If I didn't see it, I'd never believe it."

Tellio got a grin on his face. But before he could tease Kivas about a Nortian being bested by a woman, the man on the ground pulled himself up and drew his sword. Quick as a flash, the object of his attentions produced a small knife from underneath her light gown and let it fly. The big Nortian grasped wildly at his neck as he fell, once again, to the ground.

The companions of the unfortunate man recovered from their initial shock and warily drew their own weapons. Before anything more happened, however, a small dispatch of city guards surrounded the foreigners and took them into custody.

"I see what you mean, Raven," Tellio admitted.

"Who were they?" Kivas asked.

"Your fellow countrymen, of course," Sela Nadgit said, as he stopped his horse next to the front of the wagon that carried Lord Danu, Artio, and Genea. Genea, Renn noticed, now beamed with pride, whereas a moment before she had seemed upset with the strange women.

"I know who the men were, Sela. I want to know where those girls came from."

"Domeria," Artio said. "Probably from the jungle city of Tanith."

"Where is Domeria?" Harlow asked. "Is it in Lemuria? My father told me about lands across the Drbal Divide; is it across the sea or—ouch!" Renn leaned over and slugged Harlow in the shoulder, then silenced him with a stern look and a shake of his head.

"Domeria is the southernmost country in Lemuria, Harlow," Artio continued. "It's mostly dense jungle, but there are a few cities, and it has a unique system of government."

"How so?" Tellio asked.

"Women rule it."

"Women *rule*?" Kivas and Tellio both repeated, slack-jawed.

"And what's wrong with that?" Genea looked down her nose at the men. "If more women had control, this world would be a much better place to live."

"It just . . . isn't natural," Kivas stammered. "I mean, women can't govern . . . they should be cooking or . . . what about the men in Domeria? Have they no pride?"

"Men are property—slaves and concubines," Raven said, joining the conversation once again.

"Property? To *women*?" Kivas's eyes were wide, and his voice dripped with incredulity.

"That doesn't sound too bad," Olosa said thoughtfully. "I wouldn't mind cooking for those lovely ladies. No doubt they'd appreciate it more than the lot I'm slavin' for now."

The sinking sun fell behind the tall white buildings of the city, casting pointed shadows across the cobblestone roads, when Lord Danu stopped at a large inn a short distance from the palace. He arranged several large rooms for the men to share and one small room for Genea, then sent an inn boy to deliver a letter to the palace.

Renn, Harlow, Jomard, and Artio settled in one of the large rooms. After each took a long-overdue bath, they joined the rest of the group in the common room for dinner. All the soldiers except Durham sat around two tables in the middle of the crowded room, talking loudly and drinking ale. Durham sat at a booth next to the wall with Lord Danu and Raven, content to relax and watch the scene around him.

Jomard took the last remaining seat at the table of soldiers next to Kivas—it pleased Renn to see his long-time neighbor beginning to fit in and gain the trust of the others. Renn, Artio, Harlow, and Genea chose the only vacant table in the house, which sat between Lord Danu's booth and his soldier's tables.

The common room had a large fireplace built into one wall, and it radiated heat, as well as smoke, into the inadequately lit room, giving it the appearance of a tavern instead of a proper inn. Men playing cards, dice, or any other game they could gamble on occupied most of the other tables. Renn noticed Genea wrinkle her nose as she surveyed the room, but in his travels with Artio the past couple years, Renn had seen worse.

A serving girl with blonde hair, an angular face, and slightly arched brows made her way past the wanton gazes and lewd propositions of the patrons to their table.

"Welcome to the Golden Eagle. What'll you have?"

"I'd like a glass of wine," Artio said, "juice for these three, and four dinner specials."

After the barmaid left, Genea said, "That girl was pretty, Artio. Where is she from?"

"She's probably a local."

"She's an Avuman?" Harlow asked, his voice rising in pitch.

"No, but she's probably a distant relative of the Avuman."

"The Avuman aren't real. They're just make-believe," Genea said.

"That's true now," the Meskhoni agreed. "However, at one time, this land was peopled by the Avuman—before Greyfel's time. In fact, some say they were here during the war between the gods."

A loud thud and crashing noise from the center of the room made Renn jump in his seat. He turned, along with everyone else, to see what had caused the noise. The raucous inn turned quiet.

A woman wearing breeches and a shirt held her boot on the chest of a fat man who was lying on the floor with the point of her sword against his throat. Her hair was long and brown, and her skin was tan. She had a hint of the angular features found in the local people, but she didn't look like the locals Renn had seen—she was taller. She reminded him a bit of the Domerian women they saw earlier, except she was fully dressed and not quite as tall.

She glared at the man on the floor and said something too quiet for Renn to hear. Then she turned and walked to a table on the far side of the room. The fat man on the floor glared at her as he stood up. But his anger turned to embarrassment as the other men at his table started to laugh and tease him.

"He won't live that little episode down for a while," Kivas said.

"I've decided to leave the women in Achtan for other men," Tellio mused aloud as he twisted his long mustache.

The front door opened, and a tall, thin man in black hose, a black jerkin, and a forest-green cloak entered, flanked by two royal guards. The crowd noise dropped to a murmur, then died as the patrons recognized and stared at the newcomers.

As the thin man in black pulled a paper from his jerkin pocket, the fat man who was humiliated by the woman in men's clothes only minutes ago pushed by him and hurried out the door. The messenger stumbled and glared at the door as if considering whether he should send his contingency after the lout to bring him back. Instead, he turned back to the people in the room and straightened his cloak.

"I'm looking for the merchant Davon," he announced.

Lord Danu looked at Artio, who squinted as he studied the man and then nodded.

Lord Danu stood. "I am Davon of Boria City."

"I have a message from the palace regarding your request for an audience with his majesty, King Achal." He promptly withdrew a wrapped parchment from underneath his cloak, sealed with a glob of dark green wax, and handed it to Lord Danu. Then, as abruptly as he came, he and the guards turned and left.

The murmuring noise of patrons returned, and soon the room bustled again with gaming and laughter.

Lord Danu turned over the letter and studied the seal. "It's authentic," he said.

"What does he say?" Artio asked. "There hasn't been a delay, has there?"

"No, no delay. He asks for you, 'the page, Renn,' and me to see him first thing in the morning. He wants to talk with us before we pick up the special . . . cargo."

ALEAH

Aleah watched the old man and children come down the stairs and sit at the only vacant table in the main room of the Golden Eagle. The boy with sandy blond hair was probably Renn, she decided. At least she hoped he wasn't the skinny boy with black curly hair who hadn't stopped talking since they entered the room.

Aleah sat alone at a table in the back where she had a clear view of the door and the entire room. The smell of sweaty men mingled with roasting pig permeated the hazy air. She recognized Lord Danu from both her mother's and King Achal's description of him. His shoulder-length blond hair and sun-browned skin made him stand out in Achtland. His frequent smile and different-colored eyes also fit his description—one blue and the other brown. She assumed the solemn-looking dark-haired man sitting next to him was the legendary Raven. She'd never met him, but she'd heard plenty of stories from mercenaries and soldiers about him.

"Hey, wench." A whiny voice cut above the noise. "Hey, wench, I'm talking to you. Where's your dress?" A group of men a few tables away from her laughed, and she realized the comment had been directed at her. She raised her mug of tea and glared at the men as she took a long sip—she never drank ale while she was working.

"I bet you'd pretty right up in one of my missus's dresses." The man shouting at her had thinning black hair and hadn't shaved for at least a week. His round face and forehead glistened with a sheen of sweat, even though the room wasn't very hot. The men playing cards with him chuckled.

One of his friends said, "Your missus's dresses would fall right off that skinny thing."

"Why do you think I want to see her try 'em on?" the first man retorted. "What with my missus gone to see her mother, now would be the perfect time for us to get acquainted." At this, all the men at his table broke out in raucous laughter.

Worthless drylander dogs, Aleah thought as she set her mug back on the table. She wouldn't respond to vermin like them. They weren't worth the energy. She'd learned silence was usually the most powerful reproach for men like that. She could still hear voices jeering and laughing, but they'd soon tire of their sport. Instead, she watched Lord Danu's men—especially Raven.

Most of Lord Danu's soldiers weren't paying attention to anything but their ale and food. Occasionally, they'd glance around the room, but they clearly allowed Raven to be their eyes and ears. *A bad sign,* she thought. *Those soldiers are getting lazy. They're too used to having Raven watch out for trouble.*

She wondered how closely Raven watched and what would escape his notice. Perhaps a girl walking close enough to cut Renn's throat wouldn't raise his concern until too late. She decided to test it. She finished her tea and rose from her seat.

She walked forward, and Raven shifted and watched her for a moment—then apparently decided she wasn't a threat because he looked away. She headed straight toward Renn's table, but as she passed the men who were jeering at her a moment before, the sweaty fat one who started it all said something and grabbed her butt.

Instinctively, Aleah spun, pushed the man's head back, and kicked out the legs of his chair. As he crashed to the floor, his back hit with a thud, air exploded from his lungs, and he lost his wind. Before he could move, she had a boot on his chest and her sword point pressed against his throat.

The room fell silent, and she knew if she looked around, all eyes would be on her. She could feel her heart racing the way it always did during a fight, but this pompous piece of filth made it personal by touching her where she allowed no man to touch. So much for her little experiment with Raven—he'd certainly pay attention to her now if she approached Renn.

She glared at the sweaty man on the floor—he was gasping and stammering some nonsense apology, but Aleah didn't care. She would've enjoyed cutting his blubbery neck, but she couldn't afford to draw any more attention to herself.

"Touch me again and my sword will rest on the other side of your throat," she said through clenched teeth. She pushed on the hilt until she saw blood start to trickle down his unshaven neck, then calmly slid the blade into the scabbard on her back and returned to her table.

※

Soya clutched at his throat where a moment ago the girl had pressed the tip of her sword. He saw blood on his hand when he pulled it away but not much. The others at the table laughed uncontrollably as he struggled to get off the floor. His rotund stomach made it difficult to just sit back up, so he had to roll over and push himself off the ground.

"Shut up!" he hissed at the three men he was playing cards with as he righted his chair and sat back down. The other gamblers quieted a little, but even though Grylon hid his face behind his cards, his shoulders bounced up and down.

"Perhaps you should stick with prostitutes, Soya," Jonith said with a smirk.

"At least the only time they'll hurt you is if you don't pay," Grylon chimed in, and the whole table erupted with laughter once more.

Soya clenched his teeth and pounded the table with his fist, causing his stack of coins to fall over. "I said shut up!" He wiped at the sweat trickling down his round cheeks with his dirty palm and hastily gathered his coins from the table. He wouldn't be able to concentrate on cards now anyway. That wench in men's clothing was going to regret embarrassing him like that. And one way or another, he would get his way with her.

"Oh, come on, Soya," Nevon pleaded. "You can't leave now. Give me a chance to win some of my money back."

"Forget it," Soya said with more venom than he'd intended, then spun on his heels and stomped away. He could still hear them laughing as he pushed his way past the pompous royal herald and his two guards who just walked in the door.

The cool night air and the breeze off the mountains was a welcome change from the crowded room. Soya stood in the cobblestone street and considered his course of action. *There are too many people out to simply ambush the whore on the street,* he thought. So instead he ducked into the dark alley between the Golden Eagle Inn and a shop that sold blown-glass trinkets. The shadows in the alley would hide him and still allow a clear view of the street.

He thought it likely the girl would walk down the street past the alley and not the other direction, since the other way led to the poor quarters of town. Even though she wore breeches like a man, she wasn't poor. The weapons she carried were expensive; at least her sword was certainly made of fine steel and good workmanship—he had plenty of opportunity to notice that lying on his back on the floor of the inn.

He clenched his jaw and cracked his knuckles, thinking about how she humiliated him. He would enjoy forcing his way upon that girl and then killing her slowly. She took him by surprise at the inn, but he wouldn't be fooled twice. He'd wait for the right moment and grab her from behind. *We'll see how brave she is with a knife pressed against her throat.*

The side entrance to the blown-glass shop provided a great spot in the alley to hide and wait. Two steps led down to a door set far enough back into the wall to cast dark shadows. A mother cat and her kittens had already claimed the spot he wanted, but that problem was easily remedied with a hard kick that sent the animal sliding across the alley. Her five kittens soon joined her in much the same fashion.

Soya wiped his palms on his dirty breeches, then reached inside his jacket and pulled out a flask filled with rum and settled in to wait. He'd just barely stoppered his rum and put it back when he heard the door of the inn open and close. He didn't expect her to leave so soon, but she did. What astonished him more was she didn't walk down the open street.

Instead, she turned up the same alley where he hid. *What luck*, he thought. *This is going to be easier than I imagined.*

He slid his knife from his belt and wiped his sweaty palms on his pants. The arrogant girl walked quickly and confidently down the alley, but she hesitated just before she reached his hiding spot. Soya held his breath and didn't move, but she only paused a moment and then started again—he was certain she hadn't seen him.

He hurried from the shadows just as she passed and grabbed her with his left arm and pressed her back tight against him so she couldn't move. But as he tried to position his knife against her throat, she grabbed his wrist with her right hand, dug her boot into his left shin, and spun from his hold. She kept a hold on his wrist as she spun and pulled, forcing his arm to go straight. Her left arm swung upward in a circular motion and hit him under his elbow with an open-palm strike.

He heard his arm break before he felt the pain and knew he'd dropped the knife. She released her grip, and Soya grabbed at his broken arm. The girl dropped low and did a sweep kick that flipped his legs out from under him and sent him sprawling to his back.

Then she was standing over him, but something was wrong. He couldn't move. He tried to speak but only a gurgling sound escaped his mouth. He felt something warm and wet running down his neck and then saw the long silver blade of her sword.

"I warned you the next time my blade would rest on the other side of your throat," was all she said. Soya tried to reply, but he could do nothing except look up. At least his arm was no longer in pain. The girl was growing distant now . . . blurry and dark. Then everything went dark, and his pain ended.

⋈⋈⋈

Aleah shook her head as she pulled the sword from the man's throat and wiped the blood on his jacket.

"Stupid fool," she muttered as she sheathed her blade. She watched the blood pool around his head, then turned and continued on her way. She wasn't too upset about killing this man, but she couldn't help wondering if he'd had children who depended on him. After all, in the inn he'd goaded her by saying he wanted to see her in his missus's dresses—the pig might have had children with the woman. Oh well—if he did, they would be better off without him.

She hurried down the alley without another thought for the man she left behind. Before she stepped into the next dark street, she stopped in the shadows to listen and watch. This road wasn't patrolled very often, even though low-grade brothels and taverns lined the far side. Mostly thieves and unsavory characters spent their time here, and if a few of them disappeared, the throne wasn't too concerned—at least not enough to risk the lives of the guards it would take to keep it safe.

She saw no immediate danger, so she crossed the cracked, cobbled road and continued down the street. She had to step over a couple unconscious drunks on her way but didn't come across any trouble. She headed toward another alley next to the Archer's Alehouse—a rundown tavern. She ignored the giggling prostitute and her drunken customer standing at the corner and cautiously stepped into the dark.

A stairway near the back of the alley led down to a locked door. She gave three slow, solid knocks and waited. A small section of the door slid open, and a pair of beady black eyes peered out at her. The looking hole slid shut, and she heard several locks unlatching; finally, the door cracked open just enough for her to slip inside.

She walked along a narrow, dark hallway, down a flight of stairs, and through another door that had to be unlocked from the other side. The door opened to a small, dimly lit room that served as a waiting room. Two Domerian warriors stood in front of a door on the far side of the room. Each girl held a javelin, but Aleah knew both would also have several throwing knives hidden about their person—despite the lack of substantial clothing they wore. Aleah dressed that way at home, but never among the drylanders here in the north. The women bowed to her as she approached and opened the door for her.

"Ah, Aleah." A beautiful woman in traditional Domerian garb greeted her as she entered. The woman had dark, full hair and sun-browned skin, which was quite visible under the gossamer covering she wore over her short skirt and top wrap that left her tight belly completely exposed. A gold-trimmed conch shell necklace adorned her neck, and she lounged on a white chair with one leg propped over a red cushioned armrest. She absently scratched behind the ears of an old black panther that sat on her right side.

"Hello, Mother," Aleah answered with a bow.

"I see you got my message." Her mother kissed her fingertips and held them out. Aleah kissed her own fingertips and pressed them to her mother's. She motioned for Aleah to sit on an overstuffed velvet pillow next to her. "Jinwen just made a pot of cool tea . . . Would you care for some?"

"Thank you, Mother."

A bald eunuch, wearing nothing but a white robe and a thick leather headband with a large emerald set in the center, stepped from the shadows and poured a cup of tea, then handed it to Aleah with a deep bow.

"You know," Aleah said as she accepted the tea with a nod to her mother's high servant, "you really don't have to find the most disreputable spot in Achtan for lodging, Mother. After all, King Achal would be very pleased to entertain Queen Leandril of Domeria."

"Yes, I'm sure he would," the older woman replied. "Wouldn't it be great to see his face if he knew I was in town and staying in such filthy accommodations?" Her musical laugh rang out, and Aleah just shook her head.

"Strange things amuse you, Mother."

"Be that as it may, I don't want Achal to suspect who you are or that I am involved." Queen Leandril set her empty teacup on the silver platter that Jinwen held. "If he saw the two of us together, he may notice the resemblance. Or perhaps one of his servants would hear us speaking when we thought we were alone. Not to mention the fact that all palaces are infested with spies and the like. Speaking of which, does he suspect you?"

"I highly doubt it." Aleah shook her head and screwed up her face. "I think he's actually starting to like me . . . in a romantic kind of way."

"Perhaps you should pursue that. It's much easier to control a man from his bed, you know."

"Mother, that's disgusting."

The queen's musical laugh rang out again. "Why? After all, he isn't your full brother . . . just half."

"You have a very warped sense of humor, Mother," Aleah said. "You are joking . . . aren't you?"

Her mother laughed again and said, "Of course I am." Then she smiled and and got a far-off look in her eyes. "I'd love to see the look on his face when he discovers the woman he loves is his sister."

"I'd hardly say I'm the woman he loves, Mother," Aleah said with growing irritation. "He has been a bit flirtatious lately, that's all. Now, what did you come here for? I'm sure you wanted to talk about more than my prospects for romance."

"Yes, of course," her mother said. "Leave us, Jinwen."

He bowed deeply, backed out of the room, and closed the door behind him.

"The Child of the Blessing and his party have arrived," Aleah's mother said.

"Yes, I know. Achal sent me to assess Lord Danu's men. I was there just before I came to visit you . . . I assumed you'd want my judgment of them as well."

Queen Leandril nodded. "Very good. Oh that I had more agents with your foresight, Daughter." Aleah felt her face flush and was glad the lighting was dim. She didn't want her mother to know how important her praise was to her. "And what did you learn?"

"Not much." Aleah took another sip of tea. "His men probably fight well, but only Raven was alert. The rest seemed more interested in ale. Although an old man sat by Renn's side the entire time I watched them—he exuded an air of confidence."

"That would be Artio," her mother said. "He's a Mage and Renn's guardian these past years. Do you think you can convince Achal to let you join the group?"

"Is it absolutely necessary, Mother?" Aleah complained. "I really don't fancy being a babysitter for the next several months."

Queen Leandril's smile turned to a tight-lipped grin, and she nodded. "Yes, dear, the Oracle was very clear on that point. Unless you are in the party, our way of life *and* Domeria will be lost forever."

KING ACHAL

Renn had seen the palace once before but not from the inside. Last year, he and Artio had passed through Achtan during their travels. The outside was impressive enough—especially for someone accustomed to small farm villages—with its black, filigreed iron gates, lush gardens, and sky-touching, alabaster pinnacles. But the inside of the palace was magnificent.

Renn's jaw dropped the moment they walked through oak doors large enough for a horse-drawn wagon to pass through and entered the main hall. Sunlight seeped through stained glass windows that lined the outer side of the corridor and illuminated the long hallway. The colorful windows depicted the scene of a great battle fought thousands of years before between humans, dragons, and Avuman with their vibrant eyes and hair. Although the palace was centuries old, the stained glass colors had not faded.

Renn, Artio, and Lord Danu were escorted down the long corridor by two royal guards dressed in chain mail covered by forest-green cloaks that bore the symbol of their king—an eagle clutching an arrow in its claws.

Rich, deep green carpet covered the floor. Renn felt awkward walking on it because it looked so clean and exquisite. On both sides of the corridor, in strategic locations, sat hand-carved, cushioned divans. Their wooden legs and armrests were stained to a high gloss that brought out the undertones of red in the grain and contrasted nicely with the dark green cushions, which matched the green carpet exactly. The wall opposite the stained glass windows was painted plain white but decorated with beautifully framed oil paintings spaced strategically to catch the light.

Renn was so taken by the magnificent paintings he didn't notice the looming oak door at the end of the corridor until he stood directly in front of it. Sentries, armed with spears, stood guard on both sides of the ancient-looking door. One of their chaperone guards spoke to the sentries in a melodic language. The sentry on the right nodded and knocked on the solid door, which swung open quickly and silently on black iron hinges, belying its apparent mass. One of the sentries slipped through and closed it again.

Renn studied the faces of the other sentry and the guards as they waited to be admitted. Each had a narrow, angular jawline, arched brows, and pronounced cheekbones. *Maybe these people really did descend from the ancient Avuman,* Renn thought.

"It's been sixty years since I was last in this palace," Artio said to no one in particular. "It looks identical today."

Lord Danu looked around and nodded—as if he knew from personal experience what the Mage was talking about. The guards didn't respond. They looked straight ahead as though they had heard nothing.

The door soon swung open once more, and the guard who'd disappeared through it earlier signaled for them to enter. They were asked to remove their shoes, and Renn noticed the footwear of the royal guards was made of soft leather and probably never used outdoors. Their escorts took the lead once again, and Lord Danu, Artio, and Renn followed into the bright room and waited to be called forward.

Renn thought the outer courtyard and corridor were beautiful, but they did not prepare him for the exquisite beauty of the throne room. The oval-shaped room had a high, arched ceiling. Crystal chandeliers, brandishing three scores of candles each, hung in two rows of six on silver chains, adding brilliance to the natural light of the sun that radiated through stained glass murals that ran the entire length of either wall. The scene depicted on these windows was a panorama of virgin land, unmarred and untouched by mortal races. Renn thought it looked like a representation of Lemuria immediately following its creation.

Soft cream carpet blanketed the floor from wall to wall, except for a six-foot-wide path of forest-green carpet that extended from the great oak doors to the dais on the far side of the throne room. Two rows of dark-stained wooden benches were positioned in front and on either side of the intricately carved throne. The dark green cushions covering the benches matched the strip of carpet Renn and the others were standing on, which matched the color of the overstuffed cushion on the dais.

Men and women in fine clothing—nobles, Renn concluded—sat intermittently on the benches, whispering to one another and staring with unbridled curiosity at the three unlikely visitors who approached their king. A dozen guards, wearing light armor covered by forest-green cloaks, stood in strategic positions throughout the room, with two on either side of the throne.

Renn assimilated all these details in a moment's inspection, then his gaze shifted to the figure sitting on the dais. He scowled and pursed his lips. This couldn't be King Achal. King Achal had been king of Achtland for years, longer than Renn had been alive. The man sitting on the throne looked almost childlike, with soft brown hair and smooth skin, and arching eyebrows and high cheekbones that accentuated his thin, angular face.

He can't be more than twenty-five, Renn thought.

Renn looked first at Artio, then Lord Danu, with a silent question in his eyes. The first seemed to be lost in his thoughts, but Lord Danu returned Renn's look with a grin and an almost imperceptible nod that seemed to say, "I'll tell you about it later."

Then Renn noticed a woman in men's clothing standing to the left of and behind the king. It looked like the woman he saw last night in the tavern. Renn could see by Lord Danu's gaze and tight-lipped grimace that the young lord just recognized her, too.

Renn nearly jumped when a whiny voice from behind announced,

"Davon, merchant of Boria City, his grandfather, and his page wish to speak with His Highness, King Achal."

The king winced and gave the speaker an annoyed glance but, nodding his head and signaling with his hand, said, "Yes, yes. Let them approach the throne."

As they walked down the soft path, King Achal leaned toward an older man sitting to his right and said something, to which the man simply nodded. The advisor, as he seemed to be, had silver-gray hair that fell to his shoulders, and he wore a cream robe tied with a dark green sash.

"Maurer," Artio said under his breath. Renn looked at him quizzically and tilted his head slightly. "Achal's advisor," the Mage whispered. "Maurer the Wizard. He left the school about the time I arrived to study."

Renn stared wide-eyed at the man next to King Achal. He wanted to ask Artio why the Wizard looked younger than him but couldn't because they arrived in front of the king, and following Lord Danu's lead, Artio dropped to one knee and bowed his head.

King Achal sighed and impatiently said, "Rise, rise. The gods know I detest formalities."

Lord Danu grinned and in a voice dripping with melodrama said, "As you wish, Your Highness."

Achal winced and turned to a middle-aged man seated at a solid oak desk to his left. "Severin, cancel the remainder of my morning appointments. I'll be in the yard with the merchant Davon and his companions."

The secretary looked up from his books, and his mouth dropped open. "But . . . but, Majesty, you are scheduled to meet with the ambassador of Nortia next."

The young king broke into a broad grin. "Oh, that's too bad. I guess we'll have to reschedule him for next week."

The king rose from his dais, motioned for Lord Danu and company to follow, then almost as an afterthought said, "Maurer and Aleah, will you be joining us?" Neither gave a reply, but they both followed them to the inner courtyard. One of the guards who had escorted them to the throne room met them at the door and returned their footwear.

The courtyard was surrounded on three sides by the various wings of the white stone palace. A garden with stone pathways, sculpted fountains, crystal streams, colorful flowerbeds, and strong hardwood trees lay before them, stretching to the distant outer gates. The king led them past a fountain, around a bed of roses, and sat on a long stone bench underneath a large apple tree.

The king looked up, and his eyes sparkled as he smiled. "How was your journey, Lord Danu? And pray, introduce your companions to me."

"Uneventful, thankfully," Lord Danu said with a flourishing bow. "This is Artio, Mage and Meskhoni, and this is Renn, the promise of the prophecy, Your Majesty."

Renn looked around and bit his lips at this introduction. He had never been introduced as anything other than *Renn*.

"Please." Achal rolled his eyes. "Enough with the tedious titles and formality—call me Achal."

"His Majesty still isn't comfortable with the protocol of nobility," Maurer said in a deep, smooth voice. Aleah broke into an amused grin.

"I know." Lord Danu smiled. "Why do you think I insist on using it?"

"You're very wicked, *Marquis*." The young king returned the smile and emphasized the title. Lord Danu winced and scowled darkly. "Oh, I forgot," the king said in mock sympathy, "you don't fancy being called *Marquis*."

"Okay, okay." Danu held up his hands and laughed. "I'll stop calling you *Majesty* if you won't call me *Marquis*."

The king's eyebrows arched a little higher as he shifted his gaze to Renn. "So you're Renn. I've looked forward to meeting you, young man. Please, sit down."

The young king regarded Renn in an almost reverential manner that unnerved him and made him feel awkward. Why should the king of Achtland treat him so? There must be more to the prophecies, he decided, than Artio had led him to believe.

"Thank you, Your Majes . . . uh, I mean, Achal." Renn wrung his hands together and shot a glance at Lord Danu, who winked at him.

The king laughed at Renn's awkward reply, but he patted his leg as he sat down next to King Achal on the bench, making Renn feel much more relaxed.

"How does your kingdom fare these days?" Lord Danu asked, plucking a ripe apple from the tree and taking a loud, crunching bite. Renn saw a bit of juice drip down the young lord's chin. Renn could almost taste the sweet fruit in his mind, and his stomach growled.

The king shook his head. "Not as well as I'd like. The reason I brought you out here"—the king motioned at the surrounding garden—"is because I don't know who may be listening in my own court anymore."

"Spies?" Artio asked.

"Spies *and* traitors. Aleah and Maurer are the only two I trust anymore." King Achal nodded toward his advisors.

"Well, with so many nobles in that room, how do you expect to keep anything private?" Lord Danu plucked a second apple and tossed it to Renn.

"There was a time, Danu, when I could trust, without reserve, even the aristocratic elite. But Kahn Devin's influence has tainted my country."

"Do you think his spies know who we are?"

"Maybe." The king ran a hand through his hair. "That's why I sent Aleah to your inn last night—to be sure your company was safe."

"Yes. We saw her there." Lord Danu raised his right eyebrow as he looked at Aleah. "We weren't formally introduced, but she did dazzle us with her skill at swordplay." King Achal cast a questioning look at both Lord Danu and Aleah.

"I'll explain later, my lord," Aleah said, slightly flushed. After the king looked away, she glared at Lord Danu.

"Thank you for the warning, Achal," Artio said. "I assure you, we are taking every precaution to avoid trouble."

"Still, there are things you should be aware of," Maurer said in his deep voice. "The Dekla Devi and the Tiaronéa Devi are under the control of the traitor now. Crossing the grasslands of Tiaronéa will be treacherous."

"Kahn Devin?" Artio asked, and the Wizard gave a curt nod. He apparently had little regard for Lord Monguinir's right-hand man.

"When did this happen?" Lord Danu had his apple raised to take another bite, but instead he lowered the fruit and furrowed his brow. "The last report I received was that the Devi still resisted the Grand Warlock."

"Shortly after you left Basilea, Kahn Devin personally led an army of Kirocs, demon spawn, and Nortians through Dekla and into Tiaronéa. Both Devi tribes fell in a matter of three weeks.

"But that's not all. Kahn knows Renn wasn't presented during midsummer's Azur-Aven, so he assumes he is to be presented to the lore masters this winter. He has promised to greatly reward whoever finds and brings the boy to him."

Renn gasped. He felt a hand on his shoulder and looked up into Artio's concerned face.

"How does Kahn know Renn lives?" the Mage asked.

"He doesn't. But he's a careful one—he doesn't take chances. He'll have groups of Tiaronéa Devi, led by Kirocs and the like, watching for you."

"What do you suggest?" Lord Danu asked.

"And what of your sister, Princess Tristan?" Artio added.

The king creased his brow and pursed his lips. "I am concerned for Tristan, but she needs to fulfill her destiny, and I cannot think of any better escort than you. I considered sending soldiers with you, but I fear that would only make you conspicuous. But Aleah will join you."

Aleah stepped forward. Lord Danu exchanged glances with Artio and then looked at Aleah—considering her as though he were sizing up a horse he might purchase.

"I don't know, Achal," Lord Danu said, and Aleah narrowed her eyes. "I don't make personnel decisions without consulting Raven first."

"I assure you she will be of great assistance," the king said. "She is a first-rate tracker and my best warrior." Lord Danu frowned and paced.

"It would mean a great deal to me, Danu." The king stood, took Lord Danu by the shoulders, and peered into his eyes.

Lord Danu's lips drew taut, and he nodded. "As you wish," he said, and then a smile crossed his face. "I'm sure the girls will be happy to have a woman along. My men are not the best role models."

Renn wasn't sure he wanted more girls along for the journey but figured he had no say in the matter, so he remained quiet. Besides, he didn't want to say or do anything to upset Aleah. Sure, she was pretty, but she had a temper and a sword to back it up.

"Good. She'll be ready to leave when you are," the king said, smiling back. "By the way, I have people stationed in Tiaron and Menet. They'll help you as they can—but crossing the grasslands, you'll be on your own."

Artio looked up at the sky and scratched at his chin. "We'll need new disguises. It's likely some of the nobles in the king's court recognized Lord Danu, and in light of what Achal has told us, we can't afford to take chances."

"Yes, I agree," Lord Danu said. "Achal, we'll need supplies, fresh horses, and . . ." He pursed his lips, tapped his chin, and then smiled. "We'll need Kahaal clothing, armor, and banners."

"Kahaal?" The king scowled, then his eyes widened. "Ah yes, an emissary returning to Kah-Tarku. That would be a perfect disguise. They come and go all the time."

"Very good, Lord Danu." Maurer nodded and arched his brows. "Even the barbarians of the Tiaronéa Devi would think twice before crossing the council of Kahaal; their vengeance can be harsh."

"Agreed," Artio said. "Achal, can everything be ready to go by dawn?"

"Yes. Come to the palace before dawn. I have a plan that should throw off any pursuit."

PRINCESS TRISTAN

Renn watched as a group of King Achal's men dressed in the disguises that he and the others had been using for the past several weeks. The man now wearing Lord Danu's rich doublet had shoulder-length blond hair, but his eyes weren't different colors like Lord Danu's. Renn didn't think anyone would notice a detail like that anyway. A young girl who resembled Genea sat on the wagon bench next to an older man who had short-cropped hair like Artio.

Renn didn't think the boys mimicking him and Harlow looked very much like them, but at least their hair color and size were right. The men dressed in the mercenary clothing also generally looked like Lord Danu's soldiers.

The impersonating party took their mounts and wagon and left through the palace gates. Now Renn understood why the king had wanted Lord Danu's entire party to come to the palace this morning—if anybody had been watching them, they would hopefully follow the decoy northward.

Renn kept his horse, but everyone else in the company was given a fresh mount; Renn would never part with Thorn.

Two guards walked out of the palace into the inner courtyard carrying a large wooden box filled with clothing, which they set in front of the king and Lord Danu. By this time the sun was already trying to climb above the walls of the city, and Lord Danu was getting anxious to start. He passed out disguises and explained the ruse; he had already dressed as a captain of the Kahaal army, and Artio wore a rich, full-length purple tunic with eloquent gold trim. As the others dressed, he explained they were guards for Artio, whose alias was Ambassador Kosan of Kah-Tarku. Renn and Harlow would again act as pages, and Genea and Princess Tristan would be the ambassador's granddaughters.

Princess Tristan was in her fourteenth year but looked barely ten. Though she was tall, her slender body hadn't begun to develop like Genea's.

"Princess, that wreath looks lovely with your blonde hair," Lord Danu said, "but it isn't something a young girl of Kahaal would likely wear."

"It reminds me of nature and gardens." Her green eyes sparkled with excitement when she mentioned the gardens. "If anyone asks, we'll say it was a gift I received while in court at Achtland and I took a fancy to it."

Lord Danu raised an eyebrow and twisted his mouth but didn't push the issue any further.

As they finished their preparations to leave, a tall brunette wearing a rose-colored velvet dress entered the courtyard. Her tight-fitting bodice accented her breasts, drawing attention to her cleavage, and a thin, light gray sash pulled the material tight against her small waist.

Renn closed his mouth once he realized he probably looked like the rest of Lord Danu's men—like slack-jawed, wide-eyed fish. Even Raven raised his eyebrows. When she stopped next to King Achal, Renn realized who she was.

"Aleah." Lord Danu cleared his throat and straightened his jacket. "You look beautiful."

A grimace passed across her face, and she uttered a terse "Thank you." Then she turned to the king and said, "Is this really necessary? I won't be much use in a battle wearing this . . . this . . . ridiculous . . . embarrassing outfit."

Achal's smile broadened, and Aleah glowered. Even though he was the king, Renn didn't think smiling at her was a wise move. He was sure she had weapons hidden on her somewhere, although he couldn't see where she could conceal them.

"Yes, Aleah," Achal said. "It's necessary. Besides," he added, smiling even more, "this outfit makes you even more dangerous. No one will suspect you can actually fight until after he finds himself on the ground."

Aleah put her hands on her hips. "At least let me have my sword."

"That's already taken care of," he said. "You'll find it concealed underneath your cushion in the carriage."

"Carriage?" Aleah's voice rose in pitch and volume.

"You can't very well ride horseback in that—"

"How am I supposed to defend anyone from the confinement . . ." She continued complaining to the king, but Renn's attention turned to Kivas and Tellio.

"She really is beautiful," Kivas whispered to Tellio as both men continued to stare at the curves under her tight velvet bodice. "Perhaps I'll get better acquainted with her on our trip," he mused. "After all, we'll be together for a couple months . . ."

"Don't be a fool, my Nortian friend," Tellio said as he pulled at one side of his mustache. "You remember those Domerian girls we saw in the marketplace?" Kivas peeled his eyes away from Aleah and nodded. "I'd wager she's far more dangerous. She's a viper, that one. She even reminds me a bit of them—a little shorter, but just as ruthless."

Renn noticed Raven was also listening to the two men discuss Aleah. The captain's face grew thoughtful, but he said nothing.

A handsome elderly woman with a kind face entered the courtyard, wearing a dark green velvet dress with a fitted bodice that gleamed with emerald sequins. Emerald-laced cording ran from the bottom center of her bodice and fanned downward, making leaf-shaped sections throughout the full skirt. Her gray hair was done up in a simple bun and held in place with a ruby hairnet.

"Grandmother," King Achal said with a respectful bow. "Thank you for joining us."

"You don't think I'd let my granddaughter leave without wishing her well, now, do you?"

King Achal stepped aside as Tristan hurried to her grandmother, gave a quick curtsy, and embraced her.

"How did you elude your bodyguards?" Achal asked. "I should think they'd been trained well enough to keep an eye on a little old woman."

"This little old woman still has a few tricks up her sleeve," she replied with a twinkle in her dark eyes. "Artio, it is good to see you again," she said as she walked to the Mage. "You really must pay me a visit when you are finished with this journey."

"Lady Turesta," the old man said with a courtly bow, "the pleasure would be mine."

"Lord Danu." She addressed him with a subtle bow of her head.

Lord Danu bowed in response. "It's an honor to make your acquaintance, Lady Turesta. You are as beautiful as the stories say."

The queen mother laughed lightly. "And you are as impertinent as I've heard."

Once the pleasantries were taken care of and the goodbyes said, they started out. They didn't leave through the main gates. Instead, Achal and the two guards who brought the disguises led the party from the inner court into a weapons chamber, then through a hidden door that led to a downward-sloping hallway. Intermittently placed torches in black iron sconces dimly lit the hall. Renn could tell from the dust and cobwebs that the passage was seldom used.

After a half hour, they emerged into the early morning sun through a secret door hewn from a hillside outside the city walls. King Achal, flanked by his two guards, turned to face the small company and bid them a good journey. Renn thought he detected a tear in his eye and concern suppressed behind his smile, especially when the king embraced his younger sister, Princess Tristan. He and his guards disappeared back into the side of the hill and closed the door behind them. Once Renn took his eyes from the spot of the hidden door, he was unable to locate its position again.

The company traveled on the main road, which took them in a southeast direction toward the Tiarak Mountains. Although Renn couldn't see the long, narrow mountain range, which served as a natural border between Achtland and Tiaronéa, Artio informed him the road they traveled would take them through a southern pass and into the grasslands of Tiaronéa.

As they traveled, Renn watched Princess Tristan with fascination. Her green eyes sparkled with either mischief or delight—Renn couldn't tell which—and her energy and exuberance seemed unending. She talked constantly to Genea about silly things, and the girls took an immediate liking to one another. Renn was certain this would make traveling more difficult because now if he did something to upset one of the girls, he would suffer the wrath of both.

The first night after leaving the City of Avuman, Raven located a hidden clearing about a hundred yards off the main road for their campsite. After dinner, Renn walked with Harlow to a deep river that meandered through the hills. After some exploring, they found a place where it formed a pool surrounded by bushes and trees. Rocks and small juts formed natural platforms, and the water was clear and deep—deep enough for the boys to dive in and swim in the crisp, cool pool.

The next morning, Renn woke early with sore muscles. Apparently, he hadn't chosen a very good location for his bed. His first thought was of the pool that had been so invigorating the night before. The sky was beginning to lighten in the east, but dawn was still half an hour away. Renn decided an early swim, before the rest of the company rose, would be better than trying to go back to sleep on his hard bed.

He slipped out of the clearing, nodding to Tellio, who was warding the camp, and retraced his steps from the previous night. The air was cool with the brisk touch of dawn, and the grasses and bushes had a trace of dew on them.

Renn began undressing before he reached the pool, leaving his clothes on the ground as he walked. He pulled off his breeches, jogged out on a jut, and dove into the crisp water. As he hit the water, he heard a loud, high-pitched scream, and when he surfaced, someone was yelling at him.

"What are you doing? Get out of here, Renn. I'm bathing!"

Renn wiped the water from his eyes and saw Genea standing a few yards away in the pool. She spun around and glowered over her shoulder at him. In the growing dawn, he saw her back was covered with marks.

"Where did you get those scars, Genea?"

"Just go away, Renn. Leave me alone," she said, and she ducked herself further beneath the water to hide her back.

"All right, I'm leaving. Don't get so upset—I didn't know you were swimming here." He turned and waded toward the shore. "Don't watch me get out. I'm not dressed, either."

Genea's muffled crying echoed off the rocks as Renn pulled his clothes on over his wet body. Why was she so upset? Sure, he probably startled her, and he figured she didn't fancy the idea of bathing with him anymore than he did, but that was no reason to cry. Maybe it had something to do with the scars. He decided he'd never know what set her off. She was impossible to figure out. One minute she was nice, the next she wouldn't speak to him. He wondered if all girls were like that or just Genea.

⋈

During the next two days, Genea wouldn't even look at Renn. But instead of radiating petty anger as she normally did when she was upset with him, her countenance seemed sad and thoughtful.

Princess Tristan tried to cheer her, and Genea almost smiled when the young princess tied Kivas's bootlaces together during lunch the second day. The big lieutenant rose, unaware of her joke, and fell flat on his face—spilling stew all over his dark beard and hair. The soldiers and Aleah rolled on the ground with laughter. Tristan was quite proud of herself, but Genea's mood didn't lift.

That night, as Olosa cooked dinner, Renn caught Sela Nadgit stealing bits of food from the cook's stores. With a sly grin, the dirty-faced blacksmith signaled for him to come over.

"Do you want some dried beef?" he asked as Renn joined him.

"What are you doing? If Olosa catches you in his food, he'll cook *you* for dinner."

Sela put a finger to his lips and whispered, "That's why I do it." Renn's brow bunched together, and Sela's smile grew wider. "You see, that's the whole point. If it didn't make him so mad, it wouldn't be fun. Look at this." He pointed to a large wooden chest. "This is where he keeps the good stuff. He thinks someone is sneaking food, but he doesn't want to let on until he knows for sure. So he set's little booby traps on the box. But I got him figured out." He winked. "You see this little leaf on the hinge?" He pointed to a small green leaf resting on a black iron hinge on the back of the strongbox. "Watch what happens when I open the lid." As he opened the lid, the leaf silently fell to the ground. If Sela hadn't pointed it out, Renn never would have seen it. After stealing some cheese and a piece of jerky, Sela carefully returned the leaf to the exact location. "He always does something so he can tell if someone gets into it. Now we go hide behind a bush, eat our plunder, and wait for the chubby old man to show up."

"Then what?" Renn whispered as he followed Sela to a line of bushes about twenty feet away.

"Then the fun begins," he answered with a chortle, then coughed as he choked on a piece of cheese.

They sat behind the bushes, silently shared the morsels Sela had stolen, and waited. After about ten minutes Renn heard someone singing and whistling. He recognized Olosa's voice, and Sela put a finger to his lips, then scurried to peek around the side of the bush. Renn silently followed.

Olosa was examining the chest. Apparently satisfied no one had tampered with it, he opened it to get supplies for supper. When he looked in the box, he took a quick inventory, scratched his head, and counted again. He began mumbling—Renn couldn't make out his words—and slammed the lid closed. Sela backed up, almost knocking Renn over, and fought to suppress a laugh.

"Isn't that hilarious?" he whispered. "I just love watching that. It's the best trick I play on him because he doesn't know if his food is missing or if he's simply losing track of things."

"You're terrible, Sela," Renn said. "I can't wait for the day he catches you. I'm sure he'll think of some way to repay you."

"Oh, I'm sure he will. But in the meantime, I'll enjoy my little joke."

The terrain didn't change much during the first week of travel. Ever since they left Achtan, the road wound its way through low grassy hills covered with oak, hickory, aspens, and occasional pine groves. They passed merchants, travelers, and political emissaries along the way, but each encounter was minor, and Artio played his part so well no one questioned them.

Genea still wouldn't say much to Renn, but at least she giggled on occasion and talked with the princess. Tristan was something of an enigma to Renn. At times she seemed flighty and flirtatious, and then she would change and become serious and mature beyond her years. If she could stay focused, he figured she could probably become a great student of the lore. He never really felt comfortable talking to her because he wasn't quite sure how to address her or what to say. As he considered her, it dawned on him he still had questions about her brother, the king.

"Tristan, uh . . . Your Highness." He urged Thorn to the side of the carriage. Tristan giggled at his awkward approach. "Your brother, the king—he's much younger than I imagined."

"Oh? What did you imagine?" she asked through the open window. Genea sat next to her. Aleah and Artio were on the opposite seat. Harlow pulled his horse close to Thorn—he hated to be left out of any conversation.

"I don't know, I just thought he'd be older, that's all. I've heard people tell stories about King Achal as though he were always the king. In fact, I don't think I've ever heard of any other."

Tristan laughed lightly, and Renn blushed. "You silly," she said between giggles. "That's because *all* of our kings are named Achal—it's a tradition."

"Even I knew that, Renn," Genea said smugly.

Renn scratched his head. It made sense. If Achal was the same man in all the stories, he'd have to be hundreds of years old. Achtlanders did have a longer life span than most people, but not that much longer.

"Did you know that, Harlow?" Renn asked, trying to find comfort in someone else's ignorance.

"I never gave it much thought, but it explains why all the stories speak of King Achal. I like the story about the war between Nortia and Achtland best—King Achal had to fight hand-to-hand with King Druger of Nortia, and they fought for two hours before Achal finally won. That's a great story. Have you ever heard it?"

Renn waved for Harlow to be quiet and turned back to Tristan. "What was his name before he became king?"

"Torleif. That was also my father's given name," she said sadly. Tristan obviously still felt deep emotions over the death of her parents.

"What happened to your mother and father, Tristan?" Harlow asked before Renn or Genea could stop him.

"Harlow, that's a terrible thing to ask somebody," Genea said. "If she wanted us to know, she'd tell us on her own."

"I didn't mean no harm, but I didn't see them at the palace, and they didn't come to say goodbye, even."

"That's because they're dead, Harlow." Tristan frowned and curtailed Genea's imminent retort with a slight shake of her head. "It's sad because they were still young."

"How did they die?" he pressed, apparently unaware of his lack of tact.

Tristan blinked her eyes, wiped a tear from her cheek, and forced a smile. "They died in their sleep. No one knows why or how."

"What do you think happened?" Genea asked, now completely engrossed in Tristan's tale.

"Poison." She looked down to her lap. Renn and Harlow stared at the tears running down her face. Genea glared at the boys, pursed her lips, and lowered the shade of the carriage window.

Renn and Harlow looked at each other with raised eyebrows and open mouths. Renn turned back to the carriage and saw Aleah through the window on her side. She looked at Tristan with sadness, then looked out at Renn and Harlow. The way she looked at Renn was calculating and cool. Renn swallowed hard and looked away.

"C'mon, Harlow," Renn said. "Let's fall back with the others."

Without any physical signal from Renn, Thorn slowed and fell in step with the soldiers trailing behind the coach. Renn smiled and patted the big white stallion's muscled neck.

During the last few days, the company had been riding in the shadow of the Tiarak Mountains to the east. But now the terrain grew steeper, and the hardwood trees gave way to pines and firs. The dense green undergrowth of the forest and mountains surrounding Achtland was choked out by the thick evergreen canopy. Shrubs and bushes that had covered the ground during the previous days were replaced with rich brown soil blanketed by pine needles and occasional rocks. The Tiarak Mountains, even this far south, were immense and formed a formidable border between Achtland and Tiaronéa.

They came to a river that cut its way down a canyon between two peaks. Lord Danu turned the company off the main road at this point and followed the river and a less-defined road into the gorge.

Lord Danu stood in his stirrups, and his eyes swept the forest and mountains. "I don't think we'll run into the bandits who infest the mountains this far south. Most of them camp farther north, where more villages lie. Just the same, I'll be glad when we're free of these mountains. They bode ill; I don't feel comfortable here."

"Lord Danu." Raven materialized from the forest, taking everyone by surprise.

"Don't do that, Raven," Lord Danu said through clenched teeth. "You know I hate being startled."

Renn thought he saw the beginnings of a grin form on the dark-haired captain's face, but it disappeared before he could be certain.

"We aren't being followed, and I don't believe this trail has been used in more than six months."

"That's good news," Kivas said as he rode up beside the carraige.

"There's a clearing off the trail, about an hour from here," Raven reported. "It's defensible and close to the river. I suggest we stop there for the night and cross the pass tomorrow."

"Agreed," Lord Danu said. "I could use a warm meal and some rest."

Two hours later, Renn relaxed by the fire and watched the stars make their heavenly appearance like actors on a darkening stage. From the west, dark rolling clouds were enshrouding the sky in thick blackness and progressively killing the stars like an ebony-caped villain.

"A bad storm's brewing, lad," Tellio said as he worked his knife in a grinding circular motion on a damp pumice stone. "We're in for a wet and windy night."

"How soon will it begin?" Genea asked. She sat across the fire from Renn, braiding Tristan's hair.

"Oh . . ." Tellio scratched at the thick beard that he began growing the day they left Achtan, looked thoughtfully at the darkening horizon, and said, "An hour, maybe. The wind will pick up sooner than that." Almost on cue, the wind began to blow. Dust and leaves kicked up from out of nowhere, and Lord Danu barked orders at his men to secure different sections of the camp.

Micha, Radien, Julius, and Aleah—the archers of the company—ran into the clearing, clutching their bows. They had gone a short way off after supper to practice shooting but returned when they heard Lord Danu shouting orders. Aleah wore her breeches now. When they were on the road, she dutifully followed her orders to wear a dress and play the part of a lady, but once they were in camp, she changed into her preferred attire.

Renn helped Tellio put out the fire, then secured Genea and Tristan's tent with stakes and ropes against the oncoming tempest. It gave him a strange sense of satisfaction to make sure the two girls were safe. He then helped Harlow finish tying their tent between two large pine trees and laid out his bedroll.

It began to rain as Renn and Harlow turned in for the night. Renn heard the crunching sound of boots walking past their tent and Aleah complaining under her breath about the bad weather. He wondered if she regretted insisting she take equal time with the men at guarding the camp.

Soon the rain began to beat against the canvas shelter in torrents of anger. Flashes of lightning streaked through the atmosphere, lighting up the tent with its intermittent flicker, allowing Renn an occasional glimpse of the fear etched into Harlow's face. Always, following the brilliant light show came roaring thunder—close enough at times to make the earth feel as though it were shaking.

"Renn," Harlow whispered. "Are you awake?"

"Of course. How could I sleep with all this noise?"

"I'm af—you don't think—I mean, do you think we'll be all right?"

"Are you kidding?" he answered in his bravest-sounding voice. "No person or animal would be out on a night like this. And I've never known a storm that didn't pass. We'll be fine."

Another flash of lightning lit up the tent. After the thunder passed, Harlow said, "I've never heard it storm so bad. I hope it ends soon."

"Me too. Now, go to sleep. Lord Danu's going to want to travel all day tomorrow whether we're tired or not."

When Renn woke up, the tempest had calmed to a steady drizzle and Harlow was fast asleep. He wasn't certain what woke him, but then, near the flap of the tent, a voice whispered, "Renn, are you awake?"

"Who is it?" he asked warily.

"Jomard," came the reply. "Come out here; I want you to see something."

How strange, Renn thought. *Why in the world would Jomard wake me in the middle of the night just to show me something?*

"Can't it wait until morning?"

"No," Jomard whispered. "Trust me. It's important that you come now."

Renn stepped out into the rain. Jomard was wearing a dark cloak with the hood pulled over his head. He was soaked from head to foot, and droplets of water dripped from the hood in front of his face. He motioned Renn toward the trees, and Renn followed.

They walked for more than ten minutes before Renn called over the rain, "Where are we going?"

"It's a surprise. Just keep following me."

A surprise? Renn thought. *Way out here in the rain, in the middle of the night?*

The terrain became steep and slippery. Jomard let Renn pass him, then brushed the ground with a fir branch and kicked rocks over their trail.

Renn's brow creased. "What are you doing that for?"

Jomard studied Renn's face, then smiled, threw the branch aside, and hiked up beside him.

"Trust me, Renn. Have I ever let you down?" Jomard patted him on the shoulder. "Keep on this trail. I'll follow behind."

Renn studied Jomard's eyes. The man looked sincere, and Jomard was his father's friend. Renn nodded, turned, and hiked up the slippery trail.

"Jomard, we're far from camp. Where are we going?" Renn glanced over his shoulder. Jomard was bent over the trail, once again, covering tracks. Renn's heart began to race. He thought Jomard heard his question, but when the man stood, he pointed up the trail and indicated with a nod for Renn to keep walking.

Renn chewed on his lip as he hiked up the muddy trail. He slipped at one point and fell in a puddle. Jomard pulled him back to his feet, and Renn wiped mud from his eyes.

He squared his shoulders and took a deep breath. "I want to know where we're going."

"I haven't got time to explain right now." Jomard glanced behind him. "Just understand that we have to go alone now."

Renn took a step backward. "Why? What's going on?" he asked. Rain ran along his cloak, fell into his face, and rolled down his neck. "Why are we leaving at night, in the middle of a storm?"

"I promised your dad I'd take care of you, and that's what I'm doing." Jomard took Renn's arm, turned him around, and pushed him forward.

Renn *did* trust Jomard—he loved Jomard—but this didn't make sense. One thing was certain: Artio had been like a father to him. If something were wrong, certainly he would have warned him. And what about Lord Danu? He had taken care of Renn's family and had had their best interests in mind since Renn was a small boy. Jomard was a family friend, but why was he covering their tracks and looking behind them? It then occurred to Renn that Aleah had not been at her guard post when Jomard led him from camp.

"Jomard." Renn stopped and faced him. "What happened to Aleah? Why wasn't she at her post?"

"I don't know. Maybe she went behind a bush to relieve herself," he said impatiently.

Renn folded his arms. "Tell me what's going on or I'm not taking another step."

Jomard clenched his jaw, and his eyes bulged. "By Aven, I can't!" he said. "I told you to trust me."

"I'm going back to camp." Renn pushed past Jomard. "Artio will tell me what's going on."

Jomard grabbed his arm and whipped him back around. Renn's eyes widened, and fear clenched his heart when Jomard pulled him close and held a dagger to his throat.

"If you want to live, you'll shut up and do as I say."

BITTER BETRAYAL

They walked all night. Renn stumbled and fell more than once, but as Jomard would walk by, he'd grab Renn's arm, pull him up, and shove him forward. The steady rain beat a relentless rhythm against Renn's hooded cloak, which was now so wet it clung to his body like a drenched husk and hampered his labored march.

The horizon in the east slowly turned lead gray. The change was so gradual that Renn didn't know when the sun actually rose behind the overcast sky. Sheets of rain impeded his vision and blurred the path. His face was wet, a mixture of tears and rain, but he forced himself onward.

They hiked into a dense grove of pine laden with thick undergrowths of thornbushes.

"Stop," Jomard said.

Renn sank to his knees and fell gratefully to the ground. His face landed in a small pool of water, and mud caked the rim of his hood, but he didn't care. He opened one eye to see what his captor was doing.

Jomard sawed at a thornbush with a long knife. He already had a small stack of thin branches, covered with long, slender thorns, piled next to him. The tall farmer carried the limbs back to where he and Renn had entered the grove of pines.

Renn forced the muscles in his arms to raise his body off the ground, then shifted to better see what Jomard was doing. The man dug a shallow furrow across their trail using a long knife, then carefully placed the thorn branches in it. He opened his pack, pulled out a vial of sappy black elixir, and dumped it generously over the barbs. He used thin pine boughs to conceal the opening and hide the snare.

"What are . . . what are you doing?" Renn managed to ask between gasps.

Jomard didn't look up from his work, nor did his voice sound like the man Renn used to know when he answered. "Being cautious." He punched his knife into the dirt and dug another narrow ditch. "Raven might be able to track us through that storm. These traps should slow him down."

Raven? It never occurred to Renn that Raven would be sent to find him, but it made perfect sense. A drop of hope settled in his heart and rippled throughout his entire body.

"What is that black stuff you're pouring on the thorns?" Thorn. He couldn't help but think about his best friend when he looked at the sharp barbs for which he'd named his horse.

"Poison. Fast and deadly. It'll also harden the thorns, so instead of breaking on impact, they'll pierce through a man's boot and penetrate deep into the foot. It's called *Black Annis*. Pay attention; you'll be learning about things like this soon."

"What do you mean?" Renn asked.

"Come now, Renn. I thought you were brighter than that. Surely you've guessed why I'm taking you north." Jomard finished the last of three traps, threw the remaining branches into the bushes, and knelt next to Renn.

"I know you're not happy right now, Renn, but one day you'll thank me. I am taking you to a place where you'll be guided and taught to use real power." He smiled, but it was no longer a smile of friendship and love. To Renn it looked as evil as night. Jomard shoved his knife back into his belt, grabbed Renn's arm, and dragged him back to his feet.

"Let's go. We've got a lot of ground to cover, and Kahn Devin is not a patient man."

Renn jerked his arm free and glared at Jomard. "Kahn Devin?" His heart twisted into a knot as the ramifications of that name sunk in. All these years Jomard had pretended to be a family friend while he was working for their most bitter enemy.

"You let the mob kill my father." Renn pounded on Jomard's chest, and tears mixed with the rain on his face. "You were supposed to be his best friend and you killed him."

Jomard grabbed Renn's fists and pulled him forward until their eyes were inches apart. "There is a lot you don't understand."

Jomard shoved Renn backward, and he landed on his butt in the mud. "Incidentally," Jomard said, "I had nothing to do with the mob that killed your father."

Jomard grabbed Renn's cloak as he walked by, hoisted him to his feet, and pushed him forward. Renn clenched his fists and ground his teeth as he slogged through the mud. One day ago he had loved Jomard, and now he desperately wished he could kill the man.

The rain stopped. It might have been midday—Renn wasn't certain because the lead-gray sky gave scant indication as to the sun's location—but he was glad to be rid of this one bane. Still, his numb fingers were raw with cuts from grabbing at rocks and roots to catch himself from frequent stumbles.

He and Jomard came out of the dense trees into a small meadow that faced another mountain, higher than the last. Renn thought he would collapse when Jomard urged him onward. *Was there no end to this man's strength?* Renn wondered. *How and where did he learn to be so cruel?*

"I . . . I need to rest," Renn mumbled as he staggered across the grassy hummocks of the mountain meadow.

"Did you say something?"

"I need to rest!" Renn shouted, though it took incredible reserves of strength for him to do so.

"If you have energy enough to speak, you have energy enough to walk."

Renn trudged on in despair. The thought of running crossed his mind, but the lanky farmer would certainly catch him before he took ten steps. Jomard appeared unaffected by the sleepless night and endless trek in the storm.

"It may comfort you to know," Jomard said, "that we are approaching a camp of some friends of mine. We'll rest there and get supplies."

It did help. Knowing that rest was part of Jomard's plan gave Renn a second wind. He didn't look forward to meeting Jomard's friends, but anything seemed preferable to this endless, muddy march.

Renn smelled the fragrant scent of burning wood as the sun neared the western horizon. The aroma of meat stew made his mouth water, and he saw the flickering lights of cooking fires.

As they drew nearer, two men jumped down from a tree: one in front and the other behind them. Each man held a short sword, but before either could display their skill with the weapon, Jomard's hands flicked simultaneously—one forward and one back—and the two men fell to the ground, clutching their necks. They were dead almost as they hit the forest floor—their eyes bulging and small, narrow blades buried in the center of their throats. Neither knife had a handle; they were simply flat blades.

Renn looked, slack-jawed and wide-eyed, at Jomard.

"I thought these were your friends," he said.

"Not yet, but they will be." Jomard brought his finger to his lips and moved forward until they stood behind the trees surrounding the camp.

Dozens of men—mostly unshaven and dirty—lounged beside fires spread throughout the camp, laughing, talking, and holding large flagons of what Renn assumed to be some kind of alcohol. A few of them worked over kettles of food. The smell of warm stew made Renn's stomach grumble. It occurred to Renn that these were some of thieves Lord Danu had spoken of.

There seemed to be no apparent order to their camp. The place was messy and had a sort of transient permanence to it, as though the men had lived there for a while and intended to stay but had no ambition to build respectable facilities or structures.

Jomard took a deep breath, pressed his hand against Renn's back, and walked purposefully into the camp.

"Who is your leader?" he demanded as he approached the center.

The ruckus stopped. Men no longer laughed, spoke, ate, or drank. They watched their unexpected guests while fingering the hilts of their swords.

A burly man, easily twice the size of Jomard, stood—a mug of ale in one hand and his other resting on his scabbard. He wore a full black beard, but his long, stringy hair was thinning on top.

"I am. How did you get past my men?"

"My partner and I require rest, food, two horses, and a favor for which I will pay you well," Jomard replied, ignoring the large man's questions.

The company of thieves burst out laughing, some slapped their thighs, and others raised their mugs in mock solute.

One of the thieves, no more than thirty years old, drew his sword and shouted, "What makes you think we won't take your partner *and* your money and leave you dead?"

Jomard's hand flicked in the direction of the taunting man, and he, like the sentries, fell clutching his throat. This time the silence that swept the camp felt tense. Men pointed at the blade and whispered.

The leader's eyes grew wide, and he cleared his throat. "I should have guessed. Only one of you would be so bold. What is your name, Kiel-Don?" he asked.

"I am known among my peers as Jomavid." Murmurs erupted, and Renn realized they recognized this name and actually feared Jomard.

"I apologize." The leader bowed. "Had we known, we would have given you a proper welcome."

THE KIEL-DON

"Are you planning to sleep all morning?"

Rough hands shook Renn.

"Get up," Jomard said. "We're leaving."

"What?" Renn rubbed his eyes. Gradually his senses focused, and he found himself in a musty-smelling canvas tent filled with snoring men.

Renn looked past Jomard toward the dark opening of the tent. *Was it even dawn yet?* he wondered. He didn't ask Jomard about the time. He didn't want to even look at the man. He wondered how long Jomard had been living a lie. Was he always an enemy, or did Kahn recently corrupt him? And what exactly was a Kiel-Don? The very word seemed to frighten the thieves.

Renn dragged himself out of the bedroll and walked into the cold mountain air. The storm had passed, and the predawn skies were brittle and clear—as though the tempest had scrubbed it clean of any and every impurity.

Jomard walked to an unlit fire pit and spoke with the man Renn knew only as "the Leader," who held a small wooden cage with a pigeon inside. The leader nodded his head, and Jomard tossed him a small, bulging purse that made a clinking noise when it dropped in his hand.

The big man gave Jomard the pigeon and disappeared behind the trees. Jomard watched him leave and then took a small, rolled-up piece of parchment out of his pocket and fastened it to one of the pigeon's legs. As

Jomard released the bird into the sky, the leader returned with two strong horses in tow. He handed the reins to Jomard, who appraised the steeds and checked the supplies in the saddlebags. He pulled out an apple and a roll, tossed them to Renn, and said, "Let's go. This is where we lose any pursuit—these men will see to that."

The horse Renn had to ride was a pretty brown gelding, but he felt like a traitor as he climbed upon its back. He didn't have anything against the horse—he simply missed the special communion he shared with Thorn.

Jomard used a rope to link Renn's horse to his own, then set a quick pace out of the thieves' camp. Renn had to lie close to the horse's back to avoid being waylaid by low-hanging branches, but they soon came to a clearing. Renn thought Jomard would go north, deeper into the Tiarak Mountains, and choose a trail that led to the next peak as he had thus far, but the traitor made their course northwest instead.

Renn set his jaw and glared at Jomard. *He said he didn't kill Da*, Renn thought, *but he's set traps and paid thieves to kill my friends. I have to warn them somehow. I have to escape.*

Artio had taught him some defense spells, but they were only practical against magical attacks. Still, he *had* blasted a Kiroc through the wall of Artio's cottage. Maybe he could do something similar to Jomard to throw him off his horse.

Renn concentrated on Jomard. He attempted to visualize power and force it to flow through his veins, then he tried to push out with his thoughts like a fist of power to unhorse his captor—nothing happened.

He squeezed his eyes shut, pursed his lips, and tried again. This time he placed a picture in his mind's eye of Jomard being thrown a hundred yards off the horse's back and willed it to occur, but the Kiel-Don—as the thieves called him—remained on his horse. And Renn, with sweat beading on his forehead, dropped his shoulders and sighed.

In the past, his power only surfaced when he was frightened. Even though he now felt anger, the adrenaline of fear wasn't coursing through his veins.

He considered trying to call animals of the forest to attack Jomard, but the memory of the pain he'd felt when the animals had defended him against Raul made him quickly reject the idea. Raul, he remembered, had been drinking that night and probably wasn't a very good fighter anyway. A fighter as skilled as Jomard would make the animals pay a heavy toll. Eventually, Jomard would probably be defeated by them—but at what cost? Besides, Renn didn't quite know how he'd called the animals to attack Raul and doubted he could do it again.

He closed his eyes again and turned his thoughts to Thorn. *Can you hear me, Thorn?* He pushed the thoughts away from his mind and imagined them traveling through the air

Renn kept his eyes shut to help him ignore the clopping sound of his horse's hooves on the trail. He strained with his mind, desperate for a response. Nothing. The distance must be too great.

Renn would have to warn Raven without Thorn's help. The thought of him or anyone else getting hurt or killed twisted at his heart like a dishrag being wrung out and hung to dry. He would have to make a run for it.

Jomard hadn't tied the rope to Renn's horse. He had looped a rope through the harness, and Renn had no knife to cut it. He considered jumping off the horse and running but dismissed the idea before giving it any real thought—Jomard would recapture him in seconds.

Renn looked at the back of Jomard's head and bit his lip. He waited until Jomard turned to check on him. When the Kiel-Don turned back around, Renn leaned forward and loosened the horse's bridle. He then grabbed a fistful of its long brown mane with his left hand and used his right to flip the harness over the horse's head and pull the bit out of its mouth.

He jerked the gelding to the right, leaned into the horse with his left knee to turn it around, and spurred it into a run. He felt his heart beat with each fall of the horse's hoofs. He urged the horse on, kicking at its flanks to run faster across the meadow. He glanced over his shoulder; Jomard was in pursuit, but the dangling rope and harness had slowed him down. If Renn could get far enough into the mountains before Jomard caught him, he might get away.

Renn felt a spark of hope rise in his chest as he put distance between himself and Jomard. But his onetime friend drew a knife and severed the rope in a single fluid motion. His horse didn't miss a beat as it pounded after the escapee. Renn pushed his horse harder, and between his legs he could feel the poor beast quiver with the strain. Jomard had wisely chosen the stronger, swifter horse.

Renn leaned against the horse's neck to reduce the wind resistance. The forest line was so close. Once inside, he may be able to outmaneuver the larger horse and gain the advantage. But the opportunity never came. Jomard's horse raced next to him and expertly forced Renn's horse to stop.

Jomard didn't say a word. He kept one hand on Renn's foot as he dismounted—making a second attempt at escape impossible—pulled a short rope out of his supply bag, and tied Renn's hands together.

"We don't have time for this nonsense, Renn. I didn't want to do this, but you leave me no choice."

Renn wanted to scream and cry at the same time. Instead, he forced all emotion out of his voice and said, "You're a liar and a coward."

If he couldn't escape, maybe he could hurt Jomard in other ways. Maybe some part of Jomard really did care about him, and that part might be sympathetic if it could be reached.

"I saw the way you killed those thieves. I saw how much they feared you. You could've easily saved my father from the mob."

Jomard double-checked the knot he'd just tied around Renn's hands and then wrapped another rope around the neck of Renn's horse and tied it to his own horse.

"You let my father die just so you could keep the secret of who you really are—a big, fat traitor."

Jomard's face remained placid when he turned and walked back to Renn. He grabbed his shirt, pulled him forward, and slapped Renn on the cheek.

"Consider this your second lesson: respect your instructors."

"You're not my instructor," Renn said. "You were my father's friend. He trusted you. *I* trusted you. Too many people have died. You can help me end that. Let me go now before anyone else gets hurt."

Jomard shook his head, then burst out laughing. "Consider this your third lesson: Many. More. People. Will. Die."

Jomard mounted his horse and started, once again, across the meadow, northwest toward the Cragg Mountains. Renn glared at the back of his captor with a deeper, more profound hatred. Renn had never killed with a physical weapon—never thought he'd ever want to—but he wanted to kill Jomard. The Kiel-Don had stood back, probably even silently laughed, as Renn's father had been hanged from a tree.

Once more, as Renn's stallion dutifully followed Jomard's lead, he concentrated on Jomard. He focused his thoughts on his back and tried to envision the man flying through the air, mercilessly thrown to his death. But Jomard stayed on the animal's back, defying all of Renn's concentrated efforts. Renn felt angrier than ever, but his *real* power seemed only to be triggered by fear, and he was not afraid. Regardless of what Jomard had done, and despite his intended destination, Renn knew he was in no immediate danger. He hit his bound hands against his thigh in frustration. Once again, he was a child who needed someone else to save him.

A wall of flames more than ten feet tall rose from the earth in front of Jomard. His horse reared and shrieked in panic.

"Stop, Jomard." The volume and closeness of the voice caused the Kiel-Don to dive to the ground, roll, and rise in a crouched stance with long blades in each hand.

Renn looked over his shoulder, expecting to see Artio right behind them. Instead he saw three figures appear from the mountain trail and ride across the meadow toward them. Artio was in the lead, his staff held high over his head and glowing with green power, then Raven, dressed in black, and the other rider had to be Lord Danu.

"Over here!" Renn shouted, though they obviously knew where he was.

Jomard yanked him off the saddle and held Renn in front of him with a knife pressed against his throat. "Do exactly as I say or you'll die right here."

Renn went rigid and held his breath. Help was on the way, but what could they do? Jomard's knives were deadly. He would have to warn the others that Jomard was a Kiel-Don before he took them unawares.

"If you try to warn them, I'll cut your throat," he whispered hoarsely, as though he'd read Renn's thoughts.

Artio was close enough now for Renn to see that the man's face was red and lined with a deep glower. Renn had never seen the Mage look so angry—he actually felt a trace of sympathy for Jomard.

"Hold where you are," Jomard shouted as the three men came within range of his voice. "If you come any closer, I swear he'll die."

"Jomard, you pawn of filth! If you so much as harm one hair of his head, I'll do things to you the tales of which will make men cringe for centuries." Artio's voice thundered over the meadow.

Renn felt Jomard wince at the power of Artio's threat; still, he kept the sharp blade pressed against Renn's throat.

"You can't get away, Jomard," Lord Danu yelled. His voice sounded weak in comparison to Artio's, and his words slurred, as though he were laboring to speak. "Give us Renn, and we'll let you go."

"You expect me to believe that, Lordling? I'm doing Renn a favor. Drop this wall of flame and let us go, or the boy dies."

Lord Danu, Artio, and Raven slowed their horses to a walk, but they still came forward. Renn felt the knife blade push harder against his skin.

"Stop, or I'll kill him."

The three men pulled back on their reins. "I can't let you take Renn," Lord Danu said. He looked like he could barely hold himself in the saddle. Then Renn saw the bandage wrapped around the young lord's boot, and his face, which was pale with fatigue or sickness—it appeared he had fallen victim to one of Jomard's traps.

"If you refuse us, you will die, Jomavid," Raven said. Jomard inhaled sharply—probably surprised that Raven knew his real name. At the use of this unfamiliar name, Lord Danu and Artio cast a questioning glance at the dark-haired tracker.

"I thought you were more than just a simple farmer," Raven said. "The way you found our camps so easily at the beginning of our travels was unusual. But I never guessed you were a member of the Kiel-Don until I saw the traps you laid and the men you killed."

"I'm impressed, Raven. Then you should also know that I take what I want and kill those who oppose me." As Jomard made his threat, his hands flicked toward Artio and Lord Danu. Renn screamed a shout of warning—remembering what happened to the other men who'd crossed Jomard.

The blade thrown at Artio stopped in midair, six inches from the old Mage's throat, and dropped harmlessly to the ground. Lord Danu, because of Renn's warning, shifted in his saddle and ducked. Still, the blade caught him in the shoulder, and he let out a shout of pain.

Jomard reached for another knife, and Renn broke the hold the killer had on him. He ran awkwardly—because his wrists were still bound—toward Artio. He heard a low whirring sound, and then sharp pain pierced the back of his leg.

Without his hands free to break his fall, Renn landed face-first on the ground. Renn screamed and clutched the back of his leg. With all the courage he could muster, he pulled out the knife.

Raven flew past Renn like a black streak, running toward the Kiel-Don. The dark-haired captain flipped sideways in the air to avoid one of Jomard's blades and then, with a flying leap, kicked him in the chest.

Pain circled around Renn, threatening to steal his consciousness. With his wrists still bound together, he cupped them over his wound and applied pressure to stop the bleeding.

"Is that your only injury?" Artio knelt beside Renn and untied his hands.

The old man pulled out his brown leather pouch and rummaged around until he found a bottle of gray powder that he poured over Renn's wound.

"Ahh!" Renn pounded the ground with his fists at the fiery pain that shot up his leg. He blinked back tears that threatened to come, then furrowed his brows and sat up. "My leg doesn't hurt anymore."

"No," Artio said, "but this is temporary. It will slow the bleeding until we have time to properly dress the wound."

Renn shifted his attention back to the fight between Jomard and Lord Danu's captain.

Blood trickled down Jomard's cheek from a cut above his left eye. The Kiel-Don feinted for the captain's head, then tried to sweep his feet from underneath him. Raven fluidly dodged or blocked each attack and answered with twice as many of his own. Raven gracefully dove, kicked, and jabbed—as if his body were made specifically for fighting, as if he had been tempered by the gods to be a living weapon.

His palm slammed into Jomard's face, then Raven flipped backward, kicking the Kiel-Don in the head as he rotated. Jomard bled from his lip and above both eyes, and his right cheek was badly swollen.

Raven looked both unruffled and wild. His loose black shirt was still neatly tucked in, and his dark hair blew in the breeze created by the speed of his motion. Jomard, apparently realizing he couldn't win, darted for Raven's horse. Raven flipped his hand at the retreating traitor, and Jomard fell to the ground—a knife buried in his back.

Renn breathed a sigh of relief, closed his eyes, and lay on his back on the cool ground. Finally, he could relax. As he lay on the ground, he heard a low rumble, and the ground began to quake beneath him. His eyes shot open, and he sat up. The others stopped what they were doing, and they all looked toward the side of the meadow where Jomard had been trying to take Renn.

Shouts and shrieks, barely audible at first, cut through the air. The sounds grew louder until a horde of creatures and men burst through the trees.

"Kirocs!" Artio shouted.

Raven was already on his mount, hurrying to bring the Mage's horse to him and Renn. Before Raven reached their position, a sharp red bolt of light shot across the meadow at them like an arrow. Artio raised his staff, and the red bolt changed course and flew harmlessly into the sky.

Renn looked at the horde and saw a tall, thin creature in a flowing, hooded cloak walking behind them, holding a glowing red skull in one hand and a long bone in the other. The long bone pulsed red twice, and two more bolts of angry power erupted through the sky. Artio deflected this attack by raising a green shield and became locked into a duel with the creature.

"Run!" Artio shouted at Raven. "You must get Renn to safety."

But the horde was too close. Lord Danu pushed his horse forward, and he and Raven drew their swords and positioned themselves between Renn and the attackers. The first grotesque creatures to reach them died quickly as Raven—with a sword in each hand—danced from beast to beast. Lord Danu gained a second wind and hacked off the arms of those who raised swords against him.

The sheer numbers of the attackers, however, began to overwhelm them, and Renn knew he would soon be recaptured and his friends all killed.

A large man, with long, dark, sweaty hair and a thick beard with no mustache, loomed in front of Renn and grabbed his shoulders with thick, meaty hands. But his greedy smile turned slack-jawed, his eyes bulged, and he fell to the ground at Renn's feet with an arrow protruding from his forehead.

A Kiroc pulled Lord Danu from his horse and prepared to plunge a sword into his chest, then dropped to the ground with an arrow embedded in his back.

Renn looked in the direction the arrows were coming from and saw Aleah riding hard toward the battle. She pulled her bowstring back to her ear and let another arrow fly. Before the arrow hit its mark, she fluidly took another from her quiver and fired again. The rapid succession of arrows caused the attackers to pause and look around, as though trying to ascertain where all of the archers were hiding.

She positioned her horse between Renn and the mass of creatures and continued to unleash arrows. As she pulled the last one and notched it on her string, Renn shouted, "Hit the Necromancer!" He tugged at her pant leg. "Aleah, hit the Kiroc battling Artio."

She looked from Artio to the tall magic user in the dark, hooded robe standing behind the small army. Aleah pulled the string to her ear and took aim. She shook her head and lowered the bow.

"He's too far away," she said. "Raven, you're going to have to hold them alone for a minute."

She kicked at the flanks of her chestnut horse. Clumps of sod kicked up as Aleah urged her mount around the edge of the motley force. She circled behind them and headed for the Kiroc attacking Artio.

The tall magic user concentrated so much on his battle with Artio that he didn't see the rider approach or the arrow fly through the air. But he dropped his magical implements and grabbed the bolt in his neck as he fell to the ground.

Artio turned his attention to the Kirocs and Nortian soldiers. They had gained the advantage now that Aleah's arrows no longer harangued them. A dozen surrounded Raven, but he continued swinging both blades in what could only be described as a deadly dance. The ground was littered with the bleeding forms of their assailants, but Renn knew that sheer numbers would eventually wear Raven down.

Lord Danu, down on one knee, raised his sword above his head to ward off a blow from a large Kiroc. The pale red beast had green eyes. Its nose looked like it belonged on a pig, but it had a shock of black hair that looked like a horse's mane.

"No!" Renn shouted as the beast swung. Before the killing blow made contact, a burst of green light sent the creature flying backward—taking out several other attackers unfortunate enough to be in its path.

Aleah dropped her bow and drew a sword. But instead of coming back around the flank to join them, she charged her horse straight up the middle—cutting, trampling, and slicing as she progressed through the enemy ranks.

With no magic user to counter him, Artio divided the army using walls of fire and bursts of green power from his glowing staff. The horde panicked and retreated in a stampede to escape the magical assaults of the angry Mage.

The old Mage leaned against his staff and breathed heavily as he surveyed the scene. Aleah pulled up in front of Raven and glared at him.

"I thought Lord Danu told you to stay with the company," Raven said. The dark-haired captain's shirt was covered in sweat and blood, but only the sweat belonged to him. Aleah looked at the carnage of dead creatures and men strewn across the ground around him.

"You're welcome," she replied coldly.

Raven glared back at her, then nodded once and wiped his blades on the cloak of one of the dead men near his feet.

"Lord Danu, we need—" Raven stopped speaking, and lines creased his brow.

He dashed toward the young lord, who was still on his knees and leaning against his sword. His pale skin dripped with sweat from his forehead, and blood oozed from his shoulder. Raven lifted Lord Danu's head and looked into his eyes.

"Artio," Raven cried over his shoulder. "Do something, or Lord Danu will die!"

LORUM ROOT

Renn watched Artio rush to Lord Danu's side, drop his staff, and pull out his brown leather bag. Aleah came to Renn and dismounted. She pulled a flask of alcohol from one of the saddlebags on her horse and knelt beside him.

"This is going to sting," she said.

Renn nodded and clenched his teeth as she poured the burning liquid over his wound. Then she cut a strip of cloth from the bottom of her shirt and wrapped his leg.

While Aleah dressed his wound, Renn stared at Jomard, who lay facedown in the field littered with dead bodies. He was no more than a stone's throw away—a knife in his back. It didn't feel right. Even though the man had betrayed his family, and after all he'd put Renn through, it had still hurt to watch him die. Renn thought he would've killed Jomard himself if given the chance—but now that he was dead, he felt little satisfaction. *Why did you do it? Things could have been so different.*

The Meskhoni took supplies from his leather pouch and mixed odd powders and liquids together. He traced symbols in the air and mumbled strange words as he worked on Lord Danu. Renn could feel the power, but he didn't understand the incantations or how Artio controlled the aeon myriad.

"What's wrong with him?" he asked as he limped behind Artio, leaning against Aleah for support.

"Poison," Raven said. He cradled Lord Danu's head in his lap with a tenderness that was paradoxical—this man who so casually fought and killed with deadly precision now nurtured Lord Danu with the compassion of a brother. "He stepped into one of Jomavid's traps." Raven shook his head. "I should have seen it."

"You can't blame yourself, Raven." Artio re-dressed the swollen purple wound on Lord Danu's foot. "The Kiel-Don are trained killers—trained by the high priestess of Necrosys at her temple in Nortia. They are Kahn Devin's elite. Certainly Jomard was one of the best or he wouldn't have been given the assignment he had. Nobody could have known."

"I should have!" Raven exploded. "I've been trained, too—trained to recognize people like him. I should have known."

Renn had never seen Raven upset. Before now, he would have thought the man never lost his composure, but Lord Danu's need had broken through the walls of Raven's defenses.

Raven looked up at Aleah and stared her in the eye. "Thank you," he said, and then he swallowed hard. "We'd probably all be dead if . . ." His words caught in his throat, and he turned his attention back to Lord Danu.

"Don't be so hard on yourself," Artio said. "If not for you, neither Lord Danu nor myself would be alive now. We all make mistakes, Raven—even you."

Raven nodded slowly, took a deep breath, and said, "We'd better get going. The thieves Jomard sent after us are probably going to be coming soon. They're not very good trackers, but even they won't be fooled long by my little trick."

The captain looked up at the sun, apparently to gauge the hours left before nightfall. Dark clouds were forming on the horizon, and Renn could feel the temperature dropping.

Raven looked down at Lord Danu and asked, "Is he well enough to travel?"

"I don't see that we have much choice. His breathing is unlabored now, but if I don't get the antidote soon . . . Lorum root doesn't grow on this side of the Tiarak, and nothing else will stop the venom."

The look on the Mage's face made Renn realize that the old man believed Lord Danu might die.

"Artio," Renn said, "can't you change into a bird and go find some?" He'd lost too many people in his life who he loved. "We can't let Lord Danu die."

Artio looked toward the forest and scratched at the gray stubble growing from his unshaved chin.

"Don't worry about the thieves," Aleah said as though she were reading the Mage's mind. "Raven and I can elude them. We'll be safe while you search for the root."

"All right. But I'm going to keep an eye on you from overhead. If you get into trouble . . . Let me think; how can you contact me?" The question was obviously rhetorical. The Mage pursed his lips and scratched his chin. "Renn," he said, "I'm going to teach you how to mind-link. I'm not supposed to teach you things like this—the lore masters will probably disapprove—but I think our situation warrants it."

"Are you sure I can make it work? I tried to use magic against Jomard and nothing happened."

"It'll work. I probably should have taught you more before now; it would have saved us a lot of trouble. But the lore masters are funny that way. They don't like magic users being trained away from their watchful eyes."

For the next hour, Artio taught Renn how to draw on the aeon myriad, focus his mind, and slowly, with deliberate restraint, push his thoughts into another's mind. Renn tried to concentrate, but Raven made it difficult.

"Do you think you can speed this lesson up a bit?" Raven said. "In case you haven't noticed, it's started snowing and we're losing daylight."

"It would help if you'd quit pacing about like a nervous milkmaid," Artio said.

Raven harrumphed, then bent over and checked Lord Danu's pulse. Aleah sat cross-legged on the meadow grass and stared, almost trancelike, into the distance.

"One last thing," Artio said, once he was satisfied with Renn's training. "Don't blast me senseless like you did to that Kiroc two years ago. If you are excited, calm yourself *before* you enter my mind. If you aren't in perfect control, you're likely to turn me into a dawdling fool."

Renn bit his lip. The thought of accidentally destroying Artio's mind made his stomach turn. "I wish I had known how to do this a few days ago. Then I could have warned you about the traps Jomard set."

Artio nodded. "Hindsight is much clearer than foresight. Speaking of the traps, I'd better get looking for lorum root."

Artio took a step back. His staff emitted a green burst of light, and an eagle lifted off the ground where the Mage had stood a moment ago. Renn, Aleah, and Raven watched him fly east until he disappeared into the storm.

"Let's go," Raven said.

Raven and Aleah carefully lifted Lord Danu's limp form onto his black stallion. Then, balancing the young lord with one hand, Raven used the other to pull himself onto the horse's back behind him.

Renn rode Lord Danu's horse, and Aleah led Artio's mount behind her chestnut mare—the horses Jomard had secured from the thieves were long gone. They rode into a narrow gully, and Aleah handed the reins of Artio's horse to Renn.

"I think I should do some looking around," Aleah said as she galloped up to Raven. He looked at the hills surrounding them with narrowed eyes, looked back at Aleah, and nodded once.

After Aleah left, Renn tried to start a conversation with Raven, but the captain didn't help to keep it going. Renn would ask a question, and Raven would answer it simply and directly, then say no more.

Two hours later, they stopped under the protection of a large outcropping of rock. Raven carefully lowered Lord Danu to the ground and gave him water.

"There's bread in my saddlebag," Raven said.

Renn assumed that was an instruction for him to get the food. Raven mixed a little water with the bread, ground it into a pulp, placed it into Lord Danu's mouth, and massaged his throat to help him swallow.

"Get the dried meat and cheese from my bag for you and me." Raven checked Lord Danu's eyes and didn't look up as he spoke.

Renn chewed on a piece of dried meat and watched Raven care for Lord Danu.

Who is this man, really? Renn wondered. *One minute he's a deadly fighter, then a first-rate scout and tracker... then the next he's like a nurse or something.*

Renn took a bite of cheese and wondered if anybody truly knew Raven—maybe Lord Danu did. Maybe that's why Lord Danu trusted him so much.

They rode southwest down a mountain and across a river before they saw Aleah again. Renn looked up for any sign of Artio. He saw a couple birds circling high overhead, but they didn't look like eagles and Renn didn't want to risk mind-linking to find out if one was the Mage. He remembered, with vivid detail, the way he'd destroyed the Kiroc. He decided not to link minds with the old man unless he had no choice.

An hour after sunset, Aleah led them to a thicket of briars and thorns. "There's a cave behind these bushes," she said. "We can spend the night in there."

Raven raised his eyebrows as if he were impressed, but he didn't say anything.

The cave was hidden so well that Renn didn't see the opening until Raven slipped through it. It took a bit of persuasion for them to convince the horses to enter through the tight rocks, but they finally got them all inside. The cave opened into a single large cavern with a small hole in the ceiling above the far wall, underneath which a campfire had burned some time past. With the aid of Aleah's torch, Renn saw the walls were formed of brownish rock. The floor was cold and dirty, but straw and sleeping pallets rested against the back wall. Raven had already laid Lord Danu on one of them.

"What is this place?" Renn asked as he surveyed the dim cavern. "Someone has been here before."

"I've stayed in this cave," Raven and Aleah answered simultaneously as she jammed the torch in a fissure that ran along the wall. They looked at each other, both with raised eyebrows.

"I found it more than ten years ago on my way to Basilea," Raven said. "I didn't think anyone else knew of it." He pointed to a pile of deadwood stacked neatly beside the fire pit. "It doesn't appear anybody's been here since then. The wood I left and the sleeping pallets are still where I put them—I always wondered if I'd use this place again."

"I believe in leaving things the way I find them," Aleah said as she began building a fire. "I didn't know who'd used this cave before me, but I didn't want them to suspect anything if they returned. That was two winters ago."

"What if someone sees the smoke from the fire and finds us?" Renn asked.

"This . . . chimney," the captain said, for lack of a better way to describe the hole above the fire pit, "runs several hundred feet through the mountain and comes out on the other side. Even if someone sees the smoke, they'll never find the entrance."

After they ate and Raven saw to Lord Danu's needs, the captain sat next to Renn beside the waning cooking fire. He said nothing, just sat and stared into the fire.

Aleah pulled out an instrument of several small round hollow reeds tied together with twine and began to play a beautiful but sad melody. Renn listened as he lay by the fire. Aleah was as much or more of a mystery to him than Raven. She'd joined their group as a favor to King Achal, and she had saved all their lives—doing things no woman should be able to do. In fact, Raven was the only man who could even do the kind of stuff Renn had seen Aleah do that day.

"How did the three of you get past the thieves?" Renn asked. Aleah stopped playing to listen to the answer.

Raven pulled his eyes from the fire and looked at Renn as though he'd just noticed he was still there. "I knew where their camp was, so I left Lord Danu and Artio waiting behind a small hill, then charged into the middle of their tents, lighting them on fire, killed the leader, and ran off in the opposite direction." He smiled as though remembering the scene with fondness. "Of course," he continued, "they all followed, and I led them the wrong way."

"You killed the leader? Just like that?" Renn asked.

Raven turned his head and gave Renn a penetrating look, but it was Aleah who answered. "Their leader has killed, robbed, plundered, and raped innocent people for years. There's no shame in killing a man like him."

Renn turned his eyes toward Lord Danu because Raven and Aleah's gaze made him feel uncomfortable. He felt like he was sharing the cave with heroes from legends.

"You care about him a lot. Lord Danu, I mean," he said to change the subject.

Raven's forehead creased, and he looked toward the unconscious lord. "He's like a brother to me. Out here, he is my only family." Then, as if he felt too much of himself had been exposed, he stood and said, "We'd better re-dress your wound and get some sleep. We've a long way to go tomorrow."

"Where are we going?" Renn asked as he unwrapped the bandage from around his thigh and Aleah began playing the mournful tune again.

"Tiaron—the others will be waiting for us there."

During the next week, they traveled the same way. As they left the mountains, it got a little warmer, and Renn was glad to be out of the occasional snow flurries. Artio returned twice; he still hadn't found the lorum root, but he gave them information about the terrain, storms, and even where a camp of small bandits was located ahead. In this way they traveled without much difficulty.

Renn's leg healed quickly, and by the time they reached the end of the Tiarak Mountains and crossed into Tiaronéa, he could walk without limping.

The border between Achtland and Tiaronéa was obvious—as though it had been drawn and planned from the beginning of creation. Where Achtland was green, mountainous, and full of trees, Tiaronéa was a brown, hilly sea of grassy plains.

The change in landscape seemed to have an adverse effect on Raven. Lack of tree cover appeared to make him uneasy. Renn noticed him checking Lord Danu's pulse more frequently and scanning the skies for Artio more often.

"I wish that Mage would hurry," Aleah said one afternoon during the second week as she helped Raven dress Lord Danu's wound. "In another day his leg will be lost." Raven bit his lower lip and looked up to the sky.

As though on cue, a bird appeared on the eastern horizon. It grew larger until it landed on a grassy knoll in front of them and transformed into Artio—startling the horses considerably, as it always did whenever he made the change in front of them.

"I found some," he announced with a broad grin.

"Good," Raven said with noticeable relief. "I only hope it's not too late. The poison is going up his leg."

Raven gently laid Lord Danu down and Artio knelt beside him. He pulled out his ever-present leather pouch and went to work. He soaked the lorum root in hot water, making a dark brown tea that he gave to Raven with instructions to make Lord Danu drink it all. As Raven lifted Lord Danu's head and poured the tea into his mouth, Artio ground the root to a pulp and applied it to the wound. Their work took no more than an hour, and then the small company was on its way again.

When they stopped for supper, Lord Danu coughed weakly and moaned. He opened his eyes, saw the four of them huddled around him, and then smiled and fell back to sleep. Each day after that, the young lord grew stronger and stayed coherent for longer periods of time. Soon, he was well enough that he didn't need Raven's help to stay on a horse, so Lord Danu and Renn rode double.

That same day, Renn saw a faint line in the distance. Each hour it grew wider until it appeared as a blue-gray ribbon winding its way across the plain.

"It's the Wanderove Divide," Lord Danu said.

"Huh?" Renn was startled by Lord Danu's answer to his unasked question.

"That blue line you've been watching. It's the Wanderove Divide. It's the longest and widest river in all of Lemuria and divides the continent almost right down the middle."

"It travels nearly the entire length of Lemuria," Artio said. "It begins far north in Dekla—high in the Mord Mountains. Up there it is only a small stream."

"It splits into many fingers in my country," Aleah added. "One small finger runs through the courtyard of my mother's home," she said longingly.

"I wondered where you were originally from," Raven said. "You're smaller than other women I've met from Domeria."

"And you certainly don't dress like them," Lord Danu added.

She nodded and smiled almost seductively. "At home I do. But I would never parade around in front of *drylander* men like that." She screwed her face into a scowl. "I know how they drool and lust whenever a woman shows a little skin." Once Lord Danu and Raven stopped laughing, she said, "My father was an Achtlander."

Lord Danu gave her a questioning look. She shrugged. "Raven said I was smaller than most women of Domeria—that's why."

Two days later, city walls appeared on the horizon.

"Tiaronéa," Artio announced. "Let's just hope the others didn't run into any trouble getting there."

RETURN OF THE SHADOW

The first checkpoint along the road to Tiaron had been built on a hill—a wheat field on one side of the road and corn on the other. As they passed under the gatehouse, Renn stared at the soldiers in chain mail covered by red mantles with a black knight's helm in the center.

Once they passed the checkpoint, Renn caught another glimpse of the expansive city walls in the distance. It disappeared when they traveled down the gently sloping road into the fields and then reappeared—a little larger—as they topped each successive knoll.

Renn was unable to keep from gawking at the immensity of Tiaron as they approached the city gate. He had never been east of the Tiarak Mountains—even in his travels with Artio—and this city was unlike anything he'd seen.

Achtan might have been as big, but trees, mountains, and hills helped to conceal the true size of the City of Avuman. This city had nothing to hide its vastness. It sprawled out over the plains and along the bank of the Wanderove Divide like an enormous oasis of wood and rock in a sea of fields and grass.

The city walls were made of sandstone, and guards walked the parapets in synchronous intervals—but the massive oaken doors stood wide open on their rusty iron hinges, entreating travelers to enter Tiaron's rest. Like with Achtan, the closer they got to the city gates, the more and more highways merged with the main thoroughfare, and soon the four travelers were surrounded by merchants, wagons, soldiers, farmers, and people from all over the continent of Lemuria.

"Why do so many people come to Tiaron?" Renn asked Lord Danu, with whom he was still riding double. "I mean, it's like this big city just grew out in the middle of nowhere."

Lord Danu chuckled. "It's not the 'middle of nowhere.' It's the middle of Lemuria. The safest way to travel across the continent is through Tiaron and Menet. The cities are so similar to each other that Tiaron is often called the West Twin Gate and Menet is referred to as the East Twin Gate. Most travelers pass between them because travel by riverboat saves many days."

"Raven." Lord Danu turned to the dark-haired captain, who rode at their left. "Do you notice anything unusual?"

"Same thing as you, I'd imagine," he answered calmly but without a hint of sarcasm. "The flag of Valdivar is not flying."

Renn looked at the banners on the parapets—the field had two white squares and two red squares, creating a checkerboard effect. In the center of each white square was a knight's helm; in the center of each red square was a black castle with a single tower.

"What are those flags?" he asked.

"The flag of Tiaron," Lord Danu answered. "But Tiaron owes its allegiance to King Reollyn of Valdivar—every other flag should bear Valdivar's black dragon."

"I don't like it," Aleah said.

Lord Danu gave a questioning look to Artio, who rubbed at his stubbled chin as he considered the flags and then shook his head. "I don't know, but this isn't good," the old Mage said, answering Lord Danu's silent question.

As they rode through the city gates and were passing in front of the relaxed guards into the crowded city, Renn heard someone yelling in a high-pitched voice.

"Renn! Renn!" Genea ran toward them with Tristan and Harlow in tow, and the burly Kivas walked close behind. Renn climbed down off the horse to stretch, then almost wished he hadn't. Genea ran to him and without hesitation wrapped him up in a fierce embrace. When she pulled away, her face was flushed with apparent embarrassment, and tears rolled down her cheeks.

"We thought you had been killed or something." She wiped at her tears with the back of her hand. "Don't ever go off like that again."

"Yeah, Renn. We were all really worried about you," Harlow said. "I didn't even hear you leave our tent that night. Did Jomard kidnap you? Did he hurt you? Where is he now? Are you all right? I wanted to help them find you, but they wouldn't let me—"

"Yes, yes." Renn waved his hand dismissively. "I'm fine. It's not like I *tried* to scare everyone. All the same, thank you for worrying about me."

He was more than a little embarrassed by the reaction of his friends, particularly Genea, but it felt good to know they really did care about him. He thought about the comment his mother made that Genea liked him. At the time, the idea had seemed ridiculous. Now, two months later, he wondered.

He listened absently as Lord Danu told Kivas and the others about their adventure in rescuing him. Artio occasionally interjected bits and pieces to the story, but Raven and Aleah didn't add anything. Genea and Tristan were clearly impressed to hear how a woman had saved them all. Both girls beamed with pride upon learning about Aleah's skill with the bow and sword. As Lord Danu finished the tale, the two girls crowded next to Aleah and pressed her for more details.

Renn saw a white horse pulling a small wagon through the crowded square. Turning to Kivas, he asked, "How is Thorn? Can I see him soon?"

"He hasn't been the same since you left. If I didn't know better, I'd say he's depressed. We thought he might be sick, but Sela's checked him out several times and says nothing's wrong."

Renn felt a sudden wave of guilt. Poor Thorn probably thought Renn had abandoned him, but Renn would explain it to him as soon as they were reunited. "Can I go see him now, Artio?" he asked the Meskhoni.

"Is that all you can think about? Your stupid horse?" Genea's voice rose in pitch as she lost her temper. "We've all been worried sick for the past two weeks, we wait by this gate every day for you, and . . . and all you can think of is your horse. Well, that's just fine, Renn Demaris. If that's all you care about, then go see him." She spun on her heels, red-faced, and stomped off. Renn's mouth gaped open, and he watched her long, dark hair bounce as she walked away.

"What did I do?" he asked.

Lord Danu and the other men wore crooked smiles.

"You really don't know, do you, Renn?" Tristan shook her head and hurried off to catch up with Genea. Renn looked at Lord Danu and the others in confusion, and they broke out in laughter. All except Harlow. He looked as confused as Renn and simply shrugged his shoulders.

"Come on, boy," Kivas said as he slapped Renn on the back. "Climb up with me and I'll take you to him."

Thorn was so excited upon smelling Renn approach that he nearly broke through his stall to greet him. Renn hugged and patted Thorn's muzzle, climbed on the horse's broad back, and walked him out to the grassy paddock. The circular enclosure wasn't large, but it afforded them more privacy than the stable. Just beyond the wooden fence of the paddock—which had been recently mended in places—stood the inn where the company was staying, along with taverns, shops, and other buildings.

As he rode the horse, Renn tried to explain to Thorn what had happened and why he'd left without saying goodbye.

I thought you called that one 'friend', Thorn said as he listened to Renn's tale about Jomard.

I thought he was, but he lied.

I don't understand. What does that mean?

He lied. You know, tricked me, Renn tried to explain. *He pretended to be a friend, but really he was an enemy. Haven't you ever been lied to before?*

Men are confusing indeed. My kind does not . . . lie. We don't know this thing. We simply are what we are.

That would be nice. I wish people were like that. But unfortunately, they're not. Sometimes I wonder who I really can trust.

You can trust me.

A lump rose in Renn's throat. He smiled and patted Thorn's neck.

When Renn finally returned Thorn to his stall, night had fallen. He wandered across the street and stood at the door of the common room of the inn where they were staying. A large fire in a hearth on the far right wall and lanterns hanging from the rafters cast light on a room big enough to hold more than a hundred—it looked as though twice as many were there now. Seated at the bar opposite the door where Renn stood were ferrymen, merchants, and soldiers; all of them looked anxious for a woman or a fight. They talked and laughed loudly. Renn saw Micha sitting in the middle of a small group of patrons at a table in the far corner, playing his lute and leading them in a rowdy song. Coins were scattered in front of him as men threw tips to him.

The tables in the room were filled with people from all over. Most looked like westerners, and he recognized Nortians, Achtlanders, and Boranicans—he was even able to pick out some men from Kahaal by their garb. He finally saw Lord Danu and the rest of the group sitting at two long tables in the middle of the room, just finishing their meal and talking among themselves.

"What took you so long, Renn? I was about to suggest we send Genea to hunt you down," Sela teased, and the men laughed. Renn noticed that Genea pretended not to hear them, but the tops of her ears turned red—she looked like she would explode at any moment.

"Leave it alone, men." Lord Danu looked up from his conversation with Raven, Aleah, and Artio. "Kivas, why don't you join us? We've got some things to discuss."

The big, burly lieutenant sat at the end of the table, making quick work of a large stein of ale. Empty mugs littered the tabletop around him, and when he stopped to look at Lord Danu, his eyes were glazed over.

Kivas grunted and tried to stand but fell onto the floor. He raised himself up and plopped back into his seat. "I'm coming . . . Give me just a moment . . ." he mumbled, and then he passed out—sending the pewter mugs and stein crashing to the floor as his head hit the table.

"He has spirits haunting him, that's certain." Cole rubbed at one of the carved bone pendants hanging on the leather thong around his neck.

"Spirits?" Harlow asked around a mouth stuffed with bread, his eyes wide.

Renn sat between Harlow—who was next to Artio—and Sela Nadgit, who sat by Olosa. Lord Danu, Raven, Genea, Aleah, and Tristan sat on the opposite side by Cole, Durham, and Radien.

"Spirits of the deceased," Cole said. "Before Kivas fled from Nortia and joined our band, he—"

"That's enough, Cole." Durham cut him off with his deep voice. Durham rarely spoke, so when he said something, everybody had a tendency to listen. "We all have our demons . . . including me . . . including you. If Kivas wants to speak of his past, that's up to him."

A serving maid interrupted the uncomfortable silence that followed. After Lord Danu instructed her to bring Renn some food and more ale for him and Artio, he leaned toward the center of the table and spoke in a quiet voice to the group.

"That little excursion Jomard took us on has pretty much ruined our disguise," he said. "We can't very well dress Artio up to be an ambassador of Kahaal tomorrow when he rode in to town as a simple traveler today."

"It's just as well," Artio said. "There are so many Kahaalians around here. I'm certain one or more of them would know we weren't from Kah-Tarku."

"Why not just be simple merchants, like when we left Boranica?" Olosa suggested.

"Maybe that would be best," Lord Danu agreed.

"I think we should have Tristan be the princess of Achtland—like she is—on her way to Anytos to pay a visit to the king." Genea sat straighter on the bench and squared her shoulders.

"That would never work, Genea."

"Why not, Renn? Kivas and his men could be the royal guard; Lord Danu and Artio, her escorts; you and Harlow could be pages; and Aleah and I will be her ladies-in-waiting."

"I don't know that my brother would like it too well," Tristan said with a half smile toward Genea. "He didn't want anybody to recognize me on our journey. And besides, Anytos doesn't have a king—they have a duke."

"It's not a bad idea, Genea." Lord Danu smiled. "But Tristan's right. Her brother specifically asked me to keep her identity secret. He feels that her safety depends on it."

Genea turned her nose up at Renn and said, "Humph. See? Otherwise it was a good idea." Renn still thought it was dumb. If Genea was a lady-in-waiting and he a page, then she could order him about. He was certain she would make the most of that kind of arrangement.

"I think we should use Olosa's idea." Raven spoke for the first time since Renn had arrived. "We can charter a ferry in the morning, ride down the Wanderove Divide, and be in Menet in less than a week. From there we can join a merchant caravan to Anytos. We'd blend in with the crowd."

"Agreed," Artio said flatly. "Now, let's get some ale—after that bout with Jomard, I need to relax."

"Hey." Sela had a look of confusion on his face. "If we're going to . . . uh . . . the island, why are we going through Anytos? Wouldn't it be faster to cut across Tiaronéa and go through Andrika to Port Andrus?"

"Yes, it would be faster," Lord Danu agreed. "However, after talking with King Achal about Kahn Devin's endeavors over the past few months, I'd rather not risk traveling across remote areas. Out on the plains, we'd be too vulnerable to the Tiaro Devi."

"The what?" Harlow asked.

"The Tiaro Devi," Aleah repeated. "They're a nomadic group of hunters and warriors. It used to be that as long as you didn't bother them, they wouldn't bother you. Unless, of course, you had something they wanted."

"But now," Lord Danu continued where Aleah left off, "Kahn Devin has taken control of most of their tribes and they're unpredictable."

"Particularly because Kahn has told them to be on a strict lookout for Renn," Artio added.

"I see your point," Sela said. "Still, we have to travel across a lot of open plains to reach Anytos."

"But the road that way is well-traveled, and we should be able to join a large caravan," Aleah said.

"All right, it's settled. Now let's shut up about it and get some ale before this place closes for the night." Artio signaled for one of the serving girls.

Aleah took Genea and Tristan to their rooms shortly after the men started drinking. Renn figured it was for the best, because the large common room soon resembled a rowdy roadside tavern. The locals surrounding Micha bought him drinks after every song and danced on tables with barmaids to his lively melodies. The patron, a big, burly man, leaned back against the wall with his arms folded and a grin on his face, obviously pleased with the amount of business Micha's talent was bringing.

Tellio joined the party; he danced with two girls, one on each arm, and sang along as loud as he could—even though he didn't know most of the words. Cole also mingled with the party crowd, although he was much more sober and suave in his behavior than Tellio. He leaned against the bar and flirted with an attractive young brunette. Lahar threw knives at a target hanging on one of the walls, and soon Aidan and a few other men joined him. Radien, Sela, Olosa, and Durham played card games while Lord Danu, Raven, and Artio laughed and watched Julius and Beruth, who were involved in a drinking contest.

In all the commotion, Renn and Harlow were virtually forgotten, so Renn took a big swallow of ale—when Artio wasn't looking—but the taste made him cough, and he nearly choked as it burned his throat. Harlow didn't have a much better experience when he tried it either, and after a while, the two boys got bored listening to the lighthearted talk and loud laughter of the men, so they, too, decided to retire for the evening.

"Do you like Genea?" Harlow asked as they climbed the stairs and walked down the candlelit hallway to their room. "Because I think she likes you. The whole time you were missing she kept asking Kivas if he'd heard from Raven or Lord Danu yet, and she kept looking toward the mountains like she was hoping to see you ride out of them. I think she even cried sometimes in her tent at night, though I'm sure she wouldn't admit it—well, maybe to Tristan she would, but not to me."

"I missed you, Harlow," Renn said, shaking his head back and forth. "Believe it or not, I missed you." The gangly, curly-haired Harlow smiled, and his face flushed at Renn's confession.

Renn put the key Lord Danu had given him in the lock, turned it with a click, opened the door, and stopped. An open shutter on the lone window clacked against the wall from the night breeze. Moonlight streamed into the room, casting shadows from the beds and wardrobe. But the dark shadows in the far corner of the room looked unnatural—like black ink. Renn inhaled sharply and held out his hand to keep Harlow from entering the room. He could feel a dark presence nearby. He'd felt it before. Memories of the past flooded back to his mind: when he was younger, he felt like shadows were watching him from the woods all the time. Now he felt that same feeling, here in this room.

"Let's go back downstairs, Harlow." He pushed his friend back into the hall and slammed the door. His hands shook as he shoved the key into the lock and turned it

"Why? What's wrong? I don't want to go back down. I want to go to bed."

"Come on. I left something down there. We *both* need to go." He grabbed his friend's arm and hurried back down the hall, practically dragging Harlow behind.

THE WANDEROVE DIVIDE

Renn couldn't sleep with Artio snoring in the next bed over.

After Renn had pulled Harlow back down to the common room and told Artio about the shadow, Lord Danu and Raven had rushed up the stairs with drawn swords. Whatever had been in the shadows no longer haunted the room, and Renn felt embarrassed. Still, Artio insisted Renn stay in his room.

The small room had a single window in the near wall and an old wooden bureau in one corner, but the furnishings were plush and comfortable. Renn got up, walked to the window, and pulled back the shutter to look outside. In the pale dawn, he could see the paddock across the street where he had walked Thorn the evening before. The cold morning breeze combined with empty streets made the city of Tiaron feel peaceful and even innocent. Soon, however, he knew the streets would be bursting with activity and the late autumn sun would beat against the ground.

"Why are you up so early?" Artio pulled a pillow up over his face, and his gruff voice was muffled as he complained. "You're letting all the light in. Can't you let an old man get some sleep?"

"Aren't you the one who always says wise men rise with the sun?" Renn teased.

"Did I say that? Humph. Well, not when they have a headache from too much drink. Now let me get some sleep, will you? Our ferry doesn't leave until midmorning."

Renn quietly dressed in his traveling clothes—light brown breeches, a white broadcloth shirt, and a tan leather tunic—and slipped out the door.

On his way through the common room, he grabbed carrots, a piece of bread, and cheese and walked across the hard-packed road to the stables.

Thorn nickered as Renn walked in—the horse's hot breath visible in the cool air. As the horse ate the carrots, Renn rubbed hard at his arms to warm himself and wished he'd worn a jacket. He picked up a body brush and stroked Thorn's white coat. He found a rusty currycomb in a basket hanging on the wall outside the stall and used it to remove the grease from the brush.

"I can tell it's been a long time since you've been brushed," he said. "Look at all this grease. Didn't anybody take care of you while I was away?"

The one who works with fire did, but not so well as you, Thorn replied, and then he turned his attention to the water trough.

"The one who works with fire? Oh, Sela Nadgit. Why don't you call him by name?"

What's in a name? He is what he is. A name is just another thing to remember.

Renn laughed at Thorn's simplicity, until the hair on the back of his neck stood on end. He spun around to see if anyone else had entered the stable. The same eerie feeling he'd had in the room last night came back to him now.

Do you feel that? he thought to Thorn.

Yes, the horse replied. *It is wrong. Like the beasts we fought many seasons past.*

Renn remembered the Kiroc and the Demon Dog that Thorn had helped him and Artio fight several years ago and figured that must be what the horse was referring to.

Renn's heart beat faster and faster; whatever caused the sensation of him being watched grew stronger and more powerful. It reached out to him, beckoning him to join with it. Was there really someone there—physically there—or was Kahn Devin using some sort of power to watch him from a great distance?

The shadows in the corners of the stable grew dark and inky. They reached outward like fingers of smoke, beckoning him. The shadows flowed in front of the door to the stable and the gate leading to the paddock—trapping Renn inside.

He thought about getting on Thorn's back and charging out of the stable. Maybe they would catch the shadow by surprise. But then again, maybe the shadows would somehow injure Thorn. Renn didn't dare take that risk. Too many had lost their lives because of him; he couldn't bear the thought of life without Thorn. Instead he huddled in Thorn's stall and took a deep breath.

"Relax," he told himself over and over as he forced his breathing to slow. *Focus*, he thought. *Focus and concentrate. That's the key.* He consciously forced his heart and mind to relax, then attempted to use the techniques of mind-linking the way Artio had taught him two weeks earlier. He formed a mental picture of where he was and the nature of the danger, then gently pushed it out toward Artio's awareness. Renn didn't know whether the shadow wanted to capture or kill him, but the presence felt closer now than ever, so he pushed his mental picture out with a little more force.

He recognized Artio's mind pattern, despite it being muddled and sluggish. He pulled away then—he didn't want to stay in Artio's mind for too long because he needed to focus on keeping himself alive and safe until Artio could come.

He wondered whether Artio understood his message as he peeked around the edge of Thorn's stall. He couldn't see a person, but he still sensed a powerful presence and saw dark shadows. Maybe he and Thorn could escape without the dark force being able to stop them. Maybe the shadow only wanted to observe and didn't have the ability to do physical harm. He hated the uncertainty of it all.

A piercing shriek filled the air, and a great eagle flew into the stable. All of the other horses, startled by the sudden cry of the eagle, reared and whinnied in their stalls, then the bird landed and turned into Artio in a burst of green light.

The dark presence vanished.

"Boy, am I glad to see you," Renn said, stepping out of Thorn's stall. "Something was here. If you hadn't come, I'm not sure what I would have done."

"Well, we surprised him this time. I don't think he knew I was coming. Kahn wasn't able to sense your mind-link through his scrying pool. I can't believe it," the Mage said, shaking his head.

"I *told* you something was in the room last night. I'm almost glad it came again so you could see for yourself."

"That's not what I meant," Artio said. "What I can't believe is that he didn't sense your mind-link—even though he's scrying from a distance. You sent that image to me so powerfully it burned my hangover away in an instant. Kahn should have been able to sense you drawing on the aeon myriad as he watched you—but he apparently didn't."

"Is that good?" Renn asked.

Artio scratched at his chin and looked up. "I think so," he said. "Come on. Let's eat breakfast, and then I'm going to visit the local apothecary shop. I need to find a way to stop the Grand Warlock from scrying you out."

"What do you mean?" Renn stepped next to Thorn and put an arm around the horse's neck. He'd never even heard of scrying. It didn't sound like a good thing. Especially if Kahn could watch him whenever he wanted to.

"I believe the shadow you feel is a powerful Aven-Lore user scrying you—probably Kahn. It's a technique they use to watch things at a distance. If they have some of your hair or a fingernail, they can see you through a pool of water that has been infused with twisted intelligences taken from the aeon myriad. I've never heard of somebody being able to *feel* it the way you do."

"But you can block it, right?"

"It can be blocked, but I don't know the spell. It's part of their lore. That's why I need to find an apothecary who can lead me to an Aven-Lore user I can . . . convince to help us in this matter. Perhaps you should give me a bit of your hair—I think I may need it."

Artio left Renn in the common room to eat with the others. Lord Danu settled their account with the innkeep and led the group to the river.

The sun had not yet reached its zenith as it rose in the clear blue sky, but already the morning chill had burned away. Renn stood on the aft deck of a large riverboat moored to the dock. Beads of sweat were glistening on his forehead from working with Sela to get the horses and luggage on board the ferry. He wiped his forehead and looked for Artio among the crowds in and around the docks.

The streets leading to the river were narrow and dusty, but merchants didn't let that hinder trade; colorful tents and vendor carts lined the roads on every side. Riverboats arrived and left nearly every quarter hour, and boys and girls with dirt-smeared faces accosted visitors and tourists as they walked ashore, offering to carry luggage or give directions for a small price.

Renn scrunched up his nose as the breeze blew the smell of fish across the deck. Not far downriver, fishermen unloaded their catch onto handcarts that young men hauled away. At least it smelled better than the tanners' lane they'd passed on the way to the docks earlier that morning.

Renn saw Lord Danu and the riverboat captain walk down the pier toward the boat. The young lord had mentioned something earlier about trying to secure a group discount rate, but judging by the expression on his face, it didn't look like he'd been successful.

Lord Danu boarded the boat, spotted Renn on the deck, and crossed over to stand by him.

"Where are the others?" He didn't sound happy.

"What's wrong?" Renn pulled his attention from the shore and looked at the blue- and brown-eyed lord.

"Oh, nothing. I feel like I've been robbed is all. Twenty-five copper Valdins each. That's two and a half silver Valdins! The captain wouldn't budge at all. Says he doesn't care if we're all one group or not. Either way, the boat fills up just the same."

It made sense, Renn thought. Judging from all the people coming and going, it wouldn't be smart business to offer discount rates.

"Except for Artio, they're all below, settling into our cabins."

"Hmm?" Lord Danu asked as he looked over the river.

"The others," Renn stated. "They're below deck."

"Oh, yes. Thank you." He turned to go below but saw Artio walking through the crowd. Danu pointed him out to Renn, and they watched him walk up the gangway to join them.

"Any luck?" the old man asked as he leaned against the bulwark and glanced down at the torpid river.

"Not with the shipmaster, if that's what you mean."

"And the other?" Renn didn't know who Artio was referring to, but the young lord obviously did because he leaned against the bulwark next to the Mage and looked to make sure no one else was in hearing range of their conversation.

"I had worse luck with him."

"You mean you didn't locate him?" The Meskhoni raised his eyebrows.

"Oh, I found him. I just didn't like what he told me."

"What are you guys talking about?" Renn asked.

Lord Danu glanced around once more. "I met with one of King Achal's agents this morning. He didn't have good news." The last comment he made more for Artio's benefit. "One of the guards who accompanied us out of the palace through the secret tunnel was abducted last week—Achal is sure Kahn Devin was responsible. At any rate, Achal thinks Kahn knows Renn is alive. However, the guard didn't know our route, so he doesn't think the maniac knows where we are."

The old man looked up at the sky and rubbed the gray stubble on his chin. "That's unfortunate. And I'm afraid he *does* know where we are," he said, grossly understating the circumstance, as far as Renn was concerned.

"What are we going to do?" Renn wrung his hands.

"Well, there's some good news to the report," Lord Danu added. "Kahn is personally leading a small army into North Andrika."

"What in Ba Aven's name is so good about that?" Artio asked, his face turning red.

"It means he isn't here, for one thing," Lord Danu answered. "Also, he's likely concerned with other matters."

"True. However, he could be here within a day or two if he set his mind to it."

"Maybe we'd better warn the others," Renn suggested.

"Other than Raven, I don't think it's necessary at this point," Lord Danu said. "Renn, don't say anything about this to the other children. I don't want to upset Tristan. She knew the guard who was abducted. It would be better for her to hear about this from her brother."

Renn didn't like being referred to as "children," but he agreed without making it an issue.

"And wear this under your clothing against your skin." Artio handed a dark amulet on a leather cord to Renn. It felt smooth, like a small, flat riverstone, with a white rune carved into one side. Renn traced his fingers over the symbol: a long vertical line with a U-shape intersecting it near the top and a smaller horizontal line crossing it near the bottom. Renn hung the amulet around his neck, next to his father's amulet that Tavier had given him years ago.

Lord Danu raised a single questioning brow. "Did you steal that from Cole?" he said lightheartedly.

"Funny," Artio said. "This is why I'm late. I had to meet somebody in the outer city to get this made for Renn. It should stop Kahn—or anyone else, for that matter—from watching Renn through a scrying pool."

※

The days were long on the ferry, and after a while, Renn put the threat of Kahn Devin at the back of his mind. He focused instead on watching the shore slide silently by as the riverboat was propelled downstream by the current and steady strokes of the men in the galley on the deck below. But that grew tiresome, because after about ten miles outside the city walls—after the farms and villages ended—the landscape never changed. Nothing but rolling grassy plains, sage, and an occasional willow patch. He and Harlow would dangle their bare feet over the side of the boat, with their arms folded on the bottom railing of the bulwarks, and watch fish jump, but that, too, only entertained them for so long.

Kivas and the other soldiers played cards most of the day and all of the night, but Lord Danu wouldn't let them drink ale. Genea and Tristan talked a lot and sat in the sun on the upper deck, knitting or sewing. Renn didn't know one from the other, but he had no interest in either, so he and Harlow finally ended up spending most of their free time in the animal stalls with Thorn.

On the third day, as Renn and Harlow sat with their feet hanging over the side watching the shoreline slip by, more than a hundred dark-skinned men stood on the distant shore, watching them pass. They had long black hair, and their faces were painted with red and white stripes above their cheeks. They wore grass or leather loincloths, but their arms, necks, and heads were decorated with all sorts of ringlets, bones, animal teeth, and feathers. They made no threatening gestures, though they held spears and bows, but Renn felt something wrong emanating from them—similar to the feeling he'd had in Thorn's stall back in Tiaron.

"Go get Artio, *quick*," Renn whispered to Harlow.

"What is it? What's wrong?"

"Just hurry up. I'll explain later."

Harlow ran off while Renn sat still and watched. He concentrated on his mind; he cleared his thoughts and built a wall around his aura—the way Artio taught him to hide himself from mental intrusions years ago. Soon he felt a pricking sensation on the edge of his awareness. Something or someone was mentally scanning the boat. Behind the group of strange men, he saw a large, dark figure. He couldn't make out any distinctive features because it wore a long, hooded cloak.

"Renn, put up your guard, but don't make it obvious," Artio said as he, Lord Danu, Raven, and Harlow walked up to the rail and looked to shore.

"I already did. There's some type of magic user with them, but I don't recognize the others."

"The Tiaro Devi," Lord Danu answered. "They are pawns of Kahn Devin now. What are they up to, Artio?"

"They're looking for Renn. Kahn knows we were in Tiaron, and he knows we're headed for Elder Island, so he's probably having his cronies check every boat, road, and path out of the city. Apparently, the amulet is doing its job of hiding Renn from scrying."

"This is crazy," Renn said, shielding his eyes from the sun's glare with one hand as he looked up at the Mage. "For two years Kahn Devin hasn't been able to find us, and then Jomard turns out to be one of his men, we kill him, and two weeks later these . . . these . . . shadows or whatever are following me around again like they know our every move."

Everyone looked at the old magic user for an explanation. He scratched at his chin and looked at the sky. "I think, perhaps, Kahn didn't know where to look for the last two years. After we sent that Kiroc back to him and disappeared, Kahn really didn't know what had happened to us. My guess is that Jomard, somehow, notified Kahn—and gave him some of your hair, or a fingernail, or the like to use to scry you out. The only question is how."

"Maybe Jomard sent a message before he joined us that first night," Lord Danu said.

"Or maybe," Raven said, "his wife, or whoever she is, also works with Kahn."

"Before we left the thieves' camp Jomard sent a note northward on a pigeon," Renn said. "Maybe he also sent some of my hair with that."

"Why didn't you tell me that before now?" Artio asked, raising his eyebrows. Renn felt stupid for not realizing how important that bit of information was before now.

"I thought that's how he notified the army that met us," Renn offered sheepishly as an excuse. "I didn't think—"

"So, what now?" Lord Danu asked Artio. "Do you think they know we're on this boat?"

"I'm not sure. Renn covered his mind before that magic user started his search. But then again, maybe he sensed power from Harlow, Genea, or Tristan. They don't know how to mask themselves yet, and if he sensed their gifts he might guess Renn is onboard as well."

The river carried the boat away from the Tiaro Devi. Renn watched them until they turned, walked away from the bank, and disappeared into the plains.

"They left," Lord Danu said. "Maybe that's a good sign."

"Maybe," Artio said, sounding unconvinced, before he went back below deck.

Renn couldn't sleep that night. He tossed back and forth in his cot, trying to get comfortable, but comfort wasn't the problem. The realization that he was, once again, endangering the lives of his loved ones made him sick. He would leave—maybe then they'd be safe—but where would he go? Besides that, they would only come looking for him, and he remembered all too well what had happened the first time he'd tried to run away. That's when all his troubles had really begun.

He gave up trying to sleep, snuck out of bed so as not to wake Harlow, and left the cabin. He had to feel his way through the dark corridor, up the stairs, and out into the night to avoid stumbling.

A cold breeze brushed across Renn's face as he walked out on deck, and he could see his gray breath in the night air. Only a skeleton crew worked the riggings, and a single man stood on the bridge at the helm, but Renn could hear the gentle slap of oars cutting through water as the men in the galley continued to row with the current.

Renn spotted Artio leaning on the bulwarks near the stern, looking up at the full moon, so Renn walked over to join him. The old Mage heard him approach and pulled his gaze from the sky to see who was there. Recognizing Renn, he turned back around to watch the far shore slide by.

Renn walked up and stood beside him. The metal bulwark felt cold and moist against his palms as he leaned against it for support. The shore was several hundred yards away, and Renn marveled at the width of the Wanderove Divide as he watched it glide by.

Renn watched another ferry pass by them, going the opposite direction until it disappeared. He almost forgot he was standing next to anyone until Artio let out a deep breath.

"It's beautiful, isn't it?" he said.

Renn nodded, though he knew Artio wasn't looking at him. "You couldn't sleep either," Renn said as a statement rather than a question.

"No," the old man said. "I couldn't."

"What's wrong, Artio? Are you worried about the Tiaro Devi we saw earlier?"

Artio shook his head and made an attempt to chuckle. "Oh, I don't know. I'm just thinking, that's all."

"About what?"

"It's nothing, really. Just an old man's foolish sentiment. Ten years ago, I would have laughed if I could have seen myself now." He looked at the sky and pursed his lips.

"What do you mean?" Renn wasn't curious so much as he just wanted to keep a conversation going to help take his mind off Kahn Devin and his relentless efforts to abduct him.

"Well, I don't really know how to explain it. I've never been good at this sort of thing. I was just thinking about the last four years. We've been through a lot together, and I've changed. I used to treasure my solitude and freedom; I wanted to retire and close out the world. I thought I would be happy just to tend my garden, read my books, and enjoy nature until I left this world and returned to Valhasgar to wait for my next incarnation."

Artio looked at Renn and gave him a tight-lipped smile. "I never had a wife or children. I really don't even have a family. Then your father got . . . taken, and I became your godfather. At first, I didn't think I'd care for it much; I considered it my duty. You didn't always mind me well, and you almost got me killed more than once—blasted a hole in my cottage and turned me into a gypsy for two years while we hid from Kahn Devin. Not exactly the kind of retirement I had in mind."

The old man coughed and stared down at the water. Now Renn *was* curious. What was Artio getting at? He looked at the old man's stubbled face and thought the moonlight must have been at an odd angle, because it looked like Artio had tears in his eyes—but Artio never cried.

"Now I know I wouldn't trade you for the world," Artio blurted out and wiped his eyes. "You've been like a son to me. I've learned things from you I never would have understood any other way. I can't imagine my life without you in it ... Look at me, would you?" he said, and his voice cracked. "I sound like a blubbering old dolt. I guess I feel like a part of me will be lost when I leave you on Elder Island."

Renn couldn't stop his own tears; he hadn't realized how much he cared about Artio until now. Artio was like a father. When nobody else could help, Artio had come to his assistance. Even before Renn's father died, Artio had watched over him.

Renn looked up again—Artio was looking down at him with tears on his face, and Renn let go of the rail and caught the Mage in a strong embrace. For a moment they stood there like father and son. It didn't feel strange or embarrassing. It felt more like years and years of pressure were being released.

Renn pulled back and said, "I'll miss you, too, Artio."

TRUTH REVEALED

When they rowed into Menet and moored the river ferry to the dock, Renn had an overwhelming sensation of being someplace he'd been before. The similarities between Menet and Tiaron were unnerving. Small streets packed with vendors, peddlers, merchants, and travelers led from the dock into the central part of the city. The names of establishments were different and some of the buildings had changed, but the layout and activity of the two cities was nearly identical. No wonder people referred to Menet and Tiaron as the Twin Gate Cities.

Renn stood at the front of the riverboat with Lord Danu, Raven, and Artio as they waited for the gangway to be lowered and the signal to disembark from the captain.

"No black dragon flags here either," Lord Danu said to no one in particular. "I wonder what's going on. I'm almost tempted to pay a visit to Duke Nalbron and find out."

"Maybe Duke Mytton can tell us once we get to Anytos," Raven said. "I think our plan to remain anonymous until then is still best."

Renn looked at the banners on the city walls. They were nearly identical to the flag of Tiaron. "Why does the flag of Tiaron have a knight's helm in the white squares and the flag of Menet have a red diamond?"

"Very observant," Artio said. "The cities have a long history with each other and are similar in many ways. Their royal families have intermarried for centuries, so the sigils are also similar. One big difference is that Menet is the source of some of the wealthiest diamond mines in all of Lemuria. Tiaron is known far and wide for their fearsome knights and cavalry."

The ferry captain whistled loudly, signaling that they could leave the boat. The morning sun cast long shadows as they disembarked.

"Hurry up, everyone," Artio said. "I want to be to the east gate by noon. With any luck we'll find a caravan on their way to Anytos that we can join up with."

"Why do we have to join a caravan today?" Kivas asked as he dropped the crate he was carrying onto the wooden planks of the dock. "We can enjoy the city tonight and join one tomorrow. I, for one, would like to rest."

"I agree with Kivas." Sela looked up from inspecting one of Thorn's shoes. "I hear the inns in Menet are even better than those in Tiaron."

"We're not taking votes, you two," Lord Danu said as he mounted his horse. "I've already spent twice as much on lodging and travel than I had intended, and I'm not giving this city the opportunity to get its sticky fingers on my purse strings, too."

The company arrived at the east gate shortly before noon. When they rode out of Menet, they entered into a transient city of tents and wagons that stretched for a mile across the hilly plains and surrounded the city walls. Olosa set about to prepare lunch while the other men checked their weapons and the supply wagon to make sure all was ready for the one-hundred-and-fifty-league journey to Anytos. Renn and Harlow helped Sela and Durham feed and water the horses while Lord Danu and Artio set off to find a caravan for the company to join.

Just after midday, Raven rode out of the city gates driving a solid wagon pulled by a strong team of gray-flecked horses. The men stopped working and gathered around Raven's cart. Aleah didn't leave her post—she was on guard duty—but Renn noticed that she did look with curiosity toward the commotion.

"Where did you get all these spices and oils, Captain?" Lahar, the skinny, beak-nosed soldier asked.

"*Why* did you get all these spices and oils?" Kivas said.

"We're merchants. It's part of the disguise. If we have no merchandise, we'll draw suspicion."

"This must have cost a fortune," Lahar said as he tossed a vial of oil back and forth between his slight hands. "Where did you get the money to buy it all?"

"Does Lord Danu know you bought this trash?" Beruth joked.

Raven didn't answer, but he did raise an eyebrow, and Renn thought he saw the captain actually wink.

Finding a caravan turned out to be as easy as Kivas had said it would be. Late fall was a popular time for travelers to cross the lower plains of Tiaronéa, and every caravan welcomed more people into their group. The fact that Kahn Devin had effectively taken over the Tiaro Devi had put fear into most travelers, and that also made Lord Danu and his men a welcome addition to the merchant caravan. By midafternoon, they were on their way.

Lord Danu wore a rich green doublet and hose to look the part of a wealthy merchant. Once again, Artio acted as his grandfather and the girls played the role of nieces. Aleah now acted the part of Lord Danu's mistress. Renn and Harlow fell back with Kivas and his men; they were to be Lord Danu's pages, and the soldiers acted as mercenaries hired to protect him in his travels.

Renn and Harlow rode beside Durham. The stocky soldier wasn't very talkative, but he was good company.

It is good to be off the wood that rides the water, Thorn communicated to Renn. *I did not like the smell, and there was no place to run.* Renn didn't reply, but he agreed wholeheartedly.

These plains looked the same to Renn as the plains surrounding Tiaron. Farms and ranches dotted the land for about ten miles outside of the city—close enough to be protected by the city guard should they be raided. But rolling hills covered with grasses and sage met them once they rode outside of the farming district.

The caravan consisted of more than twenty wagons and a few dozen riding men. The women and children in the group rode in covered wagons. Renn and Harlow, in fact, were the only youth who didn't ride in a wagon.

Genea and Tristan rode with Artio; Lord Danu and Aleah rode in a new coach that Lord Danu had purchased in Menet; and Raven was their driver—the dark-haired captain had entrusted the wagon of merchandise into Tellio's care.

The company headed almost due east. Lord Danu lined up their group near the middle of the caravan. As they rode, Renn's eyes roamed aimlessly over the vast expanse of grasslands, and he let his mind wander. Unfortunately, Genea's high-pitched call pulled him out of his reverie.

"Renn!" she hollered as she leaned out a side window of the coach. "Come here, please."

"What is this all about?" he asked—more to himself than anyone else—as he trotted Thorn up alongside the carriage.

She gave a quaint little smile and, cupping her chin in her hands as she rested her elbows on the window, said, "Would you be so kind as to fetch some water for us?"

"What? You called me up here just to do that?" He wanted to shout at her, but he remained somewhat calm. "Get your own water. I'm not your slave."

Her lower lip dropped, and her eyes opened wide as she pouted. "Please, Renn. You *are* our page, you know."

"Oh, so that's it. You want to play the part of—"

"Now, Renn." Artio sat next to Genea. "She did say please. Besides, I could do with some water myself."

Renn scowled at the Mage. He wanted to say, "I thought you were on my side," but Lord Danu sat with a half grin on his face, and Renn knew all of them were on the verge of laughing. So instead, he pulled back hard on Thorn's reins and trotted to the supply wagon.

Why did you do that? Thorn asked, shaking his long white mane.

I'm sorry, Thorn. Genea just knows exactly how to make me mad.

But I didn't make you mad. Why did you pull me if she made you mad?

I'm sorry. It's kind of hard to explain—people are just that way sometimes. We take our anger out on the wrong person.

People are difficult to understand.

Exactly, Renn replied. *Especially girls.*

Renn unpacked an extra waterskin, filled it with water from a barrel, and trotted back to Lord Danu's coach.

"Here." He tossed the waterskin through the window onto Genea's lap. "Don't drink it all at once 'cause I'm not getting any more." He saw a look of disappointment on Artio's face as he turned and rode back toward Harlow and Durham, but he didn't care. He was sick of Genea and her little games.

"What was that all about? Why did Genea call you? Was something wrong? Did Artio want you for something—"

Renn held up his hand to make Harlow stop talking. "Her *greatness* wanted a drink to wet her delicate lips. Sometimes I wish she were a boy so I could introduce her delicate lips to my fist."

"Yeah, me too. Girls sometimes do the dumbest things," Harlow said.

Renn was surprised his gangly friend didn't start rambling again.

Durham chuckled deep in his chest, shook his head, and said, "You may not like girls too well now, but someday they'll turn into women." He squinted his eyes and pursed his lips. "Of course, you still won't understand them, and their games only get more complex."

"I'll just avoid them then," Renn said. "I don't need their nonsense."

"Me too," Harlow said. Durham didn't answer; he just chuckled his deep chuckle and kept riding.

When the caravan stopped for the night, they made a large circle with the wagons and set up their tents in a circle inside of the wagons with a fire in the center of camp. Lord Danu told Renn that without trees for cover, the strange arrangement would provide the best defense should they be attacked.

"Do you think we'll be attacked?" Renn asked.

Lord Danu looked up at the stars, which were just now beginning to fill the darkening sky, then back at Renn. "I don't know," he said. "I really don't know."

Lord Danu's admission troubled Renn. He excused himself and walked across camp to the supply wagon. The cooking fire in the center of the circle sent shadows flickering across the tents, and the firelight even reached to the covered wagons and carriages, which made it difficult to see outside the ring of their camp. However, from the edge of the ring, he could look out across the prairie and see for miles. He could see the silhouettes of Beruth and Julius outlined against the twilight sky as they stood warding the caravan.

He thought about the possibility of an attack. If one came, it would only be because he was with the group. Normally, a group the size of their caravan could cross Tiaronéa without any harassment. But with Kahn Devin looking for him, anything might happen. He thought about all the people who had been injured or killed for his sake, and—though he knew it didn't help to feel sorry for himself—he wished, for the thousandth time in his life, that things could be different. He pulled his father's eagle pendant from under his shirt, ran his thumb over the runes etched into the back, and let out a sigh.

He felt a light touch against his shoulder and jumped. His stomach knotted up with a pang of fear. He whirled around and drew the long hunting knife he'd started keeping with him since his incident with Jomard a month earlier. He breathed a sigh of relief and lowered his weapon when he saw the startled face that looked back at him.

"Don't do that, Genea. It can be dangerous to sneak up on a guy."

"Boy, you sure are jumpy," she said crossly. "And besides, I didn't sneak up on you, I just walked over normally. What are you looking at?"

"Oh, nothing," he said. "I'm just thinking, that's all."

"About what?"

For some reason, Genea was really getting on his nerves. Maybe because of the way she'd acted earlier—he wasn't sure—but he didn't want to be bothered by anyone right now, especially her.

"It's none of your business. Just leave me alone."

Genea's mouth dropped open, and Renn wished he could pull his words out of the air before they reached her ears and stuff them back down his throat. Genea looked like she was about to yell back at him; she stammered to find the right words but instead burst into tears and ran off to her tent.

Renn watched her go. He almost ran after her. He knew he should apologize and explain himself, but he couldn't make himself move. Then he saw Artio walking toward him.

Oh, great, he thought. *Now he's going to give me a lecture on my manners.* Renn turned back around to look across the plains. He didn't watch the Mage approach, but he felt his presence and knew he stood beside him, looking at the night sky and trying to decide how to begin.

"You really shouldn't be so hard on her, Renn," he said after a while. "There's something I think you should know. I've debated about whether or not I should be the one to tell you, but I think it's time you learned."

"What are you talking about?" Renn asked. He turned to look at the Meskhoni, whose hair looked silver in the pale moonlight. Artio looked up at the stars and rubbed absently at his chin.

"Do you remember near the beginning of our journey, when you saw Genea bathing?"

Renn felt his face flush furiously. He didn't think anyone but Genea, Tristan, and he knew about that. He wanted to explain that it was an accident, but instead he only nodded.

"Do you know where she got all the scars on her back?"

This time he shook his head.

"Watch."

The old man held his staff out in front of them and turned it in a circular motion. A greenish mist began to build in the air before Renn, and then a scene appeared. He saw a small, run-down shack in the center of an unkempt farm. He recognized Genea's family farm immediately—the home of the Red Bear. As he watched the vision unfold, the shack grew nearer and nearer until it seemed as though he and the Mage were actually inside the run-down home. A flood of memories ran through Renn's mind. The furniture, the sounds, even the smells took him back years, to the last time he'd been in that place.

He heard a whimper coming from the back room. He walked toward the sound. Even in the darkness, he recognized Genea's scared cry. Then the front door burst open, and light from Raul's torch filled the entire house. Genea's cry grew more fearful and intense.

"Come out, you little bitch!" he yelled as he headed for his crying daughter. "You warned them, didn't you? You told them to leave!" By this time he was standing above her, shouting at the top of his lungs. Renn could see Genea's face, white with fear but streaked red from tears.

"I—I—" She started to speak but was cut off by a hard strike from the back of his hand. She fell to the floor and began sobbing uncontrollably.

"Do you realize what you've done? That boy's a monster; someone has to get him before it's too late. Stop crying and look at me!" Genea didn't move. "Fine. If you want to sit and cry, I'll give you something to cry about."

He threw the torch down, took off his belt, and began whipping her across the back. She screamed in pain, and Renn wanted more than anything to intervene, but he could do nothing. He was an invisible witness to an event that had taken place four years earlier.

Inari ran into the room. "Stop it!" Genea's mother screamed. "You're killing her!"

"Shut up! Both of you." He threw his wife to the floor and continued hitting Genea with his belt. Renaul rushed into the room, pulled a blanket off the bed, and tried to smother the flames that had begun to spread from the torch Raul had thrown to the floor.

By the time Raul stopped beating Genea, the room was engulfed in flames, and she no longer moved. He hit his screaming wife across the face—knocking her unconscious—then dragged her and his son out of the house. Renn hurried to Genea's side and bent to pick her up, but he couldn't touch her. Tears filled his eyes as he tried in vain to save her. She was dying for saving his life—he had to do something.

Raul burst back into the room, threw Genea over his shoulder like a sack of grain, and then rushed out of the burning home. Renn could hear horsehoofs beating against the dirt and the rattle of wagon wheels as Raul fled with his family.

"She was only ten years old," Artio said.

The vision ended, and Renn found himself standing back at the edge of the ring of wagons, next to the old Mage once more. He wiped his sleeve across his eyes to dry the tears. Renn didn't speak. He knew Artio wasn't finished; he wasn't quite sure if he wanted him to finish, but he waited and listened anyway.

"Lord Danu sent scouts to find them and bring Raul to justice. Cole caught up with them near Lone Dale. When Raul saw him coming, he tied Genea to a horse and whipped the animal to make it run. Cole had to either save Genea or catch Raul. Nobody could find them after that. I suspect he took his wife and son across the northern border into Nortia."

Renn turned away and looked toward the plain once more. He didn't want Artio to see the tears running down his cheeks. He wanted to say something, but he couldn't; if he spoke now, he'd lose his composure completely. His soul ached with regret, and his heart filled with emotions he couldn't name. How could he ever face her again? She'd nearly died to save him, and he had never gone out of his way to even be her friend. In fact, he had been unfair and cruel to her many times.

"I just thought you should know." The Mage turned and walked back to the fire, where the company had gathered to listen to Micha sing songs and tell stories. Renn turned and watched Artio walk away. He felt worse and more confused now than when he'd first left Lord Danu to come sort out his thoughts.

He needed to talk with someone—someone who would listen and not judge, but he also wanted to go to Genea and beg her forgiveness. He ambled toward Genea and Tristan's tent, paused in front of it, then turned and hurried to the picket where Thorn was tied.

TIARO DEVI

Renn rode in silence the following day. Harlow tried to cheer him up, but after a while, even he gave up and stopped talking. Genea rode with Tristan, Lord Danu, Aleah, and Artio in the carriage as she had the previous day, but this time she didn't call to Renn—he found himself wishing she would.

He thought about the week they'd spent playing together as children. Renn's mother babysat Genea while Inari Lucian, Genea's mother, nursed Raul back to health. The Red Bear, as Renn and Tavier called him, had nearly been killed by the wild animals that had come to protect Renn against his wrath. During that week, Renn and Genea had grown close. He remembered the games she liked to play and how he pretended not to like them because he was a boy. But her father had put an end to their friendship—once he'd recovered from his wounds—and things were never the same afterward. The way Renn had messed things up now, they would probably never be the same again.

Once, during the day, he urged Thorn to a canter and caught up to Genea's carriage, but he lost the nerve to speak with her, so he fell back in line beside Durham and Harlow.

When they stopped for lunch, Renn watched her and Tristan as they ate and talked, but again, he couldn't muster up the courage to walk over and apologize. Genea didn't act upset, but she wouldn't look at Renn even when she knew he was watching her.

After a few days, Genea began talking to Renn and acknowledging his presence again, and that made him feel a little better. He thought that with time she might let bygones be bygones and he wouldn't have to say anything about his feelings at all; that course of action was much easier, so he decided it would be best.

Renn sat taller in his saddle, released a long breath, and gazed over the grassy landscape. The vast plains of Tiaronéa seemed endless. Other caravans frequently passed them going the opposite direction, and once or twice he caught a glimpse of Tiaro Devi in the distance. After watching one of the tribes, he turned to Durham and asked, "Which city does the king of Tiaronéa live in?"

"Valdivar," he said. Renn had heard the name of that city before, but he knew nothing about it.

"Where's Valdivar?"

"On the shores of the Drbal Divide near the banks of the Western Tiarak River," the gentle soldier answered.

"Why doesn't he do something about Kahn Devin and the Devi tribes?" Renn asked.

Kivas was riding behind Renn and had heard their conversation. Before waiting for Durham to respond, the big Nortian lieutenant spoke up.

"King Reollyn hides in his palace and cares nothing for the plains as long as the Twin Gate Cities pay their taxes. In fact, if the truth be known, he'd probably thank Kahn Devin for conquering the Tiaro Devi. The tribes have never acknowledged the government of the Valdivar kings, and the rulers of Tiaronéa have often tried to drive the Devi northward to Dekla."

"Why do the kings of Valdivar hate them so much?" Renn asked.

Kivas shrugged.

Durham rubbed his cheek. "Men fear what they don't understand," he said. "The Devi tribes are mysterious and different. Their skin is darker; they wear nothing but grass skirts, animal hide, and war paint; and they make the entire land their home. 'Civilized' men cannot tolerate such things, so they seek to destroy them."

Why does he call that which is not civil 'civilized'? Thorn asked Renn with a whinny, a twitch of his ears, and a shake of his head.

"He was being sarcastic."

"What's that?" Durham asked.

"Oh, nothing." Renn didn't feel like explaining the way he and Thorn spoke to one another, so he continued his questions. "Why won't the Devi tribes just acknowledge the king for the sake of peace?"

"I grew up in Anytos," Tellio said. "They don't bow to our king because they have their own clan leaders and even a high clan chief. The high chief is like their king. As far as they are concerned, they are a separate nation with separate laws. And like their cousins to the north and south, they lived in this land long before merchants and traders came. They think the people of Tiaron, Menet, Valdivar, and even Anytos should honor their clan chiefs as supreme rulers."

Durham furrowed his brow. "That's what is so strange about it all."

"What's strange?" Kivas asked.

"The Tiaro Devi are such a proud people. I would have thought they would fight to the death before giving in to anybody, even Kahn Devin."

"That *is* strange," Tellio said. "I have thought the same thing many times since word reached us that Kahn Devin conquered them."

During the next week, Renn felt the faint whispers of shadows searching after him. Each time it came, he shielded his mind so it wouldn't find him, but every day it grew stronger. It became so frequent he finally spoke about it to Artio and Lord Danu when they stopped to set up camp one night.

"Are you sure?" Lord Danu asked, noticeably worried as he held his hands above the fire's warmth in the center of their circular camp.

"I thought I felt something," Artio said, rubbing his chin, "but I couldn't place my finger on it. Kahn is fishing for you—I should've anticipated this."

"Don't blame yourself, Meskhoni. Besides, it could be anything."

"No, we're probably being followed," the gray-haired Mage said.

Lord Danu folded his arms and tapped one finger against his chin while he stared into the fire. "How much further to Anytos?"

Artio looked up at the cold, starlit sky and squinted. "Thirty, maybe forty leagues. We should be there in two days' time."

"Good. The sooner we leave these plains, the better."

A freezing wind blew from the northwest as they traveled the next day. During lunch, as they sat huddled in blankets and ate, the probing shadow swept the plains again. This time Artio caught its trail and followed it with his mind to its source. Renn, Lord Danu, and Raven watched intently as the old man seemed to transform into a shell with no life as his spirit traveled across the distance. Artio's face turned white, and he opened his eyes.

"We are in danger," he said as he struggled to his feet. The power he'd expended in following the shadow obviously had taken a toll on his strength.

"What is it?" Lord Danu jumped to his feet. "What did you see?"

The old man leaned heavily on his staff and wiped the sweat from his brow. "Now I understand how Kahn Devin mastered the Devi so easily. He didn't use force. He sent a Kiroc Warlock as an emissary to Sambuta, the high clan chief, and the Kiroc put Sambuta under his power. The tribes think they are still following their chief—they don't even know he's become a pawn to the Kiroc."

"*Ba Aven's breath!*" Lord Danu swore. "Are they near?"

"Very. More than two hundred of them."

Lord Danu gritted his teeth and straightened his jacket. "Jesson!" he called to the burly merchant caravan leader. "My scout spotted a large group of Devi coming our way. We need to make haste."

Jesson's eyes grew wide, and he turned and ordered the caravan to prepare to leave.

Lord Danu turned to Raven and said, "Tell the men to prepare for battle. Whatever happens, the children must make it through alive.

"Let's get moving," Lord Danu called out to the lead wagon master, and the caravan started off toward Anytos.

Renn rode beside Durham, Kivas, and Tellio with the other soldiers right behind, but he could sense the power of the one trailing them. Every few minutes, the dark, probing sensation returned with more power than the time before. A sense of urgency welled up inside Renn's chest, and he had to suppress the urge to make a mad dash for the gates of Anytos.

The caravan traveled faster now, but not fast enough for Renn. He could feel the Kiroc's power like an icy hand clutching after him in the cold air.

The lead wagon master brought his horses to an abrupt halt. Renn trotted Thorn alongside Lord Danu's carriage to see what the problem was. The young lord, Artio, and Raven were engaged in a lively conversation. The Meskhoni looked beyond the front of the caravan to a large knoll less than a league away, and Renn followed his gaze. More than fifty Devi warriors stood in a line on the crest.

Jesson, the company leader, rode up to Lord Danu and Artio. Although Lord Danu had not revealed who he and his men were, Jesson had grown accustomed to asking his advice from time to time.

"Devin." He called Lord Danu by the alias he'd given him. "What think you? Shall we turn and seek to bypass this threat, or press on and hope they mean us no harm?"

Artio answered first. "There is a much larger group trailing us with Sambuta and a Kiroc Warlock leading them. I think our best chance is to drive straight at the smaller group and, if necessary, break through their ranks and make a run for Anytos."

Jesson rubbed his finger through his coarse black beard and looked toward the threat standing on the grassy knoll.

"But do you think that necessary, old man?" he asked. "The Tiaro Devi seldom attack large caravans. Maybe the warriors trailing us and these in our way mean to fight each other?"

Raven, Lord Danu, and Artio glanced at each other. Artio nodded once to Lord Danu, who grimaced and then took a deep breath.

"Jesson," he said, "I fear I may have endangered you and your group. I did not tell you this before because I didn't think it would be necessary, but you need to know the truth."

"The truth about what?"

Lord Danu pulled a medallion that bore his family seal from underneath his tunic. "My name is not really Devin," he said. "I am Lord Danu of Basilea, and this is the Mage Artio. Allow me to introduce my captain, Raven." He pointed at the dark-haired man and then nodded toward Kivas and his soldiers. "That big Nortian is Kivas, my lieutenant. The rest of my men are soldiers, not hired mercenaries."

Kivas approached and stopped at Lord Danu's side. Kivas's dark beard had specks of frost in it now from the condensation of his breath.

"What are you doing traveling with a merchant caravan?" Jesson shouted, his eyes bulging and wild. "Are you in some sort of trouble? Is that it? You thought you could escape by hiding in our company? I should just turn you over to them if that's what they're after."

"No!" Lord Danu grabbed the man's riding tunic and pulled him next to his face. "Listen to me. The children with us are marked by the gods. One of them may even be a Child of the Blessing. They must make it to Elder Island."

Jesson's eyes grew dark. He glared at Lord Danu and pushed himself away. "I don't care about blessings and promises. All I know is you brought danger upon our caravan and a battle that is not ours to fight. Why should we—"

"Jesson," Artio interrupted. "If this Kiroc who leads the Devi takes these children, he will give the promised one to Kahn Devin. If that happens, it will only be a matter of time before *all* of Lemuria become his subjects."

"His slaves," Raven said.

Renn felt awkward being referred to as the "promised one" and spoken of as though he wasn't present.

Jesson bit his lip, ran his big hand through his dark hair, and paced. He stopped and looked toward the knoll. The band of warriors moved closer now, closing the gap at an incredible pace.

"All right. What should we do?"

"My men and I will ride up front so we can do the brunt of the fighting," Lord Danu said. "If we hurry, we should be able to break through before the warriors at our back reach us." Turning to Kivas, he said, "Get the men, inform them of our situation, and meet me up front."

"Yes, my lord."

"Renn." Lord Danu stepped toward him. "May I ride Thorn? I want you to ride with Genea and Tristan in the wagon."

Renn bit his lip and looked down at Thorn. As far as he could remember, nobody had ever ridden Thorn but him.

It's all right. I like this man, Thorn said, sensing Renn's reservations.

"Sure." Renn nodded and dismounted. He hugged the big white horse's muzzle as he crossed in front of him.

"You be careful, Thorn. And take care of Lord Danu." Thorn whinnied and shook his long mane.

"Olosa!" Lord Danu called to his cook.

The chubby man rode up and gave a quick salute. "Yes, my lord."

"I want you to let Raven use your horse. I need him and Aleah with me. You'll drive the carriage. Where's Harlow? I want him in the wagon as well." He turned to the old Mage. "Artio, you ride in the wagon also. If we do have to stop and fight, I'll lead the wagons into a circle. Make sure the children get underneath the wagon, and then you help us however you can."

Renn winced at being referred to as "the children" but let it go.

"I will be involved in my own battle," Artio said. "Someone will have to stop that Kiroc Warlock."

When the caravan leader, Jesson, heard that, he let out a high-pitched yelp. "A battle between a Mage and a Warlock? Sweet Azur, what have you gotten us in to?" He turned and ran to his carriage at the front of the caravan.

Lord Danu led the caravan with more than a dozen soldiers riding at his back. They charged forward, and the carriage bounced back and forth as they lumbered over the rough dirt road.

Renn sat across from Tristan and Genea. The two girls held on to one another, and Genea cried softly. Renn wanted to comfort them, but he didn't know what to do.

Finally, Tristan broke the silence.

"Artio, what's going to happen?" she asked.

"Hmm? Oh . . . don't worry. Everything will work out, you'll see."

"I'm scared, Artio." Genea wiped her eyes with her sleeve.

The old man reached his weathered hand over, took hold of her small hand, and patted it. "I know, dear. I know."

Renn looked out the window at the grassy plains passing by. A wave of guilt washed over him, and he felt sick to his stomach. This whole mess was his fault. If he weren't there, Kahn Devin wouldn't care about this caravan any more than any of the hundred other caravans in Tiaronéa. But now, because of him, more people would die. Even if no one in their company was injured, some of the Tiaro Devi would be. And they weren't to blame; they were simply puppets controlled by the Kiroc who led them.

Renn heard a shrill war cry from the front of the caravan, followed by dozens more. Metal clanged against metal and horses neighed. Genea buried her eyes in her hands. Renn's stomach twisted in knots, and he clasped his hands over his head.

It had begun.

THE BATTLE

Renn leaned his head out the carriage window. The dust kicked up by horses and wagons made it difficult to see the head of the wagon train.

Lord Danu and his men fought against bony, dark-skinned warriors, most of whom wore leather loincloths and war paint. The Devi warriors cried out a high-pitched war call over and over as they darted into battle, jabbing long spears at Lord Danu and his men. Although the soldiers were outnumbered two to one, they had the advantage of being mounted and armored, and the Devi warriors began to retreat over the rolling hills.

"They're doing it," Renn shouted. "Lord Danu's beating them!" Genea laughed a little through her sobs, and Tristan and Harlow poked their heads out the window to see.

"*Great Azur!*" Tristan shouted. Her eyes were as big as tea saucers, and her face turned white as a sheet as she pointed behind them. "Look!"

Everyone in the wagon turned and saw a solid line of dark-skinned, black-haired, painted warriors coming over a hill to the rear of the company. Genea screamed and covered her mouth. Artio leaned out the window and whispered, "Lord Danu, to the rear, look to the rear." Artio must have sent his words to the young lord's mind, because no sooner did Artio finish than Lord Danu looked over his shoulder and saw the other army. He made a circular motion with his arm above his head and began leading the caravan into a defensive ring.

Renn watched Thorn's stride as he bore Lord Danu on his back. He'd never realized how regal and beautiful Thorn was until he watched him carry Lord Danu—he was a perfect horse, fit for a king.

Once the caravan got in its defensive position, Artio hurried Renn and the others out of the carriage. They scurried to the ground, crawled underneath the carriage, and watched the main group of Devi warriors approach. Their shrill war cry filled the air as they raced across the grassy plains. Genea still sobbed, and even Tristan was shaking. Renn reached over, awkwardly grabbed hold of Genea's hand, and gave it a squeeze. She looked up at him, tear streaks lining her face, and sniffed. She looked down at his hand holding hers, then slid across the ground and clung to his side. It felt odd but strangely comfortable, so he reached his other hand around her shoulders and pulled her closer.

The Devi warriors were only a hundred steps away from their position now. Lord Danu placed Aleah and some of the men inside and behind the wagons and armed them with bows and arrows. The rest of his men and the merchants who knew how to use a sword were divided into four groups and were standing ready—opposite each other, inside the circle of wagons—poised to drive off those who made it past the arrows.

The Devi warriors charged at all sides of their defenses, screaming and waving swords and spears as they ran. Lord Danu raised his arm, and all the archers watched for the signal to fire.

Lord Danu waited.

Renn's insides felt bunched in knots, but still the young lord waited.

Finally, when the Devi were within fifty steps, he dropped his arm. Over the cry of the Devi, Renn heard the twang and whir of arrows as they flew toward their targets. Most of the arrows landed true, and more than a dozen warriors fell and were trampled by their own men rushing forward.

The archers fired another volley, but the arrows stopped in midair, as if they had hit an invisible wall, and dropped harmlessly to the ground.

Renn saw the Kiroc Warlock hold up a bone glowing with red power. His disproportionately broad shoulders were covered by a long black cloak. He was easily twice as big as any of the warriors and stood next to the only mounted Devi. This, Renn guessed, was Sambuta, the high clan chief. Not only was he the only one on horseback, but he also wore a large, colorful headdress of deer antlers decorated with dyed feathers, and his war paint was more elaborate than the other warriors'.

The archers fell back, and all the men drew their swords. As the dark-haired warriors attacked their position, Raven and Lord Danu burst through openings between the wagons with a few mounted men following behind. Kivas and Tellio led a group through another position, and Renn knew that on the other side of the circle Durham and Aleah were leading one group while Jesson was leading another.

Lord Danu and Raven charged through the ranks of Devi soldiers, their swords a blurry motion of death, felling all in their path. Five Devi attacked Raven simultaneously, and Renn watched as all five fell to the ground, life seeping from their wounds. The dark-haired captain emerged unscathed.

Renn looked around and saw women and children hiding underneath the other wagons in the caravan; fear was etched onto their faces, and many were crying. He wished he could do something useful; after all, this band of Devi warriors was attacking because of him. But he was helpless. He knew how to use a sword, but he would be quickly killed in the battle that was underway. And besides, he had no weapon but his knife.

A bright red light flashed from behind the Devi lines where the black-dressed Warlock stood, and a crimson bolt of lightning shot toward Lord Danu. Renn wanted to shout to the young lord, warn him to move, but by the time it would take him to form the words, the bolt would have already struck. Thorn moved graciously and nimbly through the battle, but even he didn't see the bolt come.

Despair lept into Renn's heart at the thought of losing Lord Danu and Thorn, but then a bright green shield appeared in between the lord and horse just before the bolt of red power hit. The collision of the two powers broke through the air and boomed loudly above the war cry of the

Devi warriors, knocking several to the ground and causing the fight to pause. Even though Lord Danu was protected from the brunt of the attack, the repercussion of the impact had thrown him off Thorn's back into the middle of a group of stunned Devi warriors.

An unpleasant odor filled the air, reminding Renn of the battle Artio had fought against a Kiroc more than two years ago. The red power of the Aven-Lore left a stale and acrid smell in its wake that made him cringe.

Once the initial shock of the blast had worn off, Renn saw Lord Danu buried under a mad assault of painted warriors. Raven charged into the foray and dove from his horse's back into the center of the fight; he, too, was buried by a mass of brown bodies.

Aleah charged in on her chestnut horse. She guided the animal with her knees and attacked with a sword in each hand.

Genea cried out Lord Danu's name over and over; Renn held his breath as he watched, and his mind raced to think of a way to help his friends.

A wall of green energy slammed into the crowd of fighters who swarmed around Aleah and the two men. Warriors on the outer edges of the battle scattered under its blow, giving room for Aleah to better maneuver her horse.

Now Renn could see the flashing motion of swords and knives covered with scarlet blood from within the foray. Lord Danu and Raven struggled to their feet and tried to fight their way through the mob of warriors to the path Aleah was trying to cut for them.

Renn looked toward the center of the wagon circle to discover the source of the green wall of energy that had saved Lord Danu and Raven; he figured it was coming from Artio—it was. The Meskhoni stood with his staff held high and his arms stretched out to the skies. Green energy flowed through his staff even now, and Renn noticed, for the first time, the emerald glow surrounding the entire circle of wagons like a living shield of protection. Then he looked upward, beyond the green shelter, and saw a constant red assault struggling to break through the magical barrier.

Great drops of perspiration ran down the old man's face, and Renn wondered how much longer Artio could keep up with the onslaught of the Warlock's attack. It amazed Renn that somehow Artio was able to keep his shield up and at the same time send a wall of energy to help Lord Danu and Raven.

The two men had already fought their way clear of the main force of Devi warriors when Renn looked back, but they still had their hands full, and both men were covered in blood.

Renn looked past the front lines of Devi warriors to find the dark-clothed Kiroc; he wanted to see if the creature appeared to be tiring of his relentless attack—he did not.

Sambuta rode back and forth behind the lines, shouting and waving his arms like a madman, and a dozen Devi archers pulled back their bows and unleashed a flurry of burning arrows. It looked to Renn as though they shot too high, but then he realized they were shooting at the wagons, not Lord Danu and the other defenders.

The arrows flew through Artio's barrier as though it didn't exist; apparently, his shield was only warding against the Kiroc's magical assault. The wagons that were struck burst into flames as though the wood had been soaked in pitch. Because the circle had been formed in such haste, the horses were still harnessed to the wagons, and once the wagons caught on fire, the animals reared, kicked, and ran for safety. That left an opening in one side of the circle, and the Devi began to fight toward it.

A handful of dark-haired warriors broke through the defense and ran toward Artio, who was concentrating all his efforts on his battle with the Warlock. Lord Danu and the other fighters were so involved in their own skirmishes that they didn't notice the band rushing toward the Mage.

Renn shouted a warning to Artio, but the old man couldn't hear him. A loud whinny sounded from just outside the ring of wagons. Renn looked to the sound and saw Thorn charge toward the warriors who were running to attack Artio. His white mane was flecked with blood and his coat glistened with perspiration from exertion, but he reached the old man as the first warrior raised his sword.

The Devi warrior's sword never fell; the white stallion reared up on its hind legs and came down on top of the man's head before he even knew Thorn was there. Renn felt a surge of pride as he watched Thorn fight to save Artio's life. The horse rose again. This time he landed with Devi warriors trapped underneath each front hoof, rendering both men unconscious.

The great white horse reared back a third time when warriors near the back of the group drew their bows and let their arrows fly. Thorn couldn't dodge the attack. He was already committed and was on his hind legs when an arrow buried itself deep in his chest and three more pierced his legs. As he fell, another arrow pierced his side.

Artio dropped to the ground as two arrows struck him—one in the shoulder, another in the stomach.

Horror rose from the pit of Renn's gut and tore from his throat in the form of a loud scream.

"No!" he cried, and he slid out from underneath the carriage. "No!" he shouted once more, running to his wounded friends, heedless of his own danger.

Somewhere behind him, he heard Genea calling, "Renn, come back. You'll be killed!" But it didn't register. Nothing mattered anymore. If Artio and Thorn died because of him, he could never forgive himself. They were his best friends—family.

He yelled once more as he fell beside Artio and pulled his weathered gray head into his lap.

"Renn . . ." Artio whispered hoarsely. "Come closer . . . Listen." The old man coughed, and his face grimaced in pain. Dark blood ran from his shoulder and stomach, soaking Renn's shirt and pants.

"I love you like a . . . like a son. I thank El Azur that you . . . that you came into my life. I didn't know what . . . love was. I'll die with no regrets."

"No. Stop talking like that. You're not going to die. You can't die . . . I need you . . . I love you." Renn wiped the tears from his cheek and saw the old man's blood dripping from his hands.

"Listen, Renn." He pulled Renn's ear to his lips. "Remember what I told you—never give in to the Aven-Lore." He coughed again. "I will die in peace because I'm no longer alone. I'll never be forgotten as long as you . . ." He closed his eyes. Blood began to seep from his mouth.

"Nooo!" Renn howled at the top of his lungs. A burning fire of loss and anger scorched his soul and consumed the very fiber and sinews of his flesh. He felt pure rage boiling in his veins, craving for release and hungering to take control.

"It's too much. I can't take any more!" His voice carried like thunder on the wind. The fighting paused, and everyone turned toward the young boy holding the dead Mage. He knew everyone heard him, but he didn't care how he'd made it happen. Rage consumed him, and his need to avenge Artio's death was all that mattered.

The black-dressed Kiroc raised a staff with a skull fixed onto it and hurled a blast of red fire toward him. Renn raised both hands. He caught the blast in his left hand, channeled the power through his body, and sent it back at the Kiroc through his right hand, twice as fast and powerful as it had been before.

Renn's body blazed and glowed with white radiance. He caught the warriors responsible for Artio's death in his gaze and pointed at them. White flame erupted from his fingertips and engulfed and consumed them in an instant, leaving nothing but ash where they stood.

The rest of the warriors turned to flee, but the Warlock grew to three times his normal height, and in a voice as loud as thunder said, "Capture that boy and bring him to me, or you shall *all* die."

Renn ignored the Warlock and the warriors and laid Artio's head gently to the ground, then hurried to Thorn's side. The horse breathed in quick, shallow gasps. His blood, too, had formed a pool around his wounds.

Help me, Renn. Please . . . I don't want to . . . leave you.

"No! No! NO!" Renn screamed louder than before, his voice dwarfing even the Warlock's—and each time he shouted, he pounded his fists into the ground.

"No! No! No!" The earth shook each time his fists collided with the dirt. The ground rumbled, and the grassy hills began to move as though they were waves of the sea.

Renn saw through tear-filled eyes that everyone had fallen to the ground, even the Warlock. He pounded his fist into the dirt once more and saw that his hands were buried up to his forearms. He felt a strange sensation, as if the life and energy of the soil was streaming into his body and coursing through his veins. The power was incredible and intoxicating. He believed at that moment he could do anything.

The Kiroc struggled to his feet, raised its staff once more, and began to cast another spell. Acute loathing welled up in Renn's soul for all workers of the Aven-Lore, and he whispered, "Die, you pawn of filth."

He ripped his hands from the ground, causing another tremor to shake the earth, then stood and focused his will and power on the Kiroc. White energy burst through his eyes and fingertips, but the Warlock constructed a red magical shield to protect himself. Renn's fire penetrated it like lightning through rain, and the Warlock screamed with agony as the brilliant white flame consumed his flesh.

Sambuta collapsed when the Warlock fell, and the Devi all scattered in fear and confusion. Renn's anger subsided as he watched them run, but as his rage left, the power that supported him drained away with it, and he felt helplessly weak and exhausted.

A wave of fatigue threatened to sweep him away to unconsciousness, and he fell to his knees. The weight of the lives he had taken crushed down upon his conscience like a tidal wave of guilt. In the distance, he heard Genea say, "Renn, are you all right? Oh please, Renn, wake up."

Gentle hands lifted his head, and the sky spun above him. "Hold on, Thorn," he whispered as the world faded to black. "Please don't die."

ESCAPE

The battlefield was blurry and murky. Renn ran toward Artio as the old man fell to his knees. He ran . . . and ran . . . but couldn't close the gap between them. He could see lifeblood spilling from his mentor's wounds but was helpless to stop it.

Shadows rose around him—taller than trees and with voices louder than a roaring waterfall. Thorn rose from the ground, reared up, and attacked the dark mists that surrounded Renn. The horse was swallowed by the darkness and disappeared. A shade rose in front of Renn, and he struck it down with a thought. Another rose and met the same fate, then another . . . and another.

Renn's eyes burst open, and he took a sharp breath. The bed he lay on was wet with sweat, and his skin felt cold and clammy. He was on his back and looking up at a high stone ceiling filled with distorted shadows.

Scuffing sounds to his right alerted him that someone had just entered the room, so he made a conscious effort to slow his breathing, close his eyes, and pretend to still be sleeping. He had no idea where he was, and until he found out, he wasn't about to take any chances.

He rolled his head right and opened his eyes just enough to see. The floor and walls of the large room looked as though they were hewn from rough stone. Shadows danced across the room, cast by the flickering light of a single torch in a black iron sconce near the door.

A medium-sized person stood at a desk with his back to Renn, preparing something in a basin of water. Renn couldn't see the face, and he didn't recognize the clothing. The stranger wore a light brown wool robe that clung loosely to his body and covered him completely except for his ankles and bare feet.

When the odd man turned, Renn shut his eyes. He heard him walk across the room, then felt a warm, damp cloth press against his forehead.

"How's he doing?" a deep, rough voice asked from the doorway.

"Better, I think. He should start coming around soon," the man at his side answered.

"Good. They're anxious for him to wake up."

Who's anxious for me to wake up? Renn wondered as the man's footsteps faded down the hall. What had happened to Lord Danu and Raven? What had happened to Genea? The last thing he remembered was fading into unconsciousness with his head resting in her lap.

And what about Thorn? Was he still alive, or had his horse died on the battlefield along with Artio? Oh, Artio—he groaned inwardly at the thought of his godfather. He couldn't be dead. How would he get by without the old, grumpy Meskhoni?

He had to find answers, but he didn't know who he could trust. The man treating him seemed friendly enough, but maybe he was only healing him to turn him over to Kahn Devin.

After a while, the man finished his work and left the room. Renn opened one eye, looked around, and saw he was alone. He sat up and got out of bed, then had to sit back down before he passed out once more. He was lightheaded and weak. It felt like all the energy had been siphoned from his muscles.

He breathed deeply a few times, then tried to rise again. The room swirled, and he had to grab hold of the bed for support. He took several slow, deep breaths, and the room stopped spinning.

Someone must have bathed and dressed him while he was unconscious, because he no longer wore his own clothing—besides the loose cloth robe, he wore nothing. Even his feet were naked. He knew he had to leave wherever he was, but first he would have to find better clothing. He searched for his own clothes, but all he found was a heavy woolen robe like the one his attendant wore. He gave up looking for his boots and decided going barefoot and wearing the robe might serve as a good disguise anyway.

The stone floor was cold, but he was too concerned with creeping silently out of his room and down the narrow, rock-hewn corridor to worry about cold feet. Shadows danced and flickered like demons mocking him. He didn't even know where he was or how he got here—let alone how he was going to get out. He hoped if he kept moving, a solution might present itself.

Voices echoed down the corridor, and a door slammed. Renn heard footsteps, but he couldn't tell what direction they were coming from, only that they were getting louder. He searched frantically for a place to hide before sliding into a dark corner of a doorway that was sheltered from the torchlight. As he crouched down, three large figures turned the corner up ahead.

Two of the men wore robes like the one Renn now donned, and the third looked like a guard of some kind. He was larger than the other two and wore a sword and leather armor. Renn held his breath as they passed, then waited for them to disappear around the next turn. He scurried from his hiding place and ran the direction the men had come; if the three men came in that way, he should be able to get out that way.

It dawned on him, as he hurried down the cold hallway, that the three men might be going to his room. Once they found it empty, what would they do? With that thought in mind, he pushed himself harder. He still felt weak, but the cool air of the corridor and the cold stone on his bare feet helped to fight the vertigo that threatened to overwhelm him.

He came to a flight of narrow, winding stairs that spiraled upward. He had to hold on to the stone wall for support, but fortunately, he didn't have to climb far before the stairs ended at a large iron door. He sat to catch his breath. His head spun, and his legs felt practically useless.

As he sat resting, he heard shouts of surprise from far down the corridor. The men *had* been on their way to his chamber and had found it empty. He could hear the boots of a soldier running down the stone floor toward him, and he pulled himself to his feet. He reached for the latch, fully expecting it to be locked, but it clicked when he pressed the handle, and the big door easily swung open when he pushed.

He peered around the entrance and found himself in a large assembly hall that was dimly lit with only a few torches placed intermittently on the walls. The floor was stone, like the lower level, but the walls and high, arched ceiling looked like those he'd seen in the king's palace at Achtan. Stained glass windows lined the place where the ceiling and walls met, but very little light passed through them. *It must be nighttime*, Renn thought. Wooden benches were placed in two rows down the center of the room, and the aisle between them led toward a large stone altar. The room looked like an ancient temple.

Renn saw two massive wooden doors with windows above them at the far end of the hall. One of the doors stood open to the night, and he could see an exquisite courtyard just outside. The footsteps behind him were growing louder, so Renn made a mad dash for the open door.

No one stood guard in the hall or at the open door, so Renn ran across the grassy courtyard, blessing his good fortune.

He tried to stay near trees and bushes as he made his way through the yard toward a large stone wall that circled the grounds. At one point, he stopped and turned to see if he was being followed and discovered that he had indeed been in some kind of temple. He heard muffled shouts from within the stone building and then saw torches flare up in several rooms as the complex was alerted to his escape. He still didn't know where he was, but he knew he didn't recognize the place or the people.

Renn ran to the gate. Fortunately, he arrived before the two sentries on guard duty heard the commotion in the temple; they were both sitting on the ground, leaning against the stone wall, asleep.

Whatever this place is, he thought, *they need to discipline their soldiers better.* He was glad, however, that they did not.

He rushed through the gates and found himself in a large and unfamiliar city. The streets were wide and straight, and they all seemed to lead to a central park. He continued to stay in the shadows as much as possible and decided he'd walk toward the center of town. Maybe his friends were here in the city somewhere, or maybe he could find some clue as to his whereabouts.

He walked past a tavern and two men crashed through the door, nearly bowling him over. A dozen more men stumbled closely after, yelling and cheering on the two, who were now rolling around on the street fighting each other. He looked at the men in the crowd but saw no one familiar.

He hurried down the street and turned into an alley. He thought it might be a good idea to go to the next street and follow it to the park; he'd seen about as much of this street as he needed. Halfway down the alley, he realized he'd made a big mistake. A young boy and an older man stepped out of the shadows in front of him. Both were clothed in dirty rags and reeked of alcohol and sweat. Mud and grit covered their arms and faces, and they waved daggers dangerously in their hands.

"Well, well, Silo," the old man said to his younger companion. "We got us a priest. And a young one, too." He broke into a sick-sounding chortle, and the boy smiled a toothless grin.

"Give us money, Priest, and maybe we let you live."

Renn's voice shook, and his vertigo returned. "I have no money to give you."

"I thought priests don't lie, Omar," the young boy said to the other. "Maybe I check him myself."

The boy took a step toward Renn and snarled at him like a rabid dog about to attack. Renn knew if he didn't do something, and quick, he would end up dead in this alley and no one would ever know the difference.

When the boy reached for his robe, Renn spit in his eyes. It startled the young thief long enough for Renn to kick him in the knee and shove him at the feet of the old man, knocking them both to the ground. They hollered obscenities at Renn as he fled back down the alley. He turned back on the main road and didn't stop running until he entered the central park. He looked over his shoulder and, realizing he wasn't being followed, fell to the ground behind a large bush to hide and catch his breath.

He wiped tears from his eyes; he felt so helpless and alone. Artio was dead, his friends were gone, he was in a strange city, and he was tired and hungry. He would have given anything in the world just to see a familiar face. He missed his mother and Chria and Tavier, and he wished he were back home with them. What was he supposed to do now, and where was he to go? He hugged his knees to his chest and buried his face in them to shut out the world.

He looked up as a man in black ran around a large tree no more than five yards away. Renn held his breath. He thought of running, but he was too exhausted and didn't care what happened anymore. It didn't matter anyway—Artio and Thorn were gone.

"Renn?" a familiar voice called, sounding out of breath. "Is that you?"

"Raven!" Renn pulled himself to his feet and stumbled into the mysterious captain's arms. He was so relieved to see someone he knew that he couldn't contain himself. "I've never been so glad to see someone in my entire life." He half expected Raven to be taken back at Renn's outpouring of affection, but the dark-haired captain surprised him once again by taking him in his arms and pressing him tight against his chest.

"It's all right, Renn. You're safe now." Then he turned his head and called out over his shoulder, "Lord Danu, I found him."

"Where are you?" the young lord called back.

"Behind the bushes," Raven answered. Then, speaking to Renn, he said, "We've been running hard and fast trying to catch up to you."

Lord Danu ran around the bushes. Lines of worry creased his brow, but when he saw Renn, he pulled him in with his strong grasp and gave him a long hug.

"You gave us quite a scare when you disappeared. I was worried sick."

"Where are we?" Renn asked.

"Anytos. After the Devi fled, you passed out in Genea's arms. You wouldn't revive, so we brought you to the temple, where the priests of Azur could heal you."

"But then you disappeared and sent us all into a panic," Raven added.

"I'm sorry," Renn apologized, feeling embarrassed. "I woke up and didn't know where I was. I thought I'd been captured by Kahn's men and was trying to escape. How stupid of me. I should have known it wasn't a temple of Ba Aven."

"It's not your fault, Renn. We shouldn't have left you alone," Lord Danu said. "Come on, let's get back. There's someone who wants to see you."

At that, he was reminded of another concern. "Lord Danu," he said, "tell me about Thorn. Is he . . . is he—"

"Look out!" Raven shouted as he pushed Lord Danu and Renn to the side. Men stepped around the bushes and surrounded them. Raven drew his sword in a fluid motion, but as he did, someone dropped from a tree and hit him on the head, sending the dark-haired captain to the ground like a sack of wheat. Lord Danu rolled and jumped up, swinging his blade with a furious stroke, but before making contact, he too was hit from behind and fell to the ground.

It all happened so fast that Renn didn't have time to react. He yelled for help as a heavy net fell over him. He felt a sharp blow on the back of his head and, once again, everything went black.

DINNER PARTY

A familiar, dusty smell dried Renn's nostrils and brought him out of his dreamless sleep. He recognized the smell but couldn't quite place it. His head pounded, and his muscles felt stiff and cramped. He tried to stretch but couldn't move.

His eyes bolted open in a panic, but he couldn't see. He struggled to raise a hand in front of his face but was unable to budge it—it felt like he'd been buried alive. A sick sensation twisted in the pit of his stomach, and his mind burned with the anxiety and hysteria of claustrophobia.

"Help!" he cried, but when he opened his mouth to scream, small, hard beans poured inside. Beans. That's what caused the dusty smell; he was completely buried in beans. He pushed the beans back out of his mouth with his tongue and held his teeth tight against more pouring in. He wanted to pound his fists against the barrier that held him trapped, but all his exertions only made him realize the hopelessness of his situation and served to increase his anxiety.

"Help!" he cried again through gritted teeth. "Please, someone . . . anyone . . . HELP!"

"Shut up in there." The angry voice was muffled, and Renn heard a low thud that sounded like somebody pounding on wood.

"Let me out of here!" he yelled louder than before, still through clenched teeth. "It's killing me in here. I can't move and I can't see. Let me OUT!"

He heard muffled voices speaking above him and felt the sensation of motion and the distant sound of wagon wheels rolling over a dirt-packed road.

Where was he? What had happened? He couldn't think straight; he was going crazy being trapped like this. He tried to slow his breathing and suppress his panic, but his heart pounded against his chest and sweat dripped down his back. He tried to rock back and forth, tried to kick, hit, push, and pull, but he could get no leverage; he couldn't even turn his head.

The sensation of movement stopped, and Renn listened intently to discover what was happening outside his black prison of beans. He heard voices but couldn't decipher what was being said.

"Let me out!" he yelled again. His heart beat so hard in his chest it sounded louder to him then his shouts.

This time he felt a jerking pull and heard the creak of nails being yanked from wood. Then, a hand grabbed his hair and pulled him up through the opening of a barrel. The barrel tipped over as he struggled to pull himself out, and after it fell to the ground, he rolled out and gasped huge gulps of fresh air.

He heard guttural laughter and snickering jeers. Their sneering filled him with anger. He wiped the dust from his eyes and rose to his feet. All he wanted was to hit somebody for locking him up like this, but as he looked around, he forgot about the barrel of beans and his nightmarish experience.

The setting sun combined with a ruddy glow cast by a massive bonfire, making his captors appear demonic. He caught his breath and stumbled backward. Tripping over the barrel, he fell against the wagon that had evidently been used to transport him from the city. Again, his captors burst into a chorus of wicked glee.

Renn had seen the minions of Lord Monguinir before, but never so many in one place. A dozen Demon Dogs, with their yellow fangs dripping rabid foam and their bright red eyes radiating malice, were kept at bay with chains controlled by twice as many Kirocs. The Kirocs were massive creatures. Some slightly resembled humans, but interbreeding over the past millennia had taken almost all human characteristics out of their blood.

Most now resembled giants with horns or wings, strange-colored eyes, fangs, and other gross aberrations.

Before Renn totally recovered, three score Tiaro Devi warriors materialized from behind what little foliage covered the plains. Fear rose in his chest—fear and hatred. He didn't know if these warriors had anything to do with the ambush that had killed Artio and possibly Thorn—he still didn't know what had happened to Thorn—but he felt bitter and angry toward them anyway.

"WHAT DO YOU WANT?" he shouted as he crouched behind the wagon wheel for cover. "Why can't you just leave me alone?"

Lord Danu, Raven, Kivas, Tellio, and the rest of the men wouldn't be charging over the rise to rescue him this time. Lord Danu and Raven had been knocked unconscious, and he didn't know what had happened to them. They must have been careless in their hurry to find him after he ran from the temple, leaving them vulnerable to a surprise attack. Once again, it was his fault his friends had gotten hurt.

"What have you done to my friends?" he demanded, clenching his hands into tight fists. He came from behind the wagon wheel and took a step toward his captors. None of them flinched. They acted like they didn't understand a word he said.

"Answer me!" he shouted, growing angrier and forgetting his fear.

"Tell me where my friends are, or . . . or I'll take care of you like I did the others."

"Now, now, Renn. We needn't resort to threats."

Renn spun around to locate the source of the rich, omnipresent male voice that addressed him. As he did, he saw a figure materialize inside the bonfire. The fire was reduced to red embers as the man appeared and the burning pile of wood was instantly consumed. One particularly large and almost human-looking creature kicked a couple smaller Kirocs, pointed at the dying fire, and shouted a terse, guttural command at them. They fell over each other to rush to a nearby pile of wood and built the fire back up. As the new arrival stepped forward, all of Renn's captors dropped to their knees and bowed, touching their heads to the ground.

Renn was amazed that the voice preceded his appearance. The man stood regally in front of the flames—now burning strong again—and signaled for his followers to rise.

He was a good-sized man, not as large as Tellio or Kivas, but he was tall and athletically built. His short, well-combed hair was silver-gray, and his tired yet stoic face was framed intelligently by a well-trimmed white beard. His black eyes bore a hint of dark circles underneath and were accented by dark eyebrows that rose independently of one another. His features gave him an ancient look, yet he seemed full of health, and his aura suggested he was the epitome of strength.

Like some of the Kiroc Warlocks, this man wore a long black cape that clasped about his neck, but underneath he wore a white cotton shirt tied close to his neck by a red scarf and covered by a richly woven gold-colored doublet. His pants were loose, but the black material, interwoven with gold thread, matched his cape and doublet perfectly.

"That's an interesting choice of clothing, Renn." The man pointed to the wool robe Renn wore. "Are you studying to become a priest?"

"Who . . . who are you?" Renn asked, ignoring the question. He was pretty sure he already knew the answer.

"Pardon my ill manners. I am Kahn Devin." He gave Renn a flourishing bow. "I've been trying to locate you for some time now. It's proved to be rather . . . difficult."

Renn felt the blood flush from his face and instinctively placed a hand on the amulet hanging around his neck that Artio had given him to keep Aven-Lore users from seeing him through scrying pools.

"Is something wrong, Renn? You look a bit pale." The Grand Warlock's penetrating gaze drilled into Renn's soul. "Let us sit and rest. We can chat while we have a bite to eat."

Renn shook his head. He didn't know what to do. All his life he'd been hiding from this man; now they stood face-to-face. He wasn't ready for this. He wished Artio were with him. Artio, his father, Thorn, Lord Danu . . . this man was responsible for the death and pain of every one of them, and that thought made hate and anger rise within Renn.

"I wouldn't eat with you if you were the last man on earth and I was starving to death." His voice rose in pitch and volume. "You killed my father. You killed Artio. You hurt everyone I love. I'd rather see you rot in the pit of Ba Aven's gut!"

Kahn Devin placed a hand over his heart and he closed his eyes at Renn's rebuke. "Please give me a chance, Renn. You misunderstand and misjudge me." He opened his arms and walked a step closer. "Certainly the good Mage Artio taught you that a man be given opportunity to impart his story before being condemned?"

Renn backed up, debating trying to flee. Kahn watched and smiled. When Renn didn't respond, he took another step forward.

"Do you believe I orchestrated your father's death? Do you think I wanted Artio dead? That was never my intention. You have ever been the center of my concern since the day of your blessing. Believe me, Renn, my desire is only for you to be happy."

"You have a strange way of showing your concern. If this is what you call happiness, no thanks."

"Look around you, Renn. See the creatures I work with?"

Renn nodded, though he didn't look around.

"Ofttimes they get carried away. In their zeal to please me, they occasionally go a bit too far. The mob that slew your father was not acting under my direction, and the Devi warriors that killed Artio were told only to bring you to me. If I'd have known what evil would have befallen your friends, I certainly would have prevented it."

"I don't believe you," Renn said. "You're lying to me. Artio told me you'd lie to me." But something inside him wanted to believe him. Something about Kahn compelled Renn to forgive and join the Warlock. Kahn was so civilized, so educated—he didn't seem capable of being as evil as all the stories made him out to be.

"Artio was a good man, but he didn't understand many things. You are different. You *do* believe me, Renn, because I speak the truth." The refined-looking magic user took another step closer. "Listen to your feelings. You know you belong by my side."

Renn shook his head to clear his thoughts. "Then why didn't you come to me sooner?" he shouted. "Why did you have your men jump me and hit me over the head, then stuff me in the bottom of a barrel of beans to sneak me out of the city?"

Kahn's eyes grew angry, and his brows creased together. He looked behind Renn at the two men still seated in the driver's bench of the wagon. Renn followed Kahn's gaze behind him and noticed the men for the first time. They weren't like the others; they were normal men of Anytos.

"Did you do that to him?" Kahn asked them in a voice dripping with malice.

"Look," one of them said. "You gave us a job to do, and we did it. You didn't say anything about what methods to use."

"If you'll just pay us, we'll be on our way. We've got friends back in the city waiting for their reward, m'lord." The other driver's eyes darted back and forth.

"Oh, I'll pay you." Kahn walked toward the men. "Do you realize how frightened this young boy must have been? Didn't I tell you he was special and needed to be treated well?"

"Look, we did the job you—" A bolt of red energy burst from Kahn's index finger, and the first driver was burned to a cinder. Renn felt the power of the blast in the air above his head as it passed over him—it left a residue of acrid-smelling energy in its wake.

The other driver's face turned pale. "Please, M—Mr. Devin. We couldn't get him out of the city no other way. The king had all the gates guarded, and they were searching every wagon."

He looked between Kahn and the remains of his companion with wide eyes. Kahn continued walking toward the man, who clumsily grabbed the reins and whipped the horses to a run.

Kahn transformed into a black hawk and flew after the wagon. Renn watched the bird swoop to the dirt road in front of the fleeing driver and changed back into the Grand Warlock, spooking the horses and causing them to rear back in horror.

Kahn raised a finger and pointed it at the man, who screamed with terror at the realization of his imminent fate. He, too, was silenced by a flash of red light.

Kahn's figure shimmered, disappeared, and reappeared inside the bonfire. Renn noticed that the fire quickly died down and the wood was consumed when the Warlock stepped out of it, and the smaller Kirocs quickly added more wood to the flames.

"You see, Renn, I had nothing to do with the way you were treated in Anytos. I apologize you had to witness their punishment, but it infuriates me that they treated you so poorly."

Renn wanted to believe Kahn. He sounded genuinely concerned. Something inside Renn ached to run to the Grand Warlock's side and join him. He felt his hatred and anger slip away and a desire to be with this man grow within him.

"Now, Renn. Please join me as I eat. I have ordered a feast in your honor, and we have much to discuss."

Renn's legs began walking toward Kahn Devin of their own volition. He longed to be with him; he felt compelled to run to his side. He no longer feared this man.

"That's good, Renn. You shall be my most favored pupil, and I will be your mentor."

NO! You are Artio's pupil, something—or someone—screamed inside his head. *This man has killed or hurt everyone you love.*

"No. I . . . can't . . . You're lying to me." Renn struggled to break free of the compulsion to unite with the regal man, and the desire to join him tightened around his mind. The need to go with Kahn Devin grew like a sudden storm. He *had* to give in to the need. The Kirocs and warriors moved back and revealed a table set with fine food and wine, and Renn walked forward once more.

Again, images of Artio flooded his mind. He saw the Meskhoni's face as he taught him how to make the mind-link. Then he saw Thorn running across the bloody grass to protect Artio from the Devi warriors. Next, he saw his father. He remembered sitting on the banks of the small river that ran behind their farm in Leedsdale while his father taught him and Tavier to fish.

Too much was running through his mind. A scream ripped itself from deep inside his throat. He realized Kahn was trying to control his mind, to force Renn to join him. It infuriated him.

"Make your decision to follow the light before you're ever confronted by the agents of Ba Aven." The last words his father had said to him came rushing back now. *"That way you don't have to make your choice in the pressure of the moment."*

Renn tried to remember what Artio had taught him to do when someone entered his mind. He placed his hand on the amulet Artio gave him, fought to focus and gather his will, and then pushed back with all his might and screamed, "Nooo! I won't join you. Get out of my head."

Kahn Devin's cape and head whipped backward from an invisible blast produced by Renn's will and the man flew like a leaf toward his servants. Before he hit them, Renn felt the Grand Warlock push back, and the old man landed, unharmed, on the ground.

Ruby fire flooded his eyes. He made a quick gesture with his hands, and Renn found himself encased in a ball of scarlet energy, unable to move. Kahn Devin pulled down on his shirt, straightened his cape, and walked purposefully to Renn.

"You *will* join me, Renn. I can give you power like you never knew existed." Kahn bent over, his eyes inches away from Renn's, and then he grabbed the dark amulet hanging from Renn's neck.

"This amulet is child's play compared to what I will show you." The Warlock emphasized each word, and his palm began to glow. He closed his fist around the amulet, clenched his jaw, and squeezed harder. His fist glowed more intensely, and a flash of red light exploded from between his fingers. When he opened his fist, the only thing left of the amulet was black ash. Renn watched with dismay as the Warlock poured the ash onto the dirt.

"Whether you like it or not," Kahn said with a grim smile, "you are *my* student now."

"Never. I'll die before I join you."

The silver-haired Warlock stood and smiled as though they were concluding a pleasant conversation.

"No . . . you *won't* die." Kahn stepped back, his voice deathly calm. "You are coming to the Well of Sacrifice. There you will either join me, or your soul will be sacrificed and trapped forever with Lord Monguinir."

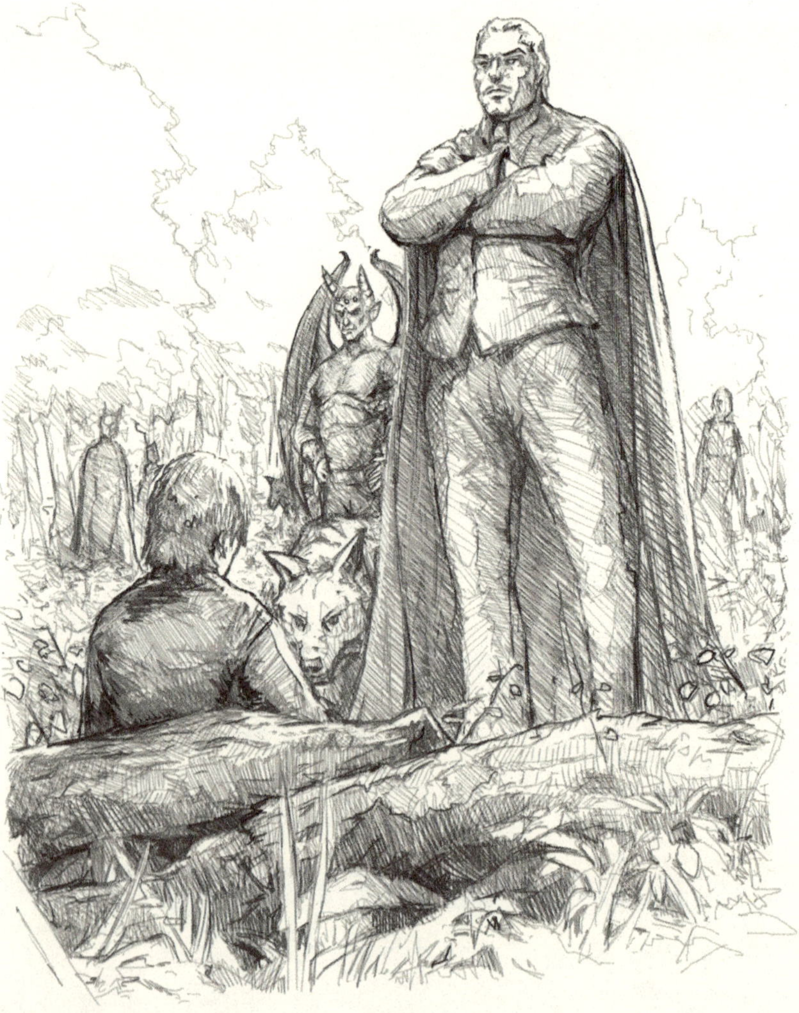

ORACLE OF TANITH

Renn watched as Kahn's right eyebrow rose and his gaze intensified. The energy surrounding Renn's body localized and wrapped around his wrists and ankles. He tried to push back using the techniques Artio had taught him, but nothing happened.

"You have great talent, Renn. It's a shame you won't give it freely to me." Kahn's mouth twisted into a snarl, and he made a cutting gesture with his hands. The Warlock turned to address his servants, but the power holding Renn remained intact. He struggled against the red ropes of energy that held his wrists and ankles together, and he tried to stand—he quickly lost his balance and fell to the ground.

"Devi tribesmen," Kahn said. "Cover our tracks and make certain no one pursues us." The dark-haired warriors dropped to their knees and brought their right fists to their hearts. Renn assumed this was their way of agreeing to serve as ordered.

Renn raised his head, and his eyes darted back and forth. The flickering bonfire threw a ruddy light over the surrounding area. Demon Dogs sat on their haunches as their handlers and the Kirocs listened to the Grand Warlock. The horses, still harnessed to the wagon that had carried Renn from Anytos, grazed on tall wild grass a short distance away.

His friends wouldn't be coming to his rescue this time. He calmed his mind and reached for the aeon myriad, but as he tried to draw the power into himself, the red bonds tightened and burned. Renn screamed, and his hold on the aeon myriad vanished.

"I'd recommend you not do that, Renn," the Grand Warlock said offhandedly. "It will only cause you pain."

"General Nishkral," Kahn shouted, and a large Kiroc with red skin stretched tightly over a muscular body stepped forward from the center of the Kiroc horde. His skeletal face was crowned with a row of spikelike horns. Despite these demonic features, the trait that was most striking to Renn was the creature's eyes. He would've expected them to be red or maybe black, but instead they virtually glowed—bright violet—in the night.

"Yes, sir," General Nishkral said.

"I want your troops ready to march in ten minutes. Those who can transform into animals will join us in the lead. The rest of the Kirocs are to clean up this mess." He pointed to the fire and the table laid out with food. "And then follow as quickly as possible." Almost as an afterthought he said, "The dogs will carry the boy."

The red-skinned general bowed his head, and then great bat-like wings unfolded from his back, and he flew above the motley army and began shouting orders in a guttural language that Renn couldn't understand.

Large green hands grabbed Renn from behind, lifted him off the ground, and dropped him like a bag of flour onto the back of a snarling Demon Dog. The animal was bigger than any dog Renn had seen before but not as large as a cow or mule. Its coarse, dark fur smelled like a rug soaked in muddy water and left out to rot.

The dog snapped and growled at the boar-faced Kiroc trying to lash Renn to the dog's back. The Kiroc used a coarse rope that scratched and irritated the skin. A tall, skinny Kiroc with a pointed face and horns like an antelope jerked on the chain wrapped around the Demon Dog's throat and issued a sharp command. The chain glowed red, and the dog yelped in pain as though it had been whipped. It howled, and saliva dripped from its fangs, but the Demon Dog allowed the Kiroc to finish tying Renn, facedown, to its back. Renn's legs hung over one side of the dog and his head hung over the other.

Renn saw red flashes of light from his peripheral vision. He craned his neck and saw that several of the Kirocs and some of the men with the horde had transformed into animals. Some had turned into birds that took to the sky; others had turned into land animals.

The Kirocs holding the leashes of the Demon Dogs removed the chains but held the dogs' collars to keep them from running. Renn saw a shadow, cast by the moonlight, of a Kiroc with large wings and heard General Nishkral shout a command from overhead. The dogs bayed, the handlers released them, and they bounded off into the night.

Renn felt nauseated because the ground rushed by so fast. He shouted at the dog to slow down, but the beast snarled and snapped at him and kept running. This felt nothing like the thrill of running with Thorn. Instead of a smooth, fluid gait, the Demon Dog darted around bushes and leapt over obstacles. Renn's stomach jolted against the animal's spine every time the dog jumped and landed.

When Renn vomited onto the Demon Dog's black fur, it was nothing but bile. He didn't know how long it had been since he'd eaten, because he wasn't sure how long he'd lain unconscious in the temple at Anytos. The bitter taste of acid clung to his tongue. He closed his eyes so he wouldn't see the ground rushing past, but the constant jostling made him throw up again.

It grew colder as the night wore on, and Renn's arms and legs went numb. When the horde finally stopped, they only rested long enough to strap Renn to the back of a different dog. It smelled the same. It ran the same. Renn vomited again.

When the sun rose, General Nishkral issued a curt command, and the small battalion stopped. Renn opened his eyes. Dried vomit clung to the side of his canine mount. He was too weak to lift his head to get his bearings. It wouldn't matter anyway. He knew they were headed northwest, toward the Cragg Caves.

He could tell by the grasses on the ground below him that they were somewhere in the Great Tiaronéa Plains. A pair of large, hairy feet with black toenails in bad need of trimming stepped into his view. The ropes holding him to the dog's back were untied, and strong hands yanked him off the animal and dropped him to the ground. His view of the clear blue sky was disrupted by a face that resembled a beakless bird, with fangs pointing upward from the edges of its mouth.

"Water," Renn whispered hoarsely.

He felt the pins-and-needles sensation of blood rushing back into his arms and legs, but the crimson energy ropes holding his wrists and ankles made it so he couldn't move into a comfortable position. The creature standing above him left. Renn closed his eyes. It felt good to lie still, and he was so weak he began to drift off. Just when merciful sleep was about to rescue him from his living nightmare, stagnant-smelling water splashed onto his face, up his nose, and into his mouth. He sputtered and spit and forced himself up onto one elbow and opened his eyes.

"Here water." The creature laughed at Renn and tossed a mostly empty waterskin on the ground next to him. Renn maneuvered into a sitting position and greedily drained the rest of the liquid. It tasted warm and fetid, but he didn't care. It was water.

A large black bird dropped from the sky. With a flash of light, the Grand Warlock smoothly transitioned from bird into man, and as his feet touched ground, he walked toward Renn. Kahn's dark eyes squinted and his mouth tightened as he looked over Renn.

"General Nishkral," Kahn shouted as he turned. Renn felt a gust of wind as the Kiroc general landed next to the Grand Warlock.

"Yes, m'lord?"

"Have you fed or watered the boy?"

The general turned his violet eyes on Renn and shook his head

"You idiot!" Kahn said. "Look at him. He's dehydrated and sick."

The general made a show of inspecting Renn's condition.

"I'll assign one of my soldiers to care for him, sir."

"That would be wise." Kahn scowled. "And wrap his feet with something. If that boy doesn't survive, it will be *your* soul I sacrifice to the demon lord."

"I understand, sir."

"Good." Kahn straightened his vest and brushed off the right shoulder of his cloak. "I've scouted behind, and no one is following. There is a herd of antelope a mile to the south. Feed everyone, and then I want you traveling again as soon as the sun goes down."

Renn was strapped to the back of another dog as the sun set, and the events of the previous night repeated themselves. In the morning, when the group finally stopped again, strong hands untied him and dropped him to the ground. The grass was wet with cold dew. Renn shivered and pushed himself into a sitting position. A Kiroc, who had been in the form of a gray wolf only minutes before, dropped a piece of meet at his feet and handed him a skin of water. Renn woodenly drank and then took a small bite of gristle-ridden meat that contained bits of antelope fur.

Renn spit out the meat. His body ached. His stomach and throat were sore from repeated vomiting, and his wrists and ankles were raw from the constant friction of the red energy that bound them together. His head pounded from bouncing up and down as the dogs relentlessly ran toward the Cragg Caves and the Well of Sacrifice.

He wondered how long it would be until they arrived. With a little luck, he would die before they got there. With that thought in mind, he considered the meat, then tossed it aside. Dying of starvation would be much better than having his soul trapped with the demon lord for eternity.

"Now, now, Renn. You must eat your food." Renn hadn't heard Kahn approach him from behind. "I want you to be alert and healthy when you meet our master, Lord Monguinir."

"He's not my master."

The Grand Warlock walked in front of Renn, crouched, and grinned. "He will be."

When the sun fell, the process began again. Sometime just before dawn, they crossed a sizeable river. The Demon Dog that Renn was strapped to bounded through the current. Each time the animal splashed into the cold water, Renn's head submerged, and he was coughing and drenched by the time they reached the other side.

The landscape changed from grasses and bushes into pine trees and undergrowth. The air cooled as they climbed in elevation. The dog's bounding was even more erratic now as it jumped over fallen logs and large boulders.

At dawn, rough hands unstrapped Renn and propped him against a fallen log. He took a drink of the water a Kiroc handed him but tossed the meat aside.

The black hawk that was Kahn dropped from the sky and stopped in front of Renn. The Grand Warlock glowered at the untouched meat on the ground.

"Nishkral!"

Renn heard flapping and felt a gust of wind as the massive, red-skinned Kiroc general landed.

"The boy is nearly dead," Kahn said. "Is this how you obey my instructions?"

"My lord, we've watered him during the nights and given him food, but he won't eat."

"Then chew it for him and shove it down his throat," Kahn said. "Get a cloak from one of your men and wrap it around the boy before he dies of exposure. He's shaking like an old man with palsy."

"Travel in the day . . . It's warmer." Renn's voice was hoarse, and he spoke so softly he could barely hear himself. Still, Kahn paused and tapped at his lip.

"Consider this your first lesson, Renn," the Warlock said. "Darkness contains the essence of K'Thrak, Ba Aven's eldest son. Kirocs and Demon Dogs draw from that power as they run."

"So . . . Aven-Lore users are weaker in daylight." Renn didn't ask it as a question but as a statement of realization. The Grand Warlock's eyebrows furrowed, and his face grew dark. He spun on his heel and walked away, giving orders to General Nishkral, who followed close behind.

"I am going to scout the area. We can't take any chances. When I return, I want . . ."

Soon the two were out of earshot, but Renn watched them until Kahn Devin turned back into a great hawk and flew away. A Kiroc walked over to Renn and threw a fur-lined animal skin at him.

"General say give to boy," the bull-faced creature accused, clearly angry. "Give back when get to cave."

Renn watched the big Kiroc stomp away. The bristly animal hide smelled of body odor and urine, but he wrapped it around himself anyway, leaned back against the log, and closed his eyes.

※

"Renn, wake up."

Renn opened his eyes and saw an ancient woman with piercing blue eyes smiling down at him. Her wrinkled face was framed by white hair as bright as lightning.

"Who are you?" Renn asked.

"Someone who can help—if you'll let me."

Renn scowled. Why would this stranger want to risk herself to help him? "I don't even know you. How did you—" He was going to say "find me," but instead he broke into a fit of dry coughs. The old woman knelt by his side and gave him a cup of hot tea.

"What . . . is . . ."

"It will help."

Her eyes drew Renn in. They were deep blue pools of concern and . . . love. He raised the cup to his lips. As soon as the warm liquid slid down his throat, the soreness and coughing stopped. His headache melted away, and he felt energy radiate from his core out to every extremity of his body.

Where did she get a hot cup of tea? Now that his mind was sharp and his body felt strong, a thousand questions came to him.

"Where did you come from?" He looked around the steep mountainside meadow at the surrounding pine trees, which reached like giants toward the crystal-blue sky. A small fire burned in a pit in the center of the sloppy camp. Kirocs and Demon Dogs lay scattered across the ground, snoring and drooling.

"Did you make everybody fall asleep?" He was beginning to think that maybe this old lady really could help him escape. He felt power emanating from her like he'd never experienced before—not even when Artio had worked his strongest spells.

"You have a choice," she said. "You can stay here or come with me." She gave him one more smile, stood, and hobbled toward the trees.

"Wait," Renn called after her. "I can't walk. Can you do something about these?" He held out his hands and nodded to the red bands of energy binding his wrists and ankles.

She turned and faced him. "No," she answered, "but you can."

"I can't," he said. "I've already tried . . . several times. It hurts when I reach out for the aeon myriad."

"That's because the Warlock instructed the intelligences in your bonds to cause you pain when you try to draw on power."

"If I can't draw on the power, what am I supposed to do?" Renn knitted his eyebrows and slumped.

"You can't draw aeon myriad from the outside and force it past those shackles," she said, "but there is aeon myriad within those bonds." She smiled encouragingly, then turned and continued walking through the horde of sleeping Kirocs.

"Wait," he called after her, but she kept walking.

What does she expect me to do? he thought. He certainly didn't want to stay here. He felt an irresistable desire to be with this old lady. *Why won't she just free me?* he wondered. *She obviously has a lot of power.*

Artio once told him that users of the Aven-Lore draw on the same power as users of the Azur-Lore—the aeon myriad. But Aven-Lore users forced it to obey their own wills rather than work in harmony with the power. He reached out his senses to the crimson energy encircling his wrists and felt for the aeon myriad. He found it immediately but sensed anger from the power. He reached with his mind and probed the intelligences within the elements that made up the magical shackles. He breathed slowly, allowed his emotions to calm, and then pushed those feelings toward the aeon myriad within the shackles binding him.

"*Act as you will,*" he whispered. "*I free you from the coercion that now binds you.*"

The red energy wavered, shifted to green, and then shot away from his wrists and ankles in all directions. He looked at his hands and feet in amazement. He was free! He rubbed at his wrists and then his ankles to increase the circulation and blood flow.

"Wait!" He stood and stumbled after the woman. "Where are we going?" he asked when he caught up to her. She smiled approvingly.

"You possessed the power to escape all along, Renn," she said. Her voice sounded younger than her face looked. "It pleases me that you found the answer with such little guidance."

Renn felt a swell of pride as he stepped around and over the Demon Dogs and past the final Kiroc between them and the trees.

"Hey! Where you go?"

Renn and the old lady turned to see a medium-sized Kiroc lumber through the trees on the opposite side of the small clearing where the group had made camp. The old woman lifted her wrinkled hand, made a circular motion with her index finger, and said a single word in a musical tone. The Kiroc paused midstride, dropped to the ground, and began to snore.

"He must've been some distance away when I arrived," she said thoughtfully. Then she turned to Renn and smiled. "We are going to my home."

They walked into the forest, but it was not far before she stopped and considered the large pine trees that surrounded them.

"This will do, I think," she said. "Renn, I want you to open the door to my home."

Renn looked around for a cottage or shack. He turned to the old woman for guidance, but her face was a mask of serenity. Her eyes studied him with an intensity that was a bit disconcerting.

"I . . . don't see a door," Renn said. *I hope she isn't just a crazy old lady.* He dismissed the thought as soon as it crossed his mind. She somehow knew who he was, she'd found him in remote mountains, she'd caused his captors to fall asleep, and she'd taught him how to free himself.

"Choose seven of the trees that surround us," she said, "and connect with the aeon myriad that runs from their roots to their tips."

Renn looked at the trees, furrowed his brow, and selected the largest and tallest pine and probed for the power that resided inside. The intelligences in the tree's elements felt . . . wise. He probed them with his mind until they recognized and acknowledged him, then he held on to that connection while he reached out to the next tree.

"Very good, Renn," the old lady said.

As he connected to each additional tree's aeon myriad, Renn felt a solid foundation of strength build in his soul. He was at peace and firmly rooted to life.

"Now," she said, "ask the powers you are connected with to converge in the midst of this small clearing to create a portal that will take the Oracle of Tanith home."

Renn didn't understand what she meant or who the *Oracle of Tanith* was, but he repeated her exact words as he spoke to the power residing in the trees.

Green mists of energy reached out from the hearts of each tree like fingers feeling for one another. The energy met in front of where Renn and the old woman stood, and when all seven fingers of power touched, a rush of sound like a strong wind blew through the trees—but the air was still. The jade-colored energy swirled together until a translucent green opening appeared in front of them.

The old lady who referred to herself as the Oracle of Tanith stepped to the portal, then turned and held out a hand to Renn. "Make your choice."

Renn didn't hesitate. He took her hand and stepped forward.

ANYTOS

Danu stood in the war room of the castle of Anytos and tapped his chin. The walls contained crossed swords, tapestries of battles, and a large red banner with a single castle tower in the center. Mytton and Kivas stood in the exact center of the room, next to a worn but solid oak table, littered with maps. Danu looked out an open window and watched Raven training men in the inner courtyard below.

"It's just poor timing, Duke Mytton," Kivas said, for at least the tenth time this week. "Now, more than ever, the cities of the plains need to be united. There are dark days ahead, and fighting among yourselves only helps our enemies."

"It's King Mytton now, Kivas, and war hasn't broken out yet," the recent duke, now king, said, without looking up from his maps. "I don't think King Reollyn has stopped entertaining long enough to notice we seceded from the kingdom," he added sardonically.

Danu rubbed at the five-day stubble on his chin and continued watching the courtyard below. The first day Raven had started the training, only Danu's men worked with the dark-haired captain. Now Bendigo Mytton's weapons master and several of his best soldiers joined in the daily regimen. Danu looked at the red banners flying proudly from the corner turrets of the courtyard with their single castle tower in the center—symbolic of Anytos's strength. No army had breached the walls of Anytos since they'd been built more than a thousand years ago. But nowhere did Danu see the black dragon on a yellow field—the flag of Valdivar.

"Don't bet on it," Kivas answered King Mytton. "The king of Valdivar relies too heavily on taxes from Anytos and the Twin Cities to simply let you walk away and create your own government."

"We aren't setting up a new government." Bendigo Mytton sounded frustrated, and he joined Danu at the window to see what Danu was looking at. "We are now three separate city-states. Nothing is changing except we no longer hold our allegiance to Valdivar."

Danu turned from the window and paced the war room of King Mytton's citadel—like he'd been doing every day for the past week.

"As far as Renn is concerned, we've combed every inch of the park," the self-asserted king said. He unrolled a large map of Anytos and laid it onto the long solid oak table in the center of the war room on top of the other maps he'd been reviewing with them.

The king was a good-sized man in his middle years. Every dark, meticulously combed hair on his head was held in place by something that looked waxy and wet. Like Tellio, who was also born and raised in Anytos, the king had a mustache he greased and turned up slightly at the ends.

"The sentries at the north, south, and central gates have been inspecting everyone leaving Anytos," Bendigo said as he traced his finger along the thirty-mile wall that protected Anytos on the west. "And we have organized fifteen hundred soldiers into a perimeter surrounding the city. In addition, we have two detachments searching the farms that lie between the city proper and the outer wall."

Danu stopped pacing and looked down at the map without really seeing it—he didn't need to study it again. He'd pored over it so many times the last few days that he had every street and quarter memorized.

"I've got to find him," Danu said for what seemed like the thousandth time. *So much depends on that boy*, he thought as he rubbed his tired eyes and turned back to Bendigo.

"I appreciate your efforts, King Mytton." Danu joined him at the table. "I'm sure if he's still in Anytos, we'll find him."

"I don't think anyone could've gotten him past my soldiers," the king said. "We sealed the gates within hours of the abduction—I sent the message by pigeon the moment you told me what had happened. And since most of my divisions are already placed in the plains, keeping the Tiaro Devi raids in check and watching for any sign of attack from King Reollyn's armies, I have notified them to be on the lookout for him, too."

Danu nodded. He'd replayed that night in his mind a hundred times. He was sure he and Raven had been unconscious for less than an hour, and then they'd come straight to the citadel, seeking Bendigo Mytton's assistance. The king had issued orders to the gates immediately upon learning of the situation. It would have been difficult for the abductors to get all the way out of Anytos's outer walls, nearly thirty miles away, before that time—but not impossible.

"I hope you're right." Danu ran his fingers through his hair and released a loud breath.

"You need some rest, Danu," King Mytton said, looking up from his map. "My men at the outskirts of the city have begun methodically closing in toward the central park. They're checking every house, inn, stable, church, and alley. Nobody is going to pass through their ranks unnoticed. We *will* find the Child of the Blessing."

Danu turned back to the window and watched Raven, who was doing pull-ups on a bar. The other men had already left the yard. "Perhaps you're right. Maybe I should rest." He walked to the solid oak door at the far end of the room.

"You will wake me if any new developments arise?" he asked as he opened the door to leave.

"Of course," the king and Kivas replied at the same time.

Danu ambled down the narrow stone stairs that led to the parapet level. His shoulder-length blond hair, which usually flowed behind him as he walked, now pressed against his head in matted neglect. He pushed a stray lock from covering his left eye and cursed under his breath.

Alternating red and green pennants hung from the ceiling of the parapet and red-and-gold-patterned carpet, about three feet wide, ran down the center of the walkway. The torches in the iron sconces on the wall weren't lit. Plenty of sunlight bathed the walkway through the large openings set in enclaves about ten paces apart from each other on the opposite wall, which overlooked the inner courtyard.

He thought of Artio as he walked. He had never fully appreciated the old Mage until he'd had to make do without him. He hadn't realized how much he'd grown to rely on his counsel over the years. He sure wished he were here now.

The war room tower dominated the southwest corner of the castle with one side of the tower overlooking Elahna's Gorge and the opposite side facing the inner courtyard. As he rounded the corner of the parapet, he saw Aleah standing at an enclave looking down at the inner yard. She wore breeches and a white tunic that gathered at the waist, but her sword and scabbard leaned against the wall next to her. She leisurely twisted her long sandy-brown hair as she gazed out the window. She was an attractive woman—though she tried hard to hide that fact. Her angular jawline and smooth skin, combined with her slightly too-small nose, high-arched brows, and big brown eyes, made her appearance both simple and exotic.

Whatever she was watching had her complete attention. She hadn't noticed Danu approach—normally she would hear an insect crawl.

"What are you watching?" Danu stepped beside her and looked at the courtyard below.

Aleah spun, and her face turned a bright shade of red. "I . . . uh . . . I was . . ." She stammered and reached for her sword, but it clanked loudly to the floor. Danu looked out the window. The only person in the courtyard was Raven—his black hair wet with the sweat of his workout. Then he understood why she was so embarrassed. Danu smiled.

"Oh . . . I see."

Aleah picked up her sword, then straightened her shoulders and raised her chin. "I was simply admiring his form and dedication."

"Of course." Danu continued smiling.

Aleah set her jaw as if to argue but instead took a deep breath.

"I was on my way to inform you that Thorn is missing."

"Missing?" Danu asked. "Did someone steal him?"

"There's no sign of a break-in." Aleah shook her head. "The stableboy just found his stall vacant this morning when he went to feed him."

Danu ran his hand through his disheveled hair and shook his head. He was tired. He looked down at his wrinkled shirt, which hadn't been changed in days. "That's curious," he said. "That horse has a strong bond to Renn. I wonder if Thorn just left because Renn is gone or if somebody . . ."

He left the thought hanging as he considered this new development. He looked back out the window and down at Raven, who was now doing handstand push-ups, then looked back at Aleah with renewed energy.

"I'm going out to the stables to look around and have a talk with the livery boy. Go to the war room and tell Mytton and Kivas about Thorn. A horse can't just disappear into thin air—someone must've seen him. Maybe the king can find something out."

Danu hurried across the parapet, down the stairs on the opposite side, and then through the door that led to the outer courtyard, where the stables were located. It smelled of fresh hay mixed with the musty odor of horsehair, but not the stench of manure that so often filled stable air. He found the stableboy brushing the king's black warhorse and whistling to himself. He was young—probably in his early teens—but obviously a hard worker. He looked up as Danu approached, and bowed.

"I'm very sorry," the boy said, "but I don't know what happened to him, m'lord."

"What happened to who?" Danu asked.

"Your white horse, sir." The stableboy set down the brush and stood next to the strong black horse. "You're the fourth one to come looking for him this morning."

Danu nodded and looked around. Everything appeared to be in order. He saw no sign of a disturbance or break-in.

"Which stall was Thorn in last night?"

"Over there." The boy pointed to an empty stall. "The gate to his stall was open when I arrived this morning, and he was gone."

Danu considered the boy's words while he studied the gate. It locked from the outside, but a smart horse would be able to open it by leaning over and using his teeth—and Thorn was the smartest horse Danu had ever known.

"Did you put oats in his stall this morning?" Danu picked up a handful of oats from a bucket hanging inside Thorn's stall.

"No, m'lord. Them 'er from last night."

Danu let the musty-smelling grain fall between his fingers and back into the bucket. It seemed unlikely that any horse would just leave without finishing them first. *But then again*, he thought, *Thorn isn't like any horse.*

"If he turns up, or you think of anything else . . ."

"I'll inform you directly, m'lord."

Danu nodded and left for the guest quarters, which were located in a solid, whitewashed building on the opposite side of the tall, square tower that housed the war room.

⋈⋈⋈

The search for Renn had turned up nothing. Every day, Danu, Kivas, Raven, and Aleah met with the king and his captain to review their progress. After six weeks, they had searched every house, building, warehouse, and alley, but they had found nothing.

At least the mystery about Thorn was now clearer. Two days after his disappearance, the supervisor who managed the north gorge lift reported a horse that fit Thorn's description had walked onto the lift with a group of merchants from Kah-Tarku and diplomats from Port Andrus. He'd thought the horse belonged to one of the groups, but when they disembarked at the bottom of Elahna's Gorge, Thorn had crossed the Andrus River alone and disappeared into the foothills of Avalian.

Danu sat at one of the large wooden tables in the great hall and nursed a tankard of ale—only halfway paying attention as Kivas, Durham, and Lahar discussed whether or not Renn was still in the city and what other actions they might take to find him. Lahar paced, picking his fingernails with a knife, listening, and stopping only long enough to make a comment now and again. Danu watched him pace over the top of his tankard. *No wonder he's so skinny*, Danu thought. *He never stops moving.*

Lahar, like all of Danu's men, worked tirelessly to find Renn. He had also fought bravely against the Tiaro Devi when they attacked on the plains, and he'd probably saved Cole's life during the fight. On the journey to Anytos, Lahar and Cole had spent most of their free time fishing. Now Cole was with Radien and Micha, searching the park for at least the hundredth time while Lahar and the others tried to determine the next place to search.

"I don't think he's here," Raven said. "We'd have found him by now if he was."

"So what do I do?" Danu set down his ale and turned to Raven.

"We still have a responsibility to get Tristan, Genea, and Harlow to the school," the captain answered.

Danu had gone over this line of reasoning in his mind before. If they didn't leave for Elder Island soon, the other children wouldn't be there in time to be presented at the midwinter festival.

Danu slammed his fist on the table, and the other men stopped talking. Even Lahar stopped his relentless pacing. "But what do I say to the lore masters when they ask about the Child of the Blessing? 'Sorry, oh great council. I lost the most important person in all of Lemuria somewhere along the way'?"

Raven didn't reply and neither did the others.

Danu dropped his head and rubbed at his eyes with his palms. "How can I face Delphia again? This one task may have been the most important thing I was supposed to do in my entire life." Danu picked up his tankard and stared at the dark liquid it held. "And I failed."

The young lord took a long drink and slammed the empty mug down on the table. He ran his hands through his hair and stood, turning to Raven and Kivas. "Begin making preparations for travel. We leave tomorrow."

WINTER'S FIRST FESTIVAL

Avaris's heart was racing. The moonless night helped to conceal him as he crept through the thick pine forests surrounding the Devi-Hold. He had to pay extra attention to where he placed his steps so as to not cause the snow to crunch or twigs to break beneath his weight.

He hadn't been on the Andrikan side of the Andrus River since his father had left him to die four years ago. Now Avaris was about to confront the man in the presence of the entire Andrikan clan. He'd imagined the scenario hundreds of times during the past weeks; he would be welcomed as a hero returned from the dead. Avaris envisioned the joy and celebration that would follow his appearance. His father would have no choice but to accept him with the entire tribe watching. Avaris stopped walking and bit his lip. *But what if they don't believe me?* he thought. *What if my father orders his warriors to kill me as an impostor?*

Earlier that week, the tribe clans had begun arriving at the hold to prepare for the first Azur-Aven of winter, and with each new arrival, Avaris's anxiety had increased. Now, as he prowled toward the open field on the southeast side of the hold—where the blessings would be held—his stomach felt as though it had an army of ants running through it, and he had to make a conscious effort to control his breathing.

Lekiah was already at the celebration, probably with Kalisha, since Akusaa would not be with his family. The high clan chief and the Meskhoni would be in a dignitary's tent at the front of the crowd, preparing for the blessings. A large wooden platform with an altar in the center, used by Mindahl for blessing the babies, would be raised in front of the tent. If things were going as planned, Lekiah should be in place close to the platform and near the guards.

Avaris went over the plan in his head once again as he stopped near the edge of the forest and peered around the cold, rough trunk of a large pine. The dignitary's tent stood a mere twenty paces in front of him—the back of the tent butting up against the forest. His father, Akusaa, would be inside, applying his ceremonial paint. Avaris clenched his fists and curled his lip at the thought.

Beyond the tent stood the raised platform surrounded by onlookers and warriors. Rather than holding weapons, many of the warriors sat on the ground, pounding a steady rhythm on animal-skin drums. Standing this close, the noise of the crowd and the drums drowned out every other sound.

He picked up a small stone and held it in the palm of his left hand. Using a spell Myrrah had taught him, he concentrated on the stone until it began to glow with a faint red light. He held the spell and used the red light to check his clothing for what must have been the tenth time since he'd left Myrrah's cottage. He wore the typical clothing of a Devi warrior, except his wooden shield bore the crest of Akusaa's personal guard—a charging black buffalo—as did his bison robe. He didn't think he'd be wearing the robe very long, but if he were discovered before he was ready, the guard's clothing would be a good disguise.

Underneath the heavy robe, he wore the ceremonial clothes of the Mordrahn family, and around his neck hung a necklace decorated with five white dove feathers. The necklace was symbolic; all warriors wore feathers to represent certain things. Some to signify bravery, a great hunt, or family heritage—but only the heir of the high chief wore five white dove feathers. Because Toci wore the feathers in a headband, Avaris chose to make his feathers into a necklace.

Assured once again that he was ready, Avaris crept around the tent, still hidden among the trees, until he came directly behind Akusaa's guard.

Lekiah stood only a few feet away, and as Avaris had suspected, Kalisha was by his side, talking excitedly and waving to friends. Seeing his sister this close brought deep emotions rushing over him like water bursting from a broken beaver dam. He wanted so badly to run and take her in his arms. Until now, he hadn't realized how much he truly missed his older sister, and it took all the control he had to remain quiet, hide behind some bushes, and wait for the baby blessings to begin.

Avaris's hands felt clammy, so he ran them through his hair and rubbed them on his robe. His heart pounded so hard in his chest he thought he'd hear it for sure if the drums and crowd weren't so loud. He peeked through the bushes and tried to count the campfires scattered across the plains. He quit counting after he reached one hundred. There must've been ten thousand fires, and each fire probably warmed a dozen or more people.

A large bonfire, surrounded by a dozen young, painted warriors, burned at the front and center of the throng of people on the far side of the platform. Avaris could smell the burning pine and see the flickering shadows dance across the faces of those closest to the fire. The warriors performed a ceremonial dance to the familiar beat being played on leather-skin drums, using carved buffalo bones as beaters. Avaris was glad Myrrah had taught him how to project his voice over great distances in preparation for tonight; he would definitely need it.

As he thought about his godmother, he wondered where she was. She had been banished by Akusaa more than ten years ago, and so she didn't come to the festival, but Avaris knew she would be watching.

Avaris waited through four more dances before the flap of the dignitary's tent opened and two of Akusaa's personal guard stepped out, followed by Akusaa himself. Avaris clenched his jaw and narrowed his eyes as he watched his father walk across the platform and approach the altar. He wore the usual ceremonial attire for his position: a headdress of eagle feathers, a necklace of bear claws, and a painted bison robe clasped loosely around his neck with a bone-carved broach. Red and black paint decorated what little could be seen of his face. He looked the same as he had four years ago—when he'd left Avaris to die—except his long, unkempt hair and thin, scraggly black beard were lined with streaks of gray now.

The crowd gathered in closer, and Akusaa held up his hands for silence.

"My fellow brothers and warriors of the Andrikan nation, welcome to first winter's Azur-Aven. I trust your separate travels have been safe and fruitful, and I rejoice to have you with us once more."

Avaris shook his head as he listened to the lies. His father hated the hassle of gathering the tribe together each month, and he only cared about the prosperity of the individual tribes because their prosperity eventually became his own.

Akusaa finished his salutation by introducing the Wizard Mindahl. Instead of walking out of the tent, he materialized with a flash of green light next to the altar. The night air echoed with silence for two heartbeats, then erupted with cheers for the strange Wizard's display of power.

Avaris wasn't sure what to think about Mindahl. The Wizard had never done anything to make Avaris dislike him, but he found the man rather odd. He wore a light blue turban wrapped around his head and a long, plain white robe. His short white beard and long white mustache looked strangely out of place among the dark-haired Andrikans. Whether that was a characteristic of all southern men or because Mindahl was old, Avaris wasn't sure. It seemed odd to him that the Wizard would serve so far away from his native land of Sarundra.

Wizards usually had their pick of kings' courts to serve in. Avaris wondered what had caused Mindahl to choose the Andrikan Devi rather than a wealthier kingdom. Myrrah often told Avaris about the untold wealth possessed by kings in Boranica, Nortia, Concordia, and even the trading cities on the far side of the Andrikan Mountains. Certainly a life of luxury in a palace would be more appealing to a Wizard than living the nomadic life of the Andrikan Devi. But of course, Mindahl was from Sarundra, and there were a lot of nomadic tribes there as well. Maybe he liked the adventure of travel and the free life the tribe had to offer.

The old Wizard finished blessing the last child, and Avaris, wrapped in thought, almost missed his cue. He rose, snuck behind the guards, and waited for Mindahl to make his final prayer to the gods.

> ". . . gods of dark and gods of light—
> Guide us all, to know your will.
> Accept our gifts presented this night—
> Let spoken promises be fulfilled."

Avaris's heart raced still, and he wiped his sweating palms on his robe. He began walking around the guards even before Mindahl spoke his last question.

"Are there any others to be presented this night?" the Wizard called out.

That was it. Now was the moment Avaris had waited for. He concentrated on two of the spells Myrrah had taught him and pulled a skull and a stone from under his robe.

Avaris stepped in front of the guards and into the light, dropped his shield, and let his bison robe fall to the ground, allowing all to see his royal ceremonial clothing. As he walked forward, he saw motion out of the corner of his eye. Some of the guard moved to stop him, but Lekiah called them back. Avaris focused his will on the stone until it shone a bright red. Then, using the power of bone, he channeled his voice through the skull so all could hear.

"I would like to be presented before the tribe." Clearly Avaris's spell was working. Murmurs arose from the crowd, and Avaris felt every eye turn to watch the young man carrying the glowing stone and wearing the ceremonial attire of the Mordrahns. Akusaa also turned to look, and Avaris saw the man's eyes open wide and his jaw drop.

Avaris walked onto the platform in front of the altar and stopped with his back facing his father to address the awestruck crowd. "My name is Avaris Mordrahn. I was lost in the wilderness, but I have returned to rejoin the tribe and warn you of impending danger."

"Avaris!" Kalisha tore free of Lekiah's grip, bolted up the steps to the platform, and ran toward her brother, tears filling her eyes. "Is that really you? We all thought you were—"

Akusaa grabbed her arm as she tried to run past him. "Shut up! This isn't your brother! He's a fraud!"

Akusaa gave her arm a shove, and the thrust of his push knocked her to her back on the hard wood. Avaris's concentration broke, and both spells dropped. He looked back at his sister, rolling over on her stomach and obviously in pain. Uncontrollable anger overwhelmed him, and he drew his sword with every intention of killing the despicable man who was his father.

Avaris took a step forward, but Lekiah jumped onto the platform, screamed the Devi war cry, and dove at Akusaa. He and the surprised clan chief tumbled off the platform and into the crowd.

A hole opened in the mass of people as the two men landed on the ground; then the group quickly closed around them. Avaris jumped off the platform and tried to fight his way through the crowd. He had to get Lekiah away before he murdered the high chief in front of the entire clan.

Before Avaris could push through the first line of onlookers, a tangle of arms seized him and yanked his sword from his grip. He tried to break free, but three of Akusaa's older and stronger personal guards held him tight, and a fist hit him hard in the stomach. Four more proceeded to fight through the crowd, trying to locate their leader. It took two more to pull Lekiah off of him.

Avaris saw Lilisha rush onto the platform and help her daughter stand. "Stop! All of you, stop fighting!" Even though a woman's voice issued the command, the warriors and Lekiah hesitated, but only for a moment. The fighting resumed, and Avaris heard Kalisha's voice above the commotion as she shouted to the Meskhoni.

"Mindahl, can't you do something? Someone's going to get killed!"

He heard the Wizard mumble in an indecipherable language, and then Avaris's body wouldn't respond to his thoughts. He could no longer kick or twist. It seemed no one was able to hit him, either, because he no longer felt fists pounding against his side and back.

He looked to the crowd surrounding Lekiah and saw that he had stopped fighting as well, although he was yelling louder than ever. A pale green light surrounded Avaris's blood brother, and Lekiah was lifted into the air above the crowd. Avaris was shocked to realize that he, too, had been lifted into the air. Both of them floated, immobile, to the platform where Mindahl stood waving his staff and mumbling strange words. Lokia must have worked his way through the audience during the fight and now stood on the platform next to the white-bearded Meskhoni—obviously upset over his son's actions.

The Wizard set the two young men next to each other on the stand and released them so they could move. Lekiah turned and tried to rush back to the fight but fell back as if he hit a translucent green wall. Avaris turned in a circle and realized that a faint green glow surrounded them both—like a wall of living power.

"Settle down, Lekiah," his father said. "You'll only get yourself in more trouble."

Akusaa emerged from the crowd. Blood ran down his face from a gash in his forehead, and his right eye and lower lip were already beginning to swell.

"What are you talking about, Lokia?" Akusaa said. "He's already in as much trouble as he can be." Akusaa's face was red, and bloody spittle dripped into his wiry beard.

"Make my voice carry over the crowd," Akusaa said to the Meskhoni.

"You may speak any time, my lord."

Akusaa turned and faced the crowd. "This is not my son." He pointed back at Avaris and glared at the crowd as if daring anyone to challenge his pronouncement. "I don't know who or what this is, but he is not my son. My son is dead. This is a pretender." He looked over the silent crowd, squared his shoulders, and folded his arms. "Lekiah has committed treason. Both boys will be sentenced at the conclusion of the festival. In the meantime, no one is to talk with them. If anyone is caught speaking with them—they will be tried for conspiracy also."

"Father, what are you—"

"That means everyone!" He slashed his arm through the air and looked sideways at his daughter. "Including you, Kalisha."

Akusaa spun on his heels and walked back into the tent behind the stage. Lokia turned toward the drummers and dancers still gathered around the large fire in front of the platform and signaled for them to continue. It took some time for the crowd to stop staring at the two boys held captive by the Meskhoni, but once the drummers and dancers began and wine was passed around the fires, the people turned their attention back to the celebration.

Mindahl moved the boys toward the hold—keeping them surrounded by his supernatural green cage. People whispered and pointed as they passed; some gave hostile looks while others stared with open mouths.

Avaris hung his head, and his soul ached. How was he ever going to win the hearts of his people as a prisoner? And what could he and Lekiah do to help them against Kahn Devin while trapped in Mindahl's green cage?

Avaris wanted to scream at the world. He wanted to cry out that his father was leading their nation to ruin, but he remained silent. He wouldn't allow the last image his people remembered of him to be a twelve-year-old boy in a rage. Instead, he walked in forced dignity with his blood brother next to him. They would face their fate as warriors—together.

PRISON

The green prison Mindahl created kept Avaris and Lekiah from getting out, but it didn't keep the cold from getting in. Avaris's fingers were numb, and his clothing was soaked all the way to his skin from lying on the snow. Being cold wasn't so bad—he'd been cold before—but the worst part was not knowing if he'd ever be warm again.

He paced and rubbed his arms. Five steps, turn, five steps, and turn. He stopped and blew into his hands while he stared out of the green prison. Mindahl had set their cell just outside the tents, next to the path that led to the west gate and the Andrus River and Mord Mountains beyond. Myrrah's cabin was in those mountains, but where was the old woman? Why hadn't she come to help them escape?

"What in Ba Aven's name are they doing?" Avaris said. "The festival is over. The other clans have surely gone back to the plains by now, so why hasn't my father come to pass judgment on us?"

Lekiah didn't respond; he simply stared off into the distance.

Avaris gritted his teeth and rubbed his hands together. "I hate not knowing what's going on. I wish they'd either kill us or let us go."

The temperature dropped rapidly as the sun set over the Mord Mountains. The few clouds in the twilight sky were painted with brilliant orange and red, but Avaris failed to see the beauty; he saw nothing but another frigid night approaching.

"I don't know if I can take another night of this, Lekiah." He sat down hard on the snow next to his blood brother. "I'm almost frozen to death already . . . I think I'm going out of my head."

Lekiah stared into the distance as though he were looking at spirits from a different world.

"Snap out of it, Lekiah. Talk to me." Avaris grabbed the bigger boy's shoulders and shook him. "Can't you see I need your help?"

"What do you want me to do?" Lekiah whispered. "We're going to die."

Avaris knew Lekiah was probably right, but hearing him say it out loud made Avaris grit his teeth and pound his fist into his hand. "What are you talking about? Why are you giving up? As long as we're together, we can do anything." Avaris grabbed Lekiah's chin, turned his face, and looked him in the eye.

"You are the greatest Devi warrior of all time. Didn't you kill the biggest Muk'gula ever? You didn't become great by giving up."

"That's different. I can fight flesh and blood. Give me a sword and a fair fight and I'd never give up, but what can I do against magic? *Ba Aven's breath*, Avaris, I haven't even got a knife!"

In the distance, a wolf howled.

"Wait." Avaris held up his hand. "Did you hear that?" he whispered.

"It's just a pack of wolves. What are you worried about?"

"Those aren't ordinary wolves. I have an eerie feeling. Something's—"

Avaris saw quick-moving shadows dart out of the trees within the walls of the hold and into the tents. A horn sounded, and as if a dam broke, creatures poured over the walls surrounding the hold. The beasts howled and shrieked with a lust for blood.

Large black dogs with scarlet eyes and dripping yellow fangs tore through the tents on the perimeter of the hold as though they were made of paper. Following on the heels of the dogs came beasts that looked half human and half animal. Some were a mixture of man, puma, and bird, while others resembled a cross between bison and deformed giants.

Women and children ran screaming out of the tents, and the Andrikan men grabbed weapons to face the assault. But the beasts came too fast and their numbers were too great. Avaris heard the cries of his people as they were torn apart by the gross savages that assailed them. He had to to escape. He had to defend his people.

Loud pounding against the wooden walls that were designed to protect the hold against attack drew Avaris's attention away from the tents. Red lightning burst the wood of the gates into a million fragmented splinters and sent them flying through the air like darts. An old woman stumbled out of her tent, her body pierced all over with splinters, and the horde that charged through the breached walls trampled her like a weed in the dirt.

Frustration and anger welled up in the pit of Avaris's stomach. He looked at Lekiah and found him frantically digging in the snow by the wall of their magical prison.

"What are you doing?" Avaris shouted.

"I've got to get out of this cage. Kalisha's out there—I've got to help her."

Avaris fell to his knees next to his friend and dug with his frozen fingers. He didn't know if they could dig under the frozen ground or not, but they had no other option.

Screams and howls filled the darkening twilight. Smoke from burning tents covered the half moon and stars, but Avaris could still see figures running and fighting, silhouetted against the many fires that raged throughout the hold.

Avaris turned his attention back to digging. His fingers bled, but he paid them no mind—he couldn't feel them anyway. A massive Demon Dog collided against the green wall in front of where they were digging, barking and baring its sharp teeth. Avaris and Lekiah jumped backward, thankful for the first time for the protection of the green shield. The beast fell back, unable to break through, but several more joined, and they circled the enclosure, hungrily searching for an entrance.

The dogs dripped rabid foam from their jaws and their eyes glowed blood-red, but a greater power drew Avaris's eyes from the beasts to the smoldering breach in the Devi-Hold's wall.

A pale-skinned man, dressed in a long black cape that clasped about his neck, marched through the opening. Unlike the beasts that flanked him, this man had a sophisticated and stoic look about him. Underneath his cape, he wore a white shirt tied about the neck with a red scarf and covered by a richly woven gold-colored doublet. His short silver hair was neatly combed, and a coarse, well-trimmed beard framed his face.

"Kahn Devin," Avaris whispered. "He's leading the Demon Dogs and Kirocs."

"How do you know that's Kahn Devin?" Lekiah looked up from his relentless digging.

"Myrrah has described him before. And I can feel his power."

The Grand Warlock strode by, then stopped and slowly turned to face the boys. The beasts following the man fell over each other to avoid bumping into him. Avaris swallowed and retreated until he felt his back press against the wall of their magical cell. Kahn's eyes narrowed and his lips pursed as he studied the green jail and the captives inside.

"You and you." Kahn pointed to two Kirocs, one armed with a spear, the other with a sword. "Stay here and make sure these two don't escape."

A horn blew from within the center of the Devi-Hold, and a chorus of howls from Demon Dogs rang out. Kahn resumed walking toward the tents of the hold, and the rest of his demonic entourage followed.

As the Grand Warlock entered the outer ring of tents, Avaris heard Kahn command his minions to find the leaders of the Devi and their families and bring them to him.

Avaris's heart raced. He fell to his knees and clawed at the frozen earth with his bloody fingers. He didn't care about his father but feared for the rest of his family. There was no telling what Kahn intended to do with them. Panic and anger welled up inside him, and as he struggled to dig, a burning feeling rose from the center of his being and continued to grow until it consumed him.

Avaris threw back his head and screamed. He stopped clawing the earth and pointed his hands at the green walls of energy that held them prisoner, and a burst of white fire flew from his fingertips. Lekiah dove to the ground as the power bounced and ricocheted off the magical barrier that kept them trapped.

"Are you trying to get us killed?" Lekiah yelled.

"I'm trying to break free. We've got to do *something*," Avaris shouted back.

"Boys no talk," the Kiroc with the spear said. "Not escape."

A green stream of power erupted above the center court of the Devi-Hold. Red flame rose to meet it, and they collided in the sky with a thunderous boom. The green power wavered until the red energy devoured it with an explosive flash of light, and Avaris and Lekiah's prison walls disappeared. Avaris figured that Kahn Devin must have killed Mindahl, but he didn't care. They were free, and he had a chance to save his family.

Lekiah charged the Kiroc holding the spear. The beast lunged to impale the Devi warrior. Lekiah turned sideways, grabbed the shaft of the spear, and kicked the Kiroc in the ribs. The creature fell into the Kiroc holding the sword, sending them both sprawling to the ground. Lekiah yanked the spear from the Kiroc as it fell and rammed it through his chest and pulled it out again.

The Kiroc with the sword rolled to his feet and swung his weapon. Lekiah used a boulder to launch himself in the air, flip over the Kiroc, and drive the spear into the creature's back. The Kiroc fell to the ground with a groan. Lekiah removed the spear, picked up the dying Kiroc's sword, and ran toward the burning tents with Avaris on his heels.

As Lekiah rounded a tent, he tripped over a dead man's body. His eyes widened, and he hesitated to turn over the corpse. Avaris felt his own stomach drop when he looked at the body lying in blood and saw the short black hair—uncommon among the Devi.

Lekiah clenched his jaw, took a breath, and rolled the man onto his back. The warrior closed his eyes and turned his head. Lekiah's father's throat had been ripped out, and his dead eyes stared vacantly at the sky.

"I'm sorry, Lekiah," Avaris said.

Lekiah placed his forehead against his father's, then reverently closed the man's eyes.

Avaris heard a sound that made his blood run cold with horror, and Lekiah jumped to his feet: a woman screaming—whether in agony or misery Avaris couldn't tell, but he recognized his mother's voice.

They rushed through the smoldering tents to the open area in the center of the hold. The scene of carnage and blood that met them made Avaris stare in horror.

Dismembered corpses littered the snow-covered ground, and pools of blood formed puddles of scarlet-colored slush. Black Demon Dogs fed eagerly on the warm flesh, devouring old and young alike.

A massive, green-skinned Kiroc stood on the platform holding Akusaa Mordrahn by the hair and forced the high clan chief to witness the slaughter of his people. Avaris's younger brother, Toci, dangled by a rope from a tree, and his mother lay crumpled on the ground beneath him.

A group of Devi youth, chained together at the neck, huddled at the side and wept. A Kiroc grabbed Kalisha from their midst and threw her to the ground in the center of the clearing, near the fire pit where Kahn Devin stood.

"I detest destroying beauty such as this, Akusaa," Kahn Devin said in an accent that Avaris had never heard before. "But you leave me no alternative."

"No, wait! I'm sorry, I'll support you . . . I promise . . . I'm sorry!" Akusaa cried.

"Groveling is unbecoming of a high clan chief." Kahn motioned a Kiroc holding two dogs to come forward. "Had you been more pleasant to my emissaries, this unfortunate incident could have been avoided."

The Kiroc loosed the animals, but Lekiah reacted like lightning. In three strides he met the first Demon Dog and drove his spear deep into its chest. The second dog changed direction midstride to confront this new threat, but Lekiah rolled and sliced the creature's belly open with his sword as it charged by.

Avaris began an incantation to create fire that Myrrah had taught him. He chanted the words and made the symbols to create flame and smiled as he felt a red glow begin to surround him. He raised his hands to shoot a ball of flame at the group preparing to attack Lekiah and Kalisha, but Kahn Devin spun around and locked eyes with him.

The Grand Warlock laughed and raised a hand, and Avaris's flame flickered and died. Kahn closed his hand into a fist, and Avaris was thrown to the ground and held there by invisible pressure.

"Now, Akusaa, you shall witness the slaying of your daughter and this hero who defends her."

Kahn kept the pressure mounting to crush Avaris and with the other hand signaled his horde to attack Lekiah. Avaris could see his blood brother ready himself for battle. The Demon Dogs attacked in a rush—Lekiah didn't stand a chance. His sword flashed like metallic death, and three dogs and two Kirocs fell to his blade before he went down. Once he fell, the dogs howled with victory and a Kiroc grabbed Kalisha from behind.

Panic and rage sprung up inside of Avaris. He felt his blood race through his veins. His vision became blurred and blinded by a bright light that consumed him.

Avaris screamed as white energy flew from his eyes and fingers toward Kahn and the creatures attacking Lekiah. Demon Dogs and Kirocs fled like sheep before a mountain lion. Kahn Devin raised a red shield to intercept the white power, but the impact hurled him through the air. Lekiah jumped up and chased the Kirocs, cutting them down as they ran.

Kahn Devin transformed into a black hawk in midair and glided to the ground, changing back into the Grand Warlock as he landed.

"Stop!" Kahn shouted.

Lekiah was oblivious to anything but the retreating Kirocs and dogs, so Kahn lifted his staff and shot a shaft of vermilion power toward Lekiah. Instead of harming him, however, the red energy formed a ball around Lekiah and pulled him back to the center of the clearing.

Kahn turned from Lekiah, though the ball of energy still held, and faced Avaris.

"I presume you are Avaris?" he asked politely, as though the scene of carnage and blood around them were insignificant. Avaris didn't respond—anger and a need for revenge surged through his veins.

"I did not expect to find you here," Kahn said. "You and I were not to meet until two more years. Is Myrrah with you?"

"How do you know who I am? And how did you know I live with Myrrah?"

"Only one other boy in all of Lemuria could have done what you just did. Since that other boy is . . . gone"—as the Warlock spoke of another "boy," his lips drew to a tight line—"I deduced you to be Avaris."

"Why did you say we weren't to meet for two more years?"

"You were to come to the caves under the Cragg Mountains when you reached the age of fourteen to begin your studies with me."

"Ha! You think I'd come to you after what you did to my people? I'd rather die."

"Avaris, you misjudge me. Give me an opportunity to prove myself to you."

Avaris listened. Even though this man had just murdered his people, he felt compelled to believe him. Kahn Devin radiated power and sophistication. It occurred to Avaris that with Kahn's help, he could become the greatest Warlock ever—then he could force people to be fair.

Avaris squeezed his eyes shut and shook his head. "Why should I trust you?"

"If it weren't for me, you wouldn't be alive."

"You're lying."

"Am I? Who do you think sent Myrrah when your father left you to die?"

Avaris found himself mesmerized and clinging to every word the Warlock uttered. He took a step closer. He forgot about the dead bodies littering the ground; he even forgot about Toci and his mother.

"Avaris, don't listen to him!" Kalisha screamed. "He doesn't care about anyone. He's lying!"

The sound of her voice broke through the trance Avaris was under. He shook his head, and once again, anger rose from the pit of his gut. He held to the anger and focused on it.

"Myrrah loves me. If what you say is true, she would have told me."

"But it is true, isn't it, Myrrah?" Kahn looked toward a clump of bushes near a tent across the clearing from where Avaris stood. "Show yourself, Myrrah. I know you're there."

The bush rustled, and the Necromancer waddled from her hiding place, her face twitching more rapidly than usual. Avaris held his breath. Had she been hiding there all along? Had she simply stood by and watched as the entire village had been murdered?

"Go ahead, Myrrah. Tell our young friend the truth."

Myrrah stared at her feet, wrung her hands together, and shifted her weight. Then she said something to the Grand Warlock in a language Avaris had never heard. He didn't understand her words, but he understood the pleading tone in her voice. Kahn snapped a curt reply in the same strange language. Myrrah shook her head, looking as desperate as a mountain cat trapped in a cage.

"Myrrah?" Kahn prodded.

"I . . . I'm sorry . . ." She looked up with tears in her eyes and reached a hand toward Avaris. "But I do love you, Avaris. You must believe that."

REVENGE

"No," Avaris whispered. He fell to his knees, clenched his fists, and screamed. "No!"

"I didn't want it to be like this," Myrrah said.

"Why? Why did you lie to me? How could you?"

"I didn't lie to you. I told you I couldn't return to Nortia, and I told you Akusaa had exiled me—both are true."

"You lied to me!" Avaris punched the frozen ground. "I thought you cared about me."

"Avaris," Kahn said, "search your heart. Myrrah has loved you and served you well."

Again, Avaris listened to the Warlock. He wanted to turn and run away, but the peculiar feeling returned and made him stay. Subconsciously, he knew the Warlock was manipulating him, but he was powerless to stop it.

"As you come to know and understand our ways, you will learn to appreciate the power of the Aven-Lore."

Avaris didn't trust himself to speak. He looked toward Lekiah and saw that the red ball of power no longer restrained his blood brother. However, he wasn't moving—nobody was. Avaris shook his head and looked at Kahn and Myrrah.

"Ba Aven is an auspicious god, Avaris, and he rewards his servants. Take

Myrrah, for example. She once fell out of our favor, but we gave her the opportunity to repent." The way he said "our favor" and "we" when he was referring to the god's generosity might have seemed a bit strange coming from anybody else. But Kahn said it so matter-of-factly that it sounded natural. "We sent her to be your guardian, and she obeyed because she was promised forgiveness and great blessings if she took care of you. She has accomplished her charge and now deserves the promised blessing."

Kahn raised his staff and chanted in a guttural tongue. He drew angular symbols in the air with his staff, and a red aura of power surrounded the old woman.

Avaris thought Kahn might kill her. But instead, a metamorphosis took place. Her stringy red hair thickened and grew long. Her short and dumpy figure thinned out as she grew taller. Soon, the Myrrah that Avaris knew was gone, and in her place stood a beautiful young woman who looked oddly familiar.

"This is Myrrah." Kahn smiled. "This is the way she really looks. Much better, don't you think?"

Avaris couldn't get over how familiar the young woman . . . Myrrah . . . looked. He knew that face . . . somewhere . . .

The drawing in Myrrah's cabin. It was Myrrah, not her sister, as Avaris always believed.

"You never loved me. You saved me because Kahn promised to give you back your beauty if you did."

"Maybe in the beginning," she said. "But I have grown to love you."

"Avaris, come back with me to the Cragg Caves. I will be the father you never had."

Kahn's offer tempted him. Even though Avaris hated the man with his whole soul, the offer pulled at his will, and he longed to comply.

Avaris pulled his eyes from the Warlock. He looked toward Kalisha and Lekiah. They stood with their mouths open as though trapped in the midst of screaming, yet they didn't move. Somehow, Kahn kept everyone frozen in time. Avaris saw the form of his mother lying crumpled beneath her baby boy, who hung from the tree; he saw the flesh and blood of those who had been slain by this man who claimed to be his friend. He looked across the clearing at the beautiful but crying Myrrah.

Avaris stood and jutted out his chin. "I will fight against you until one of us is destroyed," he hissed between clenched teeth, and he turned to walk away. He took a single step, and a blow from behind forced him to the ground.

"Then you will die tonight." Kahn increased the pressure bearing down on Avaris, making it difficult for the boy to breathe.

"Chain up the warrior," Kahn said to the Kirocs, referring to Lekiah. "I'm going to release him and the others so they can watch young Avaris die."

Avaris heard rustling feet and sobbing when Kahn released his hold of the remaining members of the tribe. A shout of alarm from one of the Kirocs distracted Kahn, but he kept enough power on Avaris to keep him down. Akusaa twisted from the grasp of his captors, jumped from the platform, and started running away.

"Bring him back!" Kahn shouted. "Alive!" It only took a moment for the Demon Dogs to catch the high clan chief. He screamed and kicked like a frightened child as the Kirocs dragged him back.

"I have forced you to watch the deaths of your wife and youngest son, Akusaa," Kahn said. "Now, because you killed my messengers and treated them with contempt, you shall live the rest of your life in contempt. Look at your wife and youngest son." The Kiroc holding him forced the pitiful clan chief to look toward the tree where Toci hung. "The blame is yours. Your daughter will become my personal slave. She will not find mercy in death. Instead, she will do everything I command and love it."

"No!" Lekiah screamed and struggled against his chains. "You *Aven* filth! I'll kill you!"

Kahn ignored him and took a step toward Akusaa. "I will not permit you to witness Avaris's death. You do not deserve the honor. Instead, the images that will live with you throughout the rest of your miserable life shall be filled by the memories of how your foolish pride destroyed this people."

Kahn pointed two fingers at Akusaa, and beams of red flame jumped from his fingertips to the clan chief's eyes. Akusaa screamed and fell to his knees as his eyes were burned from their sockets. None of the surviving tribe, not even Kalisha, seemed to be affected by the torture. Either they had seen too much already or they no longer cared about their clan chief.

"Now leave. You will live as an example for others."

The Kiroc standing behind Akusaa grabbed him by the back of his shirt and threw him off the platform. Akusaa didn't look like a high clan chief as he stumbled into the cold night. Kahn watched him go and then turned back to Avaris.

"You have one last chance to change your mind, Avaris." The pressure Kahn kept weighted against Avaris's body made it difficult to respond.

"Never . . . I'll never . . ."

"That's regrettable," Kahn said calmly, and he increased the weight pressing against Avaris. "Nevertheless, I cannot afford to let you live as my enemy." The Grand Warlock furrowed his brow and twisted his lips. Avaris, even through his pain, could see the Warlock's eyes glow bright red. The pressure turned into burning heat. Avaris tried to recall a defensive spell, one Myrrah had taught him, but his mental faculties seemed to be blocked.

As he fought against the power that held him to the cold ground, he looked around for anything that might help. He saw Kalisha and Lekiah fighting to break free. Then he saw Myrrah—young and beautiful now—standing next to Kahn with tears running down her face.

Avaris squirmed beneath the weight of the pressure and burning heat. He wondered why Kahn was taking so long to kill him when the Warlock had disposed of others in an instant. Then it dawned on Avaris that he was fighting back. His mind and will were fighting back.

Avaris struggled to control his fears and pain, then redirected the energy out and back toward Kahn. The pressure eased enough for Avaris to climb to his knees.

"Very good, Avaris, but you are not strong enough to beat me."

Kahn raised a human skull and thighbone and swirled the bone in the air. A cyclone of wind ripped at Avaris's face, and the pressure forced him back to the ground. The Warlock was too powerful. Avaris looked at Myrrah and reached out his hand as if to ask for her help. Kahn Devin laughed, and Avaris could tell he found pleasure in watching him suffer and beg.

"Myrrah," Avaris whispered. "Help me . . . please."

Myrrah looked back and forth between Kahn and the boy she'd raised. Her eyes grew wide, and she set her jaw. Kahn was so focused on Avaris that he didn't see the beautiful Necromancer pull another skull and thighbone out from under her shawl—or the bolt of red fire that leapt from each empty eye socket into the thighbone, filling it with living power until it glowed a translucent red. At the point Avaris expected to see the bone explode into tiny shards, his now-beautiful godmother raised it and, with all the force she could muster, brought it down like a sledgehammer toward the Warlock's head.

Whether by premonition or some other instinct, Kahn Devin looked up in time to see the blow coming and he dropped his attack on Avaris to raise an ephemeral shield. The release of power that emanated from Myrrah's charged skeletal implements caused them to fracture at impact, but the discharge of power sent the Warlock flying head over heels through the air.

Kahn struck a thick pine tree and fell to the ground, still encased in his red body shield and still under fire by power from Myrrah's damaged weapons. Avaris's jaw dropped when the Warlock shook off the attack, rose to his feet, and squared off against Myrrah.

"Run, Avaris!" Myrrah shouted. "I can't hold him much longer!"

Avaris hesitated. Maybe he could help and together they could destroy the dark Warlock. If he focused his will against Kahn's shield, he might be able to weaken it enough for Myrrah's power to strike him.

Avaris concentrated on the man within the shield, but Myrrah's shout broke his concentration.

"Get out of here, Avaris. Now!" She looked toward him, and their eyes locked. His godmother's gaze seemed to say, "Don't let me die in vain. Save yourself."

He looked once more at Lekiah and Kalisha, still struggling against the Kirocs who were now placing chains and shackles around his sister's ankles and wrists. He hated to leave them like that. He swore that he'd rescue them and seek revenge against this man who'd destroyed all his hopes.

Avaris ran from them, and the crunchy snow slowed him down. He couldn't run fast enough, yet each time he pushed harder, he'd slip and nearly fall. He ran past burning tents and broken bodies, past the area where Mindahl had held Lekiah and him as prisoners for three days, then out of the breach created by Kahn.

He stumbled through bushes, hills of snow, and thickets of young pine trees, then fell headfirst into the river. The biting cold of the Andrus cleared his head and brought him out of shock, but it also chilled him to the bone and reminded him how hungry and weak he was.

He climbed out the opposite bank—on the Deklan side—and started up the steep slopes of the Mord Mountains. The night sky lit up with a red burst of energy that glowed and cast a scarlet hue on the trees and snow. Avaris turned to look, and as he did, he heard a shrill scream followed by a blinding flash.

A tear ran down his cheek, and he brushed it away with numb fingers—Myrrah was gone. He could feel it in his heart. He wanted to fall down and weep. He had lost two mothers in the same night to the hand of the same man: Kahn Devin.

The sky turned dark, and in the distance, Avaris heard the baying of Demon Dogs. He didn't have much time. He couldn't outrun the dogs; he had to think of something else.

He ran in circles, around trees, through bushes, and over exposed boulders. He climbed to the top of one large rock that jutted out of the snow less than two yards from the river, then jumped as far as he could. He landed with a splash in the frigid water and let himself float with the current until he rounded the bend.

The dogs grew louder, and he could hear the shouts of the Kirocs close behind, but he figured he'd bought himself a little time by clouding his trail. However, he couldn't stay in the river much longer. His fingers were turning blue, and his muscles were beginning to cramp. Soon, he knew, hypothermia would kill him.

He kicked his legs and silently pushed himself to the Andrikan side of the river. As he passed underneath a thin, overhanging tree branch, he grabbed hold and held himself still against the current. With his free hand, he reached below the surface, pulled out a handful of black, mineral-rich mud, and smeared it on his face and in his hair. He repeated the process until black mud completely covered the skin on his upper body; then he struggled to pull himself out of the water. His drenched clothing and cramped muscles made it nearly impossible, but the thought of Kalisha and Lekiah being held prisoner by that monster kept him going when he might otherwise have given up.

He strained until he managed to get out of the river and climb up to the next limb. He stomped on the branch he'd just used to pull himself up until it broke off and floated down the river.

He climbed high up the tree and worked his way to the edge of a strong limb. He looked down and took a deep breath. His heart pounded in his chest at the thought of what had to be done. He took one more breath and jumped out as far as he could. He wanted to scream as he fell toward the adjacent tree, but he knew if he did he'd be caught for sure, so he clenched his teeth together and hoped it wouldn't hurt too much.

The first few branches he crashed through helped to slow his fall, but by the time he grabbed hold of one and stopped his descent, bruises and scratches covered his face and hands.

He ignored the pain, climbed out on the edge of another limb, and jumped to the next tree with much the same result. Tears streamed down his face, but he didn't care. Everyone he loved had been killed or taken captive. He let himself feel the emotional and physical pain. He swore to never forget how he felt at this moment in time.

"I will kill you, Kahn," Avaris whispered as he placed his fist against his chest. "I will kill you and stop all suffering caused by the Aven-Lore."

He took another deep breath and jumped to the next tree and then the next, until he stopped in one that hung over the wall of the ravaged Devi-Hold. Dull and throbbing pain screamed through his body as he gingerly lowered himself atop the wooden wall and, crouching along the parapet, waited to see if he'd successfully lost the pursuit.

The distant baying of the Demon Dogs sounded as though they were trying to decide which direction Avaris had taken. But then the howls sounded as though they were coming closer. The beasts moved fast. Their ceaseless howling grew louder and louder, and Avaris's heart beat faster and faster.

He held his breath when the first Demon Dogs appeared. They were so black you couldn't see them at night unless they were right in front of you. The first dog surged across the river, sniffing the ground for Avaris's trail as it reemerged from the cold water. It disappeared only to be replaced by five more snarling Demon Dogs. They splashed through the river and sniffed at the ground and in the air for any clue that might lead to his trail.

A smaller—but even blacker than usual, if that was possible—Demon Dog started sniffing the tree Avaris had used to pull himself out of the river. Avaris bit his lip, thanked the gods he had covered himself in mud, and waited. A Kiroc appeared on the far side and sloshed through the river, climbed the muddy bank, and stood next to the sniffing dog. After watching the animal and looking up at the tree, he gave the black beast a hard kick and, with a guttural curse, urged it onward. Had the Kiroc examined the tree more closely, he might have seen the fresh break of the branch on the trunk.

Avaris breathed a sigh of relief once the last of his pursuers left, searching for a trail that didn't exist, and he lowered himself into what remained of the Devi-Hold. He stole around burning tents and broken bodies until he came, once again, in view of the center court. With all the dead bodies, Kirocs, smoke, and carnage, he doubted even Demon Dogs would pick his scent out among the cacophony of smells here.

He hid behind a smoking tent and heard Kahn Devin. The Warlock sounded angry but controlled. Avaris stayed in the shadows and slithered onto the canvas of a nearby tent that had been trampled in the massacre. He pulled some of the excess material over his body and positioned himself better to see the clearing.

Kahn Devin was speaking to a large creature that had the body of a man, except its skin was red and its arms were disproportionately long and large. A dark hood covered its head, but a long, pointed nose jutted out from underneath that didn't look human at all. Kahn spoke in that strange language again, and all Avaris understood was his own name.

The creature replied to the Warlock's statement in a hissing, serpent-like voice, but again, the only time Avaris understood was when the beast repeated his name.

From his vantage point, Avaris could see everything in the court. The young Devi survivors looked desolate and resigned to their fate. They hung their heads in apparent depression and anguish. Lekiah, however, stood erect and proud—he, at least, refused to show fear. A tear welled up in Avaris's eye as he considered their plight, and he wished he could do something right then, but he stayed quiet.

"Gorgre," Kahn called out, and a large Kiroc with a jackal-like face, long yellow fangs, green eyes, and four arms stepped forward and jumped to attention. Kahn spoke to him and gestured at what remained of Avaris's tribe and then pointed northwest. The Kiroc nodded and hissed its reply in the same language.

Kahn Devin took a step backward and shimmered, and then a great black bird stood in his place. With a loud shriek, the Warlock lifted high into the night sky and flew northwest, toward Nortia.

Now might be a good chance for me to attempt a rescue, Avaris thought. But he quickly abandoned the idea. Still more than two score Demon Dogs and several dozen Kirocs guarded them, and Avaris's powers were too unpredictable to attack so many. And how could he know which, if any, of the Kirocs had magical abilities? No—acting now would just get him and the others killed.

Instead, he watched as his sister, his blood brother, and his people were forced to begin the long march to Nortia and the Cragg Caves. For a long time he remained still and watched from the rubble of the ruined tent. Even after the procession was gone, he lay still and waited.

Shortly before midnight, a large shadow emerged from the trees on the opposite side of the clearing. The Kiroc, obviously a powerful one, spread its mighty wings and followed after Kahn Devin.

Satisfied he was finally alone, Avaris pushed himself of the ground and approached the dead bodies of his mother and brother. Tears flowed down his face as he cut his younger brother from the tree. He didn't stop crying until both bodies were buried in a shallow grave.

At dawn, Avaris finished his work. His arms and legs trembled from exhaustion and the cold. Only the constant movement and work of digging graves in frozen ground had kept him from freezing during the night.

He stumbled up the platform and stared at the closed flap to his father's old tent—ironically, one of the few still standing. He clenched his teeth and yanked the flap aside.

He helped himself to dry clothes, grabbed a plate of cured meats and a flask of wine, and sat on an overstuffed pillow. He bit off a chunk of meat and stared woodenly at the tent flap while he chewed. He raised the wine to his lips but stopped and stared at the liquid. Red. The color of the Aven-Lore. The color of anger.

The color of revenge.

ELAHNA'S GORGE

Lord Danu sent all but six of his men back to Basilea. Genea was sad to see them leave, but Lord Danu said he didn't see any point in continuing ahead with such a large entourage, so they took their horses and supplies and set out early that morning.

Genea knew that without Renn in their group, the likelihood of attack was remote, and even if one did come, she believed Raven, Aleah, Kivas, Tellio, Durham, and Lord Danu could handle it. And although she knew they could travel faster with a smaller party, she wondered who would do the cooking on the trail. She would miss the constant playful banter between Olosa, their old, gray-haired, grumpy cook, and Sela. But more than that, she would miss Micha playing his lute by the campfire after a long day of travel.

"This is the lift your horse used," the superintendent said to Lord Danu as they walked through the stone cliff house—bypassing the line of merchants, clerics, and other travelers waiting for their turn on the North Lift, which would lower them over one thousand feet to the base of Elahna's Gorge. The cliff house reminded Genea of a large station at a river dock, except rather than waiting to load and board boats, the patrons waited to board the famous Anytos Cliff Lift. Those at the front of the line were noticeably perturbed when the superintendent led Lord Danu's group past them and out onto the waiting lift.

The lift was a solid wooden platform about eight paces wide by twenty paces long. Wooden guardrails to keep people from falling surrounded the entire platform—something Genea was extremely grateful for. The man talking to Lord Danu said he could lower and raise a full team of cattle and a loaded wagon using this strange device.

Genea looked in awe at the massive pulleys and ropes attached to the platform. The ropes were thicker than her arms. They attached at several places on the lift and were threaded through a pulley system that in turn led to enormous spools on one side of the lift house. The spools were harnessed to a single yoke of twenty-four oxen through another pulley system so all sides of the lift would be lowered or raised in unison.

"I'd heard of the famed lifts of Elahna's Gorge," Kivas said, "but I had no idea how complex and big they were."

The supervisor beamed with pride. "Yes, the engineers who designed the three lifts more than a century ago were quite brilliant. Prior to these lifts, the east and west were literally cut off from each other."

The man led them onto the strange contraption, and Genea and Tristan held hands and peered out over Elahna's Gorge. A cold winter breeze blew a strand of Genea's long, curly hair across her face, and she absently pushed it back. Tristan reached up with one hand to keep the wreath of fresh flowers on her head from blowing away—she had just made a new one this morning using flowers from King Bendigo's greenhouse. Tristan's green eyes stared, unblinking, across the Ava River to the hills and forest far below.

Genea couldn't believe how far they could see from this vantage point. The Ava River ran north to south and looked like a small winding ribbon. Genea knew from talking with Aleah that the river was actually more than a half mile wide. On the other side of the river, the rolling green foothills of Avalian were lush and inviting. Genea wondered that it could be brown and cold here up on the cliff while the valley a thousand feet below looked untouched by winter. Beyond the valley, the forests of Avalian—painted in the greens, golds, reds, and yellows of autumn—stood strong and proud. The forest went on for miles and miles until the trees terminated at the base of a tall and jagged range of snow-covered mountains.

"What are those mountains?" Harlow asked. "I wonder what's on the other side. I've never seen so many trees, and that river goes on forever. I'll bet you could travel from—"

"Those are the Kuru-Kulla Mountains," Tellio said. "Beyond is the country of Kahaal, the city of Kah-Tarku, and then the Lemurian Sea."

Harlow's eyes grew wide as he listened to the big man, but before he could ask any more questions, Genea put a hand over his mouth.

"Tellio, why is this called a gorge?" she asked.

"What do you mean?" The bald man from Anytos leaned his massive forearms on the guardrail to peer down the thousand-foot drop below them.

"A gorge is like a deep canyon," she said. "This is just a cliff."

"It's more than a cliff, little lady," he said a bit defensively. "This is where Greyfel and Elahna fell to their deaths and escaped the demons of Monguinir."

"Yeah, but it's not a gorge."

Tellio twisted his mustache. "I guess 'Elahna's Gorge' sounded better than 'Elahna's Cliff.'"

"Did the Avalians truly have a city down there?" Tristan asked wistfully as she gazed intently at the forest far below.

"Some say they still do." Aleah walked up and stood on the other side of Tristan. "A beautiful hidden city."

"Every so often," Tellio said, "a person will come along who claims to have been walking through the forest, minding their own business, when they see a beautiful city with large white spires and gleaming windows. But then it magically vanishes. I was born and raised here, but I never saw a city—or even a single Avalian, for that matter."

The lift jerked and then began to drop down the face of the cliff. Genea's stomach lurched. She felt Tristan squeeze her hand, and they took a step back from the guardrail.

It took a quarter hour to reach the bottom, and although the view from the lift was lovely, Genea was happy to be standing on solid ground again.

As soon as the lift stopped and the workers opened the gate, Genea hurried off the platform—she wanted to be sure she was safely off before it started the long trek back to the top of the gorge. She turned to call after Tristan, but she stopped short when she caught sight of the small princess.

The platform and patrons disembarking were dwarfed by the massive brown rock face of the thousand-foot cliff. Tristan and Aleah stood in the middle of the lift, holding hands, with tears rolling down their cheeks. Neither girl seemed to care if anyone noticed them—they walked off the lift and stood at the banks of the wide river, staring yearningly across the slow-moving current to the grassy hills and lush forest on the opposite side.

"Your horse walked calmly off the lift and then onto the crossing ferry," the supervisor said to Lord Danu, Raven, and Kivas as he pointed northwest across the wide Ava River. "The ferry captain also remembers him because when they disembarked, the horse left on its own and ran straight across the foothills and headed for the forest."

"That's odd." Lord Danu scratched at his chin in a way that painfully reminded Genea of Artio.

"Animals don't normally ride the lift and ferry unattended," the supervisor agreed. "In fact, it usually takes some prodding to get them on the lifts at all. So for this horse of yours to masquerade as the property of paying passengers and then run off by himself . . ." He spread his hands apart and shrugged his shoulders.

"My lord," Tellio said, "you don't suppose Thorn has gone in search of Renn, do you?"

Genea felt a stab of pain at hearing his name. She'd tried not to think about Renn because it always made her cry. She was so tired of crying. Ever since her father had beaten her, destroyed their home, and then abandoned her while he escaped north with the rest of her family, she felt like she cried all the time. She remembered crying herself to sleep every night for the first year after that. Since Renn's abduction more than a month ago, she'd been doing it again. She told Aleah and Tristan she cried for her long-lost mother and brother, but she knew they guessed the real reason for her tears. It seemed everybody knew how she felt. Everybody, that was, but Renn.

"I don't know," Lord Danu said in response to Tellio's question. "Thorn and Renn *do* share a special bond."

"Do you want me to follow him, my lord?" Raven asked.

Lord Danu shielded his eyes from the sun with a hand and gazed across the river, then shook his head.

"No. We've already spent six weeks looking, and time is running out for the other children. Next new moon is midwinter's Azur-Aven." Lord Danu released a loud breath. "Besides, the lifts don't run at night, so whoever took Renn couldn't have possibly escaped this way."

"I will follow him."

Everybody turned to look at Aleah. She wiped the tears from her eyes, but her angular jaw was set with determination.

"I'm sorry, Aleah," Lord Danu said. "But like I told Raven, there's no time."

"I'm not making a request, Lord Danu," Aleah said. "I'm making a statement."

Genea noticed others shifting uncomfortably as Lord Danu stared at her with narrow eyes.

"I know King Achal sent me along to protect Tristan," Aleah said, "but the Oracle of Tanith gave me a different task a long time before that."

"What's the Oracle of Tanith?" Harlow broke in, oblivious to the tension in the air.

"It's a she, not a what," Genea hissed at him under her breath, and she elbowed him in the ribs.

"I was sent to her as a young girl," Aleah said, "by my mother, in the jungles of Domeria. The Oracle said I must journey with the Child of the Blessing to Elder Island. She said if I did not complete this charge, the child would not survive."

"Did she say what would happen if Renn doesn't make it to . . ." Kivas whispered, as though he were afraid of the answer. Aleah turned, looked him in the eyes, then shook her head.

"She said her sight was darkened when she tried to look beyond that event. If Renn doesn't make it . . . her sight can't see beyond to what will be."

In the silence that followed, Lord Danu walked back and forth, running his fingers through his long blond hair.

"I'm going, too." Tristan stepped in front of the young lord, forcing him to stop walking.

"No, you're not," Lord Danu said without hesitation.

"But my heart is breaking through my chest and every part of my being is urging me to go into those forests," Tristan cried.

Lord Danu stared at her with one eyebrow raised and shook his head. "Tristan, that's crazy. Your brother would hunt me all across Lemuria if I let you leave this group." He pointed toward Aleah and said, "He's already going to be angry when he finds out I let Aleah abandon the task he charged her with, which was to protect you."

"I'll deal with Achal's anger." Aleah stepped between Tristan and Lord Danu. "Don't think I'm making this decision rashly. Either way, I am breaking trust and damaging my integrity. Either I defy the Oracle and leave Renn, or I defy Achal and leave my sis—I mean, leave Tristan."

Lord Danu's expression softened as he considered her words.

"And for the record," Aleah said, "you didn't let me go . . . I left despite your orders to stay with the group."

Aleah turned, picked up her bedroll, walked toward her horse, and began tying the bedroll to the back of the saddle. Genea didn't realize until now that tears were streaming down her own cheeks. It felt like her family was being ripped apart by events tumbling out of control.

Raven called out to Aleah and jogged to where she stood, finishing her preparations. As they spoke, Raven motioned toward the mountains in the distance. Aleah looked the direction he pointed and nodded. This was odd behavior for Raven, but it really surprised Genea when Raven reached for Aleah's hand and placed something in it. Aleah must have been surprised, too, judging by the way she looked at the object in her hand.

"What's this about?" Kivas asked Lord Danu, and the handsome lord stopped what he was doing and looked over at Raven and Aleah.

"Raven's been in these forests before." Lord Danu shrugged and returned to tying off his own pack and making sure all was in order. "He's likely just giving her some tips."

Kivas watched the two and pulled on his beard. He harrumphed, then picked up his pack, took the lead rope of his horse, and headed toward a waiting riverboat. Genea couldn't be sure at this distance, but she thought Aleah was . . . blushing, or trying very hard not to.

Raven said a few more words and then turned to walk back to the group. Genea watched as Aleah alternated between glaring at Raven's retreating back and studying the object in her hand.

"Time's wasting; let's get moving," Lord Danu called out, and like Kivas, he picked up his pack in one hand, took the lead rope of his horse in the other, and headed for the riverboat.

"Aleah!" Genea hiked her dress above her ankles and hurried over to her. The lady warrior stuffed the item Raven gave her in a pocket as Genea approached.

"Be careful," Genea said, and she gave Aleah an awkward embrace. "Find him and bring him back."

Aleah smiled and nodded. "Something tells me he's out there. It doesn't make any sense—I'd sooner believe it snowed in Domeria, but I can't get the feeling out of my head that he's in that forest." Aleah put her foot into the stirrup and climbed in the saddle. "Take care of yourself and watch after Tristan while I'm gone." With that she clicked her tongue, pulled on the reins, and hurried onto a crossing ferry that was nearly full and getting ready to sail.

※

Avaris's eyes flew open, and he jumped to his feet. His heart pounded in his chest, and he stumbled on the soft, overstuffed pillows that covered the floor. He caught the edge of a small ornate table to keep from falling. Something or someone had caused him to wake up.

He took a deep breath, and everything rushed back to his memory. He was in his father's tent in the ruins of the Devi-Hold. Last night he'd witnessed the annihilation of nearly the entire clan. But why could he hear the sounds of cheerful voices and the crackle of fire outside? Maybe he'd only dreamed those horrible things about the night before. The cuts and scratches on his arms and hands, however, suggested that the events had been quite real.

He crept to the tent flap and peeked out. It took a moment for his eyes to adjust to the glare of the noonday sun as it reflected off the blood-stained snow.

Mordvins, dozens of them, were gathered around several cooking fires, singing and dancing. Roasting on spits above the yellow flames were what remained of the broken and bloodied bodies of his tribe. He didn't recognize any of them—they were beyond recognition. He was glad he'd taken time to bury his mother and younger brother before going to sleep, but his heart burned at the indignity these others had to suffer.

He looked around the tent for a sword, then gave up on the impulsive idea that had formed in his head—he couldn't hope to fight against so many. Instead he peered back out the tent flap, repulsed and sickened by the scene. The smell of human flesh cooking and the sight of the Mordvins eating it caused his stomach to heave. He closed his mouth against the vomit that tried to come up, and he turned away.

He grabbed a bone-handled knife, a bison robe, and some dried meat, then crawled out the back of the tent. The Mordvins probably had enough human meat to satisfy them for a while, but he didn't want to chance letting them see him.

He made a wide circle around the tents that remained standing—being careful to avoid the common area, where the Mordvins were gathered—and hurried toward the hole Kahn Devin had blasted in the outer wall of the Devi-Hold the night before. As he approached the back of the hold, Avaris saw the place where he and Lekiah had been held prisoners. The green barrier was gone with the death of Mindahl, but the attempts the boys had made to escape were still evident in the crusted snow. He wished Lekiah were with him now. He let out a long sigh, then looked at the splintered wood lying on the cold white ground and the canvas tents that littered the snow like discarded laundry. He could do nothing more here.

He found the trail made by the Kirocs herding the young Devi captives toward the Cragg Mountains and jogged after them. No doubt Kirocs and Demon Dogs still searched the mountains for him. The last thing they would expect would be for him to head for the Demon Caves. Also, by following the same trail, his tracks and scent would blend in with the others.

The trail led across the cold Andrus River and straight up into the Mord Mountains. Avaris wondered how many of the children would be able to survive the cold night—particularly after wading through the icy river.

Avaris had climbed one mountain, down the next, and began up the second when he noticed that most of the footprints were now dragging through the snow. The captives were tiring fast. Soon, all the prints were dragging except one—Lekiah's. Avaris recognized Lekiah's tracks by the size, the depth of the impressions, and the length of his stride. His oath brother was probably exhausted like the rest but too proud to let his fatigue show. Lekiah would be looking for a way to escape. He wouldn't quit, and neither would Avaris.

Avaris only stopped once, to wolf down a piece of dried meat and take a drink from a clear stream. Just after the sun had settled behind the western horizon, he came across a small clearing where the Kirocs had stopped to camp. *They must have marched all night and slept during the day*, he thought. Judging from the tracks leaving the encampment and because the coals in the fire pit still burned, Avaris knew he was only a couple hours behind them. He considered rushing after them, but he realized he'd rather come upon them in the daylight. Coming upon them at night would be giving the advantage to the Demon Dogs and Kirocs, who could see much better in the dark. Besides, at the speed he was traveling and if they followed the same pattern as the night before, he should be able to catch up with them at their next camp around midday.

Now he'd need to figure out a way to survive the cold mountain night without freezing to death. In a dense group of pines next to the campsite, he found a large tree with lower branches that drooped to the ground. Avaris pulled one aside and nodded, satisfied with what he found: a three-by-three-foot hollow interior underneath the tree formed by the drooping boughs. This would break the wind and hide him at the same time.

He placed the rocks from the fire pit onto the coals, then used a thick, short branch to clear the dead pine needles and dig a long, shallow trench in the frozen ground beneath the pine tree. It took several hours, but when he finished, he had a two-foot-wide by five-foot-long channel. He used smaller sticks like tongs to carry hot rocks from the fire pit and laid them in the shallow trench. Using the short, thick branch again, he covered the rocks with dirt and pine needles, wrapped himself in his bison cloak, and fell asleep on his bed of hot, covered rocks.

Avaris rose shortly after dawn to follow the trail once again. A cold north breeze stole any warmth the bright sun might have otherwise imparted, and dark clouds loomed on the horizon. He wished he'd brought more supplies from his father's tent. The idea of traveling the mountains during the winter with nothing but his clothing, a bone-handled knife, and some dried meat was not something he looked forward to. He thought about going to Myrrah's cabin for blankets and more food but realized that would be a likely place for Kahn's servants to wait for him. Instead, he pulled the bison cloak tighter, took a long breath, and followed the tracks deeper into the mountains.

Shortly after noon, the tracks Avaris followed were no more than thirty minutes old, but clouds covered the sun. Light snow flurries whipped at his face, and the sky turned lead gray. He was anxious to overtake them and see how his people were holding up to the march. He darted from tree to tree as he climbed to the top of the next ridge, just in case he was closer than he thought. He peered around a tree to the gully below, and slow movement in the snow caught his attention.

He scanned the gully for danger. Tracks marred the snow where the Kirocs and their captives had lumbered. The tracks climbed and disappeared out the other side of the narrow gully. Other than the dark shape lying in the snow at the bottom, nothing moved. Avaris jumped to his feet and half ran, half stumbled toward the figure. As he got closer, he recognized Luka, a young boy barely older than himself. Luka had completed the ritual of manhood earlier that year—during the same festival that should have marked Avaris's passage to manhood.

Avaris dropped to his knees in the crusted snow by the boy and felt for a pulse. The beat of his heart was faint, but Luka was alive—barely. Avaris scanned the gully once more. The snow was falling faster than before, and the gully acted like a funnel for the storm; he needed to find better shelter, or Luka would be dead before evening. They weren't very far from Myrrah's cabin, and Avaris knew the area well. A small cave over the next mountain would offer shelter, but it was the wrong direction, and the climb would be too steep for Avaris if he had to carry the boy. Avaris saw a copse of aspen and fir trees near the back of the gully where the land rose sharply toward a small cliff, and he decided to seek shelter there instead.

By the time he set Luka down on a bed of fir branches between a large boulder, the cliffs, and a tight group of trees, Avaris's legs were trembling and sweat dripped off his forehead. The trees and cliff offered a fair amount of shelter from the storm, but Luka needed a fire and water. Avaris had hoped to avoid lighting fires, but Luka wouldn't survive without one. They were far enough off the path and sheltered fairly well. As long as he used dry wood and kept the fire small, it wouldn't attract unwelcome visitors—he hoped.

Once the fire was burning, Avaris gathered a fistful of snow and let it melt in his hand. As the water dripped through his fingers, he let it run into Luka's mouth. Avaris massaged the boy's limbs and body until Luka started to moan. Avaris rubbed harder—he wanted desperately for Luka to survive. If he could save just one captive, it would be a victory against Kahn Devin.

"Come on, Luka. Wake up," he said. "You're going to be all right."

The boy coughed a weak, breathy cough and opened his eyes. When his eyes met Avaris's, they grew wide, and he became more alert.

"Are you . . . You're . . ." he whispered hoarsely.

"I am Avaris Mordrahn. He who was thought to be dead."

"But how—?"

"That doesn't matter. You've got to conserve your energy; we have a long way to go to rescue the others."

Luka didn't answer, but he did nod and close his eyes. Avaris found several rocks and placed them in the fire. If they were to survive the cold night, they would need their combined body heat and a bed of hot rocks beneath the ground to keep them warm.

Several times before nightfall, Luka lapsed into coughing fits and thrashed around on the bed of firs. He woke long enough during one of these fits for Avaris to give him more water and a little dried meat. During these last daylight hours before dusk settled in, Avaris couldn't help but wonder if others were lying in the snow on the trail ahead. How many would not be able to keep up and would be left to freeze to death before the Kirocs reached the Cragg Caves with their captives?

Avaris looked at the trail leaving the gully, made by what remained of his tribe, and chewed on his lip. He ran his fingers through his hair and looked down at Luka. Avaris would have reached the Kirocs' camp hours ago had he not stopped to help the boy. *Oh well*, he thought as he forced himself to smile. *I can always make up the lost time once Luka gets well enough to travel.* Avaris reluctantly conceded to himself that it might be days or even weeks before Luka was well enough for that.

When next Luka opened his eyes and coughed, the sun was falling behind the mountains. He sounded worse with each gasp. Avaris briskly rubbed Luka's arms and legs again.

"Relax, Luka," Avaris said.

"Avaris," he whispered through blue lips.

"I'm here. Everything's going to be all right."

Luka shook his head and moved his mouth. Avaris leaned closer to hear what he wanted to say.

"I dedicate my arm . . . and sword . . ."

Avaris recognized the oath. Warriors said these words when a new Mordrahn came into power. Avaris swallowed back the lump rising in his throat and wiped a dark strand of hair out of his eyes. Luka was too weak to finish the vow, but Avaris was touched by the attempt.

"Don't let our people—" Another fit of coughs interrupted Luka's words, and Avaris tried to force more water into his mouth. "Don't let our people be forgotten, Great One." He settled back on the bed of fir branches, but this time, he didn't close his eyes—they simply stared blankly into the darkening sky.

Avaris sat silent and looked at the boy's face. He didn't know how long he stayed that way. He was reminded of how he felt when he saw his brother hanging in the tree two days ago. He didn't cry; he had no tears left. Instead, he gently closed Luka's eyes and completed the oath.

"You are accepted, Great Warrior. By me, Avaris Mordrahn, and the gods."

ELDER ISLAND

Genea entered the cabin room. Tristan sat on her cot, staring at nothing—something she'd done a lot since Aleah had left in search of Renn. The cramped room smelled musty, but a single shaft of light streamed through the small, round window. Genea opened the window to let some air in.

"Tristan," Genea said. "Did you notice that Aleah almost called you her sister when she was arguing with Lord Danu? Why do you suppose she did that?"

Tristan looked at her and crinkled her brow. "She did?"

Genea nodded, and the other girl shrugged her shoulders.

"Lord Danu doesn't understand." Tristan's eyes watered. "I should be going with Aleah. These forests call to my heart just like the forest of Achtland, only much stronger. It isn't fair."

Genea tried unsuccessfully to comfort the blonde princess, but after the third tearful outburst, she decided to go on the deck of the riverboat. The high cliff to the west blocked the sun as it made its westward trek across the sky, leaving the deck in shadows. But the rolling green foothills to the east were still bathed in sunlight. Genea took a deep breath of the cool air and pulled her coat tightly around herself. She couldn't stop thinking about Aleah and wondering if she would ever see her again. She wondered where she was now and if she'd found any trace of Thorn.

Harlow sat on the deck with his arms on the lower railing and his legs dangling off the side of the boat—the way he and Renn used to sit and watch the plains of Tiaronéa roll by. Harlow hadn't spoken much since Renn had been taken. And although she didn't miss his constant prattle, Genea knew he was hurting. She walked across the gently rolling planks, sat down beside him, rested her arms on the lower rail, and hung her feet over the edge of the boat. The constant river current beat a soothing rhythm against the side of the boat. The row of oars from the galley below pulled in steady unison to propel the boat north—against the wishes of the slow-moving river.

"How are you doing, Harlow?"

The curly-headed boy shrugged his shoulders and stared vacantly into the dark water. Genea followed his gaze, but watching the water glide by made her stomach queasy, so she raised her eyes and watched the forests beyond the river. She almost forgot Harlow was sitting next to her until he broke the silence.

"He was my only friend."

"Tristan and I are your friends, too," Genea said.

"Yeah." He looked at her with red-rimmed eyes . "But he's my *best* friend." Harlow rubbed his nose with his shirtsleeve. "I never had a real friend before. All the boys made fun of me growing up, and nobody ever liked me. Nobody ever made me feel like they liked me the way Renn did."

Genea almost smiled because he sounded like Harlow again, but instead she stared across the river at the forests and wondered if Renn really might be there. If Aleah believed, then Genea would believe, too.

"Renn's pretty surprising, Harlow." Genea took a deep breath and smiled. "Deep down, I know we'll see him again." She turned to see him staring at her.

"You really believe that?" He sniffed, but his eyes shined with hope.

"I can feel it in here." She placed a hand over her chest.

※

Genea, Tristan, and Harlow passed the long days on the Ava River by playing different games to amuse themselves. Genea took to going up on deck first thing every morning to see the sun rise and then watch the soldiers practice sword fighting. Raven always took the lead in training the men.

After five days, the river opened into Lake Andrus. Genea, Tristan, and Harlow all stood at the rail on the bow of the big riverboat, watching as the lake engulfed them.

"Wow." Harlow's eyes grew as wide as two tea saucers. "This looks like the Drbal Divide."

"I don't like it." Tristan had a white-knuckled grip on the rail. "So much water doesn't seem . . . natural."

"Don't worry, Tristan," Genea said. "I'm sure this crew has crossed Lake Andrus a hundred times." Just then, the boat shifted up as they passed over a large wave.

"Yee-haw!" Harlow shouted with a big grin on his face. "I hope we hit lots of waves—this is fun."

Tristan stared at him. Her face turned pale, and she gripped the railing even tighter, if that were possible.

"I'll be down in our cabin," she said weakly, and she turned to make her way to the stairway that led belowdecks. Genea watched her go and then slugged Harlow in the shoulder.

"You idiot," she said and hurried after Tristan.

"What did I do?" Harlow called out—and she knew that he really had no idea. *Are all boys insensitive and unobservant,* she wondered as she walked away, *or just Renn and Harlow?*

Later that evening, in accordance with Harlow's wish, a storm blew in from the west and the riverboat pitched back and forth with the white-capped waves. Icy rain fell slowly at first but soon turned into a downpour. A small number of the crew stayed on deck to secure things, but most of the crew rowed in the galley with all their might to keep the boat on course for the north coast of Lake Andrus.

Genea felt miserable, but Tristan looked far worse. Her fair skin had turned a pale green color, and she dry heaved into a metal bucket Genea had managed to find in the kitchen.

At least Harlow is also in his cabin throwing up, Genea thought. *It serves him right for wishing this storm upon us.* She realized it was ridiculous to feel that way, but she was miserable, and it helped to have somebody to blame it on.

The winds calmed later that night, and the pitching of the big riverboat returned to a gentle swaying. The rain changed to snow, and morning found Genea standing on deck—wrapped in a quilt and sipping hot tea—watching the white coastline of the north shore come into view, growing more distinct as they drew near.

"Perhaps we should wake Tristan and give her the good news." Genea jumped at the sound of Tellio's voice. She hadn't heard the big man approach.

"She would be thrilled to see land," Genea agreed, "but she finally got to sleep a couple hours ago."

Tellio nodded and joined her at the rail. Now that Renn was no longer with them, Lord Danu and Raven had decided disguises were not necessary. So, Tellio reverted back to wearing thick leather breeches and the colors of the Basil family under a heavy buckskin coat. Even though he wore the blue and gold of the Basils, his waxed, twisted mustache marked him a man from Anytos. A fur-lined hat now covered his bald head—it made him look more like a seasoned soldier.

"We'll reach the school in two weeks," Tellio said pensively.

Genea studied his face. He no longer had a look of stern resolve. He looked thoughtful and sad. Much the same way Lord Danu had looked since Renn had gone missing.

"It will be fine, Tellio," Genea said—mostly to reassure herself. Tellio pulled his gaze from the shore and considered Genea's eyes as if he was searching for something.

"Lord Danu says he failed," the soldier said. "But *I* feel the weight of losing the boy . . ." He trailed off and looked back to the slowly approaching shore.

"We were the stuff of legends," he said in a soft, fierce voice. "The privileged troop chosen by the very gods to bring the Child of the Blessing to his destiny."

He paused, but Genea couldn't think of anything to say, so she just listened and waited. Tellio looked back into her eyes, and she saw a man struggling with his own pain.

"I am ashamed."

"There's no shame in showing your emotions to your friends, Tellio." Genea placed her hand on his to comfort the big man.

"You don't understand, child." He slowly shook his head. "I feel fear like I have never known before. Oh, I feel fear for the boy, all right. And I pray to every god I know to protect him and guide Aleah to find him."

He took her hand from his and turned away. He walked two steps, then looked back at Genea. "But my greatest fear is how my name will be remembered in the stories and songs—that is why I feel shame . . . I thought I was a bigger man than that."

With that, he pulled his coat closed and left. Genea stared after him. She wanted to say something—anything to help. But she couldn't. Her heart ached for all of them. The weight they carried and the blame they put on themselves must be incredible.

The voyage from Lake Andrus to Port Andrus was much better, as far as Genea was concerned, because they were back on dry land. After one day of snow-covered hills and fens, they passed through the canyons of the Andrus Mountain Range that led to the seaside city of Port Andrus.

"We'll only be staying here in the city for one day," Lord Danu announced as they entered the wooden gates of the town. "I suggest you use the time *resting*." He looked pointedly at Kivas as he emphasized the word 'resting.'

"What?" Kivas said with a feigned look of innocence, and everybody chuckled.

Genea smiled. For a brief moment, the lighthearted banter made her feel like she had before Renn's abduction.

Genea and Tristan shared a good-sized room in a comfortable inn near the north end of town. Lord Danu decided to loosen his purse strings a little and get better accommodations than he had in the past before starting the final leg of the journey. Genea reveled in her warm meal and hot bath.

Tristan was finally in good spirits again, too. However, the next morning as they embarked upon a ship to cross the strait to Elder Island, she started to sob. Fortunately, this sea voyage had lasted only a little more than one day, and although it snowed constantly, it was only accompanied by a light breeze—not a gale like the storm they'd endured on Lake Andrus.

"I'm so glad that's over with," Tristan said with obvious relief as they sat around a fire Durham had built on a beach of Elder Island near the docks. His thinning blond hair blew fitfully in the wind as he stirred a pot of clam stew. Genea's stomach growled when she leaned over and smelled that aroma of salted and peppered mussels.

"I used to hunt for clams as a boy on the beaches of Mylitta," Durham said with a contemplative smile on his face. It made the dimple on his chin even more prominent than usual. Genea was a bit leery of eating sea animals that the man dug up from the wet sand, but she was hungry enough to try anything just now.

Raven and Lord Danu had gone into Aanith—the only town on Elder Island—to purchase supplies.

"I can't wait to see the school." Harlow rubbed his hands together over the orange flames. Snow continued to fall, and the entire island was blanketed in white. "I've heard it's an ancient castle, even bigger than King Boran's castle in Boria City. My da never saw it, but he said my uncle did when he was a merchant a long time ago, and he talked about all sorts of wonderful spires and . . ."

Genea only half listened to Harlow ramble on. She pulled her hood over her head and stared woodenly into the fire. These people felt like family to her—they were literally the only family she had anymore—and soon they would be leaving her, too. All except for Harlow and Tristan. She looked at Tristan and gave her a rueful grimace. *Thank Azur for Tristan*, she thought. She truly was the sister Genea had never had. At least Tristan would be with her at the school.

Just then Raven and Lord Danu rode up leading three pack mules. Durham stood and walked over to help with the animals, his thinning blond hair wisping about in the breeze. He didn't say much but was always first to start a task, and he took pride in everything he did. Genea was glad he hadn't been sent back to Basilea with the others. His solid presence was a comfort.

"We leave for the school tomorrow morning," Lord Danu announced. "We made it just in time to join a party of about twenty other students and their escorts."

"Where do we stay tonight?" Kivas stood and brushed the snow off his heavy leather cloak.

"We find shelter and pitch our tents." Lord Danu grimaced as he looked around at the snow.

"But isn't there an inn or someplace we can stay?" Tristan asked plaintively.

Lord Danu started shaking his head before she even finished. "Aanith is a small town, and both inns are already full."

"Get used to it," Durham said in his deep voice as he pulled the iron pot from the fire and poured his stew into wooden bowls for the group. "The air gets colder and the snow gets deeper the closer we get to the school."

THE CRYSTAL TOWERS

When Renn stepped through the portal he'd opened that led to the home of the Oracle of Tanith, he thought he'd entered the gardens of Valhasgar. The old lady who had guided his escape from Kahn Devin's horde laughed when he asked her if he had died and informed him that he had not. He had instead created a doorway that transported them from the forests of Dekla to the forest city of Alfheina—the home of the Avalian. Renn spent each day after that exploring the beautiful forests and gardens of this enchanted land.

If Genea were with Renn right now, she'd want to take a romantic walk through the endless gardens and reflecting pools. Or she'd want to share a picnic next to the small lake Renn loved to visit—the one that if you looked across its crystal blue waters to the falls on the other side, you could stare mesmerized for hours because the mist created a kaleidoscope of patterns as it filtered the view of flowering trees and bushes that lined the opposite shore. The trouble was . . . if Genea were here with Renn, he knew he would go along with it. This place could make a person do crazy things like that.

Renn was heading to the lake when a weeping willow with long, draping branches covered in white blossoms parted to let Arrianleah pass through. The beautiful Avalian female stopped in front of Renn and smiled. Renn had first met Arrianleah when he was Kahn Devin's prisoner. She'd come to him in the form of an old woman and referred to herself as the Oracle of Tanith. Her true form looked nothing like how she'd first appeared. The only thing more stunning than the land of the Avalians and the city of Alfheina at the center were the Avalians themselves.

Arrianleah's golden-blonde hair reached below her waist and flowed gently, as though in a perpetual breeze. Around her forehead she wore a simple yet elegant golden circlet patterned with delicate leaves and twisting vines. Her white dress looked to be little more than fine gossamer that clung to her body in places and draped strategically off it in others. She was modestly covered, but the shape of her body was unmistakable, and enough skin from her shoulders and arms showed that Renn felt his face flush with desire, which both excited and embarrassed him.

He still had to make a conscious effort to not stare at her with gaping mouth every time she came to him—even though she'd been his guide now for . . . for . . . well, he wasn't really sure how long he'd been here, come to think of it.

"You appear to be in a hurry this morning, Renn." Arrianleah's melodic voice made every sentence sound like a beautiful song.

"Yes, m'lady." Renn bowed. "The falls are the most beautiful in the morning, when the sun first breaks over the hills, and—" He stopped talking, realizing he was rambling on much like Harlow would do. Instead, he cleared his throat and asked, "Is there something I can do for you?"

"Elumniel wishes to breakfast with you this morning." Her gaze shifted to the right, and she held out her hand with her palm facing up. She looked at her outstretched hand as though she were holding a bird. Renn had seen her do unusual things like this before. If a human had her mannerisms, it would be odd. But Arrianleah moved with such beauty and grace, he barely noticed the strange interruption.

"Umm . . . sorry," he said. "Who is Elumniel?"

"He is first among us. He is the eldest."

"Am I in trouble?"

"No, my child." Arrianleah turned and started toward the beautiful willow tree, whose branches once again parted to grant her passage. Renn followed but stopped short as a thought occurred to him that made his heart sick.

"Is he sending me away?"

"No. Not yet."

Renn didn't like the "not yet" part but fell into step behind his guide. As she glided forward, flowering shrubs, greenery, and trees alike opened to create a path for her.

They came to a meandering river, and Arrianleah didn't even hesitate at the water's edge—she simply walked, and the water rose up from its unhurried journey to create a bridge for her to cross. After each step, the water behind her fell back into the river and continued its voyage as if nothing unusual had occurred. Renn stopped at the bank and bit his lip. Since she didn't turn back, he decided he was supposed to follow. He closed his eyes and stepped forward.

The deep river wasn't cold, but the shock of falling in caused him to inhale a mouthful of water. He surfaced, coughing and flailing, and was about to swim for the opposite shore when the water embraced his body, raised him up, and carried him across the river to gently set him on the opposite bank.

"Forgive me, Renn." Arrianleah covered her mouth. Renn was sure she was hiding a smile behind her long, slender fingers. "I forgot the aeon myriad doesn't respond to your passive thoughts."

Renn wiped water from his eyes. "That's all right," he said. "Do I have time to change before we go to see him?"

"We've kept Elumniel waiting for some time already," she said. "I shall remedy the situation. After all, I bear some responsibility for your sodden condition."

She looked up into the trees and pursed her lips as though she were going to whistle, but the sound that emanated from her was clear and beautiful with a songlike melody. Renn thought he heard hundreds of miniature voices join in with her song. Before he could look for the source of the voices, a warm breeze blew through his hair. It began small but grew into a strong wind that encircled his body but disturbed nothing else around him. When the breeze died down, he thought he heard high-pitched laughter fading away into the trees. He looked around but saw nothing unusual—well, in a regular forest the vibrant colors of the leaves and blossoms of the trees here would be extremely unusual.

Arrianleah smiled and arched a single brow. "Shall we continue?"

Renn felt his clothes—they were dry. He stepped over to a reflecting pool surrounded by a stone bench and flowering bushes and saw that his hair was now not only dry but also looked as though his mother had spent several minutes combing it.

Once they reached Alfheina, they followed one of the four main thoroughfares that led to the center gardens and finally the Crystal Towers. They weren't really crystal—they were actually a brilliant white—but they glistened in the sunlight, and the high spanning arches that led from tower to tower were so graceful in design that Renn could think of no better word to describe it.

Alfheina wasn't like the human cities Renn had visited. In those cities, men had forced their will upon the trees and the land and created buildings, roads, and houses to fit what they wanted.

In Alfheina, the structures worked harmoniously with the trees and flora of the land to create lush gardens and landscapes with beautiful dwelling places that rested amid the environment as if they'd grown there as naturally as any plant. The thoroughfare couldn't really be thought of as a street because the smooth white stone that formed it flowed outward from the center gardens through Alfheina and terminated at the forest like a rock river frozen in time—as though nature itself had placed beautiful smooth stone several feet wide and a mile long just for the convenience of the Avalians.

Four main pathways led from the tower through the gardens and out into the forest—one for each direction on the compass. Arrianleah lead them on the path from the east. Tall, stately trees in full blossom lined the path and filled the air with the aroma of spring.

Every forty or fifty paces, smaller paths diverged from the main thoroughfare. They were typically lined with tall flowering bushes, and the paths gently bent as they rounded their way to the next garden within the garden. One path led to rows of purple, white, and pink flowers and then on to a reflection pool; another led to dignified statuaries surrounding a majestic fountain. Others led to openings where incredible topiaries surrounded trees with ripe fruits clinging to strong branches, just waiting to be plucked and savored. The gardens were designed in this manner to make a complete circle—layer upon layer—around the towers. Renn had only explored a small portion of these grounds even though he'd spent many days lost among them.

Renn thought again that the gardens of Valhasgar must look like this. He imagined Artio was there now, contemplating his past lives and waiting to be born into another life—another opportunity to learn and gain wisdom.

Filigreed gates, gilded with gold and intertwined with silver flowering vines, opened to the tower grounds. The path leading to the tower was lined with flowers—pansies followed by a row of daisies, then a row of tulips, and behind that a row of lilies and fragrant lilacs. A row of brilliant green manicured bushes grew behind the flowers. Beyond that was a groomed lawn broken up by smaller gardens with winding stone paths that led through them. One flowering tree drew his gaze because the purple leaves were dotted with round white blossoms.

The Crystal Towers had no doors—just an open archway surrounded with glowing runes. As Renn passed under the arch, he reached out to touch its smooth surface. He could see no markings where chisel or hammer would have carved the strange white material. The walls were solid, like the hardest rock he'd ever felt, but as smooth as melting ice; they felt surprisingly warm to the touch but glistened in the sunlight as if they were towers of snow.

They walked down a brightly lit corridor that reminded him of Tristan's castle in Achtland, except instead of green carpet he now walked on a carpet of soft grass. Unlike the Achtland castle, windows didn't light the corridor, nor were there sconces holding torches or candles. Renn looked around for an Enchanter's Orb but couldn't find one. He realized then that the very walls gently radiated soft white light.

The corridor led to an inner courtyard that was encircled by the Crystal Towers as they spiraled up into the air and back down. The centerpiece of the grounds was a large marble fountain with statues of the six gods—the children of El Azur—with gilded crowns and armor, bursting from the earth and riding on the backs of flying horses. Three small rivers flowed under arches on the far side of the yard, and after cascading down small falls, they fed into the fountain to shoot high into the air from the center of the gods. The water rained down into the pool surrounding the fountain and then gently flowed out the opposite side, where a single river made its way through the courtyard and out an archway where the towers met at their lowest point.

After allowing Renn time to drink everything in, his beautiful guide led him across the courtyard to the tallest tower in the spiraling palace. Once again they entered through an open arch, but this one led to a long, brightly lit great room furnished with delicate wooden tables placed sparingly around the area. Each table had two highly polished wooden chairs cushioned with green velvet surrounding it. Plants with aromatic and multicolored flowers hung from the ceiling with vines spilling over the sides of their pots like trailers of colored light falling from one of Artio's fireworks during midsummer's Azur-Aven.

Arrianleah led Renn across the room to a grand, circular staircase on the far side. They climbed level after level until Renn's thighs burned and they reached the top, where the stairs opened directly into a bright rotunda with a domed ceiling. Gold vines made their way up the walls like branches with leaves of emeralds embedded throughout. It felt like standing underneath an incredibly large golden tree. At the center of the domed ceiling was a large, circular crystal oculus that allowed light to enter the room and amplified it so the gold and emerald adornments on the walls glimmered and shined.

Renn had to shield his eyes as he looked to the center of the room, where a striking male Avalian stood on a large golden disc embedded into the white marble floor directly beneath the crystal oculus.

He was looking up, and his milky white face was bathed with the brilliant light that poured in from the circular crystal overhead. His white hair blazed like lightning as it framed his angular but timeless face and fell just below his shoulders. His tightly fitted shirt and hose were white and stitched with gold thread, and he wore a white cape lined with royal blue silk that clasped at his neck with a delicate golden brooch. In his hand he held a staff of highly polished bleached wood crowned with a translucent orb the size of a river stone. The stone channeled light from the crystal overhead, illuminated his body, and cast a bright golden pattern throughout the room.

As Arrianleah and Renn walked forward, the light gathered back to the orb on the staff as though it were being sucked up through a hollow reed, and the blindingly bright room settled to a soft radiant glow. The man standing in its center opened his eyes to let his gaze fall upon Renn. His large eyes were perfectly almond-shaped and an ice blue that pierced like razor-sharp knives past Renn's own eyes into his heart and held him frozen in time. Renn instinctively raised the mental shield that Artio had taught him so many years ago to keep intruders out of his mind.

Elumniel smiled and said, "I'm glad Artio's lessons have become second nature to you. But I am not trying to enter your mind, Renn of Leedsdale."

"I'm sorry," Renn stammered, a little embarrassed that he'd attempted to defend himself against an Avalian—and the most powerful one at that. "I just felt . . ." Renn struggled to describe the probing he'd sensed.

"I'm considering your essence. Your soul," Elumniel said. "Tell me, child, what do you see in our land?" He gestured around them with his left hand. In his right hand, the tall staff with the clear globe on top emitted a subtle golden hue.

Renn furrowed his brow and looked around. It seemed like an obvious question, but he felt like he was missing the gist of it. He looked at Arrianleah, who gave him an encouraging smile, and then back to the eldest Avalian.

He licked his dry lips, swallowed deeply, and said, "Beauty?" It came out sounding more like a question than an answer.

Elumniel tapped at his lip with a long, slender finger and stared at Renn with his piercing blue eyes. "Yes, but what do you *see*?"

Renn scratched his head and tried again. "I see you and Arrianleah, gold vines climbing the walls and reaching to the crystal"—he pointed upward because he wasn't quite sure what to call it—"window-thing overhead that lights up the golden disc you're standing on . . ." He looked back and forth between Elumniel and Arrianleah, but the two Avalians kept silent as he struggled with his answer. "Outside I see beautiful gardens, gleaming white towers, fountains, and statues . . . Don't I see what everyone sees?" Renn asked, growing frustrated.

Elumniel raised his eyebrows and pursed his lips. "You see more than most . . . not as much as some."

"More than most?" Renn furrowed his brows at this strange answer.

Arrianleah placed her hand gently on Renn's shoulder, and he looked up at her. "Humans who pass through our forest usually see only . . . forest. Magic users see more depending on how strong they are marked by the gods. Some see gardens and not the towers; some see more. Greyfel saw more than any other human who's entered our home."

"Wow!" Renn exclaimed. "Greyfel came here? What did he do? How long was he here? The stories I've heard never tell about that? Did you know him?" Renn realized he sounded like Harlow again, but Greyfel was his favorite hero from the stories, and he'd *actually* spent time with these people.

Elumniel waved the long staff in a smooth arc, and a vision appeared in front of Renn of a man and a woman walking among the gardens. "The Wizard Greyfel and his bride, Elahna, spent sixty-seven years in our land."

The woman in the vision was even more beautiful than Renn's mother and she smiled and held her hands over her eyes as a tall man with dark, shoulder-length hair led her to a particularly beautiful fountain. Flowers and shrubs surrounded the fountain, and just beyond that was an opening of cut grass with a stone table set with a dinner for two.

"Is that . . . ?"

"Greyfel and Elahna," Arrianleah said.

"But that can't be Greyfel," Renn said. "Greyfel was over a hundred years old when he met Elahna."

"He was marked strong by the gods and was skilled in the lore," Elumniel said. "You, too, will age more slowly than other humans, Renn."

"So Greyfel and Elahna escaped the demons." Renn thought he'd never know what had really happened to the world's most famous lovers. "They *didn't* die when they fell off the cliff. How did Elahna see your land?" Renn asked. "She wasn't a magic user."

"Greyfel came to us and begged for sanctuary." Elumniel passed the staff again in an arc, and the vision changed. Now Renn saw Greyfel standing on the disc in this very room. The Wizard addressed an assembly of Avalians with Elumniel sitting on the center chair on the far side of the rotunda. Elumniel looked exactly the same in the vision as he did now.

"He asked that we touch Elahna's eyes so she could also see the land and that the two of them be allowed to live out the remainder of their lives with us. Because he'd already served our father for one hundred and fifty years and sacrificed so much for our cause, we granted his request."

"Has anybody else lived with you?" Renn asked, hoping he could stay here for the rest of his life. Elumniel gave a knowing smile and let the vision fade away.

"No. Though we do have visitors from time to time. Lore masters from Elder Island have come throughout the generations to ask a question or favor. Some are granted; some are not."

"Pardon me, brother." A tall Avalian male entered the rotunda—his hair was short but white as lightning, and his cream-and-white-colored robes flowed behind him as he approached. "It seems young Renn has a visitor who just entered our lands."

"A visitor?" Elumniel asked. "A lore user?"

"Who is it?" Renn asked with mixed feelings. The only visitors he thought could possibly find him here would be Lord Danu and his company. And if they were here, it could only mean one thing—he would have to leave the serenity of Alfheina and go back to a world where Warlocks and Kirocs hunted him.

"Not a lore user, my brother, an animal—a powerful white horse."

"Thorn!" Renn turned and started to run out of the room. He took three steps before he remembered his manners and skidded to a halt. He looked back at the Avalians, who watched him with a mixture of amusement and irritation.

"I'm sorry," Renn said. "Thorn is my best friend in the world, and I've missed him terribly. May I please be excused?"

"But we've not yet broken our fast," Arrianleah said, reminding Renn of their purpose for the visit to Elumniel.

"No matter," the eldest Avalian said. "We can dine together another time. I have learned much from our visit. You may be excused."

※

Arrianleah watched Renn disappear before she turned back to her older brother.

"Is he the one?"

Elumniel gazed up and studied the light pouring in through the crystal oculus overhead. "Perhaps . . . perhaps not." He turned his blue eyes to her. "My sight is unclear in this. As I look to his future, I see darkness and pain. I hope your interference to rescue him didn't weaken the binding of the demon lord."

"He rescued himself," Arrianleah said. "I merely guided him. I haven't felt a shift in the spell the Wizard Greyfel invoked to bind the children of K'Thrak, and my sight for the future has not changed."

Elumniel considered her words, then returned to stand in the center of the golden disc. He tapped the base of his staff three times on the disc, looked up to the crystal oculus, and raised the staff to catch the light in the orb. Bright golden rays of light filled the room, and the disc upon which he stood became translucent as the firstborn of the Avalians turned his attention to the disc of sight. He watched the events of future possibilities unfold before him for a long while before speaking again.

"In all future paths, I see heartache and darkness. Then—nothing." He lowered the staff, stepped off the disc, and moved toward Arrianleah and Omlier, the Avalian who'd brought the news of Thorn's arrival. "What does your sight show you, my sister?"

Arrianleah wiped a solitary tear from her cheek. "I see the same."

THE STAFF OF GREYFEL

Now that Renn was reunited with Thorn, he had everything he would ever need or want. As he rode Thorn through Alfheina and the gardens, the Avalians watched them with curiosity—the relationship that had led Thorn to Renn was a bond they had never witnessed before between human and animal. To discover something new and unexpected for a race of beings whose lives spanned thousands of years, as the Avalians' did, was curious indeed, Renn supposed. But nothing felt more normal and natural to him.

This day, Renn led Thorn to his favorite place in the forest—the mirrored pool. At least that's what Renn called the small lake hidden away and nestled next to the base of a cliff. A mountain rose above the cliff that reached to the sky and was capped with snow that melted to form small streams that wandered and rushed down the mountainside until they fell like curtains of rain from the rim of the cliff into the small lake below.

When one stood closer to the cliff, the waterfalls created a hypnotic roaring sound. But on the opposite side, where Renn and Thorn now stood watching the first rays of the morning sun illuminate the pool, the sound of the falls was calming.

I think I'll go for a morning swim, Thorn, Renn said to Thorn, using images and body language that were second nature to him now.

The water is cold, Thorn replied, *and you have very little hair to keep your body warm.*

Renn laughed, pulled his loose white shirt over his head, and dropped it to the ground. He sat on a boulder, took off his boots, and set them next to his shirt.

"Last one in the water is a scared pony," he shouted to Thorn as he jumped up and ran for the lake's edge. He took only a single step before he stopped and gasped in awe. The sensation flooding from the ground into his feet and through his body was a river of pure joy. The images that played before his eyes were a feast of exquisite beauty and a cornucopia of colors and elegance. For the first time in his life, he could see.

He looked down, and the grasses that had been green just moments before now vibrated with life beyond anything he had ever experienced. Renn could actually *feel* the individual blades reaching for the sun's light. They were no longer simply green—soft emerald warmth radiated with an aura of life surrounding each blade, gracing the space around them with peace. The color of their living energy sprang into the world to blend with the living energy surrounding and emanating from each and every flower, tree, and shrub. The air itself radiated vibrant and glorious life. The aromas that surrounded him were a king's buffet of scents and perfumes—so palpable he could almost taste the essence of every living thing around him by simply breathing in.

Renn heard high-pitched giggling and turned to the sound. He held out his hand—much the way he had seen Arrianleah do so many times before—and felt a thrill of joy course through his veins and into his heart as a small pixie with gossamer wings alighted on his palm and started to sing. Soon others excitedly flew around Renn in joy because his eyes were opened.

"Thorn, do you see this?" Renn asked out loud.

What do you see? the white stallion asked. Renn described the land, the plants, the vibrancy of life, and the fairy folk. *Yes,* Thorn replied, *it is much stronger in this land, but it is always there . . . Have you not seen this before?* Renn felt a little embarrassed that he could have lived in the world and never truly seen or understood its beauty before now.

"I don't think people see this way, Thorn."

"They do not, child," Arrianleah said, and Renn turned to see a row of flowering bushes move aside to clear a path for her. Three excited pixies were leading her, flying from one side of her head to the other, singing and chattering like little children unable to control their delight. "You are seeing the world as the Avalians see it."

Renn dropped to his knees and averted his eyes. Arrianleah was always beautiful to him, a being of wonder and love, but now he saw her as she truly was—a granddaughter of the creator, a literal descendant of the god he had chosen to serve.

He felt her fingers lift his chin. She was so beautiful it caused his heart to ache. He would do anything for her, and he felt hot tears streaming down his cheeks from the very thought that she chose to spend her precious time with him—a mere human boy.

"Do not worship me, Renn," she said. "We are both children of El Azur. Now rise—it is time once again for you to meet with Elumniel."

Elumniel sat on a golden throne with overstuffed cream-colored cushions in the same upper room of the crystal towers as before. Renn stopped short at the top of the landing of the rotunda. The small fairy folk had spread the news of Renn's awakening, so the domed upper chamber was lined with others of the Avalian standing in groups or sitting on green- or cream-colored cushioned divans that also had been recently added to the rotunda. As he stepped into the room with Arrianleah, the eyes of all present turned to watch.

Renn fought the urge to drop to his knees once again. He wondered why these godlike beings would not only allow him into their presence but also make him the center of their attention.

He could have stared, mesmerized by the beauty of the Avalians for days, except the room itself wrested Renn's attention from them. The gold vines pulsated with golden life as they climbed the walls, reaching to the crystal oculus high above. The emerald leaves attached to the vines radiated a soft green energy that bathed the entire room in their glow. Energy of the aeon myriad itself came from these emerald leaves.

In the center of the room, a three-foot-diameter shaft of light flowed between the crystal oculus that capped the ceiling and the disc on the floor where Elumniel had stood during their first meeting. In the middle of that light, suspended between the floor and the ceiling, was a long wooden shaft crowned with an ornament made of brass cast in the shape of an eagle in flight. Renn had seen that eagle before. He caught his breath and touched his chest. The brass eagle on the end of the staff was an exact duplicate of the mark over his right breast.

Renn's eyes locked on to the staff, and everything else became as a clouded dream—hovering on the edges of his awareness but not real enough to concern him. The staff drew him forward. It tugged at the mark on his chest like a fisherman pulling his catch to shore. Renn walked forward in this trancelike state until he stepped onto the disc and into the shaft of light.

A loud rushing noise like a raging river filled Renn's ears, and a blinding flash of light forced him out of his trance. Images flew at him from every direction. He looked down at the disc, and a flood of faces, battles, cities, and images he couldn't put names to bombarded him one after the other. He forced his eyes to look up to the staff overhead and the crystal dome beyond. Visions of flying beasts, armies, and shades of humans and Kirocs rained down on him like a driving winter storm.

Buried beneath the onslaught of images rushing at him and the sounds they carried, a distant voice called his name. He tried to close his eyes to stop the madness and clear his mind, but he could not make the images obey his will. The pictures came at him so rapidly he felt his mind would melt with the overwhelming demand to absorb it all.

One shade in the vision appeared overhead, spun rapidly in a spiral, and shot down past Renn and through the disc below. The shade joined a raging battle beneath Renn's feet and looked like the spirit of Artio. Renn felt tears form in his eyes as he tried to follow the shade but was interrupted by a flood of new images and scenes.

He caught hold of the thought of his godfather. Renn remembered one of the first lessons the old man had taught him, and he wove a shield around his mind. The images still flew at Renn in rapid succession, but now they were outside the web that protected his thoughts. The noises that sounded like raging water now became discernable—they were the sounds that accompanied each image and scene.

Renn pushed out, just like he'd done to the Kiroc that tried to kidnap him from Artio's cottage a few years before, only he controlled his push so it slowly enveloped the shaft of light and the images racing around in its wake.

The loud noise of rushing waters slowed to a gentle trickle, and Renn was now in control of the visions and scenes. He could sift through and choose those he wanted to observe and dismiss those he didn't.

He caught hold of a vision of the Wizard Greyfel and pulled it to him. The Wizard stood on the same spot that Renn now occupied and was talking with Elumniel. The Wizard held the staff with the pommel that had the brass eagle in flight. Renn saw Elumniel nod his head in approval, and then Greyfel raised the staff high above his head and in a commanding voice said, "*Lolei un ruithala variel, embrithia unlari rynthnial.*" Renn had heard Artio speak the language of the Avalians before, but now he understood the words: *To the seer's light I commend thee, safeguarded till the chosen time.* Greyfel released his staff, and it gently lifted from his hands and rose into the shaft of light until it reached the place where it now rested.

The staff pulled stronger now at the mark on Renn's chest. He released his gaze from the vision of Greyfel and looked to the staff. The wooden talisman would appear unremarkable to the unaided human eye. The old wood was worn smooth, and the grain twisted around a knot here and bent around a burl there.

Looking upon the staff with the added sight from the seer's disc, Renn saw the familiar green glow of the aeon myriad coursing and churning peacefully through every fiber, moving up and down the wood from the base to the flying eagle. The brass eagle glowed and crackled with power that begged to be released.

Renn heard a powerful voice speak. It seemed to emanate from everywhere, and it filled the entire domed room.

"Lir culmani un Greyfel lithralle, unlari rynthnial comai."

Renn hadn't spoken the language of the Avalians until now, but he instinctively knew what to say. "I am come for the staff of Greyfel; the time is now."

The energy coursing through the staff abruptly focused in the brass eagle, and green power shot toward Renn and burned through his shirt to merge with the matching flying eagle on his chest. Like a twisting cord of energy, the emerald power of the aeon myriad created a conduit of light between the staff of Greyfel and Renn. The staff rotated in the air above him and descended from its resting place of more than a thousand years toward Renn's outstretched hand.

A great flash of green energy erupted when Renn closed his grip around the ancient wood as his own gift merged with the power of the staff. In an instant that seemed to last an eternity, Renn saw the memories of the staff. The thousands of deeds done by Greyfel during his life, and many of the acts of others that the legendary Wizard observed during his life, were part of the essence of the shaft that Renn now held. Then Renn felt the memories of his own short life flow from his mind and meld with the fibers of the staff to become one with the ancient talisman.

Renn stepped out of the circle of light that surrounded the seer's disc and the green glow surrounding him and the staff coalesced to a single point of intense power and was then absorbed by the brass eagle pommel. He ran his fingers along the staff and felt the power of the Azur-Lore course through its fibers, waiting to be called forth.

Renn gazed around the room—the Avalians looked . . . surprised. Nobody spoke. They stared at Renn with wide, perfect eyes. He began to worry that he had done something wrong until Elumniel broke the silence.

"What you just did on the seer's disc takes many years to master—even for one of us." He crossed the floor to stand before Renn. "In our first meeting, I asked you to tell me what you saw." Renn nodded, remembering the strange conversation they had that day. "Now you understand. Now you truly see the world."

Elumniel ran his hand along the staff of Greyfel and then looked down at Renn's feet. Renn followed his gaze and was embarrassed to see that he'd left his boots on the shore of the lake—he was barefoot in this magnificent hall, wearing a shirt that now had a large hole burned in the chest, leaving his skin bare and revealing the eagle that was placed there by the gods during his blessing.

"Brothers and sisters." Elumniel turned in a circle to address the others in the hall. "I give you Renn Demaris, the first Earthmaster among humans."

The pixies in the hall sang and chattered one with another and flew rapidly in and out of the room. The Avalians stood as one and—to Renn's chagrin and embarrassment—bowed to him.

Elumniel placed his hand on Renn's shoulder. "I sense that another of your friends has crossed our borders and is searching for you."

Renn felt his heart drop. He didn't know which traveling companion had come looking for him, but he knew that the time had come for him to leave this paradise and rejoin the world that had brought him nothing but pain and sorrow.

THE WELL OF SACRIFICE

Shamael Daro peered from the darkness of his hooded cloak and studied the girl in the dangling cage. If it were up to him, she would have been sacrificed days ago. However, Kahn Devin had left specific instructions that no one was to harm her. But if Shamael sacrificed her to Lord Monguinir and kept her skull and thighbone for himself, it might bring him enough power to challenge Kahn. After all, she was the sister to the Mordrahn boy, one of the prophesied Children of the Blessing. Certainly the power in her bones was great. And surely Lord Monguinir would be pleased with a virgin sacrifice of her beauty and heritage.

Shamael pulled back his hood and rubbed the stubble on his head. The girl in the hanging cage crouched back as far from him as she could. He turned and walked to the black oak desk and tapped on the Grand Warlock's leather grimoire. The thought of overthrowing Kahn tempted him, but now wasn't the time. It reminded him too much of his father's bid to take control of the Thieves Guild in Valdivar thirty years ago. After the fighting had ended, the guild master had tortured Shamael's father to death while he and his mother watched. Shamael hadn't liked his father much. He'd watched the man beat his mother almost daily. But watching his father scream as he died convinced him to never underestimate his rivals.

After that day, Shamael had lived in the sewers with other boys—mostly cutpurses and beggars. He only saw his mother two times after the day his father was killed. Both times, she was working the corner of a street near the loading docks. Sailors always wanted two things when they came to shore—ale and a willing woman.

Kahn had left out an odd mix of items on his desk: maps of Boranica, Andrika, Anytos, and an old one of Tanith. It grated Shamael that Kahn didn't include him in his plans. Shamael was second only to Kahn in power and influence in the Cragg Caves. Obviously, Kahn intended to keep it that way. Shamael had been here for over twenty years and had worked his way to Second Warlock through hard work and ruthless tactics. It had paid off, too, but now he was stuck doing menial tasks for the Grand Warlock—Kahn.

For now, Shamael would pretend to admire and honor the man—even grovel before him. But the day would come when that would all change. He was good at waiting for the right moment to seize power from his rivals. The Master Thief in Valdivar never saw it coming when Shamael Daro's dagger pierced his heart. Shamael became the youngest Master Thief in the history of the guild, at seventeen years old. It had only taken him ten years to rise from boy thief to guild master. Under his short rule, the Thieves Guild had gained more wealth and influence than ever before.

When he left eighteen months later to study the Aven-Lore, he was older than most new students to the art—but he was gifted. He knew it would take longer to gain power and control in this setting than in Valdivar, but he had no doubt his day would come.

"Report," he said quietly as he raised his dark eyes from the maps and looked at the two Kirocs standing at the door on the far side of the rock-hewn chamber. The first was powerfully built, with the body of a large hairy man with long arms. However, the human resemblance ended there. His ratlike face had tusks protruding upward from his lower lip that reminded Shamael of a wild boar.

"Everything is good, m'lord." It sounded like the Kiroc's mouth was filled with saliva.

These creatures are as stupid as the rock walls of these caves, Shamael thought when the Kiroc didn't continue his report. Many years ago, the Kirocs were intelligent and powerful magic users, in the days when demons roamed these caves freely and mated with human slaves to produce the Kirocs. The Kirocs now were mostly forced to inbreed, and the sad result of that stood before him with vacant stares on their faces.

"Don't just tell me 'everything is good,' you fool," Shamael hissed. "Give me details on the armies, the new slaves, and the mining." The Kirocs backed against the walls, trying in vain to push through them to escape his anger.

The second Kiroc, as round as he was tall with beady red eyes and a snout where a human would have a nose, fell to his knees and stammered, "The armies are seventy percent armed, m'lord. And the slaves are mining ore at a pace to keep up with the blacksmiths. Within weeks we will have more weapons than soldiers."

At least this one has a spark of intelligence, Shamael thought as he considered this news. They would be ready to strengthen the Nortian army and march on Achtan soon. *If that is still Kahn's plan.* The thought irritated Shamael.

He was Kahn Devin's second-in-command, and yet he rarely knew what the Grand Warlock's plans were—and whenever Kahn did involve him, the Grand Warlock was so suspicious that he kept Shamael in the dark on key points. Instead of going out into the world to influence matters of importance, Shamael had to babysit the activities in the Aven-Lore stronghold—the Cragg Caves. The fact that administrative tasks were important was irrelevant.

"Go check the food supplies and see what last night's raids brought into our stores." The Kirocs stumbled over each other in their haste to leave and carry out his order. "And don't report that 'things are going good,'" he shouted at their retreating backs. "I want details."

Shamael traced his finger along the map of Boranica, wondering when the Grand Warlock intended to strike. He looked up and considered the girl huddled in the small cage again.

"And what are his plans for you, slave girl?" She glared at him with her dark brown eyes but didn't answer.

"And why do you need to know that, Shamael?"

Shamael spun around, dropped to one knee, and bowed in deference to the newcomer.

"That I may be of greater service, my lord." Shamael was grateful he hadn't revealed more of his thoughts out loud.

"Rise," Kahn said and sat down behind his desk. "And what, pray tell, would you have me do with her?"

"Make a sacrifice of her heart to Lord Monguinir and use her bones to make talismans of power." Shamael told Kahn the truth—this time.

"That is why I am the Grand Warlock and you serve at my whim."

Shamael bristled at Kahn's rebuke but said nothing—he bowed in deference and hoped the sweat gleaming on his bald head wasn't interpreted by his master as fear.

"You don't plan beyond the moment," Kahn said. "To be a truly useful servant, you must learn to strategize beyond next week."

"Then teach me, my lord." Shamael rose and locked his gaze with Kahn—a bold move that might earn him days of menial work or perhaps a small measure of respect. One could never tell with Kahn.

The Grand Warlock pursed his lips as his dark eyes considered Shamael. He could tell Kahn's gaze shifted to the scar that ran from his right ear and angled down his cheek ending just before the corner of his mouth—a memento Shamael Daro had to remind him of his successful coup to overthrow the man who'd killed his father.

"It should be obvious, Shamael," Kahn said with that annoyingly educated lilt in his voice. "She is bait to draw her brother to us."

It took all the reserves he could muster not to scream at Kahn. Instead, he swallowed his anger and, perhaps with a little too much edge in his voice, said, "My apologies, Lord Devin, but you did not choose to entrust me with the news that the boy hadn't been captured or killed with the rest of his clan."

The rage that flashed in Kahn's eyes and left just as quickly spoke volumes. Kahn had tried to personally capture the boys and failed. That meant that both Children of the Blessing had escaped his grasp, and Lord Monguinir would not be pleased.

A tepid knock interrupted whatever response Kahn was about to give, and two initiates entered the room at the Grand Warlock's bidding. Both wore simple hooded black robes and dropped to their knees, touching their foreheads to the floor.

"Rise." Kahn turned his back on Shamael to face the newcomers. They were both students training to reach the first level of the Aven-Lore: Demonologist. As such, they spent the majority of their time serving at the Well of Sacrifice. They protected the victims until the time of their offering—mostly from committing suicide—and when the time came for them to be presented at the well, they bathed and dressed the intended sacrifices and led them to the chamber in the bowels of the caves. Lord Monguinir also used them to communicate with the outside world. Everyone who studied the lore spent time in this service, and Shamael knew their presence here so soon after the arrival of the Grand Warlock meant Monguinir wanted to see Kahn immediately—which didn't bode well for Lord Devin. Shamael allowed the beginnings of a smile to twist the corners of his mouth.

"I presume our master wishes to see me?" Kahn's poise was admirable, but Shamael suspected the Grand Warlock was anything but anxious to address the first among demons.

"Shamael." Kahn turned back to face the younger Warlock. "I will likely be gone for several days again." He looked over Shamael's shoulder to the girl huddled in the cage and nodded in her direction. "You will give me your solemn oath that she will be unharmed until I return."

"Of course, Master." Shamael bowed his head.

"I want your sacred oath," Kahn pressed. *"Kaera tu kronos?"*

Shamael's eyes widened, and he silently cursed himself for displaying even that much weakness in front of the Grand Warlock. But the sacred oath of *kaera tu kronos*—truth of chaos—was only invoked in the most solemn ceremonies and for the deepest of commitments. This circumstance hardly seemed appropriate for that.

Nevertheless, Shamael nodded once and said, *"Kaera tu kronos."*

Kahn ignored the students and Kirocs stumbling to get out of his path as he swept down the corridors of the central cave. The jagged rock walls and red light from the Magician Globes placed on rough-cut shelves every hundred paces created as many dark shadows as light for the path. Several smaller corridors led to the right and left as he walked, but Kahn stayed on the well-worn route that led deep into the earth, to the center and soul of the caves—the Well of Sacrifice.

The two students who had come to collect him from his study followed at a safe distance. The fact that they did so meant they understood Lord Monguinir was not pleased. Kahn transformed into a hawk and flew toward the well—best not to keep Monguinir waiting.

Kahn would have to be careful with how he presented himself to Ba Aven's eldest grandson, Monguinir. The demon lord wasn't free to roam the land as he had in ages past, but he still had limited ways to view events on the surface. He'd know Renn and Avaris had resisted Kahn's every attempt to win them to the Aven-Lore. But he'd also know that Kahn had all of Nortia under his power now and that his plans in Boranica were nearly ready to be implemented. Soon they would have the armies of both nations at their disposal. Those successes would have to be enough to convince Monguinir to give Kahn more time with the Children of the Blessing.

The air grew warmer as he progressed deeper into the heart of the caves due to the eternal fire from the well, and the smell of sulfur permeated the stagnant air. It reminded him of his own service as a new student so many years ago.

He rounded one last bend in the corridor, transformed back to his human body, took a steadying breath, and pressed forward into the huge cavern. Magician Globes weren't needed to create light here. The glow from the endless pit in the center of the cavern and the three eternal wayfires located behind the Well of Sacrifice lit up the entire chamber with an unnatural dance of red, orange, and black shadows. The room was large enough to hold a small town and high enough to make it difficult to see the rock ceiling that entombed it.

Kiroc warriors with disfigured bodies and grossly misshapen faces stood guarding each corridor leading to the room, and black-robed students hurried about their duties. All of them noticed Kahn enter and quickened their pace—trying both to leave the room and not cross his path as he walked stately to the edge of the well.

Kahn had made this journey hundreds of times in his service to the Aven-Lore, but he didn't enjoy it—especially when he knew Monguinir was displeased. However, he would never let his apprehension show, particularly to new students, and so he kept his face blank and his steps measured.

As he walked, he took a skull from the large pocket inside his cloak and a thighbone from its place in a leather scabbard on his belt. Kahn didn't often use these tools to focus his magic, but the spell he would cast now required it.

The well was a round hole in the middle of the cavern, large enough in diameter to swallow a good-sized house and ringed with jagged rocks. The crimson glow emanating from the well pulsated like the heart of an ethereal giant.

Upon reaching the rim of the well, Kahn dropped to one knee and held the skull out in his left hand. He scraped the thighbone across the top of the skull and brought the skull's eyes to life with red power. He passed the thighbone over the skull in a circular pattern, drawing more and more power out of the skull. Soon, the red strength of the Aven-Lore burst through every opening.

Kahn continued to force the aeon myriad into the bone implements. Now the leg bone in his right hand radiated beams of red power from both ends as he waved it above the skull. The room turned as bright as the surface in midday, but with the thick red power of the Aven-Lore rather than sunlight.

Kahn hit the thighbone against the skull, and the red power redirected and wrapped itself around the bones, linking them together with a pulsing red flame of magical energy. In that flame, the face of a virgin girl appeared—a girl from the coast of Concordia, judging by her pale skin, blonde braided hair, and high-collared dress. She had given her life at the well sometime past, and the bones Kahn now wielded had been reclaimed from her remains. He could see fear in her ghostly eyes, but also relief that her soul had finally been released from the skull that had held it trapped all these years.

The Grand Warlock cast the skull into the well, and the girl whose life had been forfeited to create these tools screamed in horror one last time as she realized her soul was now fated to be forever trapped in the well with the demons. Kahn held the thighbone over the emptiness of the pit, and as the skull dropped into the abyss, a red cord of power tethered it to the bone in Kahn's hand.

As her scream faded into the fiery pit, another sound emerged from the bowels of the crater and climbed the rope of red power that bound the falling skull to the bone Kahn held. The sound started as a low grating noise, like rocks scraping together, but rose in volume and intensity until it rushed to the rim of the pit like a volcanic eruption, filling the cavern with plumes of billowing, murky smoke that boiled suspended in the space above the pit.

At the crest of the roiling cloud of dark smoke, a large figure emerged. His inky black skin was like a hulking shadow that absorbed all light that fell upon it, making it difficult to recognize specific features. But his eyes were ablaze with red energy, and his mouth was a raging furnace of molten Aven power.

"Why have you not brought a child of the prophecy to me?" Lord Monguinir's voice thundered through the vast chamber, and despite Kahn's best efforts to be bold, he found himself cowering on the stone floor of the chamber.

"The boy called Renn received . . . unexpected help," Kahn said. "While I was scouting, an old woman rescued him. Most likely the Oracle of Tanith."

"I don't want pathetic excuses," Monguinir roared. "I want those boys!"

"My lord, there is still time to turn one or both to your service." Kahn's voice sounded steadier than he felt. "The prophecy the Avalians place so much faith in makes it clear that the Children of the Blessing will aid in our cause and—"

"Prophecies are never what they seem," Monguinir boomed, "and our own viewings show us nothing of these children."

Kahn knew the future sight of the demons was warped by their own lust for power, but he held his tongue.

"Still," Monguinir continued, "the gods have blessed them both with great strength, and I desire them. Perhaps they are the key to breaking this prison."

Kahn stood even though Monguinir had not given him leave to rise.

"What would you have me do, my lord?"

"The first child is of the age where he can be presented at Elder Island. Most likely ten days from now during midwinter's Azur-Aven. If the Oracle *did* rescue him as you say, then he is probably in Alfheina. Elumniel will not allow him to remain among the Avalians for long. When he leaves their forest, either capture or kill him before he reaches the protection of the school on Elder Island."

"As you command, great Monguinir," Kahn said carefully. "But what shall I do if the Oracle comes to his aid once again?"

"All the better," the demon lord said. "Her interference in the affairs of man will upset the balance enforced by the godstone and weaken my prison."

"I will do as you bid, my lord." Kahn bowed deeply.

"You will return with the boy or kill him," Monguinir bellowed as he receded into the roiling cloud of black smoke. "I will not suffer another failure regarding this."

With that, the smoke and demon were sucked back into the ruddy pit as if the volcanic eruption had reversed itself. The silence that followed was deafening by contrast. Kahn stared into the red glowing pit, considering how he would deal with Renn. This time, he would leave nothing to chance. He would hit hard and fast.

THE RED BONES INN

"Ahhh . . ." Goelbak moaned. "You have magic fingers, uh . . . what's your name again?"

"Griska, Master Shapeshifter," the breeder whispered seductively in Goelbak's ear. Finding a pretty Kiroc that was somewhat intelligent in the brothels of Aven City was a difficult task for most. But Goelbak had special priority when it came to breeding.

"My shoulders have ached for days," he said. "That breeder they gave me yesterday was so weak I could barely feel my massage."

Griska had broad shoulders and thick, strong hands. She had also previously borne large, healthy Kiroc children who weren't complete imbeciles, so she was a highly sought-after female.

"That's because you have such massive muscles," Griska said with a flirtatious laugh.

"Scratch my scalp underneath my horn," Goelbak said, and Griska pressed a meaty finger between the horn where it curled around his ear and the skin of his head. It always itched him in that spot.

A brisk knock sounded on the thick wooden door, and a timid voice said, "Shapeshifter Goelbak . . ."

"Who dares interrupt me!" Goelbak roared. "Do you know who I am?"

"Um . . . yes, sir." The voice belonged to a gangly young Kiroc who resembled a lobster on two legs.

"Then GET OUT!"

"But Goelbak, er . . . Shapeshifter, sir," the young Kiroc said, "the Grand Warlock sent me to tell you to immediately meet him at his table . . . He said you'd know where that is."

Goelbak suppressed the strong desire to either pummel the youth with his fists or blast him with a stream of crimson Aven power. But Kahn didn't take kindly to those who disrespected his messengers, so instead, Goelbak shot to his feet, kicked the bed he had been lying on—sending it smashing against the wall—and shot a shower of red energy into a wooden desk resting against the far wall. The desk burned and crashed to the stone floor about the time Goelbak finished getting dressed. He snorted at the lobsterlike youth, shoved him aside, and stomped out of the room.

⊳⊰⊱⊲

Kahn sat alone at a dining table in a private room of the Red Bones Inn. The white linen tablecloth and napkins were as fine as any in Kahaal, and the room's decor was similar to what a person could expect to find in the palace of a southern king. The only element that betrayed the inn's location was the ever-present red glow coming from a Magician's Globe fixed to the center of the room where a chandelier would otherwise hang. Kahn had even paid the proprietor to cover the rocky cavern ceiling with beams, wood paneling, and plaster so he could forget he was inside a massive cave.

He watched the red Boranica wine, made deeper red by the light in the room, as it swirled in his pewter goblet. In the past, he might've sipped on Blaylok Red imported from Kahaal, but his accomplice in Basilea had given him a bottle of aged Boranica Red a couple years ago, and it had become his favorite vintage.

A knock at the door brought him out of his reverie and the aged innkeeper poked his head into the room.

"Your greatness, there is a Kiroc—"

"Out of my way, human." Goelbak spat the word *human* like it tasted filthy running across his tongue. "Master Devin is expecting me."

The door crashed open, and the fat, balding innkeep fell to the floor as a huge Kiroc Shapeshifter barged into the room.

"Goelbak, I'm pleased you answered my summons so quickly," Kahn said, to which the Kiroc grunted but also straightened his shoulders and puffed out his massive chest a bit with what Kahn assumed was pride. "Master Blithy," Kahn said to the innkeeper, who had picked himself up off the floor and was brushing off his dirty apron. "Bring Goelbak a stein of Nortian Ale, please."

"And be quick about it, *human*," Goelbak said gruffly.

"You really should consider being more kind to those who serve you," Kahn said as he pointed to a chair, indicating the one-horned beast could sit.

"What for?" Goelbak said. "Humans think they're better than me. I'm a Shapeshifter, and they'll give me the respect I deserve."

"Or they might decide to piss in your ale and smile while they watch you drink." Kahn raised his goblet to his lips to hide his amusement. Goelbak's eyes grew large, and his mouth dropped open as he considered this possibility.

The door opened, but before anybody stepped over the threshold, Goelbak called out, "You'd better not piss in my ale, human."

"I would, but my piss is too good for you, *Squid*."

Goelbak shot to his feet, sending his chair crashing to the floor.

"Norvin, you shadowsplitting weasel." The way Goelbak previously spat the word *human* was charming in comparison to the loathing that coated his words as he addressed his rival, Norvin Jixin. "What is the meaning of this, Kahn?"

"That's *Grand Warlock* to you, Goelbak," Kahn said coldly. He didn't have time for old disputes between these two.

"Perhaps Master Kahn has finally agreed to my request for a Warlock duel with you, *Squid*," Norvin said in his high-pitched, nasally voice.

Kahn sighed and shook his head. To advance from a Shapeshifter to Warlock, an Aven-Lore user had to kill another Shapeshifter to prove himself worthy. Both Norvin and Goelbak had requested to duel the other more than two years ago, but Kahn refused their request.

"Is it true, Ka—I mean, Grand Warlock?" Goelbak looked genuinely excited. "Have you decided to grant my petition to duel this human rodant?"

"My reasons for denying that particular request haven't changed." Kahn stood and stared them both into silence. "You each possess unusual gifts that I don't want to lose. In fact, the time for you to use those gifts has arrived."

Kahn removed a long thighbone from beneath his cloak and pushed energy from the aeon myriad into the bone until it glowed and emitted a red mist. He summoned a vision of Renn, the Child of the Blessing, into the mist for Goelbak and Norvin to see.

"We must find this boy and kill him before he reaches Azur's Acropolis on Elder Island," Kahn said. "If you succeed, I will advance both of you to the level of Warlock."

"Are you serious?" Norvin's red eyebrows rose. "You need me and Squid to kill a boy?"

"I'm not working with this human," Goelbak said. "And I don't want to be made a Warlock for killing a boy."

Kahn slammed the table with his fist. "You will do as I say and nothing less!"

Both Shapeshifters fell silent in the aftermath of Kahn's outburst.

"This *boy* is the embodiment of a prophecy the followers of El Azur put so much faith in. His name is Renn, and he has incredible power. I am *not* going to allow him to become a Wizard and fight against us." Kahn straightened his doublet, put the thighbone back under his cloak, and sat down. Norvin ran his fingers through his orange-red hair, and his beady blue eyes glared at Goelbak.

"So what's the plan, then?" Norvin asked when he looked back at Kahn.

"I believe Renn will be leaving the forest of the Avalians soon as he makes his way north to Elder Island," Kahn said. "You, Norvin, will scout along the north perimeter of the forest, watching for him to emerge. If he somehow eludes you, Renn will need to sail by boat to the island. That's where you come in, Goelbak. I want you to monitor the sea between the mainland and Elder Island. If that fails, I will be waiting for him on the island."

"How will we find him?" Norvin asked. "That's a lot of area to search. Do you at least know *where* or *when* he will emerge from the forest?"

"No," Kahn said. "But if he draws on the aeon myriad, you may be able to feel him."

"We'd have to be right on top of him when he draws on the power to be able to feel it," Norvin said, sounding unsure of the strategy.

"You'd be surprised," Kahn said. "When he draws on the energy, it's powerful. You can feel it from miles away sometimes. If you feel somebody drawing on the power, it will be him. If that happens, strike hard and fast."

"That doesn't sound difficult," the big Kiroc said, "and I won't *really* be working with Norvin after all."

"Not much," Kahn said, "but we must be in place in three days' time, and the only way you will get there in time is if Norvin helps you."

Norvin smiled and folded his arms.

"What—is Shadow going to turn into a birdie and carry me all the way across Lemuria?" Goelbak asked with disdain, and Norvin's brows knitted together at the mention of transporting the massive Kiroc across the continent.

"Don't be petulant, Goelbak," Kahn said. "Norvin will fly to the coast near Bremenon View and build a wayfire. You are to wait at a wayfire in the Well of Sacrifice for his signal to cross over." The Grand Warlock removed two strips of red material from his shirt pocket and gave one to each Shapeshifter. "I will scry out both of you a few times each day. Should you come across the boy, kill him and tie this to your arm so I will know it is finished."

GIFTED HEALER

Aleah took a long draw from her water bag and slowly tied it off. She pulled back the hood of her green riding cloak and scratched at her head. She ran her fingers over the horseshoe tracks in the dark, rich dirt for at least the fifth time. She was certain she'd studied this exact spot just an hour before—and an hour before that. She couldn't remember because these lush forests created a strange feeling inside her that kept making her lose focus.

It should be snowing, or at least be cold, but instead every plant, flower, and tree bloomed. The birdsong and buzzing of insects sounded like a masterful music composition, and the heady aroma of flower blossoms was intoxicating. Aleah found herself gazing at a stand of saplings or drinking in the beauty of a patch of flowers without realizing she was doing it. It was downright humiliating. She was acting like a lovesick manservant instead of the best tracker in all of Domeria. Why couldn't she stay focused?

She couldn't even remember how long she'd been following Thorn's tracks—a couple days at most, maybe a week, but certainly no longer than that.

The tracks led straight west, into those stately gardens. Strange. Aleah hadn't noticed gardens before . . . or had she? She climbed back onto her horse, intending to ride toward the gardens, but a particularly beautiful flowering bougainvillea bush on her right caught her attention, so she turned south to study it more closely.

Stop, she thought. *What in El Azur's name are you doing?*

She slapped her face—harder than she intended—and turned back to the west. There *had been* gardens there . . . she was sure of it. She jumped back off the saddle and studied some horseshoe tracks leading that direction. She was sure she'd studied them before . . . Was it an hour ago, or just moments?

The air shimmered to the west, and she thought she saw spiraling towers in the middle of the garden; that must have been a trick of the setting sun. She could no longer see towers, but she saw something else. A light moved toward her. As it approached, she realized she had been in this same place for nearly the entire day, looking at the same tracks and the same plants over and over again—like a piece of deadwood stuck in an eddy that couldn't manage to get back into the river current.

She felt a stab of anger that she could be sidetracked this way, but then the air to the west shimmered again and she forgot about her irritation. She forgot about the tracks and dropped the reins of her horse. She wasn't sure if she should cry or shout for joy. Renn, Thorn, and the most beautiful women she'd seen in her life walked toward her—and they were only three steps away.

Renn carried a long wooden staff with a brass eagle at the top. His shirt had a hole burned in it and he wore no shoes; other than that, he looked better and stronger than ever. His shoulders didn't slump like a gangly teenager's—he held them back with an air of confidence.

Notwithstanding the sudden changes in Renn, Aleah barely glanced at him. Her eyes were drawn instead to the woman accompanying him. She had long, flowing hair the color of ripe oats. She wore a tight-fitting white dress that—while modest—revealed a perfect form of female grace and elegance underneath. Normally, Aleah would have felt a tinge of jealously that another woman could be so perfect, but instead she dropped to her knees—feeling a need to follow and serve this person.

"Rise, Aleah of Domeria." The lady's voice was musical, and Aleah felt hot tears on her cheeks when the woman gently lifted her chin, causing Aleah to look into her deep blue eyes. Those eyes were familiar. She was certain she'd never seen that beautiful face, but she was just as certain she had looked into those eyes before.

"I am Arrianleah of the Avalians. I am pleased you have come, as was foretold when you were a young girl." She gestured toward Renn with her slender hand and said, "However, your journey to bring the Child of the Blessing to the lore masters on Elder Island is not yet complete, and time is running short."

A shocking recognition flooded through Aleah.

"You're Arriana, the Oracle?" Aleah whispered, and she wished she could take the question back as soon as the words left her lips. What a ridiculous notion. This goddess could never look so plain.

Arrianleah smiled. "You are perceptive, Aleah. Most do not see beyond outer appearances."

"Is this why you prophesied I must accompany Renn on this journey?" Aleah asked. "To follow him to this place?"

"You have already saved his life, as was foretold," Arrianleah said, and Aleah remembered the battle in the Tiarak Mountains to recover Renn from Jomard—who was really the Kiel-Don known as Jomavid.

"But your task is not yet complete," Arrianleah continued. "You must see Renn safely to the lore masters at the school on Elder Island."

"Will we be attacked on our way?" Aleah asked. "What is the fastest and safest route of travel?" Talk of her responsibility and being reminded of battles pulled her out of her awe-inspired stupor. She felt a little more like her normal self as she drew on her training and experience to start planning a strategy to complete her task.

Arrianleah gazed northward, and her eyes narrowed as though she were watching something nobody else could see. "There is danger ahead, regardless of the path you choose. Therefore, I suggest you take the fastest path—north, to the town of Bremenon View. There you can hire passage on a ship to Elder Island."

Renn gripped the strange staff he was holding a little tighter upon hearing Arrianleah's words, but Aleah thought his face looked resolved rather than fearful. That was certainly a different reaction than she would've expected from him a couple weeks ago.

"What if I wait?" Renn asked. "What if I wait until midsummer's Azur-Aven to be presented to the lore masters, or even longer? If Kahn doesn't know when I am traveling, it won't be as dangerous. I'm sure I wouldn't be the first to go to the school after his fourteenth year."

"Lord Monguinir will send his minions to stop you from reaching the school no matter when you go. Waiting gives him time to send more enemies against you," Arrianleah said. "But more importantly, my sight tells me that a critical event for you to realize your full power will take place on midwinter's Azur-Aven during the presentation . . . but it will only occur if you are there."

Renn's shoulders slumped. "Is there no other way?"

"I cannot see all things because the future is yet to be written. Decisions we make create multiple future possibilities. But if you wait to leave, I don't see a future timeline where you exist. I believe you will never make it to Elder Island if you don't leave now."

"I could stay here," Renn said. "Lord Monguinir's servants can't come into the realm of the Avalian."

Arrianleah shook her head and smiled sadly. "If you remain with us, I see darkness growing over the Cragg Mountains until it covers the face of Lemuria." Arrianleah's eyes glossed over, and she looked past Aleah as though, once again, she was watching something that only she could see. "Beyond that darkness, my sight is gone . . . I see nothing."

Arrianleah's eyes grew wide, and she wrapped her arms around herself. "Throughout the millennia of our existence, there has never been a time when I saw nothing." Her blue eyes narrowed, and she turned to Aleah.

"You *must* get the Child of the Blessing to the school in time for the midwinter's Azur-Aven ceremony."

"Is there nothing you can do to help?" Aleah asked.

"What if *you* take us there?" Renn said. "The same way you brought me to Avalian."

While that would make the task a lot easier, Aleah felt like she would be cheated out of her glory if Arrianleah agreed. No bard would write a song if the Avalians had to come in and save the day—great heroes must do legendary things to be remembered. But that was selfish of her. If Arrianleah had a way to get them there fast and safe, Aleah would be foolish not to accept her help.

"Yes, I do have the power to do as you ask," Arrianleah said, "but if I were free to do that, I would've simply picked you up at Leedsdale myself and delivered you to the school."

"I don't understand," Aleah said. *What good is having great powers if you don't use them in times of great need?* she thought.

"I gave you a choice, Renn, when you were Kahn's prisoner, and *you chose* to follow me," Arrianleah said. "You rescued yourself. You broke the bonds and opened the portal that brought us here."

Aleah sucked in a sharp breath and gave Renn a questioning look.

"I'll tell you what happened later," Renn said, then looked back at the beautiful oracle.

"Why does that matter?" Renn asked.

"The spell Greyfel used to trap the demons came with a price." She tapped on her chin and looked at them both appraisingly. She placed her hands on her hips and let out a sigh—a distinctly human thing to do, in Aleah's opinion. "When Greyfel first came to us, the Avalians were free to roam the land and exert our influence just as humans do today. We did many great things. But Lord Monguinir and his brothers were also free to roam the land. We healed diseases, built wondrous gardens in cities and villages, and taught people to love and care for one another. But the demons, along with the dragon Roskva, murdered, pillaged, raped, and destroyed in equal measure."

As Arrianleah spoke, the staff in Renn's hands undulated with currents of green energy, and a shaft of light burst from the eagle-shaped pommel to create a vision of the events Arrianleah was speaking about. The beautiful seeress stopped talking and watched the scene for a moment, and then raised a single eyebrow toward Renn.

"I'm not sure how I did it," Renn sheepishly said to the unasked question. Aleah gasped at the carnage in the vision, then silently cursed herself. She was a warrior and had seen bloodshed many times. Warriors don't gasp like milkmaids at the sight of carnage. But the slavery, rape, and murder that raged in the display created by Renn's magic was senseless and limitless. An enormous black dragon destroyed entire villages in a single pass and carried off livestock as the frantic people fled their homes, only to find demons and Kirocs waiting to enslave them.

Arrianleah dispelled the vision with a wave of her hand and said, "We made no progress. We built and they destroyed in such great measure that we had no hope for a meaningful future. The Godstone fulfilled its task of maintaining balance, but the balance was extreme.

"Then the Wizard Greyfel spoke with my brother of a plan to imprison the demons in their Well of Sacrifice. He planned to trap them by opening a rift in the midst of Lord Monguinir and his minions while they feasted on sacrifices in the well. The spell Greyfel used was dangerous—it created a portal to the world of the dead. In this case, however, he opened the portal on our side but not on the side that entered death's realm. Once the rift opened around the demons, he sealed it on this end, which left the demons in limbo between the two realms. Now they are connected to both realms but not truly a part of either. Much like a shadow—they can be seen under certain conditions and they can darken the world, but their power is limited."

"The Godstone still requires balance," Renn said softly, as though everything made perfect sense to him.

What happened to him? Aleah wondered. He was still a fourteen-year-old boy, but his new demeanor reminded her of somebody much older—it reminded her of Artio. Arrianleah stopped talking, and she, too, considered Renn.

"What?" Renn's face turned red when he realized they were staring at him. That, at least, *was* something Aleah would expect from him.

"Greyfel's staff has given you great insight, Renn," Arrianleah said.

Greyfel's staff? Aleah was sure she'd heard Arrianleah correctly. How and where had Renn gotten that? Aleah didn't ask just then because the seeress continued. "Do you now know why I can do very little to help you?"

"Well, I think it's because the more involved the Avalians are in the dealings of men, the weaker the spell trapping the demons becomes. The Godstone requires balance."

"Where is the Godstone?" Aleah asked. After all, if Renn could stumble across Greyfel's staff, maybe they could find the Godstone, too.

"After we used it in the binding, Greyfel hid it away. The location of the stone was forever forgotten when he died."

Arrianleah watched Renn closely as she spoke of the Godstone's location. Renn stared back at her. His blue eyes were dull in comparison to the Avalian's eyes. He shook his head and said, "The staff has no memory of that."

"The power of the El Azur is great in our land, Renn," Arrianleah said. "Connected as you are now with the land and staff, you can see and do many things. But once you leave this place, it will not be so easy for you to draw upon the staff's power. Still, remember your connection with the land. You are the first Earthmaster among humans. You can draw upon the power of aeon myriad around you when you are in direct contact with the living earth as you now are. But realize this: the life around you is not without limits. As power flows to you from the soil of the earth, you are drawing life from the living things around you."

Aleah remembered the day Artio had been killed as they'd traveled to Anytos. The ground had trembled and rolled as Renn had drawn more and more power. His fists had sunk deep into the soil as he'd pounded the earth that day.

"I must leave you now. Farewell, friends, and may our father, El Azur, light your way." With that she turned, walked away, and within four steps, she vanished from view. Aleah watched her leave, then gave Renn a fierce hug.

"Everybody has been sick with worry over you." She let him go and looked him over once more. "You'd best put your boots back on and take my spare riding cloak. It's going to be a lot colder once we leave this forest."

Renn looked at his bare feet and then considered his boots—like he was thinking of throwing the boots out. Something was different about him, but Aleah didn't have time to sort it out now.

"Quickly, Renn, I want to be a dozen leagues north of here before nightfall. We have a lot of distance to cover and only ten days to do it."

※

The first day and night of travel since leaving the beach at Aanith was miserable, but not as bad as Genea had feared it would be. She and Tristan used a trick Aleah had taught them weeks before to stay warm at night by using rocks from the cooking fires. The guide who led the group to the school was helpful—a bit strange, but helpful. He called himself Dev and was from one of the Devi tribes—that was obvious at first glance. He had brown skin and a goatee peppered with gray whiskers that hung down to his collar, but his long hair was still a deep brown with no sign of aging. He wore a permanent scowl, but that might just have been due to the way his thick eyebrows pulled down at the bridge of his nose. His most defining feature was a large mole on his forehead just left of center. He didn't talk unless he had something important to tell them, so Genea learned to pay attention whenever he spoke.

The days grew shorter the further north they traveled—the sun rose and set in eight hours. This made the trip take longer than they'd counted on, and Lord Danu was growing visibly uneasy and moody. Or maybe, Genea thought, he was dreading the fast-approaching day when he would have to inform the lore masters of his failure. Everybody seemed to expect the Child of the Blessing to arrive soon. Even their guide, Dev, had asked Lord Danu about him.

The second morning into the journey, Genea woke to find that Tristan's bedroll had already been cleaned and put away. *Strange*, she thought. *Tristan never gets out of bed before I do.* She pulled on her heavy winter cloak and cleaned and rolled her own bedding before stepping out of the tent into the cold dawn. Her breath hung in front of her like she was smoking a pipe filled with Domerian tobacco. She must have slept longer than normal because everybody else sat on logs surrounding a small fire in the center of the ring of tents, eating breakfast.

"Where's Tristan?" Kivas asked as Genea accepted a bowl of porridge from Dev. "She needs to get up and eat so we can leave."

"I thought she was out here with you," Genea said. "She was gone before I woke."

Raven stopped eating and looked around the breakfast fire at all the children huddled in their cloaks, trying to keep warm as they ate.

"Has anybody seen Tristan?" He set his porridge on the ground.

"Oh, yes," Harlow said. "I got up first because I couldn't sleep—it's so cold up here—Tristan was up, and she kept laying her hands on the trees and humming. She was acting really weird—then she told me she wanted to go for a walk to get to know the trees better. She said something like they reminded her of the forest around Achtan, but they don't look like that to me. I think—"

"She went out into the mountains in the dark?" Dev asked, and the curly-headed boy just nodded and stuffed another spoonful of porridge into his mouth.

"What's in these mountains, Dev?" Lord Danu asked.

"The Oraima Mountains are relatively safe, but there are animals in the—"

He was cut off by a high-pitched scream, and Genea knew it came from Tristan. Raven ran toward the sound with weapons drawn before anybody else had time to stand. Genea dropped her food and rushed after him. Another scream, filled with pain, pierced the morning air. Tears fell down Genea's cheeks as she tried to follow the sound.

She entered a small clearing just in time to see Raven pulling a large mountain lion off Tristan's motionless body. The lion had two arrows protruding from its neck. Genea ran to Tristan and dropped by her side in the snow.

"Tristan...Tristan?" She cradled the princess's head in her lap. Tristan's cloak was ripped, and her face and hands were scratched and bleeding. Her breathing came in quick, shallow gulps. Genea pulled Tristan to her bosom and gently rocked her.

"Tristan, please . . . not you, too . . ." she said through hot tears. The weight of her sorrow bore down on her heart. Years of loss and grief welled up inside her, and the world no longer mattered. She didn't even care that she was covered in blood and cold snow, and she hardly heard Raven tell her to let go so they could get Tristan back to camp. All she could feel was desperate sorrow and deep compassion for the girl she held in her arms. Then she felt a burning sensation borne of her emotions, and it grew in place of the grief and sorrow. Like a shadow of sound, she heard Raven telling her to let go and felt him shake her, but then she heard Dev tell him to wait and watch.

As the warm burning sensation grew, Genea thought of Tristan and her injuries. At that moment, she wanted nothing but to remove the pain and make everything better. A subtle awareness grew in Genea that warmth was somehow flowing out of her body and through her embrace into Tristan. But as Tristan's breathing slowed and grew more measured, Genea felt severe pain in her own chest. Not the burning sensation she felt before, but real physical pain. Genea's breathing now came in short, quick gasps as the pain grew more intense, but she continued to allow—no, force—the burning warmth from her body to flow into Tristan.

"Genea?" Tristan's voice was weak, but Genea knew she would be all right. Still, she kept pushing the warmth to Tristan through her embrace. She felt weaker and weaker but continued to push.

"Genea, stop." Dev shook her, but it didn't matter. She couldn't stop. "Genea," he repeated more urgently. The intoxicating flow of energy ceased—like a sharp blade had severed it. Genea opened her eyes and saw that Tristan was all right. She smiled weakly, then exhaustion overcame her. Darkness enveloped her, and she felt herself fall into Dev's arms.

AZUR'S ACROPOLIS

Avaris looked up at the waning crescent moon in the western sky from his hiding place behind a large red pine on the mountainside. He took a deep breath, pulled back the fur-lined hood of the bison coat he'd taken from his father's tent, and peered around the side of the tree. Two large Kirocs guarded the entrance to a cave in the ravine below—Kalisha, Lekiah, and the remnants of his tribe were in that cave.

One of the Kirocs had horns and a catlike face and wore metal armor that looked too small for his burly frame. Avaris had never seen anybody wear metal armor; it didn't look comfortable. The other Kiroc was short and fat, with long stringy hair, a large nose, and tusklike teeth that protruded out of his mouth. His blood-colored leather armor fit only slightly better.

Avaris had watched this pair of guards several times over the past week, waiting for an opportunity to sneak past them. The Kiroc guards rotated in shifts with three other sets every six hours. So far, he hadn't been able to come up with a plan for how he would get past them and into the caves so he could rescue his tribe. This pair was obviously the least intelligent of the bunch. They grunted at each other as they sat at a large boulder next to the entrance of the cave, playing a game with dice and cards.

The rock surrounding the cave opening had the look of an ancient arch with strange markings carved into it around the perimeter. He could see nothing past the entrance except a foreboding darkness. At least it would be warmer in there than out here. He hadn't been exposed to the elements as brutally as the captives had been, but still his knees and joints ached from the constant cold.

A black falcon flew out of the cave opening, screeched, and soared to the east. *That's strange*, Avaris thought. *I don't remember ever seeing that bird fly into the caves.* The guards must've thought it odd, too, because they stood and shouted something to the falcon, then scratched their heads and discussed it before sitting down to resume their game.

Avaris had spent most of the previous three weeks following the Kirocs and his tribe at night and watching their camps by day. During that time, five more children of the Devi had been abandoned along the trail. Like Luka, all five were either dead or had died shortly after Avaris found them.

He peered around the boulder again. The Kirocs stared down at the cards in their hands. Avaris picked up a stone and cast it into the trees on the far side of the cave opening. The Kirocs jumped up and looked toward the sound. The cat-faced one with horns left to investigate; the fat one stayed to guard the entrance.

Oh, well, Avaris thought. *It was worth a try. I guess they're a little smarter than I thought.*

The distant neighing of a horse caused Avaris to peek around his tree again. The Kiroc guards must've heard it, too, because one cleaned up the game as the other walked in front of the cave entrance to stare down the trail leading up the ravine from the southwest side. Avaris crept along the mountain, moving from tree to tree, so he could get a better view of the trail. A slender man in a thick black riding cloak with his hood pulled up to cover his face rounded the trail on a tired roan. A chain, hooked to his saddle, connected to the wrists of three staggering people behind him—two girls and a boy. They wore ragged clothing and were barely able to stand. They had unusual coloring—pale skin and hair the color of the autumn plains grass. Avaris guessed they were nearly twenty winters old.

Behind the three in chains came a group of boys and girls a little older than Avaris. They walked with labored strides—they weren't shackled, just exhausted.

Avaris worked his way closer under the cover of the noise being made by the approaching group. Several paces before they reached the cave entrance, the cat-faced Kiroc held up a hand.

The short Kiroc with long, stringy black hair called out to the horseman in a challenging tone, but Avaris couldn't understand the words. The rider stopped and pulled back his hood—except *he* turned out to be a *she* with long black hair, milk-colored skin, and eyes the color of coal. Those eyes promised death to anybody who crossed her, and the Kirocs shrunk back under her glare.

"My business is none of your concern, dog." She spat the words. "Step aside or die." For some reason, she'd answered in the language Avaris spoke.

"Come now, Kintara," a familiar voice said from within the cave, and Kahn Devin walked out of the entrance to stand behind the Kirocs, who'd dropped and pressed their foreheads to the ground at his feet.

Avaris had to make a conscious effort to slow his breathing. He wanted to use the power of bone and fire and kill the man on the spot, and at the same time, he wanted to run away as far as he could.

"You really should be more patient with our Kiroc servants," Kahn said. "After all, they're only doing their job."

"Master." The woman climbed from her horse and dropped to one knee. "I have brought initiates to be presented at the midwinter's ceremony."

Kahn Devin gave the recruits a cursory glance with a look of mild interest. "And why are you speaking the language of the savage tribes?" he asked.

"I speak in Devinese because I don't want my recruits to hear anything they shouldn't," she said.

"Ah, I see. You've always been . . . cautious. And why are these three in chains?" The Grand Warlock pointed at the two girls and man who had fallen to the ground behind Kintara.

"They tried to escape," she said, "three times."

"Hmm, they probably won't last long in the caves. Very well, carry on." He pulled a pair of dark gloves on and buttoned the top color of his cloak. "I, regrettably, may not be back in time for the ceremony—I have a pressing matter that I must personally attend to for Lord Monguinir. In my absence, I trust you to work in harmony with the other Warlocks. I shall be very put out if I return to find . . . conflicts"

"As you command, Master." She rose from the ground, but her head remained bowed.

The air around Kahn shimmered red, and the man changed into a large dark hawk. With a piercing cry, the black bird lifted off the ground and took a northeasterly flight.

As the woman named Kintara and the Kirocs watched the bird fly away, Avaris stole to a bush near the group of initiates and waited for them to start moving. His clothing was in better condition than the recruits', so he removed his coat and hid it beneath the thick foliage, ripped his shirt, and rolled in some muddy snow.

Once Kahn Devin was out of sight, Kintara pulled at her horse's reins, pushed aside the Kirocs, and entered the cave. The initiates in chains jerked forward and disappeared behind her. The others followed, and when the last one stumbled past Avaris's hiding place, he stepped out behind him and walked with the group past the Kiroc guards and into the cave.

※

Genea smelled the crisp scent of pine on cold air. That smell combined with the gentle swaying and steady creaking sound of leather on leather lulled her from sleep. She opened her eyes and lifted a hand to shield them from the blinding sun reflecting off the shimmering snow.

"I see you've decided to rejoin us." Durham's deep voice rumbled in her ear. Genea looked down and then over her shoulder before she realized she was riding in front of him on a brown-and-white horse. The soft-spoken man kept her from falling off the saddle by letting her rest against his chest as they traveled over a snow-packed mountain trail.

"How long . . ." Genea's voice cracked.

"Nearly three days," Durham said. "If it weren't for Dev, you wouldn't be here at all."

"The guide?" Genea asked.

"I think he's more than a simple guide," the soldier said. "Tristan, she's awake." That last line he called out over his shoulder.

Genea heard the soft thudding of horsehoofs galloping in packed snow, and then the blonde princess was riding by their side.

"Are you all right?" Tristan asked, and Genea weakly nodded. She wanted to fall back to sleep, but she was happy to see her best friend.

Tristan reached over and squeezed her hand. "It looks like you've got some hidden talents. Dev says most accomplished Healers who've trained for years at the school couldn't do what you did for me."

"Really?" Genea asked with a wan smile. She had no idea how she'd healed Tristan, but she hoped it wouldn't be this taxing every time she tried to heal someone. Still, she knew that if Tristan needed it, she wouldn't hesitate to do it again.

"Lord Danu even wondered if maybe you had been given extra gifts from the gods," Tristan said. "After all, you were blessed on the same night and same place as Renn."

Genea only had a moment to consider this because up ahead—where the convoy of students had already reached the end of the trail—there came excited chatter and shouts of joy. When she reached the end and rode into the open, Genea understood why. They were on an immense plateau blanketed in virgin snow. Behind them and to their west were the thick pine forests they had been traveling through and had just emerged from. To the east, the pine- and snow-covered Oraima Mountain Range continued to jut into the sky. And a mile or so in the distance, on a large hill—the only hill on the plateau—a massive and ancient-looking castle with several pointed spires, some with turrets, grew out of the earth and reached toward the crystal-blue sky. Behind the castle, the plateau stretched for probably a half mile or so and then just vanished into the blue horizon.

Tristan caught her breath, and Genea saw tears well in her eyes as she covered her mouth with one hand.

"What's wrong?" Genea asked.

"The castle," Tristan said. "It looks a bit like Achtan, except bigger."

Genea nodded as she considered the six tall, narrow ivory towers that reached above the main buildings. The castle was surrounded by a moat crossed by a great drawbridge with thick iron chains and a gatehouse, but there was no curtain wall. It looked more like a fortified palace than a castle. The outside of the edifice was covered in white instead of being left bare like the castle in Anytos, and instead of arrow loops lining the walls for archers to rain down their long bolts on would-be attackers, the massive main building was lined with row upon row of windows. Genea wondered how much it must have cost to buy so many windows. As they rode toward the school, she counted the rows—six levels in all.

Dev chuckled, watching the new pupils gawk and point at the mythic structure.

"Mr. Dev, sir." Harlow's wide eyes glistened like the snow. "Who built this, and how does it stay so white? Do you live here? How many people can that hold? I knew it was big, but wow, I never thought—"

"Slow down, son." Although Dev wore a grin, his brows still furrowed above his large brown eyes. "The castle has stood here for more than a thousand years," the guide said loud enough for everyone to hear. They all stopped talking and listened as they followed him toward the school. "The school was founded by the Wizard Greyfel, but rumor is that the Avuman built it. Some even claim the Avalians had a hand in its construction."

"That's why it looks so much like Achtan," Tristan whispered reverently.

"The facade is layered with limestone gathered from an ancient quarry in those mountains." Dev pointed to the jagged mountain range to the east of the school. "But the thing you will find most amazing is that every floor in the school has fresh running water." He paused to let that sink in.

A boy who looked and sounded to be from Concordia said, "You mean . . . we don't have to get water from a well?"

"That's correct," the guide answered, and excited chatter among the students began again.

"You use magic to do that?" Kivas raised his voice over the noise.

The old guide shook his head and smiled. "Nope. Just good old engineering—something that hasn't been done for hundreds of years, I might add."

He pointed toward the mountain closest to the hill the school occupied. "There's a spring about a quarter way up that mountain. Water is brought by aqueducts from the spring to a central location on each floor of the school. In the basement, they even have baths where the water has been heated." Genea and Tristan looked at each other with wide-eyed joy at that news.

Dev led the party of twenty pupils and their escorts up the tree-lined cobbled path on the hill to the drawbridge that spanned the wide moat surrounding the school.

"This is where I leave you," the guide said. "Phaedra will take over from here." He pointed to a tall woman standing on the top of the steps that led to the massive iron doors of the school-castle. She wore a thick blue velvet dress with a tan shawl that covered her brown hair and draped over her shoulders; on top of that was a black-and-white sash.

"Maurer, our Wizard, told me about Phaedra," Tristan whispered. "She was a lore master when he first came to the school . . . more than eighty years ago."

Genea looked at the woman waiting for them. Her dark eyes glistened with anticipation, and she wore a pleasant smile. Her face had some wrinkles, but Genea would've guessed the woman was only in her forties.

"Welcome to Elder Island," Phaedra said as the students dismounted and climbed the stairs. "This is where you will live for a time—some of you longer than others." She spread out her hands to indicate the castle and grounds. "The locals on the island refer to the school as Azur's Acropolis," she said with a broad smile. "We call it home. I am Phaedra, one of seven lore masters who will instruct you in the arts of the Azur-Lore. A week from tonight is the first new moon after the winter solstice, and we will celebrate midwinter's Azur-Aven. As you know, during that evening you will be formally presented as new students of the Azur-Lore."

Genea heard Lord Danu sigh under his breath. He looked particularly grim over the prospect of the coming ceremony.

"I will now show you to your quarters."

Tristan and Genea shared a large room with thick red carpeting and heavy red-and-gold drapes that covered a square window overlooking the main courtyard. The room also had two soft four-poster beds, a cherrywood bureau for each girl, and a vanity table with an oval mirror. Once they'd unpacked their belongings, they washed, changed into clean clothes, and hurried to the common room for supper. Lord Danu and the others had already eaten and were talking quietly among themselves and drinking ale when the girls joined them.

"What are you going to say?" Kivas asked Lord Danu.

The blond-haired lord shrugged his shoulders. "I'll tell them the truth. There's not much else I can say."

Raven held a cup of hot tea, but Genea noticed the fighter wasn't drinking it. Instead, Lord Danu's captain stared at the windows that lined the far side of the hall.

It had been dark for a few hours already—even though it was just suppertime. Kivas explained to her that as they traveled further north, the sun set earlier than it did in Boranica—at least in the winter. She pulled her wool shawl tighter and wished she'd brought a cloak with her. A roaring fire burned in a grand hearth on the opposite end of the hall—and the room wasn't cold; she just wanted to be warmer than she felt right now. Well, if truth be told, she hadn't really felt warm ever since leaving Anytos with the hope of finding Renn diminishing each passing day.

She sighed and let herself really look around the room for the first time. At the other tables, children feasted and laughed along with their escorts. Genea didn't feel like eating. The small cooked hen, spiced apples, cheese, and juice smelled wonderful, but she couldn't stop thinking about Renn. After teasing at her spiced apples, she set down her fork and sipped at her juice.

"Ooh." Tristan nudged her and pointed to the front of the room. "The lore masters are coming in."

Genea followed Tristan's gaze past the tables of other boys and girls waiting to be presented, beyond the rows of tables lined with students wearing robes with different colored sashes, and to the head table that until now had sat empty.

"*Ba Aven's breath!*" Lord Danu cursed. "They already know I've lost him."

Genea didn't need to ask how they knew that Renn was lost. One of the lore masters sitting at the table was all too familiar—Dev.

"I hope they've a lot of wine, ale, or mead at this school," Kivas said. "I'm going to need it to get through another week of this farce."

Lord Danu just shook his head, picked up his tankard of honey mead, and drained it in a single pull. "We're not going to sit here and drink." Lord Danu slammed his empty mug onto the table. "Aleah's still out there looking for Renn. I know it's a long shot, but I have a plan to give her a fighting chance."

SHADOWSPLITTER

Renn pulled the green riding cloak tighter around his neck against the cold wind and swirling snow. When they'd left the Avalian forest earlier that day, the change was sudden and drastic. The forests of the Avalians were lusher and warmer than they should have been. But more than that, the place virtually oozed with aeon myriad. The stuff of life was thick in the air. In the forest, he could sense the power from every plant and animal. It felt like being immersed in a sea of life-giving energy.

Now the trees were gone, replaced by scrappy bushes and rocky ground dusted with snow. The wind whipped from the north, causing the falling snow to swirl in the air and occasionally reveal patches of tough grass. He could still touch the aeon myriad, but he had to purposefully reach for it.

"I wish Elumniel would've let us stay in Alfheina until midsummer's Azur-Aven," Renn shouted above the pounding of horsehoofs and swirling wind so Aleah could hear him.

Aleah nodded, then pulled back on the reins to bring her horse to a stop.

"There's a good spot of grass over there." She climbed down from her saddle and rubbed her gloved hands together. "I'm not sure how much food we'll find for the horses between here and Bremenon View, so we'd better let them eat."

The female ranger unrolled a worn map, brushed snow off a rock, and sat down. Renn removed bread and dried meats from one of their bags as Aleah studied the parchment.

"I hope the horses can hold up." She shook her head, rolled the map, and put it away. "We'll have to push them hard to make it in time."

Renn watched Thorn and Aleah's mount greedily pull at the grass from the near-frozen ground. The horses had had abundant energy during the past few days; the forest practically pushed life energy into everything within its borders. But now they were visibly wearing down. Renn walked over to Thorn, took off his riding glove, and patted his best friend's neck.

How do you feel? Renn asked, though he already knew.

I wish to return to the place of tall grass and noisy water.

Renn smiled at Thorn's response. He wanted nothing more than to return to Alfheina, too. *Someday, Thorn. Maybe when I become a Wizard.*

Renn untied the leather thong holding his staff—*Greyfel's staff*—to the saddle and rubbed his hand over the ancient wood. He opened himself to the aeon myriad and drew upon a thread of power. The staff began to undulate with green energy, and the wood warmed in his hand. Renn placed his other hand on Thorn and could feel the exhaustion in the horse's muscles.

You're tired, Thorn, Renn projected his thoughts to his horse. *I wish I could help you.*

As if in answer to Renn's concerns, the green energy within the staff moved through the wood and a memory pushed into Renn's mind. The memory transported him to a cold night. Rain beat down on a muddy path. The horse beneath him was strong and fresh, even though it had been running hard for more than a day without rest. In the memory, Renn wore a dark cloak, and in his outstretched hand he held the staff of Greyfel. The staff glowed with green energy that he pulled in from the life all around, and he pushed a steady, trickling amount of that energy from the staff into the horse. As fast as the memory came, it left, and Renn was standing by Thorn with the staff in one hand and his other resting on the horse's back.

Renn bent down and touched a clump of grass. He felt for the life in the plants and then expanded his awareness to the ground surrounding the patch of grass. Even in the cold, hard ground he could feel life and power. He pulled a trickle of this life force into the staff and pushed it toward Thorn. The horse stopped eating and looked at Renn. His muscles fluttered, and he pranced in place.

Would you like to ride? Thorn asked. *I feel like running.*

Renn smiled and pushed energy toward Aleah's mount. He drew power into himself next, to replace the strength he'd expended.

"The horses look better," Aleah commented from behind Renn. It startled him because he hadn't heard her approach.

"I think we will make good time to Bremenon View." Renn nodded toward the staff.

They made steady progress as they continued north. Every so often Renn reached out his conscious toward the life surrounding them, drew energy into the staff, and pushed it into the horses. They still stopped and fed the animals whenever a good patch of grass pushed through the snow, but other than those few stops, they ran the horses all day.

"Renn, my horse's breathing is getting labored. Can you do your thing again?" Aleah had to shout for Renn to hear her above the wind and hooves beating on the snow. He nodded and reached out, feeling for the life in the soil. But he recoiled back.

"The soil feels . . . greasy." Renn looked more closely at the terrain. Nothing had changed. He tentatively reached out again—the greasy senstation rapidly grew worse.

Aleah pulled up on her reins so hard her horse reared. Thorn reacted to Renn's thoughts and also stopped.

"What's wrong?" Renn asked.

Aleah pulled out her bow and nocked an arrow. "Look at the shadows."

Dozens of dark shadows glided across the snow, coming from all directions and closing fast.

"How are there shadows with no people or sunlight?" Renn drew aeon myriad into his staff as he asked Aleah the question, and as if in reply it pulled him into another memory. He saw a large cavern with red orbs lighting the rock walls. Dozens of shadows descended on him, and he prepared to fight. The memory released him.

The shadows were closer now, and Aleah loosed an arrow at one. It stuck with a thud into the ground under the inky shade. The shadow didn't slow, but a high-pitched laugh pierced the wind.

"It's a Shadowsplitter," Renn shouted.

One of the black shapes flashed and coalesced into a laughing man with orange-red hair. Renn raised up a wall of green power between him and Aleah as the newcomer shot a burst of crimson power at them from a skull he held in his right hand. The man vanished, and in his place, a shadow remained. It continued to close on Renn and Aleah.

"I'm impressed you know what I am, boy."

Before Renn could react to the voice that materialized behind his right shoulder, a strong hand grabbed his staff and threw it far out into the snow. Aleah fired an arrow, and it whistled by Renn's head. He turned to look for his attacker but only saw a shadow on the ground and Aleah's arrow flying harmlessly into the storm.

"But knowing what I am won't help you."

Renn whipped his head around to see the Shadowsplitter standing on the opposite side of Aleah's mount. Aleah lay in an unconscious heap on the ground at the man's feet. His hair whipped about in the wind, and his blue eyes were as wide as his maniacal grin.

"Your protector is quite attractive," he said. "After I kill you, I think she and I will have some . . . fun."

Renn didn't need the staff to draw on the aeon myriad, but it took fractions of a second longer to summon without it. He shot a blast of green power at his attacker, but the man vanished, and only a shadow remained. Aleah's horse reared and ran off into the storm.

Renn looked around and saw dozens of shadows in a ring getting tighter around him and Thorn. With a thought from Renn, Thorn bolted toward where the Shadowsplitter had tossed the staff of Greyfel. Before they reached it, Thorn pulled up short. An inky shadow in the snow ahead shimmered red, and the man materialized in its place. The eyes of the skull in his hand glowed, and a stream of energy shot toward them. Renn drew on the power in time to raise a translucent green wall, but the impact when the two energies collided caused Renn to fall off Thorn and lose his concentration.

"Kahn said you were powerful." The man's voice was pinched and high. "But you are nothing compared to me!"

Another blast of angry red power split the cold air, and Renn rolled to his right—closer to where he'd seen the staff fall into the snow. He pulled in aeon myriad and sent a shaft of green energy back at his attacker, but the man vanished.

A shadow swept in front of Renn and another on each side. The one in front shimmered, and Renn stood and swung his fist at it. But instead of materializing into the man, the shadow dulled, and the man appeared instead in the shadow on Renn's right side.

Blinding light flashed across Renn's vision as the man's fist hit him on the side of the head, and Renn tumbled onto the rocky, snow-covered ground. He grabbed at his head and rolled away from his attacker, who shot another stream of red power that hit the ground where Renn had fallen a moment before.

Renn pushed against the ground to stand and his hand felt cold, hard metal—the brass eagle that crowned his staff. He pulled it from under the snow, planted it between himself and his attacker, and drew on the aeon myriad.

A green shell surrounded Renn, and the red blast from the Shadowsplitter ricocheted harmlessly into the storm. Memories flooded into Renn's mind of previous battles with Shadowsplitters, and he remembered how to fight this creature.

Renn started with the dark shadow closest to him. He used the power to feel the aeon myriad in the ground directly beneath the shadow as it passed above the earth. Then Renn caused the power to reach out and grasp the shadow, firmly holding it in place. He found a small hole in the shadow, like a thin slit running along the side. Renn poured heat against the walls of this hole and sealed it up. Now the shadow was sealed and rooted to the ground. He sent his awareness out to the next shadow and did the same, and the next, and the next.

"STOP!" the Shadowsplitter cried out. "How did you learn this?"

Renn ignored the man and contained rooting and sealing the remaining shadows against the ground.

"Wait, please." The Shadowsplitter materialized in one of the few remaining free shadows, only thirty paces in front of where Renn stood, and reached out a hand. "If you'll let me go, I can help you. I only attacked because the Grand Warlock forced me."

"If I let you go," Renn said, "you must promise to never come against me again."

"Yes. Yes, I pro—"

An arrow flew over Renn's shoulder and pierced the man's throat. His eyes bulged as he dropped to his knees and clutched his neck. Renn spun around, and Aleah advanced out of the swirling snow—her brown riding cloak blowing in the breeze and bow held at the ready with another arrow in place.

"What did you do—"

"Never negotiate with a murderous enemy, Renn."

WIND

Renn stood at the stern of the merchant boat next to Aleah and stared out at the quiet sea. Not a cloud to be seen unless you counted the storm in Aleah's eyes. Nothing but calm blue sea and crisp blue sky.

"The gods must hate me," she muttered. "Either that or they're having a great laugh at my expense."

Renn didn't have to ask what she was talking about. He and Aleah had relentlessly pushed their horses, traveling long days and into the nights in near-blizzard conditions all the way from Avalian to the town of Bremenon View. Despite the bad weather, they'd made good time and had even found a boat willing to trade them passage to Elder Island for Aleah's horse. Now, when they desperately needed a stiff wind to fill the square sail that hung limp on the single mast of the boat, it was uncharacteristically calm.

"Mistress Aleah, Master Demaris," the ship's captain shouted as he climbed the stairs and joined them. Aleah and Renn had decided it would be best for him to assume a different name once they reached Bremenon View. Kahn's agents knew the name *Renn* too well. Renn pressed the idea of using his family name. It reminded him of his father, and Renn liked the idea of honoring his father for the sacrifices he'd made.

"I know I told you we'd make the island three days before midwinter's Azur-Aven, but without wind, we'll be lucky to get there three days after." The ship's captain was a hard man, barrel-chested and strong, but he seemed fair. His hair and beard were gray and he was bald on top, but his round sun-leathered face wasn't as wrinkled as most of the sailors on board.

"My men are rowing in shifts, but it's slow going. I fear we will be delayed unless young Master Demaris here learned how to control weather during his first year at Azur's Acropolis . . ." He left the statement hanging and looked hopefully at Renn.

Aleah had lied and told the captain that Renn had completed his first year of training and that she was his older sister escorting him back to the school after a short visit to their home in Anytos.

"Thanks, Captain," Aleah answered when Renn didn't respond. "We know you're doing your best."

The captain nodded, then walked past them and looked over the railing at the rudder hanging from the stern. Nobody manned the old wooden wheel—the captain had simply locked it in position earlier that day. With no waves to fight, the rudder stayed in position, keeping them pointing north and slightly west.

"What about your staff, Renn?" Aleah whispered. She grabbed him by the arm and walked to the port side. "You told me it has memory? I'm sure Greyfel manipulated wind with it before."

"Probably," Renn agreed, "but I don't feel the aeon myriad here like I did in the forests of Avalian. It was easy there. The power practically forced itself into me."

"But what about the Shadowsplitter?" she said. "You weren't in the forest when you fought him. And when Artio died? You pounded the ground with your fists and shook the plains like they were waves of the sea. You didn't even have the staff when you did that."

Renn vividly remembered that day and the sorrow he'd felt. After he'd stopped pounding the ground, he'd looked down, and his fists and forearms had sunk deep into the soil. He didn't like remembering that day. "But there's no life out here, Aleah," Renn said. "Even if I knew what I was doing, we're not standing on land—we're standing on wood that's been dead for years."

"I'm alive," she said. Renn looked at her, his brow furrowed with confusion. "Draw on my life energy."

Renn shook his head. "I don't know how. I could hurt you if I did something wrong."

"Artio taught you how to protect your mind against mental attacks, right?"

All of his traveling companions knew the story about the Kiroc Renn had sent flying through the wall of Artio's cottage two years before.

"I don't think it works the same way," he answered, but Aleah ignored him.

"Maybe if you do the same thing you did to that Kiroc, only in reverse. Calm your mind, and then, instead of pushing out, focus on me and draw in . . . my energy."

"But what if I draw too much life from you? I could kill you, Aleah. I sent that Kiroc through a wall and destroyed its mind."

She held his chin and made him look into her eyes. "The Oracle said that I would get you through this journey. Everyone is relying on me to see you safely there. Every day we lose is another day Kahn and his agents has to find you."

"Yeah, but—"

"I trust you, Renn."

He stared at her brown eyes and bit his lip. "Demaris," he said, and she scrunched her forehead. "You called me Renn. I'm Demaris now." He turned to look back at the calm sea and then reached for her hand.

"If you start feeling pain, you must promise to let go."

Aleah nodded, spread her feet shoulder width apart, and took a deep breath.

Renn—or rather, Demaris—closed his eyes and focused on calming the thoughts in his mind. He thought of the pleasant days of his earliest childhood until he felt at peace. Next, he concentrated on Aleah's skin pressed against his hand and drew on the warmth of her touch. The life force he felt surprised him, and Aleah gasped. He tried to release her, but she gripped his hand more tightly. He opened his eyes to tell her to let go, but what he saw stopped him short. The aeon myriad surrounded him. Even out in the middle of the sea, standing on a boat, the power of life saturated the air, and the elements within this life possessed some level of intelligence. The air shimmered with subtle hints of color, as though he were looking through a prism and could see the true colors within the light. He could feel energy from the very elements in the air he breathed—the elements that were always there but that people took for granted. He gazed down, and the water looked a deeper blue than before, and he could see and feel the life teeming below the surface.

"Wow." He let go of Aleah's hand and drew in the energy from the air around him. Aleah dropped to one knee and gasped for air. Demaris directed the flow of energy into Greyfel's staff, and the now-familiar churning green power pulsed to life within the fibers of the old wood. He reached out and touched Aleah's skin again, then pushed healing life energy back into her.

Aleah stood and smiled. "I gather it's working?"

"This is incredible," Demaris said. "So much life . . . the aeon myriad is everywhere. I had no idea."

"Can you make wind?" she asked.

"No," he said with a sly grin, "but I can manipulate it."

She playfully punched him in the arm as the first stirrings of a strong breeze came across the ocean from the southeast, filling the large square sail in the center of the merchant boat.

The boat lurched forward, and Renn smiled at Aleah with relief. Now they had a chance to get to the school before the ceremony. They stood by the port side of the boat and watched the water race by. Renn kept himself open to the power as if he was a conduit for the energy itself. Part of his mind had to stay focused on pulling the wind so it would constantly push them forward.

"Trouble on the starboard side!" The sailor in the crow's nest shouted and pointed at something in the ocean. "All hands on deck! *Sea monster!*"

Sailors dropped what they were doing and rushed to the right side of the boat where the man was pointing. Aleah and Demaris ran across the deck to look too.

"What in Darlynria's name is that?" Aleah whispered.

Massive tentacle-like arms spun in and out of the water, propelling a creature forward that had a large, bulbous head with curled horns.

Aleah nocked an arrow, drew her bowstring, and let it fly. The arrow arced over the waves and hit the beast on the side of the head but bounced off its reptilian-like skin.

"Are you sure you should do that?" Renn asked. "You're just making it angry. Maybe it will go away if we ignore it."

"I don't think so." She drew back her bow for a second shot. "It's charging us."

"Mistress Aleah!" The boat captain was breathing heavily as he ran up the stars to the main deck. "Master Demaris! You should both go below. Let us handle this beast."

"Have you ever *handled* something like this before?" Aleah had one eyebrow raised as she asked her question.

"Well . . . not exactly, but I don't think it's safe up here."

"I doubt anyplace on the boat is safe, and right now you need our help." Aleah let the second arrow fly.

Renn was already connected to the aeon myriad to manipulate the wind, so he pulled in more, and the staff pulsated with green energy. The captain looked at them and their weapons, then looked at the creature, which was nearly upon them, and nodded.

"Yes, yes, see if you can drive it away." He ran off, shouting to his crew, "Stop gawking and man the harpoons!"

The sailors jumped into action at the sound of their captain issuing orders. Men grabbed ropes and ran to their various stations.

"Can you do something, Renn?" Aleah asked, frustration in her voice, presumably because her third arrow had had no effect. "These sailors are merchants, not fighters, and my arrows are useless."

The creature was only seconds away from ramming their boat. Renn opened his mind to the staff but got distracted when the sea monster dove underwater and disappeared. The sailors stopped shouting. Some ran to the port side and looked to see if the creature would surface again on the other side of the boat.

"*Brace for impact!*" Aleah shouted as she crouched and grabbed onto the railing. A loud boom sounded from below, and the boat shuttered and jerked.

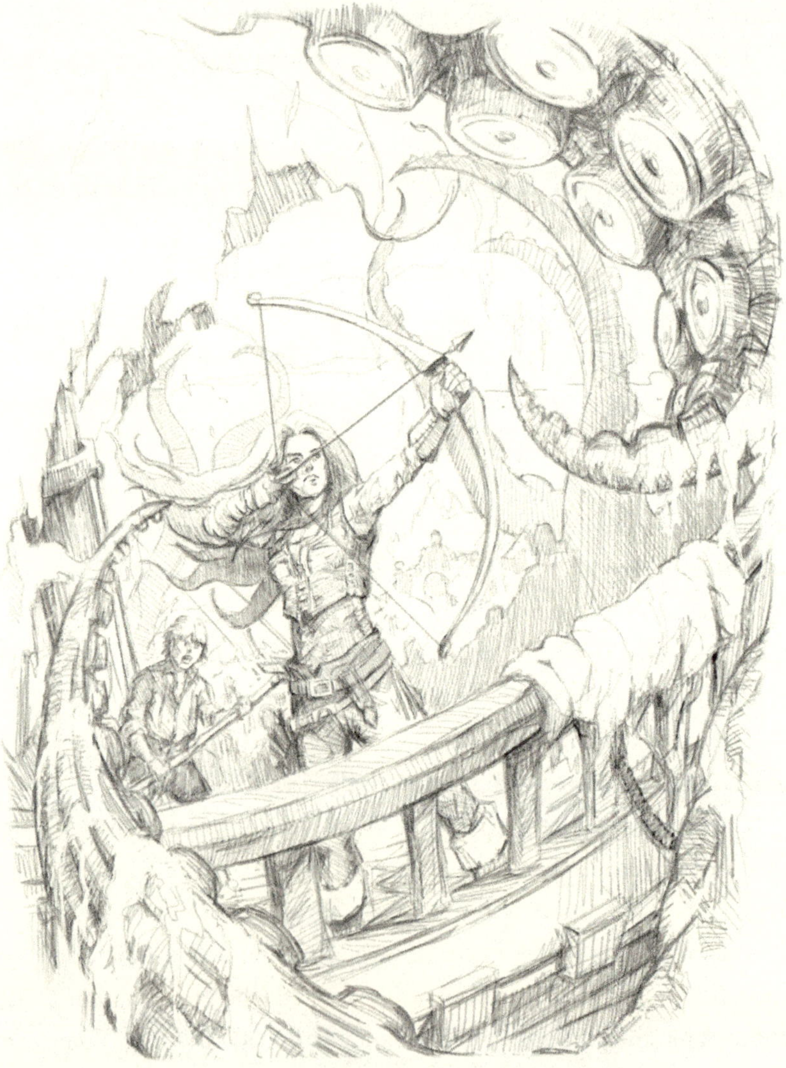

"It's ramming the hull with its horns!" one of the sailors shouted, his eyes wide and his voice cracking.

"Renn! Get back!" Aleah grabbed Renn's cloak, yanked him behind her, and pulled another arrow out of her quiver. Two gray-green tentacles wrapped around the rail on the starboard side of the boat and pulled. The boat tilted and rocked as the creature lifted itself out of the water. Its round and bulbous face had a circular maw with rows of teeth, and ram-like horns grew from the sides of its head. Its thick torso resembled a man's, with a massive chest, shoulders, and arms. But instead of legs, it had several long, snakelike tentacles with circular discs lining the underside.

Aleah let her arrow fly as the monster's head rose above the deck, but the movement of the boat caused her bolt to ricochet harmlessly off one of the beast's thick, curved horns. She climbed to her feet and tried to keep her balance while she nocked another arrow, but a massive tentacle swung over the side of the boat and swept her feet out from under her.

"Arrows might not hurt you," Renn whispered, "but this will."

He focused his mind and shot a bolt of green power at the creature's midsection. The beast roared in pain, but then a shield of red power appeared between its skin and Renn's attack.

"So, you're Renn." Its voice was deep and gravely. "I've been looking for you."

That thing can use magic! Renn thought with alarm. *And it knows my name.*

He drew on the power again, but a tentacle swept in from the side and whipped against his wrist, causing him to drop the staff of Greyfel. Renn's wrist burned and his hand went numb from the impact of the tentacle. He saw his staff slide across the deck, but before he could run after it, a thick, wet tentacle wrapped around his waist, picked him off the deck, and threw him out into the sea.

The shock of hitting frigid, dark water knocked the wind out of Renn, and he choked as he plunged beneath the waves. He kicked his legs and flailed his arms, but his thick riding cloak soaked up water and made it difficult to move. Renn's chest burned with the need for oxygen, but the light from the sun penetrating the surface of the sea fell farther away as the weight of his clothing pulled him down. Renn twisted and jerked at his cloak sleeves until he released himself from the saturated material. He looked up and desperately kicked his legs.

Renn broke the surface, gasping for breath. The cold air burned his lungs, but he was never so thankful to breathe, despite the pain. His teeth chattered, and his body felt numb. He would be dead soon if he didn't get out of this cold water. He turned to locate the boat but instead saw the spinning tentacles of the sea monster. Its torso and horned head rose out of the water as a meaty tentacle wrapped around Renn and raised him up into the air.

"I think Kahn Devin overestimated your power, child," the creature said. "Tell me, did you beat that weakling Norvin?"

Renn had no idea what the beast was talking about, but he didn't have time to consider it or ask questions, because it plunged him back under the icy water. Renn kicked and scratched at the tentacle, but it had no effect and he was growing weaker by the moment. He grabbed the tentacle and pulled with all his might to unwrap it from his body, but the beast was far too powerful. If he had the staff, maybe it would have memories of how Greyfel would've fought this threat, but the staff was on the boat, and he was drowning.

Renn kept kicking and hitting, but the realization that he was about to die filled his thoughts. But rather than cause panic, the thought made him feel calm. His thoughts were fuzzy, and the water no longer felt frigid against his skin. Maybe that was because he was too numb to feel anything. It didn't matter, and strangely, he didn't care anymore.

In the calmness of his pending death, he thought of Artio. He could almost hear the old man's voice say, "When your mind is calm, you can draw on the aeon myriad."

Renn reached out with his thoughts, and clarity and energy surged into his mind and body. The aeon myriad engulfed him. The water of the sea was filled with life and power, even without the staff to aid him. The power filling his body was intoxicating, but more than anything, he needed to breathe.

Renn closed his eyes and gave instruction to the aeon myriad surrounding him and the sea monster. *Raise me to the surface*, he thought, and the water swirled like a fountain around the tentacle holding Renn, and despite the creature's struggles to hold Renn down, both he and the beast rose out of the water and into the air.

Renn opened his eyes. He should've been terrified by what he saw, but the power of the aeon myriad supported him. His entire body glowed with green energy. He and the beast were several hundred feet above the waves of the sea, being held up by a strong fountain of water that shot them out of the depths of the ocean and now held them in the sky. As he looked down at the water, he saw the boat. It looked like a large toy from this height. Being filled with the power the way he was, he could see the looks of panic on the faces of the sailors and the look of determination on the face of Aleah as she insisted they go to Renn's rescue.

Sharp pain at Renn's waist where the water beast held him drew him from his calm observations. He looked down and saw the tentacle glowing with red power.

"Impressive, boy," the creature said, "but you aren't the only one who can work magic." The water monster wrapped two more massive snakelike tentacles around Renn until his entire body was entombed. The creature's greenish-gray skin glowed a brighter red, and it squeezed Renn until it felt like his rib cage would collapse. Renn felt his grip on the aeon myriad grow weak. He wasn't in direct contact with the water and the teeming life it held. Instead, the only thing he could feel was the evertightening grip of the creature and the burning of the red energy it pushed into Renn's skin.

He reached again for the aeon myriad that was so abundant in the waters of the sea but discovered a different source. Life still surrounded him but was manipulated and used by the creature trying to kill him. He remembered the red shackles Kahn Devin had made to hold him prisoner and how Arrianleah had taught him to give the intelligences of the aeon myriad new commands and how they had let him go.

Renn reached his mind out to the power crushing him. He could feel the anger in the energy at being forced to kill and to go against the nature of life. He reached with his thoughts to the intelligences of the aeon myriad and spoke peace to them. The pain began to lessen as the energy started to fade.

"What trick is this?" the beast said, and Renn could feel it reinforce its commands on the power. The red glowing energy brightened again and grew even angrier than before. Renn calmed his mind and reasserted himself.

I free you from this bondage. Renn imagined this thought was being delivered to the intelligences in the aeon myriad on a river of green life. He opened a conduit between himself and the energy the beast was manipulating. *You are free to act for yourselves. You are free to choose life and order over chaos and destruction.*

The red energy flickered and then turned green. Renn drew it into himself and shot it away from his body in all directions.

"Aghhh!" the horned sea creature shouted in agony. It released its grip on Renn, and they fell toward the water. Renn drew on the power, and instead of dropping into the freezing waves, he created another smaller fountain to catch and hold him up. The creature crashed into the sea next to him with a great splash. Renn continued to hold the power as the beast flailed and rose back to the surface.

"NO ONE CAN DEFEAT GOELBAK IN THE SEA!" the creature bellowed as it resurfaced. Its several tentacles glowed with angry red power as they whipped around its head. It pointed two of them at Renn and shot streams of red power like lightning at him. Renn held up a hand and let the angry power enter his body. As it touched his skin, he absorbed and made the energy his own. Renn then sent his thoughts toward the remaining power the creature held and freed it from the compulsion being forced upon it. Now, instead of being surrounded by the crackling red power of the Aven-Lore, the energy surrounding the beast turned green.

The green energy coalesced into ropes of power that wrapped around the creature's tentacles, pulling them together tightly—it reminded Renn of how ranchers in his hometown tied a calf's legs together before branding it. Renn then released the pent-up energy he had taken from the initial attack and sent it back at Goelbak, hitting the water monster square in the chest with a river of green power and sending him flying in the air and splashing down into the dark, cold water. With his tentacles tied together, the sea monster couldn't swim. The beast's eyes widened, and it cried out in rage before sinking. Renn watched the sea roil and bubble until it finally grew calm.

※

Danu went over his mental checklist for the third time as he inspected the knots on the two packhorses. The stables at the school of Azur were located on the northwest side, so the morning sun hadn't yet touched the frozen ground. Kivas cussed under his breath and pulled at the lead rope of a muscled chestnut stallion that was more interested in the pile of hay in the corner of the stable yard than he was in having a bit put into his mouth. Raven, Tellio, and Durham were inspecting a group of six strong mares—none of them saddled.

"Raven, you travel to Aanith with the last two horses and be sure—"

"You worry too much, Danu," Raven said. He was right, but it took all of Lord Danu's remaining patience to hold his tongue. Yelling at Raven wouldn't solve anything, and he'd only regret it later. Of course Raven knew exactly what to do—he'd do it better than Lord Danu himself. Danu wished for at least the hundredth time he could go with his men and leave one of the others at the school to wait, but he had to be the one to explain to the lore masters in case Aleah didn't show up with Renn before the celebration. And he needed to be there for Tristan, Genea, and Harlow when they were presented. And besides that, his right foot ached from the wound he'd received when he tripped Jomavid's trap in the Tiarak Mountains several weeks back.

"Kivas." Danu turned to his big lieutenant, who finally had the stallion settled down and was now inspecting the cinch. "You've got the final camp, so you'll have the longest wait. Stay alert. That goes for each of you," Danu said, raising his voice and turning to the others. "Watch for Aleah and Renn. If you see them coming, prepare your spare horses so the exchange can be as smooth and fast as possible. Keep your horses fed and watered so they'll be ready."

His plan was simple enough. The school was forty leagues from Aanith. Each man would set up a small camp every twelve leagues or so between the school and the town. They would have two spare horses. Raven would take two extra horses into town with him and watch for Renn and Aleah. When they arrived—*if* the arrived—they would push the horses as hard as they could and exchange horses at each base along the way. Doing that should allow them to reach the school in one day instead of the three it would otherwise take to make the journey.

"Lord Danu," Genea called from across the yard. Danu turned and wondered why she wasn't at breakfast as he watched her jog through the snow. "Um . . . I . . . I mean, Tristan, um . . . well, she wanted me to bring you an extra coat and scarf to give to Renn."

"Tristan wanted you to give them to him, huh?" Danu winked as she handed him a sturdy woolen riding coat and a knitted scarf.

Genea blushed. "Um . . . yes. She was worried he might be cold." Her faced turned a deeper shade of red and she curtsied, then ran back toward the castle. Danu watched her go with a smile. Probably the first time he'd smiled in days. They'd find Renn. They had to.

"All right, men, head out." Danu turned to the four men who were now mounted. "We have five days until the ceremony. Hopefully you meet Aleah and Renn on the trail and all of this will be unnecessary."

Danu hated the feeling of helplessness. He despised sitting around and waiting while others were out doing. He knew that most in the nobility would prefer it that way, but he'd never liked being left behind. His father, Lord Drake, had started sending him out at a very early age on errands or for training—probably just wanted to get him out from underfoot. Danu didn't mind, though. He'd never cared to be around his father. He respected him, but he disagreed with the man's approach. Drake was definitely one who liked to sit in his war room and plan while he sent others to do the work for him.

Danu took a deep breath of cold, musty air, let it out with a sigh, and watched his men gallop out of the yard. He still had five days to kill, and now he didn't even have drinking buddies to do it with.

RACE ACROSS ELDER ISLAND

Raven's black hair stirred in the cold steady breeze that blew in from the ocean, over the bay, across the docks, through the small town of Aanith, and up the snow-covered foothill he stood upon. The breeze was constant, with no change in direction or speed. He didn't like it. Wind was supposed to be sporadic and fitful—even a strong wind had eddies and flows to it as it makes its way across the world. Nature was one of the few things he trusted. He couldn't control it, but at least it followed patterns that made sense to him.

Not like people—very few people could really be trusted. Truth be told, he wasn't completely sure he trusted himself anymore. Especially after he'd opened up to Aleah when she'd left the group in the gorge to find Renn. He'd given her the protection rune necklace his mother had carved out of bone when he was a young boy. He had worn it around his neck ever since. He wasn't sure what possessed him to give it to her—well, let her borrow it. Now he felt . . . vulnerable—and not just because he wasn't wearing the protecting ward.

Very few things in this world scared him, but Aleah was one of them. Discipline, hard work, practice, duty—all those things made sense. Those ideals made a man strong and brought order to daily life. At first, Aleah was just another person in the group, just another traveling companion. But ever since she'd disobeyed Lord Danu and saved their lives in the Tiarak

Mountains, things had changed. She'd worked her way into his thoughts like a skilled thief who spent weeks gaining a person's trust before robbing them of all they possess.

He ran his fingers through his dark hair and let out a breath of frustration. Why was he even thinking about this nonsense? Letting a woman into his heart would bring nothing but weakness. He still had a lot to do, and the road he'd chosen would only get more dangerous with time. A woman could be used against him. On the other hand, Aleah was different than other women. She could probably take care of herself in times of danger. That's why he kept looking out into the bay. As foolish as it was to believe she would succeed . . . in his heart, he believed. She was special. She had a determination about her that made him believe she would find Renn and get him here on time.

But time had run out. The sun had risen four hours ago, and the children would be presenting themselves at midnight tonight. The small fishing boats had left the docks long ago, and the town of Aanith was already busy with the tasks of the day. He looked down to the cobblestone road that ran the entire length of the main thoroughfare. It had been cleared of snow and a group of women gathered in front of one of the shops. A shipment of cloth had arrived early in the morning on a merchant boat that bore the purple-and-yellow flag of Kahaal and had been delivered immediately to the shop keep. Apparently he already had several bolts of the prized material on display.

Raven scanned the other streets of Aanith—they were a mixture of mud and snow and not nearly as busy. A steady plume of smoke drifted up from the smithy and a young boy was trying to herd a group of pigs down one lane, but other than that, the town was quiet. It didn't appear that any of Kahn's agents were here. Maybe they had finally given up. Or more likely, they'd quit looking for Renn because they knew where he was—they already had him. No. Raven wasn't going to give into that line of thinking. He had to believe Renn was safe.

He started to turn back to the three horses and the fire that shared the side of the hill with him but stopped short and stared hard across the bay. A small square object appeared on the horizon and slowly grew larger. Most likely one of the local fisherman had decided to come back early, but Raven had to be sure. After a few more minutes, he realized the square shape he saw was a single large mast—he didn't recall any of the fishing boats having such a mast. This had to be a merchant cog.

He rubbed his stubbled chin and pursed his lips, then decided to put out the fire, saddle the horses, and go down to the docks. If Aleah and Renn were on this boat, they might still have a chance to make it in time for the ceremony. If not . . . well, if not, then it didn't really matter.

※

Aleah paced anxiously at the bow of the boat as the stevedores caught the mooring lines and worked to secure them to the small dock. The steady wind that Renn—Demaris, as he now wanted to be called—had created had gotten them to Aanith on the day of midwinter's Azur-Aven, but they would not make it to the school by midnight. They still needed to find a horse for Aleah before they could set out, and the only way they would make it to the school before the ceremony would be to run the horses for ten hours without stopping to rest—even up mountain trails and through snow. No horse could do that—they'd die from exhaustion. Still, she was anxious to get on land and finish the last leg of their journey. Renn wouldn't be there in time for the ceremony—that was that. But if they were just a day or two late, at least he would be safely at the school and maybe he could be presented at next month's smaller ceremony. Maybe the big event Arrianleah had spoken of was nothing more than Renn's presentation—after all, he was a Child of the Blessing that the prophecies spoke of; surely that qualified as a "big event."

Lord Danu and the others would be disappointed—everybody wanted to be there at the ceremony when the Child of the Blessing was presented. And it just seemed right that he should be presented at midwinter's Azur-Aven. Lord Danu had set aside his responsibilities for several months and had personally made the journey to participate in such a monumental event in history. But all that really mattered was that Renn—Demaris, she corrected herself again—got to the school and the protection of the lore masters and began his training as soon as possible.

She fingered the carved bone protection talisman that Raven had given her a couple weeks back but quickly let it go to fall back against the skin on her neck. Her feelings about him were another source of embarrassment. When she took a man, it would be in the tradition of her mother and Domeria—a man that would tend her house and raise her children. In spite of herself, she chuckled at the thought of the dark-haired captain in a cooking apron with a child in one arm and clearing dishes with the other.

No, Raven was striking, handsome, brave, strong—everything she didn't want in a man. These kinds of feelings made you weak and distracted, and distractions would get you killed faster than anything else.

A familiar whinny from behind made her turn in time to see Demaris leading a grateful Thorn out of the galley below. The horse had been amazingly calm during the journey, but being kept below out of the fresh air took a toll on any animal. She could barely stand being down there herself. The disorienting rocking of the ship combined with the smell of dusty hay, manure, and the cooking spices the captain was transporting on this particular voyage were nauseating.

The captain stood on the dock arguing with the dock master when Aleah and Demaris led Thorn down the gangway and off the ship. As they made their way up the rocking wooden planks, she scanned the small town. Had she come here in other circumstances, she might have thought the village to be rather quaint. A lighthouse, painted red and white, stood on a rocky bluff to the south. Aanith itself had a main thoroughfare of cobblestones, lined with small shops on either side. Fishermen's and farmers' wives were busy about their daily work—an excited bunch of them stood at one shop pointing and jabbering about something.

She didn't see a horse trader. She saw a couple inns with small stables, but it didn't look like anybody dealt in horses. "*Ba Aven's breath*," she cursed as she adjusted her saddlebags and weapons.

"What's wrong?" Demaris asked as he patted Thorn's muzzle and held an apple for the horse to eat.

"We're never going to make it," she said. "It'll probably take us half the day just finding a farmer willing to sell us a horse."

She silently reprimanded herself for not thinking of this potential problem before. A fishing town on an island wouldn't have a lot of need for riding horses. They traveled mostly by boat and probably rarely traveled more than a few miles from the town. Farmers would have workhorses, but not horses bred for riding. Hopefully one would be willing to part with a decent horse, or this last leg of their travels would be slow going.

She looked up and down the street again, and then a smile broke across her face and she had to stop herself from reaching for the bone-carved pendant around her neck again. She forced the smile from her lips—she just wished she could force her heart to stop pounding like a lovesick maiden's.

"It looks like we have a welcoming committee." She pointed with her chin toward the north end of town.

Raven was leading two horses and riding another. Demaris had dropped the wind once they'd arrived at the island, but Raven's black hair blew gently in the natural breeze as he rode. He wore his typical black breeches, shirt, and tunic, but he now also donned a thick brown riding cloak as well. He had obviously spotted them because he kicked the horses into a gallop, and townsfolks hurried out of his way as he rode through the cobbled street.

"How did you know when we'd arrive?" Aleah asked as he pulled up and climbed off his steed. "How did you even know I'd find him?"

"I didn't," he said. "I've been camped on the hillside watching every boat for the past couple days hoping you'd come through for us."

"Was there ever any doubt?" Aleah asked, trying to lighten the mood and hide the excitement she felt at seeing him again. Raven raised a single dark brow and almost smiled. Curse him for that look. It was impossible to see that and not feel anything. She silently swore at the blood rising in her cheeks making her flush. Fortunately, the old ship captain rescued her.

"Master Demaris! Mistress Aleah!" he shouted as he hurried toward them. "I'm glad you didn't get too far before I noticed you were leaving." Aleah wasn't sure why he wanted them—she'd prepaid him for their passage.

"I wanted to thank you," he said with a bow. "And young Master Demaris, if you ever need passage in the future, you are welcome at no charge—that is, if you're willing to trade passage for your services."

"Thank you, sir," Demaris stammered, obviously a little embarrassed.

The captain shook their hands and was about to say more, but shouts and curses and the splash of water caused him to look back just as a box of cargo fell into the bay. He pressed his hands against the sides of his head, cried out in alarm, and started shouting orders as he ran back toward the dock.

"Demaris?" Raven asked, looking first at Renn and then Aleah.

"I didn't want to use his real name while we traveled," she explained. "*Demaris* was his idea."

"Renn was a scared boy who was easily manipulated." Demaris turned from Thorn and locked his gaze with Aleah and Raven. "That boy is no more."

Raven raised a single eyebrow and looked appraisingly at Demaris, then shifted a questioning glance at Aleah.

"A lot has happened since he left us back in Anytos," she replied, feeling more irritated than she should. She hated it when he raised one eyebrow—it made her heart thud loudly in her chest and caused her cheeks to flush. She was not going to let any man arouse those types of feelings in her. She forced a scowl on her face, reached under her coat, and took the bone-carved pendant from around her neck.

"Here." She tossed it nonchalantly to Raven. "I won't be needing this anymore."

Raven's expressions were so subdued she had a difficult time reading his feelings with any degree of accuracy by watching his face, but for a brief moment she thought she saw a flash of pain in his eyes. Aleah repressed the feeling of guilt that tried to overtake her. If she made him feel a little pain, it served him right. She was a warrior and the daughter of a queen—not some bar wench he could win over with a raised eyebrow and a smile.

Still, she turned to her pack and busied herself pretending to check that everything was in its proper place—she didn't really want to look him in the eye right now.

Raven slipped the pendant around his neck and hid it under his shirt as if he had expected her to give it back all along—he was really starting to irritate her.

"Let's get on the road." Raven handed the lead rope of a large painted horse to Aleah. "We've set up stations with fresh horses every twelve leagues between here and the school. If we run the horses the entire way, I think we can still make it in time for the ceremony tonight."

"Wow," Aleah said as she secured her pack to the horse. "I'm impressed." She didn't want to inflate his ego any more than it already was, but forethought like this deserved some kind of thank-you.

"I'll ride Thorn," Demaris said when Raven tried to hand him the lead rope of a muscled brown mare.

"You can't ride Thorn all the way, Renn," Raven said. "He'll be dead from exhaustion before the second outpost. It's going to be hard on the horses just doing a single leg of the journey."

Demaris considered this for a moment, then turned to Thorn and began petting his neck as he stared into the animal's eyes. Thorn neighed and stomped his right front hoof a few times, and Renn smiled.

"He wants to carry me," Demaris said.

It always fascinated Aleah to watch him communicate with Thorn. She wondered if he could talk to other animals as well. "I can give him the energy and strength he needs."

Raven looked dubious as he considered Thorn. "Renn—"

"Demaris," he corrected.

"Sorry. Demaris, we will be running full speed in mud, snow, and up mountains," Raven said. "I know Thorn is special, but . . ."

"It's okay, Raven," Demaris said. "I can draw energy from the life that surrounds us and give some of it to Thorn as we ride. By the time we arrive, he'll be as fresh as if he'd had two days' rest."

Raven's lips drew to a thin line as he looked at the staff Demaris held and then the boy's face. Aleah climbed up in her saddle—it felt good to be on a strong horse again.

"We're wasting time, boys." She pulled on the reins and turned her horse. "Let's get moving."

⋈⋈

Genea pulled back the heavy curtains of the window and rubbed a small circle on one of the glass panes to clear away the frost. With no moon, the stars glimmered like a billion candles. From her room she could see across the castle yard, over the vast meadow, and to the tree line a mile south—at least during the day she could. Now she could only see dim shadows. Still, she stared long and hard, hoping against hope that she'd catch a glimpse of approaching riders.

She picked up the brush sitting on top of her vanity and absently brushed through her wavy hair.

"It's sad," Genea said.

"What do you mean?" Tristan looked at her friend's reflection through a mirror on her vanity across the room.

"As long as I can remember, I've looked forward to this ceremony. Now, with all that's happened, I'm not excited at all."

Tristan gave her a reassuring smile. "Come on," she said. "I'll help you do your hair."

Back at home, the villagers would be celebrating with wine and dancing. It would be a festive night with laughter and games. But here at the school, midwinter's Azur-Aven was a solemn ceremony. Instead of midnight dancing and music, they were led into a large, semicircular chamber on the first floor of the castle that was dimly lit by flickering torches in black iron sconces.

Seven throne-like chairs on a raised platform lined the far wall of the room. The center chair was bigger and higher than the three on either side of it. In front of the thrones sat a partition made of wood and carved with intricate designs with inlays of pewter to accent and catch the light. Behind the chairs, set in the wall, stood an arched wooden door.

In front of the platform was a stone floor, which Genea guessed could easily hold a hundred people. Twelve rows of wooden pews surrounded the stone floor. Each row raised above the row in front so all in the large hall had a clear view of the stone floor and the seven thrones behind the partition.

Lord Danu, Genea, Tristan, and Harlow sat on an empty pew in the back. Nearly every seat in the room was taken—obviously all the students in the school were here for the presentation of new students. They hadn't been sitting very long when a young man with a dimpled chin wearing green robes walked to the center of the floor.

"Students," he announced in a loud voice that echoed through the chamber, "rise and greet the lore masters of Elder Island."

The noise of shuffling feet and excited whispers filled the chamber as everyone stood and looked expectantly at the arched doorway behind the row of thrones. Although the pew was raised above the row below, Genea had to stand on her tiptoes and move from side to side to see past the tall boy in front of her.

"There's Salas, the high lore master," Tristan whispered as she'd pointed to the old man who entered first and stood before the center throne. He had long white hair with a beard and mustache to match. He wore a white robe with a multicolored sash tied about his waist and held a long wooden staff.

"He looks like a Wizard out of a storybook," Genea whispered, and Tristan nodded and grinned.

Dev walked in next. Even from this distance, Genea could see the mole on his forehead. She chided herself for noticing such things. She stole a glance at Lord Danu. He looked regal in his rich blue velvet doublet corded with gold thread and matching blue-and-gold mantel clasped at his right shoulder with a gold broach. But Genea knew the blond-haired lord didn't feel regal right now. Seeing Dev on the dais would remind Lord Danu of their failure—not that he needed to be reminded.

Genea watched as the other lore masters filed in and stood before their individual seats. Phaedra, the woman who'd met them when they'd first arrived, stood on the left-hand side of Salas. When they were all in front of their chairs, the lore masters sat in unison. The young student who announced them turned to the crowd and declared, "You may be seated."

Salas smiled and nodded almost imperceptibly to the young man, who turned and left the floor.

The high lore master squinted and looked around the large hall. He raised his staff and said something too quiet to be heard from where Genea sat, but the torches throughout the hall instantly burned brighter. With the added light, she could see that the great room they were in had a high ceiling with a row of beautiful stained glass windows high on each wall just below the peaked roof. Each window colorfully depicted various scenes and people. One was of a large battle; another of young people lounging in a forest, playing lutes, drinking wine, and dancing. She didn't reflect on them for long because the old man smiled and stood.

"That's better," he said in a strong voice that sounded rough, like a plow being pulled through gravel. "I much prefer a well-lit room—I like to see the faces of those I address." He smiled and looked over the assembly. "Tonight is a special occasion. As you know, it is midwinter's Azur-Aven and, once again, we welcome new students of the Azur-Lore." The crowd broke into polite applause at this but quieted when Salas raised his hand.

"Some fourteen years ago," the old lore master continued, "each of you being presented tonight were selected by the gods to walk this path. A path whose end you and I cannot know, but one that will surely bring great things to your life and the lives of those you serve." He stroked his long white beard thoughtfully, then said, "Tonight's ceremony is actually rather simple. You will approach the lore masters seated with me and tell us a little about yourself. After we've met each of you, you will be required to make a solemn oath to serve El Azur and his lore with fidelity and for the purpose of doing good." His eyes took on a look of steel as he surveyed the crowd again. "Do not take that oath lightly"—he emphasized each word—"for it binds you in this life and beyond. If you forsake it, you will suffer dire consequences in your life to come."

Genea felt a bit uncomfortable about High Lore Master Salas's description of the oath, but she had made this decision long ago and wasn't about to turn back now.

The old man sat down and Phaedra rose. She also wore a white hooded robe, but instead of a multicolored sash around her waist, she wore a multicolored shawl draped over her shoulders.

"We will now begin. Starting with the first rows and working our way back. Please come forward when it is your turn, address us in a voice loud enough for all to hear, and then take a seat on the first two pews to my right." She pointed to two empty pews that had been reserved. "Once you are all presented, you will rise, and I will administer the oath to you as a group."

The first to approach was a tall girl with long brown hair. She walked forward rather timidly. Genea only half listened. She looked down the row at Tristan and Harlow. She knew they both missed Renn, but the anticipation of this ceremony had been with them most of their lives, and the excitement in their eyes and on their faces was unmistakable. Lord Danu on the other hand looked dejected and sick. Genea knew he would always blame himself for Renn's disappearance.

When it was Genea's turn to approach the front, Tristan smiled and gave her hand an encouraging squeeze. Genea walked to the center of the chamber. It felt like a thousand eyes bored into her as she made her way across the stone floor—but mostly she was taken aback by the seven lore masters. Here sat the most powerful magic users in Lemuria, and she had their sole attention. She felt naked. Like her soul was being probed and judged.

A man with a bulbous red nose sat in the chair furthest to the left. A placard in front of him said "Gendul," and he was obviously from Concordia. He wore thick white sideburns that ran from his ears to the ends of his rosy cheeks, but his chin and upper lip were clean-shaven. He was bald except for the ring of white hair that met with his sideburns and circled his head. Like the rest, he also wore a white hooded robe, and he gave Genea an encouraging smile.

Next to him sat a very proper-looking woman with blonde hair and dark eyes—Tova. She, too, wore the white robe, but she had lace at her neckline and a cameo broach clasped at her throat. Next to her sat a clean-cut, thin-lipped man who looked to be all business. His name was Rana, and he was Tova's husband. Salas sat in the center, and then Phaedra was at his left. Next to her sat Devera—the guide who'd gone by the name of Dev as they had traveled. And, finally, a stunningly beautiful woman named Daria. She looked to be in her early twenties, but she had to be much older than that. Nevertheless, her dark hair was long and shiny, her full lips were red, and she had big green eyes with long narrow brows and fair skin.

Genea cleared her throat. "I'm Genea Lucian of Leedsdale . . . in Boranica." The lore masters cast a glance at one another and leaned forward. She paused because nobody else had received a reaction like this, and she thought perhaps she'd said something wrong. Then it occurred to her that Renn was also her age and from the village of Leedsdale. Most likely they were interested in what she might know about him.

"I grew up on a farm next to . . ." She wanted to say next to the one marked great but decided that might be more awkward for Lord Danu. "Next to a small river." She told them little about her family. She didn't want to lay bare her wounds in front of the entire assembly of lore masters, students, and chaperones.

When she sat down with the others, Tristan stood and approached the platform. She stood tall and erect in her white dress and crown of fresh flowers encircling her head.

"I am Princess Tristan of Achtland." Again, the lore masters looked one to another. A whispered murmur broke out among the people in the hall, and Genea could see people straining to get a better look at the princess. After telling a little about herself, Tristan glided to the pew and sat next to Genea.

Harlow was the last to present himself. The contrast between him and Tristan was so great it was both comical and sad. He stuttered and shook as he stood before the lore masters. Genea thought he would break down and cry. She had to suppress the urge to go to his side and comfort him. Finally, he finished and practically ran to the pew to sit down beside his friends.

Nobody else stood to approach the lore masters. The high master, Salas, squinted his eyes and searched the audience. Dev's elbows sat on his armrests, and he held his fingers steepled together up to his chin. His dark eyes peered over his fingertips at Lord Danu. High Master Salas leaned toward Phaedra, and she whispered something to which he pursed his lips and nodded.

The high lore master stood and walked behind the chairs of the lore masters to his left and down the three steps of the dais to the stone floor. His staff clicked with each step. "Is there no one else to be presented this night?" Salas asked. "No one at all?"

Genea suspected that few people in the hall knew anything unusual was going on. But to her, the tension in the air was so thick she felt she would choke on it. She heard a shuffling sound from the back of the large room and turned to see Lord Danu rise.

He straightened his mantle, squared his shoulders, and held his head high. Each step of his highly polished boots echoed through the chamber as he approached the lore masters. Genea marveled that the young lord could maintain such a calm demeanor as he faced what she knew he'd been dreading for the past several weeks. Salas returned to his chair, rubbed his white beard, and waited.

Lord Danu stopped in the center of the floor, took a deep breath, and bowed.

UNWELCOME GUEST

Demaris held Thorn's reins in his left hand and clutched the staff of Greyfel in his right—sending a slow, steady stream of energy into Thorn as they charged ahead. It was too dark to see the clumps of snow kicked up by the blonde mare Raven rode, but Demaris felt the cold clods hit his face. The soft thud of hoofs sounded on the snow behind as Aleah kept her horse within a stride of Thorn, so close Demaris could smell the animal's sweat.

The narrow trail rounded a large boulder and broke free of the fragrant pines, opening into an expansive mountain meadow. A castle rose majestically nearly a mile ahead on the right. Light shining from a row of small windows on the bottom floor illuminated enough of the exterior to cause the white edifice to gleam under the stars.

Finally! Demaris thought. *It feels like I've been traveling my entire life to reach this place.* A flood of relief washed over him. He would soon be safe within the walls of the castle. Once he learned to use all his power, nobody he cared about would ever suffer because of him again.

The trail broadened into a snow-packed road, allowing Demaris, Raven, and Aleah to ride abreast of one another. They covered ground quickly, and soon Demaris saw a drawbridge and six tall spires of the school castle behind it.

Arrianleah had prophesied that for him to realize his full power, he had to be at the ceremony tonight. He looked up at the sky. The outer stars of the big ladle constellation were above and slightly west of the North Star. It was at least fifteen minutes past midnight. Surely the ceremony had started.

Will it matter if I'm late? he wondered. *Will the big event still occur?*

"LOOK OUT!" Raven shouted.

The captain dove in front of Demaris and Thorn. A stream of red power—intended for Demaris—lit up the meadow and hit Raven in the chest, throwing him into Thorn's torso. The horse reared to avoid trampling the captain as the man crashed to the snow-covered ground.

Aleah had her bow at the ready in a heartbeat and released an arrow. A shot of red energy incinerated the bolt in midflight, followed by another stream of power that killed Aleah's horse and sent her sprawling, unconscious, from the saddle.

Demaris pulled Thorn's reins and scanned the meadow to locate the enemy. He thrust the staff of Greyfel in front of him and created a shield of emerald energy to intercept the river of red power that jetted toward him. The collision of the competing energies created a thunderclap of sound that echoed off the surrounding mountains. The impact knocked Demaris from his saddle, but the soft snow padded his fall. He nearly lost control of his shield as he landed on his back. The deadly crimson power crackled mere inches from his face.

Run, Thorn, Demaris sent to his horse.

But you need my help.

RUN! Demaris pushed the thought to Thorn the way he would command the aeon myriad. The horse stomped a hoof in the snow and shook his great white mane before he turned and ran toward the line of trees to the west edge of the meadow.

Demaris struggled to his knees and pushed against the power that threatened to destroy him. His shield moved forward, pushing the red energy back.

"I'm impressed, Renn." The voice boomed across the meadow.

Demaris wasn't surprised to see Kahn Devin walk toward him, a glowing red skull in one hand and a thighbone in the other.

Kahn raised the thighbone above his head. "You've grown stronger, but it will make no difference."

"I beat your Shadowsplitter and your sea monster. I can beat you." Demaris's voice sounded small, even to himself.

Kahn laughed. "They were mere Shapeshifters. *I* am the Grand Warlock!"

Demaris pushed against the fear that slammed into his mind. *How can I defeat the Grand Warlock?*

The aeon myriad twisted within the wood grain of the staff, and memories of ancient wars flooded his thoughts. He saw a thousand battles in his mind's eye and knew he needed to be on the offensive to win.

Demaris changed his shield into a lightning bolt of green power and smashed it into Kahn's attack. The roar of the colliding powers reverberated across the meadow.

Demaris leaned forward but glanced toward the castle. In the light of the battle, he saw the moat, the raised drawbridge, and the closed portcullis of the gatehouse. The safety of the school was so close. If he could hold out long enough for the lore masters to come to his aid, perhaps he could survive.

♦

"I am Lord Danu Basil of Basilea," Danu said.

The lore masters shifted in their high-back chairs. Some sat with their fingers peaked; others leaned forward on the intricately carved wooden partition.

Danu forced himself to look into their eyes. He wanted nothing more than to walk out of the castle, climb onto a good horse, and ride until he reached a small fishing village where he could hide in a nondescript tavern. But a man wasn't a man if he couldn't face his failures. He'd failed. Now he'd face it like the lord he was.

"When I left Boranica," Danu continued, "I had in my company the Mage Artio and Renn Demaris . . . the child of prophecy. Now—"

A flash of red and green light bathed the room with a dull hue, followed by a deafening boom.

The screams of new students and their escorts cut through the air, and people dropped to the ground with hands over their ears. Bright green flows of power sprang from the lore masters' staffs and joined to form a shield of protection over the room.

"Silence!" Salas's voice echoed in the chamber. The high lore master stood with one hand raised and the other holding an ivory-colored staff that rippled with green energy.

The room quieted, but then a door at the back burst open and an old man—a groundskeeper, judging by his dirty boots and ragged coat—ran into the room looking like he'd seen a horde of demons.

"A battle," he gasped. "A battle, Lore Masters, right at our very gates!"

Cries of alarm again filled the room.

"People, control yourselves!" Salas looked every inch a Wizard in his flowing white robe and long white hair and beard. "Students and guests, remain here until we return. Lore masters, with me." He ran toward the door without waiting to see if his commands would be obeyed.

Danu wasn't about to hide with children while a battle raged outside. He found Tristan and Genea among the initiates and had them sit next to each other on the front pew.

"Stay together, and don't leave this room until I return," he said. "Don't argue with me, Genea." Danu held up his hand and turned to leave. "Stay inside the castle." He drew his sword and jogged down the corridor. He ran across the inner yard and caught up with the lore masters in the great room. Phaedra looked at him and then at the sword in his right hand. Danu expected her to order him back, but she didn't object, so he fell in behind them as they ran into the large hallway that led to the main doors.

The high lore master flung open the doors to the school, and the group rushed outside but stopped short on the landing. Danu's hair stood on end from the energy that infused the air. Red and green power crackled and lit the night. It cast an eerie glow that reflected off the snow and bathed the meadow and surrounding pines.

Salas waved his ivory staff toward the raised drawbridge and shouted in a language Danu didn't recognize. The thick wooden bridge and iron chains creaked loudly in protest, but they obeyed his command.

"Lore Master Salas," Danu shouted. "Is it wise to lower the drawbridge? What if our enemies get by us and into the castle?"

"There's more than just wood and gates protecting these grounds," the old man said.

By the time the group ran underneath the gatehouse and through the portcullis, the drawbridge lay across the frozen moat so they could cross without slowing.

Danu expected to find armies and magic users at battle with one another. Instead two figures—no more than one hundred paces away—faced off, oblivious to anything except their own fight. Both wore dark cloaks, but the one standing on the north side of the meadow held something round in one hand and a long bone in the other. Even Danu knew these were implements of a Warlock. Red streams of energy shot from both objects as he faced down his opponent.

The other combatant held a single staff, and emerald power shot from its pommel. That person climbed to his feet, and his green column of energy slowly made headway against the red power.

Another thunderous boom ripped through the air, and Danu struggled to keep his balance from the shockwave it created. Rana lifted his wife, Tova, off the snowy ground. Danu helped Daria back to her feet. Phaedra had already recovered and raised her staff, crackling with green energy, above her head.

"Phaedra, wait!" Salas shouted. "Their power is locked together. You won't be able to control the direction of your assault once it joins with theirs."

A rush of crimson power burst from the Warlock's talismans and forced the green power back, causing his enemy to fall to his knees. The lore masters and Danu stood behind High Lore Master Salas, who held his arms out to stop anybody from rushing into the battle.

"You have no chance of winning, boy." The Warlock pushed forward like he was trying to force the other into submission. "I studied both lores for over a hundred years."

"That's Renn and Kahn!" Danu raised his sword and ran around Salas. Before Danu took three steps, green ropes of light enveloped him and he was unable to move.

"Lord Danu," Salas shouted, "you and Renn could both be killed if you charge in. We must wait until their streams of power break apart."

"Move closer," Danu ordered, as though he were leading his band of strangers rather than being restrained by the high lore master of Elder Island. "I want us to be in position to strike when we have an opening."

"Only attack on my direction," Lore Master Salas said, and he released Danu, who signaled for the group to spread out and flank Kahn.

"RENN!" Danu shouted. "Break your connection with Kahn!"

Demaris heard his old name and glanced toward the sound. Lord Danu and seven magic users, each holding a staff that glowed with green energy, stood in a line a mere twenty paces away.

"Break your connection with Kahn so we can help you!" Lord Danu pointed the tip of his sword at the locked streams of energy between Demaris and the Grand Warlock.

Finally! Demaris breathed a sigh of relief. *The lore masters will defeat Kahn and I'll be safe.*

Kahn aimed the skull toward the newcomers, and shards of crimson energy shot out of the skull's eyes toward them. Green shields appeared to block the attack.

"Turn your energy stream into a shield, Renn," said an old Wizard with long white hair and beard. The Wizard didn't shout, but his voice echoed across the meadow.

Demaris altered the shape of the elements of the aeon myriad into a shield, and seven green lightning-like streams of power shot from the Azur-Lore users' staffs toward Kahn. The Grand Warlock erected a red wall of power to block the attack. The sound of the opposing energies' impact was deafening. The Warlock dropped his assault on Demaris and shot power from the thighbone at the ground in front of the Wizards.

Snow rose up in response to create a wall of red ice between Kahn and his attackers that stretched the entire length of the meadow. The shield of ice pulsated with red magic as the green streams of energy pounded against it from the other side.

With his would-be protectors blocked, Demaris changed his shield back into a bolt of power. Demaris's attack collided with a thunderous crash into a stream of fire that Kahn sent to meet it. The Grand Warlock's face twisted, and he leaned toward Demaris as if he were pushing against a wall. The strength of the attack forced Demaris backward, and he dropped to one knee.

Demaris felt the fiber of the wood from the staff of Greyfel vibrate against his palm. He focused on the vibration and willed more of the magic to flow through the staff and pushed himself back to his feet.

"I've seen your staff in drawings, Renn," the Warlock said. "I don't know how you obtained it, but even the staff of Greyfel won't save you now."

Kahn made a slicing motion with the thighbone, and a stone broke free from the frozen ground and flew with incredible speed toward Demaris's head. He ducked, but three more stones flew at him. One hit the staff and another hit his shoulder; the staff dropped from his hand, and Demaris fell the other direction into the frigid snow.

He rolled toward the staff, but a bolt of red power from Kahn shot it farther away. The Warlock laughed and walked closer.

"Goodbye, Renn."

Demaris raised a shield against the power that shot from the Warlock's bone implements, but without the staff to aid him, he knew the shield wouldn't hold long. Kahn's mouth turned up into a sadistic grin. Only a thin green membrane of a shield protected Demaris. The magic of Kahn's attacking energy was so close Demaris could smell the acrid stench of the Aven-Lore.

The pounding of Demaris's heart against his chest sounded like horse-hoofs drumming against the snow. The pounding grew louder, and Demaris saw Thorn charging across the meadow. Clumps of snow flew from his hooves as his powerful legs drove him forward. He lowered his head to ram Kahn Devin, but the Warlock glanced over his shoulder and dove out of the way.

Demaris scurried to his feet and sent a bolt of green energy at the Warlock's head, but the man rolled to his knees and a red shield intercepted the attack. The wall of ice shattered, and Kahn raised a larger shield to protect himself against the streams of green lightning that shot at him from the staffs of the Wizards who charged forward alongside Lord Danu.

Kahn made another cutting motion with the thighbone, and the shield between him and Demaris hovered in the air, continuing to protect the Warlock from Demaris's attack. The Warlock pointed the thighbone to the sky and shot a thousand red shards of light over the shield he'd erected between himself and the Wizards.

He missed them! Demaris thought when the shards flew over the Wizards' heads. But as the deadly bolts of red power fell toward the snow, it lit the area behind the Wizards to reveal a large group of people who had apparently come out of the castle to watch the battle.

"BEHIND YOU!" Demaris shouted. He didn't think the Wizards could hear him above the roar of colliding powers, but they turned as the attack fell to the ground behind them and erected a shield. Unfortunately, they didn't react fast enough to protect everyone. People ran, screaming for help, and some dropped in pain. Two Wizards, both men, continued sending attacks toward Kahn, but the others ran to help the injured bystanders.

Thorn, Demaris linked thoughts with his horse, *we need to leave. Now!*

Demaris ran to his staff and picked it up at the same time Thorn reached him.

Why are we leaving your friends? Thorn's thoughts carried a feeling of disappointment.

We must draw the bad man away before he hurts any more of them. Demaris could sense the horse's demeanor change to pride. *If we run, the bad man will follow us.*

Demaris looked back as they reached the cover of the forest. A red dome of power surrounded Kahn and a green dome covered everyone else. Demaris's arm jerked backward, and he heard the thwack of wood against wood. The staff of Greyfel hit a tree as Thorn ran into the forest, and Demaris dropped it. Thorn stopped at Demaris's unspoken command, and he jumped to the ground to retrieve the staff. He inspected the wood and brass eagle for damage. The staff was whole and unscathed.

You drop the long, skinny wood often, Thorn thought. *Perhaps you should tie it to your arm like men tie wood to the ox.*

Or maybe I can teach it to come back when I drop it, Demaris thought, although he knew the horse wouldn't understand his sarcastic undertone. But as the thought left his mind, the aeon myriad twisted in the fiber of the wood and unlocked a memory. Demaris saw himself holding the staff in an ancient battle. Green power shot in torrents out of the brass eagle. An arrow pierced his hand, forcing him to drop the staff, and a boot kicked it from reach. He held out his other hand, and the staff flew back into his grip. It was as simple as ordering the aeon myriad within the fibers of the wood to return to him.

The vision closed. *I wish I had known that during my battle with the Shadowsplitter,* Demaris thought. A thunderclap sounded across the meadow, and Demaris looked back at the battle. The red dome surrounding Kahn shrank, and the Grand Warlock's body shimmered. Demaris thought the Wizards were defeating Kahn until a black bird, surrounded by a small red dome of energy, launched into the night sky. Green bolts of power ricocheted off the protective red dome as the bird flew over the meadow toward Demaris.

Time to go, Thorn.

Demaris jumped onto the horse, and they charged deeper into the woods until they came to a small clearing surrounded by large pines. Demaris slid off Thorn's back before the horse fully stopped and reached out to the aeon myriad within the trees. He calmed his mind and tried to remember every detail the Oracle of Tanith had told him when he'd created a portal to escape Kahn the last time: choose seven trees, probe until they recognize and connect with him, hold on to that connection. He felt at peace as a solid foundation of strength from the trees grew within him. He asked the aeon myriad to converge together and form a portal.

Green mists of energy reached out from the hearts of each tree like fingers feeling for one another. When all seven fingers of power touched, a rushing sound like strong wind filled the air, but the trees were still. The jade-colored energy swirled together until a translucent green opening appeared.

A burst of red energy cut through the clearing and knocked the staff of Greyfel out of Demaris's grip and sent it flying into the trees. Demaris ducked to avoid a second shard of crimson magic, and Thorn whinnied in pain. The horse dropped to his knees and struggled to regain his footing.

"I don't know what you're trying to accomplish here, Renn." Kahn Devin held a red glowing skull and stepped into the clearing, careful not to touch the portal. "But you won't live to finish it."

"My name is *Demaris*. Renn was a boy who couldn't defend himself."

Kahn raised an eyebrow. "Changing your name changes nothing."

Demaris held out his hand, and the staff of Greyfel flew like an arrow into his grip. Kahn's eyes widened with what Demaris thought was surprise, but the Warlock glared and released a flood of fiery power. A shield of translucent green deflected the Warlock's attack.

Thorn! Get into the portal while I hold him back, Demaris sent to the horse. *I will come as soon as I can—DON'T ARGUE.* He sent that last thought more forcefully than he would have liked, but Demaris didn't have time to explain right now and he could feel Thorn's resistance through their bond.

"How did you learn—" Kahn broke off his question in midsentence. His eyes narrowed into thin slits and his lips curled. He pulled a thighbone from underneath his cloak and punched both the bone and skull forward, and the energy flew harder and faster at Demaris. The air sizzled, and a loud crack split the cold night as their battle renewed.

Demaris's shield rebuffed the torrent of angry red power with ease. He still held communion with the power that flowed through the trees, and that bond fed him extra strength. He didn't have to look to see if Thorn had obeyed his order—he could no longer feel the connection between him and the horse.

Demaris maintained his shield and backstepped to the portal. He paused before entering, unsure what would happen if he entered the enchanted opening while engaged in a magical battle.

A loud screech pierced the sound of clashing energy, and an eagle, with talons extended, flew at Kahn's face. The Warlock spun away from the attack, and the bird changed into the old Wizard with the long white beard as it landed. Kahn shot a streak of magic at the Wizard, but it was met by an explosion of green light from the Wizard's staff.

"Run, Renn!" the Wizard said. "Escape through your portal."

Demaris hesitated. If he joined the battle, maybe he and the old man could end Kahn once and for all.

"Go now, Renn! I will deal with Kahn."

"You may slow me down, Salas," the Grand Warlock hissed, "but in the end, you will both be dead."

"GO, RENN!"

Demaris jumped into the portal. He barely missed the blast of crimson death Kahn had shot at him. From inside the portal, Demaris tried to raise a shield, but nothing happened. He ducked, covering his head with his hands, but Kahn's red bolt of power fizzled at the portal opening. The explosive sounds of the duel between the high lore master and the Grand Warlock changed to a muffled din; the two men blurred into dull figures. The vibrant red and green energy of their battle now looked like colors that had been exposed to the elements and dimmed over time.

Thorn! Demaris couldn't sense the horse's presence, and Thorn didn't respond.

"Thorn!" he yelled aloud. Thick gray mists swallowed his voice and bounced it back at him, but the sound returned in reverse and swirled around his head. He turned in a circle, but that disoriented him. He could feel nothing beneath his feet. He looked down and up. There was nothing but gray . . . nothingness.

"Thorn!" Demaris called again, and this time, mixed with the reverse echo of his voice, he heard a weak whinny. He moved the direction he thought the whinny came from and stumbled into Thorn. Demaris knelt and ran his hands over the horse's coat looking for the wound. His eyes adjusted enough that Thorn's body looked like a shadowed silhouette. He tried to draw on the aeon myriad to produce light, but nothing happened. Thorn nickered at Demaris's touch.

"I don't know what's wrong, Thorn," Demaris said. "This didn't happen when I used a portal to travel to Alfheina."

Demaris saw a dark spot on Thorn; it was wet and sticky. Thorn shuddered and huffed. Demaris reached for the aeon myriad again, desperate to heal his best friend. Again, nothing.

"Renn!" The swirling voice sounded like the Wizard Salas.

"Over here." Demaris felt a spark of hope. If anybody could help, it was the high lore master. "Hurry!"

"Finish the spell." Salas sounded closer now. "Tell the portal to return us to the meadow."

That's what he forgot to do, Demaris realized. He hadn't given the portal a destination.

"No. People might get hurt."

"The lore masters are prepared now." It was difficult for Demaris to understand the words because of the strange echo. "And the castle has secrets I can use to defeat Kahn."

The old man looked like a dark gray silhouette when he got close enough for Demaris to see him through the mists.

"Behind you!" Demaris shouted.

The Wizard raised his staff in time to block Kahn's attack—Kahn must have followed him. The clack of bone hitting wood swirled in the mists, but there was no accompanying green or red power or thunderous boom.

Kahn punched the old man in the face, knocking him down. "You made a mistake coming in here, Salas. The aeon myriad doesn't respond in this . . . whatever this is."

Demaris stood and swung his staff at Kahn, but the Warlock dodged and backhanded Demaris across the face. Salas tried to stand, but Kahn kicked him in the side.

"Renn . . ." Salas's voice was pinched with lack of breath. "Finish the spell . . . Take us b—"

The high lore master's instructions abruptly ended, and he collapsed from a strike of Kahn's thighbone to the back of his head.

Demaris scrambled backward and bumped into Thorn. Kahn rose to his full height, smirked, and looked at Demaris. The Warlock hit the thighbone against his palm as he walked forward.

"This isn't how I imagined it ending, Renn." Kahn stepped over the unconscious body of Salas. "So I will be generous and give you one last chance to join with me."

"I don't trust you." Demaris scrambled to his feet.

"I admit my intention tonight was to kill you," Kahn said. "But you surprised me. I'm not easily surprised. This . . . portal"—the Warlock motioned at the surrounding mists—"this place . . . what is it?"

Demaris didn't answer. The truth was, he really wasn't quite sure where they were.

"I can make you powerful, Renn." Kahn spread his hands and took another step forward. "Excuse me, I mean *Demaris*. And perhaps there are things you could show me. Think of what we could do, working together."

When Kahn had tried to persuade Demaris in the past, there was always a strong compulsion to believe him. But none of that accompanied his words in this place. "You're a liar," Demaris said. The strange reverberation of his voice made the accusation sound ominous and final. "Once you get what you need, you'll kill me like you kill anyone else who is a threat to you."

How am I supposed to finish the spell? Renn wondered.

Kahn raised an eyebrow and shrugged. "So be it." He lifted the bone to strike, and Demaris raised the staff of Greyfel to block him. The Grand Warlock feinted with the bone and instead kicked Demaris in the stomach. Demaris dropped to a knee but held the staff above his head as Kahn swung the thighbone.

"If . . . you kill . . . me . . ." The kick to his stomach had knocked the breath out of Demaris. "You will . . . will be stuck . . ."

Kahn hesitated, holding the bone above his head, and glanced around at the mists. A mirthless grin touched the corners of his mouth.

"You *will* tell me the secret of this place, and then I'll kill you."

"I'm not telling you anything." Demaris swung the staff at Kahn's head, hoping to catch the man off guard, but the Warlock blocked it with his thighbone and grabbed on to the staff with his other hand. Demaris gripped the wood with both hands and tried to yank it out of Kahn's grasp.

Kahn pulled Demaris close and whispered, "I think you will."

The Grand Warlock threw Demaris and the staff to the side, bent next to Thorn, and punched the wound on the horse's side. Thorn whinnied in pain, but Demaris knew the horse was too weak to fight.

"STOP!" Demaris scrambled to his feet. Kahn smiled and pressed his thumb against the wound, causing Thorn to whinny again. "STOP IT. Please."

"Tell me how to get out of here."

Demaris desperately reached out for the aeon myriad—still nothing.

El Azur, Demaris thought, *please help me.*

Ask the powers you are connected with to converge together in the midst of this small clearing to create a portal that will take the Oracle of Tanith home.

Demaris expected to see Arrianleah walk out of the mists. Those were the exact words the Oracle of Tanith had used when she'd taught Demaris the spell. But her voice didn't echo backward; it was crystal clear, reminding Demaris that he had to give the powers he was connected with a specific location to take him. Salas had told him to "finish the spell" before Kahn knocked the old man unconscious. Salas still lay unmoving, barely visible through the thick mists.

Thorn whinnied in pain again as Kahn twisted his thumb in the horse's side.

"Tell me, or I'll dig deeper," the Grand Warlock threatened. "Eventually, I'll come to his heart and rip it out."

Hadn't Kahn heard Arrianleah? Demaris wondered. Perhaps El Azur just helped Demaris remember what the Oracle had said to him.

Demaris closed his eyes and took two slow breaths. "Take us back to the meadow in front of the School of the Azur-Lore."

Demaris opened his eyes, and mists still obscured the silhouettes of Salas lying in a crumpled heap and Kahn torturing Thorn.

"Don't trifle with me, *Renn*," the Warlock said. "Answer, or I kill your horse."

Why didn't it work? Demaris wondered. He tried drawing on the power again; he felt nothing but frustration. Nothing—*Of course! I'm not connected with the power!*

Demaris spun in a circle, looking for the portal opening. He saw a faint glimmer in the mists and ran toward it.

"Hey!" Kahn shouted. "Where are you going?"

The Warlock's voice swirled in the mist, but Demaris focused on the glimmer of light. The light looked to be miles away, and yet a moment later, Demaris fell out of the portal door and landed, face-first, into cold, wet snow. He scrambled to his feet, held the staff over his head, and drew on the aeon myriad that still flowed from the trees, keeping the portal door open. The calm, intoxicating strength of magic flooded back into his body.

"Take us back to the meadow in front of the School of the Azur-Lore," he said.

Kahn Devin jumped out of the portal and fell to the ground. Like Demaris, he also scrambled to his feet, the thighbone glowing with angry red power. Demaris dove past the Warlock, back into the portal, and landed, once again, in snow.

The mists were gone now. Demaris drew upon the aeon myriad as he stood and looked around to get his bearings. He was back where the battle first began. A short distance away, the lore masters tended to wounded people lying in the snow. Their staffs glowed with green power as they worked.

"Thorn!" Demaris created light with his staff and looked for his horse.

I am here . . . I hurt.

Demaris was so relieved to feel the connection between him and Thorn, he nearly burst into tears of joy. He saw Thorn lying on his side in the snow. Not far from the horse, High Lore Master Salas lay unconscious.

EARTHMASTER

"Press firmly here, Lord Danu," Lore Master Daria instructed, "but not too hard."

The light emanating from her staff lit her smooth face with a soft green hue.

"I can't believe that coward would attack innocent people," Danu said as he looked around to see whom he should assist next. He grimaced when he saw Genea helping Lore Master Gendul tend to the wounded. Obviously, she'd ignored his instructions to stay inside.

"Are you truly surprised?" Daria asked, her green eyes locked with Danu's.

He shook his head and released a frustrated breath. "No," he said. "Not really."

"LORD DANU!" He jumped as his name boomed out. Danu recognized Renn's voice, but as loud as it sounded, he expected Renn to be standing behind him.

"THORN AND SALAS NEED HELP!"

"There!" Daria pointed with her staff toward the center of the meadow. Green power surrounded Renn and illuminated the immediate area. A white horse lay in the snow on one side of Renn, and a crumpled body lay on the other.

"Devera!" Daria called to the lore master closest to where she and Danu worked. "Come with me!"

Danu saw Genea stand to follow Devera. "Genea, you stay here with the others."

"But Renn—"

"Stay here."

Renn was kneeling in the snow next to Thorn when Danu and the lore masters arrived. The boy's eyes were closed, his brow was creased, and he rubbed his hand along the grain of his glowing staff. Daria and Devera knelt next to the high lore master, and their staffs erupted in green power as they began assessing his injuries.

"Can you help him?" Devera asked Daria, but Danu's attention remained on Renn. The boy's eyes opened, and he rested a hand on Thorn's wound. A green stream of power flowed into the brass eagle at the tip of Renn's staff, out of his hand, and into the horse's injury.

"How did you learn to do that?" Danu's eyes grew wide as the wound closed and the horse's shallow breathing became steady. Danu turned his head to see how the lore masters were doing with Salas when he saw someone running across the snow toward them.

"*Look out!*" Genea shoved Renn out of the way as a dark object dropped from the sky, changed into a man, and shot a stream of red power at the boy. A hole in the snow steamed at the spot where Renn had knelt only a second before. It smelled like burnt grass and rotten eggs.

Danu dove between Kahn and the children. He raised his arms to block Kahn's follow-up attack. A green shield appeared between Danu and Kahn before the red power hit the crouching lord. Although Renn still lay in the snow with Genea draped protectively over him, a green stream of power flowed from the eagle on his staff and into the shield blocking Kahn's assault.

Renn pushed out from under Genea, rose to his feet, and changed his shield into a stream of power. The resulting shock wave reverberated across the mountains as though two gods had struck war hammers.

Danu glared at Genea. "Go back to the castle before you get killed!" He drew his sword and charged Kahn, but green energy surrounded him once again, and he couldn't move.

"*Lord Danu!*" Devera shouted. "Remember what Salas said. We can't interfere when their energies are locked this way."

"Stay back, Lord Danu." Renn didn't shout, but his voice sounded above the noise of the battle. "I must attack Kahn straight-on to defeat him."

"You won't defeat me, boy," Kahn scoffed. "And rest assured, I will slowly kill your precious horse after you are dead."

"You made a mistake coming here, Kahn," Devera said as he pointed toward the castle. "You are surrounded. You can't defeat us all."

Danu saw Kahn glance in the direction Devera pointed. Phaedra and Tova had joined them, and they held their staffs at the ready, green power blazing across the wood as they waited for a break in the battle. The other lore masters were still on the east side of the clearing near the castle, attending to the wounded.

"Your most powerful Wizard lies crumpled in the snow." Kahn smirked. "I'm not worried."

The Grand Warlock kept the angry red power from the skull focused on Renn, but he swung the thighbone in an arch and raised another massive wall of pulsating red ice to block Phaedra and Tova.

"Daria, we need Salas." Devera knelt next to the dark-haired lore master. "How bad is he?"

Devera released Danu, apparently satisfied he wouldn't attack Kahn.

"He's starting to come around," she said as Danu joined them. Daria had laid the old man flat on his back and his eyelids fluttered now and again as he stared into the night sky. It was definitely an improvement from the crumpled lump he had been when they'd first arrived.

"But," Daria continued, "Salas is in no condition to fight."

Danu pulled a throwing knife from his boot and prepared himself for any break in the battle.

⋈

The magic coming from the skull in Kahn's left hand pushed against Demaris's power, forcing him to lean into the attack to stay on his feet. Kahn raised the thighbone in his right hand to the sky and shouted, "*K'Thrak, Danisyr, Necrosys, Ba Aven Kaera tu Kronus!*"

A memory of another battle in another time flowed from Greyfel's staff into Demaris's mind. The words Kahn shouted called down enormous power from the dark gods when uttered by a Grand Warlock.

Demaris's eyes widened and his jaw dropped as the air around Kahn crackled with energy. The thighbone drew upon power that materialized from the atmosphere like bolts of red lightning. Kahn's eyebrows furrowed and his lips curled. He pointed the bone at Demaris, and an immense river of power erupted from it to combine with the mass of energy coming from the skull in Kahn's other hand.

Demaris clenched his teeth and pushed with all his strength. The crimson flood of power ate away at his green stream. He slid backward in the snow as he tried to keep the Warlock's attack from overtaking him.

"Renn!" Lord Danu shouted again, "I can't help if you don't break off your attack!"

Kahn swished the bone in Lord Danu's direction, and a rope of fire wrapped around his ankles and pulled him to the ground.

A green bolt of energy shot from Devera's staff and severed the attack. Kahn laughed as Lord Danu rubbed his ankles and jumped back to his feet.

Genea ran to Lord Danu. "Are you hurt?" she asked.

"I'm fine. You need to get to safety!"

"I can't get past that!" Genea pointed at the pulsating red wall Kahn had erected.

"Then run to the forest!"

Kahn kept his attack on Demaris through the skull but sent another rope of red energy toward Lord Danu and Genea from the thighbone. The power wrapped around their bodies, pinning their arms to their sides and binding their legs. They both fell to the ground, and Kahn made a slicing motion with the bone as though he were tying their bonds into place.

Genea and Lord Danu thrashed against their magical ropes and screamed in pain.

Demaris tried to step toward his friends but couldn't progress against

Kahn's assault. He saw Lord Danu's muscles flex against his bonds. "Don't struggle," Demaris shouted. "The power will drain your life if you fight against it."

Devera sent another beam of green energy to release Danu and Genea from Kahn's ropes, but it ricocheted away like an arrow bouncing off a stone.

Kahn shot a stream of energy at the Devi lore master. Devera raised a green shield to protect himself, Daria, and Salas.

Demaris glanced at the red ice wall—it still held strong. Devera and Daria crouched behind a green shield to protect themselves and Salas while Lord Danu lay in the snow wrapped in cords of Aven power. Nobody would rescue Demaris this time. He had to face Kahn alone.

"Once I kill you, Renn," Kahn sneered, "I will kill your precious horse. But Danu and Genea won't be so fortunate. They will be sacrificed to Lord Monguinir. Their souls trapped with the demon lord for eternity."

Kahn's body glowed with angry power. Demaris held out his free hand and beckoned to the aeon myriad flowing in and around the Grand Warlock.

I release you. He sent his thoughts to the power. *I free you from the evil Warlock . . . Come to me.*

The power around Kahn hesitated in its orbit, changed direction, and wavered. Kahn sneered and made another slicing gesture with the thighbone. The aeon myriad fell back into order, and the flood of energy coming from Kahn grew more intense. Demaris held the staff of Greyfel with both hands as he pushed against the renewed fury of red power.

"Most lore users never learn what you just tried to do," Kahn said. "It's too bad you have to die."

The Warlock raised the thighbone above his head, and once again, the air around the implement crackled with red lightning. The power was like a vortex of energy being swallowed by the bone. It flowed through Kahn and rushed out of the sockets of the skull. The impact of the attack forced Demaris to one knee. Even with the staff of Greyfel, he was no match for this.

It had been a mistake telling the portal to bring him back to the castle. Renn's hands trembled and he bit his lip. How could he hope to win this fight? The lore masters on the other side of the wall of ice were too occupied with healing the injured to bring down Kahn's barrier—or too weak. *I've already lost*, Demaris thought. *I'll be dead before any of the lore masters can help.*

He fell on his back from the power of Kahn's assault. The emerald stream from his own staff grew thin as Kahn's gained strength.

Demaris turned his head and looked at Danu and Genea. Danu's jaw was rigid and his eyes alight with apparent rage. Tears streamed down Genea's cheeks, and when her eyes met Demaris's, he had to blink to keep himself from crying. He remembered the week they'd spent playing together when the Red Bear had been injured. He thought about the scars that marred her back because she had warned his family of the coming mob. The thought of Genea and Lord Danu spending eternity being tormented by the demon lord was unbearable.

"Wait," Renn said. "Let my friends go, and I'll give you what you want . . . I'll be your Apprentice."

"That offer no longer stands," Kahn said, but he held the power in check a mere finger's width from Demaris's face. "The cost to save your friends is much higher now."

Demaris looked at Genea and Lord Danu again. Genea's eyes were wide, and Lord Danu furrowed his brows and shook his head. Demaris took a deep breath, set his jaw, and looked at Kahn.

"What do I have to do?"

Kahn squared his shoulders and looked down his nose. He still held the thighbone above his head, and power continued to crackle and flow into it from the night sky.

"You are arrogant, Renn!" Kahn said. "Lord Monguinir commanded me to kill you."

"Then he'd probably rather have me than Genea and Lord Danu," Demaris said.

"Renn, no!" Genea said. "You have to live. You're the Child of the Blessing!"

"Don't do it, Renn," Lord Danu shouted.

"Silence!" Kahn glared at Lord Danu and Genea, and the ropes of power circled further up their bodies and gagged them so they couldn't speak.

The Grand Warlock looked back to Demaris, and his eyes narrowed.

"First, you will give me the staff of Greyfel." Kahn enunciated each word. He nodded as though he were contemplating the power a talisman like the staff would bring him.

"Next, you will humble yourself and bow down before me." He threw back his shoulders and shouted, "You will remove your cloak, remove your shoes, and bow before me in complete submission. You will pledge to be my slave and promise to serve in the Aven-Lore. You will kiss my ring as a witness to all present that you are mine to command for the rest of your life."

Demaris closed his eyes and took three deep breaths. Genea and Lord Danu writhed in pain, struggling against the magical bonds that held them. Demaris knew they wanted to break free so they could stop him from making this choice. But there was no other way.

"Let them go, and I'll do it," he said.

"Consider this your first lesson," Kahn said. "You don't set conditions." He pointed the thighbone at Genea and Lord Danu. Their backs arched and their eyes bulged.

"Stop!" Demaris held out the staff of Greyfel. "Here's my staff."

He let go of the staff, and Kahn split his torrential river of attacking power. A portion of his power hit Devera's shield to keep Wizards at bay, and a separate shaft encompassed the staff of Greyfel. Demaris's heart seemed to stop beating as the staff glided away from his hand and came to rest, encased in a red bubble in the air high above Kahn.

Demaris turned his head and looked away. How could it come to this? The deaths of his father and Artio meant nothing now. And what about his own life? It would never belong to him again. This was the end of his dreams.

He buried his face in his hands. He'd thought his power would one day save others. But the only way to save anyone was to give up his power. He'd never become a great Wizard and save Lemuria from evil. But he could save his friends tonight, and that would have to be enough. Maybe this would give them time to regroup and fight back. Perhaps the other Child of the Blessing would fare better than Demaris and rise to fight against Kahn.

He took a deep breath and looked to Genea and Lord Danu. They no longer arched their backs. Their eyes were wide, but they seemed to be filled with panic rather than pain. Demaris clenched his teeth and fists and stood to face Kahn.

"You are filled with pride." Kahn pointed the thighbone at Demaris. "The hatred in your eyes is unacceptable."

Demaris couldn't pull the loathing from his gaze, so he looked down at the snow.

"That's better," Kahn said. "Now, complete your rites of submission."

Demaris closed his eyes. *Forgive me, El Azur,* he prayed. *I truly wanted to serve you.* His pounding heart slowed, and warmth settled over him. Perhaps the god of creation heard his feeble prayer—perhaps not. Either way, it gave Demaris the courage to continue.

He removed his cloak and looked at Kahn Devin as he cast it aside. The Grand Warlock's lip twitched like he was suppressing a smile, but his eyes remained hard as steel swords. The man nodded once, as if telling Demaris to continue.

Demaris sat in the cold, wet snow and unlaced his boots. His wool socks were wet and crusted with ice. He shivered as he peeled them off and the wind blew against his bare skin. The thought of standing barefoot in the snow was nothing compared to the dread of kneeling before Kahn, kissing his ring, and swearing to be his slave.

Demaris stood. His feet sank into the cold snow, and his skin tingled in response.

The red flows of power surrounding the Grand Warlock glimmered with possibilities. The green shield Daria and Devera had raised to protect themselves and High Master Salas from Kahn's attack glowed like emeralds in a queen's necklace, vibrating with life.

Demaris looked at the crimson bonds holding Lord Danu and Genea and saw the intelligences of the aeon myriad struggle in anger against being forced to comply to the will of Kahn Devin.

The red power pulsating through the wall of ice that Kahn had raised to block the other Wizards glistened, but like the ropes holding Genea and

Lord Danu, the aeon myriad was angry and practically begging Demaris to set it free.

He looked down at his tingling bare feet. *Barefoot! I was barefoot with my skin touching the ground when I connected so strongly to the power in Avalian!* Demaris remembered.

The snow had numbed his feet when he first stood. But now he drew on the aeon myriad through the earth and the snow melted around him. Warm power radiated from deep within the ground, through his toes, and into his body. His fatigue gave way to vigor. The light from the stars appeared brighter, and the night air came alive with vibrant hues of blue, purple, and black. Life swirled above the forests surrounding the meadow. Demaris smiled and squared his shoulders.

Kahn's eyes widened, and his face turned red. "I should've known you wouldn't submit!"

Red lightning exploded in the sky above Kahn as the Grand Warlock drew power from his dark gods.

Interesting, Demaris thought. *I can see the flows of power as Kahn forces the aeon myriad to comply.*

Demaris stretched out his left hand and, with a simple thought, the red bubble surrounding the staff of Greyfel fell apart. The staff flew back into Demaris's grip.

The Grand Warlock leaned forward, bared his teeth, and unleashed a tsunami of angry power. Demaris directed the power into his staff and set the aeon myriad free from Kahn's coersion. The staff of Greyfel shined with the green power of raw life.

Kahn sliced downward with the glowing red thighbone. He waved it in a circle and pointed it at Demaris. Rocks rose from the frozen ground and flew through the air at Demaris from all directions.

With a simple thought, a portion of the aeon myriad that flowed in and around Demaris created a green shield to intercept the attack, causing the rocks to drop harmlessly to the ground.

Demaris looked to Genea and Lord Danu. Their eyes were wide, but instead of fear, Demaris saw hope. He pointed toward the crimson bounds that restrained their bodies. *You are free to act as you will*, Demaris thought.

Kahn must have felt his connection with the red ropes sever, because his eyebrows arched and he shot a stream of deadly energy at Demaris's friends. The red bonds turned green and formed a protective shield, causing Kahn's attack to ricochet harmlessly into the night.

Demaris pulled more aeon myriad from the earth and sent a torrential blast of raw green energy at the Grand Warlock, and the man flew backward through the air.

The snow under Demaris's feet melted as he walked forward. His body glowed with green power. The source of energy that flowed into him from the earth was limitless. Every breath Demaris took filled him with the stuff of life.

Kahn's power faltered—his river of power might as well have been twigs trying to hold back the ocean, and Kahn knew it. Demaris could see it in the Grand Warlock's eyes.

"Renn—wait." Sweat dripped down Kahn's cheeks. "Please, Renn . . . you're not a killer. I can—"

"I told you I am no longer Renn." Demaris planted the staff firmly into the ground. "Renn was a boy you could manipulate. Renn was a boy who was easily frightened. Renn was a boy whose family and friends died to protect him. I am *Demaris Earthmaster*. You are responsible for the death of my father and Artio. You have murdered the innocent, and you tried to murder me. You are guilty, and for your crimes, you will die."

A ferocious burst of green power erupted from Demaris's staff, and a gale force of emerald-colored Azur power engulfed and extinguished the red energy from the Warlock's talismans. Kahn's scream for mercy fell silent. Only a circle of scorched earth remained where the Warlock had cowered moments before. The wall of pulsating red ice cracked and crashed to the ground.

Demaris released the power he'd drawn from the earth, and his staff changed from emitting brilliant green light to a gentle emerald glow. He stood over the charred ashes of the Grand Warlock.

I killed him, Demaris thought. His hands shook as the realization hit him. He took a shuddering breath and drew upon the aeon myriad to calm himself. Kahn had been a monster and had promised to kill everyone Demaris loved. *I had no other choice*, he tried to convince himself.

When a sick puma kills for pleasure, no animal in the forest is safe. Demaris nodded at Thorn's response to his concerns. *It is better to kill the puma than to let the others be slaughtered.* Demaris turned from the blackened remains of Kahn and gave the horse a grateful smile.

The lore masters stared at Demaris in wide-eyed silence. He was relieved to see Salas sitting now. Demaris felt his hair flutter in the cold breeze. He lowered his staff, but before he could speak, a cry of anguish pierced the darkened silence.

PRESENTATION

"Help!"

Danu recognized Aleah's voice, but she'd never cried out in anguish like this before.

"Somebody . . . please . . . help!"

Not far from where the battle had been fought, Danu saw Aleah hunched over on the ground, cradling someone in her arms. Danu ran as fast as he could through the snow, stopped next to Aleah, and stared in disbelief at what he saw. He knew the lore masters had also charged through the snow and were now standing behind him, because the glow from their staffs lit the bloody scene before him in a soft emerald light.

"Raven, don't die . . . I'm sorry . . ." Aleah held the captain against her chest, and tears streamed down her cheeks. "Please, Raven, don't die."

Raven's eyes stared into the night sky, and his face was taut with pain. His breathing came in quick, shallow gasps. But what caused Danu to drop his sword and fall to his knees was the gaping wound in the center of his captain's chest. The gash in his leather armor was singed and smoldering, and the circular hole in his chest looked like ground meat.

Danu felt tears well up in his own eyes, and he shook his head in disbelief.

"Please, Raven—you have to be all right." Aleah's pleas turned into tearful sobs, and Danu placed a hand on her shoulder to comfort her. Then he heard the soft crunch of snow as someone stepped around him.

"Move aside, child." Daria gently pushed Danu back and knelt in front of Raven.

The irony of her referring to him as "child" barely registered. She looked no older than her midtwenties. But she was a lore master, so Danu knew she was at least twice that. Ironically, she looked like she could be Raven's younger sister with her long, dark hair and fair skin. Aleah didn't resist when Dariah touched her chin and raised her from leaning over Raven, but she continued to cradle his head on her lap.

Daria breathed in sharply through her teeth and said, "This isn't good. How did he get this wound?"

"He took the initial blast Kahn Devin sent to kill me." Renn had been standing among the lore masters. He stepped forward now and rested a hand on Danu's shoulder. "Raven saved my life."

Daria looked at Renn, gave a sad smile, and nodded. She looked down at Raven's wound and shook her head.

"What's this?" Daria quietly asked to no one in particular, and she reached down to examine a bone-carved pendant that hung around Raven's neck on a leather cord. The oblong-shaped piece of old bone had a simple pattern carved into it that reminded Danu of something Cole would wear. The bone was carved with a diamond shape, but the two lines that made the peak of the diamond crossed each other and continued to run diagonally upward.

"It's a protection ward," Aleah said. "His mother carved it."

Daria raised her eyebrows and traced the rune. "This saved him . . . for the moment."

"Can anything be done for him, Daria?" Salas asked.

Danu looked back at the sound of the old man's voice. He was standing next to Renn. The other lore masters began to spread out in a circle around Raven and Aleah, concern etched on each face as they watched.

Daria looked at the high lore master, then she looked at Aleah and Danu and forced a smile. "I'll do my best," she said. But her eyes said Raven was beyond saving.

"Please hurry," Aleah urged. "His breathing is getting worse."

Daria pulled a blue velvet sachet from underneath her white robe, took out a vial with dark liquid in it, and removed the stopper. She dripped a bit of the thick liquid into the open wound and then forced a few drops into Raven's mouth. Next, she picked up her staff and waved it above Raven's chest in a circular motion. Green power jumped to life as she chanted a monotonous song, and soon the dark-haired captain's chest cavity was bathed in a warm green glow. His eyes closed and his face relaxed.

Danu allowed himself to feel hope. Perhaps Daria *would* be able to save Raven. Sweat beaded on Daria's forehead and dripped down the smooth skin of her milky-white face. Soon, she began to visibly shake from her efforts. Finally, she let the power go, and Danu caught her as she fell over from exhaustion. She gasped for air and clung to Danu as he helped her to her feet.

"Are you certain he's going to be all right?" Aleah studied Raven's face. His features were no longer rigid with pain, but Danu had seen this look of serenity on the faces of some soldiers lying wounded on the battlefield—the calm look of somebody about to be released from pain by merciful death.

"I'm sorry," Daria whispered. "All I could do was ease his pain."

Aleah looked at Daria, and for a moment, Danu thought she would insist the lore master try again. But instead, her shoulders began to shake, and she buried her head in Raven's bloody cloak and wailed. Danu sniffed and wiped at his tears.

Renn walked past Danu, stood over Aleah, and looked down at Raven.

"People I loved died to protect *Renn*," the boy said. "I will not allow anyone I love to die protecting Demaris."

That was the second time tonight Renn had referred to himself as Demaris. *What happened to him?* Danu wondered. The boy stood barefoot with no cloak, and his face was streaked with sweat and mud, yet he held his head up as though he were a king.

Salas walked forward and placed a knobby-knuckled hand on Renn's shoulder. "Young man, Daria is the best Healer in Lemuria. I know this is difficult, but there is nothing you can do to save him."

Renn locked eyes with the old Wizard. "Daria is not an Earthmaster," he said.

None of what Renn said made any sense to Danu, but the boy was so confident now. He was not the same scared child who had been lost a few weeks ago in Anytos.

The staff Renn held began to undulate and flow with the familiar green glow of the Azur-Lore. The flying eagle on the pommel of the staff reminded Danu of the mark on Renn's chest that he had received the night he'd been blessed. That night seemed like only yesterday; yet, here Renn stood, using the power the gods had endowed him with a little more than fourteen years ago.

Renn rubbed his hand over the staff as if caressing the wood. He tilted his head like he was trying to . . . listen to it. His body and the staff looked like they were being consumed with green power. The snow around his muddy feet started to melt and continued melting in a circle around Renn, spreading further and further into the field. Now Danu and the others were standing in mud that only moments before had been frozen ground covered with more than a foot of snow.

Renn knelt and plunged his free hand into the muddy earth. The mud around his hand sprouted plants that grew, bloomed, and then died, leaving the ground cracked and barren. This, too, started at Renn and then radiated outward, following the path of the melted snow.

Renn and his staff glowed so brightly that Danu had to shield his eyes. The field was brighter than when the sun reflected off the white snows at midday.

Renn rested the staff across Raven's mangled chest and chanted in the same language Daria had used earlier, but Danu could tell the words were different. The green energy flowed like a river. Danu could clearly see its course as it poured from the earth, through Renn's body, into the staff, and out to Raven's chest. Within moments, the dying captain's entire body was illuminated from the inside out.

Raven's veins began to glow, making his flesh appear translucent. His lungs and heart also became visible underneath his bones and skin, and still Renn continued to pour power into him.

At first it looked to Danu that nothing was changing other than the color in Raven's body. Then veins, muscle, and sinew began to regenerate and reach across the wound in his chest to connect together. Next, the blackened skin surrounding the injury lightened in color until it turned pink and grew across the wound, sealing it shut.

Raven's breathing steadied and deepened. As Renn withdrew the green power, the captain's coloring returned to normal and he opened his eyes. He looked up at Aleah, smiled, and fell into a restful sleep.

Renn pulled his hand from the now dry and dusty earth, and the green power coursing through him and the staff vanished. He stood, and Danu was surprised that the boy wasn't sweating or showing any other signs of exhaustion like Daria had when she'd tried to heal Raven.

Danu looked around the circle of lore masters and saw that many of the students had failed to listen to Salas when he'd told them to wait behind. At least fifty more people had gathered and were standing behind the lore masters, crowding in to get a closer look at what was happening. Danu wasn't sure how long they had been there, but judging by the expressions on their collective faces, they had been there long enough to witness the miracle Renn had performed.

Thorn pushed through the circle of people, walked up behind Renn, and nudged his shoulder. Renn looked up and smiled, patting the horse's neck. Then he stepped around Aleah and Raven and walked toward High Lore Master Salas, who was now standing next to Danu.

Dropping to one knee and bowing his head, Renn said simply, "I am Demaris of Leedsdale, son of Ehrlich Demaris. I have come to present myself to the lore masters of Elder Island on this night of celebration. I humbly ask that you consider taking me as a student so I can learn the ways of the Azur-Lore."

PANDEMONIUM

As they marched deeper inside the caves, the earthy smell of dirt and rock slowly gave way to the acrid smell of the Aven-Lore. It had also grown warmer the farther they traveled, which surprised and pleased Avaris. Kintara was clearly irritated and growing impatient. Avaris watched the Warlock from under his matted hair, hoping to escape her notice.

Kintara yelled at a woman who knelt at a well in the center of the large cavern they'd just entered. Avaris thought the Warlock would be pretty if she wasn't so fierce and quick to anger. Her long black hair reminded him of his sister, Kalisha, but her smooth, pale skin was something he'd seen for the first time in his life when Kahn Devin had turned Myrrah back into her normal form. Most of the initiates also had pale skin. He blinked his eyes to stop the tear that threatened to form and run down his cheek as he remembered his sister and Myrrah. He was a warrior and would not cry. Kintara glanced in his direction while she gave orders to the black-robed students, and Avaris pressed a little closer to the group of recruits and hoped Kintara hadn't taken time during her journey to memorize each face of the captive children.

She was looking for him—or for the Child of the Blessing; she had no idea he was only a stone's throw away. Avaris had followed Kintara into the cave opening more than a week ago—at least, he thought it had been that long; he couldn't be certain in here with no sun, moon, or stars to judge the time. The eerie crimson light emanating from strange red glowing balls that bathed the corridors and caverns told him nothing of the time, and he found that unsettling.

Once inside, she'd led them to a huge, round cavern only a thousand paces from the entrance. That first cavern was so high Avaris couldn't see the stone ceiling. It reminded him of a small village. That large cave room had been divided into several sections and was tightly managed by a Kiroc named Badan. A stable close to the first cavern entrance had dozens of stalls cut into the rock for the horses and a paddock immediately in front of the stalls so the animals could be exercised daily. Across from that were soldier barracks—also hewn from the stone. There had been a large man working at a forge, sending sparks flying into the air and causing a loud clanking noise to reverberate through the chamber above the general din of other noises. Avaris had kept to the back of the recruits that day to avoid detection, but he'd stayed close enough to hear what Kintara said to Badan when they'd arrived.

"Get supplies and then continue marching these recruits toward the Well of Sacrifice—make sure those in shackles do not escape." She spoke in Avaris's language—she still did not want the recruits to understand her.

"When shall I expect your return, Mistress?" Badan asked deferentially, using the same language.

"If all goes well—soon. I just need to find one more child—an important one, who I believe is hiding somewhere in the mountains between here and Andrika."

"Will you need a horse?"

"There's no time, and I can search for him much better from the skies." After saying that, she handed him the reins of her horse and took a step away. She placed her hand on the obsidian pendant hanging from her neck, which was shaped like a bird, and the air around her began to shimmer. A moment later, a large black raven stood in her place. It let out a screeching cry and flew back down the passageway toward the cave opening.

That had been several days ago.

Kintara had returned earlier today; she returned alone and was not happy about it. She'd startled the recruits by flying over their heads to the front of the line and smoothly changing into her human form as she landed. She spoke to Badan, then sent him to the back to the large cavern where he'd met them several days earlier.

She marched them for hours at a time, only stopping for a quick meal of dried meat and water. Occasionally, Avaris caught glimpses of groups of people walking down connecting corridors. Several times he saw women carrying water or other supplies.

The corridor they traveled was wide enough for five people to walk side by side, but Kintara, leading from the front, kept them walking single file. If Avaris judged correctly, they had marched ten hours before she finally stopped at the cavern where they now stood waiting. He'd stayed in the rear during the long march through endless tunnels and caverns to avoid detection, but he wasn't sure how much longer he could go unnoticed.

Red glowing balls that hung by themselves to the cave walls lit the cavern, and in the center was a large well. A woman and two children were drawing water and filling pitchers when they arrived. Kintara said something Avaris couldn't understand, and the woman who was at the well curtsied, quickly picked up a bucket and ladle, and rushed to give Kintara a drink of water.

Avaris would need to escape as soon as he could. Kintara hadn't met him before, but he was worried she would somehow recognize him, especially now that the group was gathered in one place instead of strung out in twisting corridors. A curious expression flashed across her face as she looked at her brood of new recruits, and she handed the ladle back to the woman. She said something to her again, and the woman began giving water to the recruits. Kintara walked toward them, looking at each one and counting. Avaris felt sweat bead on his forehead, and his heart pounded so loud in his chest he was certain it would give him away.

She stopped walking and turned to look down a corridor at the far right of the cavern. She then turned and looked toward a different passageway. Avaris realized that in the distance he could hear yelling, pounding, and ... screaming. It grew louder, but he couldn't tell from which passage it came.

Then, from a tunnel directly behind Kintara, the noise became noticeably louder, and a person in a green robe, followed by a group in black robes, burst into view. Behind them came grossly shaped Kirocs and more people in black, red, and green robes. Where the cavern had been eerily quiet only moments before, it now broke into a cacophony of noise and commotion. The new recruits jumped to their feet in confusion at the sudden change. This was the perfect chance for Avaris to take his leave from the others, but he had no idea which tunnel to make his escape through.

The cavern turned brighter than a forest fire as a wall of red flame rose from the ground in front of the newcomers. The first green-robed person skidded to a halt at the sudden appearance of the red blazing curtain, but the momentum of those behind pushed him into the flames and he let out a piercing cry as his robes caught fire. Within moments, his wailing ceased, and all that remained was a smoldering pile of dark ashes.

"What is the meaning of this?" Kintara's voice echoed through the cavern. The wall of flame dropped to the height of summer grass, and Avaris realized the black-haired Warlock was controlling it.

"The Well of Sacrifice, Mistress—" a man wearing a red robe stammered as he dropped to his knees before Kintara. "It's gone dark! The demon lord is no more!"

The hall once again erupted in shouts and screams, and creatures and students began pouring in from other corridors surrounding the cavern.

"Silence!" Kintara shouted.

The wall of flame rose with the crescendo of her voice. When she dropped the flames once more, she surveyed the cave with a look that caused even the largest Kiroc beast to cower away from her.

"Now listen to me," she said through clenched teeth. "The demon lord is *not* dead, you fools. If that were the case, I would not be able to call upon the Aven-Lore so easily—nothing has changed with my power." She paused, allowing her words to sink in.

"But, Mistress, why has the well gone dark?" The voice of the man kneeling at her feet quivered. "We sacrificed a slave and offered her into the pit . . . yet it remains dark."

"Fighting has broken out," someone else shouted. "They say the Azur-Lore users are attacking us—"

"Enough!" Kintara shouted. "We are *not* under attack by the Azur-Lore. If the well has gone dark, it is because Kahn Devin is dead."

Kintara signaled for the man in the red robe to get off the ground. "You take a group of five with you and hurry back through this corridor. Tell all you meet what I have said, and let them know I am now in charge and they are to cease fighting and return to their duties or face my wrath."

As Kintara continued organizing the chaos and giving out orders, Avaris slipped away through the nearest corridor.

⌖

Shamael Daro stood in a small room that had been hewn from the stone by slave labor thousands of years ago. This room was high above the dorms, mines, and classrooms scattered among the labyrinthine caves. He concentrated on the smooth black pool of water that made up a large portion of the floor in the center of the room as he watched a scene from the court of King Reollyn of Valdivar unfold. The arrogance and wasteful display of wealth by the hundred or more guests at the party disgusted Shamael. Nobles and their wives wore hand-stitched silk clothing and costumes that cost more than most citizens of Valdivar would earn in a year of hard labor—they would most likely discard this wardrobe once the feast was over, as it wouldn't do to be seen in the same outfit twice. Minstrels played and sang while jugglers, lore users, and acrobats delighted and entertained the king's guests.

Shamael waved the red glowing thighbone in his hand over the still black waters, muttered a guttural command, and the scene changed to the king's treasury. The two men guarding the door were drunk and playing cards. Inside, King Reollyn had an enormous amount of wealth, but not as much as a year ago, and less by far than what the room had contained ten years back, when King Reollyn's father had ruled. Shamael shook his head in disbelief. Reollyn feasted and celebrated his fortune away while Menet, Tiaron, and Anytos committed treason. His father would've crushed the rebel cities long ago—of course, if his father still ruled, they probably never would've renounced their allegiance to the crown.

Shamael let the scene fade and was about to leave to visit the archives far below when an urgent pounding on the door brought him abruptly out of his thoughts. This had better be important, or the intruder would not enjoy the consequence.

He threw open the door of the scrying room. "What is so important that you disobeyed my orders to stay below?"

The Kiroc on the other side of the door stepped back, cringing, and nearly tumbled down the long flight of twisting rock stairs that led to this room.

"Mmm . . . mmm . . . m'lord," he stammered, "fight and screams come from below. A black-robe human say the pit not red anymore."

Shamael furrowed his brows and pursed his lips.

"Truly?" he said, mostly to himself, but the short, ugly Kiroc nodded emphatically. "Return and find a lore user. One who is at least at the level of Necromancer—that would be somebody in a red robe," he clarified at the look of confusion on the Kiroc's face. "Tell them to learn what has happened and meet me at my personal study.

"Don't stand there nodding, you imbecile. Go now."

The beast nearly fell down the twisted, rock-cut stairs as he jumped to carry out the order.

Shamael turned back to the scrying waters, raised the thighbone, and again brought a vision to the black pool. This time he did something he'd never dared before—he called up a vision of Kahn Devin. If Kahn felt him spying on him, he'd most likely kill him, but Shamael didn't think that would happen. The pool remained dark. Shamael tried to draw the image of Kahn to the water once more—again, the pool remained dark and empty. Shamael allowed a genuine smile to twist his lips—his suspicion was correct.

Kahn Devin was dead.

Shamael passed the glowing crimson bone once again above the waters, and now he watched the melee unfolding in a room far below—the room that was home to the Well of Sacrifice. Two lore users were bent over the dark well with skulls and thighbones brightly lit as they tried to bring the pit back to life. He couldn't see their faces to be certain who they were, but he could tell they were not Warlocks—clearly these two didn't know the ritual that would connect them with Lord Monguinir.

Of the eight remaining Warlocks, he was the only one in the caves. Well, him and Dershilek Thresher, but that blind fool was no threat. The rest were out on assignment from Kahn—other than the three high priests, who were likely at their temples in Nortia. Shamael would act quickly to present himself at the Well of Sacrifice, perform the rite of dominance, and become the key for the demons. He would soon be the Grand Warlock.

First, he would have to do something about the commotion in the caves. He used the scrying waters to systematically inspect the main halls and caverns of the caves. Most of them were in a state of pandemonium—some even had dead bodies littering the dirt floor. Slaves in the mines had stopped working because their taskmasters were nowhere to be found—it would only be a matter of time before they tried to escape.

He sucked in a breath between clenched teeth when he inspected the next cavern and saw a Warlock organizing and taking charge. To make matters worse, it was Kintara. This would cause his task to be much more difficult.

He would most likely have to kill her.

THE END

ABOUT THE AUTHOR

Perry was born and raised in the greater Salt Lake City, Utah, area. He is very happily married and has seven wonderful children and two grandchildren. His first exposure to the great world of fantasy was, of course, J. R. R. Tolkien's Lord of the Rings trilogy, when he was fourteen. After that, he read the books of Patricia McKillap, Terry Brooks, David Eddings, Stephen R. Donaldson, etc. Currently his favorite author is Brandon Sanderson. He loves the unique and interesting magic systems Brandon creates, the memorable characters, and the interesting stories.

Perry actually began writing the Lemurian Chronicles in 1993, and after more than two decades of rewrites, editing, re-editing, etc., finally decided to take the plunge and publish his epic fantasy. Don't worry; each additional installment will be released no more than eighteen months to two years apart.

Thanks for your interest in Perry and his works.

Made in the USA
Coppell, TX
18 January 2024